I0757813

A STATE SIDE
Tour of Duty

BY

Neil Mitchell

Copyright © 2024 by Neil Mitchell.

All rights reserved. No part of this publication may be reproduced, distributed, or transmitted in any form or by any means, including photocopying, recording, or other electronic or mechanical methods, without the prior written permission of the author, except in the case of brief quotations embodied in critical reviews and certain other noncommercial uses permitted by copyright law.

This is a work of fiction. Names, characters, places and incidents either are products of the author's imagination or are used fictitiously. Any resemblance to actual events or locales or persons, living or dead, is entirely coincidental.

While inspired by some actual events, this is a work of fiction. It is not intended to portray any individuals, living or dead. All military characters in this novel are composites of many people that can be met in any tour of duty.
In other words, all names, dates and places have been changed to protect the guilty.

Printed in the United States of America

ISBN 979-8-89114-041-7 (sc)
ISBN 979-8-89114-042-4 (hc)
ISBN 979-8-89114-043-1 (e)

Library of Congress Control Number: 2023924111

2024.03.22

MainSpring Books
5901 W. Century Blvd
Suite 750
Los Angeles, CA, US, 90045

www.mainspringbooks.com

ACKNOWLEDGMENTS

This book is dedicated to all those who served in a very difficult part of our nation's history. Those who did not live through the Vietnam era will never understand it; those of us who experienced it are very grateful it is over.

I wish I could thank my late wife, who supported me in this endeavor. She was a good sport about much of what is written.

I also wish to thank Maddie Nordgren, whose editing and advice were invaluable, and Vance Hawkins for his graphic design and typesetting.

Finally, I need to thank all of those individuals who provided the incredible situations where I said to others, "You can't make this stuff up." Where I took the liberty to stretch the truth, it isn't by much.

NEIL MITCHELL

CHAPTER ONE

In May of 1969, I received a letter from the Selective Service requiring me to report for induction into the military. Commonly called a draft notice, the first line read, "The President of the United States sends you greetings." It was no surprise to me that it was coming. I had held off the draft board with appeals until I was able to graduate with my college degree, but the fact that the document would eventually be received was a foregone conclusion. Some of my peers, such as Geoff Coaltrain, were in the National Guard. Those weekend warriors would never see combat in Vietnam because, in those days, the National Guard and other reservists were rarely nationalized. Back then, the National Guard was seen by many as a means of avoiding service in the war. Once a month, Geoff returned to his home state of Utah for a weekend of training, but that was it. There were others who, due to some minor physical defect, had a Selective Service classification of 4F. Then there were guys like me. My name is Norris James Moultrie—my friends call me Nick—and I had been classified as 1A for most of my senior year of college.

"It sure is nice of Tricky Dick to say hello," I said sarcastically as I looked at the Selective Service paperwork. "It's not often a guy like me hears from the White House."

"What are you going to do, Nick?" one friend asked.

"I'll serve," I answered.

"Why? I hear that Canada is really nice this time of the year."

"Yeah, but its cold as hell in the wintertime," I replied. "I won't run away."

"You're crazy! I would pack and be gone tomorrow if I were you," the kid yelled.

I looked at my fellow student and thought before speaking again. Certainly, I would have preferred to begin my post-college days with a regular job, so I had greeted the arrival of my draft notice with a bit of ambivalence. I felt a debt to my country and, likewise, a sense of duty to defend the freedoms and standard of living I had always enjoyed. However, these feelings were somewhat mitigated by thoughts that perhaps this wasn't my fight and shouldn't be my country's fight as well. Likewise, with the war raging in Southeast Asia, that draft notice represented a complete death warrant for many. To die in a war that, conceivably, neither my country nor I had any business in held some abhorrence for me. The emotions I was feeling were probably the same ones every young man had felt since the first cave men fought their neighbors over water or better hunting grounds. With the Vietnam conflict, each day there were more people talking about those who had fled the country or gone into hiding elsewhere to avoid military service, but I decided against that course of action.

"If I pass the physical, then I'll serve," I said.

"I still think you're stupid," the kid maintained.

"My father served in World War II," I answered. "Now it's my turn. I will serve."

After one graduates from college, complete with all their relevant knowledge, usually job offers are forthcoming. But that did not happen in my case. The draft notice I received was my only one. Because of it my next employment would be a government job earning eighty-six dollars and twenty cents a month and all the green clothes I could wear.

In retrospect, I made the correct decision. I gained an education I could never have received elsewhere, while the kid encouraging me to flee did indeed run away. When he received greetings from the president several weeks later, he left immediately for Canada. I later learned that he died in a traffic accident in British Columbia about a year afterward.

His death reinforced my philosophy of life. I have always believed that when your number is up there isn't much you can do about it. That being the case, if it was my turn to meet the eternities, I would rather expire in battle than die in a crash on the highway or meet some other mundane demise. Still, my feelings at entering the Army could not be described as including great enthusiasm. I would go and do my duty. The question as to whether or not my country belonged in the war would be left to the politicians and the judgments of history.

So, that's the way it all started. Among the diverse events that qualify as truly life-altering experiences are a stretch in the Army and getting married. For me, those two occasions coincided, as I would get

A STATESIDE TOUR OF DUTY

married about a year after entering the service. In some ways, those two circumstances are similar. The Army transforms you from a carefree individual with few concerns into a person with a structured and disciplined lifestyle. In marriage, you cease to be responsible for only yourself and must learn to live in harmony with another human being. Some are able to adapt and make the change while others are not. In retrospect, I am proud to say that I succeeded despite making mistakes.

Like everyone, I am a product of my environment, experiences and education. Most of the latter was obtained, in four short years, at Arizona State University. More than one professor had told me that life is, first and foremost, a learning experience. This was a rephrasing of my parents' constant claim that you never stop learning. So, in compliance, I had spent such time learning the wisdom of the ages in the classroom as my social life would allow. Despite the fact that the nightly news consistently showed rioters protesting the injustice that still exists in the world and war protesters were burning draft cards and claiming my country wasn't always automatically right, I remained a patriotic American. As a productive citizen, I realized that everyone, sooner or later, has to obtain a job and make his way in the world. Maybe the Army wasn't my first choice for an occupation, but my time there would be kept to a minimum, and I would do my best nonetheless.

Shortly thereafter, I found myself at Fort Leonard Wood in the state of Missouri. Men stationed there call it Fort Lost in the Woods in the state of Misery. There, I completed eight weeks of basic training followed by eight more of Engineer Advanced Individual Training. Not content to live on less than a hundred dollars a month, I applied for Officer Candidate School. Before my acceptance to OCS, I was transferred to Fort Meade, Maryland, where I was assigned to drive a five-ton dump truck. Shortly thereafter, I was at Fort Belvoir, Virginia, for six months of OCS. After being commissioned a second lieutenant, my next duty station was Fort Benjamin McCulloch, Texas. It was there that I met some of the very best and some of the very worst of individuals.

Everyone inevitably wishes that they knew at a previous time what they know now. The 20/20 vision of hindsight allows one to see the events of bygone years in their complete perspective. It is like looking at the pieces of a puzzle once they are connected. Prior events, which once made little or no sense at the time, form a crystal-clear picture when considered after the fact. So it was with my time spent at Fort McCulloch.

NEIL MITCHELL

The passage of more than four decades has not dulled my memory of that remote location. All of my recollections from my first night on duty, when three fatalities occurred, to the day I left as a family man twenty-two months later will forever be a part of me. When I arrived there, I was still naive enough to believe that truth and justice will always prevail. I now know that might be the case in the next life, but not necessarily in this one. That was just one of many of life's lessons I learned there.

I first arrived at Fort McCulloch during the summer of 1970. A long, solitary drive allows an individual time for contemplation and reflection. Despite the heat and monotony endured during the trip, I did plenty of both. Upon graduation from Officer Candidate School, I was immediately qualified (according to the Army) to do any job under the sun they assigned to me. Like all new officers, the Army had tried to sell me on a program called voluntary indefinite (vol-indef for short). Those who agreed to this program got sent anywhere in the world they wanted for three years, but were transferred to Vietnam for the fourth year. The program worked that way when I was commissioned. However, in the event that the Army chose to have you remain in the service, they could keep you as long as they wanted. While that scenario was unlikely, it was still possible depending upon future events and changing world situations. In other words, the four years could turn into many more. Vol-indef literally meant to volunteer for an indefinite period of time. Those of us who refused to sign up for this program would serve only two years. Unfortunately, we were told, it would be at less-than-desirable posts and would include a year in the war zone.

I will never forget the conversation I had with the representative from OPO (Officers Personnel Office) over that program just before I received my second lieutenant's bars. The man's name was Major Wilson. He was a large man with a John Wayne-like appearance and a salesman's personality.

"Well, Moultrie," he began. "Have you given any thought to the voluntary indefinite program?"

"Sir, Candidate Moultrie, yes, sir," I answered in the required officer candidate phraseology. "As you have described it for me, I can be sent to any duty station in the world for three years, and then I get sent to Vietnam."

"That is correct, Moultrie. We have some very choice assignments you can choose from. In fact, as I look at your paperwork, I see that you picked three of the best. They are Presidio of California, Yuma, Arizona, and Fort Carson, Colorado. The only way I can guarantee you one of these locations is for you to vol-indef."

"Sir, Candidate Moultrie, yes, sir," I replied. I took time to think before answering further. I suspect the major told everyone their choices were among the best, but it was obvious to him why I had chosen as I had. The Presidio was a plum assignment for anyone. Yuma was warm year-round and had excellent access to recreational opportunities, and Fort Carson, located near the Denver metro area, had access to fantastic skiing as well as breathtaking scenery. He wasn't going to give one of them up without a commitment from me. But, I wondered, where else might I be sent? I continued, "Also, in the event I decide not to vol-indef, I will receive orders for Vietnam within the year."

"That is correct," he concurred.

"Sir, Candidate Moultrie, where might I be sent to await those orders, sir?"

"There is an opening at Fort Polk, Louisiana."

Despite the fact that shivers went up my spine, I kept my poker face. I had heard horror stories about Fort Polk. I wanted to avoid that hellhole if at all possible. Those who had been to Fork Polk assured me that if the world required an enema; the device for the procedure would be inserted at Fort Polk. I changed the subject. "Sir, Candidate Moultrie," I began, "what are the odds that I will get my first choice if I vol-indef?"

"Very good, depending on a number of factors. But, you are guaranteed to receive one of the three choices."

I had always heard that the Army would not give you something you wanted unless you gave them a commitment, so I then spoke forcefully and confidently. "Sir, Candidate Moultrie, Fort Polk will be excellent, sir. As you can see, all of my choices are in the West. Since Fort Polk is west of the Mississippi River, I believe that will be satisfactory. Besides, sir, since a tour in Vietnam seems inevitable, I might as well get it over with. No need putting it off."

"You are quite sure of that, Moultrie?"

"Sir, Candidate Moultrie, yes, sir. I guess I can write my friends back home and tell them I will be assigned to Fort Polk then, sir?"

"We'll see what we can do, Moultrie. Dismissed."

"Sir, Candidate Moultrie, yes, sir."

The individual who met with Wilson right after me was from San Angelo, Texas, and ironically believed he might get Fort McCulloch, Texas, without committing to the vol-indef program, since no one else would want the assignment. Our reward for failure to cooperate with the U.S. Army (by not accepting the vol-indef program) was that he got assigned to Fort Polk, and I was sent to Fort McCulloch.

After I entered the Army, their experts took one look at my political science degree with a minor in philosophy and decided that I would be an excellent engineer. Consequently, I was sent to Fort Leonard Wood. Later, upon graduation from OCS, the Army apparently was short of military police officers, as about three quarters of my class received their commissions in that particular corps. So, that is how I wound up in law enforcement for the next two years.

Upon commissioning, I was immediately designated an officer and a gentleman. A few of the men I graduated with were such in name only. I was determined to rise to the higher standard of actually deserving the title as well as having it by virtue of some government proclamation. So, with that purpose in mind, I was now proceeding to my assignment at Fort McCulloch.

In 1836, Davy Crockett had told his Tennessee voters that they could go to hell and he would go to Texas. After traveling through west Texas, I was beginning to think that the voters had gotten the better part of the deal. As I gazed out the car window at the rocky plains and the rolling sand hills that began at the edge of the highway and stretched out as far as I could see, I guessed the temperature to be about a hundred and ten degrees. The heat waves created by this solar inferno arose from the desert floor and blurred the mountains in the distance to my left. As I continued driving, my thoughts shifted back and forth between the vast panorama of rock, dust and sagebrush that formed the most desolate area I had ever seen and the events that had gotten me to this stygian location. My eyes left the road for a few seconds. The bluish ridge of mountains in the distance appeared to dance in the heat waves. Those rocky knolls and barren peaks had joined with an occasional rain-carved ravine for the past sixty or seventy miles as the only geographic features to break the monotony of the terrain.

The hot sun and hours of driving over a highway that seemed to materialize out of some limitless source before me, had given me a headache. Rubbing the back of my head for a minute seemed to alleviate the pain, so once again my thoughts drifted back to my driving. I again marveled at the bleak surroundings. I almost suspected that driving to Hades might be an improvement.

A STATESIDE TOUR OF DUTY

The Army must have searched and surveyed southwest Texas diligently in order to find the remote area in which Fort Benjamin McCulloch was to be located. I could see with a cursory glance at my map that to reach any cities of consequential size would require quite a drive. El Paso was at least three hundred miles away, and the distance to Austin appeared to be slightly more than that. The much smaller city of San Angelo was seventy miles away, and the map indicated that there was a small town named Harrisville located just outside the post. My duty assignment was located somewhere between the middle of nowhere and the boondocks. At this point, I couldn't help but voice my thoughts aloud to myself. "What have I gotten myself into?" I muttered.

The open windows allowed a warm breeze to circulate though the car,preventing me from being overcome by the heat. However, any benefit this provided was negated by the dust and sand that came with the air currents. The dust settled on everything in the car, including, my sweat-drenched arms and face.

I now observed a high chain-link fence running parallel to the road with signs stating, "U.S. Government Military Reservation—No Trespassing." I had been aware of its presence for some time but had not noticed the signs before nor realized it was the boundary to the military post I sought. In almost any other part of Texas, distances could be easily traversed by means of a well-maintained four-lane highway. Obviously, that was not the case here. Fort McCulloch is connected to the outside world by three small highways. If the other two were as rough as this one, the local mechanics must be rich from all the car repair bills. From the different shades of asphalt, I discerned that the road had been patched many times. Apparently, though, none of those repairs had been made recently. There were potholes that must have been in the road for some time, but the road surface would still have been irregular and rough without them. Distracted by the hot sun, desolate area, and narrow rough road, I almost missed a small rectangular sign that read, "Fort McCulloch 1 Mile." At last, my destination was near, and, if you will forgive some sarcasm, I had high hopes that my great adventure was about to begin.

The last half-mile of my journey was a long dip between two hills. Atop the second hill was the approach to the main gate for which I had been searching. The gate was situated about two hundred feet from the highway. Were it not for the grotesque billboards on either side, the gate might have gone unnoticed altogether by passersby. As a child, I had been to the circus, and these signs reminded me of something I might have seen on the midway announcing freaks and extraneous acts. On the left was a large red, white and blue sign that pictured a soldier dressed in khakis who announced that Fort McCulloch was a zero-defects post where all soldiers served and saluted proudly. The sign on the right read, "Welcome to Fort Benjamin McCulloch, Home of the U.S. Army Communications School and the Largest Post in the Country." The statement was signed, "Brigadier General Oliver R. Cinch, Commander." Under the cheerful salutation was this additional statement: "Entering a U S Government Military Installation, All Vehicles Subject to Search by Order of the Post Commander." Over the sentry shack was another small sign that declared, "Fort Benjamin McCulloch, Established 1916."

As I approached the main gate, the guard motioned me through, but I needed directions, so I ignored him and stopped. When he noticed the MP brass on my uniform he saluted and said, "Good afternoon, sir. How can I help you?"

"I'm an incoming officer assigned to the 290th MP Company and I need some directions to the orderly room."

"Yes, sir. You proceed straight for two blocks and turn right. You make a left onto Humbard and you can't miss it."

"Thank you, I appreciate the information."

"You're welcome, sir. And welcome to Fort McCulloch." He saluted again. I nodded, returned the salute and proceeded.

It was a good thing his directions were so simple, otherwise I might not have caught them all. I had been looking from the corner of my eye at the guard shack, which had at least two cracked windows. In addition, a map of the post mounted on plywood was detached on one side and was hanging by the opposite corner at a forty-five-degree angle. The shack and the area around it were in great need of policing, judging from the papers and other trash the wind had blown against the fence, along with the amount of cigarette butts and gum wrappers that were lying in and around the structure.

The office of the provost marshal and the 290th Military Police orderly room were indistinguishable from the five or six other buildings that lined Humbard Street. They were all white with metal ventilators protruding from green roofs. Parked next to the one- and two-story structures were a few olive drab staff cars with a few privately owned vehicles parked in unpaved parking lots between the buildings. I quickly found the orderly room and parked beside a red Mustang. About thirty feet from where I stood was a green sign with gold letters which proclaimed, "Of The Troops, For The Troops, 290th Military Police Company." From a distance it appeared neat and well cared for, but a close-up inspection revealed it had not been painted for some time. The green background resembled a freshly dried mud puddle with cracks running in every conceivable direction. The gold letters were peeling, and any stiff breeze caused more flakes of paint to fall. In several places, masking tape had been used to replace missing spots in the lettering.

I walked into the orderly room and hesitated for a few seconds as my eyes adjusted to the dimmer light. Behind a green metal desk, a clerk was typing a report of some kind. Without stopping his typing, he looked up and said, "How can I help you, sir?"

"I've just been assigned here. I'm looking for the place to sign in."

He stopped typing and pointed with his thumb to the wall on my left near a file cabinet. "You're in the right place, sir. The sign-in sheet's over there, and I'll need two copies of your orders."

I reached into a folder I was carrying and removed two copies of my travel orders. Upon graduation from OCS, I had been given about fifty copies of orders. I left one copy at Fort Belvoir when I departed and used two copies for military hops. Now, with about 45 copies left, I wondered if everyone had this many copies left when reporting to a duty station. If so, the Army was wasting millions of dollars in excess paper. I gave the clerk the copies of my orders, signed in under someone named Staff Sergeant Warren (who had departed on a temporary duty assignment), and glanced around the room for a few seconds, sizing the place up.

"Is the CO in?" I asked.

"No, sir, but you might check with the major or colonel in the PMO next door. You'll probably be assigned there anyway."

"Why is that?"

"Only slot we have for a lieutenant is XO and Lieutenant Raymond has that," he replied.

With the chain of command of Commanding Officer (CO) and Executive Officer (XO) filled, it was clear that I would be assigned to a staff position in the Provost Marshal's Office (PMO). On any Army post, the Provost Marshal is the chief law enforcement officer. A command position is usually more prestigious than a staff position, but as I was not planning to make the Army a career, I didn't think it would make much difference to me.

I continued to try to make conversation. I thought my next question was dumb even before I asked it, but I asked it anyway as it seemed obligatory. "How is Fort McCulloch as a duty station?"

He raised his hand and tilted it back and forth in the usual gesture for mediocrity. "Uh, so-so, sir." He resumed typing before adding, "But seventy-three days and a wake-up and I'll be going back to New York, and I'll sure be glad to leave old Camp Dusty behind."

"Well, I'll probably be seeing you later." I said as I turned and left the orderly room.

As I did so, even though I was out of earshot, in my mind's eye I could still see him shake his head and say, "Just what we need around here, another second Louie."

I then walked over to the Provost Marshal's office. It was a one-story building exactly like the one I had just left. Just outside of it were hung two large, yellow, wooden, crossed pistols. I entered the building and, to my great relief, found it air-conditioned. Glancing around the room, my first impression was generally favorable. Judging from the glossy shine and circular buffer marks, the floor was obviously well cared for. There were two desks (one on each side of me), behind which were seated two secretaries. The one on the left was an attractive, big-busted blond with shoulder-length hair, while the secretary on the right (also attractive) had closely cut dark hair and was as flat as the other girl was ample. Their desks had folders and papers neatly stacked in the In and Out boxes, and various secretarial paraphernalia (staplers, hole punch, ashtrays, etc.) were lined up neatly along the outer edge of the desks. Even the leaf calendar had notes written in neat script. In the corner to my left was a coffee maker, which seemed carefully placed to balance the file cabinets in the corner to my right. They both even had little signs placed over them to add to the symmetry. One sign reminded the coffee drinker to pay ten cents a cup or three dollars a month, while the other had the federally required statement, "These File Cabinets Contain No Classified Material." The room had exits on each side and an office directly ahead, which had the name Major J. L. Receiver, Deputy Provost Marshall, over the door.

One of the secretaries stopped typing and looked up at me as I introduced myself. "I'm Lieutenant Moultrie, and I've been told I'll probably be assigned here. I was just wondering who I talk to as to my assignment and the nature of my duties?"

A STATESIDE TOUR OF DUTY

Before the young lady could reply, a voice boomed out of the office in front of me, "Right in here, lieutenant." I thanked the girl for the information she hadn't had a chance to give me and walked into Major Receiver's office. The major was a man in his mid-fifties of average height and build with reddish hair. As I walked into his office, he rose and held out his hand. We shook hands and he offered me a chair.

"Did you have a pleasant trip to Fort McCulloch?"

In the interest of diplomacy, I lied. "Yes, sir, I drove out in my POV," I stated as enthusiastically as possible and added, "It was quite a trip. The last hundred miles on Highway 132 didn't afford much to look at."

"That's a desolate stretch of road that's not too often used by very many people."

"I can see why, sir."

The major changed the subject. "What is the source of your commission, lieutenant?"

"OCS, sir." I replied. "I graduated from Fort Belvoir May 22nd and just finished the MP Officer's Orientation Course three days ago."

"Well, you'll find Fort McCulloch a quiet post and one off the beaten path. But, you'll still find just about anything here that goes on anywhere else. A good place to gain experience." At this point the major paused a second and asked, "Do you plan to make the Army a career?"

Again, I lied. "I don't know sir. I've considered it, but at this time I still haven't made a final decision."

The major then pulled an MP School correspondence course booklet from his bookshelf. He began a lengthy talk. "If you decide to make the Army a career, I strongly suggest that you attempt to gain a regular Army commission. As a Reserve officer, I can definitely attest to the fact that RA is the way to go. At any rate, it's always a good idea to take correspondence courses from the MP School at Fort Gordon. They are easy and not very lengthy, but the Army places great emphasis on them in promotions and the selection of individuals for advanced schools."

The major continued to talk for some time on the advantages of a military career and then told me a little about himself. "I was a policeman in Seattle," he began. "I first joined the Army back in 1942 for World War II. After the war ended, I was in the reserves and was called to active duty for the Korean police action. Afterwards, I left the service and, in 1963, was called up due to the escalating problems in Vietnam. So you see I pretty much come into the Army just for the wars."

He probably meant this last comment as a joke, so I smiled even though it wasn't funny. He then pushed a button on his intercom and said, "Colonel, there's a young lieutenant here that's just been assigned to us. Shall I send him in?"

"By all means, Jim. Have him come in."

The major directed me to the colonel's office and I promptly left. Walking out of the secretary's office, I entered a large room with a conference table. Some twenty feet ahead was a large wooden desk that had a brass nameplate with the name Ollie R. Prince, First Sergeant, on it. Next to the desk was the door to the colonel's office. The door was open, so I looked in, and before I could say anything the colonel smiled and said, "Come in, lieutenant, and have a seat."

I smiled as confidently as I could as I introduced myself. We shook hands and I sat in the nearest chair.

The colonel was a stocky, middle-aged man with a crew cut. He was plain and ordinary looking; it was really difficult to pick out any prominent features about him. We talked for a minute, discussing the trivia about regular Army and Reserve commissions and advancing my military career. Then the colonel changed the subject.

"I think we'll make you the assistant Operations officer," he began. "Captain Tucker leaves in September, and then you'll take his place." At this point, the colonel settled back in his chair and, after staring blankly into space for a few seconds, rubbed his top lip and nose for a second.

He then began a fatherly talk with, "You'll find that as a second lieutenant you've got a lot to learn, but it will come quickly and it shouldn't take too long to get squared away. Most of the senior NCOs will probably look upon you as just another second lieutenant who doesn't know much until you show them differently. The thing to remember is that any swinging dick that even appears to be trying to show you up or make you look foolish must be shown his place—tactfully, of course. Then you should have no problems winning their respect and confidence."

The speech appeared to be one he'd been giving new lieutenants for years. He gave no examples of what constituted an NCO trying to show me up or make me look foolish. I also did not ask for any. I just tried to look attentive and interested in the colonel's speech, as he droned on for several minutes.

Afterward, the colonel pushed a button on the intercom. "Captain Tucker, I need to see you in my office."

"Okay, colonel. I'll be there in a bit."

A STATESIDE TOUR OF DUTY

"I need to see you now, Captain Tucker," the colonel said with added emphasis. "I believe your replacement has just been assigned to us."

"I'll be right there."

As we waited a few minutes for Captain Tucker to make his appearance, I mostly just enjoyed the colonel's air conditioner and made conversation. "What will be the nature of my duties, sir?"

"Captain Tucker will brief you on all that, lieutenant. There are numerous tasks that need continuous oversight, and I'm sure you'll have no trouble remaining busy."

"Yes, sir."

Within moments Captain Tucker appeared at the colonel's door. "Captain Tucker, take the lieutenant to in-processing," the colonel commanded.

"Yes, sir, colonel." Captain Tucker extended his hand to me. "Captain David Tucker," he said. "It's good to have you on the staff."

"How do you do, sir? I'm Lieutenant Nick Moultrie. It's good to be here."

"Lieutenant, Captain Tucker will see that you get taken care of and welcome again to Fort McCulloch," said the colonel.

"Thank you, sir." The colonel extended his hand, whereupon we shook hands again and the captain and I left the building.

Captain Tucker, I learned, had graduated from LSU in the ROTC. He had delayed his entry into active duty by attending law school at Duke University, and had begun active duty as a first lieutenant. Now, nearly two years later he was about to end his military career as a captain.

As we got acquainted, I added the following comment. "I was told at OCS that when I arrived here, I was supposed to salute somebody and say, 'Sir, Lieutenant Moultrie reports for duty.' I didn't get a chance to do that, so I'm guessing that this is a rather laid-back post."

Captain Tucker's countenance remained serious as he replied, "Yeah, we don't do a lot of that formal stuff here." He then went on to explain that the weekly poker game would be held at Sergeant Peterson's apartment on Wednesday at 2000 hours, the major was an idiot, and the colonel was okay if you learned how to handle him (he volunteered no details). He then let me know that he planned to spend most of the next two months at the golf course and that I would be taking over rapidly as Operations officer.

"Ah, Captain Tucker . . . ?" I interrupted.

"Yeah, what is it?"

"Well, since I didn't vol-indef, I was told that I would only be here for a very short time and then I would receive orders for Vietnam."

Captain Tucker looked at me. "Let me guess. Major Wilson at OPO told you that crap, right?" he said with a frown.

"Yes, sir."

"Let me tell you something. Those bastards at OPO lie like hell. Wilson told me that same bull when I didn't vol-indef, and I've been here for two years. The man I replaced, Lieutenant Whitman, had gotten the same story, and the man he replaced apparently also was told the same thing. The only way you're going to leave this post is to ETS or die. Those suckers who let Wilson scare 'em and voled-indef are going to Vietnam. Those of us who took our chances will stay stateside our entire two years."

Suddenly, for the first time since I had joined the Army, I had something to feel jubilant about. I would not have to experience the rice paddies, combat and jungles of Vietnam. Maybe Fort McCulloch wouldn't be so bad after all.

We then drove to in-processing where I gave one more copy of my orders to another clerk and received a list of places to go. The first stop was the hospital where I dropped off my medical records. We then proceeded to the dental clinic where I left my dental records and to the Finance office to ensure I was paid.

"This is the most important stop you will ever make when you arrive at a new post," Tucker commented.

"No doubt about that," I agreed as I handed my records to a Finance clerk. "Even if nothing else gets done, a man has got to be paid," I said with a smile.

We then stopped at the officers' club, where I had to fill out a short form and leave another copy of orders with a gal in what looked like a bank teller's cage. She wore thick glasses with very large frames and didn't seem particularly friendly. She gave me the cheerful news that club membership was required and would cost me nine dollars a month, whether I used the club or not.

From the club, there were several other stops. The last of these was AG files. This turned out to be an office located in the basement of the extreme right wing of post headquarters. It was about the size of a large broom closet and was located in the most obscure corner of the building.

We entered without knocking and I asked, "Is this the AG files listed on my in-processing sheet?"

"Yes, it is," a very attractive girl said from where she sat behind the desk. She continued, "All we need is your name and unit."

"I'm Lieutenant Moultrie, assigned to the 290th Military Police Company," I stated as the girl wrote down the information.

"What's this for?" Captain Tucker inquired.

"This is to place him on the post OD roster," said the girl.

"Then he'll be exempt from that, since he will be on the MP duty officer roster with the provost marshal's office," Captain Tucker explained.

The girl pushed her chair back and crumpled the paper. She instinctively crossed her legs as she looked toward the trashcan to throw the paper away. I couldn't help looking at her thighs where they appeared from under her short skirt. I didn't realize I was staring until she asked, "Is there anything else you need?"

With a touch of embarrassment, I said "no" and we left. I thought it was a shame that the girl we had just met couldn't trade places with the one in the officers' club. She should be meeting the public, with the girl in the officers' club hidden in the basement.

As we began to drive back to the PMO, it was Captain Tucker who spoke first. "With the amount of time you'll be serving as military police duty officer, you don't want to get stuck on the post duty officer roster as well. That would be a big mistake," he explained. "No one needs to serve double duty."

"I appreciate that. Now what about billeting arrangements? I need a place to stay tonight."

Captain Tucker began to laugh. "The billeting office is across the street from the back of post headquarters. They can assign you a room at the BOQ, but you don't want to stay there any longer than you have to. Around here we refer to that dump as Splinter Palace."

"Splinter Palace?" I questioned.

"When you see it, you won't debate the name. I suggest you go get a room for tonight and then come to the morning briefing at the conference room tomorrow at 0800 hours. You'll want to be there about thirty minutes early."

"That's the room up front by the colonel's office?"

"That's the one. Now go get a place to stay, and we'll see you in the morning."

"Thank you, sir. I'll see you then." I shook hands with Captain Tucker and proceeded to the post billeting office. After I had acquired a room and directions to the bachelor officers' quarters, I continued to that location and quickly learned how the BOQ got its sobriquet of "Splinter Palace." It was well deserved.

The bachelor officers' quarters were a group of one-story wooden structures. They were olive drab in color and had not been painted recently. The ends of the buildings facing the road were connected by a breezeway. As I walked inside, I had to pause for several seconds while my eyes adjusted to the dimly lit hallway. The hall was not carpeted. On a stand about midway down the passageway was a phone. My room, which was the first on the left, had all the usual furniture one might expect to find in the average motel room. There was a chest of drawers, easy chair, bed, lamp, desk, and a straight-back chair.

I threw my suitcase on the bed and opened one of the drawers of the desk. As I did, hundreds of small cockroaches scattered out of the drawer. To my horror and disgust, I discovered that the room's previous occupant had left candy in the desk and the roaches had gathered to it. A quick check of the room revealed that the insects infested the place.

I stepped out into the hallway and called the billeting office. After one ring someone answered, "Post billeting office, Specialist Johansen speaking, sir."

"Yes, this is Lieutenant Moultrie. I was just assigned room number one here of building three at the BOQ. This room is overrun with cockroaches."

The specialist sighed. "I'm sorry, sir, but the previous occupant was from Ethiopia."

"Ethiopia?"

"Yes, sir. About a hundred Ethiopian officers were here attending the communications school. I swear those people must have brought roaches over as pets. We've had a problem here ever since the first ones arrived."

"Do you have anything else available?" I asked.

"I'm sorry sir, but that was the last room we had. Besides, we've been getting complaints from all the buildings since those foreigners got here. I suggest a couple of cans of bug spray and not keeping any food in the room."

"All right. Thanks for the suggestion," I replied.

I quickly drove over to the PX, where I bought two cans of bug spray. Upon my return, I closed the windows. I then cleaned the room as best I could and sprayed every nook and cranny, including all drawers, until the cans of insecticide were empty. I then walked two blocks to the bowling alley. Here I bought a couple of hamburgers, bowled a couple of games, and passed the time as I waited for the room to be completely fumigated. After a couple of hours, I returned to sweep out the roaches and air out the room. I then took a long cold shower. That was the first thing all day that cut the oppressive west Texas heat. Afterward, as I lay on the bed, I paused to reflect on the day and wondered what lay in store for the future. Despite the overly warm room, sleep came rapidly.

The next morning, I arrived at the PMO at 0730 hours. Each morning began with a briefing of the colonel with his section heads and other supervisory personnel. Around the conference table sat the major, an investigator from the PMI section, a representative from CID, Mr. Bernard (warrant officers are called mister in the Army) of the Game and Wildlife (Ranger) section, myself, SP4 Carter of AWOL Apprehension, Staff Sergeant Porter (the desk sergeant for the previous night) and Captain Bills (the company commander). Captain Tucker was in the other room flirting with the secretaries.

After introductions and a little small talk, the colonel walked in at 0800 hours sharp. Everyone rose quickly, saluted, and said, "Morning, sir," in unison. The colonel returned the salute and took his place at the head of the table. Everyone had a copy of the blotter for the past twenty-four hours and had previously perused it. As the colonel scanned the blotter, he asked a few questions, made a few comments and at length said, "Looks like a routine night."

"Very routine, colonel," answered the major. "I wish they could all be this way."

The colonel then said, "What's the status of the two patrol cars that were red-lined for parts last week?"

"Captain Tucker is in charge of that," the major replied.

The colonel then called for Captain Tucker, who replied, "Just a minute sir," from the other room.

"Captain Tucker, could you come here, please?" the colonel repeated.

"Yeah, just a minute," was Tucker's reply.

"Captain Tucker, I have a question."

"I'll be there in a moment."

This exchange continued for several seconds with the colonel appearing to get a little exasperated before Tucker appeared in the door. He leaned nonchalantly against the door frame with a cup of coffee in his right hand.

"Yes, colonel, what can I do for you?" Tucker asked.

"I need the status of those red-lined vehicles and to know when they will be returned to line duty."

"No problem, sir. I'll call the motor pool first thing and get back to you on that." Tucker then immediately turned on his heel and returned to the attention of the secretaries.

The colonel had raised his hand in a pointing gesture that indicated he had a follow-up question, but as Tucker wheeled around and left the room he clearly saw the futility of asking anything else and changed the subject.

"Does anyone have anything else?" he asked.

Everyone around the table took turns saying, "No, sir," and the colonel said, "Well, let's go to work." We all stood and saluted the colonel.

As the meeting was breaking up and everyone was leaving the room, a large man entered by the side door. The colonel said, "Lieutenant, let me introduce you to our acting sergeant major. Sergeant Prince, this is Lieutenant Moultrie; lieutenant, Sergeant Prince."

The sergeant major was just returning from leave. He was about six foot four in height and I estimated about two hundred eighty pounds in weight. He was wearing a pair of bib overalls and a straw hat and apparently had been on a fishing or hunting trip. As we shook hands, he looked around and said with a smile, "The lieutenant is probably hoping this is the new duty uniform. If it is, he's going to like it here."

"You sure are right about that, Sergeant Major." I replied. "See if you can get the colonel to approve it." Everyone had a quick laugh, and we all departed for separate areas of the building.

Walking over to the company, I next met Lieutenant Byron E. Raymond. He was a Military Intelligence Officer attached to the company and was serving as Executive Officer.

I commented about the pile of paperwork in his In box and he began to talk in length about all the official duties he had. "I'm on orders for over fifty duties, Nick. It's good to have you here. Now you can take over some of them."

"No problem, Byron. I intend to pull my own weight around here. What are you working on right now?"

"I'm completing the ammo forecast for Battalion. Next, I have to complete the historical report and there are still the re-up interviews for all of the men who are reaching their ETS date."

A STATESIDE TOUR OF DUTY

The Army lexicon is filled (like any part of the government) with overly abundant numbers of acronyms and abbreviations. I had learned them quickly. For those unfamiliar with military language, however, ETS is short for estimated time of separation and is the date one leaves the Army.

"I better leave you to your work, then. I'm still getting oriented to the post."

"Well, why don't I show you around, Nick?"

"I wouldn't want to take you away from your work, Byron," I replied.

"No sweat. I need to take a break anyway. Come on, we'll take my car."

He continued to talk about how critical the company's function was in the post's important mission, but all the talk was clearly BS. He had no trouble leaving his "important" duties to give me an extended tour of the post. As we drove around, I almost wished I had a pair of hip waders to protect me from all the bullshit he continued to pour on. Despite his talk, I suspected that the whole organization was run in a slipshod manner.

Eventually, I found myself back in the PMO. As I walked in the back door, the MP desk was straight ahead. Operations was to my right; the break room and Traffic section were to my left. Moving through the dungeon-like detention cell area, I came to the front of the building. To the right were the main offices with the secretaries, the major, and the colonel. Moving down the hall to the left, I observed three small offices. Two were unoccupied, and the sign on the door of the third indicated that it was the Game and Wildlife Preservation and Enforcement section. This was usually referred to as the Ranger section. Personnel of this section were responsible for apprehending poachers, enforcing hunting regulations, and keeping moonshiners off the post. It was rare to find anyone in this office, as the men were usually out performing their duties.

Beyond that was the PMI (Provost Marshal's Investigators) section. This was a large office with four desks. One desk was for the NCO in charge, while other personnel used the others. Beyond this was vehicle registration. A warrant officer who supervised two SP4s ran it. All vehicles that had business on post had to be registered. To comply with regulations, I filled out the requisite form and received a numbered blue sticker for the front bumper of my car. The blue sticker identified me as an officer.

About thirty yards from the company headquarters was an area fenced with a chain link fence topped with razor wire with guard towers at each of four corners. The enclosure was about forty yards square and enclosed the AWOL Apprehension facility. From Fort McCulloch, a team went out to various points in Texas to collect AWOL soldiers each week. They were brought back to Fort McCulloch either to be sent back to their unit or processed for discharge. The bunkhouse at the center of the enclosure had room for about ninety AWOLs. Next to it was the office where all the paperwork was processed.

After my tour, during which I talked in length with various personnel, I found myself back in the PMO with one more hour to kill before I could leave for the day. At this point, I walked into Captain Tucker's office. "What are my official duties?" I asked.

The captain looked up and replied, "You have to look for work. It's all around."

"Well, sir, could you give me any ideas?"

The captain thought for a second and looked at the clock. It was 1555 hours. "How would you like to pull duty officer for me tonight?" he asked.

Knowing he was about to stick me with his task, I now regretted asking about official duties, but I couldn't think of an excuse to say no— after all, I did ask. There was nothing I could do but let him dump his duty officer responsibilities on me for the evening. However, the thought did occur to me that it might be good experience.

"No problem, sir. What do I have to do?"

"Well, for openers," began Tucker, "you conduct guard mount in about two minutes and again at midnight. Then you ride with the patrols for a couple of hours and keep informed by reading the blotter."

"Sounds easy enough."

"Good," said the captain. "Go conduct guard mount." His dismissive tone of voice was such that I felt he was really saying, "Get out of here and bother someone else." I decided that would be a great idea in the future.

I walked outside, where Staff Sergeant Harris was standing in front of his relief of nine men. He saluted and said, "Second relief ready for inspection, sir." I returned his salute and quickly inspected his men. We returned to our place in front of the formation and he asked, "Who is the best MP, sir?"

I looked quickly around and decided on an individual with highly shined boots. "SP4 South," I replied. I then went to the desk and read the blotter, which had nothing of real importance. It was all routine.

"Sergeant Harris."

A STATESIDE TOUR OF DUTY

"Yes, sir."

"Here's the phone number where I'm located at the BOQ. I'm going to leave to get some chow. Afterward, I'll be there if I'm needed before I return at 2100 hours. If I don't answer the phone, tell whoever does that I'm in room number one."

"No problem, sir. We'll see you tonight."

At 2100 hours, I returned to the MP station. I again scanned the blotter and began riding with the four vehicles patrolling the cantonment area. I felt this was important since I needed to gain knowledge of the area and of the men I would be working with. PFCs Smith and Miller were Unit 11 (pronounced "One One"), SP4s Bass and Jones were Unit One Zero (10), PFC Carter and SP4 South were Unit One Two (12), and Sergeant Wallace (the patrol supervisor) and PFC Jackson were Unit One. I spent time with each patrol as they cruised around the post and gave out a few tickets for such problems as running a stop sign and littering. At 2400 hours, I conducted guard mount for the third relief and then went back to Splinter Palace and went to bed.

What happened next would set the tone for the remainder of my time at Fort McCulloch, but the details were learned from subsequent investigations and interviews with others.

PFCs Miller and Smith had arrived at the MP station at 2330 hours. They parked their squad car and went inside to turn in their weapons and their patrol report. They walked into the break room and, while Miller completed the report, Smith walked over to the drink machine. He dropped a quarter into the machine and asked his partner, "What'll it be tonight?"

Miller looked up and replied, "Pepsi." He then added, "Take a look at this report, man."

Smith took the report as he handed Miller the can of soda. He read the report and said, "Man, you write some great fiction, baby. I wonder what the old man thinks when he reads this crap." They then walked out to the desk where Miller handed their .45 caliber pistols to sergeant Harris while Smith handed their patrol report and the three Form Letter Nines (traffic tickets) written during the shift to the desk clerk. When midnight arrived, they left the PMO for their barracks, where they changed clothes and prepared to go to the EM club. They arrived at the club at 0045 hours. Despite the hour, they still managed to meet two girls who accepted their offer for a ride home. At 0210 hours, the four of them were driving down Shelby Avenue toward the main gate in Smith's GTO.

As they stopped for a stop sign on Lombard Street, a black Firebird with two men sitting on the front seat pulled up beside them on the left. The man on the passenger's side of the car looked out his window and harassed Smith. "Hi, pig," he said. "I see you dudes don't have your guns and uniforms now."

Smith looked over at the man and said, "Are you looking for trouble, man?"

The retort came, "No, man. We'd just like to see if you can handle that fancy car. You see, my buddy here says you can't drive for jack shit. However, I say how about a race?" At that point both men stared at Smith.

Smith looked back with a sneer and said, "You isn't worth my time, punk."

The driver of the Firebird yelled, "I told you those Uncle Toms had feathers." His companion began to cluck and cackle like a chicken.

At this point, the girl on the back seat interrupted with, "Hey, you guys really MPs?"

Before either could answer, the passenger in the Firebird began to heckle again. "Really proud of their jobs, isn't they? They don't even tell the broads they're with who they are."

At this point, Miller could stand no more. "Come on Jack, let's take 'em," he encouraged.

One of the guys in the Firebird said, "Now you're talking."

The girl on the back seat said, "Well, Trudy, we're going to get some real excitement tonight."

The girl in the front seat wasn't so pleased and said so. "If you're going to race, I want out," she demanded.

The confusion ended with Smith yelling for everyone to shut up.

He then turned on his adversary and said, "All right, man—out the main gate and down the highway toward town. The first one past the Burger Baron wins and the other shuts up for good." The girl on the front seat buckled her seat belt as the Firebird roared off.

Reacting a split second later, Smith popped the clutch and was in hot pursuit. The Firebird took a quick thirty-five-yard lead, but Smith's GTO had made up the distance by the time they reached the main gate. The gate was not manned after 1700 hours, so there was no one there to witness the high-speed duel. They sped out the gate with the GTO now in the lead. Both cars swung wide into the oncoming lane of the two-lane road as they made the long turn toward town. Within a few more seconds, the speedometer needle was buried at one hundred twenty miles per hour and the GTO had a substantial lead.

"Hey, we're going to win this one easy, man," Miller jubilantly shouted from the back seat.

There was no more conversation forthcoming as Smith prepared to speed toward the Burger Baron. The road had a slight turn, which was long and could easily have been made at the high rate of speed. Miller and Smith would easily vanquish their competitor and were in high spirits. Suddenly, the left front tire blew out. The car began to yaw, with the rear spinning around despite Smith's futile attempts to keep control by steering in the direction of the skid. The hope that this was only a bad dream, which would soon be over, probably entered his mind. However, the last thing Smith would see would have quickly dashed the thought.

That was a large elm tree near the side of the road that the car slammed into broadside. As it did, the left rear door came open from the force of the collision and the girl sitting next to it began a terribly violent tumble down the highway. Her battered and broken body came to rest sixty-six feet from the point of impact.

CHAPTER TWO

$\mathbf{I}$ later learned that at 0311 hours, the boredom of a quiet early morning at the MP desk had been broken by the telephone ringing. Sergeant Porter answered it in his usual official manner.

"Military police desk, Sergeant Porter speaking, sir." He paused, as the party on the other end spoke and his countenance quickly became a frown. He continued, "Yes, sir. Yes, sir. Yes, we'll need their names. Wait a minute! Say that again! Were they in a red GTO? Oh, Lord, it's going to hit the fan now. Thanks for calling. We'll take it from here." Sergeant Porter then hung up the phone. His desk clerk, PFC Caldwell, had sat silently with a quizzical expression on his face. He had not been prepared for what followed.

"Warm up your typewriter Larry, I gotta call the duty officer. This could be a long night," said Porter, as he prepared to dial my number at the BOQ.

"What's happening, sarge? What's going on?"

"Smith and Miller were in an accident. Smith and some girl are dead. Miller's in the hospital in critical condition."

The clerk's mouth dropped open. "Are you putting me on?"

"No, but I sure wish I was."

The telephone ringing in the hall woke up someone in one of the rooms closer to it and a few moments later he was knocking on my door. I opened the door and a guy in boxer shorts and a T-shirt asked, "Your name Moultrie?"

"That's me," I replied as I rubbed my eyes.

He pointed over his shoulder with his thumb and said, "You're wanted on the phone."

"Lieutenant Moultrie," I identified myself into the phone with a yawn.

"Sir, this is Sergeant Porter at the desk. I have bad news."

A STATESIDE TOUR OF DUTY

"Go ahead, sarge. What is it?"

"Two of our men from the previous shift were in an accident. There are two fatalities (Smith and a civilian girlfriend), and Miller has been transported to the post hospital."

"Since I'm not sure where the hospital is, send a unit by to transport me there. I'll call you from there to get all the details. In the meantime, check the notification chart to find out who else needs to be contacted and informed. If they need me, tell them I'm at the hospital."

"Yes, sir. I'll have a car there in a few minutes."

"Good, sarge. I'll keep in touch."

At first, as I hung up the phone, I was still a little groggy from having just been awakened. However, I realized the seriousness of the situation and quickly dressed and waited for the squad car. It was there in a matter of minutes.

The notification chart also directed the desk sergeant to call the commanding officer of the military police company, which he did, and he then met me at the hospital at 0415 hours.

"Do you have any details on what happened?" The captain asked.

Fortunately, before the captain had arrived I had called the Harrisville Police Department (HPD) as well as the desk sergeant and been briefed by them both. "Just what I learned from HPD and Sergeant Porter, sir. Apparently, Smith and Miller were provoked into a drag race with another driver and crashed about three hundred yards inside the city limits. One of their girlfriends is dead and the other wore a seat belt and survived with only a few minor scratches and lacerations. HPD is questioning her now."

Captain Bills said nothing, but instead just shook his head and stared into the distance as we both sat on a couch in the hospital waiting room. After a minute, he said, "Those bastards! I'm going to make an example of Miller and ensure none of our other men ever do this again. It makes our entire unit look bad. Can you imagine the publicity we're going to get from this?"

"I'm sure the publicity will be bad; anything connected with the military usually is," I replied. The lack of concern for the victims of the accident bothered me. I thought the injuries received as a result of their careless conduct were sufficient punishment, but I said nothing more. Shortly thereafter, a doctor entered the room. There would be no further punishment of Miller. He had died in surgery at 0418 hours.

The captain and I talked for a few minutes, getting acquainted, and then he offered me a ride back to the BOQ. As he dropped me off at Splinter Palace, we shook hands and then he suggested I arrive about thirty minutes early for the morning briefing. As I entered the building, I thought about the last sixteen or seventeen hours and wondered if they might be some sort of omen of the remainder of my time at Fort McCulloch. I attempted to sleep for about two hours before I gave up. I got dressed, shaved, had some breakfast (and a lot of coffee) at the post cafeteria, then returned to work.

When I got to the PMO conference room, the usual attendees were already arriving. I grabbed another cup of coffee and prepared to meet the day. As we perused the blotter the main topic of conversation was the fatal traffic incident. Everyone seemed to have a comment on the subject along with expressing regrets about the deaths of our two men. At 0800 hours, the colonel walked in and we all rose and said "Morning, sir," somewhat in unison.

"Morning, men. Everyone be seated."

As the colonel sat down, the blond secretary brought him a cup of coffee. "Thank you, Susan. I need this today." He said with a smile.

"You're welcome, colonel."

He began reading the blotter and directed his first question to me without looking up. "Your first night as a duty officer got started with a real bang, I guess, lieutenant. You had a hell of a night."

"Yes, sir," I replied. "Two dead troops is more excitement than I'll ever need."

The colonel did not respond to my reply. Instead he directed his next comment to Captain Tucker. "You'll want to send off a Blue Bell report to Fifth Army this morning, Captain Tucker." Captain Tucker nodded. The colonel then looked up and directed his next question to no one in general. "Who's taking care of notifying the next of kin of the deceased?"

Captain Bills spoke up. "It's already been taken care of, sir. Casualty branch is notifying the relatives of Smith and Miller and HPD informed the parents of the dead girl."

The colonel began again. "With the bad publicity we'll be receiving from this, we'll have to be on our toes to avoid any further incidents. Captain Bills, you prepare a memo to the members of the unit stating that any actions which might bring discredit to the 290th Military Police Company specifically, and the U.S. Army in general, will not be tolerated in any way." He then turned to the major. "Jim, you prepare a press release for the *Trumpet* and any local papers that might be interested, stating this is not usual or tolerated conduct in our unit, and so forth. Bring it to me as soon as you get it written."

"Yes, colonel."

"Well, let's see if anyone has anything else that's pertinent before we get to work." The colonel then began to ask everyone individually. He looked first at Prince. "Sergeant major?" he asked.

"Yes, sir, colonel." Prince said. "Sergeant Warren called from Beaumont last night about the status of the investigators and physical security personnel there. I can fill you in later."

The colonel nodded. He then looked at Captain Tucker. "Captain Tucker?" he asked.

"Nothing, colonel." The colonel continued around the table asking everyone if they had anything further to add and everyone, in turn, shook their head and said either "Nothing, sir" or "No, sir." At that point the colonel said "Well, let's go to work," and stood up. Everyone rose and saluted. The colonel returned the salute and we all left the room for our work locations or home (in the case of Sergeant Porter).

Captain Tucker had me join him in his office where he pulled some military regulations out of the top right drawer of his desk. "Did they tell you anything about SIR, Blue Bell or Blue Bonnet reports at Fort Gordon?" he asked.

I could see that he was about to delegate some more of his work to me to make an early exit for the golf course, but I also knew there was nothing I could do about it. Besides, I knew that this was probably information I would need in the future. "This is the first time I've heard of them sir," I replied. "What are they?"

"Well, read this reg and look over some of these previously submitted reports and when you understand them, I'll have you write up one on last night's incident."

Anyone who has served in the military knows that the Army will run out of weapons, munitions and supplies long before it runs out of forms and paperwork. The Army has a report or a form for every possible event, incident, occasion, happening or episode. It was clear that I was about to receive my initiation to this part of my new occupation.

Most governmental regulations are written so that it takes a Philadelphia lawyer to understand them. After you finish studying them you usually say "What the hell did I just read?" To my surprise, this regulation was comparatively easy to read and understand. In the event of serious crimes or if any incident occurred that might cause the Army or the local post some embarrassment—a Serious Incident Report (SIR report) was submitted. If the incident involved a death or other extremely serious problem (spying, treason, breach of national security, etc.), the report submitted was a Blue Bell report. Training accidents involved a Blue Bonnet Report. When any of these problems occurred, the desk sergeant would send out a flash report to Fifth Army from the post message center. This report advised them that something had occurred that they wanted to know about and that it would be followed up later by one of the before-mentioned reports. If the soldier was the subject (perpetrator of a crime or the person causing the problem), the Army expected reports to be generated until the case was fully adjudicated. If, on the other hand, the soldier was the victim of a crime and the perpetrator was a civilian, an initial-terminal report was submitted, stating what had happened. A comment was placed in the report, stating that since the subject was a civilian, the Army had no further interest and no additional reports should be expected. That seemed crazy. If a soldier killed or robbed a civilian, everyone from Fifth Army to CONARC wanted to be informed on every aspect of the case. If, on the other hand, a soldier was killed or robbed by a civilian, the Army couldn't care less. Unfortunately, I didn't create the regulations; I just had to follow them.

After a few questions of Captain Tucker, I sat down with a copy of the blotter and began my report on the traffic accident of the night before. It ran as follows:

1. Fort McCulloch, Texas
2. 14 July 1970
3. Blue Bell-Initial
4. SMITH, Jack C., PFC, 290th MP Company, Ft. McCulloch, Texas. MILLER, Clarence P., PFC, 290th MP Company, Ft. McCulloch, Texas. ODOM, Sylvia C., Civilian. JEFFERSON, Trudy, Civilian.
5. Highway 117, 300 yards inside the city limits of Harrisville, Texas near Fort McCulloch.
6. At about 0200 hours, on the morning of the 13th the above listed persons were leaving the post when they were challenged to a race by two men in a black Firebird. After some discussion SMITH, who was driving, consented. Both cars raced out of the main gate toward Harrisville at a great rate of speed. About 300 yards within the city

limits, the subject's car was involved in a traffic accident as SMITH lost control of the vehicle and hit a tree. SMITH and ODOM were killed immediately and MILLER was removed to Fort McCulloch USAH where he later died as a result of his injuries. JEFFERSON suffered minor scratches and lacerations and was treated and released at Harrisville City Hospital.

7. Because of the nature of the case and position held by the military personnel involved, some unfavorable information may result about the military and the Military Police. This may continue for some time.
8. Classified information was not involved.
9. Oliver R. Cinch, BG, Commander, Fort McCulloch, Texas.

After finishing the report, I took a moment to proofread my work before taking it to the captain. I had already learned that all military paperwork, despite its boring and routine nature had a required form and style to adhere to. This was no exception. I had simply used the example shown in the regulation as a pattern and then had Captain Tucker look over the report.

"Looks good, lieutenant. You're definitely getting the hang of this," was his only comment.

"Thank you, sir. What do I do with it now?"

"Take it up front for the secretaries to type." He handed it back to me.

"Consider it done, sir." I then walked it up to the front office for the PMO secretaries to type and send to the message center.

The next day Captain Taylor handed me a training manual the Army was preparing to print. Before it was to go to press, the Army submitted it to line units around the country for comments and suggestions. I spent over six hours reading this boring piece of tripe and by 1600 hours had written five suggestions.

On four of these, I thought the manual could go into more detail. My last suggestion was that examples could be given to help the reader better understand what was to be expected. Captain Tucker liked the last suggestion. He then put it on a report which he submitted up the chain of command.

I quickly learned that this is how the Army worked. Thousands of lieutenants like me had to read the material and submit lots of suggestions that were culled down to a much smaller number by our immediate superiors. This was submitted to Army level (1st, 3rd, 4th, MACV, etc.,) where some colonel, or general, trimmed the suggestions still further and sent them on to CONARC. Forget fun, travel and adventure. The Army had paperwork and boring duties up the wazoo. I could have voled-indef and been sent to Hawaii, Presidio of California or Europe to do this stuff. Of course, had I done so, I would hope for the war to be over in the next three years. Instead, I was enjoying the hospitality and scenery of Fort McCulloch, Texas.

The next several days at Fort McCulloch were uneventful and were followed by a weekend that was the epitome of boredom, as I quickly became acclimatized to my new job. The following Wednesday, however, saw the arrival on post of a kindred spirit—one of the few people whom I could enjoy working with for the next two years.

CHAPTER THREE

That morning I met Steven J. Bronson, an ROTC graduate from the University of Texas. He had taken Officer's Basic at Fort Bragg and completed Military Intelligence Training at Fort Holabird, Maryland. Like me, he was now assigned to Fort McCulloch, where he was now qualified to do anything under the sun that the Army required him to accomplish. His orders had assigned him to Head and Head (Headquarters and Headquarters Company), but between there and in processing they weren't sure what to do with the new lieutenant. Finally, they decided that Military Intelligence sounded similar to Military Police and assigned him to the 290th Military Police company, where he would not be doing any James Bond-type work. He was about six foot one in height, one hundred and eighty pounds and, even with his short military haircut, he had movie star good looks.

I was introduced to him shortly after arriving at the PMO, where he had been designated as a second Assistant Operations Officer. After the morning briefing, I suggested that we drive over to the post snack bar for some coffee and to get acquainted. We compared notes about our ROTC and OCS experiences and I discovered that, like me, he had not voled-indef. The conversation quickly got around to the usual trivial items.

"By the way, where are you from?" I asked.

"San Antonio, right here in the great state of Texas," was the proud reply.

I looked at him and assumed the obvious. "You must have requested this place on your dream sheet then. How did you get them to send you here without voling-indefinite?"

He looked surprised. "Hell no, I didn't ask for this place. I never heard of it until I was assigned here. I requested Fort Sam Houston or Presidio of California. Besides, even if I had heard of this place, I still wouldn't have wanted to be sent here. Back where I'm from and have gone to school, a guy can get a good piece of tail just about any night. I haven't seen anybody worthwhile around here except for that girl in AG files."

"So you noticed her, too?" I smiled.

"You better believe I noticed her," he said with his eyes opening wide. "I almost got a hard-on when she crossed her legs to throw some paper into the trash can. With a great pair of legs and a short skirt, she was easy to look at." He then added, "The rest of her was pretty good, too."

"My reaction was the same as yours. When I was there, she pushed her chair back, crossed her legs to toss some paper away just like she did for you. Do you think she's telling us she needs a good lieutenant to prevent loneliness on Saturday nights?"

"I sure hope so," he said, as he finished his coffee. "Otherwise, if this place is as bad as it looks, I've got to find a way out of here—even if I have to volunteer for Vietnam." He paused a few seconds as if in a trance, then looked at me and then corrected himself. "Well, on second thought, I wouldn't do that; but I would sure think of something."

"We best be getting back," I said, polishing off my coffee.

"I agree," he answered. "No reason to make a bad impression on my first day here, no matter how badly I dislike it."

Upon our return to the PMO, Captain Tucker informed us that the weekly poker game would be held at his apartment, that night, instead of Sergeant Peterson's and extended us a formal invitation. "By the way, you guys aren't married—are you?" He questioned.

"No," we both said, almost in unison. I then added, "Why do you ask?"

"Oh, no reason in particular," he replied and turned and went back into his office.

Not wanting to appear like we had nothing to do (which was the case), we began to look through old copies of the blotter and military police reports, searching for interesting cases. At 1700 hours, we drove to Splinter Palace, where Steve had obtained a room down the hall from mine.

At 1900 hours, after grabbing a quick bite at the snack bar, we drove to Captain Tucker's apartment, in Harrisville, in my car. Those present for the game included Captain Tucker, First Lieutenant Thomas (his roommate), Staff Sergeant Peterson, myself, Steve and CW2 Bernard. Sergeant Peterson attempted a bit of humor with a comment about being the only working man among a bunch of bosses and added, "I hope you'll take it easy on me tonight. I'm just a poor working stiff."

"People who talk like that are usually the biggest card sharks around, sarge." I noted.

"Not me, sir," he answered, holding both of his hands up as if to dismiss the observation.

We cut cards for the first deal, and Mr. Bernard won. "The game is five card draw, jacks or better to open," he stated, as he shuffled the cards. "Each hand starts with a nickel ante, with a dollar limit on raises," he added.

As I had predicted, Sergeant Peterson was the big winner after two hours, with about ten dollars to his credit in winnings. About half of that had come from me, as my wallet was about five dollars lighter. The cards had not been good to me. At this time a neighbor knocked on the door asking for Thomas. It was a woman who appeared to be in her late twenties whose face did not go with her body. She had a large bust, of which a great deal of cleavage showed over a very low-cut sweater. She also had a Jayne Mansfield-like figure with a very small waist and excellent-shaped rear end. What distracted from her figure was her face, which looked like it belonged on a horse.

Thomas looked disgusted, but left the room with the woman. While he was gone, several of the players used the break in the action for a bathroom trip to expel some of the beer they had been consuming. Since I had learned that the imbibing of alcohol can seriously impair your ability to play poker, during my college years, I was having a soft drink. I used the intermission to obtain another can of soda. I concluded that it was a good thing that I wasn't drinking, since I was the biggest loser so far. I pondered a change in strategy. I would no longer bluff and only bet on very good hands. It is always embarrassing to be the biggest loser, even if the amount you lost, in dollars, is relatively small. I planned to change the result before the night ended.

Shortly thereafter, Thomas reentered the room and talked with Tucker. He seemed a little upset and together they seemed to be planning something. As they talked, they kept looking over at me and Steve. After a few minutes, the game began again. As Tucker shuffled the cards, he said, "Jamie has been asking us to fix her up with someone from the PMO." He enthusiastically added, "She's a great person and a lot of fun to be around." The next comment was clearly directed at me and Steve. "It would only take a minute to introduce you guys to her."

"Not interested in any way," Steve snarled, as he took a long swig on his can of Budweiser.

Partly because I felt that Steve had spoken for us both, and due to the fact that I thought there was more to this situation than met the eye, I added, "I came here to play cards, not get fixed up with broads. Maybe we can discuss this another day." I rolled my eyes with a frown and added, "Another day, yeah right." I didn't know what they had in mind, but I didn't like it one bit.

At 2330 hours, the game broke up and Steve and I walked out to my car. Peterson came over to talk to us. "I think you guys have a lot of class," he said. He was noticeably under the influence of the beer he had been drinking and was acting quite chummy.

"Why is that?" asked Bronson (who had downed a few too many himself).

"Welll! Peterson began, slurring his words. "I liked the way you turned down their friend. Mosst men, and that includes mosst officers, wouldn't be sooo choosy." He clearly placed emphasis on the words "most officers."

Since he seemed agreeable to answer the obvious, I asked, "What is the story on her? They were clearly trying to pass her off on us."

"Yes, they were," the sergeant laughed as he lit a cigarette. "You see, when they moved in here, she was already living upstairs. Her husband is in 'Nam and she is looking for something better. There isn't much to do here and she has nothing to look forward to when he returns because he is a loser anyway. It seems that she developed the hots for Captain Tucker and kept coming over wearing a housecoat, with nothing on underneath, to seduce him. She claimed she loved him and wanted to divorce her husband and marry Tucker. Tucker claims he would have nothing to do with her. However, Thomas got a little too lonely one night and laid her on the living room floor. Since then, she's been coming over here and harassing them both. So, they're looking for someone she can transfer her affection and attention to. They thought one or both of you might do."

"Low-class clowns,' remarked Bronson, about our fellow officers. "I can do better than that woman at a dog fight, back home."

"No kidding!' I said. "When women are that ugly, the devil himself wouldn't touch them."

A STATESIDE TOUR OF DUTY

"Thanks for the information, sarge," said Bronson.

"No problem, sir. I'll see you later."

"Later, sarge," I said as Peterson went to his car. "Do you believe this place?" I asked Steve.

"No. I don't, Nick." Steve lit a cigarette and said, "Let's get back to the BOQ. We still have to get to work in the morning."

We then returned to Splinter Palace in preparation for another exciting day at the PMO. The colonel's briefing was routine, as usual, the next morning, except for an unusually excessive number of grammatical and diction errors in the blotter. One entry, in particular, was interesting. On the second page, blotter entry number seven, entered at 0419 hours, read as follows:

> Received a phone call from an unidentified caller who stated there was a fire at the NCO Club. Unit 10 was dispatched to the scene and reported there was a negative fire. PMI Martin was notified of the crank call and investigation continues by that office.

The major looked up and asked, "What in the world is a negative fire?"

I answered, "At the risk of being facetious, it must be the opposite of a positive fire." I could see by the look on his face that the remark was not appreciated.

The colonel then looked at me and said, "Lieutenant, I believe we will make you the blotter officer. Each morning you need to red-line the blotter, and if any mistakes such as these are in it, you need to have the clerk retype it."

Why didn't I keep my big mouth shut? I thought. My whimsical remark had just earned me a new duty. "Yes, sir," I said confidently. Despite my acting like this was no big deal, I was thoroughly pissed off at myself. This could make me very unpopular with the clerks. I didn't even bother to point out that the call was a prank—not a crank.

The colonel then called for Tucker, who was in the other room flirting with the secretaries. He had to call several times before Tucker finally showed up at the door with his coffee cup in hand. "Yes, colonel? He asked.

"Has there been any further publicity about the drag race incident of the other night?" The colonel asked.

"No, sir," replied the captain. "I think it's all over."

"Good! Submit a final Blue Bell report to Fifth Army and terminate our interest in the accident."

"Okay, colonel, I'll have Lieutenant Moultrie send one in first thing this morning." Captain Tucker then returned to the other room. As usual, Captain Tucker's insubordinate conduct was obvious and the colonel made no attempt to reprimand him. That fact was interesting.

The major interjected a comment at this point. "I see that the patrol reports are improving. No more silly nonsense like this one."

He tossed a patrol report onto the table. It was the last one submitted by Miller before his death. It was written as follows:

> This is the city, Fort McCulloch, Texas. I was doing the night
> watch out of the PMO. The boss is Colonel Cox; the desk
> sergeant is Staff Sergeant Porter. My partner is PFC Smith,
> my names Miller. I carry a badge.

The report continued like an episode of Dragnet and made the routine traffic stops and the Form Letter Nines (traffic tickets) written during the shift sound like acts of heroism. Apparently, it greatly displeased the major, although I thought it showed a sense of humor and was quite creative. I was quickly learning, however, to keep such thoughts to myself.

Sergeant Prince spoke up next. "By the way, sir, Sergeant Warren will return from TDY tomorrow and will be prepared to brief you on his section." He then said to me and Steve, "You lieutenants will like Sergeant Warren. One thing's sure—you'll hear him a long time before you see him."

The major again changed the subject. What he had to say was the dumbest thing I had heard during the time I had been in the Army. "Colonel," he began, "I've been thinking that since we have sufficient personnel in the unit now, that we should organize a goon squad. Many of the units I've been assigned to in the past have had them. That way, when a disturbance occurs with units like the 55th Infantry or one of the Engineer Companies, we'd have a group that could go over and straighten them out. If we kick some butt or bust a few heads a few times, then troublesome units will stay in line and give us less trouble. Off hand, I'd say that a member of the goon squad should be about six foot three in height or more and weigh over 240 pounds. We have several men in the company that fit that description." The major finished his comments with a question. "What do you think?"

The colonel thought for a few moments and replied, "I don't know, Jack. Why don't we talk about it later?"

"Yes, colonel," replied the major.

After the customary formality of asking everyone if they had anything further and being told no, the colonel stood up and said, "Let's go to work." We all stood, saluted and left the room.

Steve and I spent the three and a half hours before lunch further familiarizing ourselves with the various sections of the PMO. Not knowing where we might be assigned or whom we might have to work with, a thorough knowledge of the overall organization was a necessity. We therefore began learning the essential mission each section performed in maintaining law and order at Fort McCulloch. Down the hall from the main area where the colonel, major, acting sergeant major Prince and the secretaries worked was the PMI (and Physical Security) section. The large room had a receptionist's desk where a PFC named Doak sat and typed reports and answered the phone. Behind him were three other desks shared by Sergeant Warren and his six investigators. They investigated all misdemeanors, as well as thefts of less than $50. PMI stood for Provost Marshal's Investigators. All felonies and thefts involving more than $50 were handled by the Criminal Investigations Division (CID), which was located several blocks away. Steve and I had no reason to observe their operations. While a representative of CID occasionally attended the morning briefing, we rarely saw them otherwise.

The physical security portion of the PMI section involved inspections of armories, arms rooms and other secure military installations in the areas of south and southwest Texas to determine if proper security was being maintained. From there we proceeded down the hall to the vehicle registration section. When I had previously registered my car, I had paid little attention to the details involved. Now that Steve was registering his car, he was asking questions.

To begin with, all cars with business on the post were required to be registered here, and they were kept track of in several books of computer printouts. These were updated every other month. Officers' vehicles received a blue sticker that was placed on the front left bumper. The lower the number of the sticker, the more important the owner of the car was (usually). For example, blue sticker number one belonged to the post commander. Sticker number two was assigned to his chief of staff and number three was reserved for the provost marshal. Sticker numbers four through four hundred ninety-nine were for field-grade officers (majors and colonels), and numbers five hundred and up were for company-grade officers like myself and Steve. Enlisted personnel received a red sticker, civilian worker's vehicles were marked with green and commercial vehicles, such as taxis, had a black sticker. I checked and discovered that blue sticker number 500 was not assigned. Since I desired to appear as important as possible, I immediately asked the clerk if I could change my sticker number from the one I had previously been issued.

"Wait a second," Steve jokingly protested. "Since I haven't registered my car yet, number 500 should belong to me."

"We'll have to settle this the way most disputes are settled in America," I replied.

"How do we do that when they haven't issued us any guns?" Steve said with a smile.

"Better than that, we'll flip for it," I replied. Each of us took a quarter from our pocket and flipped it into the air. "Call it," I said.

"Evens," he said. Since my quarter was heads and his was tails, sticker number 500 was mine. He got number 501.

We walked back through PMI to the corridor that led to the back of the building. Here we rang the buzzer over the heavy metal door that led to the detention cell. After someone on the desk had hit the release, we opened the door and closed it behind us. As previously mentioned, the D-cell as it was called looked more like a dungeon. It was constructed of heavy metal mesh, which rose from the concrete floor to a height of seven feet and was completely enclosed. The only openings, other than the thick steel door, were several small, square openings in the top to change light bulbs. The lights remained on at all times. There were several six-by-eight-inch openings in the concrete base that allowed water to drain out when the floor of the D-cell was washed (which did not appear to be often). The door of the D-cell was a large sliding metal door, which could only be opened from the MP desk. Behind the D-cell was a rest room facility for the use of the detainees (the official name of the prisoners held there). If one of them had to go, someone on the desk pushed a button to open the door. Only one detainee at a time was ever allowed to go back to the rest room. He was under surveillance from the desk between the rest room and the D-cell when the door was shut behind him upon his return. The D-cell contained seven cots and smelled like a body odor factory. At present there were two prisoners in residence.

Next to the MP desk was another door made of the same steel mesh as the D-cell. It, too, was controlled from the desk. As we approached, the desk clerk opened it and we entered the desk area. Along the right side of the room were two smaller rooms. The larger room was the home of the Traffic section. It had three desks that were used by four men. The walls were neatly covered with charts, a map and certificates. The charts showed statistical information such as how many accidents occurred each hour of the day, which units the personnel involved served with, etc. The map was a very large map of the post which indicated where accidents had occurred by being marked with colored pins. Those accidents that had only property damage were marked with black pins. Yellow pins indicated accidents with injuries, and fatalities would be indicated with red pins. There were, at present, no red pins in the map but there were about fifty yellow ones. The most impressive items, until you looked closer, were the certificates that documented that all members of the Traffic section were qualified and certified to use VASCAR. A close inspection of the documents revealed they were doctored copies which originally had someone else's name on them. I wondered just how qualified these men were to use the equipment if they had to falsify credentials. Sergeants Foster and Mount ran the Traffic section. Their associates were SP4s Gross and Cummings. They had two cars assigned to them. One was painted white with a safety insignia on each side and was called the White Mouse. The other was a standard olive drab vehicle like all the other military police cars.

Next to the Traffic office was the break room. The MP desk was about four and a half feet high and was enclosed so those entering the room saw only the head and shoulders of the desk sergeant and clerk. Around the immediate front of the desk, extending out about three feet, was a brass rail, which made the police desk look even more imposing. To the right of the desk was the Operations office where Captain Tucker, Sergeant Peterson and the clerks were located.

By far, the most interesting section was the AWOL Apprehension section. As I have previously mentioned, this was a confinement facility that consisted of two Quonset huts surrounded by a high chain-link fence topped with razor wire. At each of the four corners of the enclosure was a guard tower. One Quonset hut had forty-five bunk beds for prisoners confined there. The other had an office in the front where Sergeant

Lippmann and three clerks ran the section. The rear of the building contained shower and latrine facilities for those in confinement.

In addition to the sergeant and clerks, the section had three men who operated the vehicles that picked up AWOLs each week in what was locally known as the Lone Star Run. The three men, Staff Sergeant Collins and two SP4s, started each Monday on a three-day trip. From Fort McCulloch they traveled to Brownsville and Galveston, spending a night in each city. While they could pick up prisoners in intervening places, these were their primary destinations before returning to Fort McCulloch. During the trip, they picked up AWOL soldiers who were collected in civilian jails at various stops.

The federal government rewarded the local police with fifteen dollars for each AWOL they apprehended. There was an additional ten-dollar payment if he was fed and held overnight in the local jail. Needless to say, every lawbreaker was checked (by means of his fingerprints) to see if he was a deserter from the military service. After the civilian case was adjudicated, he was returned to the military. The local police department then received twenty-five dollars plus any additional reimbursement due if the cost of confining and feeding the prisoner exceeded ten dollars. (Time spent confined on the civilian charges were not reimbursable.)

Each week the AWOL run made the 1200-mile run to the various cities to collect the AWOL personnel. To facilitate the process, two teams of two men each were stationed at Galveston and Brownsville. They coordinated with the local police to locate and process AWOLs and each week the bus returned to Fort McCulloch with between thirty and fifty AWOL personnel. These men were then processed to be sent back to their old unit, or given a dishonorable discharge and released from the military at Fifth Army. A hundred years ago, deserters could be shot or branded with a C (for coward) on their face and AWOLs could be whipped. Now the worst punishment anyone received (unless there were other charges) was a dishonorable discharge. It is interesting how times change.

It was then that I met Sergeant Lippmann. He was a large man of about thirty-five who smoked cigars. He gave us a complete tour of his facility, and then we listened to him tell about the types of prisoners he had seen come and go. While listening, we had some coffee and doughnuts. One of the clerks had gone out and picked up a box of doughnuts, and when Steve and I offered to pay for the refreshments we were told not to worry about it. We ignored him, and each of us tossed fifteen cents into the section coffee kitty to help out with the next doughnut run. According to Lippmann, most of the prisoners were only wanted for being AWOL; however, about one in ten was addicted to hard drugs and about one in fifteen was dangerous. This last group were those who had been arrested for a serious felony before it was discovered that he was an AWOL soldier. Therefore, policy as well as common sense dictated that, while most were not hardened criminals, you still had to be very careful around them. It was not a good idea ever to turn your back on them, especially if no other trustworthy personnel were around. Finally, the three of us began to shoot the bull in general.

"What kind of cars do you men drive—if I may ask," the sergeant asked.

I didn't see the reason for his curiosity, but I answered, "I have a '68 Camaro. Why do you ask?" Before the sergeant replied, he looked at Steve.

"I've got a '70 Bonneville," said Steve with a shrug of his shoulders.

The large sergeant took a puff of his cigar and explained, "I put in a little part-time work down at Honest George's Car Lot in Harrisville. When you get ready for some new wheels, why don't you come down and take a look? We have a pretty good selection of low-mileage cars."

Steve spoke first. "I'm not planning to trade in my car soon. I don't think I'll be much help to your business." I figured Steve spoke for both of us, so I remained silent. The less said, the better, I thought.

"Well, if you change your mind, come on down. We'll make you a good deal," replied Lippmann.

Steve and I figured this was a good time to depart from AWOL App, and our tour of the military police facilities came to an end at the company. Here we learned from the company clerk that Sergeant Lippmann's first name was George. He was in fact Honest George—the owner of the used car lot he had told us about. The CO and the XO were not around, so we played a few games of Ping-Pong in the day room. The clerk, Sergeant Satterfield, was from New York and would soon be getting out of the Army. Like most soldiers, he described it as fifty-seven days and a wake up. He had little to say about the post (or the unit) that wasn't derogatory. Shortly thereafter Lieutenant Raymond arrived. For a new lieutenant, he had money coming in from some place. He drove up in a brand-new metallic blue corvette.

"Hi Byron," I began. "I like your car. Did you get it financed through the credit union?"

"Nope! I paid cash and traded in my old red Mustang. They gave me an excellent deal," he said proudly.

I hate to admit it, but a twinge of jealously went through me. Normally I couldn't care less what others have, because a lot of possessions usually mean a lot of debt. But a guy my age had just traded in a two-year-old Mustang for a brand-new Corvette and paid for the balance in cash. I said softly to myself, "Man, how would it be."

"Come into my office, and have a seat," Raymond said, motioning for us to enter. It was clear to me that he was wanting to look busy for our benefit. He continued talking as he started looking through a card file. "I've got to get ready for an inspection of our re-up records that's coming soon. As the re-up officer, it's my duty to make sure they're ready."

"How do you do that?" Steve asked.

Raymond began writing on the cards. "Every man has to have a re-up interview every three months in which I outline the benefits of the military and try to get him to reenlist for another hitch. Rather than go to all that trouble, I just write that they were interviewed and have them sign the cards. It's easier that way."

"How many do you get to re-up," I asked. With his lack of salesmanship, I wondered if he had any success.

"Less than one percent," he admitted. "These guys are just like us. They just want to serve their time and get out."

After we left Raymond's office, we were walking back to the PMO when Steve offered an observation. "Nick, I wouldn't want this to go any further, but I think that guy is completely full of shit. I don't care how much money he has."

I couldn't help but laugh. "That explains why his eyes are brown," I added.

"I was wondering if you felt the same way," Steve concluded.

Back at the PMO, Captain Tucker had me submit the final Blue Bell report on the traffic accident that occurred the night I had arrived. He had promised the colonel he would get it out that morning, but by the time it was typed and ready for the message center another exciting day of duty at Fort McCulloch had come to an end.

After work, Steve and I went looking for an apartment so we could move out of Splinter Palace. Between stops we got a bite to eat at a hamburger joint on the main highway. The manager, who was directing a couple of employees to sweep up, was a cute gal. I was trying to think of something cool to say to start a conversation when, in a flash, Steve had introduced himself and got her phone number. I had to admit that I wished that I could move that fast. I decided to act like it was no big deal and that I wasn't impressed. We continued looking for a new residence. The locations ranged from house trailers and houses to apartments of varying desirability. We went back to Splinter Palace to discuss the possibilities.

The next morning, I looked over the blotter. There were a few typewriter strikeovers, but nothing to get excited about. Therefore, I decided that the blotter was ready for dissemination. After they had produced ten copies with the Xerox machine, the original was filed and the copies were taken up front for the morning briefing.

By 0730 hours, everyone who generally attended the morning briefing was present except for Lieutenant Bronson. It was then I was to meet Sergeant Warren, whom I had heard so much about. To find that man at any given moment, one had only to follow the deep powerful voice (and numerous four-letter words) that emanated from him. Warren was about six feet tall, deeply tanned and rather distinguished looking. His dark hair was turning white around the temples and he wore civilian clothes instead of a uniform. He was a stylish dresser. The suit he wore probably cost no less than three hundred dollars. It obviously didn't come from Sears.

Despite the initial impulse to like the man, my instincts told me to keep my distance from him. I couldn't put my finger on why, but I had a nagging feeling that this was not someone I could trust. He had charisma and sociability to match any politician, but I was happy to be on the opposite side of the table from him. Sergeant Prince introduced me to him, and after shaking hands we sat down to await the colonel.

Not being sure just how to begin a conversation with Warren, I remained silent. George Elliot had once said, "Blessed is the man who, having nothing to say, abstains from giving us wordy evidence of that fact." That seemed like good advice at the moment. The silence didn't last long, however, as Sergeant Warren began speaking.

"Listen, Top," he said to Prince (first sergeants are often called "Top" by their subordinates as well as their superiors), "you better get the word out to some of our men that if they're going to smoke pot and lay these young whores, I'm going to bust every damned one of them." He paused to light a cigarette. "Last night, we had a raid planned for the apartment at 60 Parker lane. Then, my informant gave me a list of people he knew were there and—shit!" he hit his fist on the table as he paused, "the first five people on the list were MPs." He added several more expletives and said, "If they want to screw around—fine, but if they know we have a place under surveillance, they better stay the hell away." After a moment, he added, "Or else we'll bust them along with everyone else."

Top barely seemed concerned and not overly bothered by Sergeant Warren's information. He took another puff on his stogie and asked, "Who was on the list, Bob?"

"Oh, the colonel's driver Baker was one, two men off McCall's shift (Roberts and McCoy) and those two dumb asses back in vehicle registration."

Prince calmly took another puff on his cigar and stated, "Bob, the next time any of these jokers are involved—just bring them in. Hell, they shouldn't be MPs anyway. They've been screwed up since they've been here."

"Well, Top," Warren said, "I've got a case to work, so I better take off." Turning to me he said, "Nice to meet you, lieutenant." I raised my hand and nodded and answered, "Same here, sarge."

With the exit of Sergeant Warren, Top puffed complacently on his panatela. He started talking again. It seemed he was talking more to me than wanting mutual conversation. "You'll find, lieutenant, that we've got some good men here. A few of them, though, are just plain screwed up. Now, Warren, there's a hard worker. He don't always do things by the book, but he gets results." Prince continued his talk about Sergeant Warren and how I'd probably pick up the best procedural methods with time and experience. Such advice from the front office was becoming obnoxious and was beginning to irritate me, so I threw in an occasional, "yeah," or "I'm sure he's a good man," or some other trite phrase with false enthusiasm.

About 0758 hours the major entered the room. He sat down and stated reading the blotter. As soon as he did, the colonel walked in and we all stood up and greeted him. He told us to be seated and after he began reading the blotter, he looked up and asked, "Where is Captain Tucker?"

As I had been reading the blotter while being bored by Sergeant Prince's dialogue, I hadn't been aware of Tucker's absence, but a quick glance around the room showed he was not in attendance. However, it should have been obvious to all that he was where he always was at this time. As usual, Tucker was in the other room flirting with the secretaries. However, Mister Bernard answered, "He's in the other room, sir."

The colonel called for the captain, who replied that he would be there in a minute. The briefing continued with the usual routine, including the colonel constantly calling for Tucker. Finally, at length, Tucker appeared at the door with his coffee cup in his hand. "Yes, colonel," he asked.

"Check with Mr. Cooper at the TMP and see when the two red-lined cars will be ready to return to line duty," the colonel told him.

"Okay, colonel, I'll get right on it," Tucker said as he turned on his heels and left the room before the colonel could ask additional questions.

I wondered if everyone else was as curious as I was as to how Tucker got away with his insubordinate conduct. The silly thought occurred that maybe he had caught the colonel screwing some sheep and got pictures. Of course, I knew that certain thoughts had to be kept to myself.

The morning briefing soon broke up and I went back to Operations, where Steve was on the phone. I listened to his conversation for a minute. "Can't I get transferred anywhere, sir?" Steve asked. He continued, "But sir, you say you work with quotas—don't you make the quotas? Do you have his number, sir? Thank you, good bye."

As Steve hung up the phone he shook his head. "I don't believe those clowns. It's almost like they go out of their way to make it difficult for us." He seemed almost despondent and he sure had my curiosity piqued. I let him sit staring off into space for a few seconds before I asked the question that was on the tip of my tongue.

"Who were you talking to?"

"Oh, just those jerks up at OPO. I've been on the phone since just after 0700 trying to get out of here. Each one I talk to just refers me to someone else who tells me I'm stuck here for two years. They keep telling me that once someone is assigned to a post, that's it."

"Well, good luck with trying to find another duty assignment, but I figure this place is as good as anywhere else for me. I've seen more populated posts and the crime there is terrible. I figure that I'd just be a lot busier with paperwork at a place like that, so I'll stay right here." I then changed the subject. "We missed you at the briefing this morning."

"Yeah, I should have been there, I guess, but I wanted to catch those idiots at OPO before they left to play golf. Besides, I checked with Captain Tucker and he said he'd cover for me if the major or colonel asked where I was."

"What are we going to do to keep busy, today? I asked. We were told to look for work, but that is starting to take some creativity."

He sat for a few seconds thinking and then answered, "Why don't we go over to CID and check out their operations today?"

"That's not a bad idea," I agreed. "Sooner or later we'll probably have to work with them. We might as well get to know them. Let's hop in the Camel and head over there."

The "Camel" was the nickname given to the vehicle assigned to Operations. Its official designation was MP1 and it was just another olive drab staff car like all the others on post except for the condition it was in. It was reported to have over 300,000 miles on it (the odometer no longer worked). It would not go over 35 miles per hour and shook violently if you tried to make it do so. In addition, its radiator had to be refilled with water about every thirty minutes due to several leaks. As the car's condition made it unacceptable for police work, it had been assigned to Operations for routine errands.

We were about to leave the building to drive over to CID, when the intercom buzzed. The clerk that answered it called us back and informed us that we needed to see the major.

Upon arriving at the major's office, he informed us that there were several small streets in the cantonment area that were not shown on the official map of the post. As patrolmen, on line duty, sometimes had trouble finding these streets when they were dispatched, it would be our task to take a map and fill in the names of any streets not listed.

This job probably would not have taken more than about two hours, if we had hurried. However, with coffee breaks and an hour for lunch at the officers' club (which offered mediocre food at outrageous prices during lunch) we finished in just under six hours. At 1600 hours, we presented our work to the major. He had us replace the one framed on the MP desk with our finished product.

We spent the remainder of the time until 1700 hours figuring out how much the taxpayers had paid us for creating that map. As second lieutenants, we were paid about $425 a month (exclusive of quarters and subsistence). Considering we worked forty hours a week, the government paid us about forty dollars to accomplish a task any patrolman could have prepared in the normal course of his duty. I had the feeling that this type of waste and make-work projects might become commonplace over the next two years. I hoped, however, that it might not prove to be the case.

A STATESIDE TOUR OF DUTY

That evening, after getting something to eat, I retired to my room at Splinter Palace. I lay on the bed for some time contemplating Fort McCulloch, the future and life in general. Steve obviously had no problems meeting girls and apparently knew how to really get around. In college, I remembered a few times when a roommate said that he wanted to go out with a girl who would only go on the date if he could get a date for her friend. Every time I agreed to such a double date, I discovered that the friend of the beauty (the one the roommate went out with) looked like twenty miles of bad road after a war. I swore to never again do such a favor for a roommate, no matter how good a friend they were. I was determined never to be in that position again. Also, if Steve had a girlfriend over at any given time, I would have to find company also or face feeling like a spare tire. In addition, the loneliness of single life was beginning to wear on me. It would be nice to have someone to share my thoughts with and to make goals with. At the same time, I must admit that I'm not totally high minded and altruistic: a good sex life would help, too.

I then spent a couple of hours reflecting back on my college days, before sleep overcame me. I mostly thought about someone that the stress of the almost constant training had generally pushed out of my mind for the past year. That someone was Samantha Lyn Starr. She had a body to rival the girl in AG Files. She was also my former fiancée.

CHAPTER FOUR

As I reminisced, many thoughts went through my mind. What had happened to Sam in the year since I had broken up with her? Was she doing well? Had she found someone else? Did she resent or hate me? I only knew that not getting married immediately after college was the correct thing to do. To begin a marriage on an Army private's pay would have been a recipe for disaster. Too many newly married couples fight over finances, and we would have definitely been another one. Add in the fact that we would have been able to be together only a few weeks over the past year, and the stress could easily have ended a marriage before it had a chance to actually begin. Now that I was no longer in training, with a regular income, could Sam and I make a successful relationship if we reconnected? Sam was intelligent, very attractive and, while it sounds like a stereotype, she was very intuitive. She was an excellent judge of character. She could spot a phony from a mile away. Also, and I am somewhat embarrassed to admit this—she could be very good in bed. I wondered if I should try to reconnect. Well, I decided, it would not hurt to find out. The worst thing that could happen would be that I would be told to drop dead. I decided to call her the next day to find out. In high school I had often bragged that I would not get married before I was forty. I was beginning to see that that was not a very good idea.

I had never been a guy that got around a lot, and that was by choice. In high school, I had been too cheap to take girls out and spend money on them. Besides, too many guys I knew simply saw spending a lot of money on a girl as a way to make her feel obligated to put out later. I saw that as little better than a form of prostitution. A couple of my friends had gotten married when a doctor had told them they were in love (few couples lived together before marriage in the late '60s, where I was from). Others had been treated, at times, by the county health

A STATESIDE TOUR OF DUTY

department for a little keepsake received from an amorous night on the back seat of their car. Then there were the ones who bragged about using rubbers, only to discover that a condom did not protect them from crabs. A benefit from my lack of sexual experience was that I avoided a lot of embarrassing problems. In short, the girls I met whom I would have loved to fool around with wouldn't put out; and the sleazy ones I avoided for fear of getting the clap or something worse. Before I met Sam, in college, I had got to third base with a couple of girls but that was a far as any I was with would go.

It was also my misfortune that every girl that seemed ready to go to bed with me was broken-hearted from a prior relationship. Not wanting to take unfair advantage of them, I would sit and talk with them first. I told them how wonderful they were. I also told them that there were other fish in the sea and that they were better off without the jerk. I thought we might then head off to the bedroom, but no such luck. They thanked me for being so understanding. They now knew there were good men in the world. Their faith in humankind was restored and they didn't need to have sex to enjoy spending time with a guy. Every time I headed home, part of me felt good for raising their self-esteem while the rest of me was pissed off for not having scored.

In my sophomore year at Arizona State University I meet a girl named Gloria Richards. She presented me with an entirely new problem: falling in love. I had dated other girls, but they didn't make me feel the way I did when I was with Gloria. Gloria and I went bowling, watched TV and went to the movie theater on campus. However, even though just standing next to her raised my pulse and blood pressure ten points, I could never bring myself to tell her how I felt. Falling head over heels in love presented a problem for me. I had always imagined that I'd spend the next four decades traveling the country (and hopefully the globe), having adventures like the characters on the TV show *Route 66*. I would seek my fortune and see the world. For these reasons, I was determined to keep my relationship with Gloria casual. In the meantime, I respected her and kept her on the proverbial pedestal.

One night in March of 1967 I went over to her dorm apartment for a visit. She was in her bedroom typing a term paper. I knocked on the door and she told me to enter. We talked for a few minutes while I casually looked down the neckline of her shirt to admire her cleavage. After a short time, I placed my hand on her shoulder and mentioned that I should go so she could finish her homework, but she took my hand

and pulled me toward her to kiss her. My mind started racing. Should I kiss her and let my hand slip down to the part of her anatomy I had been trying to admire? If I fondled her I could get my face slapped and ruin the moment, or would she respond favorably to such conduct? On the other hand, if she felt like I did, a moment of passion could easily lead to a very serious relationship. We might even be engaged (or married) within the year. My future plans for fun and adventure could go down in flames. The question flashed like lightening in my mind: What should I do? What should I do? At the last moment, like a coward, I did nothing. I turned away. She whispered in my ear, "I love you Nick, I really do."

I looked into her eyes. I could clearly see that she did feel like I did. What should I do? What if she decided I was not a good kisser? That could ruin such a passionate moment. I hate to admit I had such self-doubts, but I had them. Finally, I chickened out again. I said, "We'll talk later," and left. I almost hated myself for not being decisive. For the next couple of days, I debated with myself what to do. When Saturday night came and my friends invited me to join them for a night on the town, I told them I had to study. They were surprised as that was unusual, but I needed to be alone to make a decision. I had my books open for the friends' benefit but I wasn't studying at all. Finally, I decided that this was a relationship that needed to be pursued. The next morning, I would call Gloria and see if I could join her for church (always an inexpensive way to spend time with a girl). Then, while walking home, that morning, I would tell her how I felt and give her the kiss she should have received the previous Tuesday.

When you have a minor in philosophy, you spend a lot of time considering the purpose of life. The purpose of life, I now decided, in addition to being a productive citizen, was to build a future with someone special and hope your children grew up to be a Gandhi, Edison or Abraham Lincoln who might change the world. Tomorrow I would give Gloria the commitment I had been so terrified of.

A feeling of elation surged through me. I could be decisive. I would no longer let a fear of commitment control me. Ecstatic over this newfound determination, I left my room to get a late-night snack. As I passed the room of Dennis Conklin, further down the hall, I noticed his door was open and his phone was ringing. I went in and answered it.

"Hello."

"Is Dennis there?" asked a very sexy voice on the other end.

"No, he's not," I replied.

"Are you his roommate?"

"No, Jeff is not here, either. Can I take a message?"

"No, no message," she said.

Before she could hang up I quickly interjected another thought. "Since they're not here, you can talk to me. I'm here."

She laughed. "Are you sure you want to talk to me? I could be a big, ugly, fat girl." I doubted that was the case. The girls I always saw Dennis with were drop-dead gorgeous.

"Well, if that's true, fat girls are fun to roll around on and we could always go to places where it was real dark." I explained.

"You're terrible. Do you always talk to girls like that?" She laughed.

"Only on Saturday night when I'm home all alone and lonesome."

"What is your name?" she asked.

"Norris Moultrie, but everybody calls me Nick. Shall I describe myself?"

"Sure," she answered. "What do you look like?"

"I am six foot four," I fibbed. (I'm really five foot nine.) "I have dark, wavy hair." It's actually blond and straight, but I then paused. I could almost imagine her drooling. I decided to give her something to really fantasize about after we ended the conversation. "My friends say I look like a combination of Bert Reynolds and a young Cary Grant, but they are just being kind. I don't think that is true at all. By the way, what is your name?"

"Karen Parker."

We continued to talk for over an hour, during which I told her where I was from, my major and lots of other small talk. Eventually we said good-bye and I hung up figuring that I would never hear from her again (that assumption couldn't have been more wrong).

The next morning I overslept and failed to call Gloria. About lunchtime I was awakened by the phone ringing. Church was long since over. "Hello," I said.

"Hi, my name is Sam Starr. My friend Jeri Lowe and I are friends of Karen Parker and we're downstairs. She said you sound like a nice guy and we should come talk to you."

"Well, you're in luck. I was just going over to the cafeteria to grab some lunch. I'll be right down. See you in a few minutes."

When I got downstairs, there were two girls standing by the lobby phone. One was a brunette with a hard look about her and the other was a blond in a short skirt with a world-class set of mammaries. I introduced myself. "Hello, I'm Nick Moultrie."

The blond spoke. "Karen is going to be very disappointed. She thought you were much taller with dark wavy hair," she said with a smile. "I'm Sam Starr and this is Jeri Lowe."

"I guess I did fudge a bit about my appearance," I admitted.

"I believe the correct words are fibbed a whole bunch," she said with a laugh.

"Well I am tall—to someone who's five foot two. All things are relative," I explained. As to hair color, I wasn't expecting anyone to check me out and just told her what I thought she wanted to hear.

We sat down on a couch and began to talk. As we did, I noticed that the blond also had a great pair of legs. After a few minutes, the brunette made a crude comment about some of the students on campus. Something about being just off the farm. I thought if the girl enjoyed a certain amount of crudeness, I might as well give her what she liked.

"You know," I began, "there was this farm boy who was late for school. When the teacher asked for the reason for his tardiness, he explained that he had to take their cow over to the neighbors to have her bred. The teacher got irritated and asked him, 'couldn't your father have done that instead?' The boy's reply was, 'I suppose he could, ma'am, but not near as good as that bull did.'" The Brunette roared with laughter, but the blond turned several shades of red. The brunette and I traded jokes for about twenty minutes. Apparently jokes that were blatantly sexual embarrassed Sam, and the brunette and I enjoyed observing Sam's reaction. I then mentioned that I had to go eat before they closed the cafeteria and told them that it was nice meeting them.

That night Karen called. Her first comment was, "My friends tell me that you lied about your appearance."

"Yes, I did. I figured that I would say what you wanted to hear and wasn't expecting anyone to check out the story." After some small talk the girl asked, "What did you think of my friends?"

"You really want the truth?"

"Yes, I really do. But don't worry, I'll keep your opinions to myself and not tell them what you said."

I did not believe that for a minute, knowing how girls love to share information. However, I told the truth. "Jeri was a little rough around the edges for my preferences, but I thought Sam was cute. Now, I haven't met you and I'm sure you're even better looking, but I can assure you that no guy is going to kick Sam out of bed on cold, dark night." I quickly added, "Or any other time for that matter," before pausing to get her reply.

The girl laughed, "The only way you'll get her into bed is to marry her. She knows that guys don't buy the cow if they get the milk for free."

"Well, if she ever decides to give out samples, tell her to let me know." Then I added, "I'm just kidding about that." In truth, I wasn't sure that I was kidding.

Eventually, she said, "I can't be angry with you for lying about your appearance. I lied too. I am Sam. Karen Parker is just a name I made up. Last Saturday, I just opened the phone book and closed my eyes and pointed to a name. I didn't have a date and my roommates were all gone, so I thought it might be good for a few laughs. I then called the number that I had just picked out. You answered the phone."

Given the irony of the situation, we both laughed for a bit. Then I said, "Want to go out for a pizza?"

"I'd really like that."

She gave me her address and I walked to her apartment, which was a few blocks off campus. We then went to the Left Banke Pizza parlor. It was a student hangout with candles stuck in wine bottles on all the tables. Patrons were welcome to write on the plastic table cloths and many other couples had left a written mention that they had been there. After eating the pizza, we returned to her place. As I walked her to the door I said, "Sam, I enjoyed tonight." I stuck out my hand to shake hands. She pulled me toward her and again my fear of commitment took over and I turned away.

She then grabbed my collar and pulled me close and said, "Don't turn away from me."

Her sudden show of aggression surprised me and I kissed her. She really planted one on me. She suggested we go inside and soon we were sitting on the couch watching television. We began kissing again and after her roommates went to bed we were quickly in a prone position. As I had not made any commitments with Gloria (or anyone else), a little necking with this girl did not seem out of order. So, I began rubbing her back under her shirt and quickly unhooked her brassiere. I then discovered that everything she had up front was real.

"I hope you're enjoying yourself," she said with a smile, "But that's it. That's as far as you go."

I tried to ignore her and slip my hand down the front of her blue jeans but found that to be an impossibility. She was wearing a girdle that was a half inch thick and three sizes too small. I couldn't have gotten my hand down there on a bet. I kissed her passionately and whispered, "You wouldn't consider taking that off, would you."

"Forget It! I'm not going to take a chance on becoming a parent."

"Apparently, you're not a girl who goes to bed on the first date," I observed. While I admired that fact, I wasn't going to let Sam know—at least, not yet.

"I don't go to bed on the second or third date, either," she informed me.

"Can I look forward to our fourth date then?"

"Keep this up and there won't be any more dates. Look Nick, I really like you and I'll let you feel me up. But, there is no way in hell that you're getting in my pants. Below the waist is off limits. Stay away from there." The tone of her voice left no doubt that I had better comply with her instructions. "I call that girdle my chastity belt," she added.

"I can see why." After that, I was careful to stay within the guidelines she set.

After I had spent three of the next four nights making out with Sam, I began to analyze the situation. Where I had no plans to include Sam in my future, it was wrong of me to use her as an object of passion. She was beginning to tell me that she loved me and it was not good that I was keeping her from finding a real soul mate. Also, anytime Gloria came into my mind I felt guilty. I didn't like that feeling. I walked to Sam's apartment and told her that we had to talk. When she invited me in, I declined. What I had to say was best said at the door. I explained that I was in love with Gloria and that it was best that we didn't see each other anymore. It was my plan to go to Gloria and let her know that I was ready to commit myself to her for a lifetime.

To my surprise, Sam said that she understood, but added, "At least kiss me good-bye, Nick." I was expecting a quick peck to say good bye, but it didn't work out that way. She threw her arms around me and gave me the full treatment—tongue and all. That kiss was so exciting that we were saying good-bye on her couch for the next three hours.

When I returned to the dorm, anyone who saw me started laughing. "We know what you've been doing," was their comment.

When I tried to convince them that I had been shooting pool in the student union all evening someone said, "Go look in the mirror and tell us you've been shooting pool." I did. The reflection told the tale. Sam had created a row of hickeys that were all the way around my neck. I was furious. I called Sam and demanded an explanation.

He explanation was simple and to the point. "Since I know about the other girl, I figured it was only fair that she should know about me. Now we'll see if she's willing to fight for you."

I tried to hide the passion marks on my neck with turtleneck sweaters and high collars but I didn't fool anyone. Guys gave me a friendly punch and said something like, "Way to go, tiger." Girls, on the other hand, usually rolled their eyes and said something like, "Looks like you've been a busy boy."

Gloria, especially, was not impressed. After that incident, she seemed quite cool toward me. I was heartbroken. I debated going to Gloria to try to explain things, but I was afraid she would tell me to drop dead. One of her roommates even told me she was planning to transfer to another school at the end of the school year. Afraid any chances with her were gone, I began spending time with Sam. She was delighted to provide me with a shoulder to cry on.

Unlike me, Sam was not a student. She worked as a waitress. Her mother had died when she was twelve and when her father couldn't keep the family together she had lived with other relatives for three years. Finally, at sixteen, the state placed her with a family that was headed up by a philandering husband. One night when he was unable to find any of his usual girlfriends available and his wife working a night shift, he turned his attention to Sam. After his children were upstairs asleep, he cornered her in the basement and brutally raped her. Sam got her revenge. She kept track of his activities and one night when he was bedding one of his many paramours and Sam was told to keep the children away for a few hours, she stopped by a pay phone. Sam called his wife and told her that the children were sick and insisted she should come home immediately. Sam had left the front door unlocked so when the wife arrived she wound up catching her husband in the middle of his favorite activity. The woman kicked her husband out and filed for divorce. Sam continued to live with her as an unpaid baby-sitter and general slave laborer.

After the breakup of her marriage, the woman went a little crazy. Her home became the scene of wild parties and a few of the older fellows that frequented them were quick to turn their interest to Sam. However, the trauma Sam had endured had left her with an aversion to sex. Still, there would be men that she would flirt with and otherwise show affection to as long as no major physical activity was involved.

The first proposed marriage, but Sam backed out at the last moment when they got to the altar. The second also began to talk about getting married. Unfortunately, the woman Sam was living with took a shine to this boyfriend and lured him away from Sam and into her own bed. Given a choice between this easy score and Sam's rigid standards, he chose the former.

Indignant, Sam moved back home with her father and his second wife. She endured constant fights with her stepmother until after her seventeenth birthday, when she got a job, an apartment and finished her high school education at night. Sam was a survivor. Now, at nineteen, she was my new girlfriend.

When a guy is a virgin and he finds out that his girlfriend is not it is very hard on his ego. Even when the circumstances were beyond the girl's control, that is little consolation to the young man. As much as he might say it doesn't bother him, it does. That summer, Sam and I wrote to each other as I contemplated my future. I also wrote to Gloria Richards, and she confirmed that she was transferring to the University of California at Santa Barbara. It appeared that Gloria was now a part of the past.

That September, upon the return to school, I dated Sam a few times, but we seemed to have opposite opinions on every subject. We fought constantly and quickly broke up.

The next spring, I ran into Sam at a party off campus. I offered her a ride home, and after arriving at her apartment we began to make out in the car. Sam told me that she had really missed me but then I ruined the evening. I had too many beers that night and the influence of alcohol allowed me to act completely contrary to my normal conduct. In an act of total male stupidity compounded by inebriation, I ran my hand down the front of Sam's slacks, which had only an elastic waist band. There was no girdle-type chastity belt in place tonight—only a pair of bikini panties. She protested and told me to stop, but I ignored her and sent my probing fingers down inside her underpants. She screamed at me and we both sat up.

In recent months, I had observed several individuals whose conduct I can only describe as reprehensible seem to have unlimited success with the ladies. Their explanation was that most girls preferred the bad boys and enjoyed being treated like garbage. I hated to admit it but there seemed to be some logic in their reasoning. Very often when I observed a gorgeous girl, she was with a total scumbag loser. Maybe the booze was encouraging me to act like those guys in hopes of more success in my love life. That's the only excuse I can give for what I said next. After all Sam was attractive.

"What's the matter?" I asked. "You only let your regular boyfriends have it, and not us regular guys." I can't believe I said anything so stupid and untrue, but I did. She slapped me. Her next words cut to the quick.

"I always thought you were good and decent and kind. Now I find that you're no different than all the other creeps that I have to fight off." Now she was sobbing and almost hysterical. "I thought I could trust you. Damn you! You're all alike. And my roommates wonder why I don't go out much anymore."

She got out of the car and ran to her apartment. I followed, trying to apologize but it was to no avail. I knocked on the door and asked to see Sam, but her roommates told me to go away. When I tried to explain how sorry I was, they told me it was a little too late and to just leave.

The next day I sent Sam a letter. I not only told her that I was truly sorry and that her actions were completely justified, but that I was a total jerk. She deserved someone who really honored and respected her and that she should never compromise her principles. I also told her that I would respect her wishes and not bother her again.

By the fall of my senior year, I was only looking forward to graduation. Like many students, I was a member of a fraternity. Our house on Greek Row was my address for the last two years in school. One afternoon several of us were throwing around a football when I saw someone walking down the sidewalk that I never expected to see again. It was Sam. I ran over to her.

"Hi, Sam," I said sheepishly. "Remember me?"

"Hi Nick, I've never forgotten you."

"Is that good or bad?" I questioned.

"That depends on you," she said with a solemn look on her face.

Then Geoff Coaltrain walked over to join us. He clearly wanted an introduction. "Samantha Starr, this is Geoff Coaltrain; Geoff, Sam Starr," I said.

"Nice to meet you, Geoff," Sam said as she smiled. Geoff nodded and shook her hand. "Well, guys, I have to go to work. See you later, Nick." She began to walk away.

As she left our presence, Geoff leaned over to me and asked, "If you don't mind my asking, is her pair of tits the real thing?"

"Yes, Geoff, they are real. And that's a fact."

"Is she someone special, or would it be okay if I asked her out?" Geoff asked.

Yes, Geoff, she is very special." My reply to Geoff was more for Sam's benefit than mine. Geoff was famous for not taking no for an answer when dealing with girls. Sam didn't need anyone like that chasing her, regardless of whether or not I had a future with her. Then I yelled, "Sam, wait up." I then ran to catch up with her.

"What brings you to this neck of the woods, Sam?" I asked.

"I just moved in down the street," she said. "I got a job at the state school working with the mentally handicapped kids. I moved over here to be closer to work."

"Wow," I relied. "That's a bummer. "How'd you get stuck in a job like that? I'd hate to have to work with retards."

Sam became noticeably angry. "They're not retards, Nick. They are just people who are not as fortunate as we are. Those kids are the sweetest and most innocent people I've ever seen. As you try to teach them, they try their best to please you and they never criticize. Besides, I got tired of waitressing. Getting my butt pinched and having guys pretend to accidentally rub up against my breasts got really old."

As always, I had to recover from foot in mouth disease. "I'm sorry, Sam. I really am. I didn't mean it the way it sounded. I guess I'm not used to being around less fortunate people. I think you're really special to help them and you'll do a great job." As we continued to walk, I added, "Look Sam, I'm sorry that I was such a total jackass the last time we were together."

"You're a guy, Nick. What more can I say? The problem was that you were the only guy at that party that I would have accepted a ride with. I trusted you. But, as bad as you're not wanting to take no for answer was, what you said was so much worse. I almost wanted to die."

"What I said was stupid and untrue. I really didn't feel that way. I could give a dozen dumb excuses for my behavior, but they'd be just excuses. What I did was wrong, and I am sorry. Will you ever forgive me?"

"I forgave you that night," she said.

"I appreciate that Sam." After a moment's hesitation, I added. "How is everything else going, Sam? I hope you're doing well."

"I'm doing fine. I like my job." She then added what sounded like an afterthought, "And I'm not seeing anyone."

A STATESIDE TOUR OF DUTY

I now had to part company with Sam, as she had to get to work. "Sam," I asked, "can I have your phone number?"

"Are you really going to call me?"

"Yes, I will." Sam told me her number and I wrote it down. I them turned around and returned home.

A little after five that afternoon I called Sam. She agreed to go out for a hamburger. Afterward, we drove back to her place, where we sat in my car talking. It was mostly small talk until I got brave enough to say what was on my mind. "I have missed you, Sam. I have been really ashamed and embarrassed about my conduct last year. I promise that will never happen again. I've learned that booze and I don't get along very well."

She smiled and said, "Now that you've said it, I can admit that I've missed you too." That broke the ice between us as she seemed more relaxed. She stated, "In a way it might be good thing that you acted the way you did last year."

"How's that?" I asked.

"If you hadn't tried to force yourself on me and have been more patient and just made out for a while, I probably would have gone all the way with you." She explained.

"You're kidding!"

"No, I'm not. Remember that we had both been drinking. I was completely in love with you and very lonely. Anyway, sex is all you hear about these days. I'm surprised they didn't call last summer another 'Summer of Love,'" she said with a snicker. "If you had taken your time and been patient, you probably would have had me for the asking. Afterward that thought scared me and I've been really careful not to let myself get carried away with anyone ever since."

"It's just as well," I said with a sigh. "With our luck, I would have knocked you up for sure."

"If you did, you would never have known," she replied.

"Why, not?" I didn't expect to hear that.

"There is no way I'd want you to feel trapped or forced to marry me. Those kinds of marriages never work out. If you found out after the baby was born and wanted to marry me—then that would be different. But it would have to be because you loved me and not because I had your baby." The conversation now seemed to be making Sam a little uncomfortable and she changed the subject. After a few moments, she asked, "What ever happened to Gloria?"

"She got married last June. I say good luck to her and I hope she always gets the best in life. I really do," I answered.

"Oh Nick, I'm sorry I put those hickeys on your neck. You could be married to her now."

I laughed. "No way, Sam. There is no way I'm ready for marriage, and there was no way she was going to put her life on hold until I was. I need to finish school first." I then added, "Besides, that is water under the bridge; and if there is any fault, it is not yours—it's mine. I never had the guts to tell her how I felt. Also, if she wanted me she wouldn't have transferred to that school in California. Like you once said. She wasn't willing to fight for me."

"Well, just the same, she'll never have the best; because she doesn't have you." She then added, "I sincerely mean that."

"Thanks, Sam. From now on, I'll try to deserve that praise." I walked Sam to her door and kissed her good night. Suddenly, we were a couple again.

They say that opposites attract. If that's true, there were few people more opposite than Sam and myself. 1968 was an election year and we couldn't even agree on that. She was a volunteer with the "Humphrey for President" campaign. While I considered myself a political independent, I had supported Nixon ever since Rockefeller had dropped out of the race. She expressed sympathy for the anti-war movement and disapproved of people owning guns. My father had trained me with firearms when I was in grade school and had taught me to handle them properly and respect them. With the world being the way it was, I tried to explain that sometimes there might be a need for self-defense. Using a gun could be the only way someone might be able to protect themselves or their family. My personal feelings on the anti-war movement essentially were that they were a bunch of traitors and not anti-war protestors at all.

We dated all that fall and the only thing we seemed to agree on was that it was fun to make out when no one else was around. We would sit on the couch in her apartment and mostly watch television when we weren't arguing about politics. After our "political discussions" we would spend some time necking. Sam usually seemed to prefer that I be judicious in the use of my roving hands (never below the waist) but she loved me to rub her back.

That first Tuesday in November, when it was time for us to cast our first ballots in an election (both of us being 21 years of age), I explained to Sam the importance of us not canceling out each other's votes. I told her the best way to vote in all the races and issues and she promptly cast her ballot in the opposite manner in every instance. She was very emphatic afterward when she said, "Never tell me what to do again."

Needless to say, we did not spend the election night together. She joined her friends down at the Humphrey headquarters, and I watched TV in the frat house. Most of my fraternity brothers were supporting Nixon, just like me. There were a couple of hard-core Democrats in our midst, however, and they remained silent as Nixon took a commanding lead. By 9:00 PM, however, the tide had turned with Humphrey holding a one million vote lead. Those few Democrats among us were jubilant while the rest of us sunk into gloom and most went to bed. I stayed up in the forlorn hope that things would turn around, and they did. The West came in overwhelmingly Republican and by 1:00 AM Nixon had a five thousand vote lead. At that point, expecting Nixon to be elected President, I called it a night. By the time of my morning classes, Nixon's lead was about a hundred thousand votes. Both he and Humphrey had about 43 percent of the vote. The best way to describe it was that Nixon's 43 percent was a little bit bigger than Humphrey's. About 9:00 AM, Illinois (the last state to declare) was in the Nixon column and Humphrey conceded. Election night was over.

At 1:00 PM, I got out of class and went and picked up Sam for lunch. I was careful not to gloat and talked about anything but the election. She brought it up. "I listened to Humphrey's concession speech and I respect him and still think he was the better candidate."

"That's all that counts, honey. I'm proud of you for sticking up for your convictions. I guess we don't always have to agree on everything." It is easy to be gracious and magnanimous when your side wins. Later, I slipped back into my tendency to preach. "Someday, Sam, when you are not so closely connected to these events and you can look back in a more impartial manner, consider some facts. One, before the presidential campaign, the Republican Party conducted Operation Eagle Eye. They went through the voter registration lists and got over three million fraudulent names eliminated in places like New York, Chicago and Saint Louis. In Saint Louis, alone, they wiped over a hundred thousand bogus names off the rolls, and Nixon only carried Missouri by five thousand votes. If those phony names had been cast by the Democratic machines across the country, Humphrey might have won by fraud. Second, the next time you go to an anti-war rally, look at the people there. They will be waving Viet Cong flags and cheering for Ho Chi Minh. They are not true anti-war protesters. They are cheering for the other side. True protesters would not take sides. They would be against war, period—not just our part in it. Those people are anti-American and traitors to our country—"

"Nice speech, Nick," she interrupted. "You sound like you should be running for office."

I could not tell from Sam's face if I had made my point or even if she was even listening. This was something I really felt passionate about, but I decided that discretion was the better part of valor. I would save my arguments for a time when they might be better utilized. "I'm sorry Sam. What do you say we both agree to not discuss politics anymore?"

"You have a deal. Now we'll see if you can stick to it." With no further discussion of politics, the next several weeks passed peacefully.

By the time Christmas had come, Sam's family had moved to Denver and my folks had moved overseas. Our roommates all went home for the holidays, so Sam and I would be able to spend the time by ourselves.

Sam had shared the secret of her past with the female psychologist at the school where she worked. She told me how the therapist was helping her to recover from the trauma of the past event. I thought that was excellent news. In addition, we had some discussions about how many children we might have if we got together, where we might live and what kind of careers we were planning to use to finance our future with. It was nice to be talking more and arguing less.

I asked Sam to marry me and we set the date for the next summer. Meanwhile, this would be our first Christmas together. We searched the jewelry stores and found a ring Sam liked and went Christmas shopping for each other. The parents of one of Sam's roommates lived locally and she invited Sam and me over for Christmas dinner. That night I dropped Sam off at her place and walked her to the door as we talked about the future. As we stepped inside for a good night kiss I casually remarked, "I really wish that I didn't have to go home tonight."

Her answer surprised me. "You don't have to. You could stay here with me. In fact, I want you to." She kissed me very passionately as if to reinforce what she had just said.

When a man is romantically attracted to a woman, no matter how much he tells the woman he admires her intelligence or abilities, sex is always on his mind. If he says otherwise, he is a liar. When she is unaware of it (and sometimes when she is) he is admiring the curves of her body. If she is wearing a pair of shorts or tight jeans, he will check out her crotch. I hate to admit it, but that is the way it is, and right now I was as horny as a stud bull in a breeding barn. Still, I had a slight hesitation. "I'd love that very much. But, the last thing I want to do is to knock you up."

Sam smiled a sly little smile. "I've been on the Pill for the last three months. My periods were irregular and the doctor prescribed the Pill to get them regulated." She kissed me again.

My pulse quickened and my heart started pounding. No guy, at a time like this, wants his feelings to appear too obvious. He wants to appear cool and nonchalant. Unfortunately, despite my best efforts, the huge bulge in my pants gave away my true feelings. If Sam was willing, I was all set to do the honors. Tonight, we were getting laid. I asked her, "You little stinker, why didn't you tell me this before?"

"And have you trying to get into my pants every night?" She explained. "Forget it! You're all hands as it is."

"Uh, then why are you telling me now, Sam? I asked.

"Because I love you, it's Christmas and I don't want to be alone. Besides that, for one of the few times in my life I'm horny as all get out and I really want to make love to you." She gave me another French kiss for emphasis.

"You're sure we'll have the place all to ourselves tonight?"

"I'm positive," she answered.

"Okay, I'll go lock the door."

"I'll be in my bedroom, turning back the covers," She said with a wink.

I locked the door as I got a glass of water and collected my thoughts for a few moments. This might be my first time but I was determined not to act like it. I considered as to how I might do that. I quickly decided that, contrary to my immediate desires, I would be slow and deliberate and allow Sam to let me know what she wanted and when. I would take my lead from her. I then went to Sam's bedroom, where she was turning back the covers wearing only her bra and panties.

"Looks like you're ready for action," I commented.

"Not quite, but I'm getting there," she replied.

She walked up to me and kissed me again. After a few minutes of caressing and kissing I removed what little she was still wearing as she helped my undress. As I unfastened my belt and unzipped my pants, she unbuttoned my shirt. In a few seconds, I was as au natural as she. I turned off the light. She took me by the hand and we walked over to her bed where she lay down and pulled me down to meet her. Christmas

1968 was a banner day (or night in this case). We made love three times before we fell asleep in each other's arms. The small single beds in all the student apartments might seem too small for two people, but it didn't seem crowded at all that night.

The next morning, it was Sam who woke up first. She woke me up by kissing me. She mentioned that she had admired me sleeping peacefully first. She then said. "I have to be at work by nine. That barely gives me time to get a shower and fix us some breakfast. If there's anything you would like to do first, you better hurry."

"I love you, Sam," I said.

She kissed me again and said, "I love you too, and I just ended five years of chastity to prove it."

"That was a great way to do it," I commented. I smiled and said, "I have an idea."

"What's that?" She said.

I began to roll over on my back while I gently pulled her on top of me. She seemed delighted with this change as I then gently rubbed my hands all over her body as she did most of the work. After our activities, Sam showered, fixed us some breakfast and I drove her to work.

As I dropped her off, she kissed me good bye. "Pick me up at lunch. In the meantime, if you're going to get a cushy job to support us in style, you need to make better grades. Go home and study."

"Yes dear," I said mockingly. However, I knew Sam was right. My grades stank.

About noon, I drove to the IGA store to pick up some hamburger and potato chips and a few fixings. Just before one I got to the place where Sam worked. I went inside where they were just finishing up lunch. I wished that I hadn't. The older students whom I guessed to be about twelve or thirteen were making such a mess with their food that it turned my stomach. Sam, on the other hand, had nothing but empathy for them.

"Nick," she said. "It's so sad. They are totally dependent on others. We have to make sure their lives are made as well off as possible and help them learn as much as they are capable of learning." I didn't tell Sam what my first impressions had been. In fact, I felt a little guilty for having those feelings.

A STATESIDE TOUR OF DUTY

We drove back to Sam's place where we had lunch. After we had eaten, I looked at my watch. "There's still thirty minutes before I have to get you back."

She smiled at me and gave me a wink. Nothing else needed to be said. We adjourned to her bedroom where there was more of what I'd call practice for the honeymoon. We were just able to conclude our activities and get her back to work by two. Before we left, she made up her bed just in case any of her roommates came home early.

That afternoon, I picked her up at five (by having her only work thirty-five hours a week the state could classify her as part-time and pay her less than she deserved). We drove to McDonald's, where I bought us some dinner and then we drove to the frat house, which tonight I had all to myself. I gave her a general tour, stopping, of course, at my room. She admired my ribbons won in speech contests in high school and the trophy I had won in intramural sports. She turned and kissed me. I undressed her and she got into my bed. "Tonight, we'll see if your bed is a comfortable as mine is," she said as she pulled the sheet up to her neck. I disrobed and hopped into bed with her.

By eight o'clock we had made love twice. "Do you realize we've done it seven times in about twenty-four hours?" I asked.

"I can't believe you're keeping count. But then you are a guy. I guess I should expect that." Then she inquired, "Where's the bathroom in this place?"

"There are several. The closest is two doors down on the right."

"I'll be back in a moment," she said as she left the room.

Some of our fraternity members were always complaining we were too mild-mannered of an organization, since we never had naked women running through our halls. While other frats participated in yard parties (a party where the member and his date have a yard of cloth between them with which to create costumes), panty raids or were rumored to be involved in beaching, I was proud of our brotherhood for showing more class. I yelled, "Hurry back, Sam. I have a Christmas gift for you."

She reappeared at the door. "I think that would be a gift more for you—than me."

I laughed. Not only because Sam knew what I had in mind, but the fact that on this day my girlfriend was running around this place in the buff and no one would ever know. There was no way I would ever want my lusty frat brothers looking at Sam. She was all mine.

"That's the dirtiest bathroom I've ever seen in my life," Sam said. "Don't you guys ever clean it?"

"It gets cleaned every fall during rush by the pledges. That way it's a job they don't soon forget."

"Yuck, you guys live like animals! It's a wonder you don't get a disease in there. I had to wipe my feet when I left."

I lifted the covers and said. "Get in here, honey, and I'll take your mind off our dirty bathroom." Sam got back into bed with me and began to kiss me. Just as she did, the phone rang. I answered it.

"Hello."

"Is Floyd there?" A woman asked.

"No, Floyd went home for the holidays. I don't expect him back until after New Year's," I answered.

"This is his mother. He went back to school because he thought he might be able to study better with everybody gone. We expected him to be there by now. Have him call home as soon as he gets there."

"I'll make sure he gets the message." As I hung up the phone I told Sam, "My roommate's due here any minute. We better get dressed,"

"Oh no, why is he coming back so soon?"

"The big dummy thinks he has to study. Trust him to ruin our fun. Quick, get your clothes on." I never thought I'd hear myself tell Sam that. We got dressed and made up the bed. As we finished, Floyd was driving up. I gave him the message to call home as we left the frat house.

Once we were in my car, we started laughing. Despite a close call, we had had a lot of fun with no one knowing a thing. Then I said, "I think it would have been funny as hell if he would have walked in on us while we were in some erotic position."

Sam stopped laughing. "Are you crazy? I would have died of embarrassment. I could have never set foot in that place again. In fact, I'd probably move to another city where nobody knew me."

"You're too sensitive, honey," I chided. "I think it would have been titillating and exciting to have someone catch us in the act. Don't you think it would have been an interesting experience?" I teased.

"Nick Moultrie, you are sick." Then with a smile she added, "If that's what you want, when my roommates get back we can give them a live demonstration. We could do it in front of them on the couch. Better yet, we could invite them to watch in my bedroom. If you want an audience, I'm sure they would love to watch."

A STATESIDE TOUR OF DUTY

"As much as I want to take advantage of your invitation," I said sarcastically, "I wouldn't want to add to your roommates' education and destroy their naiveté."

She laughed. "Naiveté is a trait my apartment is short on, Nick. I'm sure Janie, for one, could give us plenty of advice and constructive criticism to improve our technique."

"Well, in that case, during the demonstration, maybe she could fill in for a few moments and show me some positions I could use to please you later," I joked. Unfortunately, Sam did not see it as a joke and her countenance turned very angry.

"That's not funny, Nick." She backed away and angrily said, "Are you attracted to her?"

"No," I said emphatically.

"Then why would you even say something like that? How would you like me to joke about banging some other guy?"

This was turning ugly. "I'm sorry Sam. I'm sorry! I was making a joke. I don't have any thoughts about having sex with anyone else." I was very careful to say "anyone else" and not mention any specific names. I was quickly learning that there was a limit to the type of kidding Sam would allow. It took a little while, but Sam cooled off and accepted my apology.

When we got back to her apartment, we discovered that her roommate had returned. There would be no more spending the night together. After watching television for a while with her, I simply went home and went to bed alone. I cussed roommates that night more than anytime I could ever remember.

The next day was very stressful for Sam. One of the children she usually worked with had gone into the hospital before Christmas and Sam was told that she had passed away. The child had numerous health problems in addition to mental retardation and the death was not totally unexpected, but Sam was disconsolate. I tried to help by saying the child was better off now and she was in a better place, but to no avail. All Sam could talk about was how the child was only twelve years old and always had a smile on her face. Apparently, this was one of the kids that could always brighten up Sam's day.

Sam's roommate, Martha, had a date that night and we had the place to ourselves. By eight o'clock I was tired of talking about the deceased kid (or hearing Sam talk about her) and was hoping to get down to some serious love making like the previous two days. Sam let me know that she was not in the mood. I didn't understand how after the excitement of the past two days she could not want to continue. I would coax, urge, plead, encourage, verbally coerce, beg and otherwise strive to obtain more coital activity. Finally, Sam angrily told me to do whatever I wanted and lay back on the couch staring up at the ceiling. I assumed that once we were engaged in carnal pursuits, her demeanor would change and it would be like the prior two evenings. I was wrong. I hoisted her skirt up around her waist and quickly removed her pantyhose. As I went to unbutton her blouse, she slapped my hands away and told me to hurry and get what I needed and get it over with. Her action surprised me, but I still thought that once I got started she would respond like before. She didn't. As I unzipped my pants and lay down with her, she remained motionless until I was through. She then picked up her pantyhose and went into the bathroom without saying a word. A few seconds later I could hear her crying.

I knocked on the door, "Sam, what's wrong?" I called out.

"Just go away."

"Honey, please tell me what's wrong," I begged.

"Why? You don't care. You try to act like you do but you really don't give a damn," she screamed.

"I do care, honey. I love you. I do care about you and I want to make love to you,"

"You didn't make love. You screwed me! Believe it or not, Nick, there is a big difference."

I pondered her words for a minute. In the minds of most men, the difference would be nebulous at best. Descriptions such as making love, screwing or having sex (along with coarser and cruder synonyms) are used interchangeably by most of the world's males. Clearly, in Sam's mind there was a distinct difference. Right now, she probably saw me as no better than the loser who had molested her years before. I figured that I had better learn what that difference between screwing and making love was, and I had better learn it quickly, if our relationship was to survive. I chose my next words carefully.

"I'm sorry that I'm not more in tune with your feelings," I said. "Take as much time as you need. When you come out, we'll talk. Or, better yet, you'll talk and I'll listen. Once I understand, I won't make this mistake again. At least, I'll try not to." She didn't answer, so I returned to my place on the couch. While waiting, I turned on the television.

A STATESIDE TOUR OF DUTY

As I sat there, I thought back on the psychology class I had taken last semester. At one point the class had taught that men and women do not think alike. Men, I remembered, are compartmentalized in their thinking, where all facets of their lives are separate, while women see all things as interrelated. To them, all things are part of the integral unit of life. Then it hit me. If I were to experience a bad day, I would want to do something good to compensate. Sam, on the other hand, might figure that a bad day could not be salvaged and would simply want to move on to the next day that might be better. By pressuring her to have sex on what was definitely a lousy day, she could not see it as something good. I thought about that for a minute, and finally Sam came out of the bathroom and sat down next to me on the couch.

"You probably don't even know what you did wrong, do you?" Her arms were folded and she was looking straight ahead as she talked.

"Yes, I think I do." I then began to recite the psychology information that had been part of my thoughts in her absence.

She interrupted with, "No, Nick. That's not it. There was a time when I had guys telling me how much they were in love with me and how much they wanted to show it. But the only way they wanted to show it was by having sex. Their attitudes made sex the last thing in the world that I wanted to do. They couldn't just sit and talk or hold hands. It was like I was a sex object that they needed to possess. I didn't even feel like a person. After the past couple of months where we got to know each other, the last two nights with you were nice. I enjoyed the closeness. There was no pressure and I loved it. Tonight, you were as bad as those other jerks. Only it was worse because I care about you. It was just like that night when I was sixteen again."

"Sam, that doesn't make sense. I'm your fiancé, not some predator. It's different with me."

"No, Nick, it's not. I hated what you did. I know you care. If I thought you didn't and I had to expect more of this, I might hate you too."

"Why do you love me, Sam?"

"The day we met, I had a strong, almost overwhelming feeling that someday we would get married. I thought it was crazy, since you were totally different from anyone I had ever been attracted to. But, your sense of humor, easygoing manner and the fact that under your cynical veneer you really care about people won me over. Besides, when I took you to meet my folks, you read stories to my little brother and sister and were willing to play on the floor with them. I want to marry someone who's good with kids."

"I'll try not to do any more stupid behavior, Sam. I've not been involved in too many serious relationships, so I have a lot to learn. Please forgive me."

"Of course I forgive you, you big dummy." We hugged for a while, kissed a few times and I went home.

Over the next several weeks, Sam and I made love occasionally. I was careful not to pressure her and just make the most of the times she was in the mood. Also, Sam was determined that her roommates not know about our activities, so we were always discrete. While one of her roommates might spend time in their bedroom with a boyfriend, Sam would only entertain me there if we had the entire apartment to ourselves. An excellent example was New Year's Eve.

On that night, we went out with friends and partied until two. When we got back to her place I asked if I could spend the night on her couch (her roommate Martha had gone back home for the evening). After some hesitation, since she had to be to work by nine, she said yes. She gave me a blanket and I made myself comfortable on the couch. I lay there determined to show Sam that she could trust me. After about twenty minutes Sam came into the living room. I acted like I was asleep.

"I don't believe it. You really are going to sleep on the couch," she said as she shook me.

I acted as if I had just awakened. "That's the agreement we made," I yawned.

"What the heck. Why don't you come in with me where you'll be more comfortable?"

I crawled into bed with her and we began to make out. After some extensive kissing and light petting, I adroitly got down to business. We finished the wonderful sexual excitement about four. Afterward, she said the following to say.

"I meant for us to just make out for a bit and go to sleep. I'm not going to get any sleep unless you get back on the couch. I need to be to work by nine."

"No problem, sweetie, I understand." I kissed her good night and returned to the couch. I slept well with a big smile on my face.

With my determination to make some better grades requiring the need to study, coupled with being surrounded by roommates most of the time, it was easier to keep from fooling around. Still, a couple of times a month or so we could have a good time. On some of these occasions Sam could get hotter than a branding iron at roundup time. It could happen at the oddest of times. There was no rhyme or reason to Sam's moods.

During January, we were at the drive-in, watching a double feature. The first movie was a foreign film called *A Man and a Woman*. Gloria Richards had recommended it to me before she got married as a movie you should see with someone you love. Both Gloria and I had different tastes, or the version we were seeing was severely edited. It was the most boring movie I had ever seen.

"I was hoping there would be some sex scenes in this movie to turn you on," I said with a smile.

"If there were, they would probably have the opposite effect," she said sternly.

"My frat brothers tell me that sex scenes turn their girlfriends on, and they often wind up doing it in the car. Why would it have the opposite effect on you?"

"In other words, your friends are such lousy lovers that their girlfriends need a movie to turn them on? How sad."

We said little else until well into the second feature. It was a John Wayne film called *The Green Berets*. It was a film full of technical errors and lousy acting.

I had just been sitting there with my arm around Sam, noting how disappointed I was with the movie (especially one with John Wayne), when I said, "I'm probably the only guy on campus that's never done it at the drive in."

"It's not that big of a deal, Nick"

"Is that the voice of experience talking?" I asked.

"Are you kidding? I have enough inhibitions at home in bed. The guy I almost married wanted to do it at a drive-in, but I told him we would have to get married first."

"How come you didn't get married to him?"

"When we arrived in Vegas and went to the wedding chapel, I had this thought in my head that I shouldn't marry him. He was mad as hell, but I stuck to my guns and said no." She paused for a moment. "About a year ago I found out that he went to prison for child molestation. If I had married him, he probably would have molested our kids." Sam's intuitive nature amazed me. Maybe that was one of the things that attracted me to her. She was rarely wrong about anyone.

We sat there silently for a while, when Sam gave me a French kiss. I don't know if she was bored with the movie or what, but suddenly it was okay for me to have roving hands. We lay down on the front seat. "Do you really want to do it at a drive-in, Nick?" She asked.

"Well, yeah. But, we ought to move the car back row or make sure there's no one on either side of us."

"That would just draw attention to us. Besides, the other patrons are probably watching the show or doing their own thing," Sam explained. "Anyway, thanks to the cold weather, we have a blanket with us. People would have to be real nosey to see anything."

Sam was right. With the recent cold snap, we had brought a blanket, and it was now put to good use. Hopefully, our activities didn't fog up the windows too much, but we concluded our business just in time to see the sun set in the east in the movie's final scene. We had seen most of two lousy movies but, in our case, we agreed a good time had been indulged in.

As the end of April approached, I was studying for finals. With the amount of study time that entailed, it seemed to cause Sam and me to argue more. There was a three day stretch where we didn't see each other (we did phone each other), and when I dropped by her apartment on the third evening Sam was not home. Her roommate was evasive about Sam's whereabouts. That bothered me. When I called at about ten, a roommate said Sam was in the shower. I drove over and knocked on her door. The roommate that answered it had to admit that Sam was not there. (It was obvious that the previous roommate that I talked to on the phone had lied.) Now I was pissed. I went and sat in my car in the parking lot. The longer I sat there the angrier I became. Finally, at 11:14 (per my watch) a car pulled into the lot with Sam in it. She was escorted to the door by someone I had never met. She kissed him at the door. I jumped out of the car and yelled, "Your cheater. Damn you, we're through! You can keep the ring. I never want to see you again!" I jumped into my car and drove out of the parking lot as fast as I could.

I refused to take any calls from Sam and avoided her until my graduation in early May. Shortly afterward, I left for the Army. So, after Fort Leonard Wood, Fort Meade, Fort Belvoir and Fort Gordon, Georgia, where I had four weeks of Military Police Officers' Orientation, I was now at Fort McCulloch.

As I lay on my bunk in the BOQ, the song "By the Time I get to Phoenix" was playing on the radio. Unlike Glen Campbell's traveler who was passing through, my thoughts were now centered there. I should have allowed Sam to offer an explanation. Whether or not I would have accepted it is another question. I was pretty steamed. Those who took her calls that I had ignored said she sounded very contrite and was crying. Maybe I should have talked to her. I decided to call her. The worst that could happen would be her telling me to go to hell. Where she was hundreds of miles away there could be no real harm.

I drove to the PX, where I got several dollars of coins and headed to a pay phone. I dialed Sam's old number, hoping it had not been changed. Sure enough, Sam answered the phone.

"Sam, is that you?"

"It's good to hear from you, Nick. The second the phone rang, I had a feeling it was you. Where are you?"

Before answering, the thought hit me that she probably did have such a feeling. That was her intuitive nature. "I'm a military police lieutenant at Camp McCulloch Texas."

"Congratulations. How have you been?"

"I've been fine. How are you?"

"Lonely. Other than that, I'm okay."

"Sam, I'm sorry I never listened to your explanation about the night I broke up with you."

Sam heaved a sigh and said, "Would it make any difference now?"

"Yes, it would," I replied.

Sam sighed again. "My old boyfriend came into town trying to reconnect. I decided to see if there were any feelings to reconnect with. After all, if we were going to be married the rest of our lives—I wanted to ensure that I knew you were truly the one I wanted." She hesitated and added, "And I discovered that you are. After I kissed him I knew I had no future with him. I still love you, Nick."

That was what I wanted to hear. "Sam, if I came back to Tempe— would you see me?"

"Do you still love me, Nick?

"Yes, I still love you," I replied.

"Then I'll see you."

I told her I would get a few days' leave and call her when I got to Luke Air Force Base. The quarters I had on hand didn't seem to buy much time, so we were saying good-bye before I knew it. As I hung up the phone, I decided that it was time to do what I had originally planned to do the year before.

The next morning, I went over to the company area. I went into the barracks and found Sergeant Satterfield's room. I knocked on the door.

"Come in."

"Sarge, I need a favor."

"What's up sir? What can I do for you?"

"Look, sarge, I know it's Saturday, but how quick could you type me out a three-day pass and orders for three days' leave?"

"It would just take a few minutes, sir."

"I'd need to get the CO's signature on them before he goes to play golf at eleven. Can you do it?"

"No problem, sir. This must be really important."

"It is, sarge. I may be crazy, but I'm going to Phoenix to ask a young lady to marry me."

Sergeant Satterfield laughed. "This place can make you go crazy. But usually not this fast or this badly. Be careful, sir, or they might come after you with a straitjacket."

"They probably will, sarge. But before they do, I really need that paperwork."

We walked over to the office, where he typed out the three-day pass and orders for three days' leave. It only took a few minutes. When he was finished, he handed me the documents and said, "Here you go, sir. But I still say you're either a little crazy or awful horny to do this on the spur of the moment."

"The truth be known, sarge, there might be a little of both; however, I do love her. Thanks." I shook his hand and added, "I owe you one."

"Not a problem, sir."

I went over to Captain Bill's quarters and explained what I was going to do and he signed the leave papers. "Good luck Moultrie," he said. "We'll see you Friday."

"Thank you, sir, I'll see you then."

In order to complete my plans, I coordinated with Steve. He agreed to sign me in from the three-day pass and out on leave on Tuesday. I then signed out on the pass and went back to the billets to pack a small suitcase. I then drove as fast as I could to Laughlin Air Force Base, which is near Del Rio, Texas. From there I caught a military hop (free flight) to Luke Air Force Base, outside of Phoenix. When I arrived at Luke, the last shuttle bus had already left, but one of the personnel getting off work gave me a ride downtown and dropped me off at the Trailways station.

A STATESIDE TOUR OF DUTY

I called Sam, and it was a little past seven when she picked me up in her roommate's car.

"I can't believe you're really here," she said. Then before pulling back into traffic she asked, "Why are you here?"

"Can we talk while we eat? I haven't had a bite to eat all day." I hated to put Sam off, but what I was planning needed for me to work up a little more courage.

"How have you really been, Sam? Are you sure everything's well?"

"I cried a lot and decided I was over you, until you called. Now I have all of those feelings back."

That was all I needed to hear. I had her pull into the next fast-food place we passed. We went inside and I ordered us something to eat. We sat in a little booth on opposite sides of the table. I asked, "Do you still have that engagement ring I once gave you?"

She smiled, "Why? Do you want it back?" There seemed to be some hesitation in her voice.

"No, I thought I'd see if you still want to use it."

"What are you saying, Nick?"

"I'm saying that if you still want me—we can get married now. We can go back to Camp McCulloch and have a military wedding in the post chapel or we can get married here. Whichever you want."

She sat stunned for a minute. "Wedding proposals are supposed to be delivered on a bent knee, Nick."

I suppose Sam wanted witnesses. I didn't mind that, now that she knew my intentions. I put down my hamburger and got up from the table. I stepped over to where she was, knelt down on one knee and took her right hand. Then with her totally embarrassed and me wearing my military uniform, I spoke in a loud voice. "Samantha Lyn Starr, will you do me the honor of being my wife, having my children, warming my bed and letting me worship you—not necessarily in that order." There was total silence as the other patrons turned and stared.

Sam regained her composure and said, "Yes. Yes I will. Now get up from there and let's get out of here." As I gave her a quick kiss, suddenly there was applause from all the other customers. I bowed in mock appreciation. I sat back down and said, "First, let's finish our dinner."

There were several comments from other people sitting around us. One man jokingly surmised, "That guy probably has orders for 'Nam and wants to get a little before he goes."

I put my hand on Sam's and said, "Ignore him. I don't have orders for Vietnam. I'll be stateside for the next two years." Sam seemed to be relieved.

When we left the restaurant and got into the car, Sam gave me the kind of kiss you usually only see in the movies. She then said, "Norris James Moultrie, you're not playing some game—are you? I won't stand to have my heart broken again."

"No, Sam. This time it is for real." I then explained that if we had been married the previous year we would have been dirt poor and separated for all but a few days out of the year.

"I think I could have handled it," Sam said.

"I'm sure you could, but with what I'm making now, I can really support you in a decent manner." I changed the subject. "Well, where and when do you want to have the ceremony?"

"I want to get married here, so my family and friends can be there. I would also like a reception, but my father's business is not doing too well now. I know he can't afford everything."

I took out my wallet and handed her a credit card. "Ask him to pay for what he can and use this for the rest. If we find a printer who can put out announcements in one day do you think we could set the date for, say, three weeks?"

"Yes, we can and we will. You're not going to back out again, are you?" She asked that last question with a little less confidence.

"With you holding my credit card? I don't think so."

"Where are you going to stay tonight?"

"One of the guest rooms at the frat house. Don't worry, I won't ask to sleep on your couch."

As we looked at each other, I could see that the old feelings were still there. We drove to her apartment to begin making plans.

On Monday, we found a printer that offered twenty-four-hour service and prepared a list of friends and relatives. We rented a reception hall and made arrangements for refreshments and a cake. Finally, Sam lined up some friends to serve them. Everything proceeded at a furious pace and then early Thursday morning I had Sam give me a ride back to Luke Air Force Base. Not knowing the availability of flights back to Laughlin, I figured I had better give myself plenty of time for the return trip.

As Sam dropped me off at the terminal, she kissed me and said, "I can't believe it. This time we're really going to get married."

"Oh," I said, thinking of one last thing. "On our list of people to invite, I'd like for you to add Gloria Richards to the list."

"WHY?"

"She sent me an invitation to her wedding and I felt a little like she was rubbing my nose in the fact that she didn't need me and had found someone else. Part of me wants to do the same to her. Another part of me feels bad that I never at least wrote back and wished her good luck. Anyway, why not let her know you won after all? The alumni association will have her folks' address on file. Just send it to them and they can forward it."

"All right, I can do that," she said after a moment's hesitation. The fact that Sam agreed let me know that she knew she had won and that Gloria was no longer a threat. But then she grabbed my collar like no other time since our first date. "You just get your butt back here by August 21st. So help me, if you don't show up, I'm going to hunt you down with a gun. Now, have a nice trip back to Texas." We held each other for a long time as if we were reluctant to say goodbye. However, we had no choice. Not knowing what else to say, we kissed and said farewell.

I had very good luck getting a flight back to Laughlin, and at 1930 hours I signed in at the company orderly room, one day ahead of schedule.

When I got back to Splinter Palace, I went to Steve's room to tell him he was going to have to find a new prospective roommate. With my new plans with Sam, my future was now set and I could look forward to it with newfound optimism. Meanwhile, in my absence, another military intelligence officer had arrived on post, Monday. His name was Charley Connerly.

CHAPTER FIVE

As I met with Steve, there was a slightly heavyset lieutenant, who was about an inch shorter than me, sitting in the chair by the desk. As I entered he stood up and extended his hand. "Nick, meet Charlie Connerly. Charlie, this is Nick Moultrie," Steve said as he introduced us. "Charlie has been assigned to post headquarters." The two of us shook hands.

"Charlie Connerly!" I exclaimed. "Didn't you play football for Ole Miss about twenty years ago and then have an NFL career with the Giants?" I said in jest with a big smile on my face.

"Sorry to disappoint you, but that was a different Charlie Connerly. As far as I know we're not related, either."

"Where did you disappear to the last few days, Nick?" Steve asked.

"You won't believe it, but I went back to Phoenix to ask my girlfriend to marry me. We're going to tie the knot on the 21st."

"Why so sudden?" Asked Bronson. "You don't have a bun in the oven, do you?"

"No, she was on the Pill during our last year together. I just decided it was time to stop being single and become a productive member of society."

Steve smiled. "He had his girlfriend on the Pill. Charlie, did I tell you this guy was smart—or what?"

"Man, I guess," said Charlie. "You realize you just admitted to dipping your wick before the wedding."

"Well, what can I say other than I'm a normal red-blooded male?"

We all laughed as Charlie added, "From what I've seen around here, we might be jealous of you very soon."

"What about the girl in AG files? Where you work in the same building, I'd sure make her acquaintance if I were you." I said to Charlie.

A STATESIDE TOUR OF DUTY

Charlie had a puzzled look on his face. "I didn't see a girl there. Just some dumb-ass spec four."

"You better hope she hasn't quit. She is really built. If you don't believe me, just ask Steve here."

Steve just said, "Oh yeah," as he concurred in my assessment.

"I'll have to go back down to the basement and see if she's still there," Charlie mused. "If she is still there, I'll definitely introduce myself."

"Well, Steve," I said, changing the subject, "I'm sorry I won't be living with you, but I found a better roommate. She'll probably want to monopolize most of my time. Of course, she can provide certain benefits to make it worthwhile."

"No sweat, buddy. Congratulations. I wish you well, I really do, but we get to throw you a bachelor party." Steve gave me a pat on the back.

"I may like it here after all," said Charlie. "I just got here and we're already talking party."

While the three of us relaxed and got to know each other better, another development was taking place out on Highway 142 West. The beauty of writing about these events forty years or more after the fact is that I am now privy to all the scuttlebutt, rumor and assorted information that was not available at the time. This incident on Highway 142 West was a classic example of the unbelievable nonsense that went on at the time of my arrival at Fort McCulloch.

According to the stories that were relayed to me from various individuals, Sergeants Foster and Mount were running radar in the White Mouse. The Mark VI Speedalyzer radar unit had a needle similar to a speedometer needle that registered the speeds of passing cars. The operator could either stop the needle in place manually as proof of the person speeding, or the unit could be set to stop automatically if a certain speed was recorded. The men had two girlfriends with them that night and had little desire to catch and cite speeders. Consequently, they set the radar unit at one hundred miles per hour so they wouldn't have to be bothered with having to perform their duties. From the stories that were relayed to me the entire episode went something like this:

Foster and his girlfriend were on the front seat. Her short skirt was above her hips and she was sitting astride of him. Meanwhile Mount and his companion were busy getting their exercise on the back seat. As the sergeants proceeded with their romantic endeavors, they purposefully failed to notice the radar needle as it frequently registered well over the speed limit of sixty miles per hour as other cars passed by. Foster and

Mount were both getting out of the Army in less than two months, and as their ETS dates drew nearer, this type of conduct was becoming more common. This night, however, a car that incredibly was speeding at an amount in excess of the setting on the radar unit passed them. As the car sped past them, the radar unit buzzed and the needle stopped at the one hundred-mile per hour mark on the screen. As this occurred, Mount, who was now entwined by his girlfriend's legs on the back seat profaned the name of Deity and said to Foster, "Hey man, a customer. What do you say we go get him?"

"Why the hell not?" asked Foster as he zipped up his pants. "A good chase will make it a perfect night."

Foster hit the gas and the White Mouse was quickly in pursuit of the subject vehicle. "Quick, baby, button up my shirt," Foster said to his girlfriend. She then leaned over to comply with his request and as she did her large, pendulous breasts flopped out of her unbuttoned blouse. At that time, Foster, probably found it difficult to keep his hands on the wheel and his eyes on the road.

A minute or two later, as the White Mouse raced down the highway with the blue light flashing and the siren blaring, they saw the taillights of the vehicle they were seeking just up the road. Apparently, the driver had slowed up in the intervening time, either being unfamiliar with the road or just unwilling to continue at such a high rate of speed. As the distance between the two cars narrowed, Foster slowed his speed and shortly the pursued vehicle pulled off the road.

The driver of the vehicle was a young man of twenty-two who, like many of his friends, liked to use the state highways on the post to open up their cars to see how fast they might go. Another excuse they often used was that they needed to burn a little carbon off their spark plugs to make their cars run better. As the MPs rarely patrolled these roads, it was usually safe to do so. No doubt, the driver hoped he might somehow be able to talk the patrolmen out of giving him a ticket as he drove a cab on the post during the day, and a speeding citation would not look good on his record. He hopped out of his car and began walking back to the patrol car, trying to think of something to say. Foster immediately commanded over the loud speaker, "Please stay in your car, sir."

According to reports I received, the young man started to go back to his car, but apparently noticed something was not right. Both MPs got out of the car on the same side. That was unusual, as both men were supposed to sit in the front seat and the driver was supposed to approach the subject while his partner observed from his place on the right side of the car. In addition, both the MPs looked like they had been sleeping in their uniforms. Their shirttails were hanging out and they had a disheveled appearance. In the illumination produced by the flashing blue light and passing headlights of other cars, he reported seeing a girl sitting on the front seat, and she appeared to be buttoning up her blouse. Now he decided to try a different approach than hoping he could talk them out of a ticket by being polite. It was a calculated risk, but he apparently decided to give it a try.

"I see you guys have been having a little fun. If you let me go then you can get back to it a little faster," the man said in an arrogant manner.

Since the chase was not as wild as had been anticipated, they might have let the guy off with a warning, but his attitude and tone of voice ended any chance of that.

"What are you talking about?" said Foster.

The man smiled and belligerently stated, "I got eyes. I can see you've been making it out here." He then straightened up and said confidently, "If you write me up, it could be as embarrassing for you as it is for me."

This was a challenge Foster could respond to, especially since he was shortly leaving the service anyway. "We'll find out, won't we? Get the Form Letter Nines, Dave. Okay, pal, let me see your driver's license and automobile registration."

"You're kidding!" It was clear the man was surprised by Forster's failure to back off.

"No, I'm not kidding. When I say let me see your driver's license, I mean just that. Now let me see it." Foster was very forceful in his speech and the man acquiesced.

The man grudgingly pulled his wallet from his pocket and handed it to Foster, who refused to take it.

"Please take out your driver's license and hold on to your wallet. Also, go get your registration," said Foster.

The man did so, even as he continued to complain. "I'm going to report you people for your atrocious behavior if you give me a ticket."

"Go ahead," said Mount forcefully. "Be our guest. We'll even escort you to the station so you can voice your complaints to the duty officer. Now if you'd like to return to your car while we write this up, we can have you on your way faster."

The man continued to grumble and swear as he returned to his car and got in. Foster and Mount had the girl in the front seat move to the back seat as they sat in their usual positions in the patrol car. While Foster began writing the Form Letter Nine, Mount began to talk to the girls. "Listen, girls," he began. "This guy's trying to make trouble for us. We should make sure we all have the same story. We'll say the reason you are with us is that we brought you out here to uh, uh, well . . ." (Mount stopped talking to think). "I know," he smiled. "We brought you out to Highway 142, where we were going to meet someone else who was going to give you a ride to Glendale. While we were waiting there, the radar unit was on and this guy passed by. Since he was going so fast we felt we couldn't let him go, and chased him out here. When we wouldn't let him off, he accused us of fooling around. Think that explanation will convince everyone?"

One of the girls had a reply. "That's where my aunt lives. We can say that my cousin was going to meet us here to give us a ride to her house in Glendale."

"Great," said Mount, "Works for me. Now hurry and write out that ticket fast, buddy, and let's quit for the evening before we create any more problems."

Foster gave the man back his license and had him sign the ticket. As the man continued to grumble, Foster gave him a copy of the Form Letter Nine. He then gave him directions on how to get to the PMO for traffic court. He and Mount then drove the girls to a pay phone, where they called a cab and the patrolmen gave them money to pay for the ride home.

Once the girls had left, Foster and Mount dropped the White Mouse off at the PMO. Sure enough, the man they had written up had been there and had told his story to the duty officer. First Sergeant Prince was serving as duty officer (all enlisted section chiefs who were E-7 and above were on the duty officer roster) and had taken the man's statement. He talked to Foster and Mount briefly and they gave him their account of the episode. They had gotten a call from two girls they knew that needed help getting to Glendale for a family reunion. One of the girls had a cousin who would be coming down Highway 117 after work and would take 142 to Glendale. They agreed to take the girls to the intersection, where they could meet the relative and travel on to Glendale. After they had stopped the subject of the speeding violation, the man saw the girls and threatened them with the story he recited to Sergeant Prince. They reminded Prince that if they had been doing anything improper, then they certainly wouldn't have stopped the man for speeding. They were told to go home and meet with the colonel in the morning.

At the morning briefing, the main topic of conversation before the colonel arrived was the traffic stop Foster and Mount had made the night before. First Sergeant Prince related how a civilian complained of two MPs stopping him who smelled of alcohol, had an unkempt appearance and had girls in the vehicle. In his words, the men were a disgrace to the M.P. Company, Fort McCulloch and the Army. While Prince admitted he didn't smell any alcohol and the men had a professional appearance when he met with them, the men did admit that girls were in the car but had an explanation. Prince finished with this statement: "Those two have been screwed up ever since we let 'em run that section. Now they're screwing up the whole company."

Mister Bernard offered a rebuttal. "If they were messing around out there, why in the world would they bother to stop a speeder? I think the guy was caught in a serious violation and he's trying to get us fighting among ourselves to get even."

The major then chimed in with "I'd throw the whole thing in the trash can. But, in the meantime, I think we ought to keep an eye on those two until they leave the Army."

After the arrival of the colonel, the major's reasoning seemed to carry the day. After some discussion, it was decided to appoint a traffic officer to administer and oversee the Traffic section. The question now was who to place in the job. It was not until about 1000 hours that the decision was made. The colonel, the major, Tucker and Prince had been in the colonel's office all morning while Steve and I had been at the company listening to Byron talk about all the important duties he had. He talked about the company training, the property book, Supply and who knows what else. Byron talked a good show, but I never saw him do anything. We were called back to the PMO, where we were told that since I was a trained MP officer, I would head up the Traffic section. Steve would become the Operations officer as soon as Tucker's ETS date arrived.

I found a house trailer at Donaldson's Trailer Park (the same location where Byron and his wife lived), where Sam and I could make our first home. At the same time, Steve and Charlie found an apartment on the edge of town near a small lake where they could go fishing. The apartment complex also had a swimming pool. Now we were all able to move from Splinter Palace. We were also now ready to settle into our new jobs.

NEIL MITCHELL

Lacking a basic knowledge of MP procedure, Steve was to spend the next several days studying regulations and training manuals. He was stuck at his desk in the Operations office, where day after day he fought off boredom as he learned the various forms and reports. I was more fortunate. The next few days saw me riding around the post with the members of my section. As the Traffic officer, I had the call sign Unit 15 (pronounced "One Five") for any vehicle in which I rode as Traffic officer. The Traffic NCOIC was designated as 15 Alpha and any other vehicles we had in use were 15 Bravo, 15 Charlie and so forth. As Foster and Mount were soon to be separated from the service, I chose SP4 Cummings as the new Traffic non-commissioned officer in charge (NCOIC). All traffic accident reports were to be reviewed by myself before they were sent into Operations to be approved by Captain Tucker or Lieutenant Bronson.

Each day I would ride with one of my men, observing the use of radar and VASCAR, as well as the investigation of traffic accidents. The radar unit sat on the dashboard and plugged into the cigarette lighter. A cone element hung on the outside of the window that sent a radio signal that bounced off approaching vehicles. As it did, it registered the speed on the radar screen that was calibrated from 0 to 100 miles per hour. As the needle registered the speed of the target vehicle, you could either lock it in place with a hand-held button or set it to automatically stop at a certain speed if you didn't want to have to maintain visual connection to the screen. The radar unit picked up the closest object, or in some cases the largest. It could be affected by a number of things. If the road was rough and the target vehicle bounced, then the needle might jump. It was important that the person using the unit wait until the needle was steady for a few seconds before locking it in place when that happened. That way, a true reading was assured. At any rate, on the open highway we didn't write up speeding tickets unless the violator was doing fifteen or more miles over the speed limit on a clear day. The margin might be much less on days of inclement weather and at night. VASCAR was different. It was a small computer unit mounted on the dashboard, next to the steering column. It had two buttons and two toggle switches. VASCAR was an acronym for Visual Average Speed Computed and Recorded. The first toggle switch was used to record a given distance in the machine. It was flipped on at the beginning of the distance and off at the end to record the distance. The other switch recorded the time that a target vehicle was clocked over the distance previously put into the machine. The average speed over which the target vehicle covered the distance then appeared on the unit's screen, calculated down to the tenths of seconds. The unit had a red button to clear the time and leave the distance in and a black button to clear all data out of the machine. Unfortunately, the vehicle in which the VASCAR unit was mounted was scheduled to go into the TMP (Transportation Motor Pool) for scheduled maintenance, so I would have no chance to operate it for a while.

One day Foster and I took the White Mouse out to run radar. He drove around the cantonment area for a little while, looking for a good spot to stop and observe traffic. As we talked, I was careful to avoid stupid questions—like if he was looking forward to getting out of the Army—and concentrated on questions like, "What are you going to do on the outside?"

Foster kept his eyes on the road, visually scanning the area as he spoke. "I'm going to work for my father-in-law. He's a contractor and I can fit right into his company. I plan to take it over when he retires." He stopped talking for a second and turned his head and directed my attention to an attractive black girl with large thighs wearing a short dress, was walking along the sidewalk next to the street. "That's Brenda Lou Marsh," he said. "That little girl right there is only sixteen and she's already turned pro. She gave Mount and Galloway a case of the clap."

"Did you try her out?" I asked.

"Hell no, sir," he answered. "I don't touch anything under the age of eighteen and I never deal with any pros. The way I see it, how can you arrest them when you catch them with a john if they can identify you as a former customer? Those other guys can take a chance if they like, but I like to play it safe. I don't need to be identified with someone like that and have word get back to my wife."

"Where is your wife now?" I asked.

"Mount and I sent our wives home about two months ago to get everything ready for when we get out of the service. While they're gone, we might get a little on the side every now and then, but I'm careful not to catch anything I can give to her."

"The more careful a guy is, the more he is apt to stay out of trouble," I commented. I also thought that he ought to build his relationship with his wife and not fool around so much, but I kept that thought to myself.

"You guessed it, sir," Foster concluded as he pulled the car over to the curb. He then continued, "Here in the housing area, I've always given tickets to speeders when they are ten miles over the limit and verbal warnings for those driving five miles over the limit. If there are children playing in the area, I might even write them at five miles over the limit."

After we had been sitting on the side of the road for about ten minutes, a car approached traveling at twenty-seven miles an hour. All the other cars that had passed were traveling at the speed limit of twenty miles per hour or below, which was understandable since our patrol car was visible for five blocks in either direction. As the needle rose to the vehicle's speed, Foster waited a couple of seconds to ensure that everything was correct. He then pushed the hand-held button to lock the needle in place. After turning on the blue light and looking over his shoulder for oncoming cars, he started after the clocked vehicle.

About fifty yards down the road the car pulled over to the curb. Foster stopped our vehicle directly behind it. He put on his white hat and looked behind us to check for traffic. As he got out and walked up to the other vehicle, I exited the vehicle on my side and stood by the car behind the open door. Even though I was not armed, the person we stopped would not know that. As I stood there, it appeared that he had someone backing him up. Mostly, however, I wanted to be able to hear what was being said and observe Sergeant Foster at work. He appeared very professional. He asked the woman who was driving for her driver's license and registration and walked back to our car. He picked up the microphone to the radio and said "Fort McCulloch, this is Unit One Five."

"Go ahead, One Five," came the reply.

"Fort McCulloch, do you have a fifty-one card on a White, Susan Bravo?" (All initials and letters were given, over the radio, using a phonetic code.)

"Stand by, Unit One Five," the desk clerk said over the radio. There was a pause while the desk clerk checked the files. We were not waiting long. "Unit One Five, this is Fort McCulloch," came the voice over the radio.

"This is Unit One Five. Go ahead, Fort McCulloch."

"Unit One Five, answer to inquiry on a fifty-one card for White, Susan Bravo, is in the negative. There is none on file."

"Ten-four, Fort McCulloch. Tango Yankee," said Foster.

"Ten-four, Fort McCulloch clear," said the desk.

Foster walked up to the other car and handed the license and registration back to the woman. "Ma'am, we clocked you doing twenty-seven in a twenty-mile-per-hour zone. We're not going to issue a citation; however, we would appreciate you abiding by the posted speed limit."

The woman gave a sigh of relief and said, "Oh, thank you. I'll be more careful next time."

"Okay ma'am, but remember, that often there can be a lot of children playing in the area so the next patrolman may not let you off so easy, so please drive carefully." With that, Foster turned and walked back to the patrol car. He turned off the blue light and pulled back onto the street. "Dumb broad," he said. "She had to be blind not to see the car by the road, or she had her mind on something else. That's when someone's most likely to hit a kid or something—when their mind is preoccupied elsewhere."

"Is everyone you stop, somebody who failed to pay attention, like that woman did?" I inquired.

"No sir," he replied. "We try to get those who often and flagrantly violate the speed limit. But it isn't easy. Military regulations require that we be clearly visible and not hidden. Fortunately, most people don't know that. Therefore, we often park around a curve or behind a bush or something. One night I parked with the trunk and hood up and a cardboard box over the blue light. Someone drove by doing ninety-five, but by the time I got out and shut the trunk and hood and took off the box they were long gone. Since then I don't try anything so elaborate."

During the next two hours, Foster issued two tickets. He cited a civilian for speeding at fifty-nine miles per hour in a forty-mile-per-hour zone and a buck sergeant for traveling sixty in the same area. They were given Form Letter Nines that required them to appear in magistrate's court. We also had at our disposal the Form 1498 military traffic ticket. These were used for warning tickets or for offenses that could not be tried by the magistrate's court. A copy was sent to the individual's company commander if the subject was military. If the offender was a civilian, the information was recorded on a 19-51 card and the ticket was filed in the trash can.

We returned to the PMO. As it was nearly quitting time, I prepared to go home. Before I did so, however, I went into Operations to see Steve. He was sitting behind his desk with his tie loosened. "Hey man, where the hell have you been?" he asked.

"Serving humanity and protecting the innocent people of Fort McCulloch from hardened criminals."

"Tucker wants to know if you are going to be at the poker game tonight."

"I better not. I gotta save all I can for my honeymoon. I don't feel like giving anything to those card sharks."

"I don't think I will make it either. That damned Captain Tucker agreed to fill in for Prince as duty officer tonight and then conned me into taking the job. I think I'll just go home and grab a nap so I can come in at midnight to conduct guard mount and ride with the patrols. No reason to let Tucker try and line me up with that neighbor of his again."

"Good plan," I laughed. "Tucker stuck me with a duty officer shift when I first got here. He's good at that. I hope you have a less exciting night than I did, though."

"That's when the two men got killed?"

"Yeah, I don't ever want to go through that again."

"That accident cut the black personnel in our unit by twenty-five percent," Steve mentioned, changing the subject. "Did you know that the Army is forty percent black while our unit was only just over ten percent? With the loss of those men, that percentage dropped to less than eight percent."

"Yeah, that's a problem throughout the Army," I concurred. "Most blacks try to avoid serving as MPs. I got an earful about the problem at Fort Gordon. We wind up with the perception of being a bunch of white guys enforcing the law on an Army that has a large population of blacks."

"Well there's nothing we can do about it." Steve changed the subject again. "Did you know that the hunting and fishing is supposed to be pretty good around here?"

"You're kidding?"

"No, I'm not. Apparently, the eastern part of the post, on the other side of the mountains, is forested. It's just the western part where we are that looks like hell. There was a two-star general in here earlier. Prince acts as a guide, around here, for VIPs. The story I got is whoever he takes out always gets their limit. Maybe we ought to try a little hunting some weekend. It might give us something to do."

"That might not be a bad idea, but for now, let's get out of here and go home." Steve didn't argue with that idea and we parted company.

I went home to try to get the trailer presentable for Sam. The place was a mess from the previous tenant, but with a little elbow grease I had it where I wasn't too embarrassed to call it home.

A STATESIDE TOUR OF DUTY

For Steve, however, the evening would be more complicated. Again, I am writing about the event as a result of information received after the incident.

Unfortunately, in a home in Harrisville there lived a young man who would be responsible for Steve having a long night as duty officer. According to his parents, it was his desire to eventually become an explosives and munitions expert, so to that end he had a practice of searching the artillery ranges for unexploded shells when they were not in use. The boy, who was a senior at Harrisville High School, had convinced his parents that he knew what he was doing and they did not see the danger in his hobby. He had written a term paper on the subject for school, and his parents, as well as his friends, saw his interest as the beginning of a skill which might be useful in gaining future employment.

The previous day he had made one of his trips to the artillery range and had found a real prize. It was a 155-mm howitzer shell that had failed to detonate on impact. He took it home. As his parents left on an errand he told them he would further examine the shell by cutting it so he could see it as a cross section. Apparently, to that end, he put it into a vise and began cutting into it with a power saw equipped with a special blade for cutting metal. This shell represented the largest round the young man had ever found and in his excitement, he, no doubt, vigorously pursued the aim of cutting the shell in half to examine its contents. At that point the howitzer round exploded. The boy probably never knew what happened or suffered any pain. In fact, only a few small fragments of him would ever be found. The home was demolished and neighboring homes also suffered damage as debris rained from the sky.

Harrisville police, at first, thought that the water heater had exploded and caused the accident. However, when that appliance was found intact they turned their attention elsewhere. When the boy's parents came home and mentioned their son's hobby, the police called the Fort McCulloch ordinance detachment. Investigators were immediately dispatched who recognized the blast pattern as that of a detonated shell.

The military police desk was notified and Bronson, as duty officer, spent the next several hours learning all he could about the event. He would have to brief the colonel the next morning. There would, no doubt, be derogatory publicity on the incident. Also, the boy's parents who had been stupid enough to let their son get involved in this hazardous activity already had lawyers arriving at the location to discuss the possibility of pursuing tort litigation against the Army and the United States Government.

In the future, Bronson and I would look back and swear that Tucker had to be almost psychic to know when to dump his duty officer assignments off on us new second lieutenants. Eventually we just came to the conclusion that he had just been lazy. He had conned us into taking what should have been his watches and then the most bizarre events occurred.

Tucker probably enjoyed a good night's sleep, while preparing to leave the Army, whereas we were schooled in the finer points of Murphy's law, which states that if something *can* go wrong, it *will* go wrong. Steve and I became convinced that no truer maxim had ever been spoken.

CHAPTER SIX

The next morning, the briefing began as usual. The regulars were sitting around the large oak conference table while Captain Tucker was in the other office doing what he always did. Top was cussing about stupid civilians who didn't have enough sense to keep from blowing themselves up. As he ranted on, the major was drawing something and Warren was reading a copy of *Playboy*. As usual, Warren was meticulously dressed. Today he wore a Gant sports shirt over which was a virgin-wool blue sweater.

At exactly 0800 hours the colonel walked in and we all rose to attention and said, "Morning, sir."

"Be seated," said the colonel. Having already been informed of the incident the day before, the colonel immediately began pumping Bronson for information. There wasn't much for him to add, as the cause of the blast had been determined, but he filled the colonel in on the briefings he had received. In addition to the ordinance detachment, the Bureau of Alcohol, Tobacco and Firearms (ATF) had also investigated the site. The colonel then called for Captain Tucker. As usual, the captain yelled back, "I'll be there in a minute." Today the colonel seemed more irritated than usual and demanded, "Captain Tucker, we need you now."

Captain Tucker appeared nonchalantly in the doorway and leaned up against the door frame. He had his trademark coffee cup in his right hand. "If you need someone to submit a Blue Bell on the explosion sir, Lieutenant Moultrie does those now," Captain Tucker said. He then disappeared back into the other room. The colonel then turned to me and ordered, "Have the Blue Bell report on my desk this morning as quickly as possible, lieutenant. We need to notify Fifth Army immediately."

I nodded and obediently replied, "Yes, sir."

Now the major spoke up. "Colonel," he said, "I've decided to write some patrol tips to help our men become better MPs. He held up the drawing he had just finished. It had the wording Patrol Tip Number One written across the top of the page. Under that was a picture of two men sitting in a car with the passenger holding something in front of his face. The caption read that a MP should be alert to observe anyone attempting to hide their faces as they drove by. If they did so, it might be an indication they had something to hide and maybe they should be stopped for further investigation. The drawing reminded me of the crime stopper hints that were always in the *Dick Tracy* comic strips. I thought that might be where the major got the idea. I also kept that thought to myself. After all, I was learning that such comments would just anger the major.

"That's fine, Jim," said the colonel. "How many of those do you plan to prepare."

"I don't know yet, colonel," replied the major. "I think possibly fifteen or twenty or thereabouts." He then changed the subject. "Have you made up your mind about the goon squad yet, sir? I've interviewed several men who would be excellent for it and the whole project only needs your okay."

The colonel thought for a few seconds and then said, "Talk to me about it after the meeting breaks up, Jim." He then asked each person around the table if they had anything else that needed to be discussed. When all the answers were in the negative, the colonel said, "Well then, let's get to work." We all stood up and saluted. The colonel returned our salute and most of us left the room.

I wrote up the Blue Bell report on the dead boy and the dud round that he had accidentally detonated. Since the investigation was completed, I wrote "Blue Bell-Initial-Terminal" for item number three of the report. In the unlikely event that any other information was discovered, I could always send in a supplemental report. I also wrote up a press release for all the local papers stating that dud rounds were extremely dangerous and they should never be touched or picked up. In the event one was found, it should be reported to the post Ordinance detachment at once. I gave a couple of examples how artillery rounds found many years after a war had detonated and killed or harmed innocent civilians when they were disturbed by unknowing or careless people. I took the press release up to the major, who read it and gave his approval. The rest of the morning was spent checking over accident reports and other paperwork in my office. Just before noon, I went into Operations to see if Steve wanted to join me for lunch.

A STATESIDE TOUR OF DUTY

We were just about to leave for the snack bar when Tucker called me back. "Okay, lieutenant," he began, "Now that you're the official Blue Bell reporting officer, you'll need these." He handed me a stack of manila folders with names on the tabs. "These are all of our open Blue Bell and Serious Incident cases," he continued. "If you have any further questions, you can call Lieutenant Stewart at the Fifth Army PMO at Fort Sam Houston. Here's his number. I won't be back today and you won't be able to reach me because I'll be at the golf course with Sergeant Peterson. We're too short to screw around here with office work, so don't bother us." With that he left the room.

"Let's get the hell out of here and grab some chow," I said to Steve.

"I'm ready," he answered. "Oh," he added, "I asked Charlie to join us over at the snack bar. I hope that's okay."

"Not a problem."

We got into Steve's car and headed over to the snack bar. While we drove over, *Paul Harvey's News and Comment* was on the radio. He mentioned that some 200 Americans had died during the previous week in the dead-end war in Southeast Asia. North Vietnamese and Viet Cong casualties for the same period were 12,000 dead.

"Do you believe that?" Steve asked. "We have about two hundred dead and they have twelve thousand. That seems a little hard to swallow. Do you think there's any truth in those facts?"

"Not for a minute," was my reply. "It would make sense that their casualties would be a lot higher than ours—but not that much higher." I then began to elaborate. "For example, during the Civil War there was a little battle called Falling Waters early on. In the official Confederate records, General Joe Johnston stated that his side lost two men dead and the Union loss was about ten times as high. On the other hand, however, in the Union records, their commander states that he encountered a Confederate force and withdrew after inflicting a heavy loss. He lost two men dead and he counted thirty dead confederates on the field of battle. While both sides lost the same amount of men, the two commanders inflated the losses on the other side for their own reasons. I think the same principle applies today in Vietnam." Then I added, "Besides that, it's my understanding that promotions and advancing one's military career depends on reporting a high body count of enemy dead. So, it's my best guess that those body counts may be complete and total bullshit."

"I've heard that last point a lot myself," Steve agreed. "So you're probably right." With that we pulled into the snack bar parking lot. Charlie was already there.

Charles R. Connerly was from Topeka, Kansas, and had a degree in history from the University of Kansas. Like me, he was a product of OCS. Unlike me, he had attended OCS at Fort Benning, Georgia, whereas I had gone to Fort Belvoir, Virginia. He had graduated third in his class, and that allowed him to select a branch of the Army other than the infantry. He had graduated from military intelligence school at Fort Holabird two weeks behind Steve (ROTC officers like Steve attended Officer's Basic at branch school, while OCS graduates completed a shorter officer's orientation course), and now he had the good fortune to be stationed with us at Camp Dusty. He was assigned to post headquarters, where he taught the post defensive driving course to military personnel and their dependents that had the misfortune to receive a traffic ticket or were involved in a motor vehicle accident.

As we ordered up some fries and hamburgers and several refills of coffee, we began to trade war stories and enjoy a long lunch. Steve related one story that happened while he was at Fort Bragg, North Carolina, for his initial training, after graduating from college. He described how the new ROTC officers had observed a parachuting demonstration where an entire airborne battalion, complete with vehicles, had baled out of some planes. Steve gave a hilarious account of how most of the vehicles came down too hard and were damaged beyond repair. Jeeps had their wheels break off on impact and trucks landed on their sides, receiving damage that made them a total loss. He stated that he and his comrades figured that the U S Government destroyed over five million dollars of equipment that day putting on the demonstration. "If you ever wonder why your taxes are so high, well, stupidity like that is a large part of it," he said.

"I've always heard that every piece of equipment the Army has is air drop-able—one time," I said with a smile as I held up my right index finger.

"That's right," Bronson said. "If you want to drop them a second time, usually, all you have left to drop is pieces."

Now Charlie and I began to relate our experiences about OCS. ROTC officers have the easiest road to travel in gaining their commission. As a result, Charlie and I had no difficulty monopolizing the talk once the war stories began. OCS is twenty-three weeks of pure hell, and all of it is endured as an enlisted man—not as an officer, as was the case at Steve's summer camp. The most dreaded figure at OCS is the tactical officer (tac for short). These are lieutenants who wear a black T-shirt and a black baseball cap and make the Marquis de Sade look like your kindly old grandmother. These sadistic bastards lay awake at night thinking of ways to torment the candidates (as OCS students are called) and make their lives generally miserable. Their preferred method of torture was the booney run. This was where the candidates had to strap on full field gear and run through the woods for several hours. The tacs, who carried no gear and were in excellent physical shape, insisted that everyone keep up with them. Injuries were common, and just when everyone had collapsed from total and complete exhaustion and were gasping for breath, another tac would start screaming for them to get up and move out.

At that point some men would break (it was not unknown for a few to start crying) and would be dropped from the program. Those who found the ability to draw additional strength from some source deep within them to get up and continue the run could successfully complete the program. The positive effect of this experience was that the men who survived this ordeal knew that they had seen the worst that could be done to them. They knew the program could not break them, and they were aware that they would probably graduate.

Charlie related a story about one tactical officer that everyone called Black Cloud. Black Cloud's real name was Lieutenant Jackson. He was about six foot seven in height and loomed over you like a big, black cloud, hence the name. White candidates thought he hated white people—until they saw his treatment of blacks. Then they realized that he hated *all* people. Candidates would go out of their way to avoid Black Cloud at all costs. If he was the duty officer while you were assigned to guard duty, heaven help you. He was said to scatter candidates' equipment for blocks because he didn't feel that it was put together properly or rolled tightly enough. Charlie related how he had spent several hours shinning his boots because he knew he would have to face Black Cloud on guard duty. During the guard mount, Black Cloud got his face about three inches away from Charlie's and screamed, "You call that a shine, mister?" He then stomped on the toe of Charlie's boot.

"To this day, the toe of that Corcoran boot is flat instead of round," said Charlie with a smile. "He then put his face about an inch away from mine and said, 'Connerly, do you like it here?' Of course I said, 'Yes, sir.' He then said, 'Connerly, you're lying.' Of course I then said, 'No, sir.'

That continued until he got tired and went to the next man, who got a similar treatment."

"What would happen if you admitted you didn't like it there?" asked Bronson.

"Thirty days leave and a trip to Vietnam," replied Charlie. "Nobody ever admitted they didn't like it there unless they broke you and you were dropped from the program. You then got a year's vacation in beautiful Southeast Asia."

"It wasn't easy to get the better of the tacs," I said. "But, when we did it was usually by accident rather than design. However, there was one occasion where my class at Belvoir made them real nervous." I then related the following story: "At Belvoir, before we were promoted into our junior phase of the program—called the white phase (for the white plastic tabs under our OCS brass)—we had to complete a week-long bivouac at a place called Camp A. P. Hill. It was a lot like Fort McCulloch here, with a lot of ground and few people. On the third night we were there, just as we were all getting ready for bed, they called us out into formation. Naturally, we were in various stages of undress. Some were in their underwear, others were wearing fatigue pants, some were barefoot, etc., etc."

I paused to finish my french fries before continuing. "Once they had us in formation, they began screaming that we were a disgrace because we were all dressed differently. The senior tac then said they would leave for five minutes and we had all better be SOP upon their return. Well, our candidate company commander was a guy with starch in his blood and he was very methodical in determining our SOP style of dress. Since some men were barefoot, he ordered all to become barefoot. Since some were wearing T-shirts and some were in fatigue shirts, T-shirts were the order of the evening. Some men had no T-shirt under their fatigues, so we all became bare chested. Finally, since some men were in undershorts and some were wearing pants, he ordered BVDs to be our SOP uniform. By now you can guess the obvious."

I paused before continuing. "One man who had been about to shower had no underwear under his fatigue pants. Our leader then said, 'What the hell, you know the drill. Take everything off.' We then had almost one hundred men standing under the streetlights stark naked. When the tacs returned, they began to scream for us to get dressed (probably worried about who might drive by and see us). Our candidate company commander tried to explain that we couldn't follow their orders and be dressed alike any other way. They told us that they would overlook that problem. They then had us dress and dismissed us without further harassment for the rest of the night." I waved my hands to illustrate the tactical officers' panic as they told us to get our clothes on.

We all had a great laugh over our war stories, but it was time to return to work. Before we did, however, Charlie mentioned that he had finally got to meet the girl that worked in AG Files in the basement of post headquarters. Her name was Charlotte Palmer. Charlie mentioned that he was planning to ask her out, and he agreed with us that she was a real babe. Charlie then returned to headquarters and Steve and I returned to the PMO.

Upon my return to the office, I thumbed through the pile of folders that Tucker had given me. There were twenty-two of them, in total, and none of them had any follow-up reports submitted recently. The charges included everything from murder and child molestation to armed robbery. There was no question that the reports would have to be brought up to date. However, I didn't feel like being desk-bound for the remainder of the day. I decided that I would rather go out on the road with Sergeant Mount. Knowing Steve was probably also up to his eyeballs in make-work nonsense, I invited him to go with me and observe the Traffic section in action. I asked Desk Sergeant Corley to call Unit One Five Bravo in off the road, and while we awaited its arrival Steve and I stood to the left of the desk area.

At this time a woman walked into the station. She stood about five foot five with long brown hair tied back in a ponytail. She was about average in attractiveness but very well proportioned. She wore no bra under her white shirt, and as she walked up to the MP desk her bosom bounced slightly from side to side and up and down in a continuous movement. All this time her large, brown nipples were clearly visible through the thin cotton fabric. Either through intention or oversight, two or three buttons on her blouse were not buttoned; therefore, from where Steve and I were standing we had an unobstructed view of her right breast.

She walked up to the desk and looked up at Sergeant Corley. "Is this where I come to file a complaint or have someone arrested?" she asked.

Steve and I made every attempt to look the woman in the face, as we didn't wish to embarrass her (or ourselves) by looking elsewhere. Sergeant Corley made no such effort. He stared straight at her chest as he answered, "That depends on the nature of the complaint, ma'am. Tell us what the problem is."

The woman paused to collect her thoughts. "On Saturday night I met a captain at Miller's Restaurant in Harrisville. He's here with the national guard for two weeks. He talked about how lonesome he was, and I told him that he could spend the rest of the weekend with me at my place and it would only cost him a hundred dollars." We all looked at each other in disbelief as she continued. "Well, after some drinks at the offices' club we went to my house where I fulfilled my part of the bargain. He then wrote me a check for a hundred dollars. This morning, when I went to the bank to cash the check he had written, the bank notified me that he had stopped payment on it. Anyway, I want you to arrest him."

Maybe it was the brazenness of the story or just standard male behavior, but both Steve and I were having trouble looking her in the face and not at other places. Sergeant Corley's mouth, meanwhile, had dropped open in complete and total disbelief at the story. In a few seconds, however, he recovered his composure and answered her with one word: "Why?"

The woman seemed completely surprised by his reply. She threw her shoulders back, which made her breasts bounce a little and caused her nipples to be even more visible through her blouse. Everyone's attention was drawn away from them as she snapped in an angry and almost hysterical voice, "He cheated me! He robbed me out of money rightfully due me. Isn't that grand larceny or something?"

Now the sergeant looked her straight in the face and, apparently losing interest elsewhere (at least for now), told her tactfully and professionally how it was.

"Ma'am," he began, "if someone refuses to pay another person money due for services rendered, then the only recourse the aggrieved party has is to sue. It's a civil case, not a criminal one, and we have no jurisdiction. You must go down to the courthouse and file your case in small claims court. Now, your problem is that prostitution is illegal under Texas law. If you try to sue telling the story you have just told me, then the captain can tell what services were rendered for the hundred dollars. If they fit the definition of prostitution, then you would be incriminating yourself and might be prosecuted under the law for a criminal charge of prostitution. If convicted, you might have to pay a large fine or receive jail time."

A STATESIDE TOUR OF DUTY

The woman held up her right hand to the back of her head and felt where her ponytail was gathered together, while she thought for a few seconds. Slowly, what she had been told began to sink in. Holding her hand in this manner forced the side of the blouse with the buttons to rest against her chest and caused the other side to bulge out even further than before, giving those now congregated an excellent view. She then asked Sergeant Corley, "You mean there's nothing I can do?"

"Well ma'am," said the sergeant. "If I were you, I wouldn't take any more checks."

The woman dropped her arm and said, "Well thanks anyway. Sorry to bother you." She then turned on her heels and made a quick exit. As she walked out the door she muttered a very audible "Damn."

Sergeant Corley's eyes were still fixed on the door as he sat down and said more to himself than anyone around, "I wouldn't mind writing her a few checks myself, providing I got to stop payment on them. She won't fall for that again, though."

Given the incongruity of the situation, I could not help but smile. I looked up at Corley and said, "Think your wife would mind if you did business with her?"

"She wouldn't have to know, sir," Corley replied.

The clerk, who had gone unnoticed through the entire conversation, stopped typing and asked, "Do I have to put everything that just went on in the blotter, sarge?"

"Hell, no! The front office would be mad that we didn't think of some offense to charge her with. But, everything she did was off post. We got no jurisdiction there. The less said, the better."

"Good," said the clerk. "I couldn't think of a tactful way to type it up. I still can't believe she came in here with that story. She's the first hooker I've ever met."

By this time Unit One Five Bravo had arrived. Steve and I got in. Mount keyed the mic on the radio and said, "Fort McCulloch, this is Unit One Five Bravo."

"This is Fort McCulloch, go ahead, One Five Bravo," came the reply.

"Fort McCulloch, Unit One Five Bravo is now designated Unit One Five."

"Ten-four, Fort McCulloch clear," the desk sergeant replied over the radio.

"Mount," I said. "You won't believe what just happened."

Steve, who was sitting on the back seat just laughed. He then added, "It was the damnedest thing I've ever seen. I still can't believe it."

As we described the events at the MP desk to Mount, he shook his head. He asked for a description of the woman to determine her identity, but finally decided it might be any one of several women who made their contacts out of Miller's Restaurant. Miller's had a bar where most of the higher-class hookers in the area might be found on any given night.

We spent the rest of the afternoon with Mount. He wrote a couple of speeding tickets and gave verbal warnings to a couple of other drivers, and the workday ended with Steve and me still laughing about the previous incident. If the rest of my two years here were going to be as unbelievable as the first four weeks, there might never be a dull moment.

CHAPTER SEVEN

Every Wednesday, Federal Magistrate's Court was held at Fort McCulloch. All traffic offenses, along with misdemeanors and felonies, where the maximum penalty was six months' incarceration (or a $500 fine), were scheduled before this court by our Operations personnel. Cases involving military personnel were heard at 0900 hours, while civilian cases were scheduled for 1100 hours. Many local citizens and military personnel referred to Magistrate's Court as Kangaroo Court. Most people seemed to believe guilty verdicts were automatic, and the name seemed to have stuck. The Federal Magistrate was a local judge appointed (theoretically by the President of the United States) to hear cases that occurred on the post. In actual practice, local officials would suggest a name to Washington and the suggested nominee would be rubber-stamped by the national leaders.

The reputation of Magistrate's Court was not enhanced by the setting in which it took place. An old classroom in company headquarters served as the courtroom. Before court each week, I would have a couple of men go over and arrange the desks. One desk was placed at the front of the room, where the judge could sit and preside over the proceedings. Rows of student desks would be placed in lines where the people awaiting their cases could sit. Over by the left wall another row would be placed facing the other rows. This was where observers such as myself, or other company leaders, could sit. From this vantage point we could make observations as to the appearance and presence of our personnel in order to advise them on improving their court demeanor later.

At exactly 0900 hours, Sergeant Donavon (who served as Bailiff) yelled, "All rise. United States Magistrate's Court for the San Angelo District, Military Part is now in session, the honorable Judge Hartsell presiding."

NEIL MITCHELL

Judge Hartsell would enter and gavel the court to order. The room was insufferably hot in the summer, as it had no air conditioning, and the judge's monotone voice didn't help things. He began speaking to those present, "Whereas you have been charged with offenses occurring on federal property, you have the right to have a transcript made of your case and to be represented by an attorney. If you wish to waive the first right (to have a transcript made), you can have your case heard by myself as the federal magistrate for this area. If you do not wish to waive this right, then I can transfer your case to the federal district judge who presides over this district, who is in San Angelo. If you agree to have me hear your case, the maximum penalty that can be rendered is a five-hundred-dollar fine and six months' confinement in the federal penitentiary. Please don't let that frighten you, however, as that maximum is rarely used. Now the bailiff will call your names as your case comes up, and you either agree to have me adjudicate your case or have me transfer your case to the federal judge in San Angelo. Bailiff, call the first case."

At this time, Sergeant Donavon was handed paperwork off the stack that sat to the right of the judge by the clerk, Specialist Perkins. Donavon would then read the name aloud. "Sergeant Richards," he said in a loud voice. The person whose name was read would come forward and stood before the judge.

"Do wish to have me hear your case?" The judge asked.

"Yes, sir," was his reply. He signed the waiver.

"You are charged with driving thirty-six miles per hour in a twenty-mile-per hour zone. How do you plead?" The judge then waited for a response.

"Guilty."

"Forty-five dollar fine," the judge said. "You can pay it to the clerk."

While the man wrote out a check, Perkins handed the next batch of paperwork to Donavon. "Specialist Carter," Donavon bellowed.

As the man came forward, the judge said, "Do you wish for me to hear your case?" The man nodded, said "Yes," and signed the waiver. Judge Hartsell then read, "You are charged with running a posted stop sign." He then added, "How do you plead?"

"Guilty." From the resigned tone of the man's voice, you almost expected him to add, ". . . as hell."

"Fifteen dollar fine; pay the clerk. Next case."

"Private McKenzie," Donavon said as he looked around.

A STATESIDE TOUR OF DUTY

The judge moved the cases out with assembly-line precision. Of thirty-three cases, all agreed to have him hear their case, and only two pleaded not guilty. For these two the MP who issued the ticket was called in and stated what he observed. The defendant then stated his case, and was given a chance to question the patrolman. Unless the defendant could find a problem with the MP's work, the verdict was guilty. That was the verdict rendered in both cases.

By 1015 hours, all military cases were disposed of. Another stack of cases (civilian this time) was placed next to the judge, and by 1100 hours the defendants were present. The room was usually less crowded for the civilian cases, as military personnel were often required by their company commander to bring along a squad leader, platoon sergeant or other superior to report back to the company commander. Civilian personnel generally came alone unless accompanied by witnesses or a lawyer.

"All rise," bellowed Donavon. "United States Magistrate's Court for the San Angelo District, Civilian Part, is now in session, the honorable Judge Hartsell presiding."

The judge entered and repeated his speech given earlier, explaining the people's rights, and the process of the previous hour was repeated. By 1200 hours, court was adjourned and those of us observing or waiting to testify were ready to leave for chow.

I met Steve and we joined Charlie at the snack bar. The main topic of conversation for Steve and myself during lunch was wondering what Tucker had on the colonel. We had noticed that day after day at the morning briefings the captain could give the colonel the brush-off when he needed information from Captain Tucker. For a company-grade officer like Captain Tucker to treat a light colonel this way meant that the captain had some sort of blackmail evidence on his superior officer. There was no other explanation for what was going on. Normally a colonel could put a captain in his place very rapidly. This one obviously could not. We had speculated how nice it would be to have that information before, but now Steve had a possible idea of what it might be.

"I wonder if it has something to do with the colonel's wife." Steve wondered.

"Why would you think that?"

Steve looked around, and then in a low tone of voice asked the next question. "Haven't you met her yet?"

"No, I haven't."

"Well," he continued. "She's probably less than ten years older than we are, speaks with a French accent and has a hard look to her that makes her look older than she is. Julene in the front office calls her Fifi when the colonel is not around and speculates that she might be a former prostitute. The colonel has kids, from his first marriage, that are a lot older than his new wife. He obviously left his former wife for this new one. I'm wondering if the colonel did something illegal to get her into the States or covered up information on her that might cause him to lose his security clearance. That might explain it."

I considered what Steve had said. "You have more information than I have. You've obviously been nosing around."

"Well, it doesn't hurt to know where the bodies are buried," Steve answered. "By the way, it looks like the colonel is going to set up a goon squad like the major wants. He's tired of the major nagging him about it."

"That's dumb as hell. It will take our biggest men off line duty and make us shorthanded there. We will have fewer men patrolling the post. Doesn't the colonel know that?"

Steve shrugged. "I guess that this is the only way he can prove to the major it's a bad idea."

"If I were the colonel, I would just tell the major to sit in his office, keep his chair warm and drop the subject. After all, he is the ranking officer. But then, the major might also know whatever it is that Captain Tucker knows."

"Exactly," replied Bronson. "Now you're seeing just how screwed up this place is."

"That's some place you guys work in," said Charlie. "I'm glad I'm over at post headquarters."

"Yes, we have a dandy place in which to work." I looked at my watch. "We better be getting back. I have to get over to the commo center and find out what I need to get permission from the FCC to run radar. I found out that this organization has never requested permission to do that. If anyone who was stopped for speeding (that was clocked on radar) knew that fact, they could get the charge dismissed because the radar equipment is being operated illegally."

Bronson shook his head and stated the obvious, "Why does that not surprise me? This whole place is just one big foul-up. If the Russians nuked this dump, it would be an improvement."

A STATESIDE TOUR OF DUTY

"Yeah, but until they do, we still have to work here. We better be getting back." With that, we departed the snack bar and returned to the PMO. Upon our arrival there, I got in my car and drove over to the commo center. They gave me a form to request FCC approval for our radar. I was beginning to learn that the Army and the federal government would run out of guns, bullets, gasoline and food light-years ahead of paperwork. They have an endless supply of forms for every conceivable task.

If God announced that the world was going to end tomorrow, the Army would require him to submit his proclamation in triplicate on a twelve-page double-spaced form and wait in a line somewhere.

After returning to the office, I called the company that makes the Mark V Speedalyzer and was told the frequency the radar unit operated on. With that piece of information, I then filled out the form. All the information was easy to fill in until I got to the line asking for the location of the transmitter. I thought for a minute, then typed in the following: Transmitter is in a motor vehicle and its location varies as the automobile travels from place to place. I then hand-carried the form back to the commo center, where it was transmitted to the FCC. This, I was told, would cut weeks off the approval process.

I then returned to the office, where I began to make some calls to close out some of the Blue Bell cases we had open. I was able to submit three final reports. That left nineteen folders I still had to deal with. At 1700 hours, I called it a day and went home.

After making myself something to eat and watching the news, I relaxed in front of the television until 2000 hours. At that time the telephone rates dropped to their lowest rate, and once a week I called Sam. I called at that time on the same day, each week.

I dialed her number and she picked up the phone after the first ring. She answered by singing into her phone, "Soldier boy, oh my little soldier boy!"

"Yes, it's me," I said.

"August 21st is almost here," she said, almost singing the words.

"Oh no," I said in mock alarm. "I just remembered that I forgot to schedule leave. We'll have to postpone our wedding. This is terrible."

"How badly do you want to die?" The giggle in her voice told me she could spread the bull as well as I could.

"Don't worry, honey. I'll be there. I have something for you." I paused to await her reaction.

She said, "Gee, I can't imagine what that might be."

"I'll give you three guesses and the first two don't count. If you wish, though, I can describe it for you. It is long and sort of shaped like a banana, and our marital vows will require you to allow me to use it for intimate purposes at least five times a day."

"In your dreams, lover boy. In your dreams! That will only happen in your dreams." She laughed again. "I don't want any used equipment, so just make sure you're not using it on anybody else." After a second she added, "Or I might fix it so you don't ever use it again."

"Okay, babe, but remember, that goes for you too. You better not be hot for anyone but me. I've got a lot of exercise planned for you on the night of the 21st." I again waited for her reaction.

"Oh, you talk so big. You must think you're the Fort McCulloch stud." From her chuckles, it was clear she was enjoying this. "Of course, it is a small place so you might be."

"No honey," I said. "Fort McCulloch is a very large place. There just aren't very many people here."

"Well, you know what I mean. We'll just have to see who gives up first on our wedding night." She changed the subject. "Tell me about where we'll be living."

I spent the next minute describing Donaldson's Trailer Court and our diverse mix of neighbors. While there were several officers living in the area, most of our neighbors were enlisted personnel. Staff Sergeant McPherson and his wife Jane were black. He was a clerk typist assigned to post headquarters, and he and his wife were distributors in a multi-level sales company. Sergeant Cunningham and his wife Andrea lived across from us. He was with the 375th Engineer Battalion. Most of the rest of the neighbors I knew little about yet. I ended the conversation with, "We better cut this short honey, or else I won't have any money to travel there with and we will have to postpone our wedding."

"Not on your life, pal. You get here or else."

"Okay babe, I love you."

"I love you too," she answered.

We said good-bye and ended the telephone conversation. Shortly afterward I went to bed.

The next morning was Mount's last day of duty. I wished him well on his civilian career. Since he would not be around in the future to appear in court, he had not been writing any tickets lately, and I had him in the office filing paperwork. As I looked around the office and the police desk area, I noticed how shabby the interior of the building was. It had not been painted in some time.

I went into Operations and walked over to the door of Captain Tucker's office. "Captain Tucker, what are the chances of getting some paint and having our detainees in the D-cell paint this place? It really looks like hell."

"The company Supply chief, Sergeant Davis, could get you some paint, but good luck getting any work done by our AWOL residents," the captain told me.

"Well, just the same, I'll see what I can do." Now, I stepped into his office and asked in a low voice, "Just between you, me, and the gatepost, what is it that you have on the colonel that lets you treat him the way you do?"

"What do you mean by that? What are you talking about?" His face had a shit-eating grin that told me that he knew exactly what I was talking about.

"You and I both know that company-grade officers don't give colonels the brush-off like you do every morning, unless they have something on them."

"The colonel just knows I'm a short-timer and will be gone soon. You'll probably act like this when you get short, too."

It was obvious that the captain was not going to tell me what the source of his power over the colonel was. It didn't matter when or how I asked the question, he wouldn't tell me. It was probably dumb of me to even ask. At any length, I simply left his office with a simple retort, "I doubt I'll get to act that way—short-timer or not."

I went to Supply and procured several cans of paint and some brushes and returned to the PMO. There were six prisoners in the Detention cell. I asked them a simple question. "Would you guys like to get out of that smelly place and get some fresh air?"

One man sat up and replied to me. "What do you have in mind, sir?"

"Well this place looks like hell and could use a fresh coat of paint. If you guys would like to see a little sunshine and fresh air and aren't afraid of a little work, well, we could let you out to paint."

The man got up and said, "Hell, anything's got to be better than sitting in here."

"Great," I said. "Anybody else?"

In a flash, the other five were on their feet. They all agreed with the first man, and in a moment all six were applying paint to the interior of the MP station, the Traffic office and the break room. I put Mount in charge of supervising them to ensure that none walked away, and by lunchtime the area was looking fine. Meals were brought over from the mess hall for the prisoners, and I left with Bronson to get a bite to eat. We listened to Paul Harvey's daily comments on the radio as we drove to the snack bar.

"I could have told you were wasting your time asking Tucker what he had on the colonel. I've been trying to get it out of him for some time, and I haven't had any luck either."

"I decided on the direct approach and, like you said, it was a waste of time."

"Yeah, I've asked when no one else is around, when he's in a good mood and every other time. Whatever he has on the colonel, he's not saying," Bronson stated.

"Let's just hope we can figure it out on our own. That would be good information to have."

"Don't you know it?" Bronson then changed the subject. "Sergeant Robinson wants to take me to bring-your-boss night at the NCO Club next Monday. I told him to include you and we'll make it a bachelor party. We can have most of the company over and have a good blowout. According to Robinson, those bring-your-boss nights can get pretty wild."

"Works for me," I said. "My girl and I quit drinking during my last year of college, but for a special occasion like this I might have a couple."

"You quit drinking? Why would you go and do a thing like that?"

"It's a long story," I began, but the short version goes like this . . . ." I then began to relate how during our last few weeks together, Sam and I had gone out drinking on the weekends with two married couples who really put away the sauce. One Saturday night we were about a half hour late getting to the home of the couple where we usually all met. As we arrived, the man who lived there told us that he and his wife had a fight. She had left with the other couple. He was already drunk and didn't seem to mind. He told us to make ourselves comfortable, and he had plenty to drink right there in the house. As we were deciding what to do, a highway patrolman drove up. He came to the door and asked, "Are you Mister Tanner?" The man said he was, and the patrolman said "I'm sorry to inform you sir, but your wife has been in an accident. She's been transported to Municipal Hospital and the prognosis is that she probably won't make it." Our friend was in total shock, but the patrolman assured him that he best get to the hospital right away.

Since we had not had anything to drink yet that evening, we volunteered to take Jack to the hospital. It was there that we learned that his wife had broken just about every major bone in her body. Of the other couple, the wife was dead and the husband had survived with surprisingly minor injuries. He was released from the hospital just in time to attend his wife's funeral. Jack's wife lived, but her recovery was slow and painful. After the funeral of the woman who died in the wreck, Sam and I went to the junk yard to view the car that we might have been in if we had not been late that night. The car looked like an accordion. The engine was literally sitting in the front seat, and we could not figure how anyone got out alive. I finished with the following comment, "Sam and I looked at each other and decided we had avoided that accident only through the grace of God. We made the decision that we would not drink again." I then continued, "Sam spent a lot of time helping take care of the woman while I was preparing to graduate, and our relationship fell apart. I have been pretty much on the wagon ever since."

"That's quite a story," Steve said. "Do you really think you would have been in that car if you hadn't arrived late?"

"I'm sure we would have been, Steve. Sam and Jack's wife were pretty good friends and Sam would have preferred to go with her rather than stay there at her house."

"Wow, it's a good thing you were late. Do you remember what held you up?"

"No, I don't," was my answer. "I just remember looking at that car. It hit one of the concrete supports on an overpass at about ninety miles per hour. So, you see, I might have a beer to be sociable, but I'm not going to get drunk. I've found that most people respect the way I feel, and those that don't can drop dead."

"This will be a first—a sober groom at a bachelor party," said Steve with a smile.

"Well, maybe I can help ensure everyone else makes it home alive."

We finished our lunch and returned to the PMO. Upon our return, Mount met me at the door with unexpected news. "You have a mutiny on your hands with the AWOLs," he said. "They quit working and are all back in the D-cell."

"What happened? They were happy to get out of there earlier."

"Sergeant Blanc started ordering them around and acting like a hard ass and they got pissed off and quit working," Mount explained.

I shook my head. "Now that I'm back, we'll let Blanc take care of the desk and we'll let the AWOLs answer to us." The truth be known, Mount probably didn't mind Blanc causing the trouble, because it allowed him to stop baby-sitting the AWOLs and go to lunch. I didn't say that, though. Instead, I walked back to the D-cell. "Men, I understand there's a problem. What's going on?"

One man in the D-cell spoke for them all. "Well sir, the sergeant on the desk seems to want to hard-ass us and give us a rough time. We feel like we don't have to take it."

"You're absolutely right," I said. "You don't have to take it."

The fact that I agreed with the man seemed to take him completely by surprise. He stood there dumbfounded.

I continued, "With me here, you only have to answer to me, not the desk sergeant. I can assure you, I'm not going to hard-ass anyone. If you want out of that smelly D-cell to get a little fresh air, I can help you do it. If not, that's fine too. It's your guys' decision."

The man thought for a few seconds and asked, "The desk sergeant won't bother us anymore?"

"Nope, I'll make sure he sticks to his work."

"Well, I'd just as soon be painting as sitting in here." The others agreed. Within a few minutes they were completing the task begun earlier that morning. The rest of the workday passed with no more difficulties, and at 1700 hours I was ready to depart for home.

As I was walking out of the building, Mister Garcia caught me. WO2 Garcia had recently been attached to the company, and they put him in charge of vehicle registration. Since vehicle registration was basically a SP4's job, Garcia took over the company sports program to have something to do.

I turned around as he called my name. "Yeah, Jerry. What is it?"

He asked quizzically, "You can play softball, can't you?"

I answered in the affirmative. "The Dodgers aren't scouting me or anything but, yeah, I can play a decent game. Why?"

"We have a game scheduled with the 112th Quartermaster Detachment tonight and I need a team. The 290th MP Company finished last in the first half of the season and I figure it's time to turn that around. The game is at 1900 hours at the west field. Can we count on you?"

A STATESIDE TOUR OF DUTY

I didn't have anything else to do. So, why not? "Yeah, I'll be there," I said. "You say we finished last in the first half?"

"Yes. But most of the games were forfeits because we couldn't field a team most of the time. I plan to change that right now. We've won three out of five so far during the second half, but we were lucky, and several of the guys who played are on swing shift this week and aren't available for tonight. If I can get a lineup that is pretty well set, we're going to win some games."

"Good job," I said. "Let's kick some butt tonight." I gave him the thumbs up sign.

"Thanks," he replied. He then went looking for more players.

I thought a softball game would be just the thing to get my mind off everything else going on. Besides, the exercise would be good for me. That night I got my fielder's glove and headed to the west field. Jerry had recruited just enough to field a team. There were nine of us ready to play when the umpire yelled, "Play ball!" I took my place in right field.

Right field on this particular park was a mess. The light pole for that section of the field was placed too close in, so I had to watch out for the guy-wires that stretched down from it. Any hit that did not go over the fence for a home run was invariably behind those wires, so I had to be careful not to trip over them and break a leg. Another possible danger was to run into the wires and get clotheslined. I finished the game without committing any errors or injuring myself. Unfortunately, we lost the game 10–9. As we got together to give a cheer for the 112th Quartermaster Detachment, Jerry said, "Listen guys. This team we played tonight won the first half. If we continue to play this way, we're going to beat some people. Let's hold our heads high and remember that. Thanks for coming."

The next morning, I was sitting in my office reading the paper when an article caught my eye. A man in Dallas had happened upon a traffic accident in that city about eight months ago and had saved the life of one of the participants. He was a former Boy Scout and had used first aid to keep the injured man alive until the ambulance arrived. The man whose life was saved turned out to be very wealthy and now had offered the Good Samaritan a one-million-dollar check in gratitude. The man who performed the good deed had turned it down. The headline read: Man Turns Down One Million Dollars. I was incredulous.

As I was reading, Sergeant Blanc opened the door and looked at me. He shut the door and returned to his seat on the desk, where he said in a loud voice and in a laughing manner to his desk clerk (and anyone else in earshot), "The lieutenant just stays in his office and doesn't bother anyone or rock the boat. He ain't bothering anyone."

I got up and walked slowly out to the desk. I walked up the steps to the desk where I said, "Sergeant Blanc, have you got a moment? I need to talk with you for a minute. It's very important." Blanc followed me back to my office, where I shut the door. "Listen, sarge, I don't know if you are aware of it or not, but between here and Camp Price our unit is over on our TO&E strength: two majors, a captain, two lieutenants, two warrant officers, an E-8 and bunches of E-7s. With that much extra supervisory personnel running around, we can either look for things to do or go with the flow and not rock the boat. Now, if a lieutenant (like myself) chose not to rock the boat and got the idea that he was being laughed at for choosing that course of action, he would need to look for extra duties (which could mean extra hours here at work) to impress the major and the colonel up front. If he did that, he would then need a NCOIC to assist him. That NCOIC, who would also have to work a lot of extra hours, would have to be a real sharp E-7. Do you get my drift?"

Sergeant Blanc's eyes opened real wide as my words sank in. I could tell that he understood what I was saying very well. "I'm sorry if I appeared to be laughing at you, sir. That was not my intention. You're right, though, we don't need any extra duties to be assigned around here. I think you're doing an excellent job." He paused for a second before he added, "I better get back to the desk. I also have a lot to do." He hurried out the door and back to his seat behind the desk. As he did, I heard him say, "I didn't mean to imply the lieutenant wasn't busy. He sure has a lot to do; I don't know how he gets it all done."

Now Bronson entered my office and said, "What's with Blanc? He's out there muttering something about how busy you are."

"Oh, him," I smiled. "I just had to put him in his place. He had some idea that I might not be busy doing some very essential part of the mission of this unit. I don't think he'll have any such illusions again."

"I thought we might ride around with the patrols and make sure crime is under control here in the greater metropolitan area. What do you think?"

"I think that's a great idea," I said. "However, first I have an important award to issue to a very deserving individual."

Steve's curiosity was piqued. "What kind of an award?"

"Have you seen this?" I showed him the copy of the *Dallas Morning News* that I had been reading.

"Yeah," said Bronson. "I heard about that moron on the news last night. For the life of me, I can't think of any logical reason for turning down that money." He then added, "Unless he's hoping for a larger amount in the form of an inheritance when the guy kicks the bucket. That might make sense."

As Steve guessed about the man's motivation, I was busy using a magic marker to print large letters on a sheet of cardboard. I then cut the story of the man we were talking about, out of the paper and used Scotch tape to attach it to the cardboard. I then held up the finished project for Steve to critique. The poster read: "This Year's Recipient of the Lieutenant Moultrie Dumb Ass of the Year Award Is——." An arrow pointed down to the picture of the man in the story.

"That's great! I couldn't have phrased it any better myself," Steve said.

I then took four thumbtacks out of my desk and stuck the poster on my office door. Several men in the room voiced their approval. Steve and I then walked out to the desk and had Blanc call the White Mouse in to the station. Specialist Cummings pulled up a few minutes later. SP4 Cummings was the only black soldier among the three enlisted men I now had in the Traffic section. I had named him the Traffic NCOIC over the two white sergeants, and I think it made him somewhat uncomfortable to technically oversee the two higher-ranking men. However, with Mount and Foster being such short-timers, it seemed the way to proceed, at the time. Besides, where he was already doing a sergeant's job, I thought it might make promotion more likely when he went before the next promotion board. We were out with him running radar until 1130 hours when the desk informed us over the radio that the major wanted to meet with me and Steve ASAP. Cummings dropped us off back at the PMO.

As we walked in the station, I noticed that my poster was now missing from the door of my office. I inquired as to its whereabouts and was told that the major had taken it. The stupid, dumb-ass major ought to stick to his chair-warming and patrol tips and leave my stuff alone, I thought. The desk clerk opened the door to the D cell area and we walked through to the next door, which buzzed as the desk clerk pressed the release button. We shut the doors behind us as we walked through, and went up to the front office. As we got to the door of the major's office I said, "You sent for us, sir."

Major Disaster (as Steve and I called him when he was not around) was sitting at his desk, drawing another patrol tip. This was patrol tip number three. Patrol tip number two had been posted on the bulletin board the day before and told the men to always get a description of all suspects that included height and weight. Since a person five foot nine would be a "big guy" to someone five foot one and a runt to a man six foot four, descriptions such as tall or short were meaningless. MP personnel should avoid any description that might be relative to someone else and ask for exact measurements.

"Yes, come in," said the major. He reached down beside his desk and picked up the poster I had made earlier. "First of all, Lieutenant Moultrie, I don't consider this very professional work." He held up my poster. "I'm sure the government expects you to use your time better."

"I'm sorry you disapprove, sir," I said. "It occurred to me that it might help improve unit morale. Most government studies have shown that as unit morale improves, efficiency and productivity increase also." Actually, I had no such thought. I just figured that was the type of crap the major wanted to hear.

The major sat and thought for a few seconds. "Oh," he said. "Next time find a better way to do it." He handed me back my poster. He then turned his attention to Steve. "Lieutenant Bronson," he said confidently, "I need a list of men who would be good candidates for the goon squad. They should be above average in height and weight. At least six and no more than eight men are needed, and I need the list on my desk by 1700 hours this afternoon."

"Yes, sir," said Steve. "You'll have it."

"Very good then. Dismissed."

As Steve and I returned to our offices in the back of the building he said nothing. After we had pressed the buzzer and opened the door to the D-cell area and closed it behind us, Steve busted out laughing. "Increase efficiency and productivity! Where did you dream that one up? I thought I was going to lose it on the spot when you came up with that bullshit. That was great. What studies were you talking about anyway?"

"If Major Disaster wanted studies, I could make them up on the spot. I could tell him that the National Transportation Safety Board or the New York Transit Authority spent years collecting data. He couldn't prove otherwise. Steve, my friend, if you can't dazzle them with brilliance, then baffle them with bullshit."

A STATESIDE TOUR OF DUTY

"That's a great tactic," Bronson said. "I have to admit that you're good at it."

"Thank you, I'll take that for a compliment."

We met Charlie for lunch. He told us about some of the losers that were attending the current defensive driving class he was teaching. Steve responded by telling him about our earlier meeting with the major. When Charlie heard how the major had sucked down the nonsense I had told him earlier, he laughed almost as hard as Steve had. "I've got to remember that for the next time someone is chewing my butt," he commented.

After our return to work, I reviewed some accident reports and sent them into Operations. After a few telephone calls, I was able to terminate two more Blue Bell cases and sent the reports up to the secretaries to be typed and another exciting workday ended.

The next Monday evening, Staff Sergeant Robinson had reserved a long table at the NCO club right up next to the go-go dancers for bring-your-boss night. The sergeants from various units brought their company commanders or executive officers. The post sergeant major brought Charlie (They joined us at the MP table). Sergeant Robinson had managed to obtain one hundred dollars from the unit fund, since this had been designated officially as a company party. Unofficially, it was my bachelor party. Most of the desk sergeants and patrol superintendents and other company NCOs were there, drawn by the promise of free beer. After the hundred dollars was spent, the prices at bring-your-boss night were cheap enough that one could still drink for a minimum expense.

Shortly after we got there, the go-go dancers showed up. What happened next surprised me. The statement that the bring-the-boss nights were wild was no exaggeration. There was a blond, a brunette and a red head. As the jukebox played, they twisted and gyrated to the music. They wore short skirts and frilly tops with bare midriffs. As the crowd got livelier, the girls took off their shirts to expose some bra-like halter-tops. A little while later they took off the skirts to expose some bikini bottoms. I honestly figured that was as far as they would go with the exposure. I figured wrong. Soon the red head took off her top off and exposed her breasts to the delight of those present. She received hundreds of wolf whistles and catcalls. The blond went topless next. It seemed like everyone in the place was yelling for the brunette to take her top off, which she quickly did. She then began an exercise where she was spinning each breast in the opposite direction of the other.

I sat there and thought that lots of places have topless dancers, so this wasn't that unusual. I told myself that it was no big deal. Then the blond took her bottom off. The other two quickly followed her. Now this was something I had never seen before. Three downright, sheer, buck-naked go-go dancers. They were not content to just expose their pubic hair and breasts. As they gyrated, they made sure they lifted their legs high to give everyone a good look between their thighs. Occasionally one would turn her back to the audience and bend over with her legs spread wide. Where we were only about ten feet from them, our company got quite a show.

At this time, I was very thankful that I had decided to nurse one beer a long time and remain sober. Sergeant Blanc walked up to the girls and told them something, and I saw him point over at me. Shortly afterward the blond stepped down from the go-go stand she was dancing on and walked toward me. I got up and kept a good distance from the girl. Sam would have a fit if she knew I was even watching this exhibition. There was no way I was going to do something to be ashamed of. After all, I would never tolerate her messing around with a naked man.

The girl didn't dare pursue me, as she would have quickly faced a gauntlet of grabbing hands from drunken soldiers. While she was happy to show off what nature had done for her, she apparently didn't desire to be groped. She returned to her place and danced while I returned to our company's table.

"You sure moved fast," Steve noted with a grin. "You ran like hell."

"Damn straight," I said. "If that girl had of gotten her hands on me I might have been court-martialed for conduct unbecoming an officer and have to worry about my wife finding out. That damned Blanc isn't going to get any favors from me in the future."

"I don't know what his problem is, but I'll be keeping an eye on him, too," Steve said.

Bring-your-boss night was held every six months at the NCO club. There was no doubt that this would be my last one. I knew that Sam would not want me attending these events anymore, and since I wanted our marriage to work, I would not argue with her. The marriage vows include the words "forsaking all others" and I am pretty sure that includes not viewing debauched exhibitions like the one I had just seen. In fact, I decided to just forget these gatherings existed altogether and not tell her that they even occurred.

After a while, the event broke up. As men ran out of money or just figured they had better be getting home, the NCO club began to empty.

A STATESIDE TOUR OF DUTY

Finally, the amount of time the girls had been paid to dance expired and they put on their clothes and left. Those men remaining began to file out. Steve had a few too many and Charlie gave him a ride home. Before they left, however, Charlie asked me for a favor.

"Nick, I've been reading this book on the psychology of sex. I haven't had a chance to try out what it says yet. I'd appreciate it if you would read it and let me know how well it works."

"What does it say, Charlie?"

"It has a lot of information, but I'm mostly interested in chapter three. Look, Nick, to tell the truth when I've been with a girl in the past, I seem to finish up quicker than I want to. I then have to use a little manual action to totally please the lady, if, you know what I mean." Charlie continued, "Chapter three tells how to solve that problem. I would like to know if it works before I try it."

Every man wants to be a super lover, but I was learning that many fail miserably. According to Sam, a lot of her married friends were disappointed with their husbands' performances in the bedroom. Unlike women, who will compare notes about husbands or boyfriends, men usually keep their mouths shut. I respected Charlie for having the guts to say something. I was willing to receive all the help I could get and if it worked, I would report accordingly.

I took the book. "Yeah Charlie, I know exactly what you mean. To tell the truth, in the past, I've had to use a lot more manual manipulation than I would have liked. I'll let you know how it goes." I didn't expect much but I figured you could try anything once. I went home and began to read.

The book *The Psychology of Sex* was unlike any book I had ever seen. I had seen so-called marriage manuals in the past. They were usually semi-pornographic with a lot of pictures and very little real information. This was different. There were no pictures in this book. As I started to read, the author detailed the difference between men and women when it came to dealing with sex. Men, he said, could make sex as commonplace as shaking hands (although the author did not recommend this). For women, on the other hand, sex required a major mental commitment on some level (either conscious or subconscious). I found the book very interesting, but I read rapidly until I reached chapter three. This was the chapter Charlie seemed most interested in. Chapter three was titled: The Male Trigger. Here the author detailed how the most common sexual problem for most of the male population was premature ejaculation. He claimed that the act of sex was mostly mental and with a combination of mental concentration on the act as well as certain body movements this problem could be eliminated. After I read the chapter, I reread it. I then got in my car and drove to the PMO and went into the Operations office where I xeroxed chapter three. As I was leaving, the desk sergeant commented that I was working late.

I smiled. "Just copying a training manual, sarge. I never know when I might be required to teach a class and might not be able to find the necessary field manual." After that lie I waved good-bye to the men on the desk and made the return trip home. I was getting married on Friday and I was determined to memorize chapter three by then.

Wednesday morning, I put my suitcase in the car and drove to the company area to sign out on nine days' leave. I dropped Charlie's book back off to him and promised to give him an analysis of how the information worked. I also stopped by the PMO before I left to shake hands with Steve.

"Good luck, Nick. Don't do anything I wouldn't do." He took a long drag on his cigarette and added, "There isn't much I can think of that I wouldn't do on a honeymoon, so that leaves you a wide-open field."

"Thanks, Steve. I'm hoping to get a lot of help from Charlie's book. I intend to make the MP Corps proud."

Steve laughed. "Charlie's been trying to get me to read that book and try it on a girlfriend but, hell, I figure you learn from practical application, not from some damned book."

"Well," I said. "If it works as well as I hope it does, you may change your mind. The worst that can happen is nothing. The best that can happen is you'll make a lot of women happier. If you're like me, sex is best when your partner is enjoying it, too."

"That's true. I love it when they squeal with delight, but you never know if they're faking it. Well, I'll be awaiting your report." Steve took another long puff on his cigarette and jokingly said, "Just don't make that new bride of yours too sore the first night out."

"Steve, the truth be known," I said solemnly. "She might be all I can handle."

"Then you're a lucky man," he replied. We shook hands and I was on my way.

CHAPTER EIGHT

I arrived in Phoenix shortly after noon on Thursday. My first stop was Sam's apartment. I knocked on her door and it was opened by one of her roommates.

"Sam, there's someone here to see you," the girl yelled.

"You took your sweet time getting here," Sam said as she ran out of her bedroom into the living room. She threw her arms around me and proceeded to give me a long, passionate kiss.

"Someone get some water to throw on these two," the roommate said with a grin.

Another girl sitting on the couch watching television looked over and said, "Oh, they're just getting ready for tomorrow night, I think we can cut them some slack."

"If we were practicing for tomorrow night, we would be doing something else," I said looking at the girl.

"That I really don't want to watch, thank you very much," she said with a laugh.

"Oh, come on now, wouldn't you like to know what goes on behind closed doors?"

"Not in this life, thanks," answered the girl. With that, she returned her attention to the show she was viewing.

Sam led me into her room, where she was finishing packing her things for the trip to Fort McCulloch. She had two suitcases and a half-dozen cardboard boxes, and they were all just about filled. Sitting next to her bed was a shoe rack, which contained about a dozen pairs of shoes.

"I don't think we have enough room in the car for all this stuff. Why don't you just have a rummage sale?" I said with a big smile. "The next few days you won't have much need for clothes anyway."

"The big-talking Fort McCulloch stud is at it again," Sam said as she kissed me once more. I put my arms around her and we enjoyed a lengthy embrace. After a little bit, we broke apart and I looked around at her stuff. One open suitcase had about a dozen pairs of bikini panties sitting on top of the other clothes in it. I picked up one pair of them.

"I can't wait to take these off you," I said jokingly. "Shall we close the door and let me get a little practice?"

She grabbed the panties out of my hand and tossed them back in the suitcase and closed it. "The anticipation will be good for you. You'll just have to wait until tomorrow. You will not get any previews or practice tonight."

With a big smile that showed my mock disappointment, I snapped my fingers and said, "Darn, I was so looking forward to fooling around."

"I bet you were," Said Sam. She kissed me. "Tomorrow night you can fool around all you want, as long as it's with me." She was so cute I had to give her a hug.

"I'm starving!" I said, changing the subject. "Do you have anything to eat around here, or shall I go down to a taco shop?"

"I haven't been shopping for groceries since I'm moving out tomorrow, but there are still just a few things here I can whip up for you." Sam them put her arms around me again and said, "I guess this is as good a time, as any, to tell you something and I hope you won't get mad." There was an apprehensive look on her face.

I looked into her eyes. "Sounds like bad news. Well, what do you have to tell me?" She looked away. I wondered what on earth could be going wrong now. I didn't even want to guess. "Honey," I demanded, "what is it you need to tell me?" I braced myself for the worst.

"Promise you won't be angry. I've been worried about how you're going to react to this." She was clearly worried about something.

"Honey," I said sternly, "just say it straight out. What is it I need to know?"

She looked down at the floor and in a weak voice said, "I maxed out your credit card."

There was a huge sense of relief that came over me. Compared with the amount of human folly in the world, things could be a lot worse. After all, I did give her the card. "Do you know what this means," I asked, using as irritated a voice as I could while maintaining a straight face.

"No? What?"

A STATESIDE TOUR OF DUTY

"Well," I began, "we'll be starting our married life in debt. Second, it means that in the future I'll be taking control of the money. Finally," I allowed my face to break into a smile, at this point, "what you charged up, I'm going to take out in trade tomorrow night."

Sam smiled. "I'll be worth it, honey. I can promise you that." She kissed me again. I could tell that she was relieved by my reaction.

She cooked up something for me to eat as we made small talk. Since we would be leaving right after the wedding reception, we started to pack her stuff in the trunk and the back seat after I had eaten. As we packed the last of it I asked, "By the way, what about the clothes you'll be wearing tomorrow?"

"I've kept those out," she said. Then anticipating my next question, she looked at me and said, "You'll see those clothes when I'm wearing them."

Her roommates were giving her a trousseau tea that night, so we kissed each other good-bye and I headed to the frat house. Geoff Coaltrain was still in school working on his master's. He had agreed to be the best man and he was trying to line up a few festivities for the evening. There were only a few members living at the frat house during the summer, so there would be no large party. However, any group of fraternity brothers will use any occasion to drink beer. There were about twelve guys on hand, and while they sipped suds I got to know the ones who had joined since my graduation. A few were considering service in the military and I told them all about my journey through basic training, AIT, and OCS.

"When I got to Fort Leonard Wood, Missouri, for basic training," I began, "I first met the drill sergeants who made up our company cadre. Our field first (chief drill sergeant) was Sergeant Watkins. He was a large, black sergeant first class who had about twenty years' service in the Army, and the first thing he told us was, 'If you men play ball with me, then I'll play ball with you. If you don't play ball with me, then I'll shove the bat up your ass.'" Everyone laughed as I continued. "Needless to say, I followed the rules and gave Sergeant Watkins no problems."

The evening went on with my war stories being the night's focal point. The Army is filled with people who seem more like caricatures than real people, and everyone who has served usually has no problem invoking fits of laughter from others as they tell about these individuals. Thus, it was with me. There were those in basic training (or other advanced training) who couldn't cut the program and were kicked out of the Army as unfit for duty for one reason or another. There were others you served with who became your best friends. There were also many other dedicated people who served their country proudly that you enjoyed working with. Finally, there were the losers who obviously were in the service because they couldn't find a job anywhere else. This last group was only accepted by the Army because there was a war taking place. The final group and the first group were the ones about whom it was easiest to tell hilarious stories, and I was able to keep the others entertained for some time.

Those who had draft boards breathing down their necks or thought they might serve for other reasons had many questions, and I answered them based on my experience so far.

"Look, guys," I said, "whether you end up in the service or not, one lesson I have learned is often you can go further (in life) by bluffing than you can by any other means. Let me illustrate with this story."

I then took a deep breath and continued. "While I was attending Advanced Individual Training (AIT) at Fort Leonard Wood, all our breaks between classes were taken at the position of parade rest. I thought this was just unnecessary harassment, so one morning, as we filed out of class for the break, I snuck around the corner of the building for a quick nap. I thought the noise of the men returning to class would wake me. Unfortunately, I was a much sounder sleeper than that. When I awoke, the sun was high in the sky. I had been asleep for two hours and it was lunchtime. I jumped up and peeked in a window to see if my class was still there. Fortunately for me, they were. The big problem was that a drill instructor was sitting right by the front door, and he would want to know where in the world I had been. With visions of lengthy KP or other forms of punishment before me, I decided on the boldest approach possible. I opened the door and slammed it behind me as noisily as possible. As the drill sergeant started to ask where I had been, I said forcefully, 'Morning drill, sergeant,' and headed for my seat near the front of the class."

I paused a moment for dramatic effect. "As I sat down, I looked out of the corner of my eye to see Sarge scratching his head wondering where I had been. The guy sitting next to me had the same thought and whispered that question to me. I answered back the truth, in a whisper, and he said, 'You're kidding.' I told him that I wasn't and asked where Sarge was. He looked and told me, 'He's headed this way.'

"Just as the sergeant got to my seat, the man teaching the class asked a question. I raised my hand, and as he called on me I stood and began a lengthy answer. The teacher was delighted that I was so interested in his class and asked me a follow-up question, which I answered with even more detail. As I continued to speak, Sarge became self-conscious about standing up there in the front of the class and returned to his seat at the back of the class. When he did, I finally ended my answer. We were then dismissed for chow. As I fell outside into formation, I could feel the sergeant's eyes staring at me, but I acted nonchalant and like I hadn't done anything wrong. He never asked me where I had been, and I sure didn't volunteer the information."

"It took real guts to pull that off," one guy noted. "I don't think I could have done it."

"In the Army," I explained, "the worst form of punishment is doing pots and pans on kitchen police (KP), and they would have had me on it for a week or more. With motivation like that, it was very easy to make sure that I found a way out. The point is that a good bluff will always take you a long way, because so few are unwilling to call it—if you look like you know what you're doing. Always remember that."

"That's a good lesson to keep in mind," another guy said. "I think I learned something here tonight."

I added one more thought. "Look," I said, "they taught me while I was going to school that knowing where to find information is just as good as knowing the information. This incident taught me that acting like you know something or are authorized to do something is almost as good as knowing that information or having that authorization."

"Son-of-a-gun!" the kid said. "I'll have to remember that."

"One more piece of advice I can add is this," I continued. "If you are considering going into the military, sign up for ROTC. The guys that do that have a really easy road compared to the way I did it. You go in as an officer and avoid the nonsense of basic training and AIT, and above all you don't go through the hell of OCS. I know it's not cool to be in ROTC, and you have to march around the parking lot a couple of hours a week, but it beats the heck out of what I experienced." A couple of guys seemed to think it was worth considering my suggestion.

Like any group of guys, we sat up talking late into the night. Someone asked about my not having a beer and I told the story about why I had quit drinking. Geoff knew the story and respected my decision. Still he joked, "Nick is the only frat brother I can remember who is going to his wedding without a hangover."

"Maybe I'll start a new trend," I replied.

"Don't bet on it," someone said.

"The only thing I feel really badly about," Geoff continued, "is we didn't round up a stripper for tonight to give you a proper bachelor party."

"Been there, done that, old buddy," I replied to Geoff. I then proceeded to tell everybody all about bring-your-boss night and the three strippers I had observed at Fort McCulloch. Needless to say, that story probably gained the attention of the guys more than anything I had said previously.

"Maybe I'll join the service after all!" one kid said.

"Only the best for those who serve our country!" said another.

"Truth of the matter is," one individual said between gulps of his beer, "Geoff said we probably couldn't find a girl built as well as the one you're getting hitched to tomorrow." Then he added, clearly under the influence of alcohol, "Are her jugs really as big as I've heard?"

Out of the corner of my eye I saw Geoff give the kid a look that could kill but, knowing the obnoxious slob probably wasn't used to drinking, I decided not to take offense. Instead, I just smiled and looked at the young man and quietly explained, "It's usually in very poor taste to ask another man personal questions about his fiancée. However, let me say this. The Rolls Royce Company, which makes the finest cars in the world, never gives out any horsepower ratings for their engines. They just tell you that they have adequate horsepower. Likewise, we guys must accept that whatever the lady we're with has is adequate. Hopefully, they will do the same for us."

The guy sitting to the left of the kid who asked the question elbowed him and said, "How about that, Dave? You can't find a date larger than an A cup."

The kid seemed crushed by the remark, so I tried to console him by saying, "Don't worry kid, Geoff here used to tell me, when it came to women's breasts, that anything over a mouthful was wasted."

"I lied," Geoff said between swigs of his beer. "I can definitely state that the big ones are more fun to play with than the little ones." He then looked at me, hoisted his can of beer up in a one-man toast, nodded his head and smiled. I could tell that he felt that I had done well.

Suddenly, I felt a real need to change the subject. Whereas in previous times I could laugh and tell jokes about female body parts, the thought of Sam being mentioned in such talk irritated me a lot. I decided to tell a different story. "Look guys," I related, "there was one time I fell off the wagon after I left here." Everyone seemed ready for another story so I continued with my narrative.

"At the end of Basic Training our drill sergeant, Sergeant Parker, came to me and said that since we were the honor platoon in the company we should have a party to celebrate. We took up a collection and he went and bought the beer. Drinking in the barracks being a big violation of the rules, we did what was right and went to a park. When we got there, I was all set to have a soft drink when one of the guys said he would be honored if I would lead them in a toast to celebrate the end of Basic Training.

"As the platoon guide, I had been the leader of these guys for all eight weeks and was honored he had asked, so I grabbed a can of beer and did so. After one can, I had another and then a third. About this time, I noticed that the shinsplints that I had suffered from for several weeks had disappeared, so I had several more beers. I was so happy that my legs were pain-free that I decided to run the men back to the barracks instead of walking. Most of the men in my platoon were only eighteen or nineteen years old and were obviously not used to drinking, so when we got there several were very sick from the run and began to throw up.

"As members of the other three platoons observed my men in various stages of inebriation, they decided that if the third platoon could have a party, then they could, too. Only these idiots didn't have the good sense to leave the company area. They went and bought beer, and soon the drill instructor who was CQ (charge of quarters) for the day, Sergeant Rodriguez (whom we called Sergeant R), had joined them.

"Seeing that all hell was breaking out, I had my men leave for the mess hall. After lunch, we returned to the barracks just after the CO had arrived. We walked in the front door just in time to hear Rodriguez say, 'Sir, what does this mean?' The CO yelled back, 'It means, you stupid dumb ass, that you let the men in the barracks with booze.' As we came in the door, the CO inquired of me if we had done any drinking, and I explained that we had been very careful to leave the company area to party. Also, since we were just returning from chow, we were not part of the ruckus currently in progress.

"The CO sent us to our floor and didn't bother us again as he tore everyone else a new ass. We never saw Rodriguez again. I suspect that they transferred him to Vietnam. The drill sergeant who had been selected as the new field first (that's the head drill sergeant) did not get the promotion, and two more drill sergeants were reprimanded. The only drill instructors who were not punished were our third platoon cadre. Needless to say, Sergeant Parker became the new field first. That taught me that you can be punished or rewarded for things that happen when you're not even around. The point is that you had better be sure the people you leave in charge know what they're doing, because you could be punished for their mistakes."

After I finished the story everyone was silent. I couldn't tell if they had drunk themselves into a stupor or were contemplating the moral of my story. I suppose that after so many funny anecdotes, I shouldn't have finished up the evening with a story that was a downer. Oh well, live and learn.

At that point, I decided it was time for bed, and I went and turned in. Tomorrow would be the beginning for a new chapter of my life.

CHAPTER NINE

One great thing about being in the service is you can get married in your uniform and save money on a tux. I had brought my dress blues along for the occasion. Dress blues are the formal Army uniform and are rarely worn. Usually, there are only one or two occasions during the year when they are needed. They represent an expense that most new officers resent just for that reason. Upon graduation from OCS, I was required to obtain them and they cost me $150. If I wore them to three events during my time in the service, that would represent $50 an event. Army dress blues are a very colorful and, some would say, a very ostentatious uniform. As we were trying them on after purchasing them, some of my peers at OCS commented that they looked like a band uniform. Personally, I thought they made a man look like a field-grade bellhop.

After lunch, I spit-shined my shoes to a high gloss and I was ready to go. Some of my fraternity friends kept asking if I was nervous, and I could honestly state I was not. Anxious was the more correct description. When asked what the difference was I stated, "Nervous is a state of being scared while anxious means you are chomping at the bit and ready to go ahead. The wedding was set for five o'clock and Geoff and I and the rest of the guys arrived a little early. By five thirty Sam and her bridesmaids had not shown up.

As people arrive and the start of the ceremony becomes later and later, it becomes harder and harder to smile. Five forty-five arrived and still no Sam. Some of my buddies were starting to kid me about being left at the altar. I took the kidding in stride, but the uncertainty starts to grate on you. Six o'clock and Sam was not in attendance. A million things go through your mind in an instance like this, but the only thing you can do is pace back and forth. Finally, at ten minutes after six, Sam and her attendants arrived.

"What on earth took so long, Sam?" I said as she walked in the door. Even though I knew there had to be a good explanation, I still had to ask the question.

"Laura was my best friend in high school, but we haven't been close the last couple of years, so I didn't ask her to be one of the bridesmaids. I found out that she was hurt by the slight, so we went and bought some more material and made her a dress at the last minute. We were so hurried that we had to sew the dress on her. It doesn't even have a zipper." Sam was still explaining and apologizing to everyone when I asked what I thought was a simple question.

"Why didn't she just wear a dress that she already had? That would have saved time."

Sam gave me an irritated look that showed that was not a possibility. "Nick," she said. "If she did that, she wouldn't match the others."

"But you would have all been on time," I noted.

Sam gave me another look that showed that I had best shut up and quit while I was ahead. It was clear that, for women, fashion and convention trumped punctuality. "It's no big deal," she said. "The ceremony will just get started a few minutes later."

Geoff and I went into the chapel and took our place up front. After the lengthy opening delay, the rest of the evening went on as planned. There were no more snafus. He little sisters came in as flower girls, her bridesmaids entered one by one and then there was Sam on her father's arm. Her father gave her away, I remembered to bring the ring, and Geoff didn't lose it, and Sam and I both said, "I do." Also, no one said anything in opposition. I was so happy to get it over with, I kissed her twice.

Anyone who has stood in a reception line starts to wonder where this exercise in torture originated. I have been told that President Theodore Roosevelt holds the record for shaking hands at one of these events. If so, that is a record he can keep. What I experienced was bad enough. During the three-hour duration, Sam and I got our picture taken and shook hands with a lot of people we didn't know or had not seen in years. The whole time we would rather have been somewhere else. Finally, we cut the cake, changed clothes and departed while people threw rice on us. Then we got to see what our friends had done to the car.

One side of the car had "She got him today, but he will get her tonight" written on it.

A STATESIDE TOUR OF DUTY

The other side said, "Just married—grand opening tonight," and on the trunk someone had written, "Phoenix today, hot springs tonight." Then, just to make sure that no one missed seeing us as we drove down the street, lots of junk was tied to the back of the car to make noise and draw lots of attention. Aren't friends wonderful?

I opened the door for Sam, and before she got in she turned her back and tossed her bouquet over her shoulder. Some girl caught it. Then as we drove off to shouts of "Best wishes," Sam said, "You were really handsome in that uniform. I like you in it."

"Thanks, sweetie," I answered. "And you were a very beautiful bride. Now we have to find a car wash."

"No way," argued Sam. "We have to get pictures of the car first. You can wash the car tomorrow."

As we drove to the motel, Sam had me drive down the main streets where there would be lots of people. Other drivers honked, a few guys yelled, "Sucker!" and a couple of people gave us the old Roman thumbs-up sign. Sam was all smiles. After arriving at the motel, I grabbed our suitcases and we walked to the room we had previously reserved. I set the suitcases down and carried Sam through the door, then retrieved the suitcases. Because Sam wanted to make an entrance, I took a shower first, and it was a quick one. Then Sam took her sweet time in the bathroom, while I counted the money that the well-wishers who hadn't brought a toaster, silverware, electric can opener or some other hardware, had given us. Then Sam finally made her appearance and I forgot about anything else. The slinky lingerie she had picked out for the night was an eye-catcher and it showcased her body exceptionally well. I got off the bed and walked over to her. As I did, she got a wide-eyed look and, as she ran her fingers across my chest, she asked one question. "Oh Nick," she asked. "What have you done to yourself?"

It was then that, for the first time, I was thankful for the torment of OCS. As I have said before, OCS is twenty-three weeks of pure hell. Every minute that a candidate is not in class, studying, sleeping or eating chow is spent running or doing push-ups. The change to your body is so gradual that you don't know how you've changed until someone points it out. I entered OCS weighing a soft one hundred and forty-eight pounds. Now I weighed one hundred and eighty and it was all muscle. Upon graduation from OCS an officer can run a mile in six minutes or less (wearing combat boots) and do one hundred push-ups as easily as blinking an eye. It was clear that Sam liked the change OCS had on my physique.

"You are so muscular," she said. Then running her fingers down my sides, she continued. "The way your torso narrows down in a *V* shape toward your waist—you have a great shape." It was funny that I was thinking the same thing about her. I was also thankful I had taken off my T-shirt so she could get a good look while the lights were on. She had not seen me without a shirt in well over a year, and I had not been aware the change was so dramatic.

"At Christmas, over a year ago, you asked me if I liked what I saw of your body. How do you like what you see of mine now?" I asked.

"I'm not complaining. Let's get to bed and cuddle up."

After turning off the lights, it was time to get down to the best part of any honeymoon. Men are much more practical than women about honeymoon attire. When a man gets into bed, about all he wears is a pair of jockey shorts. They cover the minimum amount of skin and are easy to remove. Women, on the other hand, wear a lot of expensive, see-through, frilly lace items. These are functional in that they cause a certain amount of anticipation and arousal for the new husband, but they don't stay on very long. That was the case tonight. As I hopped into bed I went to work removing Sam's clothes like a kid unwrapping a Christmas present. It turns out that Sam was desirous of more genteel behavior and quickly voiced her disapproval.

"Hey, hold on a second. Gees, Nick, I didn't get married so you could rape me." As I stopped doing what I was doing, she continued. "The thing I always liked about you is you took your time and were never in a hurry. You're supposed to be my loving husband, Nick, not a hungry wolf going after an injured rabbit. Act like it—a loving husband, that is."

"I'm sorry, honey. I guess I got carried away," I said with contrition. It was then that I realized that maybe the excitement of those bring-your-boss night strippers, along with the anticipation of the past few weeks, had gotten to me. I quickly changed my demeanor. I pulled her close and kissed her.

"That's better," she said. "Now we can get something straight between us."

"First, I have a little story you might enjoy," I said. I thought that might be a good way to remove any tension that might be remaining.

"What? You've got to be kidding."

A STATESIDE TOUR OF DUTY

"Honey," I said, "in the insect world the male praying mantis is only half the size of the female, and if she can catch him she will eat him just like any other bug."

"What the heck does that have to do with us?"

"Well, give me a minute and I'll explain."

Sam lay back and put her hands back behind her head to listen. As she did, this caused her boobs to protrude up higher. From the smug little look she had, it was clear she was enticing me with them. "Don't make it a long story," she said with a wink. "You're holding up my wedding night."

I continued. "Since the male praying mantis has a natural desire to create little praying mantises, and he will be eaten alive if the female catches him, he has to be careful and use a great deal of stealth in approaching her."

Sam smiled and laughed a little. I continued, "If he is successful in sneaking up on her, then he can mate with her. Or, as us humans describe it, he can get himself a good piece of ass."

Sam laughed a little more, but said nothing. She seemed to be enjoying my story, so I continued. "Only one third of the male praying mantises succeed and get away alive. The other two thirds are seen and caught and devoured alive. They become victims of the female's sharp mandibles as she enjoys a sort of wedding breakfast. Apparently, nature has decreed that only the fastest and smartest male praying mantises can breed and the others meet a horrible death."

"Don't worry, honey," Sam said. "I'm not a cannibal, so you should still be alive tomorrow morning." Then with a smile she added, "Provided you do your duty tonight very well."

"The point is, honey, that the male praying mantis wants sex so badly that he is willing to take a chance on being eaten alive. Now, just think how it would be if we humans were like the praying mantis."

"We females would be well fed," Sam said. "Most male humans aren't too bright."

I didn't let her comments take me away from my story. I continued. "Honey, if we were like the praying mantis, it would not diminish my desire for you. The only change would be that it would give new meaning to the phrase 'I feel lucky tonight.'"

"Do you feel lucky tonight, Nick?"

"Yes," I answered. "But, if I get a little too exuberant or enthusiastic in pursuing you, that's the reason. I'm sorry I got carried away before."

"I forgive you."

"Thank you, honey," I replied. "Now I'll refrain from holding up your wedding night any further."

"Good! You were getting long-winded there for a minute." Sam commented. In a few seconds I had finished removing what little of Sam's attire I had not gotten to before. She then said, "Now I'm going to let you play doctor."

"How's that?"

"You're going to perform an emergency operation called a slipthedicktome," Sam whispered in my ear with a giggle.

A few minutes later I facetiously whispered in her ear, "Honey, my religion requires that any girl I marry be a virgin. Are you a virgin?"

"You have to ask a girl that question before you start doing what we're doing. Now shut up and keep your mind on your work."

I was thankful that I read the book Charlie had loaned me. The information I learned in chapter three improved my performance over anything I could ever remember. I was enjoying my first task as a new husband when suddenly Sam grabbed the foremost lock of hair on the front of my scalp. She yanked my head so we were looking eye to eye and asked angrily, "All right buddy, who have you been practicing on?"

Her actions surprised me. "What are you talking about?"

"According to that clock on the night stand, you've been going for twenty-two minutes. You never did that before. You've been screwing somebody to improve your performance that much." The look on her face showed she was not pleased.

"No, honey," I explained. "I read a book called *The Psychology of Sex*. It gave some good information on how a man can improve his love-making. I can show you the pages I xeroxed to prove it. I studied them to get ready for tonight."

The look on Sam's face changed totally. She let go of my hair and settled back. She questioned, "You learned this in a book?"

"Yes I did, babe," I said. "Does it meet with your approval?"

She then threw herself back into the night's labors with reckless abandon, wrapping her arms around me and digging her fingernails into my back (a painful act that I didn't appreciate). She exclaimed, "As you were, soldier. Go! Go and do your duty." Like a good soldier, I complied with her orders. We made love a total of three times before the sandman arrived.

A STATESIDE TOUR OF DUTY

The next morning, I began to wake up first. Still groggy, as I rolled over to her, my mind wasn't fully functional yet. "I better get out of here before your roommates get here and catch us in bed together," I said.

She laughed, "We got married last night, Nick. You are my roommate."

That comment woke me completely up. We laughed together and then began to make out. The best thing about the morning after the wedding night is that there are no clothes to take off and you can get right down to business. Also, the light of day lets you enjoy what you're doing a lot better than the dark of night. The check out time was 11:00 AM. After that, you were technically supposed to be charged for another day. When we checked out at eleven twenty, the clerk just smiled and said he understood. We weren't charged any extra money.

After checking out, we drove back to Sam's old apartment. Her roommates had collected the gifts from the night before. In order to fit everything in the car, I had to rent a carrier for the top. While I was gone, Sam talked with her friends. Finally, after Sam had hugged her former roommates and said all the necessary good-byes and I had made sure the carrier was securely in place, we hit the road.

The American Southwest is one place where air conditioning should be a required feature on any car, especially in August. Unfortunately, my car didn't have it. With the windows rolled down and driving the speed limit, we could survive, but that was about all. When dinnertime rolled around we looked around for a restaurant that was air-conditioned, rather than picking up something at a fast-food drive-through. As we relaxed and ate our meal in a leisurely manner, Sam mentioned one of her roommates.

"While you were gone, Danae took me aside and asked me if it was painful having sex for the first time," she commented.

"What did you tell her?"

"I told her it hurt a little, but it was a neat hurt. That seemed to satisfy her curiosity. She and Tom get married in September and she's scared to death."

"Why didn't you tell her the truth? You could have told her you felt no pain because you had previous experience."

Sam's face showed a great deal of irritation at that comment. "Nick, she had no idea she was the only virgin in the apartment. I spent so long convincing others that I was, I sure wasn't going to make myself out to be a liar."

"Why didn't she just ask Janie? Everybody knew she slept around."

"She did ask, but with the number of guys Janie's had she couldn't remember the first one. She couldn't ask Martha, because she has Doug convinced she's a virgin for their wedding in December."

The incongruity of the situation in Sam's apartment was hilarious. Sam and I had been prudent in our conduct the previous year, so no one knew we had fooled around. Since she didn't want to get a bad reputation, her pretense to Danae and Janie of being a virgin was understandable. Especially after our breakup, she hadn't wanted it to appear that I had used her. She and Martha knew each other's secrets and kept quiet about them. Martha, at twenty-six, was the oldest in the apartment and had been curious enough to get practical experience in the facts of life. But after getting engaged to Doug, who was five years her junior, she also pretended to be a sexual novice. Doug had made it plain that the girl he married had to be a virgin. Since Doug's family was extremely wealthy, in addition to the fact Martha was in love with Doug, deception was the way she chose to go.

Danae was engaged to Tom, an affable, friendly Hawaiian. I had once asked Tom why there were no race riots in Hawaii, unlike the rest of the country. He just smiled and said "Hey man, that's easy. In Hawaii, agitators can't drive in from out of state." Everybody liked Tom. They had chosen to remain chaste until their wedding, and to ensure that happened Tom had gone back to Honolulu to work and save up money.

Then there was Janie. She posed as a nude model for the art students and made good money doing it. In addition, she was a full-fledged active participant in the sexual revolution and made no apologies for doing so. She was engaged off and on with numerous guys, and the so-called engagements seemed to be little more than an excuse to sleep with the same guy more than twice in a row. So, of the four girls, two pretended to be inexperienced for personal reasons, one was openly promiscuous and one apparently remained innocent. Sam's roommates showed a variety of experience, but you would expect that in an apartment of four girls.

"Did you ever think that Danae was just pretending to be a virgin, like you and Martha were?" I asked. "Maybe she was just as discreet as we were and was having fun all along. After all, no one ever caught us in the act."

Sam looked me straight in the eye and said, "I'm glad that someone besides me has had that thought. I can't imagine anyone being that afraid of having sex. Yeah, I've wondered, at times, if it was just an act."

A STATESIDE TOUR OF DUTY

"Wasn't there a time when you were afraid of sex?" I asked.

"No, I was never afraid. I just didn't want to do it because of that experience I had. It took a lot of talking with the therapist, where I worked, to get me over that."

"Good thing," I said. "Otherwise, our marriage might not have lasted very long."

She smiled. "Well, it helps that you are considerate of my feelings, patient, and usually not very demanding."

"Am I supposed to be taking notes right now?" I asked.

"It wouldn't hurt," she replied.

After we had finished dinner, we had to find a place to spend the night. Across the street from the restaurant was a run-down motel, while a newer one was next door. I went to the pay phone to call and get prices. After making the calls, I returned to Sam with my information. "The joint across the street is fifteen dollars a night while the one nearby is twenty-nine. Why don't we take the one across the street and save money?"

Sam was not impressed with my choice. "No, tightwad, we'll take the nice one."

I've always heard that newlyweds often argue about two things, money and sex. Sam gave me absolutely no reason to complain about the latter, but the former was another matter entirely. I believed money was supposed to be saved, while Sam saw a constant need to stimulate the national economy. I constantly had to explain to her that it was my nature to be frugal and thrifty. Her usual comeback was that I was cheap and chintzy.

"Nick, when we were going together you would watch my TV, eat my popcorn, make out on my couch and never spend a nickel. You were the cheapest guy I ever dated. It's time you spent a few bucks on me."

"Sam," I said. "You're a little too critical. I took you to a Glenn Yarborough concert, a Jack Benny concert, we went out for pizza once, movie on campus once, two formal dances—" At this point she interrupted me, which was good because there were embarrassingly few more things I could think of to enumerate.

"I got the Jack Benny tickets from a friend at work," she reminded. "You didn't have to buy them."

"Oh," I said. "Just the same, why don't we save a few dollars? Someday we will have a nice nest egg."

"I've seen too many of my friends spend the night with a guy in a cheap motel. Their relationships never lasted," she said.

"But, honey, we're married," I protested. "It's different with us."

"Yeah, and I want to feel good on my honeymoon. I'm not starting my marriage out in a dump like that." She gave me a determined look and commanded, "Get the nice one."

If the marital relations between men and women were a poker game, then women would hold all the aces. Common sense told me that if I did not rent the better of the two rooms, then Sam would be unhappy. That might not be good. I had always heard married men say, "If mama's happy, then everybody's happy." Suddenly, I saw things her way. "You're right, Sam, the more expensive motel would be sanitized and would make us feel much more comfortable."

Sam smiled. "Now you're thinking."

Yes, I was thinking. Having things go well was worth the additional charge. If Sam was happy, then, she was more inclined to make me happy. My ulterior motives rationalized away the additional fourteen-dollar charge with ease.

As we prepared for bed, Sam came out of the bathroom wearing nothing but a smile. "Aren't you going to wear that cute little outfit you wore last night?" I inquired.

"Why? You won't leave it on very long. Besides, you almost ripped it last night and I want to save it to show it to the daughter I plan to have when she gets married someday."

I could think of no reason to argue with Sam's logic. "May I pretend to be a farmer tonight," I asked.

Sam hesitated and then said, "Do I dare ask for the punch line?"

"That's where I do planting and fertilizing," I said, raising my eyebrows several times.

Sam lay down next to me and said, "Okay, mister farmer. Fertilize me."

Sam laughed as I said, "Okay, honey, one order of fertilization being delivered."

I turned out the light and began to give her my complete attention. The thought occurred that living with Sam at Fort McCulloch was going to beat the hell out of sharing an apartment with Steve or Charlie. Each night I was a little more pleased with my decision to marry her. She was intelligent, liked kids and had other attributes in addition to being good in bed. The next morning, we slept late and had the usual trouble leaving by the checkout time. When we did, I was grinning so much that Sam tried to act embarrassed. Though, she was probably proud of that grin. That way the world knew she was taking good care of me.

We had seven more days before I had to be back to work and five before I had to sign in from leave. That gave us some time to drive around the country and see some sights and act like tourists. The highways of the American Southwest are designed straight and wide. It is easy to develop a condition called highway hypnosis. One can pass a mileage sign saying, for example, Albuquerque 215 miles. Then, in what feels like a few seconds later, you see a similar sign which states, Albuquerque 115 miles and you do not remember the last one hundred miles. It is somewhat frightening, since you are not sure whether you were on subconscious auto pilot or if you were asleep and stayed on the road only through the grace of God. On the trip to Phoenix, I had experienced the condition and was very happy to have Sam with me on the return trip. We listened to the radio and sang along with it occasionally, and to defeat the boredom of the long ride she insisted on taking a turn behind the wheel every few hours or so. At least that was Sam's excuse for wanting to drive. She said having to be alert while driving was less boring than just sitting there as a passenger.

While we spent a great deal of time in conversation, there were times when each of us seemed to get lost in thought. During those times, we might just look at each other and smile. To me the smile was a nonverbal way of saying, "No matter what happens in the future, we will be okay and I love you." I thought that was important because I had known couples that did not smile when they looked at each other. Now I felt sorry for those people and hoped that we would never become like them. Sometimes it seems like the best communication can be nonverbal.

We spent Sunday night in Tucumcari. After checking into a motel, I was lying on the bed watching the weekend news telecast when Sam said, "You know what we haven't done in a long time?"

"Yeah, but I don't call this morning a long time."

"No, not that," said Sam. "We used to play gin rummy all the time. It's been almost a year and a half since we've played that." She produced a deck of cards and, joining me on the bed, said, "Deal."

"I'd much rather play strip poker."

"I bet you would. Forget it and deal them up for gin rummy," she commanded. Sam had always been competitive when we played card games. Unlike many other girls I had known, who intentionally lost games to me for various reasons like building my ego or making themselves appear vulnerable, Sam always played to win. She played like a shark with blood in the water and gave no quarter. She always felt that if a guy's ego couldn't take losing to a girl, then tough. She had always won her share of the games we played.

I dealt us each seven cards and we began playing. I won the first game. "This is the best two out of three," Sam said. I won the second game also. "As I clearly said, this is the best three out of five," Sam chided. I won game three.

"Do you give up? You can't beat the master," I said.

"No, smartie, this is now the best five out of nine." I smiled back at her. I knew that all I had to do was win two of the next six games. There was no way I could lose. Then Sam did something totally unexpected. Without another word, Sam got up from the bed and began to disrobe.

"That's the spirit," I said. "I was getting tired of gin rummy anyway." I started to move toward her as she removed every stitch of clothing.

"Back off," she cried. "I'm just getting comfortable. We're playing the best five out of nine. It's my deal." She sat down on the bed again and began to deal the cards.

I knew that at a time like this I had to suppress my desire to grab at her, and play cards. All I had to do was win two more games and we could move on to more enjoyable pursuits. At least I would find them more enjoyable. After each time Sam took her turn playing a card, she would lay her cards face down and lean back, bracing herself with her arms. With her legs spread wide, she made sure that I saw all of her. It was difficult to concentrate on my cards. There seemed to be no way I could keep my mind on the game the way I should. She won the next three games, to tie the score.

I regained my composure and was determined to keep my mind on my card playing, as hard as that was to do under the circumstances. Sure enough, I won game seven. Victory was within my grasp. Game eight was the closest game yet. It all came down to one final hand. As that hand proceeded, I needed one certain card for the win. The trouble was, Sam was only one card away from victory, too, and her card came up before mine. Sam won game nine going away and won the match five games to four.

"That was really unfair tactics," I complained. "Talk about dirty tricks."

With a smug look Sam said, "Show me in the rule book where a player can't get comfortable to play the game. Besides, a girl is entitled to use all her assets any way she can. But look on the bright side, honey. As the loser, you are entitled to a consolation prize: me."

"Well, that's good, because your style of play has caused me to develop a deadly Hawaiian disease," I said jokingly. "It's called lackanookey."

"You're in luck," Sam replied. "I have the cure. All I have to do is chant the magic Hawaiian word, comeonIwantalayya."

"That's good honey, because tonight I'm going to pretend to be an auto mechanic."

"Okay, mister comedian, what's your punch line?" She asked.

"I'm going to give you a front-end alignment and check your oil."

"You'll never make the tonight show with that line," Sam giggled.

"Well how about this one? Honey, how is sex like a snow storm for a new bride?

"I give up," she replied.

"She doesn't know how long it is going to last or how many inches she's going to get," I said.

Sam laughed. "You may have surprised me with how long the first time lasted after our wedding, but I knew exactly how many inches I was going to get. Now shut up and give them to me. I haven't sat around naked this long just to continue to hear you talk."

Contrary to popular opinion, sometimes in this life, there's nothing wrong with second place. I really enjoyed my consolation prize that evening. I also learned there is a time to talk and a time to shut up.

We had no set itinerary. Whatever location on the map which caught our fancy was where we went. From Carlsbad Caverns to Palo Duro Canyon, we toured the Southwest. Monday night was spent in Amarillo.

The *Guinness Book of Records* has enough taste and tact not to keep track of any sexual records. That is good, because there is no way any such records could be verified, short of voyeurism. Consequently, no one knows the world record for having sex on a honeymoon. My guess is that the record was set by someone like King Solomon, who probably honeymooned with a good many of his thousand wives and concubines. If that was the case, then there was no way a lone couple like Sam and I could set the record. That was just as well, because like all married men, I discovered on Monday night that there were a few days each month that my wife was not interested in being amorous. Just my luck that time would arrive during the honeymoon. That night we played gin rummy again and this time, for obvious reasons, Sam did not take her clothes off. Even without the unfair tactics, she won her share of the games as we played late into the night.

During the evening, we had discussed where we might live when I was discharged from the Army, how many kids we might have and so forth. For the most part, it was pleasant conversation with no apparent direction, as we changed the topic frequently. After we had finished our gin rummy competition we were just lying together, cuddling, enjoying each other's company without being intimate. This was something we had not done to this point in our new marriage. Now Sam got a serious look on her face and asked "Why did you break up with me in March of last year, Nick?"

"The truth is, Sam, I wasn't ready to get married. I was scared to death. Then when I saw you kissing someone else, I just reacted in a normal human manner."

"When you did that, I cried for three days. I was so mad with you that I was even tempted to go out and sleep with someone else to try and get over you." Then she added, "But I didn't."

"I'm relieved to hear that," I said. "Why did you decide not to do that?"

"I knew that I would only hurt myself," she explained. "I had broken a promise I made to myself by sleeping with you, and you broke up with me. I wasn't going to make that mistake again, no matter how I felt. Besides, I saw a plaque in a store that said, 'If you love something, then set it free. If it returns, it's yours. If it doesn't, then it never was yours to begin with.' I felt you would return. That night you called from Fort McCulloch, the moment the phone rang, I knew it was you. Don't ask me how. I just did."

"While we're dealing with aphorisms," I answered, "I saw one that I was impressed with, too. It said, 'Where you've been is irrelevant. What matters is where we go together.'"

"I always felt that the reason you broke up with me had to do with my past. There were times when we were making love that you had a look in your eyes that seemed to wonder who might have had me before you." She continued, "If I had one wish, Nick, that wish would be that I was a virgin on my wedding night. If I could do everything all over again, that's the way I would do it."

"To tell the truth, I have wondered how much you weren't telling me. But, at the same time, I wasn't sure I wanted to know. There were times when you said things that indicated that you might want to talk about it, but I was afraid to pursue the subject." I paused for a second.

A STATESIDE TOUR OF DUTY

"If you want to tell me all about it now, I'll listen and agree not to bring it up again."

"Do you really think you can do that?"

"Yes I can."

"I told you about what Allan did. He ripped my clothes off and said if I screamed he would kill me. Afterward he put a cigarette next to one of my nipples and told me if I ever talked, then he would burn it off." She changed the subject briefly. "That's another thing that I liked about you. You don't smoke." She returned to the subject at hand. "After I set him up and Sherry kicked him out, I met Darren at one of the parties she had. I liked him, and he told me that he loved me, but when I wouldn't do anything, he soon moved on to Sherry, who was closer to his age. And before Darren, there was Rodney. I almost married Rodney and you know about him. He told me that if you love someone then you show it. He made it sound like love was sex and sex was love. My self-esteem was practically nonexistent, so I almost swallowed that crap. But the thought of doing anything caused flashbacks of Allan. When I decided not marry him, he said some really hurtful things."

I remained silent as she collected her thoughts. She then continued. "Then, finally, there was a party where Sherry lined me up with a guy she said was divorced. I was depressed and he told me a drink would help. He kept giving me drinks until I was bombed. Then he carried me up to a bedroom and started taking off my clothes. I vaguely remember that I was begging him not to do anything, and then I passed out. When I came to, the next morning, he swore that he was the only one that spent time with me, but how can I be sure? The next day Sherry said the guy went back to his wife (it seems that his divorce wasn't final), and I shouldn't make trouble for him. Some friend she was." She stopped for a brief time then began again. "I decided that something like that would never happen again. I promised that no man would ever have sex with me again unless he was married to me. I prayed to God for him to send me someone special and then I met you. After we were intimate and you broke up with me, I figured it was because I had broken my promise. I've always loved you so much. On our wedding night, I fantasized that it was my first time."

I kissed her. "I thought sex was painful for virgins. You sure didn't seem to be in any pain Friday night."

"You scared me a little the way you started to rip my clothes off, but after that everything was great. There may not have been any pain, but I still closed my eyes and fantasized it was my first time. It may not make any sense to you, but it really made everything more special for me."

"What caused you to think about this, Sam?"

"While you were taking a shower, I was watching a rerun of *The Newlywed Game* on TV. The bonus question was what grade the husbands would give their wives for their knowledge of sex on their wedding night. Two guys gave their wives an A, while the other two gave their wives a C and an F. That got me to thinking about it." With that explanation, she paused and waited for me to speak.

"For our wedding night you earned an A+ with extra credit."

"Thank you," she said. Then, after she kissed me, she added, "But wouldn't it have been much better if we had both rated an F and got to teach each other and had all the fun of learning together?"

"Probably so," I concurred. "But, we can't change what is in the past, honey. We can only learn from it to not make mistakes in the future." I'm not sure what I meant by that, but I thought it sounded wise and intelligent. "You might as well know," I said hesitantly, "that in May, after I broke off our engagement, my fraternity brothers lined me up with Lucinda Lowell. I went out with her two or three times."

"Lucinda Lowell!" she gasped. "She's screwed every guy in Phoenix that's not gay, and probably some that are. What made them line you up with her?"

"They wanted me to have a good time, and she is gorgeous. Also, to be truthful, I was horny. Don't worry though; I used a rubber when we had sex."

"I should hope so," she laughed. "My gosh, now I don't feel so bad. She was a neighbor when I lived in the King George Apartments. I could not believe how many well-dressed, good-looking guys took her out."

"Well, good-looking, neatly dressed guys like sex too," I joked. "Look, honey, I'm not going to lie and say what I did with her didn't feel good, but there was no depth of feeling or emotional attachment, and afterward I just felt a little lonely. I would have been better off if I hadn't spent the time with her, because there's nothing she could do then that you can't do now."

Sam smiled. "Maybe you do understand how I feel."

"There's an old saying that before a girl meets the handsome prince, she has to kiss some toads," I said with a smile. "I guess it applies in your case."

"I really wish that all I had done is kiss them," Sam replied.

"Look! From what you've told me, your sexual experience was rape. Those guys should be in jail. The legal code states that if a woman is impaired from drugs or alcohol, then she is incapable of giving her consent, and sexual contact with her is rape. It sounds like everything that happened to you fits that description. One thing's for sure; you didn't get to enjoy anything."

"If I had reported the last time, I would have been laughed out of court. Most people think that if a girl gets drunk, then she is asking for it. I could have reported the episode with Allen, but I was terrified of that creep. I really thought he might kill me." She paused, and said, "I've heard of girls passing out at fraternity parties and being used by dozens of guys. If they report it, nothing happens. I felt I was lucky that I got off as easy as I did and kept my mouth shut so I wouldn't get a sleazy reputation. Does that make sense to you?"

"Not being a girl, I can't argue with your reasoning. I probably would have done the same thing you did." I kissed her and said, "We better go to sleep, since you're out of commission for the evening. That's where men are superior to women. We can perform anytime. Women can perform only part of the time."

"Oh yeah," she said, "you only *think* I can't perform." She proceeded to kiss me and ran her hand down into my jockey shorts. A short time later, with a slightly more embarrassed and subdued manner, Sam was washing her hands while I changed underwear. Never again would I tease Sam and claim she couldn't do something.

Sam's recitation of her past experiences seemed therapeutic, but we agreed that they should never be brought up again. We were beginning a new life together and what counted was the future. The next day we again barely left before the checkout time because we slept so late, having spent most of the night talking. As we were leaving, I jokingly said to Sam, "It's a good thing that no one knows what goes on behind closed doors. Since we're newlyweds, they can think we were so late getting out of here because we were warming the sheets. They don't have to know that we were just talking most of the night."

Sam looked at me and rolled her eyes as she shook her head. "All that counts is looking like a stud, isn't it? You men are so shallow." She then smiled and said, "But I love you anyway."

"I love you, too."

The next night it was I that was asking questions. After turning out the lights, I asked, "Sam, as many times as we broke up, how come you were always so quick to come back to me?"

"Because of my twentieth birthday," she replied.

"Your what?"

"Don't you remember what you did?" she questioned.

"Not really. Refresh my memory."

"Oh, Nick. I can't believe you don't remember. You were flat broke and it was my birthday. So, you wrote a special poem for me and folded it into a birthday card. You even drew a picture on it that said the entire world wished me a happy birthday. Then you found about fifteen cents to buy one of those big alligator jaw pastries at the bakery and put a birthday candle on it. When you delivered it, my roommates thought it was so ingenious and cute they talked about it for weeks."

"Oh yeah. I'm sorry I forgot."

"Well, a couple of weeks later I went to the home of a friend. It was her birthday and she was crying. She and her husband had no money to celebrate her birthday. I took her stupid husband aside and told him what you had done. I let him know that if he did that for his wife, she would love him forever."

"What did he do?"

"The stupid jerk told me that he didn't have enough time to do anything like that. So, while his wife cried to me, the worthless creep sat on his butt watching TV for the next four hours."

"You're kidding! That entire project took me less than an hour. That includes the trip to the bakery with the loose change I found in the sofa."

"Well, after that, I decided you were a keeper. After seeing how other men treat their wives and girlfriends, I was not going to let you get away. I even moved into that apartment down the street from you so we could bump into each other."

"I thought it was so you would be within walking distance from work."

"That helped. But mostly it was to see if there was any chance of reconnecting with you."

"You sneaky woman, you! You're more devious than I thought."

A STATESIDE TOUR OF DUTY

"When you want something, I believe you should go after it," she said.

We laughed, kissed and shortly afterward went to sleep.

We saw a few more sights as we traveled through west Texas, and late Tuesday night we entered Fort McCulloch on one of the back entrances through Highway 142 West. As we crossed into the post proper, I pointed out the sign that indicated we were entering a federal military establishment. "We are now on Fort McCulloch," I said.

"You mean we're almost home?" Sam asked excitedly.

"We will be in about seventy more miles."

"You're kidding!" How come it's still so far away?"

"I told you, honey, that Fort McCulloch is a big place. We live in Harrisville, on the other side of the post." A little more than an hour later we pulled into Donaldson's Trailer Park. We were home.

CHAPTER TEN

The next morning, I went to the PMO. I wasn't ready to sign in from leave yet, but I thought that I should see what had transpired in my absence. As I walked into the back of the station, I noticed six men sitting along the side of the right wall. They were dressed for duty, but seemed to be sleeping. As I walked into Operations, Steve saw me coming. He came out of his office to shake hands.

"Welcome back," he said with a smile. "Are you too exhausted from all the action to come back to work yet?"

"I'll probably sign in tonight. I'm showing Sam around the area today. Uh, what's with the men sitting around in the desk area?"

With a roll of his eyes Steve said sarcastically, "That is the feared Fort McCulloch goon squad. They are ready and poised to spring into action just as soon as a riot or other emergency breaks out."

"Shouldn't they be patrolling with the rest of the line-duty personnel?"

"If they did that, then they wouldn't be available on a moment's notice when something big happened." Steve rolled his eyes again.

"It seems to me that they would have a much greater chance of being utilized if they came in on swing shift," I noted.

"That's what I said during the colonel's briefing this morning. Starting tomorrow night, they will come in with the swing shift personnel. But I doubt if they will be needed any more then than they are now." I was about to leave when Steve said, "I thought you would like to see this. It was published during your absence."

It was a copy of the *Harrisville Herald-Messenger,* the local weekly newspaper. There on the front page was a byline which read, "Exclusive to the *Herald-Messenger* by Major James L. Receiver, Fort McCulloch DPM." The article was entitled "Dud Rounds are Dangerous." It was, word-for-word, the exact press release I had written before I had left.

A STATESIDE TOUR OF DUTY

"The major didn't even have the decency to change a single word. He just put his name on my article and took credit for it," I said in exasperation.

"Welcome to the United States Army, lieutenant. A dumb-ass field-grade officer can rip us junior officers off anytime they want and call it a privilege of rank. That's the system."

"May I take this?" I asked. "I'd like to show it to my wife."

"Be my guest. I was keeping it for you."

I went into my office to see if there was any pressing business that I needed to attend to. There was only the usual paperwork; that could wait until I returned tomorrow. I then left the station and returned home. I was planning to show Sam the area. When I arrived, Sam was cleaning the trailer.

"This place is a mess," Sam said. "I thought you said you cleaned it up."

"I thought I did." Apparently ,since my OCS days, my cleaning skills had diminished slightly. I simply waited for Sam to continue her comments.

"All you did was surface clean," Sam said. "There's a lot to be done to make this place really livable."

A little worried that an argument could soon develop, I replied, "I'll help you do that later, sweetheart. Right now, that will keep. Let me show you around the territory. We can clean later." To my relief, Sam agreed.

With that, I began to show Sam the post and the Harrisville area. I showed her the commissary, PX, officers' club, hospital and all the other facilities. We then drove around Harrisville. There were two large supermarkets, several five-and-dime-type stores and a department store, along with the usual other businesses that might be found in a town of about four thousand people. Eventually, we drove across the tracks into the black district. "The locals can't discriminate against service personnel," I said, so black soldiers can be found renting all over town." The local citizens that are black, however, seem to keep to themselves over here. I don't know if that's good or bad. That's just the way it is."

"It's too bad that different people don't associate more with each other," Sam noted. "If people got to know each other, they might find out that they're not really all that different."

"Well, that might start happening here," I replied. "There are currently two high schools in Harrisville. One is all black, while the other is ninety percent white. They are leftovers from the old segregationist system and both are falling apart. As a result, the local school board has authorized the building of one large new high school for the entire area. Maybe that will help the kids to interact more with each other."

"That should help," Sam said. She said little else as we drove through this part of town, where numerous houses that looked run down and poorly cared for were interspersed among the ones that were well maintained.

After our tour of Harrisville, we returned to the post. I drove to the Pass and ID Office, where we got Sam issued a dependent military ID card. She would need it to enter the commissary and PX as well as many other post facilities. We then went to the housing office and got on the housing list for married personnel. Sam didn't have much to say after that and soon we arrived back home.

I showed Sam the story I had written, that had been published in the local bird cage liner under the major's name.

"It's not fair for him to take credit for your work, Nick."

Even though I was a little irritated, I didn't let it show. "That's the way the system works, honey," I replied. "In the Army, we lieutenants are often little more than ghostwriters for higher-ranking officers." She made another comment about the unfairness of the situation, and then I helped her clean to get the trailer up to her standards. Finally, at 1700 hours, I went back to the company area to sign in from leave.

As I was signing in, I was told that the Tuesday softball games had been rescheduled to Wednesday due to a post FTX (field training exercise). We would be playing Echo Company of the 55th Infantry Battalion. I agreed to play.

After arriving back at the trailer, I told Sam about the game. She made us a quick supper, and by 1900 hours we were at the east field. I introduced her to the CO, Captain Bills and his wife, and a few others that were in attendance, and took my place in the outfield.

With Sam yelling words of encouragement, my performance on the field definitely improved. I didn't commit any errors and got on base three out of four times at bat on two hits and a walk. We won the game 12–6. After giving E Company a cheer with the team, I rejoined Sam on the sidelines.

"This was really fun tonight," she said. "You played a really good game."

"Thanks, babe. It helped to have you cheering for me."

A STATESIDE TOUR OF DUTY

As we headed back for home, Sam asked a question. At least, I thought it was a question.

"Do you think we should stop at Baskin-Robbins and have some ice cream to celebrate your team's win tonight?"

"I don't think so, honey. I think we need to get home so I can get ready for work tomorrow." With that, I passed the ice cream shop and headed for home. A few minutes later I became aware of an uneasy silence. "Is something wrong, honey?" I asked.

"No," she said in a very irritated laconic manner.

Apparently, I had done something wrong. "What's the matter, honey?"

"You know what the matter is," she said forcefully.

"No, I don't. I really don't."

"Well you should," she said, as she angrily looked straight ahead.

I was completely perplexed. "Honey, what is it?"

"You figure it out."

Then suddenly I remembered her suggestion to get ice cream. "Did you want to stop and get ice cream?"

"I said I did!" She sounded quite irritated.

"No honey. You asked if I thought we should stop and get some. That's a question, and I replied that I didn't wish to. If you wanted to stop, then you should have said so."

"If you loved me, then you'd know what I meant and know what to reply," She explained. That explanation was interesting to me. I guess I was supposed to read her mind.

I turned the car around and headed back to the ice cream shop. "Honey," I expounded, "I do love you but I am not a clairvoyant or a mind reader. If you want something, then you should say so. Likewise, if there is something I'm supposed to say at certain occasions, then you need to get me a copy of the script so I'll be able to say those things when you want to hear them on those occasions. Is that fair?"

"It just seems that if you really knew me you would know what to do."

At that moment, we passed a sign which stated that the speed limit was thirty-five miles per hour. I pointed it out to her. "That's like a woman replacing that sign with one that says, 'If you loved me and really knew me, then you would know how fast to drive now.'"

Sam started to laugh. "That's silly."

"No honey, it really isn't," I replied. "I love you and want to spend the rest of my life with you, but I can't read your mind." I then added, "You can't read mine either, no matter how much you love me."

"Sure I can read your mind," she said sardonically. "You're thinking about sex."

"Sorry, babe," I said with a smile. "That's not even close. You played the odds on that one, but you're wrong."

"What were you thinking?"

"I was thinking how different our thought processes were. But as the French say—*vive la différence!*" Sam laughed again, and by this time we were at the ice cream shop. We went through the drive-through and, after obtaining a treat to end the evening on, we drove back home.

The next morning, we were up at 0630 hours. Sam cooked breakfast while I dressed to go to the office. After eating the meal and kissing Sam good-bye I arrived at the PMO at 0745 hours. The usual people were gathered around the table for the morning briefing as I entered the building. As I sat down, others acknowledged my presence. Steve winked and gave me a thumbs-up.

"Morning, sir," said Sergeant McCall, the desk sergeant from the previous night.

"Morning, sarge."

"Good to have you back, lieutenant. How was the honeymoon?" Asked the major.

"Great, sir. I hated to see it end."

"I imagine so," said Warren. "When do we get to meet the missus?"

"We'll be at the fish fry Friday night," I responded. "Sam's looking forward to meeting everyone I work with." With that I began to peruse the blotter.

My first thought was one of pure irritation. We did not need the goon squad, it was a joke. Unfortunately, I didn't dare voice the thought to the major. It had been a quiet night. Except for a brief disturbance at the EM club, there was little else to read about. There were four pages of the usual traffic tickets and phone calls about window peepers and complaints about neighbors who failed to keep their dogs on a leash, as well as a few thefts and one report of a stolen car. Yes, sir, we needed the goon squad like we needed a case of the plague. I had just finished the blotter when the colonel walked in at 0800 hours. We all stood and said, "Morning, sir."

A STATESIDE TOUR OF DUTY

"Morning, men," replied the colonel. "Everybody be seated." He sat down and began to check out the blotter. "Lieutenant Bronson," asked the colonel, "how many vehicles are currently available for line duty?"

"Four, sir, and we had to borrow one of those from Traffic. Everything else is red-lined. If we don't get some new vehicles soon we are going to be in big trouble. We'll be down to walking patrols, and that's not practical on a post this size."

"Put as much pressure on the TMP as you can to get those other cars back on the road. I'll call Fifth Army and keep them advised of our situation. Hopefully they can get us some new vehicles." With that the colonel went back to reading the blotter. At length he stopped and observed, "Not much to read about; looks like another quiet night."

"That's just the way we like them, sir," commented Sergeant McCall.

"There's always calm before the storm," the major stated. "It can't be like this all the time."

Steve looked at me and rolled his eyes. This editorial comment by the major was probably a preemptive move to prevent Steve from suggesting that the goon squad be disbanded. If so, it worked because Steve knew better than to go the rounds with a field-grade officer in front of the other personnel. Steve remained silent. He probably had the intent of picking a better time to point out the stupidity of the existence of the goon squad. The colonel then starting looking around the table, asking if anyone had anything further to add. "Mr. Garcia?"

"Our company softball team is six and three in the second half of the season, sir. I think it is going to be a real morale booster and give our men a chance to associate with each other off duty," answered WO2 Garcia.

"Best team we've had since my younger days when I used to pitch," observed First Sergeant Prince.

"Good job, Mr. Garcia. Keep up the good work." He then looked at Warren for comments. "Sergeant Warren?"

"I'll be going TDY again Saturday to check on our physical security personnel as well as conduct a few inspections myself, sir. Sergeant Johnson will be supervising the PMI section in my absence."

"How long will you be gone?" asked the colonel.

"One week, sir. I'll leave the schedule of inspections I intent to conduct with you Friday and brief you when I return."

"Good," replied the colonel as he continued around the table. "Mr. Bernard?"

"The local moonshiners haven't been too active lately," stated Mr. Bernard. "The few stills we've found recently have all been abandoned. I'd like to think that this is due to our patrolling the post, but I suspect that they've found a supplier who can provide them with bonded liquor minus the taxes. If so, there would be little need to produce any rotgut. You might pass this information along to ATF. I think they might be very interested that some supplier might not be letting Uncle Sam collect his fair share."

"We'll see that your observations get passed along," the colonel stated in a matter-of-fact manner. The colonel then looked (and pointed) at the major, "Anything, Jim?"

"All goon squad personnel will be reporting to duty with the swing shift, starting tonight," the major said.

"I think that will be a good move, Jim. Swing shift is probably where they should have been all along." As this exchange took place, Steve looked at me and raised his eyebrows. It was clear he was not happy in Operations. The colonel continued around the table. "Lieutenant Bronson?"

"Nothing else, sir," replied Steve as he lit a cigarette and tossed the match into an ashtray.

"Lieutenant Moultrie, it's good to have you back. How was the honeymoon?"

Before I could answer, Warren spoke up. "Can't you tell from the way he's smiling, colonel? He's probably disappointed he had to come back to work this morning."

"Sergeant Warren, there is a time and a place for all things," I rebutted. "Right now I have a job to do and I'm just proud to be here."

"Now, now, sir, I'm sure you'd rather be elsewhere right now," Warren quipped.

"No comment!" I then raised my hand to cut off any further comments from him. I then turned to the colonel and continued, "To answer your question sir, the honeymoon was great. We toured a good part of the country and really got to know each other." I then quickly turned in the direction of Warren and added, "No cute comments or puns, please."

"Touché, lieutenant," acknowledged Sergeant Major Prince. At this point, everyone around the table laughed. Warren seemed a bit agitated at having me get the better of him in this verbal jousting and looked at his watch as if he had places to go.

A STATESIDE TOUR OF DUTY

"Well said, lieutenant, and welcome back," said the colonel

I nodded toward him and said "Thank you, sir, and I have nothing else to add."

"Well," said the colonel. "Does anyone have anything else to add?" He looked quickly around and, hearing nothing, ordered, "Let's go to work, then." We all stood and saluted and proceeded to leave the room for our individual work areas or other points of destination.

As we proceeded back past the D-cell, Scott asked, "Did you notice how the colonel no longer asks Captain Tucker to join the meeting?"

"Yeah," I acknowledged. "The captain was in the other office talking to the girls the entire meeting, and the colonel didn't call for him once."

"That's because he has me to kick around now. I sure wish I knew what Tucker has on that worthless asshole." Scott then asked, "You wouldn't like to change jobs, would you?"

"Thanks, old buddy, but I had better keep the one I've been assigned to. I'm sure the brass knows best when they make job assignments." I said that with a smile.

"That's not even funny," Steve said with a shake of his head. "I think you said it best when you made the comment that sometimes it's better to be lucky than good."

"No argument," I agreed. With that, I went into my office and began to review accident reports. There was enough paperwork to keep me busy until lunch, provided I didn't attempt to complete it too quickly. At 1200 hours I headed for home, where Sam had lunch waiting. As we ate lunch, I filled Sam in on all the office politics and let her know how our tax dollars were at work. She seemed unusually quiet. Finally, I just looked at her and said, "What's the matter, Sam?"

"The mail came," she said meekly. "You're going to hate me."

"Honey," I said firmly. "Just tell me what the matter is and let me decide what emotion I'll react with." I then said nothing else and gave her a look that I hoped would put her at ease and tell her everything would be all right.

She hesitated. "Several months ago," she began, "I saw a demonstration of a Kwick-Kleen vacuum sweeper and signed a contract to buy one. After my roommates found out, they told me I was crazy and that I could get a good vacuum for a fraction of the price. I then called the company and told them I wanted to cancel under the three-day privilege the contract gave me to change my mind. They didn't come and get the sweeper like they said, so I took it to their office and they tried to tell me that since I hadn't brought it to them within three days I couldn't return it. I told them to drop dead and left the machine there. Well, they have been sending me threatening letters, demanding that I pay $400. I thought they would quit bothering me when I left Phoenix, but this letter was forwarded to us today. They're going to take me to court and sue me. Now that I'm married, they'll probably want to get the money from you." She handed me the letter. Across the top in bold letters it said, "Corporate Collections, Inc." There was smaller print under that which stated "A division of Kwick-Kleen Industries." Sure enough, these crooks were threatening her with everything except kidnapping her firstborn child. Mostly, though, they demanded she now pay the sum of $600.

I smiled. "Don't worry sweetie, these criminals don't have a leg to stand on. They won't collect a dime from us."

"Are you sure?"

I stated yes in my most emphatic tone of voice and then tore off the bottom of the letter, which was a voucher designed to be read by some sort of computer. I wadded the paper up and then stuck holes in it with my fork. "When I get back to the office, I'm going to put staples in it and tape it to a letter I'm about to write. When it won't go through their computer they will be forced to read the letter. Get me a piece of stationery, honey." Sam quickly handed me some paper and I began writing.

> Dear Kwick-Kleen criminals and fraud perpetrators,
>
> I have in my possession three affidavits from witnesses that my wife contacted you within three days after purchase to return the vacuum one of your fast-talking crooks convinced her to purchase.
>
> She complied with the law. When the machine was returned to you is irrelevant.
>
> Also, be advised that my wife has no income and no major assets in her name. If you people are stupid enough to sue her, you are even dumber than I thought (if that's possible). You also should realize that we were not married when the transaction was made, so I am not in any way responsible to pay for the inferior piece of junk you call a vacuum cleaner.
>
> If I receive any further correspondence from you, I will consider legal action for harassment. I will also advertise for as many others that have been victimized by your predatory

business practices that I can find to file a class action lawsuit. My brother is an attorney and he advises me that we can tie you up in court for years and cause you millions of dollars in bad publicity even if we collect no damages.

Sincerely,
Nick Moultrie
2LT, U.S. Military Police Corps

"I didn't know you had a brother, Nick," Sam said with a puzzled look on her face.

"I don't, but they don't have to know that. For that matter I don't have any affidavits in my possession, either."

Sam began to laugh. "Are you serious? Can you make this go away as easy as that?" She hopped in my lap and gave me a big kiss. "You are wonderful."

"Well, right now Lieutenant Wonderful would really like to make love to Mrs. Wonderful."

"Be patient, honey, and my monthly bane will be over soon," Sam said as she gave me another quick peck on the lips. "But now, Lieutenant Wonderful, you better get your butt back to work." I looked at my watch. It was already 1300 hours. Sam was right.

Despite all the confidence in myself that I had exuded in front of Sam, I decided to get a legal opinion. I was sure I was right, but it never hurts to double-check. I quickly drove by the JAG office in order to ensure that the information I had told Sam was accurate. I quickly laid out the facts to one of the JAG lawyers and found that I was correct. While there might be some question as to whether Sam complied with the law in canceling the sale, I was not legally liable for the debt, and where Sam had no assets it would be futile for the vacuum cleaner company to sue her. I had not told the legal eagle about the letter I had planned to send. However, once I discovered that my course of action was correct, I figured sending it along would rub some salt in the wound of this corporation that would not be collecting any money. Also, stopping by JAG would give me an excellent excuse for being late returning to work, in case the major was checking.

Sure enough, as I walked into my office, there was Major Disaster waiting for me. "Afternoon, sir," I greeted. "I just dropped by JAG for a quick opinion. Captain Wardwell said to say hello."

"Thanks, lieutenant. No serious problems, I hope."

"No, sir. I had heard that some states were having problems with VASCAR tickets holding up in court and decided to check it out. It turns out there was nothing for us to be concerned with. The problem case was in California. No other states are involved, and Texas courts have no problems with VASCAR. We are perfectly all right to use it." The major swallowed the BS I was laying on him, hook, line and sinker.

"Good job," the major said. "How's everything else going?"

"Smooth as silk, sir," I replied. "As soon as I finish all this paperwork, I'm going to ride some of the patrols and determine if any additional training is needed."

The major smiled. "It's good to know that part of our operation is going well. Keep up the good work." With that the major left my office. My only thought was that it was a shame the major couldn't find something useful to do, so he didn't have to bother me. I made a memo to myself to suggest, at tomorrow's briefing, that he produce more patrol tips for the men. Maybe that would keep him out of my hair.

I put lots of staples in the vacuum cleaner bill I had brought from home and taped the letter I had written to it and put it into the envelope. I would mail it on the way home.

I then walked to Steve's office and had a seat. I figured a quick chat would get my mind off the major. Steve was signing a stack of authorizations for the weekly rewards sent out to various jurisdictions for their capture of AWOLs. The stack was about four inches thick. In addition to the rewards claimed, there were claims for refunds of damages for any destruction caused by the AWOL to the jurisdiction's property while he was in custody.

"I can't believe this BS," Steve said in a disgusted manner as he tossed the paper over to me. "The sheriff of Mitchell County is claiming $1200 of damage was done to his jail's crapper by this AWOL. Good old Uncle Sugar doesn't check anything out; he just pays the bill. Unless I have proof there is anything phony, I basically have to sign off on this."

"Couldn't you go over there and check things out?"

"That would include time off from here, some travel reimbursement and possibly a per diem if I was gone overnight. The colonel would never go for it," he countered.

"So he thinks the government should accept these claims in their usual jump-over-dollars-to-save-dimes manner?"

"Exactly. Besides," he continued, "he does have a point. I'm sure there probably was some damage done, I just question the amount. Even if there was no damage at all, they could say that it had been repaired when we got there."

"I'm sure we could tell if there had been some recent repairs," I countered.

"I'm sure they would be smart enough to at least paint the place so it would be hard to tell. Besides, I suspect that these small county sheriffs are using this as a means to keep their jails repaired and maintained at U.S. government expense."

I read though the document and, sure enough, there was a claim for precisely $1200. "Isn't it odd the repairs came to exactly an even amount? Not $1205, not $1277, but $1200 on the nose."

"I've noticed that, too," Steve answered with a grin. "It seems that AWOLs always do damage in even-numbered amounts." He then changed the subject. "I wish I could use a hand stamp with my name on it, instead of signing these damned things. I almost get writer's cramp signing all the paperwork. Unfortunately, government regulations prohibit their use. Everything has to be signed by hand."

As Steve signed his daily supply of paperwork, we chatted and otherwise made general conversation. As we talked, we made no secret of our disdain and contempt for the senior officers we served under. The Operations clerks could easily hear what we said, but we didn't care. We weren't hypocritical. We were not going to say one thing publicly and another when no one was listening. Of course, in retrospect all these years later, I realize that we should have been respectful of their positions, even if we didn't respect the individuals occupying them. I must admit that Steve and I were wrong on that account. Then Steve threw in a real bit of news. "I found out that Raymond's family name was originally Romano. His grandfather was a capo with the Genovese Mafia family. His father anglicized the name to Raymond and represents the side of the family that went legit."

I sat up straight in my chair and said in amazement, "So, our fellow lieutenant and company XO had ties to the Mafia. How in the world did you find that out?"

"Talking with an NSA investigator yesterday. Raymond has applied for a Top Secret security clearance so he can work for the CIA or NSA after he separates from the service. The guy came in and we had a long talk. He probably told me more than he should have. Apparently, even though Raymond's side of the family is legit it will be hard for him to obtain the Top Secret clearance. It looks like Secret is as high as he can get. So, I guess he'll have to find something else to do when he gets out."

"My heart bleeds for him," I said mockingly. "He's definitely not hurting for money."

"True. True enough," replied Steve. "He likes to let everyone know it, too."

I checked my watch. "Well, I better go and find ways to better protect the citizens of Fort McCulloch."

"Okay, man. Thanks for coming over and breaking the monotony."

"Not a problem," I replied. I then left Steve's office and walked out to the desk sergeant. "Call in Unit One Five Alpha and have him pick me up," I ordered.

"Yes, sir," he replied. He then keyed the microphone and said, "Unit One Five Alpha, this is Fort McCulloch."

"This is Unit One Five Alpha. Go ahead, Fort McCulloch."

"Unit One Five Alpha, ten-nineteen this location for Lieutenant Moultrie."

"Ten-four, Ft McCulloch. En route. Should arrive approximately zero five mike."

"Ten-four. Fort McCulloch clear," the desk sergeant concluded. He then looked up and said, "He'll be here in a minute, sir."

"Thanks," I replied. Shortly afterward, the vehicle drove up and I got in. I then spent the rest of the afternoon riding with Cummings. It was a routine afternoon, and at 1700 hours I left work to mail the letter and head for home.

Sam and I had dinner and, shortly afterward, we arrived at the west field at 1830 hours. I warmed up with the team as we prepared for the game and at 1900 hours the umpire yelled, "Play ball!" as we took our place on the field. Tonight we had all our heavy hitters available, and after holding the opponents to three up, three down in the top of the first, the rout was on. Every time we seemed to load up the bases, somebody would hit a home run. Everything seemed to go right that night, and the final score was a phenomenal 21–3.

We all got together and gave a cheer for the 4191st Ordinance Detachment, and we then shook hands with the opponents and thanked them for a good game. Often, when you thanked the other team for a good game it was a halfhearted gesture. This time we were sincere. For us, it had in fact been a great game—we won big.

As Sam and I got into the car for the drive home, I asked, "Do you know what would make this a perfect night, honey?"

"Going right home and going immediately to sleep?"

"No, that's not what I had in mind," I replied.

Sam put her hand up to side of her face as in deep thought and mockingly said, "Oh gee, what else could you have on your one-track mind?"

"Think real hard, honey, and the operative word is hard," I said with raised eyebrows.

"You want to sleep on the hard floor tonight. Is that it?"

"No, try again. I'm sure it will come to you. The operative word being come."

"Oh, I know," Sam exclaimed. "You want to come back to Baskin-Robbins for more ice cream to celebrate tonight's win."

"We can do that, too," I acknowledged. "I was referring to what we could do later."

"Oh," smiled Sam. "You mean much later. Like next week."

Sam's little game was beginning to get me a little irritated. A joke is a joke, but she was beginning to run this one into the ground. After stopping at the ice cream shop, I finally said, "Actually, honey, I was thinking that to make this a perfect night, I needed to go home and lie on you the rest of the night."

"And what if I don't want to be your personal couch, Nick—then what?"

"Well then," I concluded, "It would not be a perfect night." At that point I realized that I had just stuck my foot in my mouth, and corrected myself. "On second thought, honey, it would be a perfect night because I'd be spending it with you. The pleasure of your company is all I need."

"Nice save, Lieutenant Moultrie." Sam then added, "You almost got yourself in hot water right up to your eyeballs." She was quiet for a few seconds and then said, "I guess I had better give you what you want or you'll probably sulk and pout for the rest of the night, huh, Nick."

"Honey, I'm hurt," I said with sham injury in my voice. "Do you really think that I'd do something like that? I'm a brave soldier who faces hardened criminals every day. Do you really think a seasoned professional like me could possibly act like that?"

"Oh yes, Nick." She then added, "You could act like that in spades."

"Maybe I should be one of those guys I used to read about in college psychology classes who tie their partners up and inflict pain," I said in pseudo sufferance. "Then I would be much more exciting and you wouldn't tease me so much."

"Fat chance, Nick. If you were in any way into that perverted stuff, I wouldn't even be married to you."

"So you admit you got a good deal in a husband, then."

"I think I'll keep you," she said with a smile. "Now, let's talk about other things, because it will still be a couple of days before I really want to fool around."

"Good idea. I just want you to know that I'm glad you're here. We can talk about whatever you wish to."

She put her hand on my shoulder and began to rub the back of my neck. That ended the verbal jousting as I turned off the highway and drove into the trailer court.

CHAPTER ELEVEN

Friday morning began as usual. The alarm went off at 0600 hours and, if you will excuse some sarcasm, we got up for another exciting day. Sam made breakfast while I put on my uniform and prepared for another day of valiant crime fighting. In the military, the line on a uniform formed by buttoning up your shirt down to your belt buckle and then down the fly of your pants is known as the gig line, and this must be straight at all times. Also, all pockets must be buttoned and the epaulets on your shoulders must be tucked under your collars. For added elegance, one's tie is tucked into the shirt and both shirt and pants must be crisply ironed. Failure to observe these little details reflects poorly on your wife, or so Sam was told in the literature I had given her.

At Fort Belvoir, during my OCS training, wives of the candidates were given a great deal of information about how to conduct themselves as officers' wives. While I was not married at the time, I had obtained some of these pamphlets. After all, you never know what might happen in the future. I had passed this information along to Sam, who read it with interest. An officer's wife, for example, was not to use profanity. She was to dress well when she went out into public, and she was to wear white gloves for any formal or semi-formal event. I had to admit that Sam had not only read the information but also took it to heart. Since our marriage, she had stopped using profanity and encouraged me to do likewise. She also stopped wearing shorts in public. Her one complaint was that most of the officers' wives she met at the weekly teas at the officers' club were stuck-up snobs. In her words, "If being an officer's wife means that I am required to act like everyone else in the world is like dirt beneath my feet, I can't do it." Still, like everything else in our new marriage, she was adapting to her new roles. I was proud of her for making changes she thought necessary without acting like a phony highbrow.

I had always heard that once he was commissioned, a man became an officer and a gentleman by act of Congress. I don't know if that is true or not but, if so, that is the only way some could gain the description. I had met a few that might be officers, but they definitely were not gentlemen. I admit that I have my flaws. I might BS the major and be occasionally contemptuous to some superiors, but overall I did my job. I planned to deserve the title of officer and gentleman and strive to be better than those whose conduct I deplored. Above all, I was proud to have Sam as my new partner in life.

As I considered the mirror to ensure that my appearance was as it should be, with all my brass polished and straight, Sam interrupted my thoughts.

"Breakfast is ready. You can quit admiring yourself now." She then added with a smile, "I thought it was only women that stood in front of the mirror like that. Looks like men have a bit of vanity, too."

"What can I say, babe?" Then with a shrug of my shoulders I added, "If you've got it, flaunt it."

Sam gave me a hug. "You are handsome in that uniform," she said. Then after a quick kiss, we sat down to breakfast.

After a leisurely breakfast, I drove to the PMO for the morning briefing and arrived at my customary time of 0745 hours. There were the usual greetings of "Morning, sir," which I answered with a nod while saying "Morning" in reply. The senior brass arrived shortly afterward and the briefing followed the normal morning routine. At 0850 hours, I was in Steve's office shooting the bull, where Charlie joined us.

"Steve says that you're like the fat rat in a cheese factory around here, with the job you have," Charlie noted with a smile.

I gave Charlie a grimace of mock pain and replied, "I'm hurt. I battle crime daily here on the streets of Ft. McCulloch with my brave troops in the Traffic section, and this is the thanks I get." Then after a pause for dramatic effect, I looked at Steve and asked, "Do you believe that comment came from the man who teaches defensive driving over at post headquarters?"

Steve laughed out loud as he lit a cigarette. He then exhaled a big puff and said, "Hey, I'm envious of both of you. I'll trade this job as Operations officer with either one of you guys at any time."

A STATESIDE TOUR OF DUTY

At this point our conversation turned to the upcoming football season. Steve was hoping that Texas would be able to win the national championship. He was disappointed with some previous seasons as he reminisced.

"You can't imagine what we Longhorn fans have had to endure," Steve said. "For all four years I was at Austin we were expecting to end up number one. First, we had Bradley at quarterback for two years. What a disappointment he was. Then they switched him to end and we did better, but not as good as we thought we should. Finally, my senior year comes along and we went undefeated, but so did a couple of others. We claimed the national championship, but it was disputed by Penn State. This year, if we can get by Arkansas, I think we can win it all with no arguments."

"I hate to play the one-up game," I countered, "but you Texas people have nothing on us Sun Devils. The year before I got to ASU we went 9–2, and everybody was back for 1965. Ben Hawkins, Travis Williams, Max Anderson—everybody was back. It was the year we were going to make the big time. We figured to at least go to the Sun Bowl, and were hoping to get to one of the New Year's Day bowls and make a run at number one."

I continued. "The schedule had us playing BYU, the first game of the season, for a warm-up. That was supposed to be good, because the last time BYU had a winning season was just before the Spanish-American war. What they didn't know was that Brigham Young had a new football coach who was tired of losing. He sent one of his assistant coaches down to Guantanamo Bay, where the Quantico Marines were just finishing up a perfect season and all their guys were ending their enlistment. While this kick-butt team was celebrating, he went in and stated where he was from and said he would sign up anybody there to a full-ride scholarship to play college football—no questions asked. Thirty signed up."

I shook my head as I continued. "Then, in September, BYU brought what was essentially a Marine Corps battalion down to Tempe."

"What happened?" Steve asked.

I shook my head again. "They kicked our butts so badly there are probably still some of the fans from that game sitting in Sun Devil Stadium wondering what happened. The team was so shell-shocked that they quickly lost three more games to teams that we should have clobbered. Finally, Coach Kush slapped some sense into the players and they started playing like they should have. We won the last five or six in a row, but it was too little and too late. The next three years we played second fiddle to Wyoming. You have no exclusive claim to disappointment, Steve. We Sun Devil fans can sing the blues, too."

Charlie added his thoughts on the subject. "If you guys think you had problems, you should have gone to Kansas. We had one good season while I was there. That was 1968. I don't think we won five games in any other of the three years I was there. Then in the Orange Bowl the officials didn't like our twelve-man defense and gave Penn State the second chance to beat us so the '68 season ended on a loss. Jayhawk fans would kill for some of the winning seasons you guys are disappointed with. Neither one of you guys are going to get any sympathy from me."

Steve and I laughed. "Apparently, Charlie is not going to tell us how unhappy he is that his team didn't play for number one," Steve chuckled.

"Number one, hell. Kansas fans would be happy with any ranking." Charlie shook his head a few more times.

All sports fans want their team to be the best, I thought. Fortunately, most of us realize that it usually isn't to be. There will usually be no shortage of disappointing games. At least the three of us could take our teams lumps in stride.

I changed the subject. "Have you asked the girl in AG files out yet, Charlie?"

"We went out for dinner and a show last weekend."

"And?"

"Do I ask you for details of the time you spend with your wife?"

Steve laughed again. "Well, it's obvious he didn't get any."

Charlie explained, "She has almost puritanical standards. I still enjoyed her company, believe it or not. We have another date set for next Friday night."

I gave Charlie the thumbs-up sign and said, "Good luck this time around."

"Thanks," said Charlie. "I think I'll need it." Then we decided we had better get back to work, and our informal little gathering broke up.

I went back to my office and began making calls to close out as many of the Serious Incident and Blue Bell reports that I could. This involved making long-distance calls all over Texas to get the information. Still, I could finalize three of the folders I had in my possession. I wrote up the reports and took them up front for the girls to type and pass along to the colonel. The secretaries' names were Julene Davis and Susan Waymond. Julene was a brunette, while Susan was blond. It was close to noon, so as

A STATESIDE TOUR OF DUTY

I dropped the paperwork off I said, "Here's some reports for you to type up after lunch. Aren't you girls delighted with the way I provide you with job security by giving you more work?"

"We're just tickled to death, lieutenant," Julene said with a smile. "Come back, anytime, when you can't do us so many favors."

"I'm sure I'll be back," I answered. I went out and got into my car and began the quick drive home. *Paul Harvey's News and Comment* was on the radio.

"The endless war continues," Paul Harvey said. "American deaths for last week total 175. Dead for the Viet Cong and their allies totaled 14,500." Paul Harvey continued with details of national news, but I didn't follow it. I was thinking of how fortunate it was that I probably would never experience the war in Southeast Asia. But, on the negative side, when others asked me what I did during the war, I would have to answer that I was the Traffic officer at Fort Benjamin McCulloch, Texas. That would not be impressive.

As I walked into the trailer, Sam had just finished cooking hamburgers. The first thing I noticed was she was still wearing the bathrobe she had put on when she had first gotten up in the morning. That was unusual. Sam normally wore a pair of jeans and a T-shirt or, if she was going out into public, a pair of slacks and a button-up shirt.

"Hi, soldier. Welcome home," Sam said, as she placed the hamburgers on the table. She then gave me a big hug and a kiss. As I placed my arms around her, I could feel that she was not wearing anything under the robe.

After kissing her, I backed away slightly. I reached down and untied the sash around her housecoat and opened it up. "Looks like you have a surprise for me."

"That's right," she responded. With that, she did a quick toss of her shoulders which caused the robe to fall to the floor. I picked her up and began to carry her back to the bedroom. "You're going to cause our lunch to get cold," she giggled.

I kissed her and said, "Lunch might get cold, but we won't," I acknowledged. She then rested her head on my shoulder. When we got to the bedroom, I placed her on the bed where she began to turn back the covers while I disrobed. Needless to say, I was going to need to prepare another excuse for the major as to why I was late returning to work.

After our extracurricular activities and a quick lunch, I straightened my uniform and prepared to return to the PMO. As I was picking up my hat in anticipation of leaving, Sam said, "Oh, by the way, here's today's mail." She handed me a stack of envelopes.

I took them from her and began to examine the return addresses. There were several bulk mail items addressed to "Occupant" and a large envelope obviously containing a card. In the upper left-hand corner was the return address: Mr. and Mrs. Phillip Manning of Norfolk, Virginia. I had no idea who the people were, but I took the card out to read it anyway. The card proclaimed in big letters, "A Wedding Prayer for You." I opened the card and there was no written message, just some signatures in feminine handwriting. They were Phillip, Gloria and Amanda Ann. I studied them for a few seconds, pondering who they were. Probably some relatives of Sam. Then it hit me. This was from Gloria Richards.

"How nice, she's praying for us."

"Oh, Nick. That card is so sarcastic, it's sick." Then she added in a mocking tone, "A wedding prayer for you—give me a break."

"Honey," I said with a smile. "At least she acknowledged our wedding with a card. I didn't even do that for her."

"Well that was nicer than this belittling card," Sam answered. "Besides, I bet she only got married because she was pregnant. Or did you notice she's got a baby?"

I didn't say anything to answer Sam's question immediately, but that thought had occurred to me also. I had visited Gloria in March of 1968 and she was happy to see me. Then in April she wrote that she had just met someone special. I sent a reply wishing her well and in May received a wedding invitation for the first week of June. The thought occurred then that the wedding was a little rushed. I had wondered then if she was pregnant. I had never shared these thoughts with Sam before, and I didn't now. After all, that was Gloria's business, not ours. "She was married in June of 1968 and it's now August of 1970," I said. "She's had plenty of time to have a kid after the wedding. Let's give her the benefit of the doubt."

"Why? I'm sure the little wench wouldn't give us the same courtesy," Sam replied in obvious anger.

I may not be the smartest guy in the world, but I could tell that Sam was jealous. I wondered how that affected us. "Did the passionate interlude we have just experienced have anything to do with receiving this card?" I asked.

"Why would you think that?" Sam asked.

A STATESIDE TOUR OF DUTY

I didn't answer her question directly. Instead, I laid out the facts. "Sam, when she wanted to kiss me and told me she loved me, I rejected her. I then came around with hickeys, caused by another woman, on my neck. She's a woman scorned. I chose you over her. You are first prize for me. You have no reason to be jealous." Whatever my feelings had once been for Gloria, we had moved on and I wanted Sam to understand that. Sam had nothing to worry about.

"I've just always wondered if you think of her. I don't want to go through my marriage having to share my bedroom with another woman's ghost."

Determined to avoid an argument, I collected my thoughts. "The answer to the question you didn't ask is: no, I do not think of anyone else when we make love. And while I wish Gloria well, I don't think of her in any romantic manner. Our bedroom is for you and me alone. No woman's ghost will ever be here on my account."

While there may be times when people don't tell their spouses the entire truth, for me, this was not one of those times. My style of love-making required that I give Sam my full entire attention. I did not think of anyone else when I made love to her. In fact, I made the effort to only think about Sam all the time. When I asked Sam to send a wedding invitation to Gloria, I was wondering where she was and how she was doing, even though I told Sam other reasons. Now that I knew she was doing well, I was happy for her. I would do my best to never bring up Gloria's name again. Keeping Sam happy apparently depended upon that.

Sam smiled. The resolve in my voice apparently won the day. She gave me a big hug. "Like I've told you before, you'll be the last man I ever make love to." She then smiled and said, "You're the best husband that any woman could ever hope for."

"Thank you, honey." I jokingly added, "The Moultries are known for being good husbands and famous for being well hung."

She playfully swatted me on the shoulder and laughed. "Get your butt back to work. I don't want anyone to think you're late on my account," she said.

"We're newlyweds. You're supposed to keep me late for lunch. The major is just jealous because he's not getting any."

With a quick peck on the lips, Sam pushed me toward the door. "Go! Go!" she said. "You're not going to use me for an excuse. Besides, I have laundry to do."

Putting on my hat, I winked and said, "Bye, babe. See you later."

"Okay, honey," she replied. "Since we're going to the fish fry tonight, I won't have to make supper tonight."

I went to post headquarters, where I chatted with Charlie for a few minutes. It was clearly no secret to Charlie as to why I was there. "Need an excuse for the major for being late from lunch again?" Charlie asked with a smile.

"Yeah, thank heaven for JAG, you, Training Aids and the message center. I just keep rotating you on my important list of errands I have to do right after lunch."

"Well, just for your information, one person hasn't shown up for defensive driving this week." He handed me a card with the name on it. "We'll send out a courtesy reminder, and if he doesn't show up next week, you guys can bar him from the post."

"No problem," I said. "I'll pass this along to Major Disaster. Maybe it'll give him something to do."

Before returning to the PMO, I also stopped into the post safety office (it was just down the hall from Charlie's) and talked to Mr. Cooper. He was a civilian GS-14. We had to send him a copy of each traffic accident report, and any suggestions from people on how to improve safety on post was usually routed through his office to ours. Today he passed along a suggestion that had been submitted. I returned to work and went straight to the major's office. As I got to the door, I asked, "Got a minute, sir?"

"Yes, lieutenant. Come in and have a seat."

"Sir," I began, "I dropped into post headquarters on the way back from lunch. This person didn't bother to show up for defensive driving this week." I handed the card to the major. "I suggest we give them one more chance and if they aren't there next week, we issue a certificate of debarment. Also, Mr. Cooper at the safety office passed along this suggestion that was forwarded to his office." I tossed the paper onto the major's desk so he could read it also. Personally, I thought the suggestion was stupid but figured the major would probably want to institute it. I sat there in silence while he read it.

After the major had read the paper several times, he returned it to me. "Looks like Mr. Cooper's office didn't make a recommendation on the suggestion," the major noted.

"No ,sir."

The suggestion read as follows:

A STATESIDE TOUR OF DUTY

Subject: Deer Hazard on Post

Due to the number of accidents between deer and automobiles on the eastern highways of Fort McCulloch, it seems to me there is a way to help prevent them. I think that signs should be placed at all entrances to the post, warning people of the possible deer hazard. They should be instructed to turn on their four-way flashers if they see deer. That way everyone they pass would be warned there were deer in the area and would slow down, thereby avoiding accidents. I don't know what the cost of this measure would be, but it seems to me to be minimal.

The submitter of the suggestion had then signed their name.

What the major said next actually made sense. In fact, it was exactly my thoughts on the subject. "It seems to me that most people will either ignore the sign or ignore the other people's four-way flashers. Besides, with the number of deer on post, everybody's flashers will be going all the time and we will be right back to where we are now."

"Great minds think alike, sir. Those are my thoughts also. Also, there are a lot of people with older cars who don't have four-way flashers. If people pass one of those cars, they might think it was safe to drive faster, because they had the false sense of security." I then added, "Perhaps we could put larger signs at the entrances to the post warning of the deer hazard. How people react to the information would be up to them. But at least we warned them."

"Good, lieutenant. Write up your recommendations and send it back through channels." The major then asked, "I notice you do a lot of errands coming back from lunch. Why don't you return to the office and then do the errands?"

It was clear the major believed that I was using the errands to hide the fact that I was late returning from work, so I didn't argue. I had the perfect answer for him. I looked him straight in the eyes and said, "You're the boss, Sir. I can do things in any order you require. By way of explanation, though, in a management class I took in college I learned that the first thirty minutes coming back from lunch is traditionally some of the most unproductive time of the day. By using that time for errands, it helps the time to be more productive. I can then return to the office knowing I don't have to leave and can hit the ground running for the afternoon, so to speak." I then sat there in silence, so the major could think over what I had just told him. I hoped he would buy that load of crap. He didn't.

The major thought for a moment, and after what seemed like an eternity of silence he stammered, "Well, uh, well, ah, well, just the same, why don't you return to the office first."

"Not a problem, sir," I shrugged. "Perhaps that way if you need something I can take care of that, also, while I'm out." Under the circumstances, I suspected a little sucking up would not hurt.

The major smiled. "Excellent idea, lieutenant. Well, I'm a busy man. We'll talk to you later."

I left the major's office and went straight back to Operations. Walking to Steve's office door I asked, "Want to hear a good one?"

"Hell ,yeah, I could use a good laugh," Steve responded.

"I was just up in the major's office and he said we'd have to talk later because he's a busy man."

Steve burst out in laughter. "Busy? Hell, busy doing what?" As Steve asked the question he had both hands out in front of him with his palms up while shrugging his shoulders.

"If you ever find out, let me know, because I have no idea," I replied. As I turned to go I noticed that even the clerks were smiling. The major a busy man. Even they thought it was funny. His only duty seemed to be making sure I didn't return late from lunch. "Well, see you later. I have to go and make sure the streets are safe."

"Take it easy," was Steve's reply. "And if you find out what he's so busy doing all day, be sure to let me know."

"Will do." I left Steve's office and returned to mine.

I wrote up the thoughts the major and I had about the deer hazard suggestion and routed it back to Cooper. Actually, deer were a hazard only on the east side of the post, in the forested areas. On the desert side a motorist was more likely to hit an antelope. Suddenly, the phone rang. SP4 Gross answered it.

After a few seconds, he said, "I understand, sir. Foxtrot and Secord. Are you sure there are no injuries requiring medical attention? Very well, we'll be right there." With that the specialist hung up the phone. "Traffic accident, sir. I told them I'd be right there."

"Let me grab the camera and wheel and I'll join you," I said.

Quickly, Gross and I left the office and proceeded to the corner of Foxtrot Drive and Secord Avenue. It was clear what had happened as we drove up. The driver on Foxtrot had failed to yield the right-of-way, and the driver proceeding up Secord had hit him between the rear door and the left rear wheel. I quickly gave the two drivers forms on which they could give their account of what happened. Gross used the wheel to measure the skid marks. The wheel had a handle which folded out so you could push it along the skid marks. With each revolution of the wheel it made an audible click as it registered the distance. That click represented twenty-four inches. After rolling the wheel along the skid mark you could read the exact distance in feet and inches on a counter which was then reset.

I quickly asked around for witnesses and was lucky enough to find one. He quickly verified our observations. Gross quickly took pictures of the accident scene showing the location of the stop sign and the positions of the cars. While the specialist wrapped up the investigation and cited the driver on Secord for running a posted stop sign, I talked with the other driver.

"Didn't you see him coming? I asked. "You had an unobstructed view."

"Well, yes, I did, sir. But I assumed he would stop. After all, I had the right-of-way."

"There is no question that you were in the right. The trouble is, if you had been killed when you got hit, you would have also been dead right, and you have to admit that's not a good option."

The driver of the struck vehicle had no answer for me, so I rejoined Gross and we drove back to the PMO for him to write up the report. I approved the report and sent it into Steve to be disseminated to the usual suspects.

At 1700 hours, I was on my way home. Sam and I watched the news before we left for the fish fry. One of the local stations we picked up had a weatherman who called himself Cowboy Bill. He had some lead-in music which let you know that Cowboy Bill had all the weather for the local counties of southwest Texas and then he appeared in cowboy attire with the greeting, "Howdy partners." He would tell how the weather vane on the bunk house showed the wind coming from the east at 15 miles per hour, or how if you were sleeping under the stars you might get damp because the dew point was fifty-nine degrees and would take place at about 4:30 AM. I thought his entire performance was humorous as well as a good way to interest kids in the weather. Sam simply said that it was cute and agreed that it was probably geared more to children than adults.

NEIL MITCHELL

Every month or so, all company and PMO personnel got together for a Friday night catfish fry. Sam wore a good pair of slacks and a nice blouse, despite my telling her that she might be overdressed. I had been told that the occasion was strictly casual. The event was held at a pond several miles away from the cantonment area, and when we got there the grills were already set up. Acting Sergeant Major Prince was the chief cook for the evening, with a couple of the desk sergeants assisting. I introduced Sam to the colonel and his wife. Like Steve had said, the colonel's wife was probably not much over thirty, but she had a few lines developing around her eyes, which suggested she may have experienced some hard living, which made her appear somewhat older. She spoke with a French accent and had a little Pekinese on a leash. The major and his wife were there. The major's wife was a hypochondriac who seemed to delight in telling everyone who might listen about every surgery and illness she had ever had. Most people, after introducing themselves, politely moved on to more pleasant company. Captain Bills was there with his wife, and I introduced Sam to them.

I casually joked to the colonel, "If anyone wanted to rob the bank on post, tonight would be the time to do it because all the MPs are out here at the pond."

The colonel had obviously had a few drinks, because he was in a very pleasant mood. "Don't worry, lieutenant," he said. "This isn't all of us. There's still a shift on duty. The post is safe."

The cuisine for the evening consisted of a dish called scratch served with catfish. Scratch was fried potatoes and onions and bacon, to which eggs were added and steamed into the mix. Finally, a good deal of Louisiana hot sauce was added. The beverage for the event was beer, or soft drinks, depending on one's preference. The food was quite good and, judging from the laughter and casual conversation, everyone had a pleasurable time. Often, the joke was said that when higher-ranking officers threw a party, the junior officers were required to attend and were required to have a good time. Here, that was not a problem. In this relaxed atmosphere, where everyone could let their hair down, a good time really was had by all

The morning after the catfish fry, Sam and I lay in bed for some time discussing the evening before.

"You were about the only one who spent any time talking to Mrs. Receiver," I noted.

"The poor woman seemed lonely. I really felt sorry for her."

A STATESIDE TOUR OF DUTY

"What did you think of the colonel's wife?" I asked.

"I don't want to sound judgmental, Nick, but if that woman didn't used to turn tricks, then no woman ever has."

I couldn't help but laugh. "That seems to be the prevailing opinion around here, honey, so don't feel bad."

"Another thing I noticed," said Sam "was that Kathy Raymond has to be the world's biggest brownnoser. If Mrs. Bills had stopped walking quickly, Kathy's head would have gone up her butt all the way to the shoulders."

"She's just helping her husband's career," I analyzed. "That's the way junior officers are supposed to get ahead. Their wives lose to the boss's wife at tennis or golf and tell the boss's wife how great she is."

"Well, if that's how the game is played, your career is in big trouble," Sam observed.

"I also noted that you spent a great deal of time talking to the wives of the enlisted men," I said.

"They are a lot less pretentious. To tell the truth, I did enjoy talking to them a great deal more than the officer's wives." Sam paused for a second and then asked, "You don't have a problem with how I do things—do you, honey?"

"No, babe, I don't; you just be yourself. That's all I ask. After all, I married you because you're you."

Sam looked over at me but didn't say anything.

"What's the matter, honey?" I asked. "Why are you looking at me like that? Did I say something wrong?"

"To the contrary, Lieutenant Moultrie, you said something right. And now Mrs. Moultrie is going to give you a big reward."

As we then proceeded into a wonderful session of marital stimulation, my mind was racing along trying to figure out what I had said to cause my wife to react this way. Whatever it was, I was hoping that I could remember it for use at future times. The trouble, I had learned, was that what caused my wife to become amorous on one occasion did not necessarily work the same way the next time. It would be so much easier if men could read women's minds to know what they are supposed to say, how they're supposed to act and when they are supposed to speak and act accordingly. However, the true challenge in a relationship (for a man) was proceeding as best he could, knowing that would never be the case. As our morning delight proceeded, I suddenly remembered that I had told Sam to be herself. Could that have been the magic words that had triggered this great reaction? Not wanting to ruin the moment, I proceeded cautiously.

"You really appreciate the fact that I told you to be yourself, don't you?"

"Yes I do, Nick. When we got married, I accepted you just the way you were with no thought of changing you. Until now I wasn't sure you felt the same way." She then put her fingers up to my lips and whispered, "Don't talk any more. It might ruin the moment. Just continue what you're doing. Then, after we get through, Mrs. Moultrie is going shopping."

Oh great! I thought. Sam could sure pick her moments. At this point, there was no way I could try to talk her out of going shopping later without destroying these pleasurable pursuits. At least, I knew she could spend no more than what she had in her purse. That I could control. In the Army, personnel are paid on the final working day of the month. With all our bills set up to be paid monthly, I knew exactly how much discretionary income we had available for the rest of the month. A portion of that was set aside for savings and another portion was for emergencies. I gave one fourth of what was left to Sam each week for the grocery and personal shopping, along with any other incidental needs. The only rule Sam had to abide by was that she had to wait for Saturday for the next week's amount. That way we didn't run out of money before we ran out of month. I hated it when Sam went shopping, because money seemed to burn a hole in her purse. She rarely brought any back. But I counted my lucky stars that she always brought the groceries first and she was a great cook. Since I was married to her, I knew I would always eat well. So, I just remained thankful for Sam's good points and ignored her faults. After all, she did the same for me.

After our love-making activities were complete, Sam took a shower and dressed in her usual slacks and accompanying attire that she wore away from home. As she picked up the car keys to leave, I said, "Maybe you shouldn't go shopping today, honey. We might need the money for when times get tough."

"When the going gets tough, the tough go shopping." She replied. I had to laugh at her witty comment.

She then left in the car to do her part toward keeping the consumer economy functioning. I smiled as I contemplated Sam's abilities. First she stimulated me then she stimulated the economy. At least, she had her priorities in the right order.

A STATESIDE TOUR OF DUTY

I dressed and went outside. I obtained a mower from the owner of the trailer park and then mowed the little patch of grass that served as a yard around the trailer we lived in. I made everything as tidy as possible, then went inside to await Sam's return. Before doing so, I looked around. The sky was blue without a cloud to be seen. Everything was so peaceful; it didn't seem that life could be any better.

The weekend seemed to pass quickly. Sunday morning, we went to church on post and heard a sermon on kindness to others. During the nondenominational services the chaplain usually preached on positive mental attitude or some other generic topic. Due to the diversity of religious affiliations of those attending, he rarely preached any doctrine for fear of alienating or offending someone. For someone, like myself, who had taken several philosophy classes in college, this was somewhat disappointing, but I realized that was the way it had to be.

Monday morning, the briefing went like it always did. I spent the morning doing paperwork in the office and reading the *Dallas Morning News*. Then I was careful to return from lunch at exactly 1300 hours. I went to the major's office, where I announced, "I have to go over to battalion headquarters, sir. Is there anything I can do for you while I'm there?"

The major looked at his watch and said, "No, but when you return you might have some of the AWOLs in the D-cell clean off the tops of the drinking fountains. They're getting a little dirty."

"I'll do it, sir," I said as I walked away. I drove to Battalion, where I discovered that the next CBR (chemical, radiological and biological) training would start in a few weeks. It seemed the CO wanted an additional officer in the company to receive the training, and I was it. I was given a syllabus of material to prepare me for the course and I returned to the PMO. I then instructed the desk clerk to have the AWOLs shine the floors and clean off the tops of the drinking fountains. They were so happy to be out of the musty and dimly lit D-cell that a few cleaning details were no problem at all for them.

Everything seemed to be falling into place for me. In Traffic, I was pretty much left alone by my superiors. If I was not late returning from lunch, the major seemed to have nothing to bother me about. I felt sorry for Steve. He caught hell from the colonel or major about any little problem that came along. Where he was stuck in his office, I could find an excuse to go out on the road with my men. Since I was out of sight, I seemed to be out of mind.

Of course, returning to work on time was not always easy. Sam and I had fallen into a wonderful routine of making love three or four times a day, which usually included a nooner. I've always heard that if a couple, during their first year of marriage, put a penny in a jar for each time they were intimate and then removed a penny each time they made love in the years afterward, that they would never remove all the pennies. I decided to take their word for it and not try this exercise myself. But, in the future, Sam and I would have to finish our personal time at noon quickly enough for me to get back to the PMO at exactly 1300 hours.

On Thursday afternoon, I was sitting in my office reviewing paper work when I was told the major wished to see me. I left my office and went up front.

"You needed to see me, sir?"

"Yes, lieutenant. Come in. I'm a little concerned about the general appearance of the building."

That was a laugh. After having the AWOLs paint the interior of the building a few days ago the place probably looked better than it had in years. Still, I said nothing. I just listened to what Major Disaster had to get off his chest until he got to the point.

As he continued to tell me how orderliness and cleanliness were paramount in a military building, I listened. "Yes, sir," I would answer occasionally until the major decided to tell me why I was in his office.

"I'm a little disappointed," he stated. "I've mentioned a couple of times how the tops of the water fountains need to be cleaned and you haven't done anything about it."

"Sir," I responded, "I had them cleaned off last Monday."

"Not the one around the corner," he rebutted. "Now get it done, or I'll make you do it."

I didn't know there was one around the corner from his office, but I didn't argue. "I'll have them do it today, sir. Did you need anything else?"

"No, that will be all, lieutenant. Dismissed."

As I left his office and passed through the doorway to return to the back of the building, there in a dark alcove, on my right, was a drinking fountain I had not noticed before. Apparently, it was the one the major used and the only one he was concerned about. I had one of my men take time away from his duties to supervise an AWOL for an hour to police the area outside the main office and wash off the top of the major's drinking fountain. He had plenty of paperwork to attend to and reports to type, but the major's priorities took precedence over necessary work.

A STATESIDE TOUR OF DUTY

Both of us had spent enough time in the service to understand that was the Army way. He supervised the AWOL for an hour and got back to his work. It was now obvious to me that Steve couldn't take all the nonsense from the front office. Sooner or later I had to take a turn receiving some of the crap, whether I wanted to or not. That was the only rough spot in an otherwise pleasant week.

During that week, Sam had gotten to cheer me on with the team in two softball wins. Work was proceeding at a leisurely pace and I had only received one ass chewing. I considered the hellholes the government could have sent me to: such places as Fort Polk, Fort Leonard Wood, Fort Benning, etc. I counted my lucky stars that I had been sent to a laid-back post like Fort McCulloch. However, my respite from strict military regulations was about to end. This was just the calm before the storm. Soon the excrement would once more hit the fan, and this time there would be a lot of it.

CHAPTER TWELVE

s I recall my time at Fort McCulloch, this incident was one where a military policeman attempted to help a friend, with less than desirable results.

The AWOL Apprehension section personnel had decided to take a new bus out for a spin in preparation for the weekly Lone Star Run on Monday. It was sort of a shakedown cruise. Unfortunately, as they drove hell-bent for leather down the highway to return to the cantonment area, the new commanding officer for Headquarters Battalion was arriving. His name was Colonel Proctor. He could clearly see that the bus was speeding and pulled up behind it until his distance from it was constant. He checked his speedometer. His vehicle and the bus were both traveling eighty-five miles per hour. He followed the bus back to the TMP and then ordered the driver to proceed to the MP Station. Once there, he explained to the desk sergeant that he had checked the speed of the bus in a manner recognized by law and that the driver should be given a ticket for the excessive speed. The desk sergeant on duty, Staff Sergeant McCall, just happened to be best friends with the driver, Sergeant Collins. He quickly figured a way to get his buddy out of a ticket.

Sergeant Collins claimed that at no time had the speedometer registered over fifty-five. So, in his most authoritarian voice, Sergeant McCall said, "Yes, sir. We can issue Sergeant Collins, here, a ticket. However, since you have admitted to speeding yourself—we would have to issue you a ticket for the same offense also."

Seeing that the desk sergeant was determined to protect his buddy, Colonel Proctor left the building. Any elation the MPs felt in protecting one of their own would be short-lived. The 290th MP Company was a part of Headquarters Battalion. They had just pissed off their new battalion commander.

A STATESIDE TOUR OF DUTY

As these events were occurring, the Fort McCulloch goon squad was preparing for swing shift. All six of these had been complaining that the goon squad duty was the most boring job they had ever experienced. Apparently, these nights waiting for something to happen were just about to drive them out of their minds. In retrospect, they were little more than a loose cannon waiting to wreak havoc.

Meanwhile, back at home, Sam returned from her weekly shopping and proudly exclaimed that she had saved twenty dollars. She had bought ten pillows and ten laundry baskets for a dollar each, with both items fifty percent off.

"Sam," I began. "In the first place, you didn't save twenty dollars. You spent twenty dollars. In the second place, what in the world are we going to do with ten pillows and ten laundry baskets?"

Sam seemed perplexed by my reaction. "We're stocking up for the future. Now if we need then, we already have them." She then said, "If you buy twenty items that cost two dollars each on sale for fifty percent off, then you have saved twenty dollars." Sam saw no flaws in her reasoning.

"No, Sam," I said. "If you buy twenty items that you don't need for one dollar each then you have saved nothing. You spent twenty dollars. Besides, these are not necessities of life that we need to stock up for the future. We can buy them at any time."

"Not for fifty percent off," Sam protested.

I shook my head. "If we need two of each and buy them at regular price, that's eight dollars. That saves twelve dollars over buying more than you need on sale. Better yet, had you bought two of each on sale today, that would have been an expenditure of four dollars and a saving of sixteen dollars over what you spent."

"No," Sam argued. "I would have only have saved four dollars if I had only bought two of each."

"Honey, you're under the misconception that the more you spend, the more you save."

"Isn't that the way it works?" Sam asked.

"No," I countered. "If you're spending money, you're not saving money. The only way to save is to not spend."

"But they were fifty percent off. So I did save money," she said.

Sam's logic was so paradoxical and convoluted it was difficult to argue with. If everybody thought like Sam did, the whole world would go bankrupt saving money. I started to think that Sam should get a job in the governmental bureaucracy or run for Congress. Her logic would be normal there. We continued to argue as to whether Sam had saved any money and, if so, how much. Whoever said men and women don't think alike knew what he was talking about.

Finally, I decided to give up trying to give Sam an economics lesson. It was like arguing with a brick wall. The logic of my arguments seemed to go nowhere. "Sam let's agree to disagree," I said.

"Okay, but I still believe I saved money," she replied.

I shrugged but said nothing further on the subject. Perhaps Sam would think she had won, but it didn't matter. In retrospect, I thought the entire matter was funny. We stashed the pillows on the bed and found a place for the new laundry baskets and prepared for the evening. We curled up on the couch and watched television. Sam made some sandwiches and we talked and enjoyed each other's company and went to bed right after the news.

The next incident was not funny and had to be one of the most insane episodes I was ever involved with. I would be able to read witness reports and information on it for a long time. It began at about 2330 hours when a poker game at Bravo Company of the 375th Engineer Battalion broke up into a fistfight. Other men in and around the room were able to separate the participants and restore order, but tempers were still close to the boiling point. One man in the poker game was not a resident of the engineer barracks. He was from Echo Company of the 55th Infantry Battalion. While playing cards with his engineer friends, he had been drinking quite heavily and was now very drunk. The CQ on duty thought it best that the man leave, since he had been a catalyst in the fistfight, but he was also concerned that the drunken man not drive. He concluded that for the man's safety, as well as that of others, he might obtain assistance from the military police. He called the MP desk to see if they might be able to give the man a ride back to his barracks to sleep it off. The desk sergeant was in the rest room as the desk clerk, SP4 Strong, answered the phone.

"MP desk. Specialist Strong speaking, sir. How may I help you?"

"Yes, this is Staff Sergeant Stratton at Delta Company barracks of the 375th Engineers. We have a man who is quite drunk who could use a ride back to the 55th infantry. If some of your boys could give him a ride home to sleep it off, we'd appreciate it."

"Any other problems, sergeant?"

"None. He caused a big fight here a minute ago, but everything is copacetic right now. No problems."

"We'll send someone over, Sergeant. Thanks for calling."

"Thanks for your help."

Instead of calling a unit in from off the road, Specialist Strong began to explain the situation to the leader of the goon squad. After all, these guys really needed something to do. "Sergeant Harmon?" he asked.

"Yeah, what is it?" Staff Sergeant Harmon replied.

"Delta Company over at the 375th has a drunk guy who started a fight earli—"

"Drunk and disorderly at the 375th. Let's go men!" Sergeant Harmon yelled with gusto.

"Sarge, wait!" protested Strong.

Without further discussion or explanation, Harmon pressed his men into action. Strong's attempt to clarify the situation fell upon deaf ears as Harmon had his men jump into the White Mouse and MP8 (usually reserved for the major). With the blue lights flashing and the sirens blaring loudly, they then made a beeline for Delta Company. Upon their arrival, they piled out of the cars and rushed the building. The drunken soldier standing outside the building pointed to them and said, "You must be here for me. I didn't know I was so important."

The noise aroused a lot of attention. Men were looking out of windows and many others stepped outside to see what the excitement was all about. As Harmon struck the man over the head with his night stick someone yelled, "Hey, they hit that man. Get the bastards!" Seven or eight men rushed out to confront the MPs and a general melee began. As other men joined the brawl, the goon squad formed a wedge and with truncheons swinging they forced their attackers back and entered the building. Spoiling for a fight, all six men eagerly moved into the turmoil and began to bust heads with their billy clubs. This only caused the tumult to get worse, as others came to the aid of their comrades and the goon squad rapidly found themselves outnumbered. All hell was breaking loose as the engineers counter-attacked with chairs, fists and baseball bats.

Now the MPs were getting the worst of the conflict. Harmon, fearing for his life (and those of his men), took the only course of action he felt left open to him. Doing what he had observed in numerous movies, he drew his .45 caliber model 1911 semiautomatic pistol. After pulling back the slide to chamber a round, he fired three shots into the ceiling. This got the attention of the engineer troops, who quickly began to retreat. The bullets, however, went through the ceiling, which was the floor of the next level of the three-story building.

One bullet ricocheted off a pipe in the floor and went through a wall locker. The owner of the wall locker was standing next to it at the time. The second bullet went through a bunk, missing the man in it by little more than an inch and bounced off the second-story ceiling, barely missing a third man. The third bullet ricocheted out a window and into the barracks next door, causing a scare among the troops there. The fight was over, but it was only through the grace of God that nobody was killed by the warning shots. As the building's residents retreated, the goon squad handcuffed their prisoner and returned to the PMO in triumph. The goon squad members had a few bumps, bruises and black eyes, but they had given worse than they received. Staff Sergeant Harmon, who was a great admirer of the major, saw the night as the first epic of a glorious career for the goon squad. He could not have been more mistaken.

Immediately, the engineers began to contact everyone from their CO to their congressmen and relatives. All sorts of official protests and complaints of police brutality began to be filed. The Engineer Company CO called his Engineer Battalion CO, who in turn woke up the commanding general, who then raised hell with the provost marshal. Colonel Cox then contacted the MPDO to find out what had happened. The prisoner was released with apologies and was given a ride to his barracks. Still he was pissed off and filed additional complaints. Somebody's head was going to roll. The saga of the goon squad was over and they were told to meet with the colonel at 1000 hours Monday morning.

It might not have been so bad if this fiasco had not happened the same day that Colonel Proctor had been antagonized. He was still angry about the driver of the AWOL App bus not being cited for speeding. These two items together were more than he could stand. Colonel Proctor had already contacted Colonel Cox and informed him that the MP Company needed to understand that they were part of the Army. Normally this could be worked out between colonels, but with the goon squad disaster happening on the same day, the only way Colonel Cox could save his job (and his career) was to find a fall guy. He and the major met early Sunday morning with Captain Tucker and the decision was made. Captain Bills would be the victim. He would take the fall.

A STATESIDE TOUR OF DUTY

At 1000 hours Sam and I attended church services at the post chapel. When we got home at 1100 hours the phone was ringing. It was Steve. He filled me in on the details of the previous evening. It seems that Tucker had just called him and filled him in on the meeting he had with the major and colonel.

"Nick, can you believe it? The colonel and the major were going to blame me for this disaster. Tucker convinced them that it had to be someone in the chain of command, so they settled on Bills."

As he spoke, I got a sick feeling in my gut. If anyone was expendable in the provost marshal's office right now, it was me. I was probably lucky there was no way they could blame any of this on me. Fortunately, I was not in the chain of command and did not oversee Operations, but in the future, I had better be cautious. "What else did Tucker say?" I asked.

"He said we should watch our backs and cover our asses," was the answer. "He's going to ETS on Monday and be gone. He said he feels sorry for us. From what he's heard, Proctor is the battalion CO from hell and whoever is in Operations will probably get the blame for the major's stupidity." He continued, "Of course Tucker never did because he had something on the colonel. He denies it, but we both could see it. I just wish he would tell us what it is."

"So do I. It would make life a whole lot easier."

"No kidding."

"Look, Steve. Did you know that there was a drinking fountain back in the corner as you walk out of the secretaries' office?"

"No. Why do you ask?"

"Earlier this week, Major Disaster ordered me to have the AWOLs clean the tops of the drinking fountains. Apparently, they missed that one. The moron major acted like the world was going to end. He threatened to have me clean it."

"Well, Nick, the man has nothing else to do. You have to expect shit like that."

"I'll just make sure it is kept clean in the future. That will be one less thing he can bother me with."

"Good plan. If we always think ahead, we should be okay and stay ahead of those idiots."

"Yeah, and did you notice the folder on the colonel's desk this week, labeled 'Sergeant Warren's TDY to Louisiana'?"

"Yes, I did. I would give anything to look at it," Steve replied. "It might contain some clue as to what Tucker has on the colonel."

"The trouble is, Steve, old buddy, that the colonel locks his office. Too bad we can't break in and get a look at it, but that only happens in the movies."

"Yeah, if we got caught, we'd be charged with breaking and entering. So, don't even think about it. Well, I'll see you at the salt mines tomorrow morning. Take it easy, Nick."

"Okay, man. See you there." I hung up the phone. I filled Sam in on the entire goings-on, and we settled back and relaxed for the afternoon. When the national news came on that evening, there were the usual segments about the ongoing war in Southeast Asia. One reporter mentioned how it was often impossible for the troops to know who their enemies were, as the Viet Cong often posed as civilians. Funny, I thought, over here Steve and I might have the same problem. I was already looking forward to the time I would be leaving this place.

"Sam," I asked, "Have you ever left somewhere and looked back with a feeling of nostalgia or perhaps sadness?"

"Yes, I have. It's always sad to leave friends behind."

"I sort of felt that way when I graduated from school," I noted. "Do you think we'll look back in that manner when we leave here?"

Sam just looked at me and after a moment's thought said, "It's too early to tell. We'll just have to wait and see."

CHAPTER THIRTEEN

Monday, the 7th of September, 1970, was memorable for two reasons. That day saw the final, official dissolution of the goon squad and the departure of Captain Tucker. At the morning briefing, the main topic of conversation was the debacle of Saturday night. Even the major seemed a loss for words, as he was unable to defend his pet project.

At 1000 hours, the members of the goon squad were standing in the colonel's office. The colonel's voice got louder and louder as he continued his rant. After about ten minutes, he finished with, "Our mission is to protect and serve. You men have destroyed any amount of good public relations we can ever attempt to create. The post commander is putting pressure on me to court-martial the lot of you or at least give all of you Article 15's. I've convinced him that you were only defending yourselves, so starting tomorrow you will be reassigned to the patrols you were previously with."

"Sir?" asked Sergeant Harmon.

"Yes, what is it?"

"Does this mean that you're doing away with the goon squad?"

The colonel's face became bright red as he screamed. "Yes, you damn fool! You're disbanded. Now get out of here—all of you!"

The dejected members of the now-disbanded goon squad departed the PMO. As shorthanded as the military police company was, it was a foregone conclusion that none of the men would be court-martialed or relieved of duty. Everyone in the power structure just thanked the good Lord that nobody had been killed during the Saturday night disaster. If the goon squad had caused fatalities, it would have been impossible to save their butts.

Then in the afternoon, Captain Tucker ended his tour of duty at the PMO. The following morning would be his last in the Army, and he would sign out as soon as Finance paid him, but today was his moment in the sun. At 1400 hours, everyone of any rank or position in the company or the PMO assembled in the front office next to the colonel's office. The mess hall had donated a cake and about ten gallons of punch, and it was apparent that the colonel wanted Tucker to leave in style. He proceeded to talk for about ten minutes about the superlative job Tucker had done and stressed his devotion to duty. At length he finished with, "We wish you well as you begin your career as a civilian and present you with this certificate of appreciation." He then handed Tucker the certificate, which was encased in a fancy black frame, as they shook hands.

"Thank you, colonel." Tucker said. "I have enjoyed the last two years. The PMO personnel are the best and it's truly been a pleasure to work with all of you." After a moment's hesitation, he then added with a grin, "Now let's cut the cake." Everyone laughed as he reached for a knife.

As the cake was cut into pieces for all of us to enjoy with a cup of punch, everyone was all smiles. I felt that it was all just a show, however, as I looked around. Warren and Prince chatted with the CID investigators—individuals they rarely had a good word to say about. The colonel was talking with two of the desk sergeants while the major discussed troop status and TO&E strength with Captain Bills. Steve and I were sipping punch and enjoying the cake when Raymond came over and engaged us in conversation. "Have you guys been to Camp Sterling Price?" he asked.

"I know that it's part of the post complex, but I haven't had the privilege of going there yet." I admitted.

"Me neither," said Steve.

Raymond then began to tell us all about Camp Sterling Price. "The post within a post," as he called it had about seven or eight hundred personnel. There were several landing strips for fixed-wing and rotary aircraft, as well as some target ranges for Cobras and helicopter gunships. To enforce regulations, the 290th MP Company had a platoon of men stationed there. They numbered about thirty men and were led by a Captain Manning and Lieutenant Carter. Camp Price had all the necessary amenities of a military base, including a nine-hole golf course. As Brian continued his information about Camp Price, he mentioned that Phil (Lieutenant Carter) was also military intelligence. I was starting to feel like an oddball. All my fellow lieutenants in the MP Company were commissioned in military intelligence. I was the only military police lieutenant officer assigned to our MP unit. At length, both Steve and I agreed that we'd have to go out and take a look at the place. I suspected that Camp Price was just somewhere Byron and the CO could go when they didn't have anything else to do. There they would be beyond the prying eyes of the major and could probably kill a lot of time, between the golf course and the handball courts at the gym.

At about 1430 hours, the colonel's wife arrived. As I nodded my obligatory greeting and said hello to her, I noticed that her blond hair had black roots. It was pulled back in a fancy style with a series of curls, but clearly, it was time for her to apply some more dye. She said hello to everyone in her usual thick French accent, and a few minutes later she left with her husband. With the colonel gone, everyone else would have left—if they could. Unfortunately, with the major there that was not possible. As we were stuck there until 1700 hours, Steve and I walked over to wish Tucker well in his new endeavors. Tucker shook hands with us and simply said, "I really wish you guys the best."

I wanted to try one more time to find out what he had on the colonel but, knowing that was probably futile, simply said "good luck" instead. With no more official duties to keep him in the building, Tucker then made his last exit.

Steve and I then walked back to our offices to spend the last few minutes of the workday. We decided that, in the future, if one of us wanted to leave early we would cover for each other with the major. If two second lieutenants couldn't sandbag the major, then we might as well give back our commissions. No more would we be standing in Major Disaster's office explaining where we had been. With a little coordination and prior planning between us, we could take care of these problems before they happened and keep the major convinced we were both working hard. Unfortunately, Steve and I would never be able to ignore the difference in rank between ourselves and the top brass in the front office as Tucker always had. We had to at least show the major respect to his face, whether we thought he deserved it or not.

"Why don't you come over to my place for a while and shoot the breeze? I don't think you've seen my place yet." Steve said that almost as an afterthought.

"Let me check in with the boss first," I replied, as I reached for the phone. I dialed my home number and Sam answered.

"Hi, babe." I said. "Steve wants me to drop by his place and get a tour. Have I got a few minutes before supper?"

Sam hesitated a few seconds before giving a reply. "I'll have dinner on in about forty-five minutes. If you're gone any longer than that, you'll have to eat it cold."

"Not to worry, honey. I'll be there. Love you, babe."

"We'll see," Sam said. "I love you, too."

"Looks like I have about forty-five minutes. Lead the way and I'll follow you." I said to Steve.

Steve grabbed his hat, and as we walked to the door he commented, "I'm glad I'm not married and have to answer to a woman."

With a laugh, I answered him. "It's not really that bad. It's actually nice to have someone to share your life with."

Steve shrugged his shoulders as if he wasn't sure he believed me. We got in our cars and I followed him to his place. He and Charlie had a two-bedroom apartment on the west side of Harrisville. Their apartment was part of a complex that had a small, private pond about thirty yards behind it and a pool out front. Residents of the apartments were allowed to fish in the pond, which was one reason they had chosen this place to live. As we entered, Steve went straight to the refrigerator for a beer. "You want one?" he asked as he opened it.

"No thanks," I replied. "I'm still on the wagon."

"Coke, then? We've got a few of them too."

"That'll be fine, thanks." Steve tossed me a can of soda, which I opened, and we sat down and began to talk. No sooner had we done so than Charlie came through the door.

"Congratulate me, men!" He exclaimed that with exuberance, as he tossed his garrison cap on the couch.

"Why in the hell would we do that?" Steve answered as he put his feet up on the coffee table.

"I had a long talk with Charlotte down in her office in AG files today."

Steve rolled his eyes as he looked over at me. "Charlie wants us to congratulate him for talking to a girl." He then looked over at Charlie and stated, "You need to get out more, roomie. When you get her into bed, we'll congratulate you."

Charlie ignored the statement as he continued, "I asked her for another date this weekend. She's from Houston and often goes down there to spend weekends at her parents' place. Well, this weekend old Charlie's going to take her there, and we'll hit a few of the night spots that civilization has to offer." Charlie then added, "Of course, I'll be sleeping in the guest bedroom, but I'll be spending my daylight hours with her."

"Good job, Charlie." Steve said as he placed his beer down on a copy of *Sports Illustrated*. "Staying with her at her parents' place. If you sneak over to her room, like the guy in the movie *Goodbye, Columbus*, don't get caught."

"No way," replied Charlie. "I'm going to behave myself." Charlie then picked up his garrison cap, and as he walked to his room to toss it inside he paused briefly. "I've spent the past few days getting to know her, and she is definitely not somebody you move too quickly with." He then began to take off his shirt as he said, "Hey, I think I'll have a beer and then go for a swim."

"He has to go for a swim to cool off after talking to Charlotte," I noted to Steve. "Hey Charlie, I bet you can't wait to try out chapter three of that book on her. My wife enjoyed it, so I'm sure Charlotte will too."

Charlie held up his hands, palms facing out, to emphasize his point. "I'm not going to rush things. There's no hurry about when, and if, I get to chapter three, but I appreciate your letting me know it works."

Steve sat down his beer. "That's right." He remembered. "You were going to let us know if that stupid book worked. If it's that good, maybe I'll read it myself."

Charlie went into his room and returned shortly thereafter wearing his swim trunks and carrying the book, which he tossed to Steve. "Read up, man. Right now, I'm off to the pool." With that, Charlie grabbed a beer from the refrigerator and, after tossing a towel over his right shoulder, walked out the front door.

Steve settled back in his seat and opened the book. "Now that I have the place all to myself for the weekend, I definitely gotta find some company. Maybe this book will help." Steve then glanced through the book as he polished off his beer.

"The book won't tell you how to meet girls, but it sure will tell you how to make them happy once you do."

"We'll see." Steve then put the book down and with a smile began to reminisce. "You know, the scariest experience I ever had with a girl was during my junior year at Austin."

"What happened?"

"I met this pretty sophomore and asked her out." He quickly added, "That's not the scary part. Well, on our date she turned out to be the easiest lay that I ever had. I then asked her out for the next five days in a row and every night was the same thing. As soon as we were alone she was ready to put out. I was thinking that I had a great thing going."

He stopped for a second, and then continued his narrative. "Well, that Friday I was outside the library and I overheard a couple of girls talking, and they mentioned her name. Naturally, I was curious, so I got where I could hear the entire conversation, and one girl said 'Yes, she's definitely pregnant, but she's got a sucker that she's been doing it with all week. Pretty soon she is going to convince him that the kid is his so they can get married.'"

Steve shook his head as he continued his story. "Nick, I have never been so nervous in my life. All I could think about was that the girl was pregnant and I had been screwing her."

"What did you do then?"

"Well! I may have been scared but I didn't panic. I went home and called her and said that I thought we had something special. I then told her that I thought we should get married, but first I had something to tell her." He smiled as he continued. "I continued by telling her that every time I had told a girl my secret, it ended the relationship, but what we had was so special, I knew it wouldn't matter to her."

"What did you tell her?" My curiosity was piqued at this point.

"I told her that I was sterile as the result of a football injury. While I could have sex, I had a zero-sperm count, but with the special relationship we had—I knew it wouldn't matter to her." Steve looked my way with a self-satisfied smile as I roared with laughter at the story.

"What did she say to that? As if I couldn't guess."

"She said she wanted to be a mother and have kids and she couldn't marry someone that was sterile. So, I ended the conversation by telling her how heartbroken I was. She probably found another sucker to marry her. I never found out, and what's more, I didn't care."

Shortly afterward I left for home knowing Sam would have supper ready. I would have to hurry, as I was a little late. Sure enough, as I arrived at home, Sam had supper on the table.

"Not bad, honey," she commented. "You're only ten minutes late. This isn't going to become a regular thing where you spend time with the boys and leave me alone, is it?"

"No honey, it isn't," I avowed. "You're too good looking to leave alone for very long."

"Nick, you are full of BS, and I love it." She said with a smile.

A STATESIDE TOUR OF DUTY

"With all that's happening at work, Steve and I need to compare notes and if we do it at work what we say may get back to the colonel. It's just easier to talk at Steve's house," I added.

"Why not have him come over here?"

"That's not a bad idea. Maybe we can take turns meeting at our respective homes. Now let's eat."

Sam and I sat down to eat. The meal was pleasant as we just talked and generally enjoyed each other's company until I passed Steve's story along to Sam. She didn't see the humor.

"Nick that is so much like you men. All you think of is ways to get some poor girl in bed and then dump her when she gets pregnant. It's reprehensible."

"Honey," I rebutted. "It wasn't his kid. What else was he supposed to do?"

Sam then thought for a minute. "Well, you're right. That girl was just stupid. Before a girl should try to convince a guy that a kid is his, first she should ask how many children he wants to have and make sure he plans to have a family. After she finds out he wants a family, then she should tell him she is having his baby."

"Honey, are you telling me you think its okay to deceive some poor slob into raising a baby that is not his?"

Sam put her hands on her hips and in a disgusted tone said: "You men will lie, cheat, steal, and connive to obtain sex. Then when the girl attempts to provide for herself and her baby the best way she can, you men act so injured. If the guy doesn't want to get married, he shouldn't be sleeping with the girl in the first place."

Realizing that we would never see eye to eye on this subject and not wanting to get into an argument with Sam, I conceded on all points. "I guess you're right, honey. I can't argue with your logic." Of course, I could have; but I wisely chose not to. "Just remember, Sam, I married you because I wanted to; and you didn't have to be pregnant to get me to the altar."

"I know." She put her arms around me and gave me a hug. "We're lucky. We married because we love each other and when we have kids it will be because we want them."

I whispered in her ear. "Want to start working on the first one right now?"

Sam smiled and shook her head slightly in a cute sort of disbelief. "Like I said before, you'll say or do anything to get into my pants. Won't you?"

"That's true, but that's just part of my charm, Sam. It's what I do best."

"I'm glad you think so." She refuted. "What you do best better be making a good living for us. Now, if you really want to get lucky tonight, Lieutenant Moultrie, then you'll get your butt over to the sink and do the dishes while Samantha Moultrie relaxes on the couch."

Without comment, I went to the sink and began to fill it with hot water. I had always hated doing dishes, even though I know it was a necessary job. As a bachelor, my roommates and I would often wait until every single dish and utensil was dirty before someone broke down and washed them. Now as a married man, my wife could offer me certain inducements to get me to help in the household chores. The reward, in this case, was even better than food.

Meanwhile, across the post, as I learned later, Colonel Proctor was meeting with the post inspector general, Colonel David Arbon. Arbon's daughter had been cited into magistrate's court several times for speeding. In the old days, when such matters would have simply been referred to him, it would have been a simple matter to dispose of. Now that such cases were referred to Magistrate's Court, however, he was powerless to fix his daughter's tickets unless he had someone inside the PMO personally pulling the tickets for him. Arbon didn't like the new system, as he saw fixing tickets as a prerogative of rank. It had taken him many years to become a field-grade officer and he obviously felt he should be able to use that rank to his advantage or to the advantage of those around him. Their meeting probably went something like this, with Proctor getting right to the point.

"Look, Phil," he probably began. "The 290th is the biggest bunch of Keystone Cops I've ever seen. I think it's time to shape up that bunch."

"You'll get no argument from me. I don't have much use for them myself."

"In the past few days they've shot up the post, endangered others and covered their friends' butts when they've clearly broken the law. I think it's time to show them they are still part of the Army. A little discipline should bring them back to earth."

With a little more discussion, apparently it was decided that Arbon would conduct an annual IG inspection and find the 290th unprepared for inspection, whereupon Proctor would become the second of a one-two punch. He would demand that the 290th be brought up to standards, while barraging the company with unreasonable demands.

As usual, the next morning briefing began at 0800 hours. Mr. Carson was present from CID, and announced that to provide better coordination between the Criminal Investigative Division and the PMO he would be in attendance in the future. In the past, CID presence at the briefing had been sporadic, occurring only when a case in which they had interest appeared in the blotter. I found it interesting that now they decided to be a permanent fixture for these briefings. Steve and I had heard rumors about their dislike for Warren and suspected that fact might be part of the reason for their new interest.

After everyone had read the blotter, the colonel looked around the table. "Captain Bills?" he asked.

"I was notified late last night that our annual IG inspection will be held on Thursday, sir. I think we'll be ready for it."

"Good!" the colonel replied. "Lieutenant Moultrie?"

"Nothing, sir."

"Lieutenant Bronson?"

"Nothing, sir."

"Mr. Bernard?"

Mr. Bernard answered, "Yes, sir. Two things: There seems to be increased activity in poaching and also a renewed activity in cock fighting along the post boundary over in Shorter County. If we close in, the participants skip across the boundary into civilian territory. Any increase in personnel would sure be welcome."

"I wish we could help out there, chief, but the entire company is shorthanded. We can't spare any more personnel at this time."

Mr. Bernard then asked, "Is there any chance of coordinating our activities with civilian authorities to catch those breaking the law?"

"Rumor has it that the sheriff of Shorter County raises gamecocks and is the biggest cock fighter of them all, so I don't know how much help they would be. Just do what you can and let's hope the Department of the Army sees fit to send us some more personnel soon."

"Yes, sir. We'll do what we can, but there's no way we can cover the post adequately with the few men we have."

"I understand, chief," the colonel noted. "But, if you do your best, we can't ask any more."

"Thank you, sir." Bernard just nodded and remained silent at that point.

"Sergeant Lippman?" the colonel asked as he continued around the table.

"Yes, sir. I think the EM should be dropped from the OD roster."

"I wish we could," said the colonel, "but with the few officers we have, it is necessary to have E-8s and E-7 section chiefs act as duty officers also. Maybe we can take a look at it later if the situation changes."

"Yes, sir," replied Lippmann unhappily.

The colonel then looked at the major. "Jim?" he asked.

"Yes, colonel. I have prepared three more patrol tips, which I will place on the bulletin board." The major held up his latest artwork. They were patrol tips numbers four and five and six. One told the men to hold a flashlight away from their bodies when using it at night. That way, if an adversary took a shot at them, they would most likely miss. Another reminded the men to record the license number of any car they stopped. That way, if they were killed, other investigators would have an idea as to whom the perpetrator was. The last tip reminded the men to investigate any suspicious or unusual activity.

"I don't know if this is the place for it, sir, but the third patrol tip there reminds me of a joke," I interjected at that point. I realized the comment was a mistake when the major gave me a look that could kill.

The colonel, on the other hand, smiled and said, "Well, let's hear it. This place could use a little levity."

With the colonel's permission, I continued. "The story goes," I began, "that a group of robbers robbed a fast-food restaurant. As they were finishing the robbery and tying up the employees, they noticed two cops coming in, so they pretended to be the employees and waited on the lawmen. After serving the cops, the police drew their guns and arrested them. As the bad guys were being led away, they inquired as to how the cops knew they were not employees. One of the policemen then answered, 'That's easy. You got our order right.'" Everyone, except the major, laughed or at least chuckled.

The colonel especially seemed to enjoy the joke. "Well said, lieutenant. Investigate all suspicious activity." He then continued around the table. "Mr. Carson?"

"Just good to be here, sir. Nothing to add this morning."

"It's good to have you with us." The colonel then looked at Warren. "Sergeant Warren?"

"I'm getting ready to leave TDY to conduct physical security inspections, sir. I can brief you further after this meeting."

"Excellent." The colonel then looked at the sergeant major. "Top?"

"Nothing, sir," said Prince.

The colonel then said, "Okay, men, let's go to work." We all stood and saluted. The colonel returned the salute and we began to leave the room.

As we walked back to Operations, Steve shook his head. "I'm glad the major has his patrol tips to keep him busy. Maybe he'll stay out of our hair."

"Only time will tell," I answered. "Before Tucker left, he told me about a time he had to drive to San Angelo with the major in a staff car. The major made him wear his hat in the car all the way there and all the way back."

"What an idiot," Steve commented. "I hope I never have to make any long trips with him like that."

The rest of the day passed uneventfully until 1600 hours. I was with SP4 Collings, running radar in the cantonment area, when a call came over the radio.

"Unit One Five, this is Fort McCulloch."

I keyed the mic and answered, "This is Unit One Five. Go ahead, Fort McCulloch."

"Unit One Five, we have a ten-three on Highway One Four Two East, near Airfield Bravo. There are injuries and an ambulance has been dispatched."

"Ten-four, en route." I replied. "Hit the blue light, Collings, and let's check it out." Without delay (or reply) Collings turned on the blue light and pulled into traffic.

The desk sergeant concluded the radio transmission with, "Ten-four. Fort McCulloch clear."

"We'll be at Airfield B in five minutes, sir," stated Collings as he pushed the pedal down and made a beeline for the location. Sure enough, about three miles from the airfield we saw a car with its front end smashed. Near it was a motorcycle with a man lying in a pool of blood. Two telephone linesmen were standing nearby.

This was the first major accident I had ever helped investigate, so I was determined to do things right. I steeled myself so as not to recoil at the sight of the blood. "Collings, see to the injured man there. Just let him know that help is on the way if he's conscious, but don't move him. I'll see how the other people are."

"Yes, sir," acknowledged Collings as he grabbed his clipboard and put on his hat. He jumped out of the car and walked over to the injured man. I picked up a clipboard and went over to the damaged car. Two women and some children were standing there. The first woman was a white brunette, holding a little girl, while the other was a black woman. Both appeared to be in their late twenties. The white woman was crying.

"Is everyone here all right, or at least as all right as you can be under the circumstances?" I asked.

The white woman continued sobbing and said through her tears, "My little girl hit herself on the dashboard." The little girl turned toward me and I could see that her forehead was bleeding. There was something vaguely familiar about the white woman, but I couldn't place where I had seen her before.

"You'll want to take your daughter to the hospital to check the extent of her injuries, ma'am. Is your husband in the military or a civilian?"

"In the Army," she replied tearfully. "In Korea. He's a sergeant."

"I'll have a unit run you over to the hospital, then." I then realized that I needed to know who was driving. "Is this your car?" I asked the woman.

"Yes," she sobbed.

"You were driving, then?"

"Yes." Her lamentations continued. I thought it interesting that she was doing all the crying, while the other party was lying in a pool of his own blood.

"I'll need to see your driver's license and get everybody's names."

The ambulance arrived and quickly loaded the injured man and left for the Fort McCulloch hospital. While they did so, I quickly copied the information from the woman's driver's license and registration and got the names of the black woman and children, who were passengers in the car.

I asked, "Tell me what happened, in your own words, ma'am." Having said that, I then thought what I had said sounded stupid. After all, what other words was she going to use? But I could worry about changing my phraseology on future interviews.

The woman continued to talk through her tears. "I was passing another car and saw the man on the motorcycle. I tried to miss him, but he ran into me."

A STATESIDE TOUR OF DUTY

At this point, unit one pulled up to see if we needed assistance. I suggested they take the women and their children to the hospital where the little girl could be checked and the women could make arrangements for a ride home. The car was definitely not driveable. The two women and four small children were a little cramped on the back seat of the MP cruiser, but they were able to squeeze in, and in a moment they were on their way.

I walked back to our car. I keyed the mic to the radio and said, "Fort McCulloch, this is Unit One Five."

"This is Fort McCulloch. Go ahead, Unit One Five."

"Be advised that we will need a wrecker at this location, as neither vehicle is driveable. We have a '69 Oldsmobile and a Harley-Davidson motorcycle to be removed from the scene of the ten-three." I waited for the response.

"Sounds like you'll need two wreckers, sir. I don't think the Harley will fit in the cab of the first tow truck."

I chuckled. "You're right, sarge. I'll let you take care of it."

The desk sergeant cleared the radio net with, "Ten-four. Fort McCulloch clear."

As he did so, I could hear the desk clerk laughing in the background. I walked over to Collings, who was talking to the two telephone linesman. One of them was almost shouting, "He flew as high as those phone lines there."

The other was shaking his head and repeating over and over, "She just ran him over."

We asked the men if they could come down to the station to write down their statements as witnesses, and they agreed. By this time a small crowd was beginning to congregate at the scene, so I walked over and politely asked them to leave, as there was no way they could be of help. They quickly complied with my request.

Shortly afterward, two wreckers arrived. The first towed off the Oldsmobile while the second retrieved the Harley. Before they had done so, however, Collings had taken pictures of the scene, including separate pictures of the damaged vehicles. He measured the skid marks and made a number of other measurements, and we then drove back to the station, with the linemen following us.

When we arrived, it was after 1700 hours, so I called Sam to let her know that I would be late for supper. Once I explained the seriousness of the accident, she understood.

The linesmen wrote down their statements. When they had completed them, I then asked them, "Is this the truth, the whole truth and nothing but the truth, to the best of your recollection?"

They both replied in the affirmative. I had them sign their statements and then signed as the officer administering the oaths.

Our investigation revealed that the woman (Mrs. Hooper) was passing another vehicle when the motorcycle approached from the opposite direction. Instead of pulling back into her own lane, she apparently panicked and turned her car to the left side of the road, where she ran into the motorcycle (which was taking evasive action to avoid her) head on. A check of the number of the post registration sticker on the bike revealed it belonged to PFC Ronald MacDonald. Collings then called the post hospital, which verified that the injured man was indeed Private Ronald MacDonald. He had extensive injuries and remained in critical condition. He also discovered that Mrs. Hooper's daughter's injuries were superficial. No one else in the Oldsmobile had reported any injuries whatsoever.

Now came the paperwork. A blotter entry was prepared and the incident was assigned a case number (known as an MPR number), which was assigned to the Traffic section. The basic information was typed by Collings onto the form 19-32 which was attached to a form 19-68 (basic accident investigation form). To these were added a traffic accident investigator's statement stating his findings and his opinions regarding the cause of the accident. The sworn witness statements, which had been written on form 19-31s, were added to the now voluminous file. As the subject of the accident was a military dependent, all the work was prepared in four copies. One copy was retained in the Traffic files, while the remaining three were approved by myself and sent to Operations to be reviewed by the Operations officer. One copy would go to the office of the Post Safety Director, a second copy to the state of Texas Department of Public Safety and the third would be sent to a national records repository. As Collings and myself exited the office, I noticed it was 1910 hours. I reentered the office and called Sam to tell her I would be right home. I then locked the office and headed for home.

When I got home, Sam had numerous questions about the accident. I kept telling her that the woman who caused the whole thing looked very familiar, but I couldn't place her.

Sam just said, "It will probably come to you later, honey. Don't worry about it."

A STATESIDE TOUR OF DUTY

Despite Sam's natural curiosity, the idea of telling about the poor guy lying as a pile of broken bones in a pool of his own blood was not a thought I wanted to recall. Therefore, we soon changed the subject.

"Isn't there a game tonight?" Sam asked. "It is Tuesday."

"The game was already started when I left the office. I'm hungry, and by the time we eat, I don't think there will be much of the game left to play. I think they can get along without me this time."

"You usually seem to enjoy it so. I'm surprised you're not going to try and at least catch part of the game to play in."

"I just want to spend a quiet evening alone with you." I then began to elaborate. "Today the fact was reinforced that all it takes to end somebody's life is one stupid driver making a dumb move, and it could be all over. We all think that it can't happen to us, but I'm sure that the private today thought the same thing. Just in case something happens to one of us in the future, I want the other to have some nice memories. We can just sit and talk and do whatever you want tonight." I gave Sam a very long hug.

Sam smiled and said, "In that case, you can help with the dishes. You wash, and I'll dry." Sam then asked, "What was the name of the guy in the accident?"

"Funny you should ask. It was Ronald MacDonald."

Sam started to laugh. "You're kidding. Was he wearing a clown suit and being chased by a hamburglar?"

"It's not funny, Sam. The guy may die."

Sam continued laughing. "I'm sorry. I just can't imagine someone giving their child such a name."

"He probably was born and received the name before the hamburger company created their corporate character. It's not his fault they used his name for their merchandising and advertising."

"Just the same, it *is* funny."

"Yeah, I guess it is," I confessed.

After supper and washing dishes, I went through the junk I was starting to accumulate. While Sam watched TV, I found over forty copies of orders that I had never had any use for upon my arrival at Fort McCulloch. They sat there in mute testimony to the government's waste of paper. There was a bill from the officers' club that I had thrown aside without looking at before. The club had charged me a full month's dues for the first partial month I was here, plus another month's dues in advance in addition to that. The total was more than I felt I owed, so I was in no hurry to pay it. I threw away all the copies of orders except one, which I placed in my file of personal papers. Experience had taught me to keep one copy of all orders and all pay vouchers for future reference and proof of what was owed to me by Uncle Sam.

The club bill, I threw away. When I felt like paying it, they could look up the unpaid balance. It would give the clerk something to do. Sam and I had a pleasant evening as we talked about anything other than the accident, as I tossed out unwanted papers in an attempt to simplify our lives.

The Wednesday briefing had as its focal point the accident of the day before. I explained that a final blotter entry would be prepared as soon as I left the briefing. Mrs. Hooper would be cited for improper passing. In the event Private MacDonald died because of his injuries, she might also be charged with more serious offenses such as vehicular homicide.

As the briefing was about to break up, two men arrived to install carpet in the colonel's office. The carpet was a bright red and extremely thick. Whoever had approved the purchase must have authorized quite an expenditure. The carpet clearly was not cheap.

After the meeting, I returned to Traffic. Collings had called Mrs. Hooper and asked her to come by the Traffic office. She had agreed to be there before lunch. A final blotter entry was prepared, stating the charges filed in the matter. A call to the hospital revealed that Private MacDonald, while still in critical condition, was stable and improving. He was expected to live. Fortunately, he had been wearing a helmet. Therefore, he had not sustained any major head injuries. I spent the morning clearing up paperwork in the office and, sure enough, a little after 1030 hours Mrs. Hooper came into the office. Collings explained that she was being charged with improper passing and told her to appear in magistrate's court and gave her directions to get there. As they were talking, two MPs appeared at the door.

They looked in and communicated in whispered tones and left. After Hooper had left the building they came in and one of them said, "Collings that looked like Loraine Hooper that was in here."

Collings looked up and said, "It was. I had to cite her for causing an accident." He held up the accident report.

One of the men took the report and began reading it. "She ran some guy over!" he exclaimed. Both men turned and ran out toward the desk. "Hey, sarge!" he yelled. "Look at this."

Collings gave me a look that seemed to say, "What the hell?"

A STATESIDE TOUR OF DUTY

I was as dumbfounded as he, so I walked out to the desk. Sergeant McCall was looking at the report with several of his men. They were generally laughing and carrying on. One said, "They ought to hang her."

"What's going on, sarge?" I asked.

"Don't you know who this is, sir?" Sergeant McCall then added, "Lorraine Hooper is the biggest whore on post. Word is, she was in here a while back trying to have one of her johns arrested for stiffing her. She charges a bit, but she's worth it. She's really good at her profession."

Then it hit me. While her hair color had changed, Lorraine Hooper was the woman who had come into the PMO some time ago wanting us to arrest a man who had stopped payment on a check to her. I didn't know why I couldn't place her before.

McCall continued. "About six months ago, I picked her up at the NCO Club. I spent the night at her house in Harrisville. The next morning, while she was in the bathroom, I took her wedding picture out of the frame (it was just sitting on a dresser) and wrote on the back, 'It was very good, Harold,' and signed my name."

"Harold?" I questioned.

"That's her husband's name. I've known him for years. He's dumber than a rock."

My thoughts were interrupted by one of the men yelling, "Look, Margarete Allen was with her."

"Another pro?" The question was meant to be rhetorical but an answer was quick in coming.

Specialist Lightfoot just smiled and said, "Yes, sir. She and Hooper are good friends. They work Miller's together, as well as the NCO club. Hell, the word is, sometimes they even get into the offices' club. If they pick up someone who's the same race, they take them to their place. If their customer is a different race, then they take 'em to a motel. It costs a little more that way, but the neighbors don't talk as much."

While I considered myself a man of the world, I now realized I knew absolutely nothing about the sex trade. I looked at McCall, and asked, "Just out of curiosity, how much do they charge?" I then quickly added, "Not that I'm planning to do any business with them."

"Depending on how much time you spend with them, it's either $50 or $100, sir." He then added, "And well worth it, I might add. Considering they both have had two kids and have serviced half the post, they've still got the tightest twats this side of China."

"Yes, they do," affirmed Lightfoot.

McCall then went into detail about the services rendered for the hundred dollar price. He described, in detail, how the women would first perform fellatio on their customer after which they proceeded with what might be called regular sex. The length of time they spent with a customer could also depend on how much he paid. I was starting to be sorry I had asked for details.

Looking at my watch, I said, "Well, we got to get back to work." As I returned to my office, Collings took the report from Lightfoot and joined me.

As we reentered to office, Collings made the comment: "The way those guys were looking at her, I knew something was up. I suppose I should have guessed what they were talking about." With that, he got back to work at his typewriter.

"I know, Collings. Apparently this is some outfit we're a part of."

"You know it, sir." Shortly thereafter, I noticed it was 1200 hours. Time for lunch.

Upon arriving at home, I reported the morning's activities to Sam. I told how Mrs. Hooper had previously come to the MP station to have a customer arrested for failure to pay her customary fee. I then added that she was the person who had caused the accident the previous day. When I got to the details about Hooper's late-night business and the services she rendered, Sam shook her head.

"I can't believe she could be so stupid. She's lucky she didn't get herself arrested." She then continued, "To prostitute herself in her husband's absence, she must have a very unhappy marriage or have a very lonely life." After a few seconds, she added, "Or else she needs money awfully badly." As she placed lunch on the table, she winked at me and coyly commented, "Next time you get stingy with the money, at least I know where I can pick up a fast one hundred bucks."

"Sam, that's not funny." I didn't mean to sound angry but I couldn't help it.

Sam giggled. "You're cute when you get angry," she said. "Don't worry, I came into this relationship for better or worse, and you're the last man that's ever going to touch me."

I knew Sam had been kidding, so I shouldn't have snapped at her. After all, I sometimes teased her, too. "What if I should die, Sam? Wouldn't you want to get remarried?"

A STATESIDE TOUR OF DUTY

"No, I don't think I would. Once you've had the best, you don't settle for second place. I got a great guy the first time, so I wouldn't press my luck. I already know that good men are hard to find."

"I'll take that as a compliment, honey." As usual, the lunch hour passed too quickly, and I was back to work by 1300 hours.

As I walked into the building to return to work, I was notified that the major wished to see me. I was back to work on time and still I had to report to him. It was irritating. I went up front to his office to see what he needed.

"You wish to see me, sir?"

"Yes, lieutenant. I understand that you weren't in court this morning."

"That's right, sir. I saw no reason to be there, as we already have adequate personnel to act as clerk, bailiff and so forth."

"In the future, lieutenant, you will be there." He paused to light a cigarette. After exhaling a large puff, he continued, "As the court liaison officer, you are to attend all sessions and report back on any problems, as well as make suggestions about how things might be improved."

"Okay, sir. I'll be there. Will there be anything else?"

"No, lieutenant. That will be all. Dismissed."

I left the major's office and went back to Operations to talk to Steve. We talked for a while and both agreed that the major seemed to be attempting to limit any spare time we might have by adding whatever little additional duties he could give us from time to time. As I left Steve's office, I joked that the time I spent in court would be that much less time I would be dodging other tasks he had for me.

"I'll trade jobs with you," Steve offered.

"Thanks, buddy," I answered, "But as a trained MP officer I have to keep the streets safe with the Traffic section."

Steve smiled and waved as I left his office.

I walked over to the company. Since Monday, the men had been polishing floors and washing windows to prepare for the IG inspection. Today even Raymond seemed to be truly busy. He feverishly went through the files and directed the clerks to add or change paperwork, while all around other men helped make the company orderly room, as well as the nearby barracks, about as neat and businesslike as it was possible to do so. The buildings were beginning to look downright attractive (at least in comparison to how they usually looked). My time in the Army, so far, had taught me that inspections were a fact of life. You worked your butt off for several days to prepare for them. After you passed the inspection, the CO would tell everyone how appreciative he was for all their hard work. Things would then get back to normal. I didn't see any reason for this one to be any different.

That night Sam and I went to the officers' club. Wednesday night was bingo night, and I thought it might be good entertainment. It was, but we never won. Inevitably, one of us would quickly get within one square of winning, only to sit there for number after number until someone else won. We lost every game—regular bingo, the "X" game, "T" game and all other variations. Fate would tease us with what looked like an easy win, only to have us sit there in vain until someone else yelled, "Bingo!" But, what counted was we were together. We were having some laughs, and for a few hours the rest of the world didn't matter. We weren't listening to the news tell of the endless casualties in Southeast Asia. I wasn't thinking about the jerks Steve and I had to work for, and we weren't considering the uncertainty of the future. I had wanted to have a fun time with Sam, and that's what happened. We got to have a good time that evening and that was all that mattered.

CHAPTER FOURTEEN

Thursday morning Steve and I sat through the briefing, which had the usual extremely violent major crimes listed in the blotter, such as littering and shoplifting at the PX (please excuse the sarcasm). Among the prominent items listed in the daily crime wave were accounts of two stray dogs that had been apprehended and their owners cited with warnings for not having them under control. The dogs had been transported to the post veterinarian's office to await their owners. Desk Sergeant Harris was present for the morning briefing and he wasn't happy about the dog control duties.

"Sir?" Harris asked the colonel. "Isn't there something—a cage or box or something—we can get to put these dogs in when we transport them? Right now we have can only put them in the back of the cruiser, like a human. Yesterday, one of the dogs shit in the patrol car. My men cleaned it out as best they could, but it still stinks like hell in there." While Sergeant Harris obviously saw no humor in the situation, the rest of the personnel around the table couldn't help but laugh.

"Talk about your different forms of protest," I noted with a smile. "People file charges of police brutality, and dogs shit in the patrol car." I looked over at the major. As usual, the sourpuss was not smiling

"It's not funny, sir. If you ride in that car, you won't be laughing. It really stinks," Harris replied. He then directed his comments to the colonel. "We're policemen, sir, not dogcatchers. We need to find some other process for dealing with dogs."

"Right you are, sergeant! Effective immediately, no more dogs are to be placed in the patrol cars. We will have to find another option for taking care of them."

"Thank you, sir," Harris replied.

As I read the blotter, I discovered that in addition to one dog defecating in a patrol car, we had three complaints of peeping toms, two domestic disturbances and sixteen tickets issued. The tickets were for violations ranging from running a stop sign to reckless driving. Of this range of problems with which we had to deal, the ones of most concern were the domestic disturbances.

Invariably, when many people live in close proximity to each other, there will always be those married couples who don't get along very well. As these couples argue and sometimes use physical violence against each other, their neighbors eventually complain to those required to keep the peace. For the police who have to go to their home and find a way to stop the violence, it is a no-win situation. As the patrolman tries to act as a mediator, both the husband and wife often take out their wrath on him. Every policeman is aware that more law enforcement personnel are killed in these volatile circumstances than in any other situation.

I was lost in thought on this subject when I was kicked by Steve under the table. I looked up and became aware that the colonel was asking me if I had anything to comment on. I knew I had to say something other than, "Nothing, sir."

"Yes, sir." I began. "I was just thinking about all the domestic disturbances our men have to deal with. We all know that they are among the most dangerous situations in police work. I was wondering if there was any additional training available—either from Fifth Army or the MP School at Ft. Gordon—that we might use to better train our people to defuse these situations. If not, then maybe we could have a company training session where the more experienced men could tell the others what circumstances and procedures have worked best for them in the past."

Everyone around the table was silent. Most comments provided at the morning briefing were usually of a routine and mundane nature. Suggestions requiring extensive thought or of a substantive nature were rare. I looked at Steve. Even he seemed to be impressed. Deep in his intellect, he had to suspect that this was an attempt to bluff my way out of looking inattentive, but at the same time it was a suggestion that had real merit.

The colonel thought for a few seconds before answering. "That's the best damn suggestion we've had around here in a long time, lieutenant. Good job! Check into it and get back to me on that. That's something we really need to follow up on."

"Yes, sir."

"Mister Garcia?"

"Yes ,sir, if we win tonight our softball team will be 11–3. We're hoping for a good turnout from company personnel tonight."

"Colonel, I think Mister Garcia has done a fantastic job. Our softball team is the best we've had in years," Sergeant Major Prince announced.

"Good job, Mister Garcia," said the colonel. "Mister Carson."

"Nothing, sir."

"Lieutenant Bronson."

"MP 5 was returned from the TMP yesterday afternoon, sir. That gives us a little slack as far as vehicles go."

"Good! Stay on top of the situation and encourage them to get all of our vehicles back on line as quickly as possible."

"Yes, sir."

The colonel continued around the table, and those with comments or questions spoke up, and shortly the colonel spoke the words that always ended the briefing: "Well, men, let's go to work." We all stood, saluted and began to leave the room.

As soon as we were alone, Steve asked, "Where did you come up with that suggestion? I thought you were just daydreaming."

"As it turned out, I was thinking about what I suggested; but, at the same time, I had stopped paying attention. I guess the colonel just happened to ask for my opinions at the right time."

"You're either the luckiest man in the world or you sure can recover from a fumble better than anyone I have ever seen." Steve then directed me toward the PMI section. As we walked back to their office, I could see that carpet was being installed. This was the same high-quality carpet that had been installed in the colonel's office except for the fact that it was blue.

"I asked the Supply sergeant about the carpet in the colonel's office and he knows nothing about it. The order didn't go through him. I'm sure if we ask, he'll say the same about this," Steve said.

"Somebody had to pay for it. They don't give this stuff away free."

"I know, Nick. I'll bet you a year's pay, Warren is paying for it. If he is, then he is violating more regulations than I care to think about."

"I can't tell you why, but the guy has given me the creeps since I first met him. I'm starting to think my first impression was right on."

"I agree. I don't know what he's up to, but he is definitely somebody who can get a lot of people into a lot of trouble." As Steve finished his comments, several men walked through the front door carrying two air conditioners.

"Excuse me, lieutenant," said the first man. "Where do I find Sergeant Major Prince?"

"Straight down that hallway." I pointed as I directed them to the conference room.

They set the air conditioners down as the lead man walked toward the conference room. Steve nudged me with his elbow. As I glanced at him, he pointed with his thumb toward the back of the building. We walked back to Operations in silence.

Once we were safely out of earshot, Steve said what I had been thinking. "I bet the Supply sergeant doesn't know anything about those air conditioners, either."

"I bet you're right. I'll say one thing for Warren. He sure takes care of his friends."

"I don't know about you Nick, but I don't want to be one of his friends. I don't know what he's up to, but before he's through I'm predicting he is going to cause trouble for a lot of people."

"You're probably right," I concluded. "I wonder how the IG Inspection is going over at the company."

"I don't know, but I'm sure we'll hear soon enough."

It was only about a half an hour later that men began to come into the station and tell how the post inspector general had come to the company area. With Captain Bills preparing to salute and announce that the 290th was ready for inspection, Colonel Arbon had stopped in his tracks and shouted, "This unit is not ready for inspection." He and the staff that accompanied him for the detail work (checking files and records and such) then turned and walked away. All the work of the previous week had been for nothing.

Shortly thereafter, Steve walked by my office. "The colonel wants to see all section heads up front right now," he sighed.

"What for?"

"Search me. I guess we'll find out when we get there."

Steve and I walked back up front. The first thing I noticed was that one of the air conditioners that had just been delivered was installed behind Sergeant Prince's desk and was cooling the conference room. It would be nice if Traffic or Operations could get an air conditioner, but I didn't expect that to happen anytime soon. I saw that most of the people who attended the morning briefing were already present, and we took our seats among them. We didn't have to wait long before the colonel got to the point.

"I was just notified that our company failed inspection this morning. I have relieved Captain Bills of duty and he will be assigned to Head and Head effective immediately. Until a new CO is assigned, Lieutenant Raymond will be the acting company commander. I have been advised by Colonel Proctor that he and his staff will be working with Lieutenant Raymond to bring our company up to standards. I expect everyone to cooperate with them to ensure this is done. Any questions?"

Sergeant Lippman raised his hand.

"Sergeant Lippman?"

"Yes, colonel, how does this affect the personnel who have limited contact with the company? I mean, those of us assigned to the PMO usually only deal with the company when we sign in or out on leave or shoot pool in the day room."

"That's a good question, sergeant. Colonel Proctor wants us to hold a morning formation until further notice. This will require everybody sending part of their staff over to the company at 0830 hours for the formation. Also, some of our people may have to help the orderly room staff with eliminating deficiencies found by IG personnel."

"Then we can send over a different man each day for the formation, sir?"

"Yes, sergeant, you might even join the formation yourself, once in a while, to set an example."

"Yes, sir." Sergeant Lippman's tone of voice was less than enthusiastic.

"Any other questions?"

I looked around the table. It was clear that no one saw any reason to ask any more questions, and no one asked any. After several moments, Lieutenant Raymond raised his hand to get the colonel's attention.

"Go ahead, Lieutenant Raymond."

"Yes, sir." Raymond began. "I think we should look at this as a chance to improve our company. Instead of being negative, let's all pitch in and show Colonel Proctor we're all part of the battalion team. After all, we're all in this together." Raymond had a smug smile as he talked.

After listening to this bit of unbelievable bullshit, Steve looked at me. He didn't dare roll his eyes in front of others, but I could tell he wanted to. Of course, I felt the same way, too. Raymond's rah-rah crap was enough to make me want to throw up. Another quick look around the table told me everyone else was as unenthusiastic as we were.

"Good point, lieutenant," said the colonel. "Well, there is a lot to do. Let's go to work. Dismissed."

Steve and I turned to leave the room as everyone else began to mill around and discuss the situation among themselves or with Raymond or the colonel. As we walked past the secretaries' desks, Julene was filing some folders. Susan was not to be seen. I guessed she was probably in the ladies' room. Julene looked cautiously around and then caught our attention in a hushed tone.

"Lieutenant Bronson?" she asked.

As she had spoken to Steve, I remained silent and let him do the talking.

"Yes," he replied.

"I don't know if I should say anything, but this morning Colonel Proctor called Colonel Cox at 0830 to tell him we had flunked the IG inspection. From what I've heard, Colonel Arbon didn't get to the company area until nine. It's kind of weird that the PMO would hear that the company flunked the inspection before it happened—don't you think?" Before either of us could respond to her comments, the major entered the room, heading to his office.

"I'll find that information for you, lieutenant, but it will take a little time," she said. It was clear that she didn't want the major to know she had discussed the situation with us.

"What are you looking for, maybe I can help you find it?" said Susan, who had just reentered the room.

Julene hesitated, not knowing what to say.

"Nothing of importance," answered Bronson. "I'll come back for it later."

As we quickly walked back to our offices in the back of the building, I voiced my thoughts to Steve. "The company flunked the inspection before the IG arrived. That sets some new sort of record."

"Tell me about it. Looks like Tucker was right. They needed a fall guy and Bills was it. Nick, we better watch our backs. Either, or both, of us could be next."

"Raymond has to be the biggest brownnoser I have ever met. I don't trust him either."

"Me either, Nick. Apparently, he is the fair-haired boy to the front office."

When I returned to my office, I explained to my investigators, Cummings and Gross, that they might have to join in a company formation for the foreseeable future. As Cummings lived in the barracks, he agreed to be a part of the formation each morning. In his words, "I only have six more months in the Army, and a little more harassment will convince me not to re-up."

As the day progressed, it was obvious that company morale was as low as it could get. Everyone was a little quieter than normal and seemed to be just going through the motions doing their jobs. Despite the lack of spirit, however, we won our last regular season softball game. Even Sam noticed the difference in everyone's demeanor at the game. After work, I had told her everything that went on during the day, so she was aware of the office politics. Still, she wasn't prepared for the difference in attitude she had detected at the softball game.

As we drove home, she said, "Everyone seemed really down at the game tonight, Nick."

"I know honey, and you can't blame them. Everyone knows Captain Bills didn't deserve the treatment he got. What's sad is that the colonel doesn't seem inclined to do anything to help stop it. Our men feel they are going to be harassed for a while, and nobody cares."

"I noticed that one person wasn't depressed."

"Who?" I asked.

"Kathy Raymond," she answered. "Now that her husband is the acting company commander, she seems to think her ass is gold and the world is digging for it."

"She did seem unusually perky," I mused.

"Perky! Nick, the woman was downright giddy." Sam thought for a second, then added, "If she thinks I'm going to kiss her butt, she better guess again."

"The good thing is, honey, that we're both in a position to avoid them. You can stay home, and I don't have to go over to the company very often."

"Thank heaven for small favors."

Friday morning the 290th MP Company began holding the now-required company formations. I had not seen one of these since OCS. Steve and I were excused from the morning briefing to go to the company area and act as platoon leaders. By 0830 hours the men available had been formed up into two platoons of roughly twenty men each, with Steve and me standing in front of them. With a captain from Battalion observing, Raymond clearly relished his new position.

"Company!" he screamed.

He paused, apparently expecting me and Steve to yell supplementary commands—which we did not.

"Attention!" Everyone snapped to attention.

"First platoon, all present or accounted for," I said and saluted.

"Second platoon, all present or accounted for," Steve said as he saluted.

"Stand at ease, men." Raymond commanded. "I appreciate you being here this morning. Hopefully, with a little teamwork, we will quickly have the 290th up to the proper standard. Captain Tomlinson and I will now conduct an inspection of the barracks." Raymond then yelled, "Company!" After another pause he added, "Attention!" We quickly snapped to attention, after which Raymond yelled, "Dismissed."

As Steve and I were walking back to the PMO, Byron caught up with us. "Since I am the acting company commander, I was thinking it would sound more official if you guys add 'sir' when you announce the personnel status to me at these formations."

Steve was blunt and to the point. He summed it up perfectly. "Not even if you beg, Byron."

Raymond seemed put off by his curt manner. For a second he seemed speechless but quickly offered a rebuttal. "We really need to show Battalion that we are following regulations and military protocol. I think that would help. Remember, I am acting CO."

"Byron," I began to explain with irritation, "they used to tell me in OCS that rank among lieutenants was like chastity among whores. We're not going to call you 'sir,' and that's final. If you'll excuse us, we need to get back to our real work." With that Steve and I turned to return to our offices.

"I have to go conduct an inspection of the barracks. We can talk about it later."

As Raymond walked toward the barracks, Steve and I continued on our way. "Like hell we'll talk about it later." Steve muttered. "Do you believe the nerve of that guy?"

"His new position has gone to his head," I replied. "He'll get over it."

Shortly before lunch, Sergeant Reeves, the company first sergeant, came into my office. "Got time for a good joke, sir?" he asked.

"Sure, Top. This place could use a good joke. Have a seat and fire away."

"The sad thing is, sir, you won't laugh."

A STATESIDE TOUR OF DUTY

I looked at First Sergeant Reeves. He appeared older than his forty-two years of age. Hard living and twenty-two years in the Army can do that to you. The six chevrons and diamond that adorned the short sleeve of his khaki uniform probably said as much about the experience the man possessed as the lines on his face. He was the traditional type of first sergeant who believed his job was first and foremost to watch out for the welfare of his men. Right now, it was easy to see that he was not happy. I set aside my paperwork and asked, "Was the situation with the Battalion personnel that bad this morning?"

"Yes, sir, lieutenant. It was that bad."

"What happened?"

"Well, for openers, that kid they sent over from Battalion wanted to see the entire basic issue of uniforms our people had displayed."

"That's standard for an inspection. What's wrong with that?"

"Well, the first three men he came to had three pairs of fatigues on display and they were wearing the fourth. This guy starts yelling that they were issued four uniforms and he wants to see all four displayed. I tried to tell him that the men were wearing the fourth—but he wouldn't listen. What the hell are they supposed to do? Stand inspection buck naked?"

"How did Raymond react to this nonsense?"

"He just stood there making notes and saying 'yes, sir' to the guy. After the inspection, he gave me some crap about being positive and all being in this together." Reeves shook his head as he got up to leave. "Oh, and another thing, lieutenant: That kid from Battalion said we were to have calisthenics as a company each week. Just what I need to do—a couple of hours of jumping jacks and push-ups each week."

"Look on the bright side, Top. The weekend is almost here. You don't have to come back to this mess until Monday. Those idiots at Battalion don't work on the weekend."

"That's true, lieutenant. But after that, if things don't get back to normal soon, I may consider retirement."

"Hang in there, sarge. They can't harass us forever."

He shook his head slightly as he got up to leave. I couldn't tell if it was in agreement or disbelief.

Before I knew it, another workweek was over and I could relax at home with Sam for a couple of days. On Sunday, an event happened in the nearby town of Lutzville that let me know things could always be worse. I first heard about the incident on the local news that night, with further details coming at the Monday morning briefing through police reports and witness statements.

The town of Lutzville had an infamous reputation. The Triple-A Automobile Club called it the worst speed trap in America. Only ten years before, the town had speed zones featuring speed limits like twenty-one or twenty-nine miles per hour and had heavy fines for even one mile per hour of speed over those limits. State law had eliminated speed limits in increments of less than five miles per hour, so now the incorporated area stretched out for three miles on each side of town with a speed limit of twenty miles per hour. Outsiders often missed the signs as they drove along the wide road well over that speed. To lighten the wallets of those people, the Lutzville constabulary had three brand-new police cars with huge V8 engines. Sometimes the patrolman was accompanied in the car by an assistant city judge, complete with cash register and gavel. This way, tourists could pay their fines and be on their way with a minimum of interruption. From time to time there were also reports of outsiders being beaten up and robbed in some of the town's seedier bars. The local county had an ordinance prohibiting the sale of alcohol on the Sabbath, so what should have been a quiet, peaceful afternoon wound up as anything but serene.

Shortly after noon a black solder pulled his car into the local Texaco station and, after filling his tank at the self-service pump, he went into the station and asked to buy a six-pack of beer.

Unfortunately, despite the town's reputation, or perhaps because of it, he decided to show some attitude.

"I'm sorry, but we can't sell beer on Sunday," the clerk said matter-of-factly.

"If I were from around here, I bet you'd sell me the beer," the soldier sneered.

"We can't sell beer on Sunday," the clerk reiterated. "Do you want anything else that we can sell or not?"

"No!"

The soldier tossed a twenty-dollar bill on the counter. The clerk then counted out his change and placed it where the twenty had been.

"Hey! I want my change counted out in my hand," the soldier snapped as he placed his hand on the counter.

The clerk looked the soldier straight in the eyes and said in a cold voice, "Get out of here nigger, or I'll shoot you."

A STATESIDE TOUR OF DUTY

With that, the soldier grabbed the clerk by his shirt collar with both hands as he yelled, "You can't talk to me that way."

With lightning speed, the clerk grabbed a Smith and Wesson .38 Special from under the counter and with one shot put a large hole in the soldier's chest.

CHAPTER FIFTEEN

Steve and I arrived at the PMO at almost the same instant to start the new week. Common sense would normally have dictated that we go straight to the company area for the new mandatory formations, but the necessity of demonstrating to the major that we had arrived at work on time prevented us from doing so. We studied the blotter in preparation for excusing ourselves early from the meeting. The major topic of conversation was the soldier who had been shot in an altercation with a gas station attendant the day before in Lutzville. He had survived but remained in intensive care at Fort McCulloch Army Hospital.

"He should have known better," commented Mr. Carson. "It would serve the town right if the Army placed the whole place off limits."

"That's a little hard to do when you have a state highway running through the place," Sergeant Corley commented. "Besides, they would just raise the fines on everyone else passing through. All soldiers can do is stay under the speed limit and not stop."

We all stood as the colonel entered the room and said, "Good morning, sir." As the colonel told everyone to be seated, I noticed a definite tension in the air.

"Sir?" I asked. "May Lieutenant Bronson and I be excused for the company formation?"

The colonel looked at his watch. "Don't worry, lieutenant, we'll let you go in plenty of time."

"Yes, sir."

Sergeant Prince entered the room and took a seat. "I'm sorry I'm late, colonel, but I was back at the desk. It seems that the cannon wasn't fired over the weekend."

"How about it, Lieutenant Bronson?" the colonel snapped. "Why wasn't the cannon fired?"

"I have no idea, sir. Sergeant Prince was acting as duty officer this weekend, and if he doesn't know, then I'll find out."

"Don't pass the buck to Sergeant Prince, lieutenant. You're the Operations officer."

"Yes, sir. I'll find out and get back to you."

Excuse me, colonel," Prince interjected. "General Waterman will be here this weekend to do some hunting. I need to leave to line things up for his arrival."

"You're excused, Top." The colonel looked at his watch. "Moultrie, you and Bronson are also excused for the formation."

As Steve and I walked toward the company area, Raymond caught up with us.

"I've decided, guys, that when I yell 'Company' this morning that you two need to yell 'Platoon.' It will give our formation a little more formality."

"They don't use supplementary commands at less than battalion formation, Byron." I replied. "They'll think we're idiots."

"Well, I'm in command and that's the way I want to do it."

As Raymond walked away without further comment, Steve looked at me and shook his head slightly. I smiled and nodded to show him I understood.

Within a few minutes, we had two platoons formed up in front of the orderly room. Byron stuck his chest out like a rooster and yelled, "Company!" He hesitated for several seconds, looking back and forth at Steve and myself, before finally yelling "Attention!"

"First platoon, all present or accounted for," I said as I saluted.

As he returned the salute, Byron had a scowl on his face. Not only had I not given a supplementary command, but I was not calling him 'sir.'

"Second platoon, all present or accounted for," Steve stated with a salute.

"Stand at ease, men." Byron stuck his chest out again. "Men, as you know we are making progress to overcome our unit's deficiencies on the last IG inspection. To continue this progress and to ensure a high state of physical fitness in all company personnel, we are requiring everyone to attend a two-hour company training session on Thursday at 1500 hours for physical training. Now, as soon as the formation is dismissed, Captain Tomlinson and I will conduct the daily inspection of the barracks and the company area. Company!" He hesitated again for a few seconds. "Attention! Dismissed!"

Byron continued to scowl at us, but we ignored him and walked away.

"Well, I gotta go find out why the frigging cannon wasn't fired over the weekend," Steve muttered as we walked back to the PMO. "Prince was responsible for that, as duty officer, but it's passing the buck to point that out."

"Hang in there, buddy. It's always darkest before the dawn."

"Nick, if there's something I don't need right now, it's any damned platitudes."

"Sorry." I figured it best not to say anything else.

Later, as I sat at my desk to begin going through the paperwork, I noticed a copy of a flash report from the day before. As I was the Blue Bell reporting officer, the Operations clerks now gave me copies of all flash reports so I could follow them up with the appropriate reports to Fifth Army. I had noticed the item in the blotter earlier, but now I spent a few seconds more studying the facts for the Blue Bell report. Since the victim was a soldier, I could submit a combination initial-final report, but I decided against this because I wanted to find out what legal action would be taken against the man who shot him. It's not often I created additional paperwork for myself, but this time that was exactly what I was going to do. I had just begun to write when Susan looked into my office.

"Lieutenant Moultrie, the colonel wants to see you immediately."

One of the benefits of not having an intercom was not being bothered as much as I otherwise might be by the front office. They had to send someone back. "Thanks Susan, I'll be right there," I replied.

From the mood the colonel was in, I had to guess that he didn't get any the night before. He started ripping me a new rear end as soon as I got to his office. "Last Wednesday, we had five cases dismissed in court because the men who wrote up the tickets weren't available. Lieutenant, you make sure that doesn't happen again."

I had already enjoyed this conversation with the major, but I decided it was best to let the colonel continue his complaint. When he paused, I said, "Yes, sir."

"You make sure you know who is not on duty while court is in session and make damned sure they are available to testify if they are needed."

"Yes, sir."

"I don't want any excuses. Either them or their partner better be there."

"Yes, sir. It will be done. Will there be anything else, sir?"

My question caught the colonel by surprise. He ended his tirade unable to think of anything else and just said, "No. That will be all. Dismissed."

I had returned to my office for what seemed only a few minutes when Steve entered the room and shut the door behind him. He threw his hat on Collings' desk and exclaimed, "Son of a bitch!"

"I thought I was the only one having a bad day. Apparently, something's wrong?" I said.

"No shit! I'm definitely not happy." He lowered his voice. "Let's get to hell out of here, Nick, and go somewhere we can talk."

"No problem. I'll have the desk call in one of my units and we can ride around and talk."

"No, Nick. I don't want anyone else listening. Let's go get the Camel instead. I've told my clerks that we're going over to JAG to discuss some cases."

As we drove out of the company area, Steve got to the point. "Listen, Nick. The colonel has someone he wants to boot out of the Army on an undesirable discharge."

"Who?"

"PFC James—he man they have sweeping and polishing the floors over at the company. He should be on line duty. We need him, but they have him doing janitorial work."

"Why?"

"He used to be in PMI and locked horns with Warren. He wrote some letters to higher headquarters, and the front office is determined to get rid of him. Tucker wouldn't let them, but with him and Bills gone, Raymond will do as he's told. My guess is they can't stick him with an undesirable discharge, but he probably will accept a general discharge to get out of here."

"That's too bad. We're shorthanded on line duty as it is."

"Yeah, and when I questioned their getting rid of him, I was told in no uncertain terms to stay out of it."

"I don't think it's a secret that we don't trust Warren. Maybe that's why we're not too popular with the powers that be in the front office."

"You got it, Nick." He paused for a few seconds before changing the subject. "I found out why the cannon wasn't fired."

"What happened?"

"They keep a week's worth of blank rounds in a closet over at post headquarters. Somebody over at the ordinance detachment forgot to send over new rounds, and either the MPs responsible for firing it off didn't tell Prince they were out or he was too lazy to call the ordinance people to send over more. Either way, the colonel ripped my ass for it."

"I don't see how it could be your fault."

"That's not all," he continued. "He ripped my ass for the condition of the cars. MP12 and MP9 have been red-lined."

"I know," I replied. "They got one of ours."

"Yeah, and we took the major's car," he added. "The colonel said all of the cars were running fine a year ago and didn't understand why they weren't running fine now."

"You're shitting me!" I exclaimed. "Can't he understand that they have another year's wear and tear on them?"

"No, the dumb bastard couldn't figure that out." He broke into a grin. "In fact, when he asked what the problems were, I told him transmission problems and they needed to have the muffler bearings replaced."

"There is no such thing as muffler bearings, Steve."

"Hell, Nick! Don't you think I know that? But, that dumb bastard didn't."

Now we both began to roar with laughter. "We have to have the dumbest bunch of leaders the world has ever seen. Weren't you afraid he might know the truth when you said that?" I asked.

"I figured the worst that could happen was that I might get transferred out of here," he said. "Besides, if he can't understand that cars wear out, how much could he know about them?"

"Still," I said, "I don't see how he can figure that any of this is your fault."

"I don't either, but that's not the way he saw it. He claimed I was inefficient and uninformed. He said I had better be on top of things more in the future." Steve hit the steering wheel with his fist. "I tell you what, Nick. It will be a cold day in hell before I let anyone talk to me like that again. I don't care if he is a colonel." A few seconds later he added, "Lord, I'd do just about anything to get out of this place."

"Well, Steve, I don't think there's any chance of that, but I know what we can do."

"What's that, Nick?"

"We need to start keeping a notebook of things that aren't kosher. In other words, start a little unofficial investigation of our own. We might uncover illegal activities by Warren that might be used for a court-martial. If not, maybe we can find something that will allow us to skate along like Tucker did. We both know that he had no problems with the colonel and his cronies."

"Nick, old buddy, you have a deal." He extended his right hand over and we shook hands. Neither of us said much else. We knew that we would have to proceed cautiously, but proceed we would.

As we pulled back into the PMO parking lot, Steve added one more thought. He had a great big grin on his face when he did. "Oh, and we don't have to go to those stupid formations anymore, either."

"Why not?"

"I told Raymond to have a couple of sergeants fill in for us to give the status reports."

"And he went for it?" I was dumbfounded. "How in the world did you sell him on that?"

"It was easy, Nick. I reminded him that he could get them to call him 'sir.'"

I couldn't help but laugh. "Give me five!" Steve slapped his hand across mine and we returned to work. Maybe things were starting to improve.

The idea of proceeding with some unauthorized detective work to get the goods on Warren was an exciting prospect, but first I realized that the required work would have to come first. I had the Operations clerks prepare me a list of all the cases each patrolman had pending in magistrate's court for Wednesday. These were typed onto a disposition form (DF) and posted in the break room and on the company bulletin board. I then called each man that was off to remind him that either he or his partner had to be available, if the subject pleaded not guilty.

Meanwhile, Steve was working to ensure there would be no more problems with the operation of the cannon. At 0700 and 1700 hours, as the large American flag was raised and lowered at post headquarters, two MPs would show up to fire off the cannon located there. The ceremony included the appropriate bugle call being played over the loud speaker while the flag was raised and lowered. To ensure that nothing interfered with this observance in the future, Steve had several extra blank rounds delivered to the company arms room. This way, there were a few rounds in reserve in the event that the supply at post headquarters was depleted again. Steve even went the extra mile and requested that the ordinance detachment inspect the cannon to insure it was in proper working order.

The next day, I again reminded all personnel who had cases in the weekly magistrate's court of the necessity of being there. That night, after we had beaten Echo Company of the 375th Engineers in the first round of the post softball playoffs, I again reminded those present, who had cases pending, to be available for court the next day. By Wednesday morning, we were ready for the tribunal.

At 0900 hours, Judge Hartsell slammed down his gavel and brought the court to order. As usual, he proceeded with his usual conveyor-belt justice, and shortly after 1000 hours the room was cleared. No cases were dismissed due to patrolmen not being in attendance, and a couple of personnel accompanying the accused persons saw humor in the speed of the proceedings. Judging from their facial expressions, Kangaroo Court continued to live up to its nickname.

At 1100 hours, the judge brought the civilian proceedings to order, and again everything went without a hitch or problem. That is, until the last case.

"Danielson," called out the bailiff.

"Here, sir." A man stepped forward, accompanied by a woman (I presumed she was his wife).

"You are charged with traveling eighty-six point four miles per hour in a sixty-mile-per-hour zone. Speed checked by VASCAR. How do you plead?"

The mention of VASCAR gained my immediate attention. We had no personnel certified to operate it, and until the proper training was completed, I had given instructions that it was not to be used to issue tickets.

"Not guilty, Your Honor." The man pulled a folded piece of paper from his shirt pocket and continued. "Your honor, the night I was stopped, we had friends in the car who witnessed the fact that I was not speeding. They wrote up this statement which I had notarized. I would like you to take a look at it."

"I'll look at it, but I'm afraid it would be considered hearsay and be inadmissible as evidence," replied the judge.

"Oh."

"But, Your Honor," interjected the woman, "I swear my husband wasn't speeding."

"Who was the patrolman who issued the citation?" the judge inquired.

"Thomas," responded the clerk.

A STATESIDE TOUR OF DUTY

"Send in Thomas."

Within a few moments, Thomas stood before the judge.

"Sergeant Thomas, were you on duty the night of August 31?"

"Yes, Your Honor."

"In the course of your work, did you happen to stop this man?"

"Yes, sir."

"Please tell us in detail what led you to stop him and why."

"Your Honor, that night Sergeant Gillman and I were on patrol and we proceeded to operate VASCAR on Highway 142 East. During the evening, we clocked this man driving eighty-six point four miles per hour."

"There has to be a mistake. I can assure you that I was not speeding," the man insisted.

"Where is Sergeant Gillman?" asked the judge.

"His term of service ended the next night, Your Honor. In fact, he was the one who operated the VASCAR unit. I only signed the ticket, since he would not be here for court due to his ETS date."

I could not stand any more. Since most people claim to be innocent of any charges, such claims should be taken with a grain of salt. But in my gut, I felt that these people might be telling the truth.

I stood and asked the judge. "Your Honor, may I confer with Sergeant Thomas?"

"Yes, lieutenant."

Thomas walked over to me. In a low voice, I said to him. "Sergeant, I think Gillman may have screwed up and left you holding the bag."

"How's that, sir?"

"Well, to begin with, he was not certified or authorized to use the equipment. In a civilian court, that alone would invalidate the ticket. We're under federal jurisdiction, though, so we may be okay. Tell me how he clocked this man."

"Gillman drove over a distance and set the information in the computer. He then got off the road about thirty yards from the road, halfway between the two reference points to observe cars. This guy was the first one who passed. We then went back to regular patrol duty."

"Gillman didn't know what he was doing. You never use two angles when you check the speed of target vehicles. It makes it very difficult, if not impossible, to get an accurate reading."

"I don't know anything about VASCAR, sir. I just thought Gillman knew what he was doing. From what you've told me, this guy might really be innocent."

I contemplated Thomas's words. Obviously, this ticket should never have been written. Some nitwit, wanting to obtain additional experience, had used equipment he was unqualified to use and was now long gone, so he would not have to face the consequences. I would have to choose my words carefully. "Your honor," I began. "Sergeant Gillman was neither certified or authorized to use the VASCAR unit, and from what Sergeant Thomas has told me it is possible that errors might have occurred in its use. If that is the case, we can't prove guilt beyond a reasonable doubt. If Sergeant Thomas has no objection, I would recommend that these charges be dropped."

"Sergeant Thomas?" asked the judge.

"No objection, Your Honor. I really didn't want to be part of this case, but had no choice since Gillman was leaving the Army."

The judge then looked at the accused and said, "Very well, then. I hereby find you not guilty." He slammed down his gavel. Court was over for another week.

As I was leaving the building, Mr. Danielson and his wife stopped me in the hallway. He extended his hand to shake hands while he thanked me. "Thank you, lieutenant. Thank you very much." His wife was repeating similar words as he spoke.

"You folks are welcome. Under the laws of our country, people don't have to prove themselves innocent; we must prove them guilty beyond a reasonable doubt. Given the circumstances, in your case, that was not possible."

"Lieutenant, I swear to God that I was not speeding."

I replied with a smile. "For the record, Mr. Danielson, I believe you. But, even if I didn't, the judge still said 'Not guilty.'"

"Thanks again, lieutenant."

"You're welcome."

I returned to the PMO and prepared a DF (disposition form) for the bulletin board stating that uncertified and untrained personnel were not to use the VASCAR unit. I was going to make sure we didn't have any more tickets dismissed due to lack of evidence. I then headed home for lunch.

"My husband is a regular Perry Mason," said Sam as I related to her what had happened in court.

"Like Perry, I'm interested in liberty and independence for all, along with truth, justice and the American way," I replied.

Sam laughed. "What you just described is Superman, not Perry Mason."

"Who knows, after a few more court appearances maybe I'll be able to leap tall buildings with a single bound, too. But remember, Sam, it's my job to find people guilty. Perry always got them off. Today was an exception."

"You couldn't sit back and allow an innocent person to be convicted, though, could you?"

"No way; things have to be done right."

"Then, I'm proud of you. I'll bet there are others you work with who would have allowed an injustice to take place," she commented.

"That's right, but we won't mention any names, will we?"

After lunch, I suggested to Steve that we go over to the post Personnel office. The warrant officer in charge, Mister Swanson, often put in some time with the ranger section at night. He figured the experience would help him land a job with the Texas state Fish and Game Department when he retired in a couple of years. The state wildlife personnel seemed to hold him in high regard, so Steve and I figured we could trust him. As we arrived at his office the door was open, so he motioned for us to come in.

"Come in, gentlemen. What can I do for you?"

I got right to the point. "Well, Larry. We are hearing some rumors about Sergeant Warren around our company and, frankly, they are starting to effect morale. We wouldn't ask you to disclose any confidential information, but if there is anything you can tell us, then we would appreciate it."

"Why? What have you been hearing?"

Steve answered him. "Nick and I don't trust him any further than we can throw him. While we may not be the best judges of character in the world, a few senior NCOs have come right out and told us he is a crook."

Swanson said in a low voice, "Between you, me and the gate post, those NCOs are right. They know what they're talking about."

The fact that he had lowered his voice to prevent anyone around from hearing, and the frown on his face, left no doubt that the subject of Sergeant Warren was very serious indeed. After a few moments' hesitation, he added, "Wait here for a moment." Swanson got up and left his office for a few minutes. When he returned, he was carrying Warren's 201 file, which he tossed on his desk. "I don't wish to spread unsubstantiated gossip or rumors, so I won't discuss Warren. I have to leave for about ten minutes. I trust you won't disturb anything on my desk while I'm gone."

"Not me," Steve said with a smile.

"I'm an officer and a gentleman. I'd never look at anything I was not authorized to look at," I added with obviously satiric tones in my voice.

"Good. That's what I'm counting on." With that he left his office.

Steve and I grabbed the 201 file and what we read in it confirmed every rumor and bit of gossip we had heard. Warren had been involved in the Army's massive NCO club scandal in Vietnam. As an E-7 in Vietnam, he had been assigned to MACV headquarters. There, he kept his partners in the corruption aware of all investigations as they misappropriated millions of dollars in funds, equipment and merchandise earmarked for the Army's NCO club system. After a lengthy investigation had finally proven the wrongdoing and the massive scope of the operation became public knowledge, Warren had avoided a court martial by feigning insanity and voluntarily resigning from the Army. Although he had somehow managed to rejoin the Army as an E-6, he had no security clearance, and there was obviously no way the government would ever grant him one.

"Someone way up the chain of command of Fifth Army had to be involved to get this bastard back in the Army," I said. "He definitely has friends in high places."

"More to the point, Nick, how in the hell can this clown conduct inspections at locations which require at least a Secret clearance? He has no security clearance at all."

"Search me. I think we better put that back. We've probably seen enough."

"Nick, old buddy, we may have already seen too much."

We placed the file back on Larry's desk, just as we found it and sat back in our chairs. A few moments later, Mr. Swanson returned to his office. "I trust you boys didn't disturb anything on my desk while I was gone," he said with a smile.

"Not a thing," replied Steve. I just smiled and shook my head.

"Good!" He then lowered his voice. "But to answer your earlier question, Warren is not someone I would trust with the sweat off my ass, let alone anything of value."

"Thanks, Larry. We appreciate the information." Steve said, as we got up to shake hands with him. Neither of us said anything else until we were in the car.

"Nick, I have a feeling this place is worse than I ever imagined."

"No kidding. I believe that what Tucker had on the colonel probably had something to do with Warren. That guy is capable of anything," I said.

"Yeah, including lining up accidents for nosey second lieutenants."

"Don't think that hasn't crossed my mind, Steve. Why don't we stop in at CID? They don't like Warren. It might be smart to let them know that we're on their side?"

"Good idea! Let's go see Pike. I think we can trust him," Steve concluded.

As the Operations officer, Steve had dealt with the CID personnel and had gained a respect for Pike. Since I knew nothing about CID personnel except that they sometimes attended the morning briefing, I decided to follow his instincts on this matter.

A short time later we were talking to WO2 Pike, one of the few CID personnel we had any confidence in. After some small talk, I got down to business. "We were wondering, Mister Pike—"

"Call me Ken."

I smiled. "Well, Ken. It is common knowledge around the PMO that Warren has no security clearance."

"It is?"

"Yes, it is. We were wondering how it is possible for Warren to conduct inspections at Secret or Top Secret sites with no security clearance."

"Sounds like you men don't trust Warren."

"Let's just say that we think he is big trouble," Steve countered.

I added, "We wouldn't be unhappy if he was to depart the provost marshal's staff, and we wouldn't really care how that departure took place."

Pike thought for a moment. "To answer your question, the Top Secret sites fall under the control of NSA. Warren's people can't get close to them. The Secret sites, he sends his people (who have clearances) into. He's smart enough not to go in himself. Warren only inspects ROTC and

National Guard arms rooms. If we had our way, he wouldn't see those either."

"You mention arms rooms," I noted. "I've noticed a lot of break-ins of arms rooms reported in the blotter around our area of responsibility."

"Yeah, and it's always shortly after Warren conducts an inspection," Pike noted.

"Have any of the weapons turned up?" Steve asked.

"Some have been captured from guerrilla groups in South and Central America. But you didn't hear that from me."

"We understand," Steve agreed.

"Are there any theories you can share on how the weapons are disseminated into South America?" I asked.

"The best guess is, whoever is collecting them here is shipping them to a port in the Caribbean—probably in Haiti. From there they would go to Cuba to be distributed to their surrogates further south. But that's conjecture."

"Also, whoever is collecting the arsenal here is probably paying top dollar for the arms room information," Steve added.

"You got it," Pike said. "Again, that is conjecture you could have reached on your own."

"We appreciate your time," I said. "If anyone asks, just tell them that we came by here because we didn't have anything else to do. Our superiors will believe that."

"Okay. But look, guys. I want to get Warren as badly as anyone. But I won't move without solid evidence. The man has friends—if you get my drift."

"We do," I concurred. "Again, thanks for everything."

On our return to the PMO, it was Steve who spoke first. "Nick, this place is a damned can of worms."

"A can of worms would be an improvement."

"I tell you what, Nick. We better watch ourselves. I don't see anyone around the PMO we can really trust."

"You're right. Anyone who has their career to worry about is going to be more concerned with their job than getting Warren. Also, we can't really turn to CID because Pike is the only one worth a damn there and he is a career man. I don't see him rocking the boat."

"I know. Pike may be a good man, Nick, but he knows this place is a dead end for CID investigators. CWO Jarvis, who heads the office, is a failed Sears appliance salesman and I've heard that most of the others are equally incompetent. Pike just wants to get transferred out to a location more conducive to his career."

"Let's just keep our ears to the ground and hope something turns up."

"Okay, Nick, but we better be careful."

"Agreed. I'm just glad that I get to go home at night, cuddle up with Sam and forget this place."

"Hey, I forgot to tell you!" Steve blurted out. "I met a gorgeous girl named Barbara. She teaches English at Bradshaw High School."

"Good. Sounds like you can get your mind off this place, too."

"You got it, Nick. With Charlie gone this weekend, I've invited Barbara over. I'll put a couple of steaks on the barbecue, chill a bottle of wine, put some soft music on the stereo, relax and let nature take its course."

"Steve, my boy, sounds like you have the situation under control."

"Let's just say the situation is improving and let it go at that," he countered.

CHAPTER SIXTEEN

Thursday night saw the 290th Military Police Company win in the second round of the post softball playoffs. Our turnout for the game was the best of the year. We had at least fifty spouses, friends and other observers. Even the colonel and his wife were there. All the camaraderie and good feeling that permeated the event seemed in contrast to the undercurrent of mistrust and animosity that was so evident during the day at the PMO. As we gave our opponents a cheer to end the game, everyone's spirits were elevated and company morale was as high as I had ever seen. Somehow, I knew it couldn't last. As we drove home, it was evident that even Sam had experienced the emotional high that the game had produced. "That was fun, Nick. I wish every night could be like that. I could even tolerate Kathy Raymond tonight."

"Did you get to talk to her very much?" I asked.

"No, she was too busy brownnosing the colonel's wife to bother me. We just chatted briefly, and she told me how her husband was so busy getting the company in shape. She then parked by the colonel's wife for the rest of the evening and bothered her."

"When I came off the field between innings, I noticed they were giving you the evil eye for spending so much time talking with the enlisted men's wives," I noted.

"Do you want me to play Kathy Raymond's game, Nick?"

"No. You do what you feel comfortable doing. I just want to get out of this place. I don't plan on making the military a career, but I do plan to spend my life with you. To heck with what my superiors think."

"I've never heard you say 'heck' before, Nick. Turning over a new leaf?"

"I don't know, honey. I feel so great tonight maybe I'll add 'dang' and 'shucky darn' to my vocabulary, too."

A STATESIDE TOUR OF DUTY

Sam laughed. "That would be a nice change," she said. "Then I could start calling you Opie."

"After a threat like that, I probably never will stop swearing," I laughed.

Friday morning, during the colonel's briefing, we got some interesting news. "In response to our pleas to Fifth Army for more personnel," the colonel began, "we will have forty new men assigned to the company the week after next. They will be coming directly from basic training at Fort Hood. Before we can assign them to duty, we must train them in a manner equivalent to AIT. Fifth Army has left the method of training to us. I think that three weeks of class work and one week of OJT will be the best way to proceed."

"Sir," I asked, "where AIT lasts eight weeks, wouldn't it be to our benefit to give them more than three weeks of class work? That way their 201 files would reflect training equal to what they would normally receive. Then there would be less risk of us ever being criticized for having insufficiently trained personnel."

"Their 201 files will simply state that they have had four weeks of intensive training, lieutenant. Therefore, that issue can never come up," the colonel said curtly.

"Yes, sir," I acquiesced. I should have known better than to even bring up that point. The week of OJT would be little more than an effort to get the men on the job quicker. Everyone knew that. They also knew that the colonel would get his way.

The colonel began again. "Lieutenant Moultrie! You and Lieutenant Bronson will coordinate with Sergeant Major Prince in setting up the curriculum. Have Major Receiver review and approve it and bring it to me."

"Yes, sir," Steve and I said almost in unison.

"Sir," I began again. "I was due to begin CBR training next week—"

"Your participation in CBR training will be postponed," the colonel interrupted. "This takes priority."

"Good, sir," I answered. "How quickly do you want the schedule of classes and instructors on the major's desk?"

"Have it to him by noon Wednesday," the colonel commanded.

"Yes, sir."

As the meeting broke up, Steve and I figured we had better get to work on the class schedule for the future MPs we had to get trained. We approached Sergeant Prince to have him join us, but he declined.

"You lieutenants go ahead and get started. Maybe I'll join you later," Sergeant Prince said. "I have other things to do right now."

As Steve and I got to work, we took a standard AIT class schedule and began to customize it for our purposes. The first thing we did was to eliminate the physical training portion. That way the eight weeks of class work could easily be reduced to three.

"We'll just tell them to go to the gym," Steve said caustically. "It will be their duty to keep in shape."

"Good idea. Once they begin regular service work, they will be on their own anyway," I concurred.

The assignment of instructors was relatively easy. I would teach the classes on traffic points, accident investigation and radar and VASCAR. Pike, from CID, would teach basic investigative techniques. Captain Warren (no relation to Sergeant Warren) of JAG would provide some legal training. Desk sergeants would teach classes on how the various forms and paperwork should be filled out and give insight into basic police work. Finally, we provided for each department head to be scheduled for an hour to explain what their assignments were, and what duties their personnel were responsible for. About 1100 hours Steve suggested we take a break.

"Let's go up front and see what Prince is so busy doing," he said.

"Good idea. I bet he is answering the phone, just like usual," I commented.

Together we walked up front. Prince was sitting behind his desk ,which had stacks of papers between two telephones, each of which had four lines. He was alternately answering the phones, which were ringing constantly.

"Provost Marshal's Office, Sergeant Prince speaking. Thanks for calling; we'll take care of it." Then grabbing the other ringing phone, he would answer, "Provost Marshal's Office, Sergeant Prince speaking. I'll brief the colonel as soon as possible, thanks for calling." Then he would grab the other, and after the preliminary greeting he would add, "Yes, I have the paperwork right here. I'll get back to you. Thanks for calling."

I asked, "Sergeant Prince, do you want to look at what we have so far?"

"No, sir," he replied. "I'm far too busy right now. It will probably be Monday before I can get with you."

"No sweat, sarge," I agreed. "We'll get with you Monday"

A STATESIDE TOUR OF DUTY

As we walked back to our end of the building, Steve said what I was already thinking. "I'd sure like to know who the hell he has making all those phony calls. The phone rarely rings when he isn't here."

"I know. The colonel has got to be able figure out he is only pretending to work," I agreed.

"If Prince looks busy, I doubt he cares," Steve concluded.

Steve and I finished our training schedule just in time for lunch. As we were leaving, we ran into First Sergeant Reeves. He saluted, and Steve and I both returned it.

"Well, we finally have good news, sirs," he stated.

"What's that, first sergeant?" I asked.

"We have finally corrected our IG deficiencies. We passed this morning. I guess our company is finally out of the shit house," he said with a smile.

"You're right, sarge, that is good news," replied Steve. "Maybe things can get back to normal now."

"I sure hope so," replied Reeves. "They've sure harassed us long enough. You men at the PMO are lucky. You got to avoid most of it."

Steve and I didn't argue with him on that last point; we just went to lunch. Upon my return, I began to prepare some supplemental and terminal Blue Bell reports. About 1620 hours, I took the last one up front. The major was sitting on a chair outside his office, looking up at the clock. He was holding his hat in his left hand.

"If there isn't time for either of you to type this before five, don't hesitate to leave it for Monday," I said as I placed it on top of the In box of Julene's desk.

"Don't worry, lieutenant. I'm sure one of us can get to it today," replied Susan.

"Thanks, ladies, I appreciate it," I said.

About 1650 hours, I again walked up front to talk with Sergeant Prince. As I did, I noticed the major sitting exactly where he was a half-hour before. He was just sitting outside his office, holding his hat, looking up at the clock. Then it hit me. He was waiting for 1700 hours, when he would leave. Even though he had nothing to do, he felt it was his duty to stay until quitting time. I could see through the door into the main office that Prince was already gone, so I decided to chat with the secretaries. Sure enough, at 1700 hours the major put on his hat and said, "Well, let's go home."

As he proceeded to the door I said, "Good idea, sir."

Once he was gone I asked Susan, "Is he always like that?"

"Yes he is, lieutenant. It's enough to drive you crazy. Even if he has nothing to do, he will sit there waiting for quitting time. We feel like we need to stay busy while he is sitting there. That's why we didn't mind that last report you brought up."

"Well, I'm glad I was able to help," I said as I turned to go. As I did, a thought entered my mind which came to me often at Fort McCulloch. That thought was—what a place to work.

The weekend that followed, was routine for me, but not for Steve. This weekend would prove to be a catalyst for changes in job assignments around the PMO.

Steve's new girlfriend, Barbara, was spending the weekend. Steve had already told me about the steaks and bottle of wine he had bought. Charlie was out of town with Charlotte, so Steve was expecting a pleasant, idyllic weekend.

Steve was also the duty officer that weekend. This meant he had to leave for an hour to conduct guard mount and read the blotter every eight hours. Except for those brief absences, the rest of his time would belong to Barbara. What happened next is a matter of supposition and guesswork for me, but I am sure it went something like this: After a beautiful candlelight-with-wine dinner, Steve and Barbara, no doubt, began to proceed with the evening's entertainment, which consisted of giving each other their full attention. After a little necking on the couch, she probably got up and walked seductively to the door of his bedroom. There she began to unbutton her blouse. Steve quickly joined her and they hurriedly began to undress each other. When Barbara was naked, she lay down upon the bed where Steve was about to join her, when the telephone rang. Steve would have reluctantly (after all he was the duty officer) walked back into the living room and answered it.

"Hello."

"Lieutenant Bronson?"

"Yes, this is Bronson."

"Sir, this is Sergeant Harris at the desk. We have some people in here that want to see the duty officer right away." His voice had an obviously anguished tone.

"What is it about?" asked Bronson.

"Well sir, they're screaming about entrapment and unfair police practices. One is even threatening to call his congressman."

"Have we done anything illegal?"

"No sir, not that I know of," Harris continued. But, they are still pretty upset. They're demanding to talk to the person in charge, and right now that's you."

"Okay, sarge, I'll be there shortly." At that point Steve would have sighed and walked back to the bedroom. "I've got to go the MP station for a little while. That stupid sergeant can't seem to do his job," he would have said.

Remember, I am guessing here, but Steve never denied this happened when I teased him about being late to the PMO that night. Barbara, I'm sure, turned over so she was facing him. With his body perpendicular to hers as he stood facing the bed, she probably slowly spread her legs, and with a coy smile said, "Are you sure you want to go to the MP station right now?"

For Steve this would have created a terrible dilemma. He could complete his duties at work at the risk of insulting his companion or place pleasure before profession obligation. At critical times, an officer is required to make important decisions, so there is no doubt in my mind that Steve made one. Taking off his shorts, which would be the last item he was wearing, he would have joined Barbara on the bed. Knowing Steve, he would have jubilantly said, "War is hell," before doing so. He arrived at the PMO an hour and twenty minutes later. Again, I admit that the previous episode included a lot of guesswork, but I don't think it is very inaccurate. Later, I joked with Steve that it was Barbara—and not a flat tire— that made him so late to work. He never denied it.

The problem that required Steve's attention was that Gross had been running radar on Highway 142 East in the White Mouse. He had opened the trunk as he sat on the side of the road, in order to appear like a motorist in distress. This obscured the blue light and the tendency was for drivers to speed on by. As he pulled out quickly to pursue speeders, the trunk would close and he had no trouble writing up a large number of tickets. Several had taken exception to the tactics and had registered vociferous complaints with the desk sergeant. By the time Bronson arrived at the PMO, only one complainant remained. The others had become impatient and left. After being advised of the situation, Bronson began to talk with the man who by now was angrier than a grizzly bear with an ass full of buckshot.

"I see that you were cited for traveling seventy-seven miles per hour in a sixty-mile zone. Do you dispute the speed we clocked you at?"

"No," said the man. "The speed is not the issue. It was the trickery and deceit that was used to catch me."

"If you had not been speeding, you wouldn't have received a ticket," Bronson reminded him.

"But, there's the question of ethics. To hide and pounce on unsuspecting motorists is not right. A police car should not be hidden."

"Why not?"

"I just said why not! It's entrapment! It's taking unfair advantage of the public." The man continued his tirade for a while until Bronson gave his final word.

"Look, all I can do is back up one of my men, and have you present your case to the judge. The only way for the ticket to be invalidated is for the man who wrote it to do it," Bronson explained.

With that the man turned on Gross. The two of them went into the Traffic office to continue the argument. As the dispute continued, Bronson began to talk with Sergeant Harris.

It's been like this since I called you sir," Harris began. "I thought the guy was going to drive us crazy. What happened, sir? You sure took a long time getting here?"

"I had a flat tire. I then found out that my jack was defective. Fortunately, I was able to flag down someone who had a hydraulic jack and I got the damned tire changed. Sorry I was so late."

"Well sir, I was about to give up hope. I've seen a few countries where they would have just shot this guy and forgot about it. I was really starting to envy those countries." The exasperation in Harris' voice was evident.

At length, Gross walked out of the Traffic office. Bronson asked, "How'd it go Gross? Did you just tell the guy to take it to court?"

"No, sir," came the reply. "I got tired of hearing that guy bitch and let him go."

"I wish you hadn't done that," Bronson replied. "The guy was a prick."

Gross thought to himself for a few seconds. Then with a grimace on his face and holding up his hands in resignation said, "I wish I hadn't let him go, myself, now. But, I got so tired of arguing with the guy I just had a weak moment and tore up the ticket."

"Look, Gross," said Bronson. "Next time, just tell the guy to tell his story to the judge. Your attitude should be that once a ticket is written, it's out of your hands. If the guy thinks he has a valid point, he should bring it up in court."

A STATESIDE TOUR OF DUTY

"Yes, sir. I'll remember that. Right now, I think I'm going to call it a night."

Steve probably wished he could do the same, but with the lateness of the hour that was not an option. He read the blotter and the desk log and conducted guard mount at midnight. Finally, at about 0030 hours he would have returned home. I'm sure Barbara was asleep, so he probably set the clock for 0700 hours and joined her.

By Monday morning, several people had filed complaints through official channels, about the police car not being clearly visible as Gross wrote tickets the preceding Saturday night. Ironically, one of them was the man Gross had let go. The colonel was angry with Bronson for not getting to work quicker and calming the situation. He was angry with me for letting my men use subterfuge to catch speeders. In addition, a sign that I had ordered from the post engineer sign shop for Magistrate's Court had come to us with the wording "Commissioner's Court" on it. The name of the court had only been changed a few months previously and someone at the sign shop had incorrectly used the former name. Of course, the colonel blamed me for the error.

The colonel decided that Steve would be assigned to the company as XO (a new company commander was due to arrive soon), and Raymond would become the new Operations officer.

I suggested that I might change jobs with Steve, but the colonel refused. In his words, Raymond had done such a good job correcting IG inspection deficiencies that he deserved the Operations slot. I then asked to be assigned as chief of AWOL Apprehension or Company Supply Officer. Again, the colonel refused. He said, "You will remain in Traffic." It was clear that he was determined to break up the comradeship that Steve and I shared and make it difficult for us to work together.

That afternoon, I showed Prince the schedule Steve and I had prepared, and he made some minor changes. He moved some morning classes to the afternoon and shifted the afternoon classes to the morning. I didn't argue with him. I just passed the schedule along to the major, who then added his input by shifting most of the classes back to where they were in the first place. The trainees would arrive in the next two or three days, and training would begin in exactly one week. I began to prepare my lesson plans.

Tuesday night, the 290th MP Company defeated Head and Head (Headquarters and Headquarters Company) 12–6 in the post softball semi-finals. Head and Head had led the league for much of the second half of the season and had been heavy favorites to defeat us. We had a large contingent of fans on hand with air horns and other noise-making devices, and everyone was in high spirits. If we could win on Thursday, we would be the Fort McCulloch softball champions for the 1970 season.

Meanwhile, Steve was learning his official duties as the company executive officer. One of the more important duties he received was that of property book officer. In this role, he was required to sign for all the equipment held by the company. All the equipment and supplies were listed in a document know as the property book. Before signing, Steve began to take inventory. Among other items were thirty-three radios of various makes and models. Most of these were mounted in vehicles or at the MP desks in the PMO or at Camp Price. An additional seven were listed as being on hand in the supply room. A check of the supply room failed to locate them. Everything else the company had in the way of equipment was accounted for. Raymond, as the outgoing property book officer, attempted to get Steve to sign as the new property book officer without seeing the missing radios. In his words, "The radios were around and would eventually turn up."

"No way," answered Steve. "Either you produce the missing radios or you can pay for them."

Within three hours Raymond returned with a box of miscellaneous radio parts and broken odds and ends. "Here are your radios," Raymond said with a confident smile.

"To hell with you," Steve replied. "The property book lists seven radios, not a lot of broken crap."

Now Raymond stopped smiling. "Look, these are the radios. Just sign the damned property book."

"No way," Steve countered. "You get me those radios or we'll drop them from the property book and survey them against you. It can come out of your pocket."

Raymond was now visibly angry. "Look, you son of a bitch! If I can't make you sign, the colonel can."

Steve was not to be bluffed. Even if Raymond's threat had been real, the worst penalty Steve might face was being transferred to another unit. With anger and determination very evident in his voice, he leaned forward and practically snarled in Raymond's face. "Call me a son of a bitch again and I'll smash every tooth out of your damned head. Now, first," (he held up his index finger), "if the colonel orders me to sign and

A STATESIDE TOUR OF DUTY

I refuse, his only option is to court-martial me for failure to obey a lawful order. That will never stand up."

"Why not?" Raymond backed away slightly as he asked the question.

"Once the radios aren't produced in court, it will show that the order wasn't legal. And second," (he held up a second finger), "I have thirty days to inventory the property book, by regulation. There are twenty-eight days left. If I don't have the radios by then, we will survey them against you and you can pay for them. Now, get your ass out of my office and get me those radios."

Raymond's entire demeanor now changed. With a smile, he said, "There's no reason why two reasonable officers should argue like enlisted men. We need to work together—"

"That's right," Steve interrupted. "You bring me the radios, and I'll sign the property book."

With that, Raymond turned and walked away. He would have the missing radios to Steve within the next two days.

Wednesday morning, we were introduced to our new 290th Military Police Company commanding officer. His name was George W. Lynch. He stood about five foot four and tended to walk around in a Napoleonesque manner with his nose elevated and his right hand inside his shirt. Byron had just taken over Operations, and his first official duty was to introduce Lynch to the PMO staff.

As they walked into the Traffic office, I shouted, "Attention," and I, along with my two investigators, rose to attention. This formality was only used for visiting dignitaries and changes of commanders.

"Please be at ease, men," Lynch said.

"Captain, let me introduce you to our Traffic officer and his men," Byron began. "This is Lieutenant Moultrie" (we shook hands) "and Specialists Gross and Cummings" (he shook hands with them also). "Everybody, this is Captain Lynch."

"It's very good to be at Fort McCulloch and to meet you men," Lynch acknowledged.

"Same here, sir," we all said pretty much in unison.

"I could be in the area at any time, so there's no need for formality. Just proceed to work and, again, it's good to be here." With that statement, Byron and the new CO left the room. My one overwhelming thought was that I finally was meeting someone more arrogant and pompous than Byron E. Raymond.

On Thursday evening, we met the 112th Quartermaster Detachment on the west field for the post softball championship. Just about everyone connected to the company was present. Even Steve was there, accompanied by a very beautiful companion.

"Hey buddy," I said, "are you going to join us on the field tonight?"

"I'll be an observer, thanks," Steve replied.

"He's just afraid he might commit an error in front of all these people," his friend added.

"Nick," Steve interjected, "this is Barbara Parry. Barbara, this is Nick Moultrie."

"It's wonderful to meet you," Barbara stated as she held out her hand. "I've heard so much about you."

"Something good, I hope," I said with a smile.

"Very good." She looked around to ensure there were no eavesdroppers and continued. "In fact, you're one of the few people he works with that he has anything good to say about."

At this time I called for Sam to come over. "Sam, I would like to introduce Steve Bronson and his good friend, Barbara Parry. This is my wife, Samantha, the person who keeps me civilized."

Sam shook hands with them and said, "It's so very nice to meet you, Barbara. Steve, Nick has told me so much about you, and it's all good."

"You mean there's something good about this guy?" Barbara said with a laugh, as she gave Steve an elbow.

"Oh yes! Steve is one of the few people Nick really enjoys working with." Sam placed emphasis on the word *really*.

Barbara changed the subject. "What do you do, Sam?"

"Besides picking up after this guy and keeping him in line," (she put her arm around me) "I'm planning to become a future generation specialist."

"Which is?" asked Barbara.

"I plan to be a stay-at-home mom and raise kids. That is, providing this guy will do his duty and provide me with them." Sam pulled me a little tighter to her.

"Hey, I'm doing all I can. The rest is up to you," I said defensively. Everyone laughed.

Shortly thereafter the umpire yelled, "Play ball!" and the game began. Despite our best hopes and high spirits, it did not go well. The quartermaster detachment had a lengthy undefeated streak in the second half of the season, and despite our belief that we could end that streak, it was not to be. Their batters were constantly able to place their hits between our fielders, and their fielders made continual big-league catches and great plays. We lost 16–7, and the game was not that close. Many of our fans left before the game was over.

On the way home, Sam did most of the talking. "Mrs. Lynch is a sweet lady. I don't know how she stands that husband of hers."

"They say that opposites attract, Sam. I guess they're Exhibit A."

Sam didn't acknowledge my comment. She just continued, "Barbara seems like a fantastic person. I hope she and Steve get married. I can tell that she wants to."

"I think Steve will have something to say about that. I'm not sure he wants to get married."

Sam continued, "If she plays her cards right, she'll catch him. I can tell that he likes her, too."

"You haven't mentioned Kathy Raymond yet, honey," I chided.

"You mean Mrs. Brown Nose. She just sat between the colonel's wife and Mrs. Lynch. She was way too good to associate with us ordinary folks. Even Barbara thought she was a stuck-up snob."

"You really like Barbara, don't you?"

"Yes, I do. She's down to earth, like us. Did you know she teaches English at the high school?"

"I do now."

"Anyone that teaches is special," Sam added.

"I will be teaching some classes to our new OJT personnel the next three weeks, honey. Does that mean I'm special, too?"

Sam smirked. "Of course, dear. You're always special—just like the kids I used to work with at the state school." She laughed.

"Now I'm insulted," I laughed. "You can't compare me with those kids."

"Why not? When I have to pick up after you, I sometimes get the feeling you might be handicapped, too."

I decided to change the subject. "I'm going to miss working with Steve. I wish the colonel hadn't split us up."

"Don't worry, honey. Your buddy is only a building away. You can still get together."

"That's true." I changed the subject again. "Right now, I want to forget work and go home to work on that future generation you were talking about earlier."

"Oh my," Sam laughed. "I was wondering how long it would take for my husband's one-track mind to get around to that."

I smiled. "I don't have a one-track mind, Sam. I also think about food, sports, history, politics and a lot of other things."

"It seems to me that the thought of sex quickly pushes those other thoughts out of your mind," she rebutted.

"Its important to keep the world populated, honey. Besides, you know you love me," I said.

"Well, let's just say that I'm not going to trade you in any time soon," Sam agreed as we arrived at home.

By Saturday, a total of forty-three men, who had recently graduated from a Fort Hood basic training brigade, had arrived for the OJT class to begin on Monday. I had been spending most of my time preparing my lesson plans for the classes I would have to teach. At home, on Saturday afternoon, I practiced my teaching techniques on Sam.

"Remember, honey," Sam would continually remind me. "You're teaching classes, not giving speeches. Be sure to call for questions and get your students involved."

"That's good advice, honey. Where did you learn that?"

"Believe it or not, Nick, I did attend school once. The teachers I hated the most were the ones who just lectured and bored me to death. The good teachers were the ones who got students involved. They always taught me the most."

"You may not have a college degree, Sam, but you're smarter than a lot that do."

"I'm glad you figured that out. For a man, you're pretty smart," Sam said with a smile.

"The fact that you agreed to marry me also shows you are intelligent, and have great taste in men," I added.

"It's getting deep in here, Nick. You better open the door and let a little of the BS flow out."

At that point, I began to make sure my brass was polished and my shoes were shined to a high gloss. Where the students had just come from a basic training unit, they would be expecting that. Finally, my lesson plans were completed, my uniforms were ready for Monday and the day was just about over. That night Sam and I relaxed on the couch to watch the nightly news. As usual, the bulk of the news involved the war in Vietnam. There were the usual graphic pictures of combat and wounded soldiers being medevaced out by helicopter. All wars give people a lesson in geography, and this one was no different. The news had a lengthy list of geographic places that were mentioned each night, such as Saigon, Hua, Danang and the Mekong Delta. As we watched, Sam held me a little tighter.

"Oh Nick, I thank God every night that you don't have to go over there," she said.

"Someday, people will ask me what I did during the Vietnam War," I replied. "It won't sound too impressive to tell them I was the Traffic officer at Fort Benjamin McCulloch, Texas."

"I don't care, Nick. The facts are that you answered your country's call and served. That's all that matters." At that point she kissed me, and we ignored the rest of the news.

CHAPTER SEVENTEEN

Sunday morning Sam and I went to the post chapel for the morning service. Frankly, I would have preferred to sleep in, but Sam insisted otherwise. If you will forgive some sarcasm, since I was an obedient, dutiful husband Sam got her way. After returning home I quickly changed into casual wear and began to read the Sunday paper I had bought at the PX. I looked up and noticed that the bedroom door was open. Sam was standing in front of the full-length mirror in her underwear. This was unusual, as she was usually the first one to change clothes when we got home from church. I got up and walked back the length of the trailer to her. She seemed to be in deep thought.

"You better get dressed in case we have company. You don't want to entertain visitors like that," I commented. "Although you're dressed perfectly to entertain me."

She ignored that comment when she spoke. "Nick, do you see anything wrong with me?" she asked, as she turned to face me.

"No! Why on earth would you ask a silly question like that?"

"Then why would you want to look at a magazine like *Playboy*?"

Yesterday, I had told her about a joke I was going to start my class with Monday morning, and it included a centerfold from *Playboy*. She had objected to the joke, but I had explained that many military instructors usually start a class with a risqué joke. She had let the subject drop then. Why was she bringing the subject up now? "Sam, *Playboy* is just a harmless men's magazine. It's no big deal." I said in my defense.

"It's a big deal to me!" she interrupted. "If my husband feels the need to look at silicone-injected bimbos, it makes me feel inadequate as a woman. Besides, everyone knows that those pictures are just touched up to make them look perfect. You can bet that they don't look like that in real life."

"Sam, there is an old joke that says; 'when a man gets married he goes on a diet, but he still gets to look at the menu.'" I had hoped a joke would calm things down, but I was wrong.

"Women are not a menu, Nick! We're human beings," she exclaimed. "How would you feel if I posed in one of those magazines? I'm sure I could make some money putting these on display." She reached with both hands up to the bottom of her bra and jerked it up so her breasts fell out at the bottom. "If *Playboy* is harmless, why don't I pose? You could show the magazine to other men and brag about your wife. Here's my wife, Sam; she's double-D and all natural with no silicone."

"Sam, please stop!" I yelled. "I could not stand to have a bunch of sick perverts lusting over pictures of you. Besides, Sam, I truly believe that if a woman is willing to take off her clothes and pose naked for pictures for one sum of money, then she will prostitute herself for a higher sum. She is just waiting for the right amount to be offered."

"Then why would you want to look at such a magazine?"

I shrugged as I struggled for words to say. Sam was angry and I did not want to fight. I didn't understand her anger and I just wanted to have a quiet afternoon. "Sam, if a man avoided looking at *Playboy* his peers might see him as a wimp or queer or something."

"Does what other men think mean more to you than what your wife thinks?" Sam exclaimed.

"No! That's not what I mean."

"Then what is the problem?"

"If it means that much to you, honey, I'll gladly forget about magazines like *Playboy* in the future. I love you, Sam, and you are more important than anything else."

"Do you really mean that? What about your joke tomorrow?"

"Look, honey, if it means that much to you, then after tomorrow, I'll only tell clean jokes. I don't know any, so you'll have to help me find some. Sam, the night we met you had a friend that really liked dirty jokes, why do you have so much trouble with them?"

"She has also caught the clap several times," Sam smiled. "Do you really want me to be like her?"

"Hell, no!" I said. "I guess the bad jokes will have to go. Sam, I know I have a few rough edges and can be a little crude—"

"Sometimes you can be uncouth," Sam interrupted.

"Then I will happily look forward to you helping me improve my social skills and teaching me some couth."

With that commitment on my part, Sam smiled and the rest of the day passed peacefully. Sam seemed to usually win the arguments, but it was worth it to have her happy.

The OJT classes began at 0800 hours, Monday morning. Captain Lynch filled the first hour of class work by recounting the history of the Military Police Corps. He went into considerable detail about how the motto was "Of the troop, for the troops," described the official qualifications for military police service and generally bored the new men to death.

Finally, at 0900 hours, it was my turn. I had already set up an easel with my training aids, so all I had to do was walk into the room and take my place at the podium. "Good morning men," I said in a loud voice. "I'm Lieutenant Moultrie. I'll be your principal instructor for the next three hours. We'll be discussing traffic points—day, traffic points—night, radar and VASCAR use and the forms involved in traffic accident investigation. First, men, since we are in the Army, I believe a review of weapons is in order." I then turned the first sheet of paper (which announced the subject of the class) over the top of the easel to expose a *Playboy* picture of a very beautiful and very naked woman. "Men, here we have the M1A1 Russian Hand Grenade." As I continued with the joke I used a pointer to point to certain parts of her anatomy. "This weapon is readily identifiable by the prominent hand dials located here. Also of interest is the short fuse canal. This is important, men. You might want to take notes. This weapon is highly reactive to heat and may be hand-operated."

The class roared with delight after I recited my punch line. Their reaction was quite different from Sam's the night before. When I had told her that joke, she had let me know that she didn't appreciate it. I had agreed to avoid such jokes in the future, but I couldn't resist using this one.

After the good start, I was able (with only a ten-minute break at about 1100 hours) to continue until lunchtime. The men were then taken by bus to the battalion mess hall for lunch. After lunch, Captain Warren of JAG would begin to educate them on the finer points of the law as it pertained to searches and informing people of their rights.

After lunch, I spent some time talking to Steve, who had now set up his office in the supply room. The Supply sergeant, Sergeant Winters, had a large supply of pornographic magazines in his desk and Steve had borrowed a few of them. As I walked into their office, Steve was leaning back in his chair with his feet propped up on the desk. "Come in," he said over his magazine. "Welcome to my new habitation."

I quickly inquired, "Why aren't you using Byron's old office? You traded jobs with him."

"I want to stay as far away from little Napoleon as I can," Steve answered matter-of-factly. "By the way, I heard that your classes went very well this morning."

"Thanks! I take it that you don't care for our new CO."

Steve threw the magazine in a desk drawer and sat up in his chair. "That little nut case probably makes his wife stand at attention and inspects the bedroom after sex. He spent most of the morning walking around the orderly room complaining about dust." He hesitated a second and then continued. "I convinced him that we need an additional mail officer for the company, so you will get to go take the mail room personnel test with me tomorrow."

"Just what I always wanted to do—" I said sarcastically, "take a test and obtain an additional duty."

"The test is open book and you have a copy of the mail regulations with you, so how hard can it be? Besides, it will give us a chance to continue working together on our pet project," Steve explained.

I paused for a second and then asked, "What time is the test tomorrow?"

"That's the spirit!" Steve stopped to light a cigarette. "1400 hours at the post testing office tomorrow. This will give you an extra excuse to get out of the PMO occasionally."

"Let's hear it for extra duties!" I concluded.

The next day, Steve and I met at the testing center to take the mail room personnel test. The plan was for Steve to be the company mail officer and for me to be the assistant. As Steve had said, the test was open book and each of us was supplied with a copy of the regulation. Unfortunately, the test was so voluminous that it was not practical to look everything up, as we only had an hour to complete the test. When the results were released two days later, they revealed that Steve had flunked the test and I had passed.

I was therefore the new mail room officer for the 290th Military Police Company. Steve denied it, but I suspected that he deliberately failed to avoid the extra responsibility. I didn't care though, as I was required to make periodic inspections of the mail room. This required me to go over to the company, and while I was there Steve and I usually managed to play a game or two of pool or Ping-Pong in the day room.

The unit fund paid for subscriptions to several magazines. Most of these magazines were immediately placed in the day room for the benefit of the soldiers to read. There were two exceptions to this rule. *Playboy* and *Penthouse* tended to disappear quickly from the day room. Therefore, these magazines were kept in the desk of the mail room officer (or the mail clerk) and checked out to those desiring to read them until the next month's issue arrived. The older copies were then placed in the day room with the other magazines. The first person to read these sexually oriented periodicals each month was either myself or my mail room clerk. Since Sam objected so strenuously to the magazines, I allowed him to keep track of them. I told him that since he was around the mail room more than I that would make sense. He agreed. After he had "read all the good articles," they were then available to be checked out by others.

Raymond kept control of the unit fund, but the fifty or so other duties were reassigned to either me or Steve. One morning Steve was called into the colonel's office. (Steve filled me in on the details afterward.) The colonel got right to the point. "Lieutenant, the PMO has some property which I understand has not been picked up on the company property book. I want you to remedy this problem immediately."

"No problem," said Steve. "What property are we talking about, sir?"

"The carpeting in my office and that in the PMI section, as well as the two new air conditioners," the colonel said flatly.

"I'll be glad to add them to the property book, sir," replied Bronson. "Who currently owns them?"

"What do you mean?" the colonel asked suspiciously.

"Well sir, we'll have to list the source that supplied them when we add them to the property book." Without waiting for the colonel to comment, he asked, "Do they currently belong to you, sir?"

"No!"

"Do they belong to someone in PMI?" Steve then added, "Sergeant Warren, for example?"

"Sergeant Warren only—," the colonel stopped, thought for an instant and said curtly, "No, they don't belong to Sergeant Warren, either. Just pick them up on the property book. I have another appointment. Good day, lieutenant."

"Yes, sir." Steve then left the PMO and went to the office of the post property book officer. I accompanied him, as there was a good chance that I might have the property book duty sometime in the future. We learned that almost anything can be picked up on the company property book as "found on post." The only exceptions were sentry dogs and weapons.

As we drove back to the PMO I asked the one question that came to mind. "Who do you think really owns that carpeting and those air conditioners?"

"I do now," said Steve. "At least I will as soon as I pick it up on my property book."

"Do you want to know what I think?" I looked over at Steve to await his reaction to my question.

"Yeah, what do you think? Your opinion is one of the few I care to hear in this hellhole."

"I think it's clear that the carpeting and the air conditioners were gifts from Warren. If the colonel got caught accepting gifts from subordinates, he could be court-martialed. That's why he was in such a hurry for you to put it on the company property book. Now, it's no longer a gift to him. It belongs to the MP Company."

"That is the only theory that makes sense," agreed Bronson. "I would sure like to know what Warren's game is. You can be sure that he is up to no good."

"I agree. At least we're not the only ones who think so. Warren now knows that CID is out to get him, too." I had to add that detail since I wasn't sure if Steve was aware of that fact yet.

"How do you know?"

"Warren won't let CID have access to his files and he won't coordinate any of his activities with them. The tension is so thick at the morning briefings that I'm no longer allowed to attend unless I'm the duty officer."

Now Steve's interest was aroused. "When did this happen?" he asked.

"This morning, Raymond informed me that they were reducing the number of personnel at the morning briefings. I am no longer an attendee. If I have something that needs to be discussed, I must submit it through channels. In other words, I tell him and he brings it up in the meeting."

"I'll bet it breaks your heart not to have to attend those meetings," Steve commented.

"Oh, and one more thing: The Department of the Army is sending a manpower specialist to ensure that we need the extra men that are being assigned to us. All the section heads will need to justify the number of men assigned to them."

"When does that guy get here?" I asked.

"He is due here Monday." As we pulled into the PMO parking lot, Mr. Garcia was just leaving his office. He immediately came over to us.

"If you guys are going to enter the weekly football pool, I have the sheets ready in my office," he said.

"We could just give Sergeant Dee our money now and avoid the suspense," I said.

"Think positive, Nick. Remember, everyone has the same chance," Garcia noted as he walked away.

WO2 Geraldo (Jerry) Garcia would be coaching the post basketball team, in addition to his PMO duties, when that season began. Now he spent his time with the company flag football team (which was undefeated) and organizing the weekly football pool. Each week he printed off sheets listing fifteen college football games. To enter, you simply circled the teams you expected to win and picked the score of the fifteenth game as a tie breaker. You then gave your entry to the vehicle registration personnel, with a dollar. The person with the best record of prognostications won all the money. That person, more often than not, was the new Operations sergeant SFC Walter de la Vega. Most of the personnel called him Sergeant Dee, while the Operations clerks sometimes referred to him as the Frito Bandito (but not to his face).

De la Vega seemed to be the one person among the PMO staff that Warren was afraid of. Shortly after Sergeant Dee (he seemed to prefer that name) was assigned to the PMO, Warren had entered the Operations office and was told by de la Vega to stay the hell out of his area. To the surprise of all, after a short protestation about "the need to work together," Warren left like a whipped dog. Since that time, if he needed anything from Operations, he sent one of his clerks to get it. Sergeant Dee likewise avoided the PMI section.

After parting company with Steve, I went into Operations. Byron was not around, so I thought this might be a good time to talk with Sergeant Dee. He was busy with the pile of paperwork that cluttered his desk. I asked, "Got a moment, sarge?"

The sergeant put down his pen and looked up. "Sure thing, sir. Have a seat. What can I do for you?"

A STATESIDE TOUR OF DUTY

Instead of getting to the point, I asked, "I was just wondering if you might share your secret for winning the football pool."

The sergeant smiled. "Oh there's no secret, sir. I just compare who the teams have played and follow my hunches. Good luck takes care of the rest." He looked around and in a quieter tone stated, "But, you aren't really here to discuss the football pool, are you?"

I smiled. "Is it that obvious, sarge?"

"Yes, sir," he replied. "What's on your mind?"

I saw no reason for additional small talk. I got right to the point. "Look sarge, I think Sergeant Warren is bad news."

He sat back in his chair and smiled. "You figured that out all by yourself?"

"It wasn't hard to do," I replied.

"Look, sir," Sergeant Dee began again. "You realize that curiosity killed the cat. Sometimes it isn't wise to ask too many questions."

"Well, if something bad happens, I would hate for good people to be taken down with the crooks," I explained.

"Let me tell you something, lieutenant. If the good people get too close to the crooks, then they deserve to be taken down with them. In my opinion, they have ceased to be good people." He paused for a second before adding, "Close the door for a second."

I got up and shut the door to his office and sat back down. "Apparently, there is more you want to tell me," I said.

"Just this, lieutenant. There are personnel whose job it is to investigate people like Warren. Sooner or later the law of averages will catch up with Warren, and the investigators will apprehend him. You should let those people do their job and you do yours. Warren has friends, if you know what I mean. I suggest you put as much distance between Warren and yourself as you can, and leave him alone."

"You talk like you've known Warren for some time," I interjected.

"We crossed paths in 'Nam. On the record, that's all I'm going to say on the subject." He then added, "Off the record, lieutenant, I wouldn't trust Warren with the sweat off my balls."

"I appreciate the advice and input, sergeant." With that, I got up to leave.

"Anytime, lieutenant." Sergeant Dee then added, "I trust that we won't be discussing Warren again."

"Consider him forgotten, sarge."

"Well, have a good day then, lieutenant," he replied.

I returned to my Traffic office and finished the paperwork that occupied my desk. Just before quitting time, I went over to Supply to pass along Sergeant Dee's advice to Steve. His reaction was about what I had expected.

"The investigators he was talking about was the CID," Steve acknowledged. "We both know that our CID detachment couldn't find their ass with both hands."

"That's true," I replied. "However, it might be wise for us to be patient for a little while and keep our misgivings to ourselves. Like Sergeant Dee says, the law of averages will catch up with Warren sooner or later."

"Let's hope it's sooner rather than later," said Steve. "Charlie says this place is worse than the outfit in *Catch-22*. I'm starting to believe he's right." With that, we both headed for home.

I spent the rest of the week preparing for the manpower specialist that Steve had informed me that the Department of the Army was sending. His job was to ensure that the men recently assigned were indeed needed and to see that they were properly allocated among the various sections of our staff. I instructed my men that we were going to convince this pencil-pushing bureaucrat that we were very overworked and therefore obtain additional personnel for the section. By the time the manpower specialist arrived on October the 5th we would be ready for him. The reasons for my plan of action were purely selfish and ego-related.

Where I was a lieutenant in a job designed for a sergeant, my ego dictated that I have a more prestigious job. I was determined to increase the size and scope of the Traffic section and make it a higher profile position. Since the manpower specialist was scheduled to meet with me on Wednesday the 7th, I directed my men to be out of the office until then, thus allowing the paperwork to pile up on our desks.

In college, I had once heard of Parkinson's Law. This theorem, which is often called the Law of Bureaucracy, states that work expands to fill the time allotted. In other words, a member of a bureaucracy will build his influence (and power) by expanding his staff and generating paperwork to make himself appear more important. The time on the hands of his staff members will be filled with make-work projects and unnecessary paperwork in order for the entire organization to appear invaluable and indispensable. In retrospect, I hate to admit that I acted in such a manner, but history has shown that it is normal human nature.

A STATESIDE TOUR OF DUTY

On Wednesday morning, Sam told me that she needed the car, so I had her drop me off at work. I explained that I would work through lunch and she could pick me up at 1700. She would bring me a sandwich at noon, since my overwhelming workload would prevent me from coming home for lunch. As I kissed her good-bye, she shook her head and said with a smile, "I can't believe you would try to snow somebody like this."

My reply to her was, "We all have to do our best in this time of crisis. After all, honey, my country is counting on me."

She laughed. "No comment, honey," she said. After telling her I loved her, I went into the office.

My court duties kept me busy all morning, as I ensured that all necessary people were there and observed the proceedings. Then, at noon, I went to the office to begin taking care of the paperwork that was piled up on my desk. At 1300 hours, Cummings came in off the road and joined me with the manpower expert.

"As you probably know," I began, "Fort McCulloch measures almost ninety miles in length and about sixty miles in width, and we must investigate all traffic accidents that occur within its boundaries, regardless of the time they occur. This means that one of my men has to be on call at all times between 1700 and 0800 hours."

"It is a big post," the man agreed.

"Yes, sir." I then continued, "We are also responsible for radar and VASCAR enforcement on the state highways. This is a necessary deterrent to keep speeds down in the outlying areas and help prevent accidents."

"Sir," Cummings added, "don't forget the amount of time we need to fill out all of the paperwork and answer the phone."

"Good point, Cummings. If we're not here, then the desk personnel have to take our calls, and that distracts them from their duties overseeing the patrols." I was proud that I could say that with a straight face. We probably didn't get ten business calls all day, but this guy didn't need to know that.

About every five minutes, the phone would ring and Cummings would take a message and tell the caller that he would get back to them. I had learned this trick from First Sergeant Prince. I could have Gross make continuous calls as needed to make the point that we were very busy, also.

"As you can see, sir, we get a lot of calls from the post safety director, the DMV and others requesting information during the workday," I explained.

"So I see, lieutenant," he agreed.

As we showed the staffing expert all the charts that we maintained, he did indeed seem impressed. At 1700 hours, we were still detailing all our duties. Even the most mundane of tasks required some time to accomplish, and we made sure we listed them all.

"Thanks for your time, lieutenant," the man said. "This has been most informative. As I have told everyone else, my findings will be available in about ten days."

"You are very welcome, sir. If you need anything else, just let me know," I said as we shook hands. "Well, my wife is waiting, so I better be going."

"Okay, lieutenant, I understand." He then added, "You definitely need additional manpower. We'll try to see that you don't have to work through lunch again."

"That would be nice. Thank you again, sir." With that, I closed up shop and, after shaking hands with the manpower expert, I joined Sam in the car.

"How did it go, honey?" she asked.

"Very well, I think. I'm hoping for one or two additional investigators. But you never know how these things will play out." I then asked, "How was your day?"

"Pretty good," she said. "In fact, I've decided that you're going to take me out tonight."

"Why? What's the occasion?" I protested.

"We haven't gone out to a restaurant since our honeymoon, and I think it's time for my tightwad husband to take me out." She continued to look straight ahead as she turned the car toward home. "We will go home long enough for you to change and then we'll have a nice dinner out."

"Where do you want to go?" After a slight hesitation, I teased her with, "I understand Miller's is a nice place." In reality I had no intention of taking her there.

"Where the hookers hang out, Nick? I don't think so."

"Honey," I countered, "The hookers are in the bar, not in the restaurant."

A STATESIDE TOUR OF DUTY

"Just the same, Nick, we'll go to the officers' club. Then we can stay afterward and play bingo."

That night we had a nice candlelight dinner in the dimly lit dining room at the officers' club. When I remarked that it was probably dimly lit so that we couldn't see the food, Sam made a stern comment. "It's nice and romantic, Nick; please don't spoil it." I deserved that reaction, so I let it go. I also decided to keep any other caustic or comical remarks to myself, as they would be out of place. We then proceeded to have a nice, leisurely dinner where Sam did most of the talking. After the day I had experienced, I was happy to just listen.

After dinner, we went to the main ballroom to play bingo. As usual, we didn't win anything. Finally, we arrived back home a little after 10:30 (2230 military time). As we undressed for bed, Sam said, "You haven't asked me why I needed the car today, Nick."

"I supposed you just wanted to do some shopping, or not be stuck in the house all day."

"Actually, honey, I went to the hospital for a pregnancy test," she replied.

"And? What did they say?" She had my attention now.

"I'll get the results on Friday, Nick. I don't know yet, but I think I am."

I grabbed her and gave her a great big hug. "That is wonderful, Sam. I think I'm the happiest man in the world. Wow! I hope it's a boy." In my mind, I could see myself throwing around a football with my son in the front yard in a few years. If it was true, I couldn't wait to pass on the information to Steve. Sam just smiled at my reaction. She knew that I was a happy man.

The next day, I was scheduled to teach traffic accident investigation all day. As usual, I began with a joke. Sam had protested so vehemently against crude sexual jokes that I had searched for some she might not object to. "Men," I began, "an atheist was walking down a path at Yellowstone National Park. He verbally pondered all the beautiful surroundings that had been provided by the accident of creation. He admired the vistas of lakes, mountains and meadows and wondered how some people could believe in God when they should be enjoying the beauty of nature. Suddenly he was attacked by a grizzly bear. At that point he shouted out in fear, 'Oh God, help me!' Suddenly the bear was motionless and a light beamed down and a voice said, 'You deny all my work as well as my existence, and now ask for my help?' The atheist replied, 'I don't wish to be a hypocrite and tell people that I've changed my mind, but could you please make the bear a Christian?' God said,

'Done,' and the light disappeared as the bear returned to life. The bear then bowed his head and folded his paws and said, 'Dear Lord, for this food I am about to eat, I am indeed thankful. Amen.'" As usual, the joke was well received. I suspected that maybe the jokes didn't have to be risqué after all.

With accident investigation, as with all facets of police work, you first learn to search for answers to *who, what, when, where, how* and *why*. After impressing that fact on my students, I went into some actual cases. The point I was trying to get across was always look for all possible factors involved in the accident and don't ignore anything. After lunch, we set up a staged traffic accident. The cars were parked as if an accident had happened and the students were given a list of the hypothetical damages to each vehicle. In addition to the drivers, each car had one passenger, and there were three onlookers who claimed to have seen the whole thing. Of course, the onlookers all gave different and contradictory accounts of the accident. The class was divided up into eight teams of five or more men and told to sort it all out. After two hours, they returned to the classroom to compare notes and critique each other. The feedback I received from those who observed my classes, over the next few days, was all positive.

On Friday, I dropped in at Post Engineers. I had requested some signs warning of the deer hazard to be posted on Highway 142 East. The man in charge of the office was sitting with his feet on the desk. When I inquired as to how long it would be before they would be placed, I got an answer I didn't expect.

"This is our busy time of the year, lieutenant," he said. "I'm not sure how long it will be before we can place those signs. I wish we could give you a date, but this is our busy time of the year."

I wanted to laugh. With his feet on his desk, this guy looked less busy than the major. I didn't laugh, though. I knew better. I simply said, "Well, just do your best," and left. I suspected that once the signs were ready, it would be some of our MPs that would have to place them.

Also, on Friday, I finally got the news I had been waiting for. About 1600 hours, the office phone rang. I answered it, "Military Police Traffic Section, Lieutenant Moultrie speaking, sir." It was Sam.

"Guess what, honey?" she asked.

"Don't hold me in suspense, babe," I said. "What are the test results?"

"The rabbit died." She paused, and when I didn't say anything she added, "The baby is due Memorial Day."

I sat back in my chair. "That's great, honey. That is fantastic! I want to go and tell Steve, babe. I'll see you in an hour."

Sam then said, "See you at five, honey. 'Bye."

I went over to the company to tell Steve the good news.

"You guys work fast," he said with a grin. "Most people usually wait a couple of years."

"Why wait?" I replied. "The sooner we have kids, then the sooner they are raised and on their own. We'll be able to enjoy our grandchildren while we're still young."

Steve smiled. "You're really happy being married, aren't you?"

"Yes, I am." I continued. "It's really nice to have someone to share your life with. If I didn't have Sam to go home to, this place would probably drive me crazy. She helps keep me organized and is a good cook as well as being a good advisor to the lord of the castle."

"How's that?" Steve laughed.

"A man's home is his castle," I explained. "All rulers, monarchs and potentates always had their grand vizier, chief advisor or counselor to give good advice. Sam fills the bill for me." While waiting for Steve to reply I added another thought he might relate to. "You know, Steve, when I asked Sam to marry me; I probably didn't see past idea of having sex all the time. Well, I now know what I should have known all along. That is that there are some times when a woman is just not in the mood. But during those times we can still hug and cuddle up and talk. It still makes for a good time."

"I don't know," Steve said. "I can't imagine having a good time with a woman without sex."

I laughed. "Look Steve, let me explain it this way. How many hours are you and Barbara together when she spends the weekend?"

He thought for a moment. "Probably thirty or so," he answered.

"But, I'll bet, you probably only spent three or four hours actually having sex."

"Four hours would be a bit on the high side," he admitted.

"Right! You spent the rest of the time talking, having a candlelit dinner and enjoying each other's company and getting to know each other." I continued to explain, "The same principle applies in marriage. I've even watched an occasional soap opera episode with her where she explained the plot. Likewise, I explain the finer points of a sport to her if we are watching a game of some sort." I then added an admission. "Look. I sometimes show her attention in the hope of receiving a reward. For those times when she isn't in the mood, I show her extra attention so I can get a little extra next time. She knows what I'm doing. She always laughs and says, 'You're a man, Nick; I have to expect that.'"

Steve broke out in a laugh. "You have a great philosophy, buddy. A great philosophy."

At this point it was quitting time, so Steve and I parted company and I left for home. When I got there, I knocked on the door instead of entering. As Sam opened it she looked surprised.

"Nick, why in the world did you knock?"

I tipped my hat to her in a comical manner and said, "Good afternoon, madam. I'm from the Fort McCulloch Stud Service. As one of our clients who has recently been bred, I'm here to follow up and see if your services received were satisfactory."

From Sam's facial expressions she was doing everything possible to keep from smiling. "I suppose it was okay," she smirked. "But frankly, it could have been better."

"If the service was not outstanding, ma'am, you are entitled to a refund. Unfortunately, the company doesn't allow sales representatives to carry cash, so you'll have to take it out in trade. My many satisfied customers can vouch that I'm the best. The International Studs Union has me rated at triple-A"

"Don't you mean triple-X?"

"Whatever. By the way, what was your complaint about our previous supplier?"

"Well," Sam began, "he seemed to talk too much."

"You're in luck, lady. I'm the silent stud. Your wish is my command, and services are guaranteed. If not completely satisfied, you get triple service next time—free of charge."

Sam grabbed my tie and pulled me toward the door. "Get in here, Nick, before the neighbors think you've lost your mind."

Once inside, Sam was unable to suppress her urge to laugh. In addition to laughing, Sam was positively beaming. I put my hands on her stomach. "How long before I can feel the baby move?" I asked.

"That will take a while, honey." Sam was already starting to cook supper and she returned to that task. "When do you find out if you will get additional men?" she asked.

A STATESIDE TOUR OF DUTY

"The findings of the manpower study should be known next Friday. That will be just in time for the new men to start their week of line duty training the next Monday."

"You haven't told any more disgusting jokes in your classes have you?"

"No, Sam. You would be proud of me. I'm looking around for some clean ones."

"Good! That grenade joke is not acceptable for any public setting."

I did not argue. Then, after the early supper, Sam and I watched television as we discussed names for the baby. I have always suspected that most women prefer to have a daughter first and began to concentrate on girls' names. It turned out that I was right. When I began to suggest boys' names, Sam told me a masculine name would not be appropriate.

"Our baby is going to be a girl, Nick," she said.

"How in the world can you know that?" I asked.

"I don't know. I just do. In my heart, I know I'm carrying a girl."

I was disappointed. I decided, however, that I would not let it show. In my mind, I had a couple of girls' names in mind but hoped they would not be needed. "We could name the baby after our fathers, if it is a boy," I suggested.

"My father has never been too thrilled with his name," she replied. "If it is a boy I want to name him Norris James Moultrie Junior."

What could I say to that except, "That works for me." Maybe it was ego, but I liked the idea.

With Sam insisting that the baby was going to be a girl, I decided to let the subject drop. If it was a boy, a name had been chosen and there was little left to do.

After the nightly news, which contained a few references to what I still dubbed as Lyndon Johnson's War (even though he was no longer president), Sam was reading a library book. I decided to go to bed. Sam had not been too amorous the last couple of days, and I figured it had something to do with her being pregnant. She said, "I have a couple of more chapters to read, honey, and I will be along shortly."

"That's okay, sweetie," I replied. I was asleep in a matter of minutes.

I have no idea how long I had been asleep, but Sam woke me up by gently shaking me and rolling me onto my back. "Hi there, soldier," she said. "Are you new in town?"

"Yes," I mumbled. Then, the realization that Sam was completely naked caused me to become completely alert. She put her fingers up to my mouth as a sign to remain quiet and placed her left leg over me to get astride of me.

"Soldier," she continued. "Are you qualified with the M1A1 Russian hand grenade?"

"No," I laughed. "I think I need more training."

"Well, let us proceed with that training." She ran her hands up my sides and took hold of my hands. She then placed them on her breasts. "First, soldier, you have to adjust the prominent hand dials to the proper settings while I load the short fuse canal. It is very important, soldier, that you know that this grenade is very hot and does not desire any hand-operating."

It does not sound like a very masculine reaction, on my part, but about all I could do was giggle and smile. I did not say a word. I knew that on that night, Sam was in charge. I remained silent as Sam continued with what she referred to as "training." It was past 3AM when she announced that I had qualified as expert with the M1A1 Russian hand grenade.

As we continued to lie there holding each other, I contemplated her incongruous behavior. It was clear that it was okay for Sam to say things that I should not. A year before, when I had described her father as dumber than a box of rocks, she had become very angry. Then, as I pointed out later that she usually felt the same way about him, she exclaimed, "He's my father, Nick. I can say it—you can't." I now realized that the same principle applied to her body. She could describe her private parts any way she wished. However I had to be more judicious and circumspect in describing female anatomy and careful about repeating jokes associated with the subject.

I also remembered that she had described the Russian hand grenade joke as unacceptable in any public setting. Since this activity had been very private, apparently she thought differently about it.

I fell asleep before 4:00 AM. We then slept past noon the next day.

CHAPTER EIGHTEEN

Early October saw the arrival into the 290th MP Company of two additional sergeants. Perhaps the most notable thing about these men was the contrast in ability and competence they displayed. SSG Jacque Bingham was the epitome of professionalism and efficiency. His counterpart that arrived that day was SGT Joseph R. Katone. The latter would not be a useful addition to our company.

Mr. Swanson at Personnel had given us a heads-up that Katone would be assigned to us. He said his Personnel file was filled with reprimands and comments from former commanding officers suggesting that the Army would be better off without Katone. According to Mr. Swanson, "If the Vietnam conflict was not occurring, the Army would have gotten rid of Katone long ago." Steve had gone to Personnel to review the file in order to know what to expect.

According to Steve, the list of reprimands and police reports was extensive. Joseph R. Katone was one of the U.S. Army's Project One Hundred Thousand. Under this experimental project, the Army allowed the enlistment of 100,000 men who did not meet the educational or intelligence requirements of the Army, the idea being that the Army could train them to rise above their deficiencies. The venture was an abject failure from the beginning. Most of the men had been given dishonorable or bad conduct discharges within weeks of their entrance into the Army. That a handful of these mentally deficient individuals, like Joe, made it through Basic Training was a minor miracle.

In his third week of Basic Training, at Fort Leonard Wood, Joe decided to sneak off post for a quick tour of Waynesville. When the MPs made a routine check of off-limits establishments, that night, they found him at Rosa's Chicken Shack. He was just leaving after spending time with one of the prostitutes when he was informed he was under arrest.

After shedding a few tears and swearing he didn't know the place was off limits (after all, the bulletin board did have a map showing how to get there), Joe got off with a reprimand.

During the fifth week, at the rifle range, several deer wandered into the beaten zone. Despite a call of "cease fire" from the tower, Joe emptied his magazine and killed two deer before the SDI (Senior Drill Instructor) could grab his weapon. Joe received an Article 15, but his greatest disappointment was when he learned that the mess hall would not be allowed to serve the venison to the platoon.

In his fourth week of AIT, Joe had better luck. He got picked up at a bar called The Mark Twain, by a young lady who allowed him to drive her car. As soon as they were on a straight stretch of highway she began to perform fellatio on him. In his excitement, Joe wrecked the car. After explaining the situation to the police, the lady was cited for interfering with the driver. Still, Joe's commanding officer put a note in his 201 file stating he didn't believe Joe would ever be a decent soldier.

Finally, toward the end of his final week of AIT, Joe was in the PX. He lit a cigarette and tossed the match toward a large butt can. Unfortunately, the match landed in the trash can next to it. The trash can contained some flammable items and quickly burst into flame. This, in turn, set some curtains on fire. Before the flames were extinguished, several thousand dollars in damage had occurred.

Also during AIT, Joe went AWOL three times. Fortunately for Joe, the battalion commander was striving for a special unit citation. One of the requirements for this award stated that the unit only have a minimum number of AWOL personnel during the training. Once this number was reached, the commander simply stopped reporting anyone AWOL. Consequently, Joe's violations were never reported, contrary to his company commander's wishes.

After AIT graduation, while most men were packing up to move on, Joe and some of his friends in the barracks were practicing their "indoor baseball." This involved using a pair of rolled-up socks for a ball and an entrenching tool for a bat. When it was Joe's turn at bat he took a round house swing, which caught his platoon guide (who was walking up from behind) in the side of the head. While the platoon guide recovered from his concussion in the hospital, Joe was allowed to move on and become someone else's problem.

He was sent to Germany. There, on his first night of guard duty, he was sent to secure the motor pool. During the night, he thought he observed an intruder and decided to scare the individual by driving toward him in a five-ton dump truck. In the process, Joe wrecked the truck. Joe was reprimanded and scratched from the post guard duty roster.

Next, Joe fouled up on KP. The mess sergeant had a large recirculating fountain in the foyer of the mess hall in which he kept his prize tropical fish. Joe was assigned to paint the outside of the fountain. He wanted to speed up the job and decided to use a sprayer instead of a brush. The result was that he got a lot of paint in the water and killed all the fish. The mess sergeant threatened to kill Joe if he ever set foot in his mess hall again. Joe was placed on separate rations.

Finally, Joe was sent to Vietnam. Apparently, it was there he could feel at home for the first time in the Army. Being in a combat zone, he paid no income tax. If he was horny, there were plenty of hooch maids available to satisfy his needs. In his words, "Those girls would lay for a quarter." Consequently, behavior which would be questioned anywhere else on earth was acceptable there. He was quickly promoted to buck sergeant.

After a soldier finished a tour of duty in Vietnam, they could remain there for a second year if they requested it. After the second year, they were rotated back to the States. Somehow Joe was allowed to remain in Vietnam for a third straight year. No one ever found out how he accomplished this, but at the end of his third year he was involuntarily compelled to leave Vietnam. By all accounts he had to be forcefully carried onto the plane (while literally kicking and screaming) to be returned to the States. Now Joe was a member of the 290th Military Police Company. Steve was not optimistic as to how well he would fit in.

In total and complete contrast to Joe Katone, SSG Bingham's record was exemplary. Historically, new lieutenants serving as platoon leaders seek to have an outstanding NCO as the ramrod to assist them in running the platoon. No one could have ever found a better qualified man for the job than Bingham. Bingham showed up for work each day with shined boots and a pressed uniform that would make a drill sergeant envious. Katone usually arrived for duty looking like a slob. A steady diet of beer and junk food had caused him to start developing an expanding girth and his uniform, which was usually stained by some part of his last meal, looked like it had been slept in.

NEIL MITCHELL

SSG McCall would be transferring out to Japan in a couple of weeks and Bingham was to take his place as desk sergeant. Katone would be the new patrol superintendent for Bingham's shift.

I met both of our new NCOs as they worked the day shift on Monday. I was amazed at the difference between the two men. One was clearly intelligent and articulate, while the other had a vocabulary that was mostly limited to four-letter words. I wondered how the two would get along.

The final week of class work for our new OJT class began with each section leader coming in and telling about the responsibilities and tasks performed by the personnel under their leadership. My turn came at 1030 hours. As luck would have it, I followed Warren. He had come in dressed to the nines and played the proverbial big shot. As he spoke, I thought he should have a manure spreader to provide an even coat of BS around the room. It was getting so thick that I wanted to tell everyone to grab a shovel. You would have thought that the entire Army revolved around the provost marshal's investigators and physical security section.

When my turn came, I walked to the podium. Warren hesitated at the door to watch my presentation. As always, I began with a joke. "Men," I began, "we have some outstanding personnel here at Fort McCulloch and we work together very well. In fact, some time ago a bunch of us drove down to the Gulf of Mexico to go swimming at the beach. One of our sergeants started complaining that the girls were ignoring him. I told him to go to the produce stand across the road and buy a big cucumber. I said that if he would drop it down his swim trunks, the girls would pay attention to him. He did that, but the girls continued to ignore him. In fact, they gave him disgusted looks if he tried to talk to them. That's when I explained that he had to put the cucumber down the front of his trunks—not the back." I waited a few seconds for the hysterical laughter to subside.

"Men," I began again. "I'm not going to try to snow you or blow smoke up your butt. Most of what happens here at Fort McCulloch is routine and basic stuff, but I insist that it be done right. That way, anyone who spends much time here will be prepared for police work just about anywhere else."

At this point, I introduced Cummings and Gross. They each told a little about the Traffic section duties, with heavy emphasis on the accident investigations. I then mentioned that once the new personnel were assigned, all the section would be certified to operate VASCAR. After

A STATESIDE TOUR OF DUTY

a few questions, there was a ten-minute break, and Sergeant Lippman then began his presentation about the AWOL Apprehension section.

As I walked down the hall from the classroom, I passed by Supply, where Steve motioned for me to enter. "Well, did you catch my presentation to the new men?" I asked.

"I was standing behind Warren and caught most of it," he said.

"What did you think?" Maybe I was fishing for compliments, but I wanted to know his opinion.

He gave me the thumbs-up sign. "Outstanding!" He leaned back in his chair. "Warren didn't seem too happy, though. I think he thought you were belittling his speech and making fun of him."

"I was," I said with a smile.

"That's what I thought," he replied. "Keep up the good work."

After I returned to my office, Warren came into the Traffic section. "I don't mean to be critical, lieutenant, but I think your entire operation is a little flaky."

"How's that, sarge?" I waited for his answer.

"Well for one, you need permission from the FCC to operate your radar unit legally—"

"You mean like this document," I interrupted. I handed him the authorization I had received from the FCC some weeks before.

"Well, yes," he answered as he scanned the paper. He changed the subject. "And another thing, if it gets out that your men are not certified to operate VASCAR, you could have trouble making charges stick in court."

"We haven't issued any tickets using VASCAR since I've been in here, sarge." Of course, I didn't mention the one we had dismissed earlier in court. I pushed my chair back from my desk and continued. "I already have the necessary training lined up for week after next through the Texas Highway Patrol. Then, we'll be checking speeds with VASCAR and issuing tickets."

"Yes, well, I'd love to stay and chat but I have cases to work. I'll see you later, lieutenant." He turned and left the office.

"Anytime, sarge," I replied.

Shortly afterward, Bingham (the new desk sergeant) entered my office. He would be starting on swing shift that afternoon and had come in to talk with Sergeant Dee. "Warren left here like you shot him in the butt, lieutenant. I don't know what you did, but good job."

"We were just discussing my management skills here in Traffic," I explained. "I hope to have the same discussion with him again in about six months. Then we'll see whose operation is flaky."

Bingham shut the door to my office. "I'll tell you what, sir. Warren has to be one of the biggest con men I've ever seen."

"How so, sarge? Tell me about it." Bingham had just arrived the previous Friday night. It was incredible that he already had Warren pegged. My opinion of this man was rising by the minute.

"Well, sir," he began. "I came in last night to get acquainted with the men I'll be working with, and McCall left the desk for a couple of hours to ride with his men. Warren calls me up and tells me that, starting at 1900 hours, he wants me to call him at the colonel's quarters every fifteen minutes."

"Why did he want you to do that?"

"That's what I was wondering, sir. But I did as he requested, and the moment I got him on the line he would say something like 'I'm aware of that' or 'Okay, keep me informed' or 'I'll have my men give me a full briefing in the morning.' In other words, Warren was trying to con the colonel into thinking he is a lot busier with his case load than he is. The man is just a hustler and a con artist."

"Well, sarge, that doesn't surprise me a bit. I really appreciate the information."

Bingham continued. "Well, there's more. When McCall got back, I told him and he admitted that Warren does that about once a week. I guess Warren pulls a lot of weight with the front office, so McCall figures that it's to his benefit to help him out. If that's the way they do things around here, lieutenant, I won't be a good member of the team."

"That might be the way Warren works, but there's a lot of us that don't work that way. It's good to know you take pride in your work, sarge. It's good to have you here." I stuck out my hand and we shook hands. After he left my office, I added our conversation to the information I was compiling on Warren.

I don't wish to sound like a hypocrite. I had employed the same tactic Warren had used earlier to have more of the new men assigned to me. I did it as a one-time event, whereas for Warren it was constant activity. I suspected, also, that Warren would use the tactic to rip off more money from the government somehow. Warren had seven investigators working for him in addition to a clerk. Only two of those investigators now worked with Warren out of the PMO. He had two men living in

A STATESIDE TOUR OF DUTY

Brownsville, one in Houston, one in Beaumont and one in Shreveport. These men received twenty-five dollars per diem plus ten cents a mile, in addition to their regular pay and allowances. The U.S. government was paying a lot to keep Warren's men in the field. It seemed to me that the government was getting very little in return. In the past six months, there had been eleven separate break-ins of arms room at National Guard armories or ROTC buildings (all unsolved cases). This seemed to be of little concern to the physical security section. Their reports always ended with the statement, "Case closed for lack of investigative leads."

Wednesday, the blotter detailed the latest break-in. An ROTC arms room at a high school was the latest victim. Thirty M14 rifles had been taken. The subjects had simply chopped through a wooden door to gain entry. It was evident that the school had not complied with regulations. It was a joke to think that Warren's people were on the job.

Friday morning, Steve made one of his rare appearances at the PMO. He came into my office with the results of the manpower study in his hand. The CO was gone for a week on leave and, as acting CO, Steve was the first to receive the completed report. "Congratulations, Nick," he said. "You won the manpower lottery."

"How's that?" I asked.

"Turn to page four, old buddy. You will love what you read." He tossed the document on my desk.

Cummings came over to my desk as I turned the pages and began to read. "The Traffic section is responsible for all accident investigation on the military reservation. A detailed examination of records indicates an accident frequency of .74 accidents per day, occurring at all hours around the clock. Consequently, with one TI (traffic investigator) on call at all times the personnel are stretched quite thin. This diminishes the amount of speed enforcement available on the state highways, resulting in higher average speeds which, no doubt, results in more accidents. . . ."

"Hot damn, sir," Cummings exulted. "Do we do good work, or not?" We gave each other a high five.

"You're not to the best part yet," Steve insisted.

I scanned down the page of the detailed list of duties we had assigned to us and quickly found the expert's recommendation. I continued to read. "The Traffic section should be enlarged to a minimum of four investigators, with a clerk to type reports and file paperwork. This will allow for the investigative personnel to make optimal use of their time."

Cummings was beside himself with joy. "Four men? This is great!"

"Minimum of four men," Steve reminded.

"Wait a minute, there's more," I stated.

"More?" Cummings asked.

I continued to read. "It is the opinion of this manpower specialist that the section also should have an NCOIC to assist in the supervision of personnel. This will free up the officer in charge to ensure that proper training and readiness levels are provided for and guarantee that all federal regulations are complied with by section personnel."

The look on Cummings' face showed that he was not happy with that recommendation. That would drop him to at least third place in the section as senior investigator. "Now, Cummings, you will only have to be on call once every four weeks instead of every other week," I reminded him. That made him a little happier.

Steve now drew my attention to another part of the report. "Look on page seven, under administrative personnel," he said.

When I read the recommendation, I couldn't believe it. Civilian secretarial staff was to be cut from two to one. "That will piss off the colonel," I noted.

"I figure that Julene is gone," Steve surmised. "Susan takes the colonel coffee, while Julene calls his wife Fifi. Even if the colonel doesn't know that, he still shows favoritism toward Susan."

"Will Julene lose her job?" Even if I didn't know Julene very well, I still hated to see anyone become unemployed.

Steve's retort was, "Are you kidding? Julene is civil service. Those people never lose their jobs. She will just be reassigned, probably to Headquarters."

With that, my thoughts came back to the Traffic section. "This news for us is great—"

Steve cut me off. "I was supposed to show this to the colonel first," he said. "When you next hear about this, you have to pretend that you're hearing about it for the first time. Remember, you never saw this before."

"You got it, pal," I said. "I'll swear on a stack of Bibles that I never saw that before."

With that, Steve left. It was about 1500 hours before the colonel called a meeting of all section personnel and desk sergeants.

In addition to the changes in the Traffic section, the rangers would obtain five new men. The PMI section would be enlarged by three, each relief would be expanded by four men, the orderly room would gain another clerk and our satellite garrison at Camp Sterling Price would gain twelve additional troops. Vehicle registration and AWOL Apprehension were the only PMO sections whose personnel requirements would remain unchanged.

As the meeting broke up, Sergeant Corley caught me in the hallway. "Sir," he began, "the colonel mentioned that the Traffic section would be getting an NCOIC. I would like to volunteer for the position."

"Great, sarge. I'll let the colonel know that you're interested." If the truth were known, I would have preferred Sergeant Bingham, but Sergeant Corley would be a very capable man for the position. Corley likewise knew a good deal when he saw it. He would leave the shift work of line duty and gain the regular 0800–1700 position in the Traffic section. A cushy position like Traffic NCOIC was something to go after.

I caught up with Bingham a little later. I offered him the position. I was a little surprised by his answer.

"I appreciate the offer, sir, I really do," he began, "but the job will probably be mostly administrative. All patrol activity is coordinated by the police desk, and I like being where the action is. If you don't mind, sir, I'd like to remain on the desk. But, again, I really appreciate your asking me."

That was enough for me. With Bingham turning me down, I would recommend Corley's name to the colonel for Traffic NCOIC.

That night I gave Sam the good news. She was excited for me.

"My husband, the empire builder," she teased.

"I had no idea of my own persuasiveness," I bragged. "I was looking for another man to supervise, and wound up getting an additional four instead."

"Watch out, honey. If you let your head get any larger, it won't fit through the door of our trailer. You'll have to sleep in the car." She playfully hugged me.

"Honey," I objected, "there is no conceit in my family."

"That's because you have it all," was her comeback.

Despite her teasing, I knew that Sam was happy for me. I should be the Operations officer or company XO, but Traffic officer would do just fine. I could conduct traffic studies, coordinate with the post Safety office and Post Engineers and oversee Magistrate's Court. Byron and Steve might be my superiors on the official organizational chart, but my job would be one of much higher profile than theirs. Also, I could spend time on the road with my men, away from the prying eyes of the major.

Steve and Byron would be desk-bound most of the time, with superiors constantly able to look over their shoulders

After filling Sam in on the events of the day, I turned my attention to her. I listened as she told me about the friendships she was developing among the neighbors. Byron and his wife lived on the other side of the large trailer court, so Sam never had to run into Kathy Raymond. Since she was an officer's wife, the women who lived around us had been slow to warm up to her. As their husbands were enlisted men, there was a normal reaction to shun her. Slowly, however, they began to see her as someone who cared for the individual, irrespective of what that person's station in life was. It seemed that the most often repeated phrase she heard was, "You're not like other officers' wives. You're down to earth and normal and not snooty." As usual, Sam accepted this for the compliment that it was.

"I invited Andrea and her husband over to play canasta tonight. I hope that's okay," Sam said.

"No problem, sweetie. It sounds like fun." In the Army, officers and their wives traditionally play bridge, while enlisted men play canasta, pinochle or hearts. Sam resisted learning to play bridge. I don't know if she was intimidated by its complexity, or just wanted to avoid a game she felt was played by elitist, snotty people. Either way it didn't matter. "I'm happy to see that you're making friends, Sam," was my only additional comment.

Sergeant Cunningham and his wife, Andrea, came over at 7:00 PM sharp. He seemed a little uneasy at first and called me sir.

"Please call me Nick," I said. "If you ever run into me on post, in uniform, then you can call me sir. But around here, I'm a neighbor first and an officer as a distant second."

"Call me Tom," he said as we shook hands. With that, he relaxed and the rest of the evening was fun. Sam had popped some popcorn and bought some soft drinks and they didn't leave until after midnight.

"Next time, you guys need to come to our place, so we won't have to pay a baby-sitter," Tom said as they were leaving.

"We'll consider that an invitation, then," I said.

"Good, we'll have a rematch next Saturday, then," he said.

As we went to bed, Sam was still asking if I had any reservations about having our enlisted neighbors over. My answer was to the point. "Not at all, honey. I thought it was fun."

A STATESIDE TOUR OF DUTY

"Good," said Sam, "because we're going to take them up on that invitation to go over next Saturday night."

On Monday morning, the week began with a torrential downpour. The cantonment area of Fort McCulloch didn't often receive a great deal of rain. When it did rain, it made up for the remainder of the time. Rain usually meant accidents, and with this deluge there would be a lot of them. The week did not seem to be beginning well.

Thirty minutes after arriving at the office, Sergeant Corley came into the Traffic section. Right behind him was his former patrol superintendent, Sergeant Brown, and Private Byrd from the OJT class.

Corley got right to the point. "They are going to be allocating the new troops this morning at 1000, sir. Before they do, I wanted to make some suggestions."

"Please do, sarge."

"Well, sir. Since the Traffic section generally requires a little more expertise and experience than line duty, I think we ought to bring Brown in. He's been a patrol sup. Also, Byrd here finished at the top of the OJT class. I think he ought to be the fourth investigator. Whoever they give us for a clerk won't matter, as long as the guy can type."

Sergeant Corley's advice made sense. "I like your thinking, sarge. Let's go talk to Operations."

Corley smiled. "Sir, I've already suggested it to de la Vega. He thought it was a great idea and will see that it gets done. I told him that I had already talked with you."

"Well, sarge, next time make sure you do talk with me first. Let's make sure that we always do things right." While I did admire Corley's initiative, it still irritated me a little that he didn't check with me first. After all, I was the officer in charge.

Within the hour, I was notified that the personnel assignments Corley had suggested had been implemented. In addition, Private Moss had been assigned to us as a clerk. I had Brown work with Cummings and Byrd assist Gross for the remainder of the day. There were only two accidents (each with no major injuries), so each pair got to investigate one. I spent the day with Sergeant Corley and Moss, getting them familiar with the reports we had to submit and showing where everything was filed.

Wednesday, after court, I dropped in to see Steve. He had moved out of the supply room and into another office. He was looking at one of Sergeant Winters' pornographic magazines. It featured one thousand pictures (at least that's what the cover said—I didn't count them).

"Those of us that don't have a hot little wife to go home to have to make do with visual stimulation," he said with a grin.

"Visual, hell," I replied. "I've seen the girls you go out with. Don't give me that visual crap."

"That's on weekends, Nick. The rest of the time, this is all the action I get. But you're right. The girls I go out with sure beat these dogs. If these women weren't naked, I wouldn't even look at them." He threw the magazine in a drawer. I smiled because I suspected that as soon as Steve gained a full-time girlfriend, he would have to forget those magazines. Sam would not tolerate me looking at them, and if Steve gained a steady companion—she wouldn't either.

Suddenly, Sergeant Winters entered Steve's office. Men in the military have a reputation for coarse language, but of all those acquaintances I've made, Winters was one of the worst. When he opened his mouth to speak, the plethora of obscenities that issued forth was the foulest I had ever heard. His utterances constituted a complete verbal rape of the world in general and all femininity in specificity. After only a few minutes around Winters, your ears began to burn. If it was possible for someone to be a connoisseur of the profane, the honor belonged to Winters. It was no wonder that Steve had found another office.

In between all of his cuss words, Winters asked Steve, "Care to go over to Self-Service sir? I need to pick up a few things."

"I have to finish a report, sarge," Steve responded. "Lieutenant Moultrie here can probably go with you though."

I could have guessed that I shouldn't have agreed to go. Steve's passing up a chance to leave the company area was a dead giveaway that this errand was not one I should undertake.

Without thinking of that, I said, "No problem, sarge. Let's go." It would be the first and only time I would ever ride in the same vehicle with Winters.

As he drove down the street, Winters would stick his head out his window and administer a wolf whistle or yell a suggestive or risqué comment at every female that we passed.

"Hey, baby! Sit on my face tonight," he yelled at one woman.

He whistled and yelled, "You have a nice set of tits," to another.

After my initial shock, I angrily snapped, "Knock that off, sarge; you're attracting too much attention."

"It's okay, sir," he said between yells. "Women love compliments."

A STATESIDE TOUR OF DUTY

"I don't think they take those comments as compliments," I said. "That's more like an assault."

"You're too uptight, sir. This is 1970," Winters continued. "You have to change with the times, women today—" He turned his attention to two black teenage girls walking on the sidewalk. He yelled, "Hi ,you gorgeous pieces of ass, let's have a threesome."

In my whole life, I have never been so embarrassed. If I could have shrunk myself down and crawled into the ash tray, I would have done it. Again I demanded Winters stop his verbal escapades. "Damn it, sarge! Ignore the girls and keep your mind on your driving. You'll get us into an accident if you keep this up," I said angrily.

Winters was definitely a man in denial. He saw nothing wrong with what he was doing. "You need to relax, sir. Women love it even though they pretend not to." Winters then turned his attention to a young lady in a very short mini skirt. He yelled between wolf whistles, "Bend over and show me your pussy." She angrily showed him the middle finger of her left hand instead.

That shout was the most disgusting yet. It was the lowest of the low. I sank down into my seat hoping no one would see me. I also found myself wishing I could have fit into the glove compartment. I would have spent the entire ride there if I could have.

Finally, we reached self-service. This was a military-style hardware store where cleaning supplies, paint and other items for routine maintenance were obtained. All the post units had an account there and could charge up to a certain amount each month. I helped Winters round up the supplies he needed and get them into the car. Then came the delightful return trip to the company area.

Winters continued to be oblivious to my attempts to have him shut up as he shouted his "compliments" to women on the sidewalk. Our drive back to work seemed to be one of the longest I had ever taken. I kept bending over, pretending to dust off my shoes or to pick up items on the floor so my face would not be visible in the passenger-side window.

After our return, Steve had an ear-to-ear grin that looked like the cat that swallowed the canary. He asked, "Enjoy your ride with Winters?"

I shook my head. "Steve, no offense, but sometimes you can be a bastard."

Steve continued to laugh. "When I rode with him, I kept trying to crawl under the seat, but I couldn't fit. Did you have better luck than I did?"

"No I didn't fit either." I continued my commentary. "For one of the few times in my life, though, I wanted to die. I'm never riding with that son of a bitch again."

"No kidding," Steve agreed. "If I have to go somewhere with him, I just tell him I'll meet him there and drive over in my car."

Like most men, I learned all the cuss words at an early age. I'm not a prude. A little profanity doesn't bother me. But Winters' lexicon was so horrendous that I tended to avoid the supply room. Many of us will use a little profanity to emphasize a point, but Winter's language was a vulgar overload that desecrated all humanity that heard it.

The next two days that followed, I had my men get as much practice on the VASCAR unit as possible. The highway patrol would test us for certification that next Monday.

At home, Sam had occasional bouts of morning sickness, but she didn't let it affect her day. In fact, there was a nice side effect. Being pregnant seemed to increase her sex drive. Almost every night she came to bed in the buff and showed me a very good time. Often, after making love, I would kiss or rub her belly and look forward to the time when it would get larger.

"Nick!" she would protest. "I can't believe you would want me to get fat."

"You won't be fat," I explained. "You're pregnant. Pregnant women are supposed to have a big belly. Pregnant women are the only ones in our society who can go around showing off the fact that they're sexually active. Like Bill Cosby once said, 'The husband gets to go around saying, "Look what I did."' Everyone will know that Lieutenant Moultrie got at least one good piece of tail."

"Nick, I swear that's all you think about," Sam commented.

"No it isn't, honey," I said in my defense. "But it is a great start. Besides, you love me anyway."

"Sometimes, I have to wonder why," she said playfully.

"Maybe it's because I like the beautiful glow you have about you since you became pregnant," I answered. She put her arms around my shoulders and gave me a big kiss.

Friday, the 23rd, another lieutenant was assigned to the 290th MP Company. Steve brought him by my office as they made the rounds introducing him to everyone. His name was 1LT David W. Geoffrey. A few inches below the lieutenant's bars on his shoulders, his khaki uniform sleeve had the telltale marks where NCO chevrons had once been sewed.

A STATESIDE TOUR OF DUTY

The man was a former E-7. After our introduction, Geoffrey went up front to meet with the colonel while Steve stayed behind to talk.

I asked Steve, "What in the world are we going to do with another lieutenant around here? We're way overstaffed on officers as it is."

"The word I get," answered Steve, "Is that they will move Raymond into PMI and make this guy the new Operations officer. You may find this hard to believe, but the guy has a Ph.D. in criminology from the University of Maryland."

"What is he doing here?" I asked.

Steve thought for a second. "I guess he's just lucky. Kind of like us."

I later found that after finishing his last tour in Vietnam, Geoffrey had completed his doctorate and had received a direct commission to first lieutenant. Even though Geoffrey had landed initially at Fort McCulloch, the Army probably had great plans for him.

Unfortunately, it was not to be. His military career would soon be derailed, as he would shortly become the next victim of Sergeant Warren.

CHAPTER NINETEEN

As the duty officer for the week, I had to attend the morning briefing. I had almost forgotten about this little duty since Raymond had become Operations officer. But Warren was not in attendance and the meeting was short. I was careful not to make any facetious remarks to irritate the major, who had completed five more patrol tips, and by 1000 hours I was in my office.

Texas Highway Patrol trooper Samuel H. Grant met me at that time. He was the man responsible for training and certifying people in the use of VASCAR for our region of Texas. While federal personnel were not required to be certified, I knew that doing so would eliminate an opportunity for people to contest speeding tickets. Grant had previously provided me with the necessary training materials for my men, so all he had to do was test our ability.

We calibrated our equipment and Grant explained that everyone would check his vehicle's speed a total of fifteen times. There would be five times following, five approaching and five clocking from the side of the road. As we did so, he would be recording his speed and our difference should not average more than .5 miles per hour. Grant then stated that since there was no legal requirement for my men to be certified and since some of my men were very new to this equipment ,he would pass us even if our rate of difference was as high as .75 miles per hour. I would be the first one tested.

After my fifteen checks, my average difference was .38 miles per hour. "You passed with flying colors, lieutenant. Let's hope your men do as well," Grant said.

I spent the remainder of the tests riding with Grant in his vehicle and kept touch with my men via walkie-talkies. Operating VASCAR is an exercise in timing, depth perception and intelligence, and our practice paid off. Sergeant Corley did the worst with an average difference of .77 miles per hour. "You guys usually give a leeway of ten to fifteen miles per hour, don't you?" asked Grant.

"Yes, we do," I replied.

"List him as .75 then and I'll pass him," Grant said. "I suspect that you and he will probably not be using VASCAR very much anyway."

Grant was right. The chance of Corley and me writing tickets was slim to none. "You got it," I replied.

The rest of the men tested at between .51 and .68 miles per hour difference. We could now use the VASCAR unit with no questions asked. As Grant looked at the results he had two comments. "It looks like you did a good job, lieutenant. Your men were ready. Also, I've always believed the man in charge should be the best at doing the job. You can clearly do that."

"Thanks, I said. I appreciate that." Grant would deliver our certificates of proficiency for VASCAR in a few days, but we could write tickets immediately.

Like Steve and myself, in the past, 1LT Geoffrey spent the first few days at his new assignment getting acclimated. He toured the law enforcement facilities and got to know everyone. Warren was out of town, but he met with all the other section chiefs and desk sergeants. Geoffrey was about five foot ten inches tall and had wavy blond hair. He seemed to be of an affable, friendly sort.

Wednesday morning several of us were seated around the conference table awaiting the colonel's arrival when Warren walked in. As he spotted Warren, Geoffrey's smile disappeared and his mouth turned into a snarl. As Warren pulled a chair away from the table to be seated, his eyes met Geoffrey's. Warren paused for a second with his posterior hovering over the chair, as he seemed unsure whether to sit or remain standing. The two glared at each other briefly and Warren regained his composure first.

"I've got a case to work," said Warren. "I'll see you later." He then stood erect and proceeded hastily out of the room.

With anger in his voice, Geoffrey asked, "How in the hell did that man get back into the Army?"

"Apparently, you know Warren from a previous duty station," I stated.

"Vietnam," he said in a matter-of-fact manner. "He was a part of Wooldridge's NCO club scandal. I spent a lot of time on that case before I got commissioned."

"Warren's a changed man, lieutenant," Prince interjected. "He was allowed back into the Army and he's working hard to put the past behind him."

Any further discussion of Warren was cut short by the arrival of the colonel. We all stood and said, "Morning, sir."

"Morning, men. Be seated," said the colonel, as he picked up his copy of the blotter and Susan brought him a cup of coffee.

The morning briefing went as usual until the end, when the colonel asked for questions or comments around the table. When it was Geoffrey's turn, he took a moment to answer. Geoffrey seemed to have some difficulty enunciating his question. It was clear that he had no use for Warren. "Sir, I, uh, met Sergeant Warren earlier. What is his position here?"

A puzzled look came over the colonel's face as he answered the question. "Warren runs our PMI section and does an excellent job, lieutenant. You'll probably find him easy to work with."

Prince then added, "Warren is a hard worker and doesn't bear any grudges. I'm sure you'll be able to work together, lieutenant."

Geoffrey straightened up in his chair. "I see," was his only comment.

After that, Geoffrey and Warren seemed to avoid each other. Warren was not to be seen at the morning briefings and Geoffrey avoided PMI's wing of the building. If Warren had occasion to frequent the desk area, Geoffrey was suddenly preoccupied with something in Operations. If Warren needed something from Operations he sent the PMI clerk with written instructions from him.

If Steve and I tried to talk to Geoffrey about Warren, he simply said curtly, "I have nothing to say on the subject of Warren." The relationship between Warren and Geoffrey reminded me of an uneasy truce in the middle of a war.

With our now expanded Traffic section, two new desks were brought in. Sergeant Corley put his directly across from mine. Private Moss had his across from the equipment closet and the four investigators shared the remaining two desks. Brown and Gross shared one with Cummings and Byrd using the other. With Corley directly supervising the men, I now turned my attention to other matters. I began to prepare a plan for observing and checking speeds from aircraft and investigated the possibility of starting some public relations programs such as calibrating speedometers for the public. I also checked into moving Magistrate's Court to more dignified surroundings. In addition, Corley and I could now cover for each other if one of us left early or was late getting back from lunch. In these cases, if someone (such as the major) asked for our whereabouts, we simply stated that the other had just stepped out and would be returning shortly. If we thought it necessary, or if we were asked, we had a list of places which corresponded to different days. So, if it was Wednesday, for example, and I was asked where Sergeant Corley was, I would inform the inquiring party that he had gone to Battalion. That way, if the interrogator asked Corley where he had been, he knew what to say without my informing him what I had said. In addition, if one of us came in after 1700 hours to accompany one of our men while they patrolled with radar or VASCAR, there was always compensatory time available. Also with the additional manpower, there was always someone in the office to talk to while I did paperwork. The new arrangement was working outstandingly well.

Saturday night was Halloween, so Sam and I postponed our canasta appointment with the neighbors to pass out candy to trick-or-treaters. As one group of costumed kids left the trailer, Sam commented, "I can't wait until our children are big enough to do things like that."

"You better wait until we have some kids before you start wishing them to be half grown," I replied.

"Oh, Nick! You know what I mean," Sam said.

I did indeed know what she meant, and to tell the truth I felt the same way she did.

I couldn't remain at home for long. Being duty officer on Halloween means extra hours. That is one night when every vandal and practical joker assumes they have the right to wreak havoc. The MP desk gets about ten times the number of calls it does on a regular Saturday night, and a good many are prank calls. At times like this, an experienced desk sergeant is worth his weight in gold. He can quickly prioritize the calls and cull out the obviously phony ones. In addition, he knows that would-be troublemakers usually call in a bomb threat or report a nonexistent disturbance to keep law enforcement personnel away while they create their mischief. While an experienced desk sergeant does send a police unit to the location the caller identified, it is only one unit. The others are dispatched to other potential trouble spots. Many would-be pranksters have had their trouble-making interrupted, or prevented, by this tactic.

To keep problems to a minimum, the post commander had required all trick-or-treaters to be completed with their rounds by 1900 hours. He also declared a curfew of 2200 hours for all children under the age of 17. The only exceptions were those accompanied by parents or those who were out due to employment. These rules were rigidly enforced and were a big help in preventing trouble.

Still, it was a busy night. By the time Steve came into the PMO shortly before 2400 hours to take over as duty officer, I was ready to go home. I was up behind the desk reading through the desk log and the blotter as he entered the building.

"You should have been here earlier. You missed all the fun," I said sarcastically to Steve.

"I'm sure there will be more before morning," he replied.

As he came up the stairs to the back of the desk to check out a side arm, he smiled and said, "I trust you kept the citizenry safe and maintained law and order tonight."

"The post is still on the map, so I guess we did some good."

We continued to talk as we walked back out the main entrance. The relief coming on duty was forming up for guard mount, so while he performed that chore I headed for my car.

After the long night, Sam and I slept late Sunday morning. With most of the businesses closed in Harrisville, many people seemed to dislike Sunday. I had heard many complain that the day was boring, with nothing to do. For me, that made for a perfect day. I didn't have to go to work and there wasn't a great deal of traffic on the roads, so it was a nice, relaxing day. If Sam and I wished to go for a drive or go on a picnic, we could take our time. The nights were becoming cooler, and Sam and I sometimes just went for a stroll. It was nice to go for a walk, holding hands like a couple of kids. Of course, any walk that took place on Sunday night had to be over in time for us to get home for my favorite TV program, *All In The Family*.

While most people watched the program to enjoy the one-liners of the lovable bigot played by Carroll O'Connor (Archie Bunker), the character I paid the most attention to was the Meathead, played by Rob Reiner. His character (Michael Stivic) was an academic idiot whose half-wit brain only allowed him to parrot the latest left-wing rhetoric spewed out by his college professors.

I figured that by watching the show I would be kept current with the latest moronic oratory being taught in the ivy towers of America's academia. I have always believed that one should know his enemy, and the universities of the United States were producing the Students for Democratic Society (SDS) and other anarchistic groups, which were definitely my enemies. I figured that my viewership of that television show would allow me to know what I might expect from them. I was not disappointed by that assessment. According to the Meathead, the United States used the doctrine of Manifest Destiny to steal Texas from Mexico and "The Star-Spangled Banner" was a terrible song that glorified war. Never mind that the Texans had revolted from the despotic rule of Santa Ana after he had rescinded the Mexican Constitution of 1824 and ruled as a dictator. Never mind that Hispanic residents of Texas had fought shoulder-to-shoulder with their Anglo counterparts in fighting for their rights. And, of course, never mind that Texas had only requested statehood after nine years as an independent country, during which they were constantly threatened with aggression from the south. In the minds of all left-wing politicos, anything done in history by the United States has always been automatically wrong. Watching that TV show reminded me that those people existed in the world. I would have to do whatever I could to counter their arguments or logic whenever I encountered them.

Equally irritating was the idea that our national anthem glorified war. Those who have studied history know that a few heavily outnumbered and out-gunned Americans at Fort McHenry, Maryland, in 1814 managed to stand off the entire British navy. Then the next morning, as the sun was rising, the Americans raised a giant flag, in defiance, to meet the dawn. The words "conquer we must, when our cause it is just" set a standard for the world. While I had ambivalent feelings about the conflict in Southeast Asia, certainly our cause was infinitely more just that those of the Communist warlords we were fighting. When I thought of the courageous men who raised that flag in 1814 and inspired the writing of "The Star-Spangled Banner," my service at Fort McCulloch seemed so insignificant.

Monday morning, I was making some calls to close some of our Blue Bell cases. As I went through the pile of manila folders, I came to the case involving the soldier shot in Lutzville.

I looked over at Sergeant Corley. "I guess I had better call down to Lutzville and find out what their local county officials did with this case. How do you think it went for the kid who shot the soldier, sarge?"

"Hell, sir," replied Corley. "Why call? We can probably drive down cheaper than what the long-distance call would cost. Besides, the nice drive will give us something to do this morning."

"Let's go," I replied.

Two of our investigators were filling out paperwork, so we had a vehicle available. With Corley driving we were soon headed down the road for Lutzville. Within twenty minutes we were approaching the Lutzville city limits. As we did, Corley quickly slowed the car down to twenty miles per hour. Corley filled me in on some of the local history as we drove into town.

"About two years ago, sir, one of the local politicians wasn't getting his share of the graft, so he contacted the FBI and let them know some of the illegalities that were going on around here. Before the federal people could meet with him and get his official deposition, his wife shot him six times with a single action-revolver. The local coroner ruled it an accidental shooting."

"You've got to be kidding," I said in amazement.

"Not at all, sir," he continued. "Apparently, the guy and his wife weren't getting along very well. I figure the people in charge gave her permission to shoot him. That got him out of their hair, and she could try to collect his life insurance."

"Do you know if she was able to collect it?"

"Well, sir, the last I heard, the insurance company was fighting her. The local judge ruled in her favor but the insurance company appealed the case. As I understand it, the State Court of Appeals reversed the decision, and her lawyers are now trying to get the case before the State Supreme Court," Corley explained.

"Sounds like Lutzville and the surrounding county is a wonderful place to call home," I said with a shake of my head.

"Oh, you don't know the half of it, sir. On election day, people who have been dead for years wind up voting. It's worse than Chicago." Corley paused in his narrative for a few seconds. I wasn't sure if he was just collecting his thoughts or letting me contemplate our destination.

Corley continued. "About a year ago a tourist was beaten and almost killed there. The governor put up billboards on both sides of town, warning travelers not to get caught in a speed trap or robbed in a clip joint. He then had state highway patrolmen guard the signs with shotguns."

I asked the obvious. "Are the signs still there?"

"No, sir. It was costing the state over a thousand dollars a day to maintain them. The state finally gave up and let the locals change the billboards." Corley then added, "When the local political boss gives a barbecue, big shots from several surrounding counties show up for it. He swings a lot of weight in this part of the country."

A STATESIDE TOUR OF DUTY

Corley's account of local events was over by the time we reached the courthouse. We parked the car and went inside. We entered the county attorney's office, and on the other side of the counter several men were sitting around a desk talking. One turned out to be the sheriff. The others were the county attorney, coroner, and several other local officials.

We identified ourselves and, after the usual pleasantries, I told why we were there. "I have to send in a report to Fifth Army about the soldier who got shot a while back here in town," I began. "I just needed to get some information about how the case was adjudicated."

"Well," the county attorney began. "The grand jury meets this afternoon to indict the shooter, and the trial will be tomorrow."

"Then you will have a barbecue tomorrow night to celebrate his acquittal," Corley said with a big smile. I gave the sergeant a quick and not-so-subtle kick in the side of the leg.

"I don't know if his family has anything like that planned, but the chances are good he won't be found guilty," the local official continued. "After all, the young man was acting in self-defense and he did shoot the soldier in the foot."

I was dumbfounded by that last comment, but Corley couldn't pass up a chance to say something. "No. Haven't you heard? He shot the soldier in the heart and he died." I kicked Corley in the side of the leg again.

A young lady who couldn't have been over twenty-two years of age had been typing at a desk over on the left side of the room. After Corley's remark, she suddenly jumped up and in a hysterical manner exclaimed, "No. He can't be dead. Matt just shot him in the foot. He can't be dead. He just can't."

At this point, I figured it was time to go. The soldier had been shot in the chest, just above the heart. He had survived, but just barely. Between Corley's fib and the girl's hysterics, I just wanted to stay out of trouble. I thanked the men for the information and wished them a good day. Corley and I then headed back to Fort McCulloch.

"They have it figured out," Corley said. "Once he gets acquitted, double jeopardy will prevent him from ever being tried again. He's practically home free."

"That must have been his girlfriend that was typing," I surmised.

"Girlfriend or sister. She was related or involved with him somehow," Corley said. "I still can't believe that they said he shot the man in the foot."

"What was the purpose of those comments you made back there?" I asked. "Were you trying to get us killed?" Corley's previous story definitely had me spooked.

"No, sir," Corley said slowly. "I figured with two of us there, and one of us an officer, our chances of getting out okay were pretty good. I thought it was worth seeing the look on their faces."

That night, I told Sam about my travels earlier that day. She could hardly believe it.

"That sounds like something you see in a movie, Nick." She then asked, "You're not exaggerating, are you?"

"No, honey, I'm not." I then added, "I don't think we are going to travel through Lutzville, if there is any way we can avoid it."

"I think that would be a very good idea," she agreed.

I then tried to put her mind at ease. "As soon as we get Texas tags for our car, we probably won't have anything to worry about anyway. As I understand it, the Lutzville cops mostly just stop people with out-of-state tags."

The next Thursday afternoon, Geoffrey and I were walking back to the PMO from the orderly room, where we had a meeting with the CO. We approached the building just as Warren and one of his investigators were leaving. Warren nodded and said a quick greeting, "Afternoon."

The man with him, a fat dumpy SP4 named Devers, asked, "How you fellas doin' today?"

Geoffrey turned on his heel and snapped, "The word's 'sir.'"

Warren and Devers were both surprised by Geoffrey's anger. They turned and listened as the lieutenant continued his rebuke. "Wearing those civilian clothes might allow you to avoid saluting officers, but you still call us sir."

Warren took off his sunglasses and put them in his pocket. Having had a few seconds to think, he commented, "Make a man an officer and it sure goes to his head."

"We know each other, Warren. Remember! So, don't try to get to me with that old put-down," Geoffrey countered.

Warren simply said, "Yesss, *sir.*" He stretched out the yes and placed added inflection on the sir to indicate his annoyance. The two then eyed each other for a few seconds before Warren asked, "Will that be all, *sir*?" Again, to show his irritation, he placed a heavy emphasis on the word "sir."

Geoffrey hesitated for a second before answering, "Yes, that will be all." As they walked away Geoffrey turned to me. He had one question.

"By the way, is it true that those clowns conduct their physical security inspections in civilian clothes?"

"I haven't witnessed the inspections personally, but that is my understanding," I replied. "Why do you ask?"

"Because it's against regulations." Geoffrey smiled before his next comment. "I think it's about time someone notified CID that they're not doing everything by the book."

"Well, you have an office where you can shut the door and avoid eavesdroppers," I advised. "I certainly wouldn't know anything about it."

Nothing else was said as we walked into the PMO, but within the hour CID received a tip that the PMI physical security inspectors were working in civilian clothes. They made a few calls to verify that was indeed the case, and at that point WO3 Jarvis put in a call to Commanding General Cinch. Once the general was apprised of the situation, he called the colonel and ordered him to end the practice of inspecting military sites in civilian clothes.

The next morning, the colonel met with Prince and Warren. It was Julene's last day at the PMO before joining the staff at Headquarters, and she later filled me in on what happened next. According to her, the colonel came quickly to the point. "Sergeant Warren, the post commander called me yesterday and ordered me to terminate the practice of conducting physical security inspections in civilian clothes. Will that hamper your operations?"

Without hesitation, Warren answered, "Yes, sir. We'll do what you say, but you know as well as I that if some officer sees a spec four coming that he won't pay as much attention as he would to a fellow officer. If the inspector is in civilian clothes, they don't know what rank the inspector is and they are more apt to listen."

The colonel thought for a moment before speaking. "That's true," he mused. After pondering for a few seconds more he stated, "You do what you think is necessary, and I'll handle the general." Even though any of the inspected sites could have informed CID, the colonel apparently assumed the tip came from within the PMO. He asked, "How is this information getting out, anyway?"

"Well, sir," Warren began. "I'm not one to bad-mouth anybody who is not around, but I've had trouble with Geoffrey lately. We knew each other in 'Nam back when I had that trouble, and he seems to be the kind who doesn't forget. I know that I've made mistakes but, dammit, I've paid for 'em. Now I think they ought to be forgotten."

"Right, sarge," the colonel replied. "What has Geoffrey done?"

Warren paused for a second. "Well, sir," he began. "He's tried to harass me and my men. He makes a big deal out of wanting to be called 'sir' and be saluted. I think getting that silver bar has gone to his head."

Sergeant Prince then interjected a thought. "Maybe you should have a chat with Geoffrey, colonel. He used to be an NCO, so he should know better. I'm sure you could explain the facts of life to him."

"No," replied the colonel. "Let's watch him closely and see how he acts from now on. If he is a troublemaker, we'll let him hang himself."

Julene finished the story with, "I couldn't believe that the colonel would take a chance defying the general."

"Remember, Julene, he can always claim that the PMI personnel are ignoring orders and put the problem back on them," I replied.

I guessed that as the meeting ended, Warren knew exactly how he'd take care of Geoffrey. He would set him up Monday morning. The colonel always arrived promptly at 0800 hours for the morning briefing. Warren probably figured that if he timed things right, Geoffrey would be out of his hair permanently.

As the week began, Sam and I were having breakfast when the phone rang. Sam answered it.

"Hello?" she said, before handing it to me. "It's for you, honey."

I took the receiver and answered it. "Hello, this is Lieutenant Moultrie."

It was Steve. "Nick, you won't believe this, but Warren is wearing his uniform. I'm filling in for the CO at the briefing this morning and Warren is dressed like a regular soldier. I thought you might want to hurry in and see this; it might be the only time it ever happens."

"Warren's wearing a uniform?" I repeated. "Are you talking about a military uniform?"

"Yep," he answered. "Regulation fatigues with E-6 chevrons and everything."

"What's the special occasion?" I wondered.

"I don't know," he replied. "But, Warren's definitely up to something, Nick. This is the first time I've ever seen him dressed like this."

"Thanks, buddy. I'll have to go up front and check out that sight this morning." As I hung up the phone, I knew something was going on. I just didn't know what it was. Fortunately, Steve filled me in later.

At the PMO, as each section chief arrived, Warren steered the conversation toward the subject of working together and mutual cooperation. In his words, "Everyone is a member of the 290th Military Police Company first and foremost, and a member of a subordinate section last." He reiterated his opinion that such a policy would promote better organizational unity and improve law enforcement. No doubt Warren had been practicing this spiel all weekend.

As Geoffrey entered the room, Warren went into the second phase of his plan. He began, "One thing that bothers me though, and I'm not saying it happens around here, is when someone lets their position go to their head and causes dissension in the organization."

With considerable irritation, Geoffrey asked, "Why don't you say what's really on your mind, Warren?" Geoffrey had taken the bait and was falling into the trap.

With a smile, Warren said, "I beg your pardon, sir." Everyone noticed Warren was uncommonly polite.

"You're referring to the fact that I expected you and your personnel to comply with military discipline. Aren't you?" The two were now staring at each other.

"I didn't say that, sir," Warren said as held up his hands in semi-surrender.

"Well," Geoffrey replied. "We all know what you meant. The fact is that if those in positions of authority don't require the correct military courtesy, then they won't receive the proper respect, and the entire military organization will go down the drain."

Apparently, Warren had one of his men stationed outside the PMO. When the colonel's car was a short distance away, the man entered through the side door and walked through the room. As the man did so, Warren went into the final phase of his plan.

Warren became completely acquiescent. "You're right, sir. That's a damned good point." He rose from his chair. "Well, I have to go; I've got cases to work." He then started to leave through the side door. As he was starting to depart, he turned and asked Geoffrey, "Have you got a moment, sir? I'd like to talk to you."

"I guess so," replied Geoffrey. He got up from the conference table and followed Warren out the door.

As he did so, Warren spoke in a voice loud enough to be heard by everyone in the room, "I'd like for us to be able to work together and get along, sir."

I learned what happened next a week later when I played a round of golf with Geoffery, who had been reassigned to the golf course. He was totally dejected that he had let Warren set him up as he had. He told me that this is what happened next:

As the door closed behind them, Warren turned and spoke in a low voice that only the two of them could hear. "The fact is, you worthless asshole, you're a good-for-nothing jerk, and neither I nor my men will ever call you sir or salute you again. Not while I'm around. You better just accept that fact, shit head." He then turned to walk away.

Warren's sense of timing was perfect. At this moment, the colonel's car was pulling into its parking place. As the colonel arrived, Geoffrey reacted exactly as Warren had hoped he would.

The remark was more than any officer should or would stand and was particularly infuriating to an experienced military man like Geoffrey. "Don't walk away from me, sergeant!" he yelled. "You salute right now. You're wearing a uniform and I'm an officer. You're not Mister Warren, you're Sergeant Warren and you better acknowledge that fact right now."

Hearing the commotion outside, everyone looked out the window to witness Geoffrey's apparent tirade against Warren. Likewise, the colonel got out of his car just in time to see what looked like harassment of Warren by the company-grade officer.

Warren continued to taunt and provoke. "I can't salute anyone that I don't respect," he said in a low voice.

"You salute now, and that's a lawful order!" Geoffrey screamed.

"Why would I want to salute an idiot?" Warren scoffed.

Geoffrey got madder. "Idiot, huh? Just salute and get out of my sight—now!" Geoffrey's voice went up several decibels at that point.

Warren snapped to attention and, while saluting, said in a voice loud enough for all to hear, "Okay, sir. Like I said before, sir, I just want to be able to work with you and get along."

Geoffrey emphatically stated, "Just stay away from me, Warren. I don't want anything to do with you."

As Warren walked hurriedly away, the colonel called out to Geoffrey. "Lieutenant! Come here. I want to talk with you," he said in a disgusted tone.

A quick look around let Geoffery that he had been had. To all the witnesses it clearly appeared that he was the aggressor, and an unreasonable one at that. He had two options. He might humble himself to the colonel, beg forgiveness and apologize to Warren. That might possibly allow him to salvage a position at the PMO, but he would lose the respect of all. The other option was to stick to his convictions and wind up somewhere else on post. Either way, he knew his military career was over. He walked over to the colonel, straightening his shoulders and back as he did. He told me that he kept his pride and did not grovel.

"What was all that about, lieutenant?" the colonel asked.

Geoffrey's explanation got right to the point. "Sir, no man is going to insult me and call me an asshole and then walk away without me explaining the way it is to him."

The colonel asked sternly, "And what way is that, lieutenant?"

"Whenever Warren or his men are around, I'm going to expect them to pay the proper military courtesy due to myself and my position," was the reply.

The two eyed each other for several seconds before the colonel spoke. "I'm relieving you of duty, lieutenant. You'll be reassigned to Headquarters and Headquarters Company. You can report there tomorrow for your position and duties."

"Very well, sir," Geoffrey said with dignity. "If you don't want to know all the facts, I'll just go. I suggest you watch out for Warren, though. That man will end your career too, if he gets a chance."

"Dismissed, lieutenant," the colonel said sharply.

In the coming days, Steve and I felt badly for Geoffrey, but around the PMO he was rarely mentioned. He spent most of the time improving his golf game as manager of the post golf course. Raymond was reinstated as Operations officer, and Warren disappeared from the PMO, spending most of his time TDY on the coast.

Whenever Steve or I had occasion to speak with the colonel, we noticed the folder lying on his desk that had SGT Warren TDY Vouchers written on the tab. We discussed breaking into the colonel's office to get a look at the folder, but we knew that was not an option. While the contents of the folder would, no doubt, incriminate Warren, if we got caught we would be charged with breaking and entering. The fictitious officers in *M.A.S.H.* or *Catch-22* might be able to conduct such activity with impunity, but not us in the real world. Steve and I had this conversation before and the result was the same. We could not break the law to catch a lawbreaker. We would have to wait for Warren to make a mistake.

Days passed, more cases in PMI went unsolved and were closed for lack of investigative leads, and two more National Guard armories were broken into. Over one hundred M-16 rifles, ten M-60 machine guns, twelve M-79 grenade launchers and other equipment were taken. Steve and I both felt that when the FBI solved these break-ins they would find that Warren had something to do with them. We just wished we had some evidence to go with our suspicions.

On Thanksgiving Day, Sam and I had Steve and Barbara over for dinner. It was a nice, leisurely day. After the feast, Steve and I relaxed to watch the Oklahoma and Nebraska football game on television while Sam and Barbara sat at the table and had a nice chat. As a Texas alum, Steve hated Oklahoma, so I joined him in rooting for Nebraska.

"The Southwest Conference can mop the floor with the Big 8 any day," Steve boasted.

"That's because the Big 8 is only a two-team league," I commented. "After Nebraska and Oklahoma, the rest of the league has six cream puffs."

"Don't let Charlie hear you say that. He might make jokes about Kansas football, but he still thinks their league is the greatest there is," Steve noted.

After the game, Steve and Barbara thanked us for our hospitality and left. After they had driven off, Sam made the following comment. "Barbara really wants to get married, Nick. I think you ought to let Steve know how great it is to be married." She gave me a little hug as she spoke.

"I'm not sure Steve is the marrying kind, honey," I replied. "Besides, I think we should just mind our own business and let them make their own decisions."

"Well what did you guys talk about while you were so engrossed in the game?" Sam asked.

"Oh, a lot of things," I replied. "At one point Steve commented that before Geoffrey left, he predicted that Warren would end the colonel's career. We both believe that is one prophecy that will come to fruition."

CHAPTER TWENTY

The evening of payday, I was going over our finances and making out checks for our bills. Usually Sam's input was minimal, but tonight she insisted on having a larger say in how our money was spent. "Christmas is coming," she said. "If you insist on not buying on credit, you need to budget in enough to cover everyone that we need to buy a present for."

"Okay, honey, I'll see what I can do," I said.

"No, Nick! I mean it," she said forcefully and sat down at the table by me. "And another thing." She put her hand on my writing hand. "Any money I need for myself has had to come out of what you allow for food and household expenses. That's not fair. I need some money to do with whatever I want."

I could see a fight coming. I decided to pick my next words carefully. "Sam, I have seen people who are deeply in debt. Their lives are hell and they are no better than slaves. I never intend to live like that. I know you think I am a miser, but I'm not. Someday you'll see the wisdom in how I conduct our finances."

"Listen to yourself, Nick. It's how you conduct our finances. Am I your partner or not? Don't I get a say in how things are done?

"Well, yeah. You always agree when I give you the money each week. We're always on the same page."

"No, Nick, we're not. You hand me the money and say, "Here, honey, don't spend it all in one place. It's like, take it or leave it, honey. You call that being the same page?"

As Sam continued to complain, I realized that I had better proceed carefully. Sam had a temper. There had been a couple of times when our disagreements had become shouting matches. Fortunately, those times had been on a Friday or Saturday night. We had argued until the early hours of the morning. Afterward there had been some very hot sex to make up, and we had slept most of the next day. This was a Monday night, and I could not risk falling asleep at my desk the next day regardless of how good the make-up sex might be. "You're right, Sam," I said. "Let's go through this line by line." I showed Sam my leave and earnings statement.

"I appreciate this, honey," she said.

"Okay, Sam," I started, "You can see here that I get four hundred seventeen dollars and sixty cents a month. Out of that, Uncle Sam has got his share of forty dollars and eleven cents. That leaves three hundred seventy-seven dollars and forty-nine cents. To this is added our subsistence and housing allowances, which are non-taxable. The housing part goes straight to our rent. That leaves four hundred twenty-five dollars and thirty-seven cents that we have for the month. I was hoping that Sam would get bored with the numbers and go away—but she didn't. She nit-picked over every item. She insisted on more money for groceries. She also insisted on an amount that would be hers—to spend how and when she wished. She was determined to get her way.

"Okay Sam, you can have ten dollars," I said.

"Are you kidding? That's an insult. I need at least thirty," she responded. We agreed on twenty-five.

I had always budgeted for ninety dollars for groceries. She demanded a hundred and twenty. We settled on a hundred fifteen. The bills were all set amounts, so there was no discussion there. Then we discussed the proposed Christmas expenses. The final amount we agreed upon reduced the usual savings a little, but the debates were over. I wrote Sam a check for the twenty-five dollars she could cash when she went shopping in the morning. I thought the money discussion was over. I was wrong.

"Why are you so dictatorial with the money, Nick? Sometimes, you make me feel like a kid asking her parents for money."

"Honey," I replied. "I've watched you spend money. You tend to impulse buy and buy things we don't need. Besides, I'm scared to death you will be like your father."

"How's that?" There was noticeable anger in her voice.

"Sam, you know as well as I that the man has never paid a bill on time in his entire life. And, we won't discuss his penchant for writing bad checks."

Now I had done it. Sam was very defensive about her family. "My father has had some terrible luck," she screamed. "Nothing ever seems to go right for him. I'm sorry that you're so high and mighty that you can judge him."

I tried to keep my voice down. I didn't want the neighbors to hear us fighting. Finally, after about another half an hour, I apologized. I had started this one and I wanted to end it. With contrition, I made peace.

"Sam, I'm sorry. Things didn't come out the way I wanted. The point is that when bills are paid late there are late fees and usually interest charges, which can double what is due. I never want to pay more than I have to." I paused. She calmed down. "I will be the first to admit that your father is a nice old guy that would give someone the shirt off his back if they needed it. However, you know as well as I that sometimes he doesn't use the best judgment. All families have problems, and I'm sorry I pointed out one with yours in our personal discussion."

"I understand, Nick. But I'm not my father. You need to give me a chance. Maybe I have a lot to learn about money and budgeting, but you need to allow me to learn it."

"Okay, honey. I guess tonight has been a good start," I concluded.

"It has, Nick. You're the chief financial officer of the family and I'm the foreman of household management, right?"

"Right, honey," I agreed.

"Good, you do the dishes."

As I have previously mentioned, the greatest benefit of writing about things which happened many years ago is that I am now privy to all the investigations, probes, inquiries and rumors which were subsequent to the episodes. As such, I am justifiably proud of the small part I was to play in the ensuing events.

In retrospect, if there was one point when it could be said that Warren's fortunes had started to change, the day was December 2, 1970. On that day, Warren's assistant, Johnson (a buck sergeant), had conducted an inspection of an air defense artillery site on the coast. After finishing his assigned duties, that afternoon Johnson went to the NCO club, where he remained until early evening, consuming the finished product of brewer's art.

At that point, Johnson became loud and obnoxious, and the master-at-arms requested that he leave. Johnson then began to brag that he was a military policeman and he would do whatever he pleased. The master-at-arms immediately placed a call to the security police and informed them that a man claiming to be an MP was causing a disturbance. When they arrived, Johnson showed his identification and, as a professional courtesy, the security police offered to give him a ride to the local BEQ barracks to sleep it off.

As they left the NCO club, however, Johnson quickly jumped into their jeep, which had been left running, and drove off. He didn't get far, though, due to his inebriated condition. He quickly drove off the road through a ditch and crashed into a fence about a hundred yards down the road.

Fortunately for him, Warren was staying at a resort about twenty miles away, and Johnson used the phone call he was allowed to call him. Two hours later, a man who identified himself as Colonel Robert E. Warren (a bird colonel, no less) arrived and asked to take possession of the prisoner. The young captain on duty was apprehensive at first, and hesitated. Warren began to reassure him.

"Don't worry, captain," he said. "The damage to your jeep will be surveyed against Johnson here. You route the 19-32 detailing the charges of drunk and disorderly conduct and misappropriation of government property to me, and I'll insure that appropriate punishment is administered."

Warren then began to berate Johnson. "You'll be washing dishes in the battalion mess next week as Private Johnson. So, keep your mouth shut and avoid the stockade. I don't want any excuses out of you. Understand?" His voice was loud and determined.

"Yes, sir," Johnson said meekly.

The captain relented and released Johnson to Warren's custody. As they left the police station, Warren was still scolding Johnson loudly for all to hear. However, as they drove off in Warren's car, both broke into a laugh.

"Damn, sarge," Johnson chuckled. "You almost had me thinking you were a colonel. You play the part real good."

"You ain't off the hook yet, you dumb bastard," Warren said. "I've got to intercept that 19-32 report when it gets to the mail room and make sure they get the money for the damages to that jeep. What in the hell were you thinking, anyway?"

"I just needed to unwind. I guess I drank too much and got carried away," replied Johnson. "Think you can take care of everything, sarge?"

Warren's answer would have been in his usual authoritarian voice. "Shit, yes! You just do as you're told and don't cause anymore trouble, and I'll take care of you."

A STATESIDE TOUR OF DUTY

Fortunately, when the paperwork containing the Form 19-32 came to the 290th mail room, it was addressed to Colonel Robert Warren and not to the provost marshal, chief of staff or Operations officer. That way, Warren was able to convince the mail clerk that the colonel part was a joke written by a friend. He then had one of his other men pose as a Finance clerk and deliver an official-looking check to the motor pool at the ADA site for damages to the jeep. He also sent a report to the captain he had dealt with, detailing the severe Article 15 (non-judicial) punishment received by Johnson. Everything looked official and no questions were asked. Warren just had to be sure they didn't send Johnson to that location again.

Benjamin Franklin once said that three people can keep a secret, provided two of them are dead. In Johnson's situation, one person couldn't keep a secret. Johnson told somebody he had sworn to secrecy about his misadventures. That person told someone else whom he could trust not to tell anyone else, and so it went. Within a week, Colonel Warren was the worst-kept secret in the 290th Military Police Company.

I heard the rumor from Sergeant Corley. While we were talking, PFC Byrd confirmed the rumor. "Sir, he began, last night Cavanaugh and I were coming out of the post theater when we saw Warren trying to make time with some local teenyboppers. As a joke, we said, 'Evening, Colonel Warren.' Later, he thanked us because he had told the girls that he was a colonel and he appreciated us corroborating his story."

At that point, I decided to go see Steve. Maybe now we might have enough evidence to move against Warren. First, I went to the mail room. My clerk told me about the large envelope that had come addressed to Colonel Warren some time before. This complicated the situation. Maybe the rumor had gotten started as the result of a friend putting the title of Colonel Warren on a piece of correspondence as a joke. I had to face that possibility.

As Steve and I began to compare notes, he let me know that he had heard the Colonel Warren rumor also. However, the version he had heard included a wrecked jeep. The version I was privy to only had Warren impersonating a field-grade officer. I then passed along what Bingham had said about calling Warren at the colonel's quarters and making it appear that the sergeant's case load was greater than it was. While pretending to be overworked was not an offense under the UCMJ (Uniform Code of Military Justice), it did show that Warren was disingenuous at best and fraudulent and untrustworthy at worst. However, the other charge, that of impersonating an officer, was a serious illegality. If we could find someone willing to sign witness statements attesting to Warren's transgressions, his days in the service were numbered. We decided to proceed accordingly.

First we met with Bingham. When we told him what we wanted, his first comment was, "Well, sir, pretending to be overworked is not any kind of crime or chargeable offense."

Obviously, he had a point there. Even I had done that on occasion, but I wasn't going to tell anyone. Still, I said, "We realize that," I said. "But it does show the man's character."

"The problem I would have, sir, is that it would be my word against his," Bingham replied. "Knowing what he did to Geoffrey, I wouldn't want to get into a pissing contest with that man without a lot more evidence against him. If you can get someone that has witnessed a real crime to provide you with a sworn statement, then I might reconsider."

Next, we approached Byrd. Again, we were disappointed. His concerns were similar to those of Bingham.

"Warren would just deny it, sir," Byrd said. "Or, he could just say that I misunderstood what he said. Unless someone else can verify his impersonating an officer, I'd rather not stick my neck out."

"That's the problem," Steve explained. "Where no one wants to be the first to come forward, Warren keeps getting away with all the crap he pulls."

Byrd's next comment was one we couldn't argue with. "I'm just a brand-new PFC around here, sir. Warren is an E-6 and the colonel's right hand man. I wouldn't dare be the first to try to bring him down."

The reactions of Bingham and Byrd were disappointing, but we understood. Steve and I would have to remain patient. In our hearts, we felt that it was only a matter of time before we got rid of Warren. We didn't realize that his departure from the PMO would come sooner rather than later.

Since Julene had left the PMO to do clerical work at Battalion, the workload was more than Susan could handle. Therefore, a former desk sergeant, SSG Stephen Tate (who was an excellent typist), had been brought into the front office to pick up the slack.

On the afternoon of December 11, Raymond and the colonel were in a meeting at post headquarters ,and the major was gone to tend to some personal business. My telephone rang.

A STATESIDE TOUR OF DUTY

"Military Police Traffic Section, Lieutenant Moultrie speaking sir," I said as I answered it.

"Sir, this is Sergeant Tate up front. Since you don't have an intercom in your office, this is the only way I could call you."

I pushed my paperwork aside. "Okay, sarge. What can I do for you?"

"Well, sir. There's a Captain Knapp here to see whoever is in charge, and with everyone else gone, right now that's you," the sergeant said.

"No problem, sarge," I said. "Send the captain back."

Tate hesitated for a second. He then said, "Uh, sir, this is a Navy captain."

"I understand, sarge. I'll be right there," I said.

For those not familiar with military rank, there is an enormous difference between a Navy captain and a captain in the Army, Air Force or Marines. A captain in the three latter services barely outranks a lieutenant. A Navy captain is the equivalent of a bird colonel in the other services. The man in the front office had a lot of horsepower, and I didn't intend to keep him waiting for long.

I hurried up to the front office. The captain was talking to Tate as I got there. "Sir, Lieutenant Moultrie," I said. "What can I do for you?"

"Well, lieutenant, it's probably just an oversight, but since I was headed this way I thought I would stop and check it out," the captain began. "We have a reserve armory down on the coast that your people are supposed to inspect, and since it moved to a new location about a year and a half ago it hasn't been inspected."

I had wanted to look at Warren's files for weeks, but didn't dare, knowing how close he was with the colonel. Now, with everyone out of the office, I had my chance. "Let's go back to the physical security section and check this out, sir. We'll find out what's going on very quickly," I said.

Accompanied by the captain we walked back to Warren's section, where only Doak was present at the time.

"Specialist, we need to look at your files," I said.

Doak looked up and replied, "Sir, do you have permission from Sergeant Warren to look at our files?"

I pointed to the gold bar on my shoulder. "This says that I don't need Warren's permission, specialist." Then pointing back over my shoulder with my thumb, I added, "But, if you want to argue with me, there's a full bird here you can argue with, too." I smiled as I said that.

"Yes, sir," Doak said sheepishly. "I have to go back to vehicle registration anyway, sir. Help yourself."

I knew Doak was going to use the phone in vehicle registration to call Warren. I decided to move quickly. Opening the drawers, I found the manila folder with the location the captain was concerned about and opened it up. "According to this they inspected the location twice in the past year, sir." I gave the documents to the captain.

"This gives the address of the old location," the naval officer said. "According to this, they gave a clean bill of health to an armory that isn't even there."

I quickly grabbed the phone and dialed CID's number. Pike answered it.

"Mister Pike, this is Moultrie at the PMO. I think I have just discovered fraud on the part of the Physical Security Section. You people better get over here quickly to impound the files."

Pike asked, "What have you got, lieutenant?"

"Proof of inspections that were never conducted, and a Navy captain who can verify what I'm saying," I answered. "I suggest that you people get here quickly. If Warren gets here first, I can't guarantee what might happen to the evidence."

"We're on our way, lieutenant," he replied and hung up the phone.

Within ten minutes, three cars of CID personnel were parked outside the PMO, and the PMI/Physical Security files were being carried outside in anticipation of the arrival of a truck that had been ordered from the motor pool. While they worked, I talked with the captain.

"Looks like I stirred up a hornet's nest," the captain said with a smile.

"No problem, sir," I replied. "If something's not being done right, we want to get it corrected. By the way, you said earlier that you were coming this way en route to somewhere else?"

"I have to attend a conference at Buckley Station, up near Denver," he replied. "I needed additional hours to maintain my flight status so I'm flying myself and five others up there. I decided to stop off here on the way. I'm glad I did; I haven't had this much fun in years."

"I'm glad I could help out, sir," I replied. "By the way, where are your passengers?"

"I left them over at the officers' club," answered the captain. "They'll be sorry they missed out on watching the fur fly."

A STATESIDE TOUR OF DUTY

I shook hands with the naval officer and left, while CID took the captain's statement. I figured it was time to depart. As I walked past the D-cell, I ran into Steve.

"What's happening, Nick? I've heard that the shit is hitting the fan," he said.

"Major league, big time, my friend. Come into my office and I'll tell you all about it," I said. "You are going to enjoy this."

I filled Steve in on all the details and he was thrilled. He couldn't believe that everything we had worked on for so long had finally come to pass. I relished being the one to give him the good news.

Steve elatedly asked, "You mean all dumb-ass CID had to do was to check Warren's files and see if the work was really being done?"

"Yeah. But remember, the colonel wouldn't let them do that because he felt they were harassing Warren," I reminded.

At that moment Tate appeared in the door. "The colonel just returned from post headquarters, sir. He wants to see you right now."

A chill went up my back but I was careful not to let any nervousness or apprehension show. "Let's go talk to him," I said. As I walked up front my brain was working overtime to have a good explanation prepared for the colonel.

As I walked into the colonel's office, Raymond was standing to the right of the colonel's desk. I knew that if he had met with Captain Knapp, he would have concocted an explanation and Warren would still be in business. I would get no help from him.

"What in the hell is going on, lieutenant!" The colonel's voice was loud enough to be heard all the way down the hall. "I leave for a little while and the whole place goes to hell in a handbasket."

"Sir," I began. "At USAMPS they taught me a couple of things. First, protect evidence and, secondly, protect those you work with. When Captain Knapp arrived with proof of illegal acts, I was required by law to secure the evidence. If I had not, and Sergeant Warren had destroyed those files, then he might have attempted to implicate others, including you, in those acts. I felt the need to protect yourself and the other good workers of the PMO."

"I see," said the colonel. He sat back a little in his chair.

"Also," I continued. "I have received information about Sergeant Warren, and Lieutenant Bronson is a witness to this, that led me to believe Warren might be the type that would destroy the files if he got a chance." Without naming names, I passed along the information I had received from Bingham and Byrd. I then added further explanation. "Those facts, without sworn statements, were just hearsay, and I didn't dare to pass along the unsubstantiated information. However, in the face of real illegality, I had to proceed in haste to secure the evidence against Warren." I then reiterated my conclusion with, "Everything I did was necessary to protect the provost marshal and the good members of his staff." I then shut up to allow the colonel to comprehend what I had just said.

After what seemed to be an eternity, the colonel said, "Good job, lieutenant. I'll have to relieve Warren of duty, pending CID's investigation. Dismissed."

"Yes, sir," I said. I hurriedly went back to my office.

That night, as I told Sam the good news, some interesting developments were taking place on post. It seemed that when the colonel called Warren to tell him about the day's events and relieve him of duty, Warren had news of his own. I learned the following events from subsequent investigations.

As it turned out, the colonel and Warren had met at a restaurant to discuss business on several occasions, and the colonel had allowed Warren to pick up the check. To accept gratuities from subordinates was a serious offense under the UCMJ. Now, Warren made it clear that he had documented evidence of these facts and unless the colonel helped him get out of his difficulties, Warren would take the colonel down with him. "Unless this goes away, General Cinch will receive the evidence in the mail," Warren threatened. "By the way, colonel," he added. "I gave Sergeant Major Prince a Smith and Wesson .38 as a gift. Tell him I would appreciate any help he might render also."

I'm sure the colonel didn't care about Prince. He only wanted to save his own career. He checked Warren's desk and those of his men, and it was later discovered that he broke into Warren's off-post apartment, searching for the evidence. He apparently didn't find it.

Monday, December 14, was rainy and cold. After the hot summer I had just experienced, it hadn't occurred to me that this place could get cold, but it could. The entire Traffic section staff was in the office. Officially, we were all dealing with paperwork. In reality, we were having a general bull session.

Byrd was discussing his work checking vehicle speeds by radar the previous Saturday night. In his words, business was terrible. "I don't know what the problem was, but nobody was speeding enough for me to give them a ticket," he lamented.

I leaned back in my chair. "Look at it this way, Byrd," I said. "At least you were doing your job. That's all that counts."

"That may be true, sir. But when the only person speeding is the provost marshal, it still seems like a waste of time. I sure didn't want to give him a ticket," he added.

"What!" That comment really caught my attention.

"Oh yes, sir. I clocked the colonel doing forty-nine in the twenty-mile-per-hour zone leading to the housing area, just a little before midnight," he responded.

"Are you sure it was the colonel?" I asked again.

"You bet, sir," He replied. "The car had blue sticker number three, and I recognized the colonel as he drove past under the street light."

Unless he was on leave, the colonel rarely drove his own car. Usually, he had his driver take him wherever he needed to go in a staff car. I wondered what would have the colonel out so late at night and so distracted that he would be speeding that fast. I had no way of knowing, at the time, that the colonel was returning from Warren's apartment after looking for the evidence Warren had threatened to use against him. My thoughts were interrupted by the desk sergeant entering the room.

"Sir, we have a report of an accident at the corner of McArthur and Secord," he stated.

Gross and Brown headed out the door to handle the investigation, as the sergeant added, "And another thing, sir. The colonel needed a unit to ten-one-nine with him at his office, but we don't have anybody available. Could your guys take this?"

"No sweat, sarge," I said. "I'll go up and see what he needs."

I walked up to the colonel's office. He seemed unusually worried about something. "Sir," I told him. "I understand you need a unit. Tell me what you need, and I'll send two of my men to take care of it."

"No, lieutenant," he replied. "You can handle this. Go to my quarters and have my wife give you the brown attaché case Sergeant Warren left there last month. My wife sleeps late and usually doesn't answer the door before ten. I'll call and wake her up so she will know you're coming. Bring that case back to me immediately."

"Yes, sir, I'll bring it back immediately," I replied.

No doubt the colonel was irritated at himself for not remembering the briefcase before. If the evidence was there, he could have saved himself a lot of trouble and effort.

I had Byrd join me, and we went straight to the colonel's residence. The house was on Sheridan Circle, where most of the field-grade officers lived. These houses had large, well-manicured lawns and were the largest and nicest on post. The rain was now a fine mist as we rang the door bell. The colonel's wife opened the door and asked us to come in. It was clear that she had just gotten out of bed, as her hair was in disarray. However, neither Byrd nor I was prepared for the manner in which she was dressed.

She had a housecoat draped over her shoulders, but it was not closed by the sash that hung from its sides. It should have been, because what little else she wore amounted to almost nothing, so her body was completely exposed.

The other garment she wore was a thin negligee. It hung low at the top, showing a lot of cleavage and ended with a thick fringe about halfway down her thigh. The sheer fabric in between was so thin that her big, brown nipples and triangular dark patch of pubic hair were clearly visible. She also wore furry blue slippers, making her feet the only part of her that was completely covered.

I was stunned that she would answer the door dressed in this manner, let alone parade around before two men she didn't know. Suddenly, I began to believe the supposition about her previous employment. I could easily imagine this strumpet lounging in a cathouse waiting for her next customer.

My only thought was to be professional. After my initial shock, I would look her straight in the eyes when we talked and ignore everything else. Thinking of Sam at home made this easy to do. For a nineteen-year-old unmarried kid like Byrd, apparently, that was not so easy to do. He didn't seem to be able to take his eyes off her. He followed her every movement as I glanced elsewhere around the room. She retrieved the case from a closet and brought it to us. She could have handed it to one of us. Instead, she bent over to place it on the floor before us. As she did, it was possible to look down the loose open neckline of her negligee at her overexposed body. I looked away to some pictures on the wall instead.

"Here you are, lieutenant," she said. "You can take this to my husband."

"Thank you, ma'am," I said. "I was just admiring the beautiful paintings on your wall."

"Thank you, lieutenant," she replied. "We bought them in Switzerland."

After a little more small talk about the paintings, I said, "Yes, well, the colonel is waiting. We had better hurry to get this back to him. Thank you."

I picked up the case, and with Byrd following we quickly left the premises. As we got into the car, Byrd spoke first. "Damnation, sir!" He exclaimed. "I was getting a boner so big I didn't think I'd be able to walk. I had to hold my hat in front of me the whole time we were there. I'd sure like to get a little of that."

"Getting a little of that could get you some time in the stockade or Fort Leavenworth," I explained.

"But it might be worth it, sir," Byrd replied. "Don't you think so?"

"No, I don't," I said emphatically. "I wouldn't touch that woman with a ten-foot pole. I'm happy with my wife and I'll let the colonel keep his."

We returned to the PMO. It was raining hard again and another traffic accident had been reported. Byrd left to handle the investigation as I walked up front to deliver the case to the colonel.

"Here you are, sir," I said.

"Thank you, lieutenant. That will be all," replied the colonel.

As I left, the colonel closed the door to his office. I thought that was odd, as he had never closed it before during business hours. I returned to the office. I knew that Byrd would be informing everyone upon his return as to the colonel's wife's manner of dress (or undress, as it were) when she had answered the door.

Behind his closed door, there is no way to know exactly what happened. I'm guessing that the colonel proceeded to force the lock open on Warren's attaché case. He probably did not find what he was looking for. No doubt the colonel began to collect his thoughts as to how he could deal with Warren. There is no way to ascertain what he believed his options to be. Perhaps he could reason with him. While he might not be able to help the sergeant avoid all punishment, he could ensure that the penalties for his former subordinate were as minimal as possible. That would probably be his primary bargaining position. If the colonel was removed as provost marshal, Warren would lose his most highly placed ally. If reasoning with Warren didn't work, maybe Prince had something on him they could use for leverage. A little counter blackmail could sure help right now. The soon-to-be former section chief might back off, if it meant avoiding an even longer prison sentence. However, that is all supposition on my part.

If the colonel was considering his options, events were happening elsewhere that would render them moot. Those events would end the colonel's military career and topple the current PMO power structure.

In the CID inspection of Warren's files, twenty inspection reports were pulled at random and twelve were found to be fraudulent. The locations in question had not been inspected. With fraud this extensive, Warren was in very big trouble. To compound the problem, an informant for the FBI reported that there was a plot being formulated to rob banks and kidnap the commanding general of a southwestern Army post. This last item had been Warren's escape plan. If his informants at Fifth Army tipped him off that his arrest was imminent, then he would strike first. With the proceeds from the bank jobs and holding the commanding general as a hostage, Warren would commandeer a plane and fly to a country that might grant him asylum.

It was a grandiose scheme at best, and any chances it had for success depended upon Warren being alerted by his friends at Fifth Army and being at Fort McCulloch where he could assemble his team and proceed without delay. One Navy captain dropping in unannounced while Warren was over three hundred miles away on the coast had thrown a monkey wrench into the works. Since the events happened locally, Warren had no chance to be warned from higher headquarters, and with those who might have protected him out of the office, Warren was finished. It was as if the stars had aligned perfectly to bring about his downfall. But now the noose tightened.

After being warned of his rights, Warren insisted that the bank robbery story was a lie told by someone who was out to get him. He then asked for two weeks' leave to obtain and confer with legal council and to get his affairs in order. When the leave was granted by orders of the colonel, most of us couldn't believe it. Fortunately, Warren was forced by CID to surrender his passport and his leave location in Shreveport, Louisiana, would be monitored. If it was the colonel's hope for Warren to flee the country, there were others who would make sure it didn't happen.

With their leader gone, the other PMI personnel were finished. They were read their rights and, faced with phony reports signed by themselves, each began to attempt to get the best deal he could. Graves and Devers asked for legal representation and refused to say anything further. Johnson asked for a deal, saying they would testify against Warren in exchange for immunity for himself. The CID refused. He, Williams, Doak and the others then spilled their guts. They each gave sworn statements, attempting to minimize their involvement with Warren and putting as much blame as possible on their former boss.

Williams' statement went as follows:

> I, Robert C. Williams, went on leave 19 April 1970 for two weeks to New York City. While there, Sergeant Warren called and told me that since I was doing such a great job, I should stay an additional week and he would take care of the paperwork for the additional leave. When I returned, he had a TDY voucher filled out instead for the additional week. He said everyone did it and that I deserved the money. He hinted that I might get in trouble for being AWOL if I didn't sign the voucher. After signing, he produced phony inspection reports to document the work the voucher supposedly covered. If I refused to sign them, I was told that I could be court-martialed for misappropriation of government funds.
>
> At that time Sergeant Warren threatened to court-martial me unless I followed all of his orders from then on. I countered that if he did that, I would blow the whistle on his entire operation and he never asked me to do anything illegal again.

Williams signed the statement and, after attesting an oath that it was true, asked, "May I be allowed to leave?"

"Go ahead, sergeant," said the lead investigator, "but do not leave the post without prior permission from me. Have the Supply sergeant issue bedding, and you will sleep in the company barracks. You can retrieve your personal belongings from your off-post apartment later."

Sergeant Williams nodded his head and left without further comment. He had been planning to join the U.S. Marshall's service after he finished his time in the Army. There was no chance of that now. A promising career in law enforcement was over. Those of us who observed Williams' final departure from the PMO felt sorry for him. He had done the least wrong of all of Warren's personnel, but between his failure to report the section's wrongdoing and his own less-than-intelligent actions, he would still pay a price.

As the extent of the fraud in the PMI section became known and additional evidence verified Warren's former contingency plan to rob banks and kidnap General Cinch, both CID and the FBI decided it was time to pick the errant sergeant up for questioning.

When the FBI found he was no longer at the address he had given as a condition for leave, Warren's name was sent out by the NCIC to all jurisdictions in surrounding states. Despite CID's insistence that he be monitored, he had slipped through the cracks again.

As it turned out, Warren was still in Shreveport. He was checked into room 16 of the Westside Motel under his real name. Apparently for the time being he had decided against trying to leave the country. What happened next is pieced together using records of the Shreveport police and the interrogation the FBI had with his wife afterward (to everyone's surprise he got married).

According to her, Warren lay on the bed in their room appearing to be depressed. I figure he was considering his alternatives. He clearly knew that it was only a matter of time before military authorities issued a warrant for his arrest, so he would have to act quickly. He had been in this situation before when he was in Vietnam. There he had feigned insanity and avoided prosecution while others were sentenced to terms in the Military Confinement Facility at Fort Leavenworth. To use the same defense again would be risky, but it had worked before. He would have to do something unusual. It would have to be something very drastic and done in a convincing manner to make sure a claim of insanity would be believed.

In the top drawer of the dresser that was next to the bed, next to the obligatory copy of the Holy Bible was a large envelope he had ordered his girlfriend to mail in the event anything happened to him. Also in the drawer were a 9mm pistol and a .38 Colt revolver. He had assured his companion that they were for self-defense. He probably thought that those were friends that would help him get out of the predicament he was in. I'm guessing that he figured they were the only friends he had. All the time, he was probably thinking of what he would do or say in any given circumstance. While he was lost in thought he had ignored the girl in the room

His companion, Joy Parker, was twenty-four. She was tall (about five feet seven), with a slightly dark complexion. She was slender, the figure required in her brief career as a model, and very attractive. Normally, Warren would be directing all his attention to her, but the stress caused by his present problems apparently had caused him to lose interest. These times of temporary depression were interspersed between periods of confidence when he was, no doubt, sure he could beat the rap. The more he thought and plotted, however, he probably experienced far fewer of those confident moments.

Joy told how she had noticed the change in his behavior. She had become used to having this dashing soldier around who was the life of the party. She had no way of knowing that the stories he enthralled others with were essentially embellished lies. She just enjoyed being on the arm of this distinguished-looking man with the graying temples, soaking up the attention that came her way when she accompanied him. Now these periods of melancholy and depression where he ignored her were a source of irritation. What added to these feelings of irritation were the feelings of jealousy that came with the feeling that she was no longer at the center of his thoughts. The following account comes from her statement to the FBI and information from the Shreveport police.

She lay down on the bed next to him. "Bob," she said softly in his ear.

Warren continued to lie there in his trance-like state.

"Bob," She repeated.

"Huh?" Replied her companion, looking at her.

"Bob, forget your work and spend time with me. Let's do something fun." She then said the magic words that normally bring any man to life. "Want to make love?"

To her surprise, he asked, "Want to do something really rash instead?"

"Like what?" This was more like the soldier she was so attracted to. She asked again, "What have you got in mind, Bob?"

"Let's go get married," He replied.

"You're kidding!"

"No, I mean it. Let's go get married," He repeated.

In the five months she had known Robert Warren, Joy had been impressed with the amounts of money he always had available. She was in awe of the authority and control he seemed to have over others and the way he seemed to dominate any conversation he joined into. She knew men like Warren usually avoided marriage, so she hadn't expected their relationship to move beyond the shack-up phase. She was now thrilled, and with a feeling of conquest she said, "Yes."

"Grab your shoes and a jacket and we'll go to the courthouse," Warren said.

The woman was overjoyed as she checked her hair in the bathroom mirror. She had no way of knowing her prospective bridegroom was taking the two pistols from the dresser drawer and placing them in his belt, hidden by his brown sport coat.

They drove to the courthouse, where they obtained a marriage license and found an official available to perform the civil ceremony. Afterward they went to a nice restaurant for a late lunch. It was a little past two in the afternoon when they returned to the motel. As they pulled into the motel parking lot, Warren noticed a police car parked on the curb near the motel office.

"Baby, go get us some cigarettes," Warren said. "I'm all out."

"Why don't you get them while I get ready for you?" she asked with a wink.

"Don't argue, doll," Warren countered. "Old Bob has a big surprise for you when you get back. There's a machine in the office, so you won't have to go too far."

She didn't argue and, after giving her new husband a quick kiss, she went after the cigarettes. As she did, she noticed the policemen getting out of their car.

Police officers Billings and Zacharius had been on routine patrol when they received the call to be on the lookout for Warren. It had been a slow morning, so they began to check out the local motels in their area. They didn't expect to find their suspect in this manner, but to their surprise found he had checked into the Westside under his real name. It had been only the fifth motel they had checked. Finding the occupants were not at home, they decided to wait for their return. Since the man in question was a military policeman who was only wanted for questioning, they saw no need for backup. They had been waiting forty minutes, when a man answering Warren's description pulled into the stall outside room 16.

Billings reached over and tapped his partner on the arm. "There's our man," he said.

"Yeah, I see him," Zacharius said. "I wonder what they want to question him about."

"Hell if I know," Billings replied. "If I know the Army, he probably forgot to make his bed before he left on leave."

"Let's go see him," Zacharius said as he got out of the car and put on his hat.

A STATESIDE TOUR OF DUTY

The patrolmen walked up to the room in silence. Joy passed them as she went into the office to buy the cigarettes, but didn't give them any thought until she saw through the office window that they were stopping at her room.

The patrolmen stationed themselves on either side of the doorway and Billings knocked with his left hand. "Robert Warren?" He called out.

"Yes, who is it?" Came a voice from inside.

"Shreveport Police," said Billings. "We need to talk to you."

"Okay guys, just a second," Replied the voice inside the room.

The casual answer put both men at ease, and Zacharius even leaned against the building. They were both unprepared for the next move. With lightening quickness, Warren jerked the door open. He began firing with both pistols as he yelled, "I'll kill you all."

CHAPTER TWENTY-ONE

Of Warren's first two shots, one hit Billings in the side. As he fell, he still managed to draw his weapon. The other shot missed. Without hesitation, the seemingly crazed gunman turned and fired at Zacharius. Again, one shot missed the policeman's head, but by only about an inch. The second shot grazed his shoulder. Zacharius lost his balance and fell backward as he grabbed for his gun.

The sergeant turned again on Billings, who was lying on the ground with his gun unholstered. Billings instinctively knew he had to return fire as quickly as possible. I'm sure that the knowledge that failure to do so might be fatal negated the burning pain in his side.

Warren's fifth shot hit the sidewalk about eight inches from the policeman's head, and chips of the concrete peppered the right side of Billings' face. Almost simultaneously with that fifth shot, Billings got off a shot hitting Warren in the left arm. The soldier spun around from the force of the blow, shooting wildly twice more.

Zacharius fired twice, hitting Warren in the leg and side. In desperation, the wounded gunman raised his gun to fire once more. Before he could shoot, however, Billings got off the last shot of the confrontation. It was aimed at the soldier's chest. However, the bullet hit Warren's gun hand, which was in the trajectory of the bullet. This bullet broke the sergeant's wrist and creased his neck before ending up in the wall of the motel room. Warren now collapsed from his five wounds.

The entire battle had lasted less than four seconds. To the stunned policemen, however those few seconds probably had felt like an eternity. Now that they had gained control of the situation, their attention turned to each other.

Zacharius asked, "You okay, Don?"

"I'll live," Said the other cop. "I think it's only a flesh wound. Hell's bells! Can you believe this guy was an MP?" Billings held his side.

"You never know what to think," Said Zacharius. "I'll go radio for an ambulance."

As the shooting ended, Joy rushed to her husband's side. Billings picked up the two pistols and stepped back. The woman most likely had a sense of disbelief permeate her entire body. She probably felt a surge of bitterness toward the two policemen and the desire to scream in uncontrollable rage at them. She didn't. Instead, she knelt over Warren and started to cry. What only minutes earlier had been the happiest day of her life was turning into a nightmare.

While his partner radioed for help, Billings searched the motel room for additional weapons. His search turned up the large envelope addressed to the Army CID.

"What is this?" he asked the woman still sobbing over her husband. He held up the envelope.

"My husband told me to mail it if anything happened to him," The woman said through her tears.

"It's addressed to the Fifth Army Criminal Investigations Division at Fort Sam Houston, Texas," Billings told his partner (who had just returned). "I guess we better see that they get it. I think something just happened to him."

A few minutes later the ambulance arrived. Mrs. Warren rode to the hospital with her husband, accompanied by a policeman. Billings and Zacharius followed the ambulance to the hospital, where they were treated for minor wounds and released.

Warren regained consciousness, but refused treatment for his wounds. Joy persuaded him to reconsider the decision, and after a half hour he changed his mind.

The envelope found in the motel room was in the hands of CID personnel within a matter of hours. The contents of the envelope documented the gifts and gratuities the colonel and Sergeant Major Prince had received from their subordinate. Prince had thrown the handgun received from Warren in the river and tried to claim it had been a gift from someone else, but a photograph in the envelope showed otherwise.

That night, the information on Warren reached Fort McCulloch. It came through the message center, and the clerk quickly relayed the data to the general's chief of staff, Colonel Rulon.

NEIL MITCHELL

Rulon then relieved Colonel Cox of duty. Major Receiver was notified that he would be acting provost marshal for the interim period and he then relieved Prince of duty. For Colonel Cox and First Sergeant Prince, their careers in the Army were over. Pending a full investigation, they would be allowed to retire.

Reports of the wrongdoing had been coming into post headquarters from Fifth Army CID for some time (bypassing the PMO, who would normally be informed of any investigation in progress). While the major hoped to become the permanent provost marshal, those hopes were in vain. As a member of the staff where an incident of this magnitude had taken place, he would not get the job.

Despite the lateness of the hour, the major went to the PMO, where he personally typed a Blue Bell report detailing the colonel's being relieved for dereliction of duty. I found the report several days later and was amazed at the spelling, punctuation and grammatical errors in it. Had I not known better, I would have thought that the major had less than a third-grade education. Perhaps it was the late hour, and he was just fatigued. Maybe the major couldn't contain his joy at having the top job (no matter for how short a period), or maybe the major was semiliterate. All I knew was that if I had sent off any paperwork as sloppy as the major's, I would have caught hell.

The following morning, I walked into the PMO totally unaware of the events the day before. "The major needs to see you immediately this morning, sir," The desk sergeant said.

"Okay, I'll go up in a few minutes," I replied.

"You probably ought to see him now, sir. There have been some big changes since yesterday," The sergeant stated.

Not knowing the gravity of the situation, I responded in jest. "Oh yeah, what happened? They rewrite the SOP's?"

"No, sir. Warren shot it out with some guys in Louisiana. They shot him five times with a .357 Magnum. He's in critical condition."

Now I could tell that the sergeant wasn't kidding. "Sounds like either they need target practice or Warren was damned tough. They couldn't kill him with five shots, huh?"

"I guess not, sir," replied the desk sergeant. "But word is that he may lose an arm."

I headed up front, where the major was directing the morning briefing. He was sitting in the colonel's usual place at the head of the table.

A STATESIDE TOUR OF DUTY

"We need you to submit some Blue Bell reports, this morning, lieutenant," said the major. I had barely walked into the room before the major was giving me the instructions.

"Yes, sir," I said. I picked up the blotter and began to read. Among other offenses, Warren had been charged with assault on police officers and attempted murder. The colonel and Prince were relieved of duty, and the entire PMI/Physical Security section was awaiting the outcome of an Article 31 proceeding (Article 31 is the military equivalent of a civilian grand jury indictment).

"As you all know," stated the major, "we now have no PMI section. Lieutenant Raymond, you will oversee reorganizing that section. Choose a man from each of the four reliefs, one from AWOL App and one from Traffic. After you pick some personnel, there is as lot to do. Keep me informed of all your activities. There will be no per diem payments for TDY service without prior approval from Colonel Rulon." The major turned to me. "Lieutenant Moultrie, you will take over as Operations officer immediately."

"Yes, sir," I replied.

After the meeting broke up, most of those present began to discuss the gossip involving Warren. I had no time for that. I had to get back to my office and prepare the reports for Fifth Army. I carried the copy of the blotter back with me. Once there, I called the Shreveport Police to verify the facts the blotter contained and began to work. As I wrote up the reports, I thought back on the past few months. Warren had been arrogant, obnoxious and unorthodox. He had bragged incessantly about how his operations were a paragon of police procedure. According to him, his men had an outstanding record of solving cases. In reality, most cases had simply been passed along to the CID. Those that had not been were simply closed out by listing a suspect for the offense that had been convicted of a greater crime. The government would never waste resources prosecuting someone for a misdemeanor who was already incarcerated for a felony. This tactic effectively closed many cases. The remaining cases were simply closed for lack of investigative leads.

I also thought back to his comments that my section was flaky and lacked investigative expertise. In view of the past couple of days, that comment was now hilarious.

By 1100 hours, I had all the reports finished and took them to Susan to be typed. The major then signed the reports and they were sent to the message center.

NEIL MITCHELL

When the FBI searched Warren's off-post apartment, they found automatic weapons, grenades and maps detailing plans to rob the post Finance office. Also, there were more details on the plans to kidnap the commanding general as a hostage for safe conduct out of the country. The plans called for five accomplices, but no names were given. There was no way to determine if there had been an actual danger of the plans coming to fruition or if the plans were the product of a fanciful mind. Even if the plans weren't real, the weapons were. They had been stolen from a National Guard armory six months before.

I walked over to the Operations office. Sergeant de la Vega was assembling stacks of paperwork for my signature. "Lieutenant Raymond cleared out of here two hours ago, sir," He said. "His office is yours now."

I looked at the stack of paperwork. It was nice of Byron to leave all his work for me. Fortunately, or unfortunately in this case, orders had been cut some time before designating me as an acting assistant adjutant general. The piles of paperwork were all mine.

As I began to sign the papers, I reflected on a lesson I had learned in OCS. That lesson stated that you never signed anything without reading it first. That was wonderful advice, but it was not practical. To read all this material would take the fastest speed reader until Judgment Day. I had to have it signed and out of the office by 1700 hours.

I now remembered another piece of information I had heard in Basic Training. One drill sergeant told me not to be too impressed by all the ribbons and awards someone had on their chest. In his words, the most decorated man in any outfit was usually the company clerk. This was because the clerk could place a recommendation for an award for himself in a large stack of paperwork. The commander, who did not have time to review each piece of correspondence, simply signed everything, and the clerk had an award for heroism or some other commendation. Now I realized that fact was probably true.

After some contemplation, I decided to read every tenth document. The other nine I would simply sign and trust the competence and honesty of my clerks. I hated to do it that way, but I didn't see any alternative. Using this tactic, I cleared all paperwork off my desk by 1600 hours.

Before going home, I walked over to see Steve. I told him of my dilemma. He began to joke around.

"What, you didn't read every word on every single document?" he chided. "Call the FBI! Call CID! A major outbreak of lawlessness has occurred. It's your duty under your oath as a military officer in the

A STATESIDE TOUR OF DUTY

United States Army to read every single word of all the crap that gets put on your desk." He broke out in a big smile as he pretended to rant on.

"I can take it, then, that you were never derelict in your duties and always read everything," I replied. I added, "Remember, you're under oath here."

"Like hell I am," He laughed.

"Seriously," I said. "How did you handle all of the voluminous paperwork when you were in Operations? I read every tenth item and just signed the rest. They all looked about the same anyway."

"You were more conscientious than I ever was." Bronson put his foot on one of the drawers of the desk and leaned back in his chair to light a cigarette. "I just read about every twentieth one and scanned every tenth. If you read all of that crap you'd never get to go home and probably go crazy in the meantime."

"That's about what I thought," I admitted.

"What in the hell are we going to do around here for fun, now that the colonel and Warren are gone?" Steve asked.

"Search me, buddy," I answered. "But if the last six months are any indication, we'll find something."

That afternoon I did indeed find something. A message from Fifth Army indicated that the Traffic Institute of Northwestern University at Evanston, Illinois, was offering a class in traffic accident investigation for military officers. The class would start on the 18th of January and last three weeks. This would be a TDY assignment where participants would receive a per diem of $25 a day, plus mileage both ways.

I collected my thoughts and prepared arguments for the major about why I should be allowed to go. It was imperative that PMO personnel be as well trained as possible for all contingencies. With the difficulties we had recently encountered, I would argue that it was even a greater necessity. As it turned out, no great argument was necessary. The major gave his permission for me to take the training. My Operations clerks filled out the necessary paperwork, and I was ready to go back to college, if only for three weeks.

I next submitted a request for leave for Christmas. Sam and I would spend the holidays at my grandparents' home in Rogersville, Tennessee. The leave was for the days of December 21 to 25. As usual, we would leave after I got off work on Friday, the 18th. Steve would then sign me out on leave on Monday and Sergeant Corley would sign me in from leave late Christmas Day. Sam and I would then arrive back on Sunday the 27th. That way I would be charged for five days' leave while being gone for nine.

When I got home that afternoon, Sam told me that there had been an announcement that the local news would be expanded to an hour. This was due to a news conference that General Cinch was giving to answer questions about the local difficulties. The speech and following questions from the media would be aired on all three stations. The morning's newspapers had been filled with news about Warren, and this was the best way to answer local inquiries.

Sure enough, at six o'clock the local news cut away to a live speech by the general. He told of Warren's activities, including plans to rob financial institutions, such as the post Finance office and local banks, and kidnap the general or members of his family. The speech was only about five minutes long. The general reassured everyone that the lawbreakers were in custody and everyone was safe. His obvious desire was to put to rest all the rumors that were circulating about Warren, but I suspected it might be counterproductive.

Sure enough, as soon as the speech was completed and the media began to ask questions, our phone began to ring. Everyone Sam or I knew on post was calling to find out more about what was going on. I felt like just telling them, "Watch television and you'll know as much as I do." But I didn't. I was polite and recounted what I knew. I also tried to reassure everyone that the one bad apple had been removed from the barrel. I don't know if I told more than what I should have or not. There was a part of me that wanted to just say, "No comment," or, "I'm not at liberty to say," to each caller, but that would sound like I was hiding something. I wanted to prevent such a feeling and was as open and forthcoming to each caller as possible. In my heart, I knew this would all blow over quickly but, in the meantime, it reflected badly on everyone connected with the military police at Fort McCulloch. I was happy to be leaving the area for a week.

Rogersville is a beautiful little town in northeastern Tennessee. It's like myriad other towns throughout the Deep South and Midwest. The people are friendly; the neighbors know each other and life seems almost idyllic. Having seen *Gone With The Wind*, Sam was expecting everyone to have homes like Tara. She was disappointed to find that my relatives lived in houses like those in other parts of the country. When she expressed these feelings to my grandfather, he laughed.

A STATESIDE TOUR OF DUTY

"The Yankees burned those fancy houses down about a hundred years ago, sweetie," He said. "After the fires, these more modest homes were about all we could afford."

As we spent the week visiting relatives, Sam found that my grandfather's dry, wry sense of humor was typical of Southerners. She enjoyed the hospitality and friendliness, along with the humor. She had never appreciated my sense of humor before. Now she knew where it came from. Christmas is a day designed for friends and family, and I was happy to be away from Fort McCulloch. Unfortunately, all good things must come to an end.

On the trip back to Fort McCulloch, we had to take plenty of rest stops. Sam was only four months along in her pregnancy, but it was beginning to have some definite effects. At least every hour or so, we had to find a rest area where she could relieve herself and walk around for a while.

"Honey," I teased, "think of the women who crossed the country in a covered wagon a hundred years ago. Pregnant women back then were tough and didn't have to stop all of the time."

"That's because those women got to take their time and walk all day," she replied. "Besides, when they had to pee; they could just step behind any rock or tree. The whole country was their rest area."

I chuckled and didn't argue with her. I had to be patient, and we returned to Fort McCulloch late on the afternoon of the 27th.

The week of January 1st was the major's week to serve as MPDO. We had suspected that since he was now acting as provost marshal he might skip the duty, but he didn't. I joked that it was easy for the provost marshal to be debriefed by the duty officer when they were the same person. Besides, considering how quiet the week was, the major couldn't have picked a better week to be duty officer. For me, it was a week of transition. I was now desk-bound and tied to the office with all the paperwork that went with being Operations officer. While I was still officially the Traffic officer, it was a title I now held in name only. It didn't matter, though. Sergeant Corley was more that qualified to run the section. It was actually a sergeant's job anyway.

When I gave him the news that the section was all his, he rubbed it in a little bit.

"Don't worry sir," he said. "We'll be thinking about you while we're out on the road. Just make sure to get the paperwork done, so the Army will continue to function."

"Sarge, if I know you, the only paperwork you truly care about is what Finance does to ensure you get paid," was my retort.

"No argument, sir," He replied as he and Byrd left the office.

Tuesday morning, I had to go over to JAG to check the disposition of the prosecutions against the PMI personnel. Captain Warren (no relation to the former MP) informed me those would start in late January. While there, I admired the courtroom in their building.

"I have another question for you, captain," I said.

"I'll probably have an answer for you, too, "He replied.

"Would it be possible for us to hold Magistrate's Court over here on Wednesday mornings?" I couldn't think of a reason why I hadn't thought of this before.

He smiled. "We would have to clear it with the colonel, but yeah, I can't think of a reason why you couldn't hold Kangaroo Court over here."

"Unfortunately, that sentiment seems to be universally held around here, sir," I said.

"Maybe holding it here will provide a little class and help dispel those feelings," he commented.

As I left, I noted that it sure couldn't hurt.

Upon my return to the PMO, I relayed my thoughts to the major, who promptly called the colonel at JAG. Beginning January 20th, Magistrate's Court would be held in the JAG building courtroom.

Thursday night, Sam and I attended a gala at the officers' club, where we celebrated the arrival of the new year. If our patrolmen had positioned themselves outside the officers' club that night, they probably could have arrested most of the celebrants for DUI (driving under the influence). Of course, the same could be said about the NCO club or the EM club. The amount of booze consumed that night was staggering. Fortunately, for those commemorating the occasion, the only drivers the MPs can concentrate on are those so inebriated that they are unable to keep their car on the road, or those who got into an accident. It is a busy night.

Sam and I enjoyed the dancing and had a good time. Having a good time while remaining sober seemed to be a secret the others had not heard of. Shortly after midnight we decided to leave. I told Steve and Barbara of our decision.

"We're going to leave," I said. "The pregnant lady needs her rest, so I have to take her home."

A STATESIDE TOUR OF DUTY

"Don't blame me," Sam interjected. "The pregnant lady is just fine. You're a homebody who doesn't care for big crowds."

"Do you want to stay, then?" I asked Sam.

"No. I'm ready to go, too," She admitted. "I just didn't want you putting all of the blame on me."

"This way," I told Steve, "we can go home and celebrate in our own way." Barbara and Steve laughed as Sam rolled her eyes.

The next afternoon Steve and Barbara came over. Steve and I watched the football games while Barbara and Sam talked. Steve had gotten his wish, and the Longhorns had gone through the season undefeated. Now they were playing in the Cotton Bowl to confirm their number one rating against Notre Dame.

If Steve was suffering any hangover effects from the night before, he didn't show it. He was in high spirits as the Sugar Bowl ended and I switched the channel for us to watch the event of the day—the Cotton Bowl. Steve's high spirits soon turned to depression.

Notre Dame came ready to play that day. The "Fighting Irish" dominated the game, and Steve remained fairly quiet as his team went down to defeat. "Maybe next year," was his frequently repeated comment.

As the game ended, he and Barbara left. I switched the television back to the Rose Bowl, which was late in the second half. "Is watching football all you're going to do today?" Sam complained.

"It's New Year's Day, honey," I countered. "By tradition there is nothing else to do." I patted the couch next to me and said, "Come sit down next to me and we can watch the games together."

Sam continued to complain about not being able to watch anything else but football, but she reluctantly sat next to me on the couch. Before doing so, however, she got a book to read. We then enjoyed some family togetherness. I was watching the game; Sam was reading her book.

"Barbara really wants to get married," Sam said. "You ought to encourage him to do that."

"Honey," I said. "We've had this conversation before, and I have told you that the last thing one man does to another is encouraging him to get married. He must make that decision for himself. If it doesn't work out, I don't need him blaming me."

Sam dropped the subject and went back to her book.

Shortly after Stanford had finished off Ohio State in the Rose Bowl, the Orange Bowl began. I was rooting for LSU to beat Nebraska and enjoying a great end to the day. Sam looked bored as she continued to read her book. Her next comment caught me off guard.

"Let's make love," She said.

The thought of making love while watching a football game was pure ecstasy. I could enjoy my two favorite pursuits at the same time. Sam let me know that was not possible.

"We can make love, or you can watch this stupid game," she said. "But," She continued. "Since I would want your undivided attention, you would have to turn off the TV."

"Okay, honey," I said. "Wait until halftime."

Sam forcefully said, "No! It's right now or not at all. I'm not talking about a quickie. What I have in mind should take a couple of hours."

Talk about being on the horns of a dilemma. If I chose the football game, Sam would probably feel rejected. I might not only miss a great evening in the sack, but Sam might hold a grudge for some time. On the other hand, if I chose an erotic night, I would miss a game I wanted to watch.

"Make your decision now, buddy boy," Sam reiterated, "Me, or the game."

The United States Army trains its officers to make wise, though difficult, decisions. In this moment of coercion, I made one. I got up and turned off the television. Sam's face broke into a big smile.

"A wise decision," She said. She got up and walked over to me. As she gave me a passionate kiss she asked, "Do you want to start here or in the bedroom?"

"It's your call," I said. "You're the one who planned the evening's activities."

CHAPTER TWENTY-TWO

The first thing I did Saturday morning was to drop in at the PMO and find a newspaper. As I looked at the sports section, the desk sergeant asked, "Did you catch that game last night, sir? Nebraska's going to be national champs now."

"I missed it, sarge. I dozed off early and got a good night's sleep," I lied.

"You're kidding! You missed a great one," the sergeant explained. "Nebraska barely pushed in a touchdown late in the game to pull it out."

After reading about the game, I picked up some books Sam had asked me to return to the library on my way home Thursday afternoon. I had set them aside in the office and forgotten to do as she had asked. As soon as I had arrived at home New Year's Eve, she had asked, "Did you return my library books?"

Not wanting to admit I forgot, I suggested, "I better go pick up some milk and bread, we probably need some."

"You did forget," she had exclaimed. "The big, brave, competent Army officer couldn't remember to take my books back."

"Okay, rub it in," was my comeback.

"For once, we have plenty of milk and bread," she had said. "We're going to the officers' club tonight, so you can get them the next time you go to the office."

Now it was Saturday morning, and I was finally retrieving the books. I checked the due date. My lapse of memory would cost me a small fine.

As I came out of Operations, I noticed that the door of the Traffic office was not locked. I considered locking it, but decided that since I no longer maintained a desk there it was not my responsibility. Besides, one of the investigators might be working this morning and would lock it when he returned. Instead, I hurried to return the library books and go home. I have always heard that one should follow their instincts. My initial instinct was to lock the Traffic office door, and I didn't. I would soon regret that decision.

About 11:00 PM that night the phone rang. Sergeant Katone was calling from the PMO. "Sir, the major needs you in here right now. He's madder than hell."

"What about, sarge?" I inquired.

"We have a bunch of escaped prisoners. They got out through Traffic and the major wants to know why the door wasn't locked," Katone replied.

"How did they get past the metal door by the D-cell?" I asked.

"Apparently, it was left open, sir," was the answer.

"What in hell for? That door is always supposed to be closed," I stated.

"I don't know, sir." He changed the subject. "The major needs you right now."

"All right, sarge, tell him that I'm on my way." I hung up the phone and without changing into a uniform I left immediately for the PMO.

Upon my arrival at the PMO I learned that Bingham had left on leave the Monday before and Katone was filling in as desk sergeant. Apparently, the large metal sally port door by the desk had been left open and all six prisoners in the D-cell had gone through the Traffic office and out its back door to freedom. The major was asking why the Traffic office was left unlocked, when the question should have been why the prisoners hadn't been better secured and observed in the first place. To reach the Traffic office, they first had to get through the door to the D-cell then through the door by the desk. Both had obviously been left open. When I pointed this out to the major, his anger subsided a bit.

"Sir," I continued, "I suggest that I begin an immediate investigation into this matter. It is apparent that routine security standards have not been observed. After all of the facts have been discovered, we can take appropriate measures to ensure this never happens again."

"Good idea, lieutenant," said the major.

"Also, sir," I continued, "have civilian jurisdictions been made aware to be on the lookout for these men?"

The major glared at Katone. "How about it, sergeant? Have you spread the word that we're missing prisoners here?"

"No, sir. I'll do that right now." Katone picked up the phone and began to call the surrounding police departments, giving them the names and descriptions of the escapees.

I then talked with SP4 Boyd, the desk clerk, and got his deposition. In his words, they had gotten busy with a rash of calls about 2200 hours. He was sure the escapes happened about that time or shortly before the prisoners were discovered to be missing. After all, he did check on them periodically as the SOPs required.

Sergeant Katone's statement was like Boyd's. In a moment when desk personnel had been distracted by a number of calls, the prisoners had obviously left in a united escape. He was sure it was just a few moments before the disappearance had been discovered.

"Why was the door to the D-cell left open?" I asked.

"The prisoners had to pee a lot tonight, sir," replied Katone. "I guess that when one of those times occurred, the phone rang and we forgot to close the door behind the prisoner."

"Why was the door beside the desk left open, sergeant?" I asked.

"We had the prisoners waxing the floor earlier, sir. Between them having to go back and forth and the PMI people coming through several times, I guess we just forgot to close it once."

I looked at Sergeant Katone. I didn't believe a word he said, but I decided not to challenge his recall of the facts at this point. It was now early Sunday morning, and I just wanted to go home.

"Thank you, sergeant. That will be all," I said.

"Yes, sir," he said and left.

As I drove back home, I continued to be amazed at how there never seemed to be a dull moment at Fort McCulloch. Things seemed to go wrong with even the most mundane and routine of tasks. I was beginning to believe that we did have men assigned here that could screw up a wet dream or foul up a proverbial excrement sandwich. The facts would prove me right.

When I got home, I told Sam of the night's events. She was incredulous.

She asked what should have been the evident question. "How in the world can they blame you, if two other doors were left unlocked and the one in question is no longer your office?"

"Search me, honey. As near as I can figure, the men on the desk passed the buck, and the major wasn't smart enough to call them on it."

I then added, "Don't worry, though. I have control of the investigation, and I'll make sure the fault gets placed on the right people."

As we spoke, two of the escapees were hitchhiking to San Angelo. The duo, Tom Haskell and Mark Haslem, had the misfortune to be standing on the side of the road when two off-duty MPs drove by. SP4s Harding and Trout recognized the men as prisoners from the PMO's D-cell. They stopped and, even though the patrolmen were in civilian clothes and unarmed, they quickly convinced the men to return with them to custody. This was accomplished by reminding the men that they were not currently facing any major charges. Also, by returning peacefully, things would go better than if the authorities had to apprehend them later. By 0200 hours they were locked back in the D-cell without further incident.

Two other escapees made the mistake of traveling through Lutzville. Tim Soward and Jeff Enlow were questioned by the local cops as soon as they got to the city limits, since their descriptions fit those of the escapees they had been told to be on the lookout for. By 0400 hours, four of the six were back in custody.

A fifth escapee, Ted Sorrell, was panhandling in Fort Worth when police approached him Sunday evening. He was not having much luck and, being tired, and hungry, he admitted who he was. AWOL Apprehension would bring him in on the Lone Star Run the following Wednesday.

Monday morning, I walked up front for the morning briefing. The major truly relished having the place at the head of the table and prolonged the meeting as long as possible by asking about insignificant or irrelevant details about every item on the blotter. He had been the duty officer, so there should have been no reason for the questions. My investigation of the Saturday night escape would begin after I left this meeting. For now, I just drank my coffee and endured this exercise in futility along with the others. As I returned to my office, I looked briefly at the morning paper. The item that first caught my eye was the fact that Lieutenant William Calley's court martial was about to begin at Fort Benning, Georgia.

Most people had an opinion about Lieutenant Calley. Personally, I saw him as a scapegoat. The news media had presented most of the facts to the American people. On the 16th of March 1968, Calley's platoon had swept through the village of Mylai in South Vietnam. Several hundred people, mostly women, children and old men, had been rounded up and forced into a ditch, where they were shot. By the time the story had become public on 30 November 1969, most of the soldiers had been discharged and, as civilians, were beyond the Army's reach. Those still in the Army had been coerced into testifying against Calley in exchange for immunity.

The company commander, Captain Medina, avoided prosecution, as did the battalion commander. The platoon sergeant, SSG Mitchell, was black. As the military saw blacks as an enormous reservoir for recruitment, the Army made only a half-hearted attempt to prosecute him, and he had been acquitted. With everyone above and below him in the chain of command exonerated, the full weight of the United States prosecution fell on the hapless lieutenant.

What most people had not been told by the media was that Calley was an honor graduate of the Fort Benning OCS program. He was an intelligent, capable leader who truly believed he was responsible for the welfare of his men. The second platoon leader who served in Calley's company had become a tactical officer at Fort Belvoir after his tour in Vietnam. He had nothing bad to say about Calley, although he would say (always off the record) that the Mylai incident technically fit the definition of war crimes. He would never elaborate.

"Looks like they're going to hang Calley out to dry," I said to Sergeant Dee.

"That's exactly what they're doing, sir," the Operations sergeant agreed. "A man does his duty, and thanks to a few newsmen who want a story he's on trial for his life."

Having no combat experience of my own, I thought this might be an excellent opportunity to hear from someone who had seen the result of battle. Most men who had been involved in hand-to-hand fighting usually got real quiet when the subject came up. Now that sergeant Dee seemed agreeable to talk about it, I made the most of the situation.

However, I did take an indirect approach. "I understand war is never a clean and tidy exercise, sarge," I began, "But, Calley's legal problems stem from the fact that he did order the execution of those civilians." I used the term *civilians* rather than *people* to improve my chances of getting a response from De la Vega. It worked.

"Let me tell you something, sir. Those weren't civilians. Not really." He paused for a second. "*All* the people in Viet Cong–controlled areas were killing our men. I have seen nine-year-old children fire RPGs at patrol boats on the Mekong River. I have seen babies left behind in abandoned huts, connected to trip wires so when an American picked the infant up to take care of it, he was blown up. Women and old men like to ambush our men. Then when we counterattack, they hide the weapons and sit around smiling at us. When asked who was shooting at us, they know nothing." He threw the ballpoint pen he was doing paperwork with down onto the desk in disgust and sat back in his chair.

"I'm guessing you lost a few friends over there," I replied.

"Yes, I did," he said. "They were all good men. Most of them were killed by booby traps set by those so-called civilian noncombatants."

I continued to probe for information. "Now that you mention it, I understand Calley's unit was taking heavy casualties in the Mylai area."

"Yes, they were, sir. So Calley gave the enemy a taste of their own medicine. It was okay for their women and kids to shoot our men, but we return the favor and it's a war crime."

I was prepared to continue doing paperwork, but Sergeant Dee apparently found venting a little rage to be therapeutic. He continued without any prodding from me. "You know what really pisses me off, sir?"

"What's that, sarge?"

"This whole Mylai episode began when some helicopter pilot reported the incident. People up the chain of command had the good sense to pigeonhole the report, but the asshole went to the news media that searched the world to find some guy who would corroborate the story."

Sergeant Dee was correct. Some helicopter pilot, from the relative safety of his aircraft, had observed the action. With no knowledge of the realities of combat for ground personnel, he had felt a need to protect the murderous Mylai residents, who killed our troops with such relish, from the avenging American troops. Many combat veterans felt the villagers at Mylai deserved their punishment. In fact, it was a well-known detail that after the reprisals, the number of ambushes against American and ARVN (South Vietnamese soldiers) troops in Viet Cong–controlled areas dropped precipitously. By holding the Mylai residents accountable for their actions and administering retribution, other hamlets had gotten the message.

Having gotten his gripes off his chest, Sergeant Dee went back to work. We had no more discussions about the war, and I got to work on my official investigation.

My first order of business was to interrogate the prisoners. Steve agreed to join me in conducting the investigation. Together, we met with

Haslem and read him his rights and he waived them. I had him write his statement down. It went as follows:

> I, Mark Haslem, was in custody in the Fort McCulloch detention cell on the night of January 2, 1971. Someone else asked to get a drink of water and the desk sergeant opened the doors so he could go out to the water fountain. After getting a drink, the guy walked out the front door. I decided that since the guy got away, I could do the same thing. I asked to get a drink and was told to go ahead. After getting a drink, I walked out the front door also. I was hiding behind the building next door when, a short time later, Haskell came out. We then left together.

I then said, "do you swear that this is the truth, the whole truth and nothing but the truth?"

"I do," Haslem said.

"Okay, go ahead and sign the statement," I said. "Why did the men on the desk not see you go out the front door?"

"They were watching *Mission Impossible*," he replied.

"*Mission Impossible*?" I asked.

"Yeah, they had a TV right there on the desk. The dudes were watching it and never saw anything else," he elaborated.

"Do you know the name of the first man that left?" I asked.

"No, sir. He was the last guy they put in the D-cell. A blond guy. I never learned his name. He kind of kept to himself."

I continued the interrogation. "When the first guy left, did he have any trouble convincing the men on the desk to open the door to the desk area?"

"No, sir. The sergeant had his feet propped up on the desk and just leaned back in his chair and pressed the button with his billy club. He didn't even look back."

"Did the desk personnel ever close the door entering into the desk area?" I further inquired?

"No, sir. As far as I know it was never closed before I left."

"Thank you, I appreciate your cooperation," I said. From the description, I guessed the first escapee to be Sorrell. I would have to wait until AWOL App returned him to verify that fact. I decided to question Haskell next.

NEIL MITCHELL

After warning Haskell of his rights, he wrote his statement down, and after subsequent questioning from me and Steve, verified everything Haslem had said. Their stories were fairly consistent. In addition, Haskell identified the first escapee as Sorrell. My hunch had been correct.

We talked to Jeff Enlow next. His statement went as follows:

> I, Jeffery R. Enlow, departed the detention cell on the night of January 2, 1971. After four other men had walked out the front door unchallenged, I decided I might as well go, too. I walked to the side of the MP desk and saw the open office to my right and cut through there. As I was walking past the main gate, I found Soward hiding there. We decided to hitchhike south toward Mexico. Our first ride dropped us off just north of Lutzville. We were walking through town when the cops arrested us. We were turned over to military authorities and back in the D-cell before morning.

I administered the oath, and Enlow signed his statement. I now had a clear picture of the events. Also, through the process of elimination, it was clear that the last man to leave was Kellogg. All four men were clear about several facts. One, the desk sergeant and desk clerk had been derelict in their duties. They had been watching television since about 1930 hours. *Mission Impossible* came on at 2000 hours, and everyone agreed that the boob tube had been in use for at least a half hour before that.

Second, the first four men had walked out the front door. The fifth had left through the Traffic office. The sixth, I hadn't talked to yet.

Third, given the spacing between escapes, it was clear that all six were probably gone at least an hour before Katone had reported the escape to the major.

The sixth and final escapee, Bill Kellogg, had gotten as far as his home in Albuquerque, New Mexico, before he was apprehended. The biggest mistake deserters from the Army usually make is heading for home. This is the first place the authorities go to look for them. Kellogg made the same mistake. Once we were advised the Albuquerque police had our sixth man in custody, Mister Swanson flew two of our men there to pick him up. By Friday morning all six escapees would be accounted for.

After AWOL App brought in Sorrell on Wednesday, Steve and I warned the escapee of his rights. "Do you understand these rights as I have explained them?" I asked.

"Yes, sir," he answered.

"Do you agree to answer questions?"

He thought for a few seconds and said, "Yes, sir."

Everything he said agreed in the main with the other four men we had questioned. After we had asked our questions, I asked him if he would like to make a written statement. He picked up the pen, but after a few seconds he said, "Sir, I'd rather not make a written statement."

"No problem," I said. I supposed that, since he had been the first to go, he was afraid that a written statement might come back to haunt him. He didn't need to worry. To prosecute him and the others for this escape would bring considerable embarrassment on the military police company. The quicker we shipped these men out to Fort Sam Houston to be returned to their units or discharged, the better. I informed Sergeant Lippman that the five escapees could be shipped out Thursday morning.

By Friday afternoon, I had finished my interrogation of Kellogg. As the last to leave, he had escaped before 2100 hours and he had gone through the Traffic office. I was now prepared to complete my report. About 1500 the major informed me, via the intercom, that he wished to see me.

"You asked to see me, sir," I said as I walked to the door of his office.

"Yes, lieutenant, I understand that five of the men who escaped have been shipped out by AWOL App," he stated. "Who allowed that to happen?"

"I did, sir. I was finished with my investigation and since you hadn't told me otherwise, I saw no reason to incur additional expense to the Army to keep them here."

"But what about pressing charges for escape to make an example of them to others?" the major asked.

"Sir," I explained, "to attempt to prosecute those men for escape would make the 290th Military Police Company and the Fort McCulloch Provost Marshal's Office the laughing stock of the Army. Fortunately, they committed no felonies while they were free, so no Blue Bell reports need to be submitted. We can take care of this here and not bother Fifth Army. I recommend that we take corrective action to ensure this never happens again and let it blow over. You will have my final report in one hour"

The major was visibly impressed with my explanation. "I see," he said. "Very well, lieutenant. I'll await your report."

At this point, Lieutenant Raymond came into the major's office. "We don't have all of the escapees, Nick," he said.

"All six are accounted for," I said. "How do you figure that we don't have them all?"

"What about Monteer?" he asked.

I shrugged my shoulders. "Who's Monteer? I never heard of him?"

"I don't know," Byron said, "but he disappeared off the desk log at 1900 hours on New Year's Eve." He held up the desk logs for the past week.

I took the papers from him and began to examine them. Sure enough, the 1800 entry read, "Checked D-cell and Monteer, Sorrell, Jones and Carter accounted for." The 1900 entry only had Sorrell, Jones and Carter accounted for, in the D-Cell. As I continued to go through the logs, I saw where Jones and Carter had been picked up by their first sergeant. They were charged with DUI and were cited into Magistrate's Court. Over the next two days the other five men who had been involved in the mass escape had been added, but there was no explanation for the disappearance of Monteer.

"Well what about it, lieutenant?" The major demanded. "What happened to Monteer?"

"Sir," I replied, "you were the duty officer who signed the log." I showed the paper to him. "You should have a better knowledge of that than I."

The major's face went white as he looked at the desk log I held in front of him. He sputtered and stuttered and acted like he was about to choke. He then said, "Lieutenant, since Lieutenant Raymond is the head of PMI you can turn your information over to him to conclude the investigation. Escape does fall under PMI's dominion."

"Yes, sir," I said with glee. "I'll go get my material and bring it up to him right now."

I went back to my office and got the statements from all the prisoners, along with the questions I had asked and their answers. I xeroxed the material to ensure that I kept copies. I then took the originals back to Byron in PMI.

"You shouldn't have done that to the major," he said. "Making the boss look bad is never a good policy."

"He signed the log," I snapped back. "I'm not going to take the blame for his error."

A STATESIDE TOUR OF DUTY

"Half the time, the duty officer signs those logs without reading them, Nick. You know that," he said. "We all get busy or in a hurry. You know how it is."

Yes, I knew how it was. A brownnoser like Byron Raymond would probably go to the top of some government agency or other bureaucracy with ease. Perhaps I should have been more tactful with the major, but his attitude and tone of voice was a little more than I was going to tolerate. I was not going to be a fall guy or scapegoat for his incompetence. I didn't always read the logs in totality, as the duty officer, but I did at least scan them. Hopefully, I would have spotted a man who disappeared with no further explanation.

I walked over to the company, where I informed Steve of the latest developments. He became almost hysterical with laughter. "I wish I could have been there," he roared. "The dumb-ass major wants to chew somebody's butt for losing a prisoner, and he turns out to be the person that lost him."

While Steve hooted, guffawed and snickered at the total irony of the situation, I suggested that there might still be work to do. I suggested that we talk to Boyd about the last missing man. That way, we would have all the facts in case there was any more fallout about these latest developments. After a few more chuckles, he agreed.

We sent one of the company clerks over to the barracks for Boyd. Shortly before quitting time he came over to see us.

"You needed to see me, sir?" Boyd asked.

"Yes, Boyd, this should only take a few minutes," I replied. "Have a seat."

Boyd sat down. "What can I do for you, sir?"

I showed the log to Boyd. "Look, Boyd, I just need to know what happened on the desk on New Year's Eve. If something improper was done it's Katone's butt, not yours, that is in a sling."

"I don't want to get anybody in trouble, sir," he hedged.

"Boyd," I began. "Katone is a loser. I'm sure that his days as a patrol supervisor or acting desk sergeant or in any other supervisory position are over. I just don't want to see you go down with him. We can help you, but we have to know the facts."

"Well, sir, now that you mention it, I did think it was kind of strange."

"What was strange?" I asked.

"Well, we got behind. It was New Year's Eve and it was busy." Boyd then continued. "About six o'clock I started filling in the log. I did about a page and a half at once. I just retyped what was already entered; it rarely changes. Well, I then called out the names of the men in the D-cell and one didn't answer. We had four names and only three men. Katone then erased the missing man's name and said to forget about him."

I thought for a moment. With the recent PMI debacle, we had lost a few men. I didn't want to lose any more. We could quickly become shorthanded again. "Look, Boyd," I began. "As soon as possible, I need you to tell this story to Lieutenant Raymond at PMI, and don't tell anyone else. In the meantime, if you need advice, then get with Sergeant Corley over in Traffic. He's been around and he can tell you what else to do. Also, tell Corley that if any help is needed keeping you out of trouble, then Lieutenant Bronson and myself will do anything we can. Remember, except for Lieutenant Raymond and Sergeant Corley, don't talk to anyone else about this."

"Thank you, sir. I appreciate it," Boyd said.

After Boyd's departure, Steve really began to laugh. "Can you picture it?" He chuckled. "They call out the man's name and he doesn't answer. Do they check it out? Hell, no! They just say 'Piss on it; he ain't there,' and erase his name."

"Steve, my friend," I said. "We need to put a tent on this circus and charge admission."

"I have a better idea," he replied. "Let's call the *Ripley's Believe It or Not* people. There is no way in hell they would ever believe what goes on around here."

"I agree. Let's go home," I said. "If I didn't have Sam waiting for me at the end of each day, I don't think I would survive this place."

"You know, Nick," Steve said. "Barbara really wants to get married. I don't know if I'm ready for that. You seem to be doing okay though, huh?"

"We have our disagreements and arguments," I said. "But, the making up sure is fun." I thought for a second and then added with a smile, "I have no overwhelming complaints."

Steve didn't reply to that. He just said, "I'll see you Monday."

When I told Sam about the latest happenings at work, she shook her head. "They should turn that place into a soap opera—," she said, "*Another World in Fort McCulloch*."

"A better title might be *The Guiding Dumb Asses*," I speculated.

"I don't think the script writers would go for that one," she concluded.

Friday night we went to the theater to watch *Catch-22*. The movie was based on the book, of the same name, by Joseph Heller.

A STATESIDE TOUR OF DUTY

Unfortunately, the movie was part of a new genre of movies where directors concentrated on realism over acting. Placing squid on actors' stomachs simulated graphic belly wounds from combat, and some sex scenes left little to the imagination. Likewise, even though this was a comedy, many of the scenarios depicted were too ridiculous to be taken seriously. A scene where American officers receive payment from the Germans to bomb their own American airfield comes to mind. As we drove home, I brought that fact up to Sam, and she began to explain the film from a more artistic point of view.

"It's a satire, honey," she explained. "They're satirizing the free enterprise system and how the desire to make money can even be more important than a war effort."

"I know what satire is, Sam. It's just that what was depicted is so far from reality as to make it impossible."

"That's what makes it funny, Nick. You ought to know that. You're the one who went to college."

"I guess so. It's just that . . . ." Suddenly I lost my train of thought.

"Think about the bureaucrats you tell me about, that you deal with every day, Nick. Can't you imagine them doing stupidly insane things?"

Now I had to laugh. Sam was right. Civilian workers with their feet on the desk telling me how busy they were, paperwork being returned for minor typos and people searching for obscure regulations to enforce were common occurrences across Fort McCulloch. However, since I considered her question to be rhetorical, I did not answer.

"Seriously, Nick! What is it you always tell me about the place where you work?"

"I know. If they put a tent over the PMO, it would be a circus. I've said that."

"Exactly! So, if you exaggerated a little, it would be as funny as that movie we just saw."

"Honey, where I work is funny enough now. I don't need to exaggerate."

"Well," said Sam. "As long as we're agreeing on things, how about I pick the next movie."

"Why, honey?"

"I'm tired of movies with sex and gore. That seems to be all you ever pick."

"How do you figure that?"

Sam began to count on her fingers. "*M.A.S.H.*, *Patton* and *Catch-22*. Is that a trend, or do you detect a theme here?"

"There was no sex in *Patton*," I corrected.

"No," she admitted. "Just a lot of combat and killing. It's getting a little old."

"Okay, babe," I agreed. "You get to pick the next one."

Saturday night we went over to Tom and Andrea's to play canasta. They were still asking questions about Warren and his activities, and I did my best to trivialize everything that had gone on. I reminded them that Jesus had Judas among his twelve apostles so there was always one bad apple in every barrel.

"This episode has given us a chance to clean house," I said. "All of the bad apples are gone."

While it was easy to maintain an outward appearance of total confidence, my gut instincts let me know that I wasn't so sure.

Sunday morning, Sam forced me out of bed to attend services at the post chapel. The chaplain delivered a sermon about loving your fellowman and forgiving others. For the most part, everything he preached seemed to be good advice. I guess it is okay to love your fellowman, but trusting them is another thing entirely. My instincts had told me not to trust Warren, and they had been right on. While his friends had claimed he was a changed man who had paid the price for his mistakes, I had been wise to have my doubts. Warren's friends had been dragged down with him. Those of us who kept our distance had survived.

Monday afternoon, Raymond turned in his finished report about the escape to the major. Somehow, he had gotten the idea that Enlow had left before Soward, but his report was mostly a rehash of mine. His recommendations were also what mine would have been. Katone would no longer serve as patrol supervisor. Also, new SOPs (standard operating procedures) were drafted, stating that television sets and other distracting items would not be allowed on the MP desk. Also, it was made clear that negligence such as had happened the night of the escape would never be tolerated again.

Wednesday, after court, I returned to the PMO. As I walked in the door, Specialist Byrd said, "Sir, they got that last guy that escaped."

I smiled at the good news. "You mean Monteer? Where did they find him?"

"New Orleans, sir," he replied. "It turns out that he took off late Wednesday night, the day before he disappeared off the log."

I was stunned at the news. "You mean he was gone for twenty-four hours before Katone erased him from the board?"

"Yes, sir," he replied. "Sergeant Corley says it's the funniest thing he has ever heard of."

I reviewed the news in my mind. A prisoner had escaped and was never missed until a full day later. Then, someone simply deleted his name off the record and failed to report the missing man. Things were worse than I had thought.

CHAPTER TWENTY-THREE

I was sitting at my desk, preparing to leave the next day, when Mr. Garcia came into my office. "This is yours, Nick," he said. He dropped twenty-two dollars on my desk.

"What is this?" I asked.

"The last football pool for the bowl games. I'm sorry to take so long, but with Christmas leave and coaching the post basketball team, I just barely got around to figuring the winner."

"You mean Sergeant Dee didn't win one? That's a switch."

Garcia laughed. "Nope, it's all yours."

I looked at the money. The Nebraska-LSU game had been the tiebreaker. When I missed that one, I figured I had lost. As it turned out, I had picked enough of the other games right. The tiebreaker was not a factor. I cheerfully put the winnings in my pocket and headed for home.

On Friday, the 15th, Sam and I took off for Chicago for the three weeks of training at the Northwestern University Traffic Institute. The institute is located just off the university campus in the suburb of Evanston, and that was our exact destination.

The farther north we drove, the colder it got. Suddenly the morning lows of twenty-five or thirty degrees didn't seem so bad. In northern Illinois, those were often the high temperature for the day this time of the year.

We spent the first night in Missouri. As usual, we had a disagreement about where to spend the night. Sam wanted a nice, sanitized location and I wanted to save a few bucks. As was the case most of the time, Sam won the argument. By Saturday afternoon we had arrived at our goal. We found a hotel and settled in for the evening.

Sunday, we did some sight seeing and I discovered that Fort Benjamin Harrison was within commuting distance. We drove there and checked into the post guest house. The apartments there had kitchen facilities and would only cost us two dollars per day. While attending the Traffic Institute, I would receive a per diem of $25, since the military was not providing quarters or meals. Now I had to consider the ethics of the situation. The military was not providing the facilities outright, and I had to go out of my way to find them. We quickly discovered that another couple next door was thinking the same way.

First Lieutenant James Leavitt and his wife, Sharon, were from Fort Carson, Colorado. After reconnoitering the area, they (like us) had found Fort Benjamin Harrison and had taken up residence in the guest house. This would give Sam someone to spend time with and allow me to carpool back and forth to class. Also, I would have a companion to study with. Our neighbors, likewise, had considered the morality of using government facilities and had decided, as we had, there was nothing illegal or unethical about it.

For the next three weeks, I received an in-depth course of study about traffic accident investigation, details about tires, insurance, effects of alcohol consumption and other diverse subjects the United States government considered germane. In sum, the trip was well worth it. I saved my notes and course material to share with the traffic investigators back home. This was material they should be aware of.

The class consisted of thirty officers ranging from a light colonel down to numerous lieutenants. We came from posts all over the United States. We compared notes about the problems we encountered and the resources we had at our disposal. Some of the men from posts nearer to large metropolitan areas had to deal with anti-war demonstrations, and many of the other posts had occasional murders—something I had not had to deal with at Fort McCulloch. I kept the more unusual details about Fort McCulloch to myself. The location I was assigned to might be a joke in many ways, but I wasn't going to let any else know that. As others discussed their problems, I just nodded knowingly and said that I understood.

A couple of the officers who were members of a fraternity decided to stay at the frat house of the local chapter on the Northwestern University campus, where there would be no charge. They changed their mind after one night. It seems that as they were sitting down to dinner the first night there, a food fight broke out. They rapidly found other accommodations.

Jim Leavitt and I took turns driving to class, while Sharon and Sam did their daily sight-seeing. On the weekends, the four of us relaxed and enjoyed touring the area. Until the end of the second week, that is. That weekend Sam and I both became deathly sick. The temperature in Chicago plummeted to twenty below zero and Sam and I were ready to return to southwest Texas. With Lake Michigan so close, I expected the area to be humid, but it wasn't. The air was so dry that it seemed to suck the moisture right out of our bodies, and we were constantly thirsty. I placed pans of water on the radiators to try to put humidity back into the air. With Sam's pregnancy, I tried to be the one who took care of us, but by Sunday afternoon I could barely even stand up. I was a little embarrassed that it was Sam who drove us both to the post hospital that night. I don't know what the doctor gave us, but between the medicinal prescription and a long night's sleep, I could go to class the next day. Sam spent Monday in bed. I brought home some hamburgers that night, and again we retired early. By Tuesday morning, whatever we had been afflicted with was past.

By the time the class had ended on February 5, I can sarcastically say that a heat wave had swept into northern Illinois and the overnight low was a balmy two degrees above zero. Sam and I were both happy to bid that area good-bye.

We spent the night in St. Louis, and by late Saturday afternoon I was signing in from TDY back at Fort McCulloch. It was sixty degrees in Harrisville as we arrived at home.

Monday, everyone seemed happy to see me. Byron was happy that he could turn the paperwork of Operations back over to me. Steve was happy to have a kindred spirit around, and the major had someone whose shoulder he could look over.

During my absence, we had welcomed a new provost marshal. After being relieved of duty, Colonel Cox had been reassigned to Headquarters while his retirement paperwork was being processed. The new boss was Colonel Sherman. The major was now relegated back to writing patrol tips and bothering me. I spent part of the morning briefing the colonel and the major on the subjects I had covered during the past three weeks and how I would like to incorporate them into the weekly company training. I was impressed with Sherman. He clearly desired to end the Keystone Cops reputation the Fort McCulloch law enforcement personnel currently had.

About 1500 I was summoned to his office. "Moultrie," he began. "I like your ideas."

"Thank you, sir," I replied.

A STATESIDE TOUR OF DUTY

"Technically, the major is between the two of us in the chain of command; however, any thoughts you have on how to improve the quality of our personnel and advance better public relations can be brought directly to me. You don't have to feel obligated to get the major's approval on them first."

"I understand, sir. I'm guessing that I should be tactful in routing everything around the major, though." After less than two weeks, the new colonel had already pegged the major for what he was: a bureaucratic drone with limited competence and few meaningful assigned duties.

The colonel smiled. "I see you understand the system. Anything that is of limited importance and it isn't of an urgent nature can be sent through channels and routed through the major. You don't need to bypass him with everything," the colonel smiled and added, "just the important things."

"Yes, sir. I understand," I said.

"Well, it's good to finally meet you and have you back on the job, lieutenant. Carry on." We shook hands and I walked back to my office.

I almost felt sorry for the major as I left the colonel's office. It was clear that the colonel had no confidence in him. The other junior officers and I would serve as the colonel's right-hand men ,and the major would be largely left out of the loop.

Once in my office, I began to plow through the pile of paperwork that was now coming to my desk. By 1700, I had pretty well cleared it out when Steve dropped in.

"Welcome back, vacation man," he said.

I stood and shook hands with him. "Vacation, hell! I've been going to school."

"I wish I could have traded places with you," he replied.

"I see you were able to keep the place together while I was gone," I chided.

"Barely," he said. "Just barely." He paused for a second, then asked, "How would you and your wife like to attend a basketball game Friday night?"

"Who's playing?"

"Barbara's brother plays guard for Central Valley State. They play their big rival, Lamar Tech. Barbara's parents won't be able to attend, so she has two extra tickets available. I thought it might be a nice evening for the four of us."

"Steve, my friend, you have a deal. By the way, how's her brother's team doing on the season?"

"Only lost two games. Averaging ninety-five points a game. It should be a great game."

"Sounds great, Steve. I'll look forward to it."

When I got home, I gave the news to Sam. She was less than enthusiastic.

"Don't you think you should have checked with me first, Nick?" she said.

"What's the problem, honey? It will give us a nice evening out."

"You know I'm not a big sports fan, Nick. Besides, you're just excited about the free tickets. You see it as a cheap date."

"Honey, we can get dinner at a restaurant afterward. It will be nice."

"All right, tightwad. We'll go to the game." We gave each other a hug.

"You'll enjoy it, honey. It will be an exciting game."

Tuesday morning, the blotter contained a charge of assault with a deadly weapon. As I read the entry I wasn't sure who the victim was. It seems that a soldier who had been drinking at the EM club had one too many. He had gone to the rest room and, while sitting on the toilet, he had passed out. When the PFC (private first class) came to, he found that another soldier had crawled under the wall of the bathroom stall and was performing oral sex on him. In apparent disgust, he had pulled a knife and stabbed the pervert.

The man who had passed out was about five foot six, while the man seeking the momentary diversion was about six foot two. After being warned of his rights, the attacker had made a statement that he was terrified, since the other man was so much larger, and he had resorted to using a knife out of fear.

"If you're dumb enough to drink until you pass out, you deserve whatever happens to you," Mr. Garcia chuckled.

"The poor guy still didn't deserve to wake up and find some dirt bag blowing him," Sergeant Corley said with a smile.

"I can't help but think that I might have stabbed that creep, too, if I had been in the little guy's place," I interjected. "However, we can't let people go around stabbing each other, regardless of the justification. Our whole society would become chaos."

"That's right, lieutenant," said the colonel. "I presume you'll have a Blue Bell out on this case."

"I'll do it the first thing this morning, sir," I replied.

A STATESIDE TOUR OF DUTY

In fact, the report would be a SIR (Serious Incident Report) instead of a Blue Bell, but I wasn't going to correct the colonel in front of everyone else. If the charge had been agg-assault (aggravated assault) there would have been no report at all. However, the use of a deadly weapon, in this case a switchblade knife with a six-inch blade, made for a more serious charge and, consequently, more paperwork for me.

"You know men, this reminds me of a joke," said the colonel.

As we all gave the colonel our undivided attention, he began a joke I had heard in Chicago and had told to him the day before.

"Two men decide to go on a hunting trip," began the colonel. "They drive into the mountains, hike twenty miles into the foothills and then canoe twenty-five miles upstream. At that point, one needs to relieve himself and just as he's taking a leak a big rattlesnake strikes and bites him right on the end of his male anatomy. The second man has him lie down and remain comfortable while he goes to consult a doctor. The second man then canoes downstream, hikes back down the trails and then drives back into town. He goes to a doctor's office for advice and explains that a large rattlesnake has bitten his friend. The doctor explains that this man must go back and make incisions deepening the fang puncture wounds and suck out the poison. When pressed for an alternative, the doctor explains that must be done quickly or the unfortunate man will die. This second man then drives back into the mountains, hikes the twenty miles into the foothills and then canoes twenty-five miles upstream. As he approaches his companion the first man yells, 'What did the doctor say? What did the doctor say?' The second man says very enthusiastically, 'The doctor said you're going to die.'"

As everyone laughed I realized one of the realities of military life. The amount of laughter that followed a joke was directly proportionate to the rank of the person telling the joke. The higher the rank of the joke teller and the more subordinate the listeners, the more laughter that was produced. If I told a joke to a group of lower-ranking enlisted men, my chances of getting a good laugh were much better than a joke told to my peers or superiors. While the colonel had enjoyed the joke the day before, the response to his rendition was better than anything I had been able to create when I told it.

As the laughter subsided from the joke, Mr. Bernard commented, "That's definitely a time when you find out who your friends are."

"I'm not sure I could be that good of a friend to anyone," Sergeant Harris chuckled.

With Colonel Sherman in charge, the morning briefings were more relaxed, but kept the format we were used to with Colonel Cox. At the end, everyone was asked for final comments and we departed for our respective offices.

Upon returning to my office, I began to sign the daily pile of paperwork. After completing my necessary tasks, I walked over to the company, where I discussed with Captain Lynch the possibility of incorporating the information I had received at the Northwestern Traffic Institute into the company training. Steve joined us in the conversation.

"That's an excellent idea," said the captain. "This is information all of our men should know."

"Since Lieutenant Bronson is the training officer, should I just turn my material over to him, sir?" I knew what the answer would be, but I asked the question anyway.

Before the CO could answer, Steve interjected with, "You're the one that's familiar with the information, and it would make sense for you to teach the classes."

"But you're the company training officer," I protested with a smile. "I wouldn't want to usurp any of your duties."

"Since he is the company training officer, I can see where he might want to schedule you to teach the classes. Therefore, it's all yours, lieutenant," the captain said as he ended our mock argument. "By the way," he added, "you're also our new income tax officer."

"Income tax officer?"

"Yes, lieutenant," Lynch said. "If anyone has problems filling out their tax forms, they come to you for help. We cut the orders while you were in Chicago."

I thought that was just wonderful. A guy leaves for a couple of weeks and since he's not around to defend himself, he gets another duty. I left the CO's office before he could add any more.

Wednesday morning, I went with Sergeant Corley to court to observe the proceedings. I made notes so I could critique the men on their presence in court later. SP4 Jacobs was called to testify against someone who was disputing the ticket they had received. He described how he had observed and checked someone's speed before writing a ticket. Everything was going well until he inadvertently reached down and briefly scratched his groin.

A STATESIDE TOUR OF DUTY

As we sat in the observer's area to the side of court, Sergeant Corley gave me a slight elbow. He bent over to me and whispered, "We need to tell Jacobs not to scratch his balls in court."

I whispered back, "Yeah, I see him. The trouble is he doesn't even know he's doing it."

Sure enough, when I talked with Jacobs the next day, he swore he had never scratched himself in court. Even when Sergeant Corley verified my observation, Jacobs was sure we were mistaken. All I could do was pass the information along and hope he would not be so oblivious to his surroundings the next time.

Friday evening, Steve and Barbara picked us up at six o'clock. With the workweek ended, Steve and I were in high spirits, and a great sporting event was just what we needed to make it a perfect night.

As I read the sports pages the past few days, the sports writers had made it clear that the Central Valley State and Lamar coaches didn't like each other. In addition, the Valley State coach stated that if Lamar played a zone, then he would stall to make Lamar change to man-to-man defense. The Lamar coach likewise claimed that if his opponent stalled, he would play a zone. To say there was no love lost between the two coaches was an understatement. Not only were these guys bitter rivals, but their feelings for each other seemed to border on hatred. Steve assured me that it would be a great game. Unfortunately, the press buildup that preceded the game was hyperbolic.

We got to the gym and found our seats. Sam and Barbara sat next to each other with Steve and me on either side. It was clear that Sam and Barbara intended to talk about other things than the game, so Steve and I concentrated on the game, but not for long. The game was hideously boring.

Valley State controlled the opening tip and Lamar Tech dropped back into a tight zone. For the next five minutes, the Valley State guards stood at three-quarter court, bouncing the ball back and forth to each other. The fans didn't like it and booed like crazy. It was to no avail. Finally, the fans simply settled back in their seats and either went to sleep or chatted with whoever was next to them. With six minutes to go in the half, one of the Valley guards tried to penetrate the defense and dribbled the ball off his foot out of bounds. I had never seen anything like it. Fourteen minutes into a college basketball game and the referees were blowing their whistles for the first time. We had the girls move over one seat and Steve sat between me and Sam. It was a good move. If Steve hadn't been there to talk to, I would have dozed off completely.

With two minutes to go in the half, a Lamar player got the ball a little too close to an opponent and a jump ball was called.

"Wow!" I said. "Finally, some action."

"You call this action?" Steve commented. "I've seen more action from the major when he's sitting in his office."

"I'm sorry, you guys," Barbara lamented. "This was really supposed to be a great game."

"You don't need to apologize, Barb, it's not your fault," Sam noted.

"I still feel bad about it, though," Barbara said.

Valley State got the jump ball, and with thirty seconds left in the half, called time out. Just before the half, Barbara's brother took a shot and missed. The center from Valley State rebounded the ball and put it in at the buzzer. Half-time score: Central Valley State 2, Lamar Tech 0.

"As near as I can tell," Steve noted, "the referees made about forty dollars each time they blew a whistle."

"If I didn't know any better, I'd swear that they had been playing baseball, from the score," I noted.

I have heard of hard-headed, stubborn people before, but these two coaches set new standards for it. The second half started out exactly like the first. Lamar played a tight zone and Valley State held the ball. With the players mostly standing around, the fans began to boo like crazy again, but to no avail. Many began to file out of the gym in disgust.

With ten minutes left to play, Valley State finally took their third shot of the game. It missed. Lamar rebounded the ball and three minutes later tied up the game.

"I don't mean to belittle your brother's team," Steve said to Barbara, "But this game sucks."

"This game is a disgrace to the sport of basketball," I commented. Sam leaned forward and stared at me. One look in her eyes told me not to say any more. I guessed what she was thinking. Poor Barbara was feeling bad enough without me adding comments like that.

At that moment Barbara's brother hit a jumper to put his team up 4–2. There were four minutes to go and the torture would soon all be over. At Arizona State, I had seen games where both teams had scored close to, or over, a hundred points—classic games with New Mexico, BYU, Utah, Wyoming, and the Wildcats. If any of those teams had ever played like this, their coaches would have been lynched. But I remained quiet, not wanting to incur Sam's wrath for making Barbara feel bad.

With less than two minutes to go, Lamar Tech tied up the game again at 4–4. Central Valley then played for the last shot. With Lamar keeping in their zone defense, the Valley boys had no choice but to fire up an outside shot, which missed with about five seconds to go. Their center again rebounded the ball and was fouled hard by his opponent. In a normal game, a foul like that might have triggered a riot as both benches emptied—but not tonight. In a game like this, first you would have needed to wake up the guys on the bench. There were a few coarse words passed back and forth between the players, but the referees kept control. The Valley center would shoot two free throws.

"You can do it," I yelled. "Make them both." I clapped my hands and whistled to make my point.

"It's nice of you to cheer like that for Barbara's team," Sam whispered to me. She had moved to the other side of me to ensure that I didn't say anything she disapproved of.

"I just don't want this damned thing to go into overtime," I whispered back. Sam elbowed me. She did it with a smile.

The player made both of his free throws and the Lamar boys missed a long shot from back court as time ran out. Final score: Central Valley State 6, Lamar Tech 4.

As we made our way out of the quickly emptying gym, most conversations centered on whether this was a record for the lowest score for four-year college basketball games. I guessed that it probably was.

As we got to the restaurant, Barbara was still apologizing for the game.

"You don't have to apologize, Barbara," Sam said. "You weren't playing or coaching. If these big sports fan guys of ours can't handle a low-scoring game, then it's their problem. Not yours."

"Thanks, Sam," she said. "I appreciate that."

Steve and I quickly changed the subject. The four of us then passed the rest of the evening, over dinner, with pleasant conversation.

Monday, Colonel Sherman was his usual relaxed self. His morning briefings were so much more laid back than Colonel Cox's had been that it was incredible that both men were from the same army. Despite his casual manner, Sherman was a leader who went by the book, and he expected things to be done right. I considered it an honor to serve under the man.

Historically, in the annals of the Army, there are those commanders who order their men to charge in battle and observe from a safe distance. That is called leading from the rear. Other commanders yell, "Follow me!" in the same scenario and lead the charge. Soldiers prefer to serve with the latter. I honestly felt that Sherman was the kind of leader who would lead a charge rather than watch from the rear as his men attacked an enemy. At the same time, he was down to earth and downright likable.

Steve stated that Sergeant Winters had finished an inventory of the supply room and would require all personnel to keep possession of anything they had checked out. In the past, some personnel had checked out equipment and then loaned it to someone else. Accountability had been lax and would no longer be tolerated. The conversation then centered around how it was necessary to keep all documentation for military property that one signed for and how failure to do so might cause that individual to have to pay for the equipment.

"You know, men," the colonel began. "After I got commissioned, my first duty assignment was the Canal Zone. I signed out the biggest motor I could find and put it on a boat to go out on a lake for some fishing. As I started the motor, it kind of dug a hole in that lake, and boat, motor and Sherman went down that hole." He motioned with his hands to emphasize his point.

He leaned back in his chair to continue. "Well," he said. "After a minute, Sherman popped up. The boat popped up. But we never did find that motor. So, for the next six months I spent a lot of time hanging around that equipment room. As a spare part like a gas tank or propeller showed up, I got it. When I got enough parts, I screwed them together and turned it in. Fortunately, they never checked to see if it would run. If I had to pay for that motor on what I was making as a brand-new second lieutenant back then, I'd still be paying for it."

I couldn't help but chuckle at the story. No matter how much one follows the rules, self-preservation comes first. When you consider how congressmen and bureaucrats waste money, only a fool would not find a way to legally avoid paying for that motor, as Sherman did.

We also got a replacement for Sergeant Prince. Sergeant Major Humpheries liked to skydive on weekends, and unlike Prince, who had phones ringing all the time, he seemed to sit at his desk and twiddle his thumbs. Over coffee on Wednesday, Humpheries passed on some information about the colonel. The information allowed me to understand how highly esteemed he was by Fifth Army.

A STATESIDE TOUR OF DUTY

"Lieutenant," he began. "Sherman was in line to become the Fifth Army provost marshal down at Fort Sam Houston. He had been working for that for years."

"No kidding?" I replied. "How did he get sent to this armpit?"

"The commanding general at Fort Sam decided he needed to send his top man here to straighten this place out. Sherman is not too happy about it. From what he has told me, I think he may retire soon."

"That would be a shame, sarge. I enjoy working for him."

"Yes, lieutenant, he's the best provost marshal I've ever seen."

Even though I didn't have the years of service Humpheries did, I had to agree with his assessment. It seemed par for the course, though. We finally get a provost marshal worth having and, like many others stationed here, all he wants to do is leave. I just resigned myself to doing my job and letting the time pass. In just fifteen more months, I would be leaving Fort McCulloch. I was thankful that I had Sam with me to pass the time. Marrying her had been a great decision.

On Thursday, Sergeant Brown dropped into the office. He was one of the men who had been reassigned to PMI after the personnel in that section had been brought up on charges.

"How is it going?" I asked.

"Just fine, sir," was his reply. "You know, sir, I enjoyed working with you in Traffic, but Lieutenant Raymond does things in a completely opposite manner from the way you do them."

"How's that, Brown?"

"Well, sir, you always joked with us before we got down to work, but once we needed to get things done, you were all business," he said.

"Isn't that the way Raymond does things?"

"No, sir. He's all business before we go to work and jokes and enjoys himself afterward. For example, the other day we inspected the arms room over at Charlie Company at the Engineer Battalion. He pulled out obscure regulations no one had ever heard of to gig them with. As I wrote up the violations, he was as serious as a heart attack. He kept noting how these violations needed to be corrected as soon as possible and such. Then when we had driven off, he broke out in laughter and said 'We tore them a new ass.' He definitely enjoys his work. He laughed and joked all the way back to the PMO."

"What kind of violations did Raymond gig them for?" I asked.

With a smile, he said, "The sign on the door was one inch less in width than the regulations called for and was not completely centered on the door; shit like that, sir."

"Sounds like Raymond is keeping the world safe for democracy," I laughed.

Brown continued, "He has found regulations no one ever heard of. Raymond says that when everyone corrects these, then he'll find some more."

"How do you like working for him?" I asked.

"Well, sir, he is different. Most of the time he seems to view us enlisted men as lesser beings. It's like he is descending from on high to endure our presence. But after he clobbers some unit with an unsatisfactory inspection, he laughs and jokes like he is one of us. I don't know what to make of it."

I thought for a moment. "If I had taken more psychology classes in college, Brown, I might be able to give you an analysis of Raymond's behavior, but I didn't." I continued, "But if it's any consolation to you, Raymond doesn't seem to like the presence of other officers either, unless they're a higher rank. I suggest that when he is friendly, you just enjoy the moment and give him his space the other times."

"Thanks, sir. Well, I better get back to work."

"I appreciate you dropping in, Brown. It's good talking to you. I really miss the Traffic section."

As Brown walked out the door, he looked back and added, "I think Sergeant Corley misses you too, sir. He can't get away as much as he used to. The major expects him to be around all the time."

After he left, I pondered as to why Brown had stopped in. I wasn't sure if he had been looking for advice or just wanted to past the time of day. Either way, I was glad he stopped in.

Two weeks later Steve came into my office. "We went to the wrong ball game," he said.

"How's that?" I asked.

"Saturday night, Valley and Lamar played again, and Valley won 95–89. Barbara's brother scored eighteen points."

"Why the big difference from the night we attended?" I asked.

"I guess the booster clubs threatened the coaches," he replied. "If they ever play like that again, they'll never find another coaching job."

Suddenly, Charlie showed up to get a list of the people who would be required to attend his defensive driving class that would start the next day. "This is just like old times. The three of us shooting the bull in this office," he said.

"Before, it was Steve behind the desk instead of me," I noted.

"This is not the piece of cake the Traffic section was, is it?" Steve asked.

"To be honest, old buddy, I do miss the Traffic section."

The three of us chatted for quite a while. Charlie was getting serious about Charlotte, Barbara wanted Steve to think about marriage and I let them both know that I had no complaints about being married. Eventually we got around to the obligatory discussion about the current NCAA basketball season and other subjects we were more comfortable talking about and, before we knew it, quitting time had arrived.

After arriving at home, I let Sam know that I had offered all the encouragement I dared for Steve to marry Barbara. A guy can't be too obvious about these things, and I was subtler in my encouragement than most. Sam didn't approve.

"Aren't you happy being married?" Sam inquired.

"Yes I am, honey. I have no complaints."

"Well, then, why don't you let Steve know that and tell him to marry Barbara? He's liable to lose her if he keeps dawdling around."

"Sam," I said, "one man can't tell another what to do with his love life. I can let others know that I'm happy and hope they profit from my example, but that's about it."

Sam did not approve of the overly subtle way I dealt with the situation, but she knew better than to argue. We ate supper and watched the news. The war in Southeast Asia was winding down as the ARVN (Army of the Republic of Vietnam) troops took a greater role in the war. However, that didn't seem to make any difference to the war protesters around the world. They still raised hell that we had any part in the war at all.

"I can't believe I ever agreed with those people," Sam commented as we watched the news. "There is no violent means that they won't stoop to."

"Like I once said, honey: While many of those people may be sincere, the leaders are not war protesters—they're traitors. They only want to destroy this country." Sam didn't disagree with my appraisal of the situation.

I had had no problems at work for some time. Maybe life was getting easier. As we got into bed that night Sam made her usual inquiry as to whether it bothered me that she was getting fat. I had my usual reply ready for the occasion.

"You're not fat, honey; you're pregnant. There is a big difference. Pregnant women are the sexiest women in the world. They're the only women in our society that get to show off the fact that they're sexually active without offending people or breaking a law of some kind."

Sam laughed. "You are just trying to make me feel good. And, for the record, let me say that I love it."

"I'm just telling the truth, Sam." She gave me a big kiss.

As we lay in bed I ran my hands over her belly and observed the baby's reaction as I did so. From the inside, the baby kept hitting where my hands touched, as if the unborn child disapproved of my actions.

"Junior is very active tonight," I noted.

"The baby is a girl, Nick. I keep telling you that."

I put my hand gently to the side of her head and said distinctly, "Think boy."

She smiled. "I can think any thing you want, but the sex is already determined, stud. It's a girl." She then added, "As the father, you are responsible for that. I learned that fact in high school biology."

"No, no," I said in a facetious manner. "It's your fault that your egg didn't reach out and grab a male sperm."

Sam laughed out loud at that. "The egg just floats, Nick. The first sperm cell to get there wins. It is not my fault if your female sperms swim faster than your male ones."

While I continued to hope our baby was a boy, in my heart I suspected Sam was probably right. She was rarely wrong when it came to these things.

As I continued to gently rub my hands across her belly, Sam said, "Want to fool around?"

I looked at Sam. "It's only March, so you can't say 'April fool' if I say yes?"

"Don't worry. I just suspected that my husband might be getting horny, since it's been a couple of days."

I gave Sam a peck on the lips, and said, "I'm always horny, babe, you know that."

Sam Laughed. "I know. There have been times when I thought you could screw me to death if I let you."

I gave her another quick kiss and a wink. "Just think, Sam. What a great way to go."

She laughed again. "I'm glad you think so. But, I want to be around to raise our daughter."

A STATESIDE TOUR OF DUTY

"Well, just for the record there are times when you are all I can handle," I commented as I continued to rub her abdomen.

Sam smiled. "You better proceed while I'm in the mood, and I'll try to make this one of those times." She followed the comment with a French kiss.

When your wife is six months pregnant, love making requires extra concentration to be careful not to harm the baby. Despite your best efforts, however, the baby still doesn't like it and makes its displeasure known. While the passion continues, the baby does more somersaults and flips than an Olympic gymnast performs. This distraction seems to add to the fun, and afterward we drifted off to sleep in each other's arms. As slumber approached, I could only think about how everything was perfect. The situation at work had improved and Sam and I had a wonderful life. I was beginning to think that we didn't have a care in the world.

My illusions were shattered about 2:00 AM. I woke up to find that Sam was absolutely hysterical. She was sobbing uncontrollably.

"Sam, Sam, what is the matter?" I asked, as I put my arms around her in a consoling gesture.

"I'm going to die, Nick! I'm going to die!" She repeated that statement several times. She was disconsolate.

Despite my best efforts at reassurance, she kept saying, "I'm going to die, and our baby will grow up without her mother."

CHAPTER TWENTY-FOUR

When you are awakened from a sound sleep, your first thoughts are those of confusion. It takes a few moments for you to orient yourself and assess the situation. This moment was particularly surreal. With Sam crying hysterically and my wondering if this was a dream, my mind was in a complete muddle. It only took a few seconds for me to emerge from this disorganized state, but it seemed much longer. I pulled Sam close and, holding her with my left arm, I began to wipe away tears with my right hand. She gradually calmed down and I was able to reassure her, "You're not going to die, Sam. Why on earth would you think such a thing?"

"I saw the baby's delivery in a dream," she explained. "There were complications. I died."

"Honey," I comforted, "it was just a bad dream. Everybody has them sooner or later. It doesn't mean a thing. If there are complications, the doctors will know what to do. I promise everything will be fine."

"You can't promise that, Nick. You're not God!"

"I know, honey, but this is 1971. You will have the best medical science at your disposal—"

"You haven't seen that hospital, Nick. Everyone jokes that it was antiquated when George Washington was president. During our OB appointments we're herded around like cattle." She continued to cry.

Now I understood. A few people had made unkind remarks about the hospital and its staff and, in her delicate condition, the result was bad dreams. I tried to choose my next words carefully.

"You're a loving mother who is worried about her child, honey. It's only normal for your concerns to cause a few bad dreams. But, that's all they are—bad dreams. They don't represent reality."

A STATESIDE TOUR OF DUTY

My efforts to placate her and explain away her fears fell on deaf ears. She stopped crying, put her hands up to my face and stated her case more forcefully.

"Nick!" She said loudly. "I saw the entire operating room. My spirit was hovering near the ceiling as they declared me dead and wheeled me away. I died. Do you hear and understand me? I died."

I thought for a moment. My reasoning would have to take a change of direction.

"Okay, honey. Assume for a moment that everything you saw in your dream is going to come true. What would be the point of your having the dream? If we can't change anything, the dream is useless and only serves to upset you. I can't see any point to that. Therefore, it must be a warning of what *might* happen. Now that we know the fact that there might be problems, we can warn the doctors so that they will be ready when the problems occur. You will be fine. I know it in my heart."

Sam lay back on the bed. "It's not a case of there *might* be problems, Nick. There *will* be. But you're right. The dream is a warning. Now that I know what is coming, I can make plans to be prepared."

"That's the spirit, honey. There is nothing that we can't face together. We will raise our baby together. You're not going to die."

Now she seemed relaxed. She cuddled up next to me and I began to rub her back.

"That feels so good," she said. "Keep rubbing."

"Want to fool around?" I asked as I massaged her back.

"No!" She stated emphatically. "I can't believe you would even suggest that at a time like this."

"When a man is cuddling with his nearly naked wife, it's a normal thought," I said. "And, you have to admit that I'm normal."

"Typical man! You already got it once. So shut up and rub my back, especially the small of my back. The baby is really active right now. I swear she's wearing combat boots tonight."

"I'll keep rubbing until you and her both go back to sleep," I reassured.

Sam kissed me. "Thank you for finally admitting it's a girl," she said.

While I didn't feel that I was admitting any such thing, I did keep gently rubbing her back until she was asleep. I then went to sleep confident that Lieutenant Moultrie had come through in the pinch and solved another crisis. I couldn't know then how wrong I was.

As the alarm sounded to begin the day, Sam seemed to have regained her composure and forgotten the nightmare of only a few hours before. She got up and began to make breakfast while I dressed for the office. Since Sam no longer appeared to be concerned about her dream, I didn't bring up the subject, either.

At noon, I returned home for lunch. Sam had it already prepared and on the table as I arrived. "I'll need to take you back to work," she said.

"Oh! Why is that?" I asked.

"I'm going to go over to the hospital and make sure everything is okay with the baby."

"Good idea, honey," I replied. Now I was convinced that Sam had understood that I was right. The doctors could tell her that there was nothing to worry about, and our lives could get back to normal.

After work, Sam seemed to be in high spirits when she picked me up. "Everything okay with the baby?" I asked.

"The doctor says everything is fine. We should have a healthy baby," was the reply. She then continued, "From the heartbeat, the doctor thinks it is a boy, but he's wrong. We are going to have a girl." She said that last part with a smile and a lot of conviction in her voice.

I smiled, too. Hopefully the doctor was right. "See, sweetheart, I told you everything would be okay. Lieutenant Moultrie always has the answer."

She laughed. "Maybe we should go to Las Vegas. If you always have the right answer, we could win a lot of money at the roulette wheel."

"Sorry, honey. Gambling is not my forte," I countered. "I only have the answers when it comes to questions of life."

She continued to joke. "Oh great! You only have the answers for stuff we can't make any money on."

I was glad to see Sam back to her usual self. The rest of the afternoon and evening was going as usual, when at about eight o'clock Sam finished reading a novel she had checked out of the post library. "Honey," she commented. "I just noticed that this book was supposed to be back today. Maybe you better go drop it off."

"No sweat, babe. I can take it back tomorrow."

"Honey," she countered. "You're an officer. It wouldn't look right for you to turn it in late."

I decided not to argue with her. "Want to go with me?" I asked.

She rubbed her belly. "No. The baby is acting up. I'm going to lie down."

"Do you want me to check out any more books for you?" I asked.

"No. Maybe we can go over tomorrow and I'll find something. I'm going to go lie down for now."

I kissed her and drove over to the library. After turning in Sam's book, I looked around for a little bit. I checked out a copy of *The Carpetbaggers*, a book which I had heard was inspired by the life of Howard Hughes. I didn't know if Sam would like it or not, but I checked it out anyway.

When I returned home, Sam was already in bed. As I walked into the bedroom, she was listening to music on the radio but seemed to be in deep thought. I sat on the edge of the bed and after a moment asked, "You okay, honey?"

"I'm okay." After a few seconds of silence, she added, "Please don't be mad at me, but I called my dad while you were gone."

"No sweat, babe. It's good to keep in touch with your family every now and then. Is that why you sent me to the library? To sneak in a long-distance call?" I smiled. I knew she thought I was cheap, but I didn't mind her calling her folks occasionally.

"No!" She hesitated for a few more moments. "I've decided to have the baby in Phoenix."

"Phoenix? What the—"

"Hear me out, Nick."

"Honey, you're not thinking this through—"

"Yes, I am, Nick. I spent the entire day working out the details."

"Honey!" I argued. "Everything will be fine. Don't let a silly dream bother you."

She sat up in bed and raised two fingers for emphasis. "You have two choices, Nick. You can raise our baby by yourself after I'm dead, or we can raise her together. What's it going to be, mister?"

"Of course I want you to be with us. What kind of a question is that?"

"Then, I'll give birth to our daughter in Phoenix."

In a college psychology class, I once read about primitive people in the Amazon or New Guinea who arrive at a doctor's office and say that they will die when the sun goes down because the witch doctor says they will. A quick check-up shows them to be in perfect health, and despite reassurances from a medical doctor to the contrary—sure enough—they die when the sun goes down. Their belief in the witch doctor's power is that strong. If Sam truly believed she was going to die if the baby was born at Fort McCulloch, that might indeed happen. Like the primitive people I had read about, maybe there was a real danger of a self-fulfilling prophecy. I searched my brain for the words to convince her otherwise, but it was no use. I found myself wishing I had studied more in that psychology class. Maybe then I would be able to find the words necessary to get this silly idea out of her head. Her next statement ended the stalemate.

"For once in your life, Nick, please sit still and shut up."

Knowing I would be unable to convince her that her feelings were unfounded, I meekly complied with her orders, but my brain continued to search for ideas.

"First, the doctor said he will okay me to fly for two more weeks. After that he advises against it."

"Well, then—"

"Don't interrupt me, Nick."

"Okay. Continue."

"My folks have moved back to Phoenix. I can stay with them until the baby comes. It won't cost you anything."

"I thought you hated your stepmother," I protested.

"I was a kid them. With both of us being adults, there should be no problem. We'll get along fine."

"Well, uh, I—" I was at a loss for words.

"When the baby is due, you can get a few days' leave and be there," Sam continued. "Afterward, we can return here together."

"We're practically newlyweds, Sam. We shouldn't be apart like this."

"It will only be for three months, Nick. Then we will have the rest of our lives together."

At this point, there was little else to say. "Are you sure this is what you want, Sam?"

"It's not what I want. It's what I need to stay alive."

"When will you be leaving?"

"A week from Friday."

"Well," I mused. "For a couple of months I'll get to bach it and act free-wheeling and carefree."

Sam playfully grabbed my shirt collar and pulled me closer. "Not too free-wheeling, mister. You remember that you belong to a wife who will be returning soon with your baby." We gave each other a long hug and remained silent for a while.

I wanted Sam to be well and happy, and if this is what it took to insure I would continue to have her as well as a healthy baby—so be it.

The separation might be a little inconvenient for me, but I could live with it. After all, if I was sent to Southeast Asia, we could be separated for a whole year. Fortunately, under the current military situation that would not happen.

As I got up to get ready for bed, I mentioned the novel I had picked up at the library. "I checked out a book for you tonight. I hope you like it."

She smiled. "I'll find out tomorrow. Thanks for thinking of me."

The next Wednesday, before court, I went over to the company to chat with Steve. He had his feet propped up on his desk as I entered his office. "What's happening, Nick? Pull up a chair and park the body," he said. "You look like you need to talk."

"Well, Sam has decided she wants to go home to Phoenix to have the baby," I commented as I sat down in the closest chair. "I've tried to talk her out of it, but it's no use."

"Can you blame her?"

I quickly explained the situation. "I think she's being unduly worried. She's afraid she is going to die if she has the baby here."

"I can see her point." He took a big last puff on his cigarette and put it out in the ash tray, on his desk. "Have you been in that place?"

"Only to drop off my medical records," I confessed.

"Go on sick call sometime. The place is a dump. You're liable to trip over a loose board or something."

"It can't be that bad!"

"Oh, yes, it is, sir," Sergeant Winters chimed in as he entered the room. After a few cuss words the sergeant added, "My last kid was born down in Houston. I have an aunt that lives down there. My wife stayed with her for a couple of weeks and had the baby there. CHAMPUS took care of the bill and it only cost me twenty-five dollars."

"That's the voice of experience talking," Steve said. "That horny bastard has six kids."

"I'm only doing what comes natural, sir." After a moment, the sergeant added, "If the good Lord didn't intend for me to use it, he wouldn't have given it to me." He then picked up some forms from Steve's Out box and left the room.

"You might consider what Winters said. I can't blame your wife for being concerned." With that, Steve started signing more paperwork and placing it in his Out box.

I must admit that I was starting to feel better about Sam's decision after hearing what they had to say. "Well, I gotta get to court," I said as I got up to leave. "I appreciate the information."

"Not a problem, buddy. Best of luck."

I then drove over to court and took my place in the observer's section. The morning was routine, until a case came up involving a Captain Rasmussen. He was an infantry officer and the guy was an absolute slob. He was wearing fatigues that looked like they had been slept in for several days, and his shirt tail was hanging out in the back. The captain pleaded not guilty to speeding, but the patrolman who issued the ticket laid out the facts and, despite Rasmussen's best arguments, he was found guilty. He wrote a check and left the courtroom muttering and cursing to himself.

I made some notes as I observed the proceedings and at noon headed for home. Sam had lunch ready.

She kissed me and said, "Welcome home, soldier."

"You're in high spirits!"

"Yes, I am," she answered.

"Is that because you'll be leaving me soon?"

She looked hurt by the comment. "The three months we're apart will be the longest and loneliest of my life. But if we're to have a life together afterward, it has to be. I love you, Nick, but I also want to live."

"I want you to live, too."

"Then it's settled." As we sat down, she added, "I've been reading that book you checked out. It's nothing like the movie."

"Books are always better than the movie."

She smiled again. "How would I know? My cheap husband doesn't take me to the movies very often."

"Fine, Sam. We'll go to the movies Saturday night."

"The Cunninghams are coming over for canasta Saturday. We'll go to the movies Friday night."

I laughed. "How am I going to keep my social calendar straight while you're gone?"

"All you have to do while I'm gone is get lots of sleep and watch television."

"No, honey," I protested. "I prefer the exciting life. I'm sure Steve and I can find other things to do."

"Such as?"

"Oh, I don't know. I'm sure we can find something." I paused for several seconds and added, "Like watching a ball game."

She patted her stomach and commented, "Spoken like a true family man. Just remember the two of us are waiting in Phoenix."

I smiled. Sam knew full well that I would never be unfaithful. Neither of us would ever tolerate such conduct from the other.

We ate lunch in silence for a few seconds, then she said, "I hope you eat something besides hamburgers and french fries while I'm gone."

"Sweetie," I replied, "if hamburgers and french fries are good enough for the rest of America, they're good enough for me."

"Nick, you need to eat some vegetables occasionally."

"Potatoes are vegetables," I countered.

"You know what I mean, Nick."

"We can discuss it later, honey. For now, let's just enjoy the next few days together."

"Okay."

With that we changed the subject to other small talk. The coming separation seemed to keep us from any more arguments or disagreements.

Friday night we went to the theater to watch *Love Story*. After our last trip to the movies, I had agreed that Sam would pick the next movie for our viewing pleasure. This was her choice. I found it melodramatic, overly sentimental and totally predictable, but Sam thought it was the greatest thing since the invention of the camera. She even sighed as she kept quoting the line of half-baked pop psychology that advertised the movie.

"Love means never having to say you're sorry. Isn't that beautiful, Nick?"

I snickered. "Beautiful, hell! I don't even know what it means. It's illogical, poorly thought-out drivel to me. Since I'm in love with you, I should never apologize if I do something wrong or hurt your feelings and vice versa? I don't think so."

"Oh, Nick. What am I going to do with you? You're so unromantic."

Worried that I might have hurt her feelings, I quickly said, "Okay, honey. You explain the meaning of the phrase to me. Maybe I missed something."

"When two people love each other, they're in tune with each other's feelings and they don't have to apologize verbally. They know each other's emotions."

"That's a little naive, Sam. No matter how much love two people share, some oral communication is always needed to avoid life's difficulties. Humans are not clairvoyant."

"I still say that a couple can learn to know what each other thinks and be in touch, heart and soul."

More meaningless platitudes, I thought. But, not wanting to start an argument, I decided to find a way to concede a few points and let Sam have her way. Two strong-willed people like me and Sam have enough arguments. I was not going to fight over something this trivial. "I suppose that, as a couple ages and spend more of their lives together; they can come to be more in tune with each other in the manner you describe. However, until they reach that point of omniscience, they need to talk and let each other know how they really feel, Sam."

"Then that is what we need to strive for. I love you, Nick."

I smiled. "I love you, too."

Having made her point, Sam said little for the rest of the drive home. Once home, she read her novel while I watched the news. As usual, the news was dominated by Lieutenant Calley's court-martial and combat in Southeast Asia. As I continued to watch, Sam laid her book aside.

"I'm so glad you're not over there," she said.

"I know, Sam, but sometimes I feel I'm not doing my fair share of defending the country by being here. When I talk to men who were over there, I frequently feel inadequate, knowing that I've never had to prove myself in combat."

"Don't even think that way, Nick."

"I know it's silly, babe. Especially since many of the troops who have been there haven't seen combat either. Most serve in support jobs or fairly secure areas."

After a few seconds, she changed the subject. "How'd this stupid war ever get started in the first place?"

"It's a long story, babe. But like you said—it was mostly the result of stupidity."

She smiled. "Well, I still have a few days to listen if you wish to give me the benefit of your vast knowledge."

"Just what I need—a sarcastic wife."

"A sarcastic, pregnant wife," she added.

She sat closer to me, and I paused to notice the movements of the baby within her. As I moved my hand slowly across her belly, the baby seemed to protest with a series of kicks.

A STATESIDE TOUR OF DUTY

"Junior is not happy with dad touching your stomach," I observed.

"Our baby is a girl, Nick."

"Only time will tell." I got up and turned off the television. I then sat back down and added, "But I can tell you how this war got started."

"Go ahead, professor. Your class is in session."

"Well," I began. "Prior to World War II, Vietnam was part of an area known as French Indochina, and Ho Chi Minh was a nationalist leader trying to free his country from colonial rule. A few months into the war, France surrendered to the Germans, and their Japanese allies then took over the French colony. That made Ho and his followers our allies against the Japanese."

"You mean that the people we're fighting now used to be our friends?"

"Yes, and Ho was a dependable and loyal ally. Unfortunately, when Japan surrendered in 1945, France wanted their colony back. The Truman State Department thought it was more important to please France than to honor any commitments to Vietnam, so they backed France."

"That doesn't seem fair. Vietnam was our ally for the entire war while France spent most of the war siding with the enemy."

"You're right, honey, but the world is rarely fair. However, we digress." I caught my breath and continued. "After nine years of revolt, the French pulled out in 1954, largely because they had no popular support in Vietnam or France."

"So how in the world did we get involved?"

"Well, to fight the French, Ho had obtained weapons and supplies from Red China. He was then seen as a Communist ally of one of our worst enemies."

"Was he really a Communist?"

"Nobody knows. Most nationalistic leaders had always asked Communist countries like Russia or China for support against colonial masters, with comrade-style rhetoric, but some turned out later to be anti-Communist. Chiang Kai-Shek is a good example. What is known is that before this, China was an ancient enemy of Vietnam."

"So we drove a dependable ally into the arms of one of our worst enemies who had previously been their enemy also?"

"Isn't international relations fun?" I mused.

"Don't get funny, Nick. You still haven't explained how in the world we got into this mess."

"Well, when the French pulled out, Indochina was split four ways. Ho got half of his country while the other half was given independence with the hopes that it would have a democratic style government. Laos and Cambodia were also given independence. Ho then set about to conquer the southern half of his country."

"Okay, but how did we get involved?" Sam was clearly getting impatient with me.

"Well," I continued, "The new leader of the South was an anti-Communist guy named Diem. He came to Washington for help and became friends with a young anti-Communist Senator named Kennedy. Kennedy and his friends in Congress pressured President Eisenhower to send military aid to Diem. Eisenhower refused to get involved in another war in Asia, but he agreed to send some limited aid in the form of equipment and money. After Kennedy was elected, he sent a few military advisors to South Vietnam to train Diem's troops."

"A few? We have a lot more men than that there now."

"Yes, we do. That's because as the North escalated the conflict, Kennedy had to send more advisors to help Diem's army. But by this time, Diem was persecuting the Buddhist majority in Vietnam and his government was shown to be very corrupt."

"Why didn't we pull out at that time?"

"Some people think that Kennedy might have done just that, but that's debatable. He was assassinated, so we'll never know. It is known that Kennedy did have a lot of reservations about how the war was going."

Sam just shook her head as she waited for me to continue.

"Once Johnson took over, he decided to send in combat troops. He also claimed that our Navy had been attacked in the Gulf of Tonkin. With that lie, he persuaded Congress to pass a resolution allowing him to proceed with the war, and we then took over the bulk of the fighting."

"Take over the fighting in someone else's war? Where's the sense in that?"

"Well, honey, Johnson was an idiot and the biggest crook the country has ever seen. He wanted to be like his idol, FDR, and be a wartime president. What else can you expect?"

"I'm glad I was not old enough to vote for him in 1964. Otherwise you could blame me for him being president."

"No, baby, he fooled a lot of people. He won by millions of votes, honey. Unfortunately, as president he dictated all military strategy and policy out of the White House and tied his commanders' hands to where they couldn't conduct the war properly. I've heard that he even chose all bombing targets from the White House. He was quoted as saying that the military couldn't even bomb an outhouse without his approval. Our field commanders were totally unable to do their jobs."

"What you have just described is the most screwed-up policy I have ever heard of, Nick. It sounds like we haven't done anything right."

"That about sums it up, Sam. We haven't done much, up till now, that makes sense."

"What are we doing now?"

"After Nixon took over, he decided that the war would be turned back over to the South Vietnamese, and that our boys would gradually be pulled out. That's the policy we're using now."

"Why don't we just totally leave now and cut our losses?"

"Two reasons. The domino theory that says that if South Vietnam falls, all of Asia will follow like dominos to Communism. And second, if we just cut and run and leave our South Vietnamese allies unable to fend for themselves, no one else in the world will ever trust us again. Besides, Nixon's policy of bombing the North has forced them to begin serious negotiations in the peace talks. While Johnson was in charge, they argued with us for three years over the shape of the conference table."

"Are you serious? We argued for three years over the shape of the table while our men were dying in combat?"

"Yeah, but Nixon changed that. In fact, if it wasn't for our news media and the war protesters, North Vietnam probably would have surrendered to us by now."

"What did the news media do?"

"In 1968, the enemy conducted their annual Tet offensive. We were ready for them and slaughtered them. It was one of the greatest victories American troops have ever won. The enemy was destroyed as a fighting force. However, our news media reported it as just the opposite. Don't ask me why, they just did. The media made it sound like we were being overrun or were just barely hanging on. They convinced the public that the Viet Cong were invincible and could do as they pleased. As a result, popular opinion, which had been in favor of winning the war, reversed itself, and afterward a majority of Americans opposed the war effort. There is probably no way for us to win a military victory now."

"Are you sure most Americans supported the war before that, Nick?"

"No question. All public opinion polls verified the fact that they were a majority. Nixon called those people the silent majority. Unfortunately, the anti-war movement convinced the enemy that if they held out a little longer we might quit. Once the media turned public opinion against the war, the fact that we would eventually pull out became academic."

"How long do you think it will be before we're out of there?"

"I figure by the next election we will have a negotiated settlement where we will either be out, or the plans for the pull-out will be made public."

"How sad. A war that could have been avoided will have lasted twenty-seven years."

"That won't be the end of it, Sam."

"Why not?"

"The aggression of the North against the Republic in the South will continue. They will do what they did in 1954. For a while they will pretend to follow the peace accords. Then, without us there, Ho's forces will conquer the South."

"You really think so?"

"Yes! Everyone I've talked to has said the ARVN (that's the South Vietnamese forces) won't fight unless we're there to lead them and hold their hands. With us gone, it's just a matter of time."

"Now I'm really thankful you won't have to go over there."

"If we would just have backed Ho against the French, in 1945, Vietnam might very well be an American ally united against the Red Chinese today. That would have prevented what will ultimately be probably thirty years of war and over a million dead."

I put my arm around Sam. It suddenly occurred to me how we complemented each other. Our conversation was beginning to sound more like an interview, but the fact that she was inquisitive and I was long-winded probably made us perfect for each other.

There didn't seem like much to talk about after that. We held each other for a while. Then Sam and I went to bed and slept late in the morning.

About six o'clock Saturday evening Tom and Andrea Cunningham came over to play cards. They were barely through the door before Andrea began to tell me about the post hospital.

"Sam says you aren't too happy about her decision to have the baby back home in Phoenix, Nick."

"I just think she's being unduly worried, but I've agreed for her to go."

"Listen, Nick," she continued, "that place is so rickety and ram-shackle that it almost falls in when the wind blows. I think Sam is doing the right thing."

"That seems to be the consensus around here," I conceded.

After that, the four of us proceeded to enjoy a pleasant evening of canasta. We knew it would be our last for at least three months.

The final week before Sam's departure was spent packing and making plans. We would call each other every Sunday night, with no other calls except for emergencies. She kept encouraging me to eat something other than fast food while she was gone and, before we knew it, I was driving her to the San Angelo airport Friday afternoon.

After a very long embrace, she departed at 3:12 PM. I watched her plane climb out of sight, and then I began the long, lonesome return trip home.

CHAPTER TWENTY-FIVE

After I returned home, I just sat around and watched television. I had told Sam to call me as soon as she reached her parent's home so I would know she had arrived okay. It is amazing how slowly time can pass when you are waiting. About 6:00 PM the phone rang. Expecting Sam to be on the other end, I answered it.

"Hello, this is Lieutenant Moultrie."

It was Steve. "Nick, we're having a poker game over here. Care to join us?"

"Sorry, man. With a kid on the way, I can't afford to lose anything."

"You're more domesticated than I thought. With the old lady gone, you should let your hair down."

"Well, let me get a rain check for another time. I told Sam to call when she got there, and I'm waiting for her to call now."

"Okay, next Saturday a bunch of us are going to the roller derby. We'll be expecting you."

"Roller derby?"

I could tell that Steve had had a few. "Roller derby's a great sport," he said. "Watching the rednecks in the crowd is almost as much fun as watching the skaters."

I chuckled a little. "I've never thought of roller derby as a sport."

"You don't want to say that to the participants. You'd probably get your head busted."

I snickered again. "Okay, pal. Roller derby next Saturday, it is. I'll go."

"That's the spirit. Well, talk to you at work next week."

I said good-bye and hung up the phone. Over the next two hours, there were two wrong numbers, and finally, a little after 8:00 PM, Sam called.

"Hello."

"Hi, honey."

"Well, I was wondering if you had made it. Was your flight okay?"

"Everything is fine, honey. I called a little while ago and the phone was busy."

"Oh, that was just me planning my busy social schedule while you're gone," I joked.

"Very funny."

At this point I figured I had better be more serious. "Steve called and wanted me to come over and lose some money. I told him no."

Sam giggled. "I'm proud of you. Keep this up and you'll become a responsible adult."

"I'm working on it," I admitted.

We had a conversation in which we both admitted to missing each other, and after a while we said our good-byes. After hanging up, I quickly realized how much I did miss Sam. The trailer was a lonely place being by myself. But I fixed myself a sandwich, watched the news and went to bed.

The next morning, I slept late. There was a basketball game on the television that afternoon. I didn't care about the teams, but I watched it anyway. Afterward, I began to read the book I had checked out for Sam some time before. By 7:00 PM Sunday night I had finished it. It was then the phone rang again.

"Hello, this is Lieutenant Moultrie."

"Sir, this is Sergeant Lippman. I have a favor to ask."

My first thought was that if it didn't involve buying a used car, I would try to help him out. "Sure, sarge. What can I do for you?"

"Well, sir, the colonel wants an officer or senior NCO to accompany the men on the Lone Star Run once each month, and I'm scheduled to go tomorrow. Trouble is, something has come up and I'm trying to find somebody to take my place. Lieutenant Bronson suggested that you might be available."

I could think of no reason not to. "Yeah, no sweat, sarge. I can do it."

"I really appreciate it, sir."

"No problem."

I said good-bye and hung up. I then called Sergeant de la Vega. He picked up the phone after the first ring. "De la Vega residence!"

"Sergeant Dee, this is Lieutenant Moultrie. I need a favor."

"I can probably help you out, sir. What is it?"

"Well, sarge, Lippman just called and needs me to fill in for him on the AWOL run tomorrow."

"Lippman must have a customer tomorrow for some used cars," he replied. I detected a little contempt in his voice.

"Probably! At any rate, I need you to fill in for me at the morning briefing for the next three days. And be sure the colonel knows I'm doing Lippman a favor."

"Will do, sir. Have a nice trip."

"Thanks, sarge. Bye."

After hanging up, I called Sam. As I got her on the phone, she sounded almost jubilant. "Hi, honey. You must really miss me to talk twice in two nights."

"Yes, I do, sweetie, but that's not the reason I'm calling."

"What's the matter, honey? Do you need to find out how to turn the stove on?"

"Very funny!" I paused as she giggled. "Actually, I have to go on the AWOL run tomorrow. I'll be gone until Wednesday. So, if you have an emergency, you can call either the Company CQ or the MP desk and have them get in touch with me." After giving her the phone numbers and a little more small talk, it was time to say good-bye.

"I miss you already," she said sadly.

"I miss you, too. Just take care of yourself. Make sure we have a healthy baby."

"I will, honey. Bye."

"Bye-bye, sweetie." After I hung up the phone, I quickly packed some clothes and a towel along with my razor and toiletries in an overnight bag. Then, after leaving to buy a hamburger, I came home and went to bed. The next morning would start early.

The alarm went off at 0400 hours. I hadn't awakened at an hour this early since OCS. I staggered out of bed and grabbed a bowl of cereal and got to the company area shortly before our departure time of 0530.

Altogether, there were four of us in two vehicles. PFC Gallway drove the bus, with Sergeant Powell accompanying him as a guard. Powell was armed with a 12-gauge shotgun and Gallway had a .45-caliber pistol. Sergeant Collins and I preceded them in a van. Both vehicles were equipped with police radios so we could communicate with each other during the trip. If we had troublemakers who needed to be separated from the others, they would be placed in the van. Collins also had a .45 pistol. Both vehicles had a steel wall-like barrier dividing the prisoners' compartment from the police personnel. The wall in the bus had a door, while the one in the van did not.

The 446 miles to Brownsville would take about nine hours in military vehicles if we drove straight through. However, with a stop in San Antonio to eat lunch and pick up three AWOLs from their county jail, we didn't arrive in Brownsville until 1630 hours.

We placed our three prisoners in the local jail to join the seventeen we would pick up the next morning. After getting something to eat we then drove to the house rented by the local AWOL Apprehension team. Specialists Foote and Parker rented a two-bedroom home with a large living room. The four of us making the run would bed down there. We drew straws to see which of us would get to sleep on the two couches. The other two would spread out blankets on the floor. I lucked out and drew a long straw for one of the couches.

Specialist Foote checked their answering machine for messages left when they were out. After the prerecorded message, which stated, "This is the Brownsville, Texas, U.S. Army AWOL Apprehension team; we're not in right now, please leave a message," there were two or three calls which were sprinkled with profanities. The next message said, "We have three AWOL WACs who need to be picked up. Meet us at the corner of Fourth and Main tomorrow morning."

As Foote erased the prank calls, he looked over at me and rolled his eyes as he explained, "We get a lot of this crap. For every legitimate call, there are twenty of these."

"It just comes with the job," I commented.

"Yes, sir. It sure does," he agreed.

Actually, the apprehension team had it good most of the time. Their job was pretty much eight-to-five, Monday through Friday, and the rest of the time they could dress in civilian clothes and relax far from the rules of the military post. They had a staff car, which they could use to retrieve AWOLs from the surrounding counties, and they had to be in uniform when they drove it, but most of the time they could act like civilians. Their job did have its risks, however. Foote mentioned one of them.

"About five months ago, we did have an AWOL WAC, sir. The only one I've ever seen. She and a boyfriend went AWOL together to go on a crime spree, robbing some banks and gas stations."

"No kidding?"

"No joke, sir. Parker and I had to go to Laredo to get them. They were real hard cases. We kept them handcuffed with their hands behind their backs during the entire trip back here. They bitched like hell about it, and called it brutality, but we would be dead now if we hadn't done things that way."

"How's that?" I asked

"When we dropped them off at the Brownsville jail, they had a matron do a body cavity search of the WAC before they placed her in a cell. The matron found that the woman had a .380 automatic hidden up her vagina."

"My gosh!" I exclaimed. "That's one hell of a big pistol."

"Yes, sir. But, I guess she had one hell of a big snatch. If we hadn't kept them hand-cuffed like we did, we probably wouldn't be here today."

"What happened to the couple?" I asked.

Foote continued. "Two of their robberies were in Brownsville, so the locals decided to prosecute them and not give them back to us. They're guests of that big hotel the state of Texas runs now."

"The one you don't get to check out of," I mused.

"Yes, sir. At least, not until your time is up."

After a few more war stories, we all decided to get some sleep. The next day would start at 0500.

By 0700, we were picking up our prisoners at the Brownsville jail. One of the deputies gave me a briefing on our prisoners. All were wanted only for being AWOL from the Army except one. The exception was Steven R. Schrade, who had originally been arrested for murder. Instead of trying him for his crime, the county was just turning him over to us. That surprised me.

"Why isn't he standing trial for murder?" I asked.

"His victim was a local scum bucket we're better off without," a deputy sheriff explained. "Also, a trial will cost the county thousands, so the prosecutor's office figured they would just pass him on to someone else and avoid the expense while collecting the reward money from Uncle Sam." After a few seconds the deputy added in a sarcastic tone, "And while he's been here he's found God."

"Don't they all?" I asked in a dismissive tone.

"Yes, and the worse their crimes, the quicker and louder they proclaim their newfound faith," he stated.

That paradox was not surprising to me. I admit I'm a cynic. If a person professes religious convictions before he gets into trouble, he may be sincere. If he does so afterward, I figure he's looking to reduce his time of incarceration. At any rate, I quickly informed my men of the new development. Schrade would ride in the van.

The prisoners were shackled together, in pairs, with leg irons. One individual on the bus and our guest in the van got their own personal pair of leg irons. As the prisoners were moved from the jail onto the bus, a few had relatives on hand to say good-bye. However, this was done from a distance. No personal contact was allowed between the prisoners and anyone else. This prevented the risk of someone passing them a weapon or other contraband.

As the prisoners filed onto the bus, there were comments from onlookers about how sad it was that their friends or relatives were being treated like common criminals. The thought occurred to me that these men were lucky. Most would be back home with a dishonorable discharge in a few weeks or returned to their units. A hundred years ago, they could have been shot for desertion or branded with a hot iron in some grotesque manner. These men were fortunate to be living in the latter twentieth century.

As soon as everyone was aboard, we headed up the road to Corpus Christi. There we ate lunch and picked up eleven more prisoners. Then, it was on the road again, this time to Galveston.

It takes a certain type of person to enjoy constantly driving on the open road. Most people know a few truckers who are content to spend weeks at a time driving freight across the country. Most seem to enjoy it and each of these AWOL Apprehension personnel appeared to be just that type of individual. Personally, the tedium and monotony of constant driving would drive me crazy. I had to make constant small talk with Collins to stay awake.

"You really like working with AWOL App?" I asked.

"Oh yes, sir," Collins replied. "Out here on the open road—nobody bothers us. Besides, where I'm gone two nights a week, the wife seems to appreciate the time I'm home more. If I was gone more, I probably wouldn't like it. But, as it is, it works out well. Besides, the extra money comes in handy."

"It is possible to get by on less than twenty-five dollars a day out here," I noted.

"Yes, sir. And the extra is tax free."

"Good point!" I agreed.

For their service on the road, these men drew a $25 per diem. By keeping expenses to a minimum, they could accumulate a tidy sum of extra money over a year's time. We continued to pass the time with conversation and arrived in Galveston about 1600. We had fifteen more AWOLs waiting for us there.

In Galveston, the small apartment of the AWOL App team would not accommodate us. A reasonable motel had been found, and the military had a standing reservation for two rooms on Tuesday nights. After checking in, I looked in the phone book for an old college friend who was from the area. Sure enough, he was in the book. I quickly dialed his number and he answered.

"Hello."

"Is this the Stan Wright who managed to finagle a degree in business from Arizona State?" I asked.

"For any good it's done me, yes, it is," was the answer.

"I'm with the State of Arizona Board of Regents and we've found some irregularities in your academic record. You'll need to return for some more classes or else we'll have to rescind your diploma."

"Who in the hell is this?"

"This is Nick Moultrie."

"Nick! He said with a laugh. What in the world are you doing in Galveston?"

"I'm a military police lieutenant down here picking up AWOL troops and deserters. While I'm in town tonight, I thought I'd give you a call."

"Wow!" He commented. "If the Army takes reprobates for officers, then this country is worse shape than I thought."

"Yes, it is," I joked. "But imagine how much worse it will be when guys like us take over completely."

He changed the subject. "Are you coming by? It would be great to see you again."

"I'd like that. Tell me how to get to your place."

He gave me directions to his home and I wrote them down along with his phone number in case I had trouble following them. The other men were about to go across the street to a restaurant for chow, so I borrowed the keys to the van and headed to Stan's place. I had no problem following his directions. I was there in a matter of minutes. His wife was about to cook supper as I arrived.

"Have you eaten yet?" my buddy asked.

"No, I haven't. But I don't want to be a bother."

"Nonsense. It won't be a bother at all." He then called to his wife. "Honey, can you set an extra place for Nick?"

A STATESIDE TOUR OF DUTY

His wife walked into the living room. She was a real beauty. Stan seemed to have done well for himself. "No problem, Stan. I kind of planned on it when you invited him over."

"I really don't want you to go to any extra trouble," I reiterated.

"It's no trouble, Nick," she said again. "Besides, I need to find out if all of the stories my husband has been telling me about you guys are true."

"You realize the Constitution of the United States provides me with the right to avoid self-incrimination?" I noted.

"As much as my husband has already incriminated you, I think you'll probably want to defend yourself," she rebutted.

Now my friend regained control of the conversation. "Nick, this is my wife, Kathy. Honey, this is Nick Moultrie."

"How do you do, Kathy? It's a pleasure to meet you," I said. She held out her hand and I shook it.

"It's nice to finally meet you, Nick." She hesitated for a second, then said with a smile, "Is it true that you and my husband stole the toilet paper from all of the dorms on campus in one night?"

"Stan exaggerated," I corrected. "It was only the men's dorms, and we didn't have time to hit them all before the sun rose. A couple of dorms still had toilet paper when we got through."

"From what my husband has told me, you guys and your fraternity brothers broke every rule the state of Arizona had," she commented.

"Again, Stan has stretched the facts. We broke all but one," I said with a smile

"Which one was that?" she asked

"We never killed anybody." I smiled to await her reaction.

"But we did threaten a few," Stan interjected with a laugh.

Kathy shook her head. "Oh, you guys. How did you two manage to stay out of jail?"

"We never lost our nerve and we got some occasional good advice from the law students," I explained.

Kathy shook her head in disbelief and returned to the kitchen.

The two hours after dinner were pleasant as my friend and I relived some old times. His wife concluded that most of the stories she had heard were true.

I had about decided to leave when I asked, "How's Andy doing these days?"

A dejected look came over his face. Then with a voice choked with emotion while obviously holding back tears, he replied, "Andy is dead, Nick."

That answer stunned me. Stan's older brother, Andrew, was about four years older than we were. He had received both an MBA and a law degree from Southern Cal and planned to be the CEO of a Fortune 500 company before he was thirty-five. Everyone who had ever met Andrew figured he would be running the country someday.

"What happened?"

"It was murder, but we can't prove it," he replied.

"I'm sorry, Stan. I didn't mean to dredge up hurtful memories," I apologized.

"Its okay, Nick. You didn't know. Besides, if telling the story prevents anyone else from getting killed, it will be worth it."

I remained silent as Stan regained his composure and began the story. It was unbelievable, but I was glad I heard it.

"About a year and a half ago, Andy was selected by the board of directors of a corporation up in Seattle to head up their company. He had no sooner taken over, when he was asked to sign an application for three quarters of a million dollars of life insurance on himself, with the corporation as the beneficiary. They call it key man insurance. My brother had reservations, but they told him he was more valuable than he knew. The rotten bastards weren't kidding."

At this point, Stan got up and went to get a drink. "Can I get you anything, Nick?"

"No. I'm good, thanks."

Shortly, he returned to the living room with a glass of bourbon and 7Up for himself and a glass of wine for Kathy. "Are you sure I can't get you anything?" he again asked.

"No way, buddy. After that great dinner Kathy cooked, I'm okay. Besides, I'll be driving."

"Tell that husband of mine to pay a compliment on my cooking once in a while," Kathy said.

"You know, Kathy, Sam has the same complaint about me. I guess men aren't used to paying their wives compliments on their cooking. I'll change that when I get home."

"You're smart. Stan could take a lesson from you, Nick."

Before I could answer Kathy, Stan continued his story. "Well, about four months later the company had a big party on Puget Sound where the big shots went out water-skiing. While they did so, there supposedly was an accident and Andy wound up on the bottom of the sound, where they couldn't find his body."

I shook my head in disbelief at what I was hearing. Then, after Stan took a sip of his drink, he continued. "After the insurance company paid the death claim, they audited the company. They found the company had desperate cash flow problems before the accident, but afterward, with the big infusion of money—they were doing just fine. The police tried to investigate, but the other corporate officials refused to talk or to cooperate with the investigation in any way. Their lawyers just made public announcements about how they were shocked that their clients could be suspected of anything. After all, they were pillars of the community."

"That is unbelievable," I noted. "But there must be something you can do."

Stan took another sip of his seven and seven and concluded his story. "Not really. The lead detective told our family that they are sure it was murder, but they can't prove it. And with that wall of lawyers around them, they have us outgunned in court. What pisses me off the most is that they didn't even have the decency to leave his family with a body to bury. Of course, there was a big group policy that paid his wife and kids some money, but it was nothing compared to what he would have earned over the next thirty years."

"If anyone ever wants to purchase key man insurance on me, I think I'll tell them to drop dead," I said with conviction.

"That's right, buddy. Me too." Stan took another sip of his refreshment and added this comment. "I've worked for Ameri-Tex Oil for over a year now, and I can retire in twenty-nine more. In the years I have remaining, I swear, I'll never agree to any such nonsense."

I was sorry to bring up such sad memories for Stan, but I also figured the experience made me a much wiser man. The world could definitely be a perverted place. A man had to proceed cautiously and not let it drag him down or destroy him.

After saying good-bye to my friends and returning to the motel, I decided to cover my tracks on the unauthorized use of the military vehicle I had enjoyed. All three men were watching TV in the room next to the one I was in.

I walked in and tossed the keys to Collins. "Here you go, sarge. I don't guess anything needs to be said about my borrowing the vehicle for a couple of hours," I said with a laugh.

"You never borrowed the van, sir," Collins replied.

"How's that?" I asked in surprise.

"You've been sitting in that chair watching TV with us all night. I'm sure of it." Then Collins added with a big smile, "In fact you were a great conversationalist. You never interrupted any of us even once."

I couldn't help but laugh. I gave him the thumbs-up sign and said, "Thanks. I appreciate it."

Shortly afterward, we all hit the hay to prepare for the trip home the next day.

The next morning the four of us walked across the street to the nearby restaurant to have breakfast. Everyone seemed to be in high spirits. The trip had been largely routine and uneventful and by afternoon would be over. By 0700 we were loading our prisoners (now numbering forty-six) onto the bus. They were a diverse collection of new recruits and veterans, each with a different excuse for being AWOL. One said his little daughter was sick and foolishly thought he could do more at home than he could at the post where he was stationed. Another thought his wife was having an affair. And then there was Schrade, whom we separated from the rest.

As I opened the back of the van to allow him to get in, he remarked, "I forgive you, sir."

"You forgive me?" I asked. "You forgive me for what?"

With a big smile he said, "For being a person with malice in your heart. I hope someday God can help you to want to do good in the world."

While making sure to remain more than an arm's length away from him, I replied, "Look soldier, I don't want to call you a liar, but you might try finding God *before* you get into trouble. When you profess a faith after you're arrested, it's clear you might have ulterior motives, and I have to doubt the veracity of your statements."

"The what?" he said with a perplexed look.

"Veracity means truthfulness, and I doubt your words contain much of it," I answered.

He replied, "I pray to God that your cynicism will subside and you might be born again with a new spirit, sir." He then took his place in the van.

A STATESIDE TOUR OF DUTY

Deep down you want to give people the benefit of the doubt. But with this guy, I felt everything he said was only empty words. I didn't trust him any more than a venomous snake.

Soon we were on the road. According to Collins, who had made the trip many times, we were now 419 miles from home. The trip continued to be uneventful. At noon, we stopped to get some more fast food for ourselves and passed out C rations to the prisoners. C rations are meals in a can, which are fed to troops in the field. The date the item was canned is stamped on the bottom, and if you were fortunate to get one less than fifteen years old, it is practically brand new. The rations can be eaten either hot or cold, and I can personally attest to the fact that they are more palatable when warmed up. However, we had no field mess or any other way to heat them, so this day they were served cold. This just gave our prisoners one more thing to complain and bellyache about.

By 1600 hours, we were pulling into the company area. The prisoners were placed in the confinement facility, and we went over to Finance to turn in TDY vouchers for the past two and a half days. The per diem amounted to $62.00. The six meals I had purchased on the road had cost me $17.12. In addition, my share of the room we had rented the second night set me back an additional $9.00. So, that left me with $35.88 I could put in the bank tomorrow. If a guy didn't mind being away from home two nights a week, this could be a profitable job. After Warren's escapades, the AWOL App drivers were the only ones in the company receiving TDY pay.

Friday afternoon, I was in my office when Collins dropped by. "You were right about Schrade, sir," was his first comment.

"How's that, Collins?" I replied.

"We just got word that he knifed a guard at the Fort Sam Houston Stockade last night in an escape attempt."

"No kidding? Then the guy was just as big a hypocrite as I thought," I commented.

"Yes, sir. No doubt about that." Collins continued, "They were going to send him back home to Arkansas, where he's wanted for several crimes. He was looking for a chance to escape all along. We just didn't give him one."

"How's the guard he knifed?" I asked.

"Critical condition, but they think he'll live."

As Collins left my office, I reflected on the past trip. Especially how some in Brownsville had thought we were unduly harsh on the prisoners.

If we had not been careful and followed the rules, it might have been me or one of my men that was now lying in the intensive care ward of a hospital. Instead, some poor guard at Fort Sam Houston had bought into Schrade's Christian conversion routine and had nearly paid with his life for that mistake. Two thoughts came to mind over the experience. One was that you should try to give people the benefit of the doubt, but never turn your back on them. The other was that no good deed ever goes unpunished.

As I was leaving to go home that afternoon, Steve reminded me of our roller derby plans for the next day. We would meet at his house at 1700.

"Who all is going?" I asked.

"Woolhouse, me, you, Riegals, Malone and Charlie," he replied.

"Three officers and three enlisted men. That's a good mix."

Steve smiled. "When we get there, you'll be glad we have the big guys along."

I didn't know much about roller derby, but the Amarillo Bombers had scheduled several of their competitions in San Angelo. That night they were playing the Nashville Renegades. As I looked around at the crowd, I understood what Steve had meant the day before when he said I would be glad to have the others along. The three enlisted men accompanying us were some of the biggest men in the company. The grandstands, on the other hand, were filled with the worst rednecks and assorted riffraff I had ever seen. They looked like any of them might pull a knife at any moment. If we got into a fight, our comrades were men who could handle themselves.

"You'll notice that roller derby draws a high-class crowd," Steve said with a smile.

"I was just noticing that," I said in reply. "We should have brought Winters. He would fit in well with these people."

"I don't go anywhere with Winters," Steve commented. "You, of all people, should know that."

"What if he was riding in the trunk?"

Steve thought for a moment. "No, not even then. He would still embarrass us when we let him out."

"You have a point there," I agreed.

In roller derby, the participants skate around a track and score points by skating past their opponents. I didn't understand it all (and didn't try to) but it seemed to be a combination of professional wrestling

A STATESIDE TOUR OF DUTY

meets Lil' Abner's Dogpatch. Each team had an equal number of men and women who skated in different heats and beat the hell out of each other while doing it. Steve had been right. It was almost as much fun to watch the crowd as it was to watch the competition. As the night wore on, the drunker they got. I don't remember what the score was, or even who won, I just knew that the experience could be called slumming. I also had Steve give me his car keys. Since he was enjoying numerous cans of beer, I would drive us home.

After the roller derby, Steve and the others wanted to go to a nearby bar to get one for the road. Everyone ordered a beer except me. Since I was driving, I ordered a Coke.

A local yokel at a nearby table looked over and chided, "I don't think anyone who orders a Coke is much of a man."

I turned around in my chair and replied, "Since I never said otherwise, there's nothing to argue about—is there?" I thought that might calm the situation and allow everyone to start minding their own business—but it didn't. They just got more belligerent. To be honest their verbal harassment was getting on my nerves. I was starting to get irritated.

I was about to suggest that we leave, when one of the hecklers said, "Look at them their short haircuts. They're probably some of them baby killers back from Vietnam." The others voiced similar comments.

Woolhouse and Riegals then got up and went to challenge our detractors. As they did, the bartender pulled a baseball bat from under the bar and pointed it at us as he bellowed, "Take it outside. There will be no fighting in here."

As we went out the back door into an alley I quickly evaluated the situation. There were six of us and six of them. Even odds, I thought. I had never been in this type of situation before, and I must admit that I was scared. However, I was careful not to show that emotion. I thought about trying to step aside and avoid conflict but my pride prevented that. These guys were real mouthy with the insults, and I was not going to look like a coward. My instincts told me it was best to hit first and ask questions later. I picked out a guy about my size and just as we got outside, I quickly decked him. He went down and didn't get up. As I stood over him I thought, "That sure was easy."

Suddenly, I was clobbered by a fist to the right eye next to the temple. That blind-side hit stunned me and knocked me against the side of the building. Somehow, I kept from going down, too. Before I could recover,

Malone had taken care of my attacker. I recovered my wits as quickly as I could and rejoined the brawl. Shortly thereafter, it was all over. Our opponents were all sprawled out, moaning, on the ground.

"Let's get to the car before any of their friends come to help them out," Charlie suggested.

We did just that and a few minutes later I was driving us toward the highway home. My companions were jubilant.

"Hot damn, we sure showed them!" Woolhouse shouted.

"I guess you've never been in a bar room fight before, sir?" Riegals asked.

"How did you know that?" I inquired (I thought I had done well).

"Well, for one thing, sir, you don't stand there and admire your work after you hit somebody. You look around for the next man to fight."

I began to explain my actions. "There were six of us and six of them so I guess that I figured I had done my share."

"No, sir!" Malone answered. "Nobody's share ain't over until all of the other guys are out of action and lying on the ground."

"I learned a good lesson, then," I concluded. It was also a lesson that I never intended to use again, if I could help it.

It was a good thing that Sam was out of town. If she could see the shiner I had now, she would give me a lecture on maturity that would never end. This incident would be filed away under things best not talked about. I also knew that my time as a roller derby fan was over.

CHAPTER TWENTY-SIX

As I arrived for the Monday morning briefing, someone asked me, "What does the other guy look like, sir?"

"I got hit by a door," I explained. "It was stuck, and as I pulled on it, it came open and hit me in the head." Steve was filling in for the CO at the briefing this morning, and winked at me as I told the story.

After his arrival, the colonel sat down and immediately noticed the shiner that I was sporting. "I hope the other guy is worse off than you are, lieutenant," he said with a smile.

I kept to my story. "The other guy was a door, sir. It's none the worse for wear."

The colonel smiled. "Uh-huh. You sticking with that story?"

"Yes, sir."

"It reminds me of my younger days," the colonel observed.

After the meeting, Steve and I walked back to my office together. "If it's any consolation, the men were impressed with your right hook," he commented.

"Impressed by what? The fact that I was the only one to wind up looking like he'd been in a fight, or is it the fact that I was brawling like a teenager. I'm really embarrassed."

A big grin came across Steve's face as he chuckled. "Don't sell yourself short, Nick. You knocked that other guy flat on his ass. Besides, you were the first to throw a punch. The men noticed that. They know you can take care of yourself."

I took some solace in the fact that I had shown everyone that I was no pantywaist. However, I had to point out the obvious. "If we had been arrested for brawling, can you imagine the trouble we would be in now, Steve? Embarrassment would be the least of our worries. I'm just glad no one lost any teeth or had any permanent injuries."

"I know," Steve replied. "That thought has occurred to me, too. We can't do that again."

"I'm just glad that my wife is out of town. She would never let me forget this."

Steve laughed again. "She won't find out from me, buddy. Well, I should get to work. See you later."

I went to my office as Steve returned to the company. As the clerks began to snicker and cackle, Sergeant Dee had the first comment on my appearance and it was funny.

"Sir, Mohammed Ali is on line one. He wants to schedule a bout with you," de la Vega said with a big grin on his face.

"No can do, sarge," I replied. "I promised Joe Frazier and Ken Norton I would fight them first. Tell Ali—maybe another time."

One of the clerks then said, "We're planning a fight at the EM Club Saturday night, sir. You're welcome to join us."

"I wish I could help, but I've decided to become a lover instead of a fighter," was my retort.

"With that eye, I can see why, sir," Sergeant Dee replied.

I figured that I deserved the teasing I was getting. After all, it was good-natured, and so I continued to dismiss their remarks with jokes. Besides, I supposed that I enjoyed the attention to some degree. Soon I was left alone to review and sign the mountain of paperwork on my desk.

At lunchtime, Steve and I joined Charlie at the post snack bar. It was just like old times. We talked about sports, politics and the war. Finally, I changed the subject. "Have you decided to ask Charlotte to marry you yet, Charlie? Looks like that's the only way you'll get her into bed."

"Hey!" Steve interjected. "Don't do anything to cause me to lose my roommate."

"To tell you the truth, Nick, I'm really crazy about her," said Charlie, "I am considering asking her to marry me."

I was only half serious when I asked the question. Charlie's answer surprised me. I didn't realize they were that serious in the relationship.

Steve shook his head. "Another one of us is about to bite the dust. I'll be the lone holdout."

"With a great girl like Barbara chasing you, you don't need to be a holdout for long," I pointed out.

"Barbara does want to get married. It just scares me, though. I've seen a lot of my friends from college get divorced."

A STATESIDE TOUR OF DUTY

"Maybe they got married for the wrong reasons. I know Sam and I don't have any major complaints. We have our disagreements, but that's normal. And this is coming from a man who used to be scared of marriage, too."

Charlie held up his coffee cup in a mock salute to me. "You're the inspiration for us all, Nick," he joked.

"Thanks," I said. "Nothing like putting pressure on me."

"You used to be afraid of getting married?" Steve was obviously very surprised.

"Big-time, Steve. I once swore I would never get married until I was forty."

"What happened?"

"I finally figured out that waiting so long was a bad idea. After a while things just seemed right to get married. Before that, I was just like you are now."

"Well, I'll be damned." Steve shook his head in disbelief.

We all laughed and returned to work. In addition to my other duties, I now had men coming into my office asking me to help them file their income tax forms. After all, I had been designated the 290th MP Company tax officer by Captain Lynch.

At first, I told the men I was busy and I would get to their tax returns later. After they left, I would read the necessary instructions and regulations. After learning what forms were required and how to fill them out, I would put everything back exactly the way they left it. When they returned, and inquired if I had finished their 1040's, I would snap my fingers and say, "Sorry, it slipped my mind. Let's do that now." I would then fill out the forms with ease.

Often a man would observe, "You sure are smart to be able to fill out those complicated forms so quickly, sir."

With my usual modesty, I would reply, "Hey, that's my job. The Army teaches me these things." They, of course, never knew that I had just discovered how to complete the task.

Within a few days, my reminder of the earlier fight I had been in was gone. I passed the time reading and watching TV. One night, while buying some groceries, I walked over to the liquor section in the store. The thought came that a few drinks might help pass the time. I picked up a bottle of vodka. I thought about Sam and the agreement we had made to stop drinking and then I thought about the friends whose lives had been so terribly changed by alcohol. I decided to save the money and put the bottle back. That was the last time I had the desire to drink. Despite my loneliness for Sam, one week became two and the two quickly merged into three, and the month of March was over.

On March 31, 1971, the news announced that Lieutenant William Calley had been found guilty of the charges against him and was sentenced to life in prison. Now, numerous soldiers began to sport Free Calley in Illness signs on their cars. These were usually painted with water-base paints on a side or rear window.

The U.S. Army has regulations against controversial or otherwise passion-provoking signs, and the commanding general quickly directed the provost marshal to require all military personnel to remove the words from their cars. Unfortunately, there are limits to free speech on a military base.

My men and I took no pleasure in ordering men to wash these expressions of free speech off their cars. Most of us were sympathetic to Lieutenant Calley. Unfortunately, orders are orders and they did follow them. However, I thought it was ironic that the men whose job it was to defend American rights and values were denied the right to fully express the right of free speech.

The local radio stations played a song called "The Battle Hymn of Lieutenant William Calley." This was to the tune of the more famous Civil War song by Julia Ward Howe. It started, "My name is William Calley, and I'm a soldier of this land." It then went on to explain how a young leader was determined to end the bushwhacking of his men by a vicious enemy. While many stations across the country refused to play the song—which many believed to be glorifying a war criminal—the stations around Fort McCulloch played it constantly.

I was happy that I had not been serving in his place in the unpopular war. To have the decisions made under the pressure of combat reviewed and critiqued by bureaucrats and other Monday-morning quarterbacks who have no idea what is going on seemed absurd. No one had arrested General Sherman after his army had plundered and raped the South during the Civil War. None of the generals in the various Indian Wars had their careers ended by a prison sentence for using brutality to force the various Native American tribes to live in peace on reservations. Even when Indians were treated unfairly and peaceful Indians were massacred at locations like Bear River, Ash Hollow or Sand Creek, the victorious military leaders were not punished. But it seemed that times had changed. Our government expected American forces to follow rules that no one else in the world took seriously. The Viet Cong and NVA (North Vietnamese Army) certainly didn't follow the rules. They could murder and torture Americans with impunity. That double standard in judgment bothered me. While I would never want us to follow the horrible examples of our enemies, I felt our soldiers should not be required to act like Boy Scouts, either. If a little high-handed treatment helped end a war—then so be it. That is the nature of war.

The highlight of each week came on Sunday night. I would make a lengthy call to Sam at 7:00 PM. Without fail, later in the week Sam would call to discuss some perceived emergency. It was clearly something trivial that could have been mentioned in a letter, but I didn't get angry about the unnecessary expense. After all, it was obvious that Sam missed me as much as I missed her. Both of us looked forward to the arrival of the baby, when we would be reunited.

April 6 was noteworthy for two reasons. On that day, President Nixon freed Lieutenant Calley from the Fort Benning Stockade and changed his punishment to house arrest while his case was being appealed. That brought howls of disapproval from war protesters. If Calley had been an officer in the North Vietnamese Army who had massacred Americans, the war protesters would have considered him a national hero. That irony was not lost on me.

The second event of April 6 was the assignment to the 290th MP Company of Captain Richard Marsden. He had just returned from Vietnam and only had about six months left in the Army. He would have the pleasure of spending those six months at Fort McCulloch. As soon as orders were cut designating him an acting assistant adjutant general, he took over as Operations officer and I went back to Traffic.

About two weeks later, another captain was assigned to the PMO. James "Buffalo Bob" Barker had an uncanny resemblance to the character on the old *Howdy Doody* show of the fifties and early sixties, and thus the nickname. Of course, no one called him that to his face. He was given the title of Military Police Public Relations Officer. Since I believed it would be difficult for "Buffalo Bob" to find enough work to keep himself busy in his new job, I suggested to the colonel that he be given the additional duty of Blue Bell reporting officer. The colonel agreed, and I turned over the folders containing the open cases to him. He set up shop in an unoccupied office up front, and soon he was constantly on the phone to cities all over Texas to find out the disposition of the various cases. The best thing about the arrival of these new men was the fact that now there were two new additions to the MP duty officer roster. That was good, since the colonel had agreed to drop the enlisted men from the OD roster and the duty came around more often.

As I rejoined my old staff in Traffic, Sergeant Corley was happy to have me back. "Welcome back, lieutenant. We've missed you," he said with enthusiasm.

"Thanks, sarge. It's good to be back." Of course, in my heart, I knew that without the Operations paperwork to deal with, and after dumping the Blue Bell reporting on "Buffalo Bob," I would now have to search for work to do. But it was quick in coming.

On April 14, the colonel informed me that there would be a major encampment of Boy Scouts out on the busiest of the state highways. This jamboree would be held the second week of June. As Traffic officer, I would have to ensure their safety and coordinate with their leaders to provide for ready access of vehicles in and out of the area. Sergeant Corley and I drove out to the area to make some preliminary plans.

The encampment would be far out on Highway 142 East, in the forested area of the post. The forest was composed mostly of cottonwood trees mixed with elms and stands of spruce trees. Unlike the largely barren landscape of the western side of the post, this area was perfect for a large powwow-style convention of Boy Scouts. There were large, clear areas on both sides of the highway, and there was a bend in the creek, which formed a small lake and came within a hundred yards of the highway, where canoeing and other water activities could be held. I quickly began to make some notes. The speed limit on the highway was sixty miles per hour. However, during the brief residence of the visitant scouts, it would have to be reduced to only thirty to provide for their safety. Signs would have to be placed at least a quarter of a mile each way from the encampment, warning motorists to reduce speed. Also, there would have to be increased patrolling of the area by our personnel.

After surveying the area, Sergeant Corley and I returned to the PMO. I went to the colonel's office to brief him on the situation. As I passed along my observations, the colonel was silent until I suggested thirty miles per hour as the reduced speed during the camporee.

"Lower the speed limit to twenty-five while those kids are camped there," the colonel ordered.

"Twenty-five, sir?"

"Definitely!" The colonel stated. "And strictly enforce it! None of those kids are going to get hit by a car on our watch. Not if we can help it."

"Yes, sir. That's the way we'll do it," I agreed.

"Good, lieutenant," said the colonel. "Now what about the signs?"

"I'll get them ordered immediately, sir. I was promised we could have them available one week before the encampment. If there are any more developments, I'll keep you informed."

"Keep up the good work, lieutenant."

"Thank you, sir." I left the colonel's office and returned to my own. There, I made a call to the local Boy Scout council office. They assured me that all other logistical support (civilian ambulances, medical personnel, etc.) was already provided for. I now turned my attention to other items.

With Sergeant Corley, I began to set up a schedule where people could have their speedometers calibrated. We decided the third Thursday afternoon of every month would be set aside for this service. I also submitted a work order for white lines to be painted across the highways, at quarter mile intervals, in several locations. From a helicopter or airplane, motorists could have their speed checked by a military policeman with a stopwatch. We then compiled a chart of speeds, with the corresponding times required to travel a quarter of a mile, to facilitate the process. The speeds were in five-miles-per-hour increments, so if a time fell between two speeds on the chart, the motorist was given the benefit of the doubt and the lower speed was charged.

While we waited for the post engineers to paint the white lines, we began to experiment by clocking cars with various types of aircraft. The first attempt was in a large Huey helicopter. The windows by where we had to sit allowed for limited observation, and with the altitude we had to maintain, constant observation of the cars was impossible. We next tried a small, fixed-wing aircraft—what civilians call an airplane. Again, with the altitude we had to maintain, the job was difficult. If you took your eyes off the target vehicle, even for a second, it could be difficult to spot them again if numerous vehicles were on the road. Finally, we tried a small bubble-top helicopter, the kind used to medevac injured people to a hospital. It was perfect for the job.

This helicopter could fly just above the tops of the trees and telephone poles and, with a clear field of vision, the target vehicle was under observation always. There was no chance the personnel on the ground would stop the wrong vehicle. If necessary, the helicopter could fly just above and behind the car being clocked until it was stopped. With a walkie-talkie, the man in the helicopter was in constant communication with his comrades on the ground. Also, with the number of pilots on the post that needed hours to maintain their flight status, we would have no problem maintaining aerial surveillance any time we wished to do so. In addition, with the number of aircraft flying around the post at any given time, motorists could not be sure whether they were being clocked or not. The signs that would be placed around the post stating, "Speed Checked by Aircraft," would, no doubt, keep many from speeding—at least during daylight hours.

For the most part, I enjoyed being back in Traffic. With Marsden being such a short-timer, he would cover for me with the major any time I wished to take off early or come in a little late in the morning. Of course, with Sam gone, I often spent the evenings observing my men running radar or VASCAR. I was satisfied with the professionalism they exhibited in the performance of their jobs and knew that any tickets issued would stand up in court. The patrolman working late could come in later the next day to compensate for the evening work. Likewise, Marsden agreed that I was also allowed compensatory time for my after-hours work. When I was not working, I was often visiting with Steve and Charlie at their place or finding something interesting to read at the library. Meanwhile, things at work continued to be routine.

The week of April 9, I was the duty officer. On Tuesday night, I was riding with the patrol superintendent, Sergeant Woods. As we proceeded down Leonard Wood Road, suddenly a man bolted from a phone booth and ran between two buildings. We both saw him at the same time.

"I bet he just rifled that phone booth, sir," Woods said as he pulled the cruiser over.

"We'll soon know, sarge," I said as we got out of the car.

Sure enough, the coin box of the pay phone was pried open, and the metal bar apparently used in the theft was lying on the floor.

"Don't touch anything, sarge," I cautioned. "That piece of metal should have his prints on it. Go call CID. I'll make sure nobody comes along and disturbs the crime scene."

Within minutes, CW3 Jarvis had arrived. As soon as he looked into the phone booth, the first thing he did was to pick up the steel bar. "What's this?" he asked.

A STATESIDE TOUR OF DUTY

I was irritated. "It's probably what he used to rip open the phone, and you could have checked it for prints if you hadn't handled it."

"Well, I didn't know that," Jarvis retorted.

I shook my head. "Why don't you just wait here, and maybe he'll come back here and confess. Then, you can solve the crime," I said with disgust.

"I don't care for your attitude, lieutenant!"

There was irritation in my voice as I replied. "Whatever! Let's go, Woods. Our work here is through." I had wasted my time keeping people away from the phone booth.

As we drove off, Woods said what I already knew. "Everybody knows that CID is the biggest bunch of dumb asses around, sir. Every time I see them in action I get more and more thankful that most people are law-abiding. If they weren't, we would all be in big trouble."

"I know, Woods. Most of those clowns wouldn't be able to solve anything."

On the evening of April 22, I was watching the national news on television when my blood began to boil. A former skipper of a PBR (Patrol Boat, River in military nomenclature) in Vietnam was testifying before Congress. The man was leading a group called the "Veterans Against the War," and recounted numerous war crimes and atrocities by American soldiers in Vietnam.

When one senator noted that the man had only spent four months in the combat zone and questioned how he could have observed so much in so short a time, it became obvious that the man was simply passing along gossip and shithouse rumors. It appeared that he had seen none of the things he was talking about.

To have a fellow officer from the United States military make such statements seemed almost treasonous to me. There was no mention of the mistreatment of our men in enemy captivity, the summary executions the Viet Cong carried out on a daily basis, or the other enemy behavior. It was made to seem that only Americans did anything improper or criminal. I knew in my heart that I would never forgive this treacherous individual for his actions. In anger, I turned off the television and wrote a letter to Sam. I had to get my mind off what I had just heard.

On April 30, a soldier was robbed of four hundred dollars—at gunpoint—near the EM Club. A sketch artist had made a drawing of the subject and CID had distributed copies around the post, but none of us expected an arrest to be made. On Friday, May 14, the subject struck again. This time another soldier was robbed of over five hundred dollars. The robber used a .38-caliber snub-nosed pistol, and his description matched the one previously given.

At the briefing Monday morning, CID proposed a plan to catch the armed robber. We would work in three teams. An MP would go into the EM Club and order a beer. He would then leave on foot. He would walk around while we kept him under surveillance, hoping the robber would strike again. If not, a second man would do the same thing with a second set of surveillance personnel. Then a third team would do the same thing.

I was with the first team. As our decoy left the EM Club, I was in one of two POVs watching from distant locations. As he proceeded to walk around, we would leapfrog to different locations, keeping our eyes on him constantly. We coordinated our movements via walkie-talkies. The robber never struck, and by midnight CID had called off the effort.

At 1800 hours on Tuesday, we were preparing to do it again. As we were being briefed for the night's operations, this time I interjected my thoughts in the hopes that the robber would be caught. I quickly discovered my suggestions were not wanted.

As CW3 Jarvis asked for questions before we got started, I stated, "The robber has always struck before on Friday night. Maybe we should be doing this on a Friday night."

"Armed robberies can occur on any night of the week, lieutenant."

"True," I replied. "But it seems to me that the robber will stick to his MO, since it has been successful for him."

"You let us do the thinking, lieutenant."

"Another thing," I pointed out. "All of the men who were robbed flashed a roll. If you want this robber to strike again, you need to show a roll of money to motivate him."

Jarvis laughed. "Then we might entrap someone else into committing a robbery who was just enticed by the money. Besides, that would be a good way for us to lose our money, if the guy got away."

"For the so-called entrapped man to pull off the robbery, he would need a gun. That means he was probably planning a robbery to begin with. Also, we could use green-colored paper with a couple of bills on either end to look like a roll of money." After a second, I added, "And with all of us around—the subject can't get away if we're doing our jobs."

A STATESIDE TOUR OF DUTY

"We don't tell you how to run Traffic, lieutenant. We'll do this planning; you just help with surveillance."

"Okay," I said with resignation. I knew it would be a wasted night, but no one was going to accuse me of not helping. However, I decided this would be the last night I would participate unless changes were made.

Sergeant Corley and I were manning one of the surveillance cars that night. Corley said what I had been thinking. "You should have known better than to suggest CID do anything on a Friday night, sir. By then, those guys are looking forward to the weekend."

"I know, sarge. This all seems like such a waste of time. You know as well as I do the guy won't strike tonight."

"You know it, sir. But at least they can't say we're not team players. We're helping as best we can."

Sergeant Corley was a professional soldier who knew the system. Do what you're told and don't rock the boat. That was the way to a long and successful career, and he did it well. As we continued our surveillance, he began telling war stories.

"Before my tour in 'Nam, lieutenant, I was at Fort Jackson. One night I caught a mess sergeant hauling an entire station wagon of steaks and other groceries off post to sell."

"What happened to the guy?" I asked.

"Well, I took him back to the station and took pictures of the car with all the food he was stealing and filled out the paperwork, complete with blotter entries. By the next day, all the paperwork and pictures had disappeared and the blotter had been retyped to delete the entries. "I was mad as hell and went to see the colonel—a Colonel Wight. He was the provost marshal there. He told me that I had done my job, and if anything improper had occurred or a criminal got away—then it wasn't my fault."

"Sounds like the guy had been paid off," I commented.

"Probably! But, I knew that if I tried to go over his head, I would be the one who would lose. Like it or not, sometimes there's nothing you can do about a situation except wait for things to change."

Sergeant Corley was right. I had heard stories at Fort Gordon about investigators being told to close a case (one where he had the subject dead to rights) by a superior. The investigator could do as he was told and have a successful career, or he could attempt to go over his superior's head to attempt to pursue the case. Those who did the latter usually spent whatever time they had left in the Army in some monotonous dead-end job with no chance of promotion.

Suddenly, a man approached our decoy. As he did, Sergeant Corley reached over and tapped me on the arm.

"I see him, sarge. Start driving up the road real slow," I instructed.

I then grabbed the walkie-talkie. "This is Delta Two; we have a possible fox approaching the pigeon. Over."

"This is Delta One," came the reply. "Sighting confirmed. Approach slowly, but do not reveal yourself unless 10-19 is in progress. Over."

"Ten-four, Delta One. We will observe. Delta Two out."

"Delta One out."

We drove up the road past our decoy. As we did so, the other surveillance car passed us going in the opposite direction. The two men on the street seemed to be talking in a friendly manner with no robbery in progress. When we were about thirty yards from the men on the street, we made a U-turn and proceeded back. The two men we were observing had now parted company. As we came to our decoy individual, we pulled over to the side of the road and Corley yelled, "Excuse me sir, but can you direct us to the PX?"

Specialist Garrett, the decoy, approached our car as he stated in a loud voice, "Yes! You go three blocks, make a right and it's on the left. You can't miss it."

"Thanks," replied Corley. As Garrett got closer, Corley spoke in a softer voice. "I guess that wasn't our man?"

"No," said Garrett. "He just asked for the time, but I gotta tell you guys that I was nervous as hell when he first walked up."

"I don't blame you," I countered. "Well, just keep going and we'll be watching."

"Yes, sir."

As Garrett proceeded, we moved to a position where we could observe him as I picked up the walkie-talkie.

"Delta Two to Delta One, over."

"This is Delta One. Go ahead, Delta Two. Over."

"The subject only wanted the correct time. We are continuing surveillance. Over."

"Ten-four, Delta Two. We will continue to observe also. Delta One out."

"Delta Two out," I concluded.

A STATESIDE TOUR OF DUTY

The rest of the night was just as big of a waste of time as I had predicted. There were no attempted armed robberies of any of our decoys, and by midnight the operation was called off and everyone had left for home.

Wednesday morning, I was advised of bad news. Sergeant Warren, who had been confined to the psychiatric ward at Walter Reed Army Hospital in Washington for observation, had escaped. Suddenly, I was delighted that Sam was not here. If Warren attempted a return to Fort McCulloch to exact revenge against myself or anyone else, I didn't want her in harm's way. Right now, I was thankful and relieved that she was in Arizona.

When the clock showed 1700 hours that afternoon, I just headed for home. I had already let CID know that I would not be available for their decoy operation that night. Two wasted nights were enough for me. As I arrived at home, I began to pack for my trip to Arizona that weekend. I was looking forward to seeing Sam and becoming a father. I had scheduled leave from Monday the 24th to Sunday the 30th. There was no way I was going to miss the birth of my first child. As I packed, I reflected on the world situation in general. While doing so, the approaching birth of my child kept me from being depressed about how irrelevant my service seemed to be.

Just eighteen days previously, on May 1, war protesters had attempted to shut down the city of Washington, D.C., with widespread protests in the streets. They had failed, but they did disrupt the capital for several hours. With the war continuing, it seemed that headlines were being made everywhere except Fort McCulloch. The thought occurred that I might spend my entire life in anonymity as just another average Joe. I quickly dismissed those depressing thoughts with the decision that if I was to be another unknown citizen, I would be the best husband and father I could possibly be. That way, when my life was over, I would have children and grandchildren who might remember me with fondness. Besides, I thought, we can't all be a Washington, Lincoln or Douglas McArthur. Those men only came along once in a century when the stars were properly aligned.

I tossed clothes into my suitcase as I continued my ruminations and reflections about my life and job. It came to me that no one has an exciting life all the time. Washington had been a surveyor and Lincoln a backwoods lawyer. McArthur had spent years behind a desk before World War II. Their lives had been boring much of the time, too. Those who chose to have a constant life of continual excitement usually burned out quickly. The case studies for continual excitement had been the deaths of Jimmy Hendrix and Janis Joplin the previous year. They had made it big, but so what? Their lifestyles had destroyed them, and they never got to really enjoy the celebrity. Not for very long, at least. Then I remembered that even Albert Einstein had produced his theory of relativity while he was a low-level clerk in an office somewhere. Maybe anonymity wasn't all bad. Each of us can only be the best we are capable of being. If a chance for greatness comes along, we can take it. If not, then you don't make the world a worse place for your having been here.

My thoughts then turned to another decision I had made. Sam would not accompany me on the return trip unless I knew that Sergeant Warren was back in custody. My excuse for not bringing her back would be simple. After the birth of the baby, it would be better if there was someone around to help her for awhile. With me at work all day, that wasn't possible at Fort McCulloch. Sam did not need to know the truth. If Warren was after me, I could buy a gun. I figured that my marksmanship was as good as his was. But there was no way I was going to let Sam, and the baby, be in danger. Our separation would have to continue a little longer. I finished packing the suitcase and set it aside. When Friday came, I would be ready to go.

I turned on the TV, but I ignored it. I was lost in thought as to what might happen if the baby wasn't born by the 29th. Sam seemed sure that the baby wouldn't wait until the original due date of the 31st, so I had planned accordingly. If the unforeseen happened, I decided that I could call the Red Cross. I had been told during all phases of my Army training that they could help a soldier obtain emergency leave for such situations. I felt that I was prepared for any future problems.

Thursday morning, I was reading the newspaper when my eyes caught an article germane to my work. The United States Supreme Court had just ruled on a case called California v. Byers. In this case, a man named Byers had been involved in a motor vehicle accident resulting in property damage. He had been charged with hit-and-run and found guilty. His defense was that if he were required to stop and report the accident, it would be a violation of his Fifth Amendment rights. Incredibly, the California State Supreme Court had bought the argument.

As I continued to read, I discovered that the decision of the California Court was reversed by a 5–4 decision. The two Nixon appointees had joined with three others to form the majority. I was disgusted by the thought that if Hubert Humphrey had been elected President, he might very well have put two more liberals like Douglas on the bench. Had that happened, then hit-and-run would now be legal, and there would be no recourse for charging those who tried to avoid responsibility for their automobile accidents. How on earth anyone could have accepted the Byers argument was beyond me. Sometimes it seemed that the entire world was only one step from going completely crazy. I tossed the paper aside.

As we took care of the day's paperwork, I made conversation with Sergeant Corley; it took my mind off that recent court case. "Well, do you think you can handle things in my absence, sarge?" I sarcastically asked.

Sergeant Corley took a long drink of coffee. He then answered, "Believe it or not, sir, while you were in Operations, the Traffic office remained open. We were able to write tickets and everything." He took another swig of coffee and smiled as he said, "Come to think of it, sir, we never knew you were gone."

"Touché, sarge. Touché," I replied.

"Well, sir," Corley continued, "part of the job description for a good senior NCO is to keep junior officers from getting a big ego and a swelled head."

"Mission accomplished, sarge. Now why don't we go out on the road and keep the streets safe for the populace."

"The what?" Corley asked with a puzzled look.

"Populace means the common folks, the multitudes, the regular citizens," I explained.

"Then why didn't you say so?" Corley asked.

"Well, sarge, part of the job description for a good junior officer is to use big words and keep senior NCOs scratching their heads."

"And you do it well, sir."

We spent the next two hours driving along the state highways looking for some spots to run VASCAR. We needed locations where the clocking vehicle could be hidden and the two reference points were easily seen. We also needed locations further down the highway on either side where the chase cars could be placed. In order to comply with regulations, they were placed on the right side of the road, in the direction they were facing, about a mile and a half apart. That way, as speeders slowed down while approaching them, they would think it was safe to increase their speed once they were past. We found several excellent spots. When I returned from Arizona, we would teach some speeders a lesson they wouldn't soon forget. Many of the people who bragged about the high speeds they achieved out on the state highways would be paying for that privilege.

Friday I just spent in the office tying up loose ends. I had called Sam and convinced her not to return with me. Since I would not be bringing Sam home, I agreed to go on the Lone Star Run the first week of June. After all my mundane tasks were completed at 1600 hours, I went over to the company to talk with Steve.

He, also, was looking forward to a weekend—only he had a different reason for doing so: Barbara would be spending it with him.

While my leave didn't officially start until the 24th, I would leave after work. Steve would need to sign me out on leave sometime Monday morning. I sure hoped he wouldn't forget. He had always been dependable before, and I was sure he would be this time. Still, I couldn't help but be nervous about these things.

"Welcome, Nick, to my humble headquarters," he said as I entered his office.

"You're in high spirits," I observed.

"You bet your life. Charlie will be out of town and Barbara will be spending the weekend."

"In all your romantic endeavors, you won't forget that favor I need, will you?" I asked.

"No way, buddy. Unfortunately, I must return to work Monday. I'll do it then. It won't interfere with any love-making."

"I really appreciate it," I said.

"No problem. That's what friends are for. You and Sam come back here with a healthy baby."

"I'm not bringing Sam back here until Sergeant Warren is captured again," I said.

"That's good thinking, Nick. After all, you were one of the ones responsible for the termination of his career." Then with a hint of admiration in his voice, Steve added, "I just wish it could have been me that did it. That was good work."

"Thanks," I said. "But now I have to look over my shoulder until Warren is in custody again."

"True, but remember there are a lot of people looking for him. He has a lot more to worry about than you."

Steve's words were comforting because he was right. While he was on the run, I was probably the last thing on Warren's mind. I changed the subject. "I am so anxious to see Sam and find out if my child is a boy or a girl, I can't stand it," I said.

"You have looked like you've been a little preoccupied all week," Steve replied.

"Yeah, I keep wondering how things will change, now that another person is dependent upon me." I looked at my watch. "I'd better get going."

Before I could leave, Steve passed on an observation. "I've noticed, Nick, that when Barbara is around I drink a lot less. When I'm with her we might have a couple of glasses of wine, but when she's not around I can kill a six-pack real quick. Come to think of it, when Charlie is with Charlotte—I don't think he drinks at all. It is amazing what having a woman around can do."

"Well," I grinned, "there are women available who can have the opposite effect on us."

"No man with a brain would want one of those around for very long," he commented. He then said, "Good luck, Nick."

"Thanks, man."

Steve and I shook hands, and I returned to lock my office for the day and prepare to leave.

It was 1700 hours, and I didn't even go home. My suitcase was already in the car, and I headed over to the Personnel office. Mr. Swanson was flying to an Air Force base near San Antonio for a conference of some sort, and he had offered me a ride. From there, a flight to Luke Air Force Base should be easy to obtain. I left my car in the Personnel parking lot, and together we drove out to airstrip number three. It was ironic that I had to fly east first to get a flight west, but it was a quick and pleasant trip. Mr. Swanson was happy to have some company for the flight, and I was delighted to be on my way to see Sam.

CHAPTER TWENTY-SEVEN

As soon as Swanson landed the plane in San Antonio, I went into the terminal and discovered that the next flight to Luke Air Force Base would be at 0900 the next morning. We got rooms at the base BOQ for the evening, and early the next morning we parted company after breakfast. He went to his conference and I headed back to the flight line terminal.

"Thanks again for the ride, Jim. I really appreciate it," I said as we shook hands.

"You're more than welcome, Nick. I was happy to have the company. Best of luck to you and your wife."

"Thanks again. I'll pass that along."

My flight was on time and, even with a brief stopover somewhere else in Texas, we landed in Arizona shortly after noon. By 1:00 PM Sam and I were together again for the first time in almost three months. She was huge. If the baby was a boy, I suspected he would be big enough to start football practice the day after he was born. I wisely decided not to say anything about her size. I just kissed her and gave her a big hug.

"I'm sorry I've gotten so big," was her first comment.

"Honey," I explained. "You're not big. You're pregnant. I've told you before how pregnant women are the sexiest women in the world."

"I love it when you lie," she said as she kissed me again.

I feigned a hurtful look and said, "Honey, I'm an officer and a gentleman. Do you seriously think I would lie to you?"

"Yes, Nick, you would. And for the record—thank you very much." It was then that she noticed the bar on my shoulder was now silver instead of gold. "You've been promoted. When did that happen?"

"It was official two days ago. You are now married to a first lieutenant instead of a shavetail."

"Oh honey," she groaned. "I wish I could have been there."

"Don't worry. The colonel says that when you return, we can all pose for a group picture of you and him pinning on the new bars. No one needs to know that it was taken a few weeks after the fact."

"That is so neat," she said, running her finger across my new bars.

"Yeah! Now Steve and I are the same rank again. He got his promotion a couple of weeks ago."

"How come?" she asked?

"Because he received his commission before I did, that's why. Remember, he was ROTC. He was commissioned the same day he graduated from college."

"Well, just the same, you deserve a reward." She then gave me a passionate kiss.

Her doctor had encouraged her to get some exercise, so we spent much of the remainder of the day walking around the neighborhood. Sam couldn't walk very fast in her condition, but that didn't matter. I just patiently accompanied her as I held her hand and listened to her tell me how great it was for us to be together again.

"It was really boring to have to do this by myself, Nick, but I've been doing it every day."

"I'm proud of you, honey. Most women would have just sat around and watched soap operas."

"I've watched my share of them, too," she admitted. "But, I spend as much time as I can stand doing this." She waved to a neighbor who returned her wave.

"Now that you're here, everyone can be sure I'm really married." She waved to some other neighbors as I nodded to them. "I think some of these people were starting to think I was an unwed mother."

"It's good to clear up any misconceptions," I said with a smile.

As we walked, I wondered if Sam's enthusiasm for exercise had anything to do with avoiding her stepmother. Despite the cordial treatment they accorded each other, I could tell that they weren't close. During my college days, I had met more than my share of sorority girls who believed that their ass was golden and their shit didn't stink. Sam's stepmother seemed to be the older prototype from which those girls were designed. However, I kept those thoughts to myself. I just kept telling her to concentrate on having the baby and thinking positive.

By 5:00 PM Sam was in labor. We hurried to the hospital, only to be sent home. They thought it was a false alarm. Somehow, the word had gotten around that I was back in town, and as we arrived back at her house some friends showed up to recruit me for a softball game.

I started to explain, "Sorry, guys. I can't go. My wife is in labor— "

"Go, Nick. Believe me it's okay," Sam interrupted.

I was surprised at her reaction, but suddenly I understood. All afternoon I had been offering words of encouragement and telling her to think positive. I thought I was being helpful. Unfortunately, by this time I guessed that Sam was probably to the point of thinking she only had one nerve left and I was standing on it. "Are you sure, honey?" I asked.

"Yes, Nick. Right now, you're just making me nervous. Go play softball."

I hadn't been playing on the company team this season, so I thought a game would be fun, and I wouldn't be annoying Sam. I agreed. I borrowed a glove and joined my buddies. I returned from the game about 10:00 PM. There was no change in Sam's condition. She still claimed to be in labor. While I was no doctor, I figured she was right. The way her abdomen constricted every seven or eight minutes seemed to confirm that.

"Want to go to the hospital again?" I questioned.

"No. Those people will just send me home again. I'll wait until the contractions are closer."

We then went to bed, but Sam had a restless night. Sleep in her condition was hard to obtain. She seemed irritated with the ease with which I drifted off to sleep and kept waking me up to rub her back.

By Sunday afternoon, I suggested we go for a walk, but Sam declined. "Take me back to the hospital," she ordered.

I quickly found out why my wife wouldn't go for a walk. Her pace was so slow it took forever just to get her out to the car. Once we got to the hospital, the pains were timed at five minutes apart. But there was no dilation. After two hours, they sent us home again.

Once we were home I suggested that Sam take a hot bath to relax, but she declined. She was afraid her water would break and we wouldn't get to the hospital on time. So we spent another night of her tossing and turning and me rubbing her back whenever she would wake me up. She seemed irritated that I didn't stay awake as much as she did.

By Monday night, it was back to the hospital. By now the pains were less than five minutes apart, and Sam dug her fingernails into the back of my hands with each one. I suppose it was a psychological attempt, on some level, to use me as a surrogate for the pain. This attempt to transfer the discomfort to me didn't seem to help her much, though. I suspected that this could also be a vain attempt to let me know what she was going through or simply a means to cope with the torture she was experiencing. Whatever the reason, I bit my lower lip and didn't complain. I could see that her pain was much greater than mine. Besides, to endure the pain of her twisting my fingers and drawing blood on the backs of my hands without complaint made me feel like more of a tough-guy he-man. A silly thought, when I compared it to the anguish she was experiencing.

The night proceeded at an agonizingly slow pace. Sam was a real trouper. While I could hear women in surrounding rooms cursing their husbands or threatening to amputate their male anatomy, the most Sam did was groan in agony.

To some of the nurses, even these moans and groans were too much and they would tell Sam to be quiet. To hear them tell it, she was the only one in the hospital expressing cries of pain. I couldn't believe they could tell such falsehoods with a straight face. It was like they thought we were deaf. The lady in the room next to us was using language only Sergeant Winters or a Basic Training drill sergeant or some drunken sailor could appreciate. She also sounded menacingly close to completely eviscerating her husband. I could hear other women who were expressing similar complaints, but the nurses told Sam to be quiet.

Medication seemed to diminish the pain, but as I observed the massive needles it was administered with, I wasn't sure how. One procedure was called a saddle block, and it hurt me just to watch. The needle and syringe it was administered with were huge.

As the night wore on, Sam attempted to rest while the medical personnel began to discuss the possibilities of a Cesarean section. I just kept wiping Sam's forehead with a cool cloth and holding her hand. I suspected that the scars I would bear on the backs of my hands from this night would be a reminder of the experience, but I kept telling myself that it was nothing compared to what Sam was enduring.

The other women who were complaining so loudly had arrived after us and delivered their babies soon afterward. However, we were still there. I could not understand why it was taking so long. When we had first arrived, I had attempted to add levity to the situation by chanting, "Have that kid," like a cheerleader and cracking jokes. Now, I was starting to really get worried. However, this was a new experience for me and I had no idea what to expect. So, to not add to the anxiety of the situation, I kept my thoughts to myself.

Finally, with the morning came some change in the situation. Dilation of the cervix was beginning and Sam's water broke. Still, the process seemed incredibly slow. I really envied the couples who came and departed in much shorter periods of time.

Then came a surprise. As the expected time of the delivery got closer, I was told that the hospital was experimenting with a policy of allowing fathers in the delivery room. Most men, when given the choice, elected to wait in the father's waiting room, and that was my first thought. I asked Sam what she preferred.

"Would you want me to be in the delivery room, honey?"

With a painful grimace, she sank her fingernails into the back of my hand again and uttered an emphatic, "Yes!" Through clenched teeth she then added, "You didn't mind being there to start this kid; now you can welcome her into the world."

"Yes, dear."

Within a few minutes, I had scrubbed my hands and arms with antiseptic soap and was dressed appropriately for the delivery room. Finally, with me at her side, Sam was wheeled into delivery.

The best way I can describe the birth of a baby that other men might relate to it is this: go to the bathroom and try to pass a watermelon. As I watched I was very happy to be a male. The pains were coming rapidly now, and after about forty minutes in the delivery room, the baby's head popped out face down. Sam was told not to bear down until the doctor had cleaned out the baby's nose and mouth. Then as the doctor extricated an arm, Sam asked, "Is it a girl?"

"It's difficult to tell from this end," the doctor joked. Then with one more push, the entire baby slid out. It was a girl.

Sam heaved a big sigh of relief, and then exclaimed, "I'm having another pain."

The doctor then checked and said, "It looks like another head coming."

"What does that mean?" I asked.

With a glare, Sam looked over and said, "What do you think it means? Use your brains, Nick!"

To rescue me in this time of bewilderment, the doctor replied, "It means, Dad, you are going to be the father of twins."

Twins! The word hit like baseball line drive to the head. Suddenly, I was responsible for *four* people in this world. A feeling of euphoria then overwhelmed the feeling of massive responsibility. The second child could be a boy, I thought. That would be great. I kept thinking to myself that I should be positive. Think boy! It didn't help. Five minutes later the second baby girl was born. The disappointment of not having a son was cancelled out by the thought of twins. The feeling of elation I felt with twin girls overwhelmed the disappointment of not having a boy.

Within a few more minutes, the placentas had been expelled also. All my life I had heard jokes about how the afterbirth was supposed to look like a pizza. The jokesters had been wrong. Neither of these things looked anything like a pizza. After seventy-two hours of labor Sam said with delight, "Look honey, I'm starting to have a flat stomach again."

I just smiled and looked at the clock on the wall. It was 5:17 in the afternoon.

While Sam was in recovery, I went to the nursery to admire our new girls. They were beautiful. I was given pictures of the girls, and after I left I would show them to anyone who would take a moment to look at them. Before I left, though, I made sure I got a chance to hold them. Knowing Sam had given birth to almost thirteen pounds of babies; it was easy to see why she was so miserable. The other, single-birth babies were between five and eight pounds.

After a couple of hours Sam was wheeled into a room to get some much-needed food and rest. She shared a room with another woman who described the ordeal of delivering a five-pound baby after five hours of labor. After hearing about Sam's experience, that woman's husband had less sympathy for his wife. Now I decided it was time to leave so Sam could get some rest.

"I'll see you in the morning, sweetie, after you've had a good night's sleep."

"Okay, honey," she replied. "I really love you."

"I love you, too." I then added, "I'm proud of you. I don't think I could have handled what you went through."

"That's because you're a man," she said with a wink.

Before I left I returned to the nursery to admire our girls again.

The next morning, I went first to the hospital to see Sam and the girls. I held one daughter and sang to her as Sam nursed the other. Now we began to discuss names. Sam wanted names that implied power and strength. I thought that was a great idea.

"Well," I suggested. "We could name them after famous rulers. That would be names like Catherine the Great, Elizabeth, Mary, Isabella, Victoria, Anne, Charlotte—" I paused to add a witticism, "Spain even had a queen named Joanna the Mad."

"Forget her!"

"Well, how about Mary Anne?"

"You've been watching *Gilligan's Island* too much, Nick. Try again," she said.

"How about names that rhyme?" I suggested.

"Like what?"

"I don't know," I admitted. "I never was much of a poet."

Sam smiled as if having a bit of inspiration. "How about Tracy and Stacy?"

I couldn't think of any real arguments against those names, so with a shrug I answered, "Works for me. Now, what about middle names?"

"We'll use our grandmother's names. Amanda and Angelena."

"As in Tracy Angelena and Stacy Amanda?" I guessed.

"No. We'll make it Tracy Amanda and Stacy Angelena."

"Okay, honey. Put that on their birth certificates."

So it was that Tracy Amanda Moultrie had entered the world at six pounds one ounce and had blond hair. Stacy Angelena Moultrie showed up at six pounds fourteen ounces and had hair with a more reddish tinge. Tracy measured eighteen inches long, while her sister was seventeen and a half inches.

I spent much of the day talking with Sam or walking around the hospital floor with her as we talked and admired our new children. I also asked the one question that had been bothering me. "Why didn't they know that we were giving birth to twins, Sam?"

"We didn't give birth to the twins," she corrected. "I did."

"I stand corrected, honey. How come they didn't know twins were on the way?"

"The doctor thought he heard a double heartbeat a couple of times, but he just thought the baby was extra active and moving around. Besides, I wasn't gaining any weight. I was just getting so big I thought I was going to pop."

I suspected then that someday medical science would come up with a device that would show when multiple births were imminent, but during the summer of 1971 such things were still in the future. Surprise was still the order of the day.

Then Sam said, "It's too bad you men can't know what it's like to give birth."

A STATESIDE TOUR OF DUTY

"Maybe we have had the experience, but just don't remember it." She gave me a quizzical look as I continued, "All it would take is for us to have been a seahorse."

"If this is another of your stories, I think I need to lie down first."

After I got Sam back into her bed I, continued. "A lot of the world believes in reincarnation where people return to earth after death as an animal of some sort. Right?"

Sam shrugged and said, "Okay."

"Well, I think those people have it all wrong. I think humans are the highest form of life. It would be absurd to have us return after death as a lesser form of life. Imagine if God had created our spirits by having them evolve from lesser forms. For example, he might have created us as one-celled creatures, which after that life might have come back as two-celled organisms. After that we might have been a form of plant life, say a Venus fly trap. From there we became higher forms of life until we became the human spirits that were born into this life. If that were the case, our learning and growth would have required all of us to have spent time as a seahorse."

"Why is that?" Sam asked.

"The seahorse is the only creature on the earth where the male gets pregnant and bears the young. So, if we existed together as seahorses many eons, of years ago, then you got to enjoy knocking me up while I gave birth to the thousands of offspring. Of course, the male seahorse never travels more than a few feet from home, while the female roams far and wide looking for other mates. Therefore, I'm hoping that you were not a naughty little seahorse and stayed close by and faithful."

While Sam began to giggle, the woman she shared the room with almost became hysterical with laughter. "Girl, is that husband of yours for real?" she cackled.

"He comes up with stuff like this all the time," Sam replied. "Continue, honey," she said to me. Then she said to the other lady, "I promise it gets better."

"So," I continued, "When this life is over and we are up in heaven remembering all our experiences as different forms of life, because I had to give birth to all our progeny of seahorses, you'll know that I fully understand what you went through having our kids. That will be part of the way God will make all things fair and equitable."

As the women laughed, Sam said, "Nick, how in the world did you ever obtain bluish-green eyes?"

"Genetics, honey. You know that," I replied.

"I have never figured out how your eyes didn't wind up dark brown," she stated.

"Why dark brown?"

"Because, Nick, you are so full of shit."

The other woman continued laughing, "Full up to the top of his head."

"Sam," I said, pretending to be shocked. "I thought you had quit swearing."

"Believe me, Nick, that is the only way I can describe it."

Sam's roommate said, "It sure is." The two of them continued to laugh.

"If nothing else, Sam, you can always be thankful that you are not an elephant. That poor female endures a pregnancy of two full years and gives birth to a baby that weighs a quarter of a ton. So things could always be worse." At that point I departed and left Sam and her roommate talking and laughing with each other.

As I was leaving, the roommate said to Sam, "I sure hope you and me had as much fun with those male seahorses as our men seem to have with us." Sam's only reply was to continue laughing.

By Friday night, Sam's roommate had been discharged and she had the room to herself. It was then that she and I were sitting in her hospital room as the nightly national news came on the television. The commentator began his story with:

> This morning the subject of a national manhunt was killed in a shoot-out in Keokuk, Iowa. Staff Sergeant Robert Earl Warren, who has been sought since his escape from the Walter Reed Medical Center May the 19th, was killed in a gunfight with federal agents shortly after dawn at a Keokuk motel. Fred Anderson, from our Davenport, Iowa, affiliate, reports from Keokuk. . . .

"Nick, isn't that the guy from Fort McCulloch?"

"Yes, honey. It was. Apparently, he's dead now. Let's listen to the news."

Sam ignored me. "Is that why you didn't want me to go right back with you? Why didn't you tell me he was loose?"

"I didn't want to upset you. You had enough on your mind."

"But, Nick, he might have been coming back to kill you. You were one of the people responsible for his downfall."

A STATESIDE TOUR OF DUTY

"No, Sam," I reassured. "After the CID personnel and FBI agents, I was probably way down on his list. Besides, he was responsible for his own downfall."

I kept trying to listen to the news report, but I couldn't hear a thing. Sam was angry that I didn't tell her about Warren's escape.

"I have a right to know if my husband's life is in danger, Nick."

"Honey. After what you've been through, you need a couple of more weeks with people around who can help you constantly. I must be at work all day and can't be there all the time. That's why I wanted you to stay longer. Maybe I should have told you about Warren, but he's dead now. It's academic. It isn't worth arguing about."

"Yes, it is, Nick. I'm your wife. I have a right to know about these things. Don't ever keep me in the dark again."

With Sam continuing the argument, I missed the rest of the news story. It didn't matter, though. With Warren dead, a matter of great concern was eliminated. I decided to acquiesce on the matter.

"I'm sorry, Sam. I should have told you, but I've always been taught that it's a man's job to protect his family. You had more than enough to worry about. Again, I'm sorry."

I paused to get her reaction.

"All right, Nick. Apology accepted. But remember, I'm your wife and partner. I have a right to know these things. I'm not a child, and I don't appreciate being treated like one."

"Okay, baby. I am sorry." As I spoke those words, it suddenly struck me that they sounded paradoxical and ironic in reply to what Sam had said. If she noticed it, though, she didn't respond to them. She continued with her current line of thought.

"Just don't let it happen again." Sam smiled and added, "You are cute when you play the big tough man, though. I do love you."

"I love you too, babe."

Shortly afterward, I returned to Sam's parents' home, where they too had heard the news report, which included a mention that Warren had been assigned at Fort McCulloch.

They had numerous questions about Warren's activities and how I was involved in the case. As I filled them in on what information I was privy to, they listened in stunned silence. Afterward, we continued with general small talk. Our conversation lasted until the early hours of the morning and I didn't get to bed until after 1:00 AM.

I slept late the next morning and was awakened only when Sam called shortly before 10:00 AM. I got dressed and was able to check her out of the hospital shortly after 11:00. I would have to leave the next morning, so we spent the rest of the day mostly greeting the well-wishers who came by to see the twins. During those moments when we were alone, we just talked about when we would be able to be together again and enjoyed each other's company. I began to feel that life was perfect. Unfortunately, each time I had that thought, it seemed disaster was about to strike. This time was no different.

About 6:00 AM Sunday Sam awakened me. She was lying in a pool of blood. I got up from the bed as she pulled the sheet up around her like a diaper and ran into the bathroom. I lay back down thinking I was in some surreal dream. Then after a few seconds I opened my eyes and looked around. Sam was not there, but a big blood spot was. Then, remembering what I had seen, I jumped up and ran to the bathroom. I knocked on the door.

"You can come in, Nick."

I opened the door and Sam was sitting upon the toilet holding what appeared to be a liver.

"What is that?" I asked.

"A big blood clot. I just passed it." She looked at me. "I'm scared, Nick. Something is wrong."

"I'll go grab you some clothes. We're going back to the hospital right now." After we quickly dressed, she wrapped the blood clot in some wax paper so the hospital personnel could see what we were dealing with. I got the keys to her stepmother's car and we went back to the hospital.

A pelvic exam failed to reveal any problems, and Sam was told to remain in bed for the next couple of days. Above all, if she had any more problems, she was to return immediately. Now I had to make another decision. Should I return to Fort McCulloch, or should I remain with Sam? She told me to go.

"Are you sure, Sam? I can request more emergency leave."

"Go, honey. Everything will be fine. If there are any more problems, I can call you. Right now, there's nothing else you can do here."

I thought for a second. "Okay. But if anything happens, call the Red Cross immediately. They can contact the MP desk or the company and authorize emergency leave and I can return in a flash."

"Even if you're gone on the AWOL run?"

A STATESIDE TOUR OF DUTY

"Our MP personnel know where we stay. They can give the Red Cross a number where I can be reached."

"Okay, honey. Go defend our country."

"You're sure?" I was feeling very apprehensive.

"Yes!" she said adamantly. "If you don't hear from the Red Cross, call me as soon as you get back to Harrisville Wednesday night."

With that, her dad gave me a ride back to Luke Air Force Base. Again, I gave him the numbers at Fort McCulloch that the Red Cross could use to get in touch with me if necessary.

I was unable to get a flight to Laughlin until the early afternoon, and from there I caught a ride into Del Rio, where I bought a bus ticket for Harrisville. It was 4:00 AM Monday when the bus arrived in Harrisville. I went to a phone booth and called the MP desk and asked for a unit to come into town to pick me up. I was then taken to the Personnel parking lot to retrieve my car, and I arrived at the company area a little after 0500 hours.

Knowing I might be late, I had called ahead for the CQ to sign me in from leave at 2400 hours. Upon my arrival, I rushed into the orderly room to insure my instructions had been complied with. As I entered the building, Specialist Tanner was running a buffer over the floor to shine it up.

"No sweat, sir. You're all taken care off," he laughed. "You're not AWOL."

"Thanks, Tanner," I replied. "I appreciate it."

"No problem, sir. That's what I'm here for. How's your wife and baby?"

"We had twins, Tanner. The babies are fine. It's my wife I'm worried about. There may be complications, so if the Red Cross calls, give them the number where I can be reached. Right now, I have to leave on the Lone Star Run."

"Good luck, sir. If they call, I'll give them the number."

Since it was Memorial Day, only the line-duty personnel were working in the PMO and only the CQ was on hand at the company. Unfortunately, the Lone Star Run left every Monday—holiday or not. I went outside, where the AWOL Apprehension personnel were getting ready for the weekly run. I threw my suitcase into the van and hopped into the shotgun position accompanying Sergeant Collins.

"Welcome back, sir. You must have drawn the short straw again," Collins commented.

"Yes, and I haven't had much sleep in the last twenty-four hours, so you are going to have to talk like hell to keep me awake." Then with a yawn I said, "Let's go."

This was one trip when I was appreciative for a talkative companion like Sergeant Collins. He kept up the conversation all the way to Brownsville. I got a little dozy but I remained awake.

Meanwhile, I could not have imagined the problems that were occurring in Phoenix. Shortly after my departure, Sam had begun hemorrhaging again. She was rushed to the hospital, where it was discovered that the loss of blood had reached critical levels. Sam's blood type was the very rare B negative. With very little of that type on hand, the hospital began a desperate search for donors.

As the situation worsened, Sam's parents were told to prepare for the worst. In my absence, her father gave permission for a medical procedure to be performed that the doctors referred to as a D and C. This removed the final tiny piece of placenta that was causing the problems. However, with compatible blood for Sam in short supply, the prognosis was grim. As I was a soldier on active duty, the hospital then called the emergency number for the Red Cross. It was Sunday, but with a little determination they were eventually able to get the home number for the local director. Apparently, he was not happy to receive the call. It wasn't until later that I learned what had happened. I learned from doctors and Sam's family about his abominable attitude. Also, I was told that from the way he slurred his words, he was apparently quite drunk. I was told that the conversation went like this:

"Pinnock residence," the man said, answering the phone.

"Are you the local director for the Red Cross?"

"Yes," he snapped. "What do you want?"

"This is Doctor Platt at the Phoenix Regional Medical Center. We have a patient who will probably die this evening."

"So, what do you want me to do about it?" the bureaucrat scolded.

The doctor was stunned by the callous way this director of the local charity acted, but simply stated the facts. "Her husband is an Army officer on active duty, and you need to contact him immediately."

"It's Sunday, buddy. Tomorrow is Memorial Day. Call back on Tuesday during business hours. I'll take care of it then."

Now the doctor was angry. "Look, his wife won't last that long. It's your duty to contact him tonight. He needs to know what is happening."

"Don't tell me how to do my job, doctor. I have twenty-nine years' service. You people think you're gods and everything is an emergency. You give me a pain."

"Look, you son of a bitch—," the doctor yelled.

"Call back during office hours or go to hell," the soulless bureaucrat interrupted, before the doctor could continue. He then slammed down the phone. The charitable functionary probably then reached for a half-filled bottle of booze.

It is hard to understand some people's justification for their actions. I can only imagine that while pouring another drink he muttered to himself, "Damned officers and doctors think they're so special. I'll call him when I'm damned good and ready." Whatever the rationalization, he did not call the post that day at all.

Against all odds, on Tuesday morning Sam was still breathing. As she slipped in and out of consciousness, it was pure conjecture on the part of the nurses and doctors in the intensive care unit as to what was keeping her alive. The best guess was a determination not to leave her daughters without a mother. At 9:00 AM, Doctor Platt called the local Red Cross Office once more. Again, what happened was related to me later.

A secretary answered the telephone. "American Red Cross. How may I help you?"

"This is Doctor Platt at Regional Medical Center, I have a woman here in critical condition and we need to get word to her husband who is in the military—"

"Hold, please!" The woman pressed the hold button on her phone. She then spoke via an intercom to her boss. "Sir, there is a doctor on line one who needs to get in touch with someone in the military. Can you take the call?"

"Yes." He replied as he picked up the receiver. "Mr. Pinnock speaking. How may I help you?"

"Yes, there is an Army officer at Fort McCulloch, Texas whose wife is here in critical condition. You need to get in touch with him to get emergency leave." The doctor then stated slowly and emphatically, "She could die at any moment."

"This is the woman who was going to die on Sunday?"

The doctor later gave me a statement that he felt his blood begin to boil as he continued to deal with this incompetent, uncaring, drone-like individual. He stated that he struggled not to raise his voice or lose his temper. "By some miracle, she has survived until now, but we don't know how much longer she will live."

"Okay, Doc. Give us his home number. We'll notify him. He can then call the local chapter, who can call us for verification and authorize the emergency leave."

"He is not at home. He is on temporary duty elsewhere in Texas," the doctor explained.

"How are we supposed to contact him, then?"

Once again, the doctor must have found it incredible that someone so inept and completely stupid could be conscious. Again, the doctor spoke slowly. "You can contact his unit, and they can tell you how to get in touch with him."

"I have a budget to live with. I can't be making a lot of unnecessary calls and running up our telephone bill."

Later the doctor stated how he somehow resisted the desire to scream obscenities at the seemingly insensitive individual on the other end of the line. "Look, just call his unit and they can get you in touch with him." He then repeated my name and the phone number for the 290th orderly room.

"I'll do it," Pinnock said. "Anything else you need?"

"No, that's it," said the doctor, ending the call.

Pinnock then dialed the number he had just been given. Our company personnel would later relate this conversation to me.

As the phone rang in the orderly room, the first sergeant answered it. "290th Military Police Company orderly room. First Sergeant Reeves speaking, sir."

"This is Tom Pinnock with the Red Cross in Phoenix, Arizona. I need to contact Lieutenant Moultrie."

"He is TDY until Wednesday afternoon, but we can give you a number where he can be reached tonight," Reeves said.

"That won't be necessary. When he gets in Wednesday, let him know that we called."

"Is this an emergency?" Reeves asked.

"No sergeant, it will be okay if he calls us Wednesday. Just give him the message."

"Okay, sir. Thanks for calling."

As Reeves hung up the phone, the CO and Steve were both only a few feet away. He said, "That was the Red Cross calling Lieutenant

Moultrie. They asked us to give him the message that everything is okay. I asked if it was an emergency and they said no."

"Tanner said that the lieutenant was worried about his wife," the CO said. "Better call Foote and Parker's place and have them give the lieutenant the good news. That will be a load off his mind."

"Yes, sir," replied Reeves.

A local Phoenix newspaper reporter later discovered that after placing the call to Fort McCulloch, the local Red Cross director left his office to play golf with the United Way chairman. He needed to get his budget increased for the next fiscal year, so he was out of the office the rest of the day.

As we approached Brownsville, a rod in the bus engine began to knock loudly. I called the transportation motor pool and requested another bus be sent down so the one we had could be repaired. The wait for the new bus would put us one day behind schedule. We would spend the extra day helping Foote and Parker process paperwork and rounding up any extra AWOLs we were notified were in confinement in the surrounding counties. We would all draw an extra twenty-five dollars for the inconvenience, so there was a silver lining to the problem.

After we arrived at the home of our personnel in Brownsville, I got the good news (incorrect though it was) that everything was okay with Sam. After getting something to eat, I grabbed a blanket and pillow and made myself comfortable on the floor. I didn't even wait to draw straws for one of the couches. I got my best night's sleep in several days.

Meanwhile, Sam's condition continued as critical. The hospital continued to call the Red Cross and was told that until the local Red Cross Chapter at Fort McCulloch or myself called them back, there was nothing that could be done. A couple of times the doctor calling apparently lost his temper, which probably didn't help much.

Somehow in all the confusion, Sam's dad lost the paper with the telephone numbers on it. Between that fact and the belief that everything needed to be coordinated with the Red Cross, I was never notified. Wednesday morning, the hospital received several pints of blood that were compatible with Sam's blood type, and by some miracle she improved enough that Wednesday night her condition was downgraded from critical to serious.

In Galveston, Wednesday night, I called Stan to tell him about the birth of the twins. Before I knew it, he and his wife Kathy had come by the motel to take me to a restaurant to celebrate. Despite my best efforts to pick up the check, they refused. I then insisted that they come to Fort McCulloch sometime in the future so I could introduce Sam and reciprocate. If that was not possible, then the next time I was in Galveston it would be my treat. They agreed.

Except for the one-day delay, the AWOL run was routine. As always, there was one troublemaker whom we shackled hand and foot and placed in the van. But, with that minor exception, nothing else notable happened. We even arrived at the company area on Thursday over an hour ahead of the revised schedule—at 1445 hours. As I signed in from TDY, I again got the message that the Red Cross had called. Again, I was told that everything was okay and I could call them back at my convenience. Since there was no hurry, I went to Finance with my men to turn in our vouchers and draw the per diem payments we had coming.

I then went home and called Sam. Her dad answered the phone. "Hello Harvey," I said. "Let me talk to Sam."

"Nick, it's about time. Sam has been in the hospital since you left. She almost died. If the hospital hadn't gotten some of her blood type yesterday morning I don't think she would be alive now."

"What!" I was stunned. I could hardly believe what I was hearing. "Why didn't the Red Cross contact me? I would have been there in a heartbeat."

"The Red Cross kept telling us that you couldn't be reached. Those worthless chair-warmers were as useless as tits on a boar hog. The doctors called them everything except human beings. I've never heard doctors use language like that before."

A rage was building up within me, but I didn't take it out on her dad. It was not his fault. "How is Sam now?" I asked.

"She was able to walk around today. They think she will be strong enough to be released on Saturday."

"Give me the number for the hospital. I'm going to call her. Somebody's head is going to roll for this."

My father-in-law gave me the number. He then added, "She's in room number 314."

"Thanks, Harv." I then dialed the number for the hospital and asked for her room.

"Hello," Sam answered.

"Honey, I just found out that you're back in the hospital. Your dad said the Red Cross refused to help."

"Yeah. The doctors were really mad about it. It was unbelievable."

A STATESIDE TOUR OF DUTY

"Are you okay, now? Do I need to come out there?"

"No, the worst is over. I get out on Friday. Maybe sooner if I continue to improve like I have today."

"No, you stay until the doctors are sure everything is fine. I don't want to take a chance on losing you again. What was wrong anyway?"

"A tiny piece of afterbirth. Smaller than the end of my little finger. If I had delivered at Fort McCulloch, I never would have made it, honey. I would be dead now."

"Are you sure I don't need to come to Phoenix?"

"No, honey. I'm going to live. I'll come home two weeks after I get out of here."

"You're sure?"

"Yes, honey."

We continued to talk for some time. I told her about our vehicle problems that delayed my call by one day, and she convinced me that my presence in Arizona was not needed. That was very good, because if I had traveled there, I would probably have gone to the Red Cross office and killed that bureaucratic half-wit and gotten myself arrested for murder.

I looked at my watch. It was 1745 hours. Phoenix was on Mountain Time. It would be an hour earlier there. I called Information to get the Phoenix Red Cross number. I then dialed it.

"American Red Cross, how may I help you?" asked a woman who answered the phone.

"My name is Lieutenant Norris James Moultrie and I'm calling from Harrisville, Texas. I want to talk to the dumb ass that refused to get in touch with me while my wife was in the hospital in critical condition."

The woman gasped. "Hold, please." The phone went quiet as I was put on hold.

As the woman contacted her boss, I'm sure she informed him, "Sir there's a very rude person on the line. He used the term dumb ass."

"This is Tom Pinnock," the man said angrily. "Who is this calling?"

"This is First Lieutenant Norris James Moultrie calling from Fort McCulloch, Texas. I'm the one you didn't bother to get in touch with when my wife was in the hospital, and whose company orderly room you called to let them know my wife was fine while she was in critical condition. You're not only a dumb ass; you're a stupid, inept son of a bitch! I'm going to have your job for this!"

NEIL MITCHELL

The man screamed at the top of his lungs, "I don't have to take this shit from some two-bit lieutenant. I have twenty-nine years of service!" He then slammed down the phone.

CHAPTER TWENTY-EIGHT

Friday, June 4, the weather was very hot. As it turned out, the meteorological condition wasn't the only thing that was steaming. I had been telling everyone about my experience with the Red Cross, as I passed out cigars to announce the arrival of my daughters. I had also decided to file a complaint with the national director of that organization. I was composing several letters to collect evidence and pursue that aim when I received word that the major wished to see me.

Like so many times before, I walked up front to talk with him. "You needed to see me, sir?" I asked.

"Yes, lieutenant. Captain Marmol from the post Red Cross office just called. He complained that you used abusive language to one of the Red Cross officials in Arizona."

"I sure did, sir," I admitted. "My wife almost died and he didn't even have the decency to contact me. I intend to see that the man is fired. I'm going to make as much trouble for him as possible."

"You are at the bottom of the power structure, lieutenant. You don't make trouble for people in positions of authority. They make trouble for you. You'd be wise not to rock the boat."

"I appreciate the advice, sir, but let me give you the details of what happened."

"I don't have time, lieutenant," replied the major. "I'm a busy man. I told Captain Marmol you'd be right over to rectify the problem. I suggest you do it. Dismissed."

"Yes, sir."

Before driving over to see the captain, I took the badge that read "Federal Reservation Enforcement" out of the glove compartment and hung it from the left pocket of my uniform. It had been issued by the major when I arrived at Fort McCulloch. Colonel Sherman had ordered that their use be discontinued upon his arrival, since they were non-regulation. Now all of our patrolmen wore the regulation MP armbands instead. In order to project as much authority as possible, I was temporarily adding it back to my uniform. I would remove it before returning to the PMO.

I then drove over to the post Red Cross Office. Not knowing what kind of reception I might receive, I considered several different ways I might discuss the problem. I could ask the captain how he might feel if he were in my place. I might let him give me a lecture and then leave and do as I pleased, since I was leaving the service in a few months, or I could tell him to shove it. I decided against the last option. Even though I was feeling both nervous and angry, I was determined to not let either emotion show. I would play the situation by ear. I walked into the building and entered a large room with six desks. To the right was another large office, outside of which a staff sergeant was seated at one of the desks. "Can I help you, sir?" he asked.

"Yes. I'm Lieutenant Moultrie from the provost marshal's office. I need to see Captain Marmol."

"The captain is expecting you, lieutenant. Please go right in."

As I entered the captain's office, it was clear that Captain Marmol believed he was Captain Marvel. He had a massive oak power desk with a huge brass nameplate sitting on the edge that proclaimed in large letters, "DON F. MARMOL, CPT AG." He had a large American flag to the right of his desk, with a Texas flag on the left. A thick throw rug was placed on the floor in front of the desk, with a massive picture of President Nixon hung behind the desk. The office looked more suitable for a senator or congressman than a lowly captain.

"Lieutenant Moultrie, sir. I understand that you wished to see me?"

"Yes, lieutenant. Have a seat." He pulled out some papers from the top drawer of his desk. "I have an official apology you need to sign to Mr. Pinnock in Phoenix, Arizona. I'm sure there will be no hard feelings once he receives it."

"I am not going to sign that paper, sir."

The captain was taken aback. He looked stunned. "What do you mean you're not going to sign it?" he said angrily.

I was very forceful in my tone of voice. "Just what I said. My wife almost died and he refused to get in contact with me. He told the doctors to go to hell. I'm going to try to get the man fired."

A STATESIDE TOUR OF DUTY

The captain smiled. "I understand there may have been a little misunderstanding. We're all human and sometimes mistakes are made. We have to realize that."

"What I realize is the man is an incompetent fool who should not retain the job that he has. I need the name and address of the national Red Cross director so I can file an official complaint against Pinnock."

The captain sat up straight in his chair. "I won't give you that information."

"The name and address of the national director is a public record which I am entitled to. If you refuse to give it to me, I will have to write my congressman and both senators from Arizona as well as the congressman from this Texas district and let them know you refused to supply me with the information. Unless you want to be dealing with congressmen and senators, I suggest you provide me that name and address, which I am politely requesting. Now, may I have them, or not?"

It was clear that the captain was not used to being challenged. He thought for a second, and then opened the drawer to his right. He pulled out a printed sheet of paper which listed not only the national director, but all the regional directors as well. He tossed it my way. I folded it and put it in my pocket. "Look," he said, "as your superior officer, I suggest that you sign this apology and let the matter drop. Things can be made difficult for you."

I looked down at the law enforcement badge that hung from my left shirt pocket while I briefly touched it with my left hand. "Sir," I smiled, "do you walk to work, or do you drive a car?"

"Are you threatening me, lieutenant?"

"Not at all, sir," I said cheerfully, "I'm just making conversation as one officer of the United States Army to another."

The captain now changed tactics. "Look, lieutenant," he said with a friendly smile. "The man in Arizona will turn sixty-five in two years and retire. Let's just let the senile old bastard go in peace. A more competent person can then take his place."

"In the meantime, more soldiers might have their wives die and be denied emergency leave to attend the funerals."

The captain threw his hands in the air as he exclaimed, "But your wife didn't die!"

"No, sir. But the next man's wife might. No one else is going to go through this if I can help it."

With resignation in his voice, the captain asked, "So, you still refuse to sign this apology?"

"Yes, sir, I do."

He sat back in his chair. "Very well, lieutenant. I'll have to pass along the information that you're not a team player."

"I fully understand, sir. Will there be anything else?"

"No."

"Have a good day, sir" With that, I got up and left his office. As I walked out of the building, the sergeant came running out and said, "Sir, you forgot to salute the captain before you left."

With a smile, I said, "Oh! I'm sorry, sergeant. Give my apologies to the captain." I then walked to my car. I never saluted the colonel or the major when I left their offices. There was no way I was going to salute the two-bit office boy I had just dealt with.

After I returned to my office in Traffic, I grabbed a typewriter and finished the work I had begun earlier. I typed up the entire situation with a time line detailing my dealings with the Red Cross. I also typed up letters to the doctors and my in-laws asking for witness statements verifying that my account was accurate. Finally, there was an official complaint to the national director of the Red Cross, which would be sent after all supporting documents were received.

At noon, Captain Marsden announced that he was going to get a bucket of chicken and would return later. I worked through the lunch hour. Marsden did not return. As I continued to prepare the letters I was going to send, Steve dropped in.

"Nick, I hear that you've ruffled some feathers," he said with a smile.

"Like whose?"

"The CO has received calls from Proctor at Battalion and Colonel Rulon, the post chief of staff. You've pissed off two bird colonels in one day. Good job! Give me five!" He held out his hand and I slapped it in a clapping motion. I then held my hand out palm up so he could reciprocate. "What the hell did you do?" he asked.

He sat down as I described in detail what had transpired over the past couple of weeks. I then showed him copies of the letters I was preparing. He agreed that what I was doing was right.

As he placed the papers back on my desk, he added his two cents. "It's no secret that the Red Cross gets most of its work done by volunteers, while a majority of the money it collects goes to salaries of the officials who run it. If any other charity had most of its money going to overhead, they would face a national investigation. They've got problems."

I sat back in my chair. "That's why after they collect money for emergencies, they have to collect still more money after the disasters happen." I pondered.

"I'm sure that's part of it. Of course, there are a lot of people who don't want to hear that. You're making some of them very unhappy. They say you're not a team player."

"Screw them!" I said.

"I don't want to," Steve laughed. "Barbara wouldn't like that. Besides, those asshole colonels would probably enjoy it too much"

We both laughed. It was great to have Steve to work with. With Sam still in Arizona, if I didn't have him around to talk to, I probably would have gone stir-crazy. We passed some more time before he decided to return to the company. "See you later, Nick," he said. "And good luck."

"Okay, buddy. Thanks for the heads-up."

I decided to go up to the front office and talk with the colonel. As I entered the secretary's office, the major was sitting in the chair next to his office holding his hat in his left hand. He was staring at the clock. It was 1635 hours. The major clearly had nothing to do and was waiting for 1700 hours so he could leave. "Is Colonel Sherman in?" I asked.

"No, he's not, lieutenant. He won't be back until Monday," Susan said.

"Okay, I'll see him then." As I stood facing Susan with my back to the major, I pointed with my thumb as if pointing through myself toward the major. Susan rolled her eyes. If I thought I had it bad dealing with the major, the personnel in the front office had it a dozen times worse.

I returned to my office and wrapped up my activities. At 1700 hours, I left for home. I mailed off the various letters, except for the one to the national Red Cross director. I would wait until I got my supporting evidence before that one was sent. One letter was to *The Arizona Republic*, a Phoenix newspaper. It suggested that they conduct an investigative report on the matter and see if other soldiers had experienced problems similar to my own.

At 8:00 PM, when the rates changed, I called Sam to see how she was and let her know what I was doing. Of course, we had a lengthy talk about the babies. I sure wished I could see them. "What will you do when the girls are teenagers and some guy like yourself wants to take one of them out?" she asked.

"I'll have him sit in a straight-backed chair with a bright light overhead and grill him as to his intentions," I replied. "I'll probably be cleaning a shotgun at the time."

"Oh, Nick! What would you have done if my father had done that?"

"That was different. You were on your own when we met and your father could tell that I was a keeper."

She laughed. "I think I'll ask him and see what he thinks about that."

"Now, Sam. Don't you think you got a keeper?"

"Yes, I do, but I don't know what he thought."

We then got back to the problem at hand and I told her what I needed. If her family would help get the information I needed, I could conclude this matter as quickly as possible.

Through the weekend, I continued to polish up the letter I was going to send. The weekend was over before I knew it.

After the Monday morning briefing, I met with Colonel Sherman to brief him on the preparations we had made for the Boy Scout jamboree that was to start the next day. He seemed satisfied with everything I had done. After my presentation, he paused for a few seconds and then said, "Look Nick, I don't want to bury you with work, but I need your help this week."

"You can count on me, sir. What do you want me to do?"

"Well, to begin with, Marsden told Sergeant de la Vega he was going to get a bucket of chicken for lunch Friday, and nobody's seen him since. Barker's on leave this week, so I need you to cover Operations until one of them returns."

"Not a problem, sir. I'm still on orders as an acting assistant AG, so I can still sign any of operation's paperwork."

"Good!" He hesitated a second, then continued, "Shut that door, Nick."

I got up and shut the door to his office, then returned to my seat.

The colonel drummed his fingers on his desk for a second then continued. "The dumb-ass major has placed a notice in the *Daily Bulletin* stating that we are looking for men willing to cross-train and OJT as military policemen. I've instructed him to send them through Operations first. Operations can cull them out and send the best to me. In reality, Nick, if Operations approves them, I don't give a damn what the major thinks. Do you know what to look for in prospective OJT candidates?"

"I believe so, sir. Before someone can OJT, they would need to get permission from their company commander. If they can get that, then we probably don't want them. The only exception would be if that unit has a surplus of good men in one particular MOS."

The colonel slammed his fist down upon his desk in delight. "Right, by Jove! I wish that you had the oak leaves, Nick, and that idiot had the silver bar. It would make my life a lot easier."

"Thank you, sir."

The colonel then changed the subject again. "One more thing. What is this ongoing battle I hear that you have with the Red Cross?"

"Well, sir," I began, "I can give you the Cliff Notes version or let you read the entire story." I then placed a folder containing the correspondence (sent or planned) on his desk.

As the colonel read the information I had given him, he began to shake his head. "Why does this not surprise me?" he asked. After reading the material, he looked at me and said, "I don't blame you for pursuing this, Nick. I would be mad as hell if I was in your position. But, I should warn you. A lot of generals and colonels see the Red Cross as the source of high-profile, high-paying jobs after they retire. This can make you some enemies."

Suddenly, I had another thought. Until now I had only been thinking of myself. I had not considered how this might affect anyone else. I respected Colonel Sherman and did not want to adversely affect his career. Also, I thought this might be an excellent time to find out just how much support I had in this matter.

"This won't cause you any problems—will it, sir?" I then added, "I can drop the whole matter, if it will." I'm not sure how sincere I was when I said that, but, as it turned out, it didn't matter.

The colonel laughed. "When I retire, Nick, I'm going fishing. I don't plan to work for the Red Cross. You do what you have to do and I'll support you one hundred percent."

"Thank you, sir. I appreciate it." That sealed the deal. There was no turning back now.

The colonel continued. "This next bit of information is just between us, Nick."

"I won't tell a soul, sir."

"I will be retiring on October the 31st. That won't be public knowledge for a couple of weeks."

"I understand, sir."

"From what I've seen of this place, Halloween is the appropriate time to leave. This place is such a joke." I smiled as he said that. He continued. "You need to conclude this business with the Red Cross by then. I don't know who my successor will be, but it could be someone who will yield to pressure from above and make your life miserable."

"I appreciate the information, sir. I'll make sure that I'm finished with this project by then."

"Good!" said the colonel. "If you can do that, the whole thing may be blown over by the time I leave. I can't help you once I'm gone."

"I'll take that to heart, sir; and, again, I'm really thankful for the information. Is there anything else?"

"No, Nick, that's all. Let's go to work."

While rising from my chair, I brought my right hand up to my forehead to salute as I said, "Thanks again, sir. Also, I'd like to say that it is an honor to serve under your command."

He returned the salute with a smile. "Thanks Nick. And, it's good to have a couple of lieutenants like you and Bronson around who can give me the information and facts I need rather than being kiss-ass brownnosers."

As I left the colonel's office, I suspected that the last comment was directed toward Raymond. Unfortunately, I knew most people in authority were not like colonel Sherman. Thus, in any hierarchy, the kiss-ass brownnosers usually rise faster through the ranks than those of us who tell it like it is. But such is life. It has always been that way.

In college, I had learned that, in ancient times, messengers who brought an emperor in China bad news were executed. Those who arrived with good news were rewarded with gold and silver. Consequently, no one ever brought in bad news. Like the messengers of old, Raymond was a good-news man. I suspected he would go far.

I went first to Operations. Sergeant Dee was putting a pile of papers on Marsden's desk. "I'll be back in a couple of hours, sarge," I said. "If Marsden is still gone by then, the colonel has asked me to fill in for him."

"That's great, sir. The paperwork is really piling up and the clerks are starting to panic. We'll see you after a while." With that, Sergeant de la Vega returned to his own work.

I then went with my men from the Traffic section to pick up the temporary signs I had ordered from Training Aids. They were large cardboard signs that read, "Scout Encampment Ahead. Speed Limit 25." I had planned to tape them over the permanent speed limit signs, but Sergeant Corley had a better idea. Using heavy, wide-headed nails, we found that the cardboard signs could be nailed over the permanent signs. The nails could be driven right through the permanent metal highway signs.

"This way, we can just tear the cardboard off on Sunday afternoon after the kids leave," Corley stated. "We can leave the nails. Nobody will notice them."

As we finished our work, I could see that the local Scout personnel were already setting up the tents to welcome and process in the jamboree participants as they arrived. We stopped in to reassure them that there would be regular patrolling of the area by police vehicles. We were told that over 1,000 Boy Scouts were expected to join in the festivities.

I hurried back to the PMO and went directly to Operations. I sat at Marsden's desk and began to review and sign the mountain of paperwork that had collected there. For the second day in a row I worked through lunch. By 1600, I had finished with all the paperwork that Operation's clerks had generated to that point. I sat back in my chair. It was time for a break. I walked over to the company, where Steve had more than his share of problems. Captain Lynch had just left for a week's leave. That meant that Steve was now the acting CO. He had his own paperwork to deal with.

"How's the pressure of command?" I said in jest as I entered his office.

"Not worth a damn!" he replied.

I sat in the nearest chair. "What seems to be the problem?"

"Taggert and Gray have been AWOL for three days."

"I know. Graveyard has been shorthanded because of it. It's a good thing that the nights have been quiet. Otherwise, we would be in a world of hurt." I then added the obvious, "So, give them an Article 15 when they return. That will teach them a lesson."

"I can't!"

"Why not?"

"If I write them up I'll have to give Marsden an Article 15 also. The nit-wit has been gone since Friday noon, with no explanation whatsoever."

I shrugged my shoulders. "So, have the colonel give Marsden a company-grade officer's Article 15. It might teach that jerk a thing or two."

"The CO would never go for it. He feels like it would give our unit a bad reputation to have one of the officers receive that punishment."

I laughed. "How can the reputation of this unit be any worse?"

"Lynch would argue that an officer getting non-judicial punishment would make it worse. And he's right, although I hate to admit it."

"Well, why don't we go play some Ping-Pong and forget our troubles?"

Steve threw his pen down on the desk and said, "I thought you'd never ask. Let's go."

We went into the day room and proceeded to play Ping-Pong until quitting time. I won three games, Steve won one.

As we were leaving the building, I asked, "Does it make you feel guilty that we played Ping-Pong for an hour that the government was paying us to work?"

"You have got to be kidding," Steve snorted. "Major Disaster is sitting over there watching the clock. At least we're doing something to improve our dexterity and timing." Steve smiled as he added, "Ping-Pong makes us better officers."

"Sounds good to me. I couldn't agree more."

I then went by the MP desk to remind the desk sergeant to make sure the highway through the Scout camp was patrolled. While I had been told that most of their activities didn't start until tomorrow, I had been advised that early-arriving kids were pouring into the area.

I usually didn't think about work as I headed for home, but this time I couldn't help it. Three people who deserved an Article 15 would escape punishment because one of them was an officer.

An Article 15 is non-judicial punishment. It can consist of anything from being reduced in rank (for an enlisted man) to forfeiture of pay or days of extra duty, as well as confinement to quarters for a length of time. The person being punished may refuse the punishment, however to do so is to risk a court-martial.

If the offender accepts the Article 15, then a court-martial proceeding is impossible due to the constitutional guarantee against double jeopardy. Ironically, though, since it is non-judicial, a person could be given the Article 15 after a court-martial for the same offense, if the individual was stupid enough to accept it.

Perhaps the most unfortunate misuse of the Article 15 provision of the UCMJ (Uniform Code of Military Justice) was to build a case for kicking someone out of the service. If a soldier received an inordinate number of these punishments (more than three), he could be discharged. There were also commanders who used the constant threat of the Article 15 to keep their lower-ranking personnel in line. At the other extreme were units like the 290th Military Police Company. We wouldn't use the punishment because the CO thought it would make us look bad because one of the offenders was an officer.

A STATESIDE TOUR OF DUTY

After arriving at home, I made myself a sandwich and watched the news. After a few minutes, I turned it off. The country seemed to be going to hell in a handbasket. I drove over to Steve and Charlie's place, where the three of us proceeded to watch *Monday Night Football*.

Usually, I avoided *Monday Night Football* like the plague because it featured color commentary by Howard Cosell. This loud-mouthed fool was the epitome of elitism. It was clear that he believed himself to be the smartest person in the world and that he felt his ass was gold and the rest of the world was digging for it. I voiced my complaints to the others.

"Everyone hates Howard," Charlie said. "That's part of his appeal."

"Yeah," said Steve as he opened a beer. "Every football fan in America is watching this game hoping that he has a heart attack or chokes to death on the air."

Charlie put his feet up on the coffee table. As he sipped his beer he added, "Wouldn't that be nice. I bet that Frank and Dandy Don would have somebody just drag him out of the way and continue the broadcast. They probably hate him as much as we do."

"But by watching him, everyone is driving up the ratings and making him rich," I rebutted.

"That's life, Nick," Steve said philosophically. "There's nothing you can do about it."

"Yes, there is," I argued. "I normally don't watch this. I'm here because my wife is gone and I didn't have anything else to do. I mean— let me rephrase that."

"Well thanks, buddy," Charlie laughed. "We enjoy your company, too."

"I'm sorry, Charlie. I didn't mean it that way." After verbally putting my foot in my mouth, I fumbled for the words to try to improve the situation. Charlie's reply got me off the hook.

"It's okay, Nick. Steve told me what you're going through. It's gotta be tough."

"It is," I admitted. "I really appreciate your friendship. I don't think I could make it otherwise."

"No problem, Nick. That's what we're here for," Steve interjected. "We figure you'd do the same for us."

"Yes, I would," was my reply.

Tuesday, I continued to run Operations. Wednesday, I attended court in the morning and again filled in for Marsden in the afternoon. The double duty continued Thursday. On that afternoon, I was finishing up the day's paperwork. It was 1545 hours when one of the clerks, Dobson, notified me that a Sergeant Hooper would like to see me.

"Sure, Dobson, show him in," I said.

Staff Sergeant Harold L. Hooper was a slightly heavyset man with a crew cut. He walked into my office carrying a folder, and I offered him a chair. "Thank you for seeing me, sir," he said.

"What can I do for you, sarge?"

He handed me the folder. "I saw in the *DB* where you were looking for men to become MPs through on-the-job training. I would sure like to do that. There's my paperwork."

I examined the papers in the folder. There was a letter from his engineer company commander, releasing him from duty there, if we accepted him, and several letters of recommendation. Everything looked good.

"I see that your company commander is willing to release you," I noted.

"Yes, sir, I just returned from Korea and the unit has a surplus of squad leaders."

"Why do you want to become an MP?" I asked.

"Well, sir, I worked for the sheriff's office for two years before I joined the military. Police work was my first choice of a career. Uncle Sam had other ideas and made me an engineer—which has been good— but I'd really like to get back into law enforcement."

I asked a few more questions, which were mostly small talk, before I said, "Well, sarge, everything looks good. I'll pass this on to the brass in the front office. If they decide to use you, they'll get back in touch with you."

"Thank you, sir." With that he left my office.

I was preparing to write up a disposition form and route the information to the major, when Dobson appeared at my office door again. "Do you know who that guy is, sir?" he asked.

"I don't have a clue, Dobson. I've never met him before."

Specialist Dobson smiled. "Remember Lorraine Hooper, sir?"

I sat back in my chair. As I pointed toward the door, I asked the obvious. "You mean that he's her husband?"

"Yes, sir," he answered.

That put an entirely different light on the subject. Normally we would do a background check on the man, but now I saw no reason for that. With half of the soldiers on post banging the man's wife for the past year, I wasn't going to give him a gun and a badge. That would be a disaster waiting to happen and our military police unit had enough trouble without asking for more. I turned around and dropped Hooper's file in the trash can. "Thanks Dobson. I appreciate the information."

He smiled. "You're welcome, sir." He then returned to his typewriter.

Suddenly, I remembered the major. He was probably already planning on using Hooper on line duty. I couldn't tell the major the reason I was rejecting Hooper. He would want details that I couldn't supply. Details like which of our MPs were consorting with prostitutes and how long such conduct had been going on. I didn't want to know that information, let alone be required to investigate such matters. I thought for a minute, and then decided I should be very tactful in giving a reason for Hooper's rejection.

I then hurried up to the front office. I paused at the major's door. "Sir," I said, "I just interviewed a Sergeant Hooper as a possible OJT."

The major eagerly looked up. "Yes, lieutenant! What did you think?"

"Sir," I hesitated, "I think we ought to pass on this man."

"Why is that?"

Again, I hesitated thoughtfully. "Well, sir, there's nothing I can put my finger on, but I have a real bad feeling about him. I sense there could be trouble from him."

I expected the major to overrule me, but he didn't. After a few seconds, he simply said, "Okay lieutenant, that's good enough for me."

"Yes, sir," I acknowledged. I then went back to work.

Later that afternoon, I received a call from a reporter from *The Arizona Republic*. As I answered the phone, I identified myself in the customary manner.

"Military Police Operations, this is Lieutenant Moultrie, sir. How may I help you?"

"Is this the Lieutenant Moultrie who sent the letter to us about the Red Cross?" the newsman asked.

"Yes, it is. What can I do for you?"

"This is Matt Percy, with *The Arizona Republic* in Phoenix, lieutenant. I should tell you that I have called the doctors and your wife's family at the numbers you gave and I think we have ourselves quite a story."

"Did you call the Red Cross guy in Phoenix?" I asked.

"The one with twenty-nine years' service?" he sneered.

"That's the one. What did he have to say for himself?"

"He was a real piece of work. He threatened a lot of trouble for you. Do you still want me to pursue this?"

"Indeed I do," I insisted. "I plan to have a letter mailed off to the National Red Cross director by tomorrow documenting everything Pinnock did, and I'm sending copies to my congressman and senators. I'm not backing down on this."

"Good! I'll call the National Red Cross Office first thing in the morning to get their comments." He continued, "If I were you, I would send that letter registered mail, where they have to sign for it."

"I will. Thanks for suggesting that."

"No problem, lieutenant. I just had to see how serious you were before I continued with the story."

The next day I mailed off the letters. As Percy had suggested, the one to the national Red Cross headquarters was sent registered mail. It cost a little more, but I was convinced it was worth it. There was no turning back now. My fight with the Red Cross functionary back home was now underway. In military parlance, the battle was joined. I knew that what I was doing would make me no friends, but I didn't care.

Friday, Marsden finally showed up. He claimed that he was due the leave and simply forgot to submit the paperwork. The colonel turned over the job of verbally ripping him a new one to the major. Barker then replaced him in Operations and Marsden took over Barker's job. He was so delighted with the reduced workload that I doubt that he saw it as a punishment. Also, Friday was Raymond's last day on the job. After some punch and cake in the front office, everyone bid him good-bye, and he and Kathy drove off in their shiny, blue Corvette.

After work, I had one of the patrols take me out to the Scout encampment. We had very few complaints about speeding motorists all week, and nothing had gone wrong. I couldn't help but be proud of the way the coordinating had gone so smoothly with the civilian agencies. I wished everything could always go so well. However, I knew that was wishful thinking.

There was one more item of note that happened on Friday the 11th. We received new cars. Fifteen model 1971 cars that had been purchased the year before for recruiters in the south Texas area were turned over to us. It was about time. The cars we were using were on their last legs. The TMP was working overtime to keep some of them on the road. The recruiters would get new vehicles, and we were given theirs. It didn't seem to make much sense that a line-duty unit responsible for maintaining law and order had to play second fiddle to a bunch of recruiters, but that was the system. There was nothing we could do about it. Our men were just happy to have something dependable to drive, for a change.

CHAPTER TWENTY-NINE

On Monday, the 14th, Master Sergeant de la Vega was reassigned from Operations to the PMI section. He replaced Raymond. Staff Sergeant Bingham then became the Operations sergeant. It surprised me that Bingham would take an administrative job, but the word I got was that he couldn't stand to work with Joe Katone any longer. The transfer to Operations got him away from baby-sitting Katone. His complaints to Captain Marsden about the patrol supervisor he had for an underling had been ignored. Fed up with the situation, he took the position in Operations.

On Tuesday, I received a notice from the post engineers. They informed me that the cost of the white lines I had ordered painted on the highways would be $1,500. They requested additional paperwork from me to justify the expense. I showed the letter to Sergeant Corley.

"I thought you ordered white lines painted on the highway, lieutenant, not solid gold ones," he said.

"I did, sarge. How much do those guys get paid anyway?"

"Apparently, it's a hell of a lot more than you and I get." He then contemplated, "I think I'll apply for a job with Post Engineers when I retire."

"Between you and me, sarge, I think somebody is getting a kick-back on the side. That's the only way a figure like this amount could be arrived at."

"You're probably right, sir. But don't waste time submitting any more paperwork. I have a better idea."

"What's that?"

"Let's go to Self-Service and get a couple of rolls of masking tape, some buckets of paint and brushes and have our people paint the lines.

A STATESIDE TOUR OF DUTY

We can measure the distance between the lines with a car odometer. I bet we can get it done for a damn sight less than fifteen hundred dollars."

I smiled. "Ideas like that are why I keep you around, sarge. Let's go do it."

We drove to Self-Service and obtained the supplies, along with a hundred-foot measuring tape. I then had the desk call my men in from off the road and we drove to the first of the locations where I had ordered the lines painted. It was a quick process to put down tape and get a line painted by two men while two others measured off a quarter mile with the measuring tape. Corley double-checked the measurement with a car odometer, and the result was close enough for our purposes. Any difference was so slight that we could just use the odometer reading on the car for further measurements and save time.

"Lieutenant, you've heard the phrase, close enough for government work?" Corley asked.

"Yes, I have."

"Well you've just seen it in action," he joked.

By our official quitting time of 1700 hours, we had all the lines painted. As Corley and I drove back to the office, I calculated the cost of the project. Figuring a five-day workweek, I divided what I and each of my men were paid per month by the twenty-two workdays in the current month and added in the supplies. It had cost the United States government just under two hundred dollars to get the lines painted on the highway. I told that information to Sergeant Corley.

"What in the world were they going to do to cost the additional thirteen hundred dollars, sir?" he asked.

"I don't know, sarge. But, I suspect that's why defense contracts cost the government so much. Somebody is getting rich."

Corley pondered the situation for a second and sighed. "We're in the wrong line of work, sir."

"You're not kidding," I noted. "Soldiers risk their lives while somebody else makes a bunch of money."

"That's just the way it is, sir. It's called life."

I couldn't argue with Corley's assessment. I thought he was right on.

Wednesday morning, Corley and I went over to observe traffic court. Everything was routine until the last case in the civilian part of the judicial proceedings. I was very happy that it was the last case. I would have been very embarrassed if very many people saw what happened.

"Scalora, Sterling C.," called out the bailiff. Two men stepped forward. Both were dressed in suits.

"You are charged with driving seventy-five in a sixty-mile zone," said the judge. "How do you plead?"

"Not guilty," Your Honor.

The judge asked, "Is Sergeant Katone available?"

The bailiff called for the presence of Katone, who quickly came forward.

"Your Honor," one man said. "This is my friend, Grant Smith, who was in the car. He can verify my story is correct."

"That would be inadmissible," said the judge. "Besides, the police officer could just counterbalance that account with that of his partner. I'll get your account in a moment. Let's hear what happened, sergeant."

I observed Katone's appearance. He looked like a slob. It appeared that he had worn his uniform for several days. His shirttail was out in the back and part of his last meal stained the front, as always.

"Well, Judge," he began, "last Monday I saw these guys speeding down the highway and followed them. With my speedometer, I clocked them going seventy-five miles per hour. In fact, they didn't stop until they had reached a place where Boy Scouts were camped. The speed limit there had temporarily been reduced to twenty-five. I should have charged them with a much more serious charge of seventy-five in a twenty-five-mile zone."

The man casually stated, "The speed limit wasn't changed until that afternoon, Your Honor."

Corley leaned over to me and whispered, "We put those temporary signs up that morning, sir."

"I know," I acknowledged. "Katone better say that."

Katone never challenged the man's statement.

"Let's hear your version, Mr. Scalora," the judge said.

"Well, Your Honor," the man began reverently, "I was just driving along, minding my own business, when my friend here noticed a car coming up behind us swerving all over the road. I was a little scared, so I did speed up a bit to try to get out of the way. Then I saw a blue light come on and realized it was a police car and pulled right over. I guess that the sergeant made an honest mistake and thought the speed he was going as he sped up behind us was the speed I was going also."

"That ain't true!" yelled Katone.

A STATESIDE TOUR OF DUTY

"Sergeant, relax and don't interrupt," admonished the judge. "Is there anything else, sir?" the judge asked.

"No, Your Honor, I believe that's it," the man said.

"Do you have anything you'd like to add, sergeant?"

Katone was so mentally disorganized that all he could say was, "No, Judge."

The judge paused for a moment the ruled, "I have to conclude that reasonable doubt exists in this case. Therefore I have to rule not guilty. Bailiff, are there any more cases for today?"

"None, Your Honor."

The judge tapped his gavel down and declared, "Court is now adjourned."

Corley and I then went to Sergeant Katone, who whined, "Sir, he lied. I wasn't weaving all over the road—*he* was. That's why I spotted him in the first place."

"Why didn't you tell the judge that?" I asked.

"I don't know. I guess I didn't think it would matter what I said." As Katone continued to complain, Corley and I excused ourselves and walked away.

After lunch, I went to Bingham and told him exactly what had happened in court. I explained that Operations needed to provide Katone with a lot of additional training, counseling or both. Bingham was not surprised.

"Sir, I left line duty because of that moron. I've talked to him until I'm blue in the face."

"Very well, Bingham, I'll talk to the CO and the colonel and see what else we can do with him."

Bingham looked around to make sure no one was listening to our conversation. "You shouldn't bother talking to the major, sir. I have, and all he ever says is to carry him or help him and don't rock the boat."

Bingham was just telling me what I already knew. I had no plans to deal with the major on this subject.

That night I called Sam to have a long discussion about the girls and get her flight information. Tomorrow she would be returning to Fort McCulloch, and I was very much looking forward to her arrival.

Thursday afternoon, at the Hooper residence in Harrisville, a chain of events began which would make for a day we would all remember for a long time. I would learn of the events from blotter entries and subsequent investigations.

Somehow Sergeant Hooper had apparently learned about his wife's career choice as a prostitute during his year in Korea. Maybe some neighbor had told him the bad news. Maybe he had noticed that the furnishings she had bought in his absence cost much more than the allotment of money he had sent home could purchase. Maybe it was a combination of such factors. Whatever the source of the information—he knew.

An intelligent man would have moved out and filed for divorce. With the evidence he could accumulate, he could probably not only be granted the divorce, but would probably be granted custody of his children also. Unfortunately, Hooper could not be considered an intelligent man.

He began to beat his wife. Amid the chaos, Lorraine Hooper screamed out a window to a neighbor who was hanging out clothes on a line to call the police. She screamed, "My husband is going to kill me," and she was probably telling the truth.

The neighbor screamed back, "I'll call them now."

With the police on the way, Hooper left the house. He spent the next two hours at a local bar getting drunk. When he was totally inebriated, he heard another customer say something about the hookers that frequented Miller's Restaurant. He picked up a chair and hurled it at the man. As others tried to break up the fight, Hooper broke a beer bottle and began to threaten everyone with its jagged edges. The bartender called the police.

Again, warned that the police were on the way, Hooper ran for his car. As he fled, the bar patrons got his license number. He went to the NCO club on post, where he ordered a pitcher of beer. There, he started a disturbance and the bartender called the MP desk. When the MPs arrived, Sergeant Tony Lightfoot (who had recently been promoted to buck sergeant and been made patrol supervisor) was the first in the door. He recognized Hooper and, being unaware of the previous events happening off post, simply walked over to him.

Putting his hand on Hooper's back he said, "Come on, Harold, you've had enough. We'll see that you get home. We don't want you to get into trouble."

Hooper screamed some foul expletives about what he thought every man in Texas had been doing with his wife and hit Lightfoot over the head with the half-empty pitcher of beer. If he had hit Lightfoot hard enough, the blow might have been fatal. But, in his drunken condition, all he did was knock him down. He quickly knocked down Lightfoot's partner, Kelly, who was not expecting such a rage, and ran out the door. He then drove out of the parking lot with Lightfoot and Kelly in hot pursuit.

While Kelly drove, Lightfoot called for backup as he rubbed his aching head. The chase continued across the post, reaching speeds in excess of 100 miles per hour. Two more units joined in the chase, but as Hooper sped out the main gate, the additional units discontinued the high-speed chase. Instead, Harrisville police cars (alerted by the MP desk) now took their place. The Harrisville police cruisers registered 115 miles per hour as the speeding continued through town.

As they left the Harrisville City limits and zoomed through the small community of Midway, the part-time policeman there (who was also a county deputy sheriff) joined in the chase. Shortly afterward, a vehicle from the Texas Highway Patrol joined in the pursuit as they raced toward Lutzville.

Now, with four jurisdictions (or five, depending on how you count them) chasing him, the Highway Patrol set up a roadblock about eight miles north of Lutzville. As Hooper approached it, he attempted to drive around the blocking cars and got his vehicle stuck in some sand. He jumped out of his car with a tire iron in one hand and a knife in the other. As he lunged at the numerous law enforcement personnel surrounding him, he was quickly knocked to the ground. Once he was down, he was disarmed and handcuffed.

With the excitement over, the next question became who would prosecute Hooper first. It was quickly decided that it came down to federal charges (those on post) and state charges (those off post). Since the latter were more numerous, the state of Texas would stand in line for first prosecution. Either way, the list of felonies and misdemeanors were almost too numerous to list. Hooper was looking at a dishonorable discharge from the Army and at least a couple of years of incarceration somewhere.

When I arrived for the Friday morning briefing, the blotter entry on Hooper ran on for four pages. Among the charges were assault on a police officer, flight to avoid arrest, drunken and disorderly conduct, reckless driving, driving under the influence, speeding one hundred in a twenty-mile-per-hour zone, running five stop signs, reckless endangerment and many others. It was unbelievable.

After the colonel picked up his copy of the blotter ,he exclaimed, "My gosh, we had a one-man crime wave!"

"You might be interested to learn, colonel, that Sergeant Hooper had applied to be an OJT with us, and the lieutenant here turned him down," the major commented.

The colonel looked at me. "What made you decide to reject him, lieutenant?"

Once again, I didn't dare tell the truth. I was more tactful. "Like I told the major, sir, there was nothing I could put my finger on. I just had a gut instinct that we shouldn't take him. Something told me that there might be trouble."

"And right you were," said the colonel. "That's good police work. A man should always follow his hunches."

As the briefing ended, the colonel asked for final comments. When he got to me, I said, "I have to drive to San Angelo this afternoon to pick up my wife. I'll need to be excused after lunch to do that."

"No problem, lieutenant," said the colonel. "How are your wife and kids?"

"The twins are great, sir, and my wife is getting much better." I then added, "Also, I've talked with a reporter from the paper in Phoenix and I believe I'll get this matter with the Red Cross concluded quickly." The major frowned as I said that.

"Excellent," said the colonel. He began to reminisce. "After I joined the Army in '41, the Red Cross started selling military personnel cigarettes and candy bars. When we opened them, there would be notes saying the products had been donated for military use by Camel or Hershey." He frowned. "I've had a few complaints about the Red Cross myself. They do a lot of good work, but they have made some mistakes in the past."

He then continued to ask for comments around the table and soon the meeting was over. As I was leaving the front office, Susan said, "Lieutenant, this man called from Phoenix while you were in the colonel's briefing. I told him you'd return his call." The name on the note was Matt Percy.

I went to my office to return the call. When I got Percy on the phone, he said, "Lieutenant, I have good news and bad news."

"Give them to me in that order, then," I said.

"It seems that once the National Red Cross office learned that our newspaper was doing a story and that the locals in Texas couldn't get you to back down, they forced the guy here to announce his retirement. He departs July 31st."

"What's the bad news?" I asked.

A STATESIDE TOUR OF DUTY

"With the man retiring, my editor has decided we no longer have a story. I can't prove it, but I believe there was a deal made."

Wow, I thought, it's over. It was almost anticlimactic, but I was glad it was finished. I mostly just felt relieved. "Well," I said to Percy, "as long as the man no longer has that job—that's good enough for me."

"I was hoping you'd see it that way, lieutenant. At least he won't be able to treat any other soldiers like he treated you."

"I appreciate that," I said. "Thanks for your help."

I then began to approve a stack of accident reports on my desk and take care of some other paperwork. When noon came, I left for the day.

I drove to the San Angelo airport and, shortly afterward, Sam's flight arrived. She had lost weight and was a little gaunt, but she was alive. She was holding one of the twins in each arm. It's difficult to hug a woman while she is holding two babies, so I took one of them and we had a group hug. I kissed her and admired the little ones and then we walked to the car. As I got her luggage placed in the trunk and fixed the babies a bed on the back seat, I gave her a real hug and a long kiss.

"I really missed you, honey," she said. "You don't know how much."

"Yes, I do," I countered, "because I missed you, too."

As we made the drive back to Fort McCulloch, I wished that my car had air conditioning. I stopped to get Sam something cold to drink and then headed home.

As we drove, I began to fill her in on everything that happened in her absence. When I mentioned the events of the previous day, she shook her head. "Those poor Hooper kids now have a father who is a felon and a mother who's a whore. What kind of life can they have?" she asked.

"As good as they make it, honey," I speculated. "A lot of people come into this world in less than perfect circumstances. Some rise above it. Some don't. Hopefully, people will remember that the kids are not responsible for what their parents did."

"You know better than that, Nick," she said. "Those kids will suffer with that stigma for a long time."

"True enough," I agreed. "But, they can still rise above it. They get to make their own choices, the same as their parents did. Besides, you had it tough and came through it okay."

"Not that tough, Nick. My dad and step mom didn't break any laws. Oh, I almost forgot!" Sam then exclaimed. "Pull over before you see this. I don't want you to wreck the car."

"Huh?"

"Just pull over, Nick."

I pulled over to the side of the road, and Sam handed me the copy of *The Arizona Republic* that she had purchased just before she had left Phoenix. On page two of the local section was the headline, "Local Charity Director Announces Retirement." Sure enough, the object of my scorn would retire from the Red Cross at the end of July.

"He should have been shot, Nick," Sam said angrily.

As I continued to drive, I told Sam the details of my fight with the Red Cross. The facts that I could only force him to retire two years early and cause him to receive a few less dollars a month in pension remuneration were small victories, but they were victories. "Besides," I added. "He probably won't get any major awards at his retirement ceremony. I suspect they will be happy to see him go."

Sam looked at me. "He still should have been shot," she said.

I smiled. "True enough, honey. But that was never an option, even though it should have been."

The rest of the long drive was spent with Sam bottle-feeding the babies while we discussed the future. After we got home, there was a constant parade of neighbors coming over to welcome Sam home and see the twins. Between the *oohs* and *aahs* was a lot of "they're so precious" and "you're so lucky" and "they're beautiful" from the onlookers. The Cunninghams even brought over a casserole dish so Sam wouldn't have to eat my cooking. Eventually, after the twins had been held and rocked by about twenty people, we were alone.

As we prepared to go to bed, Sam picked up her red flannel nightgown. "I don't need this, do I?" she asked.

I laughed. "No. After what you've been through, I won't try anything."

It had been an unwritten rule, since we had been married, that if Sam wanted to be left alone at night, she wore that monstrosity. After witnessing her ordeal with the birth of the twins, I agreed with the medical wisdom that she should wait six weeks before indulging in love-making again. "Besides, it's too hot around here at night for that," I added.

"Sleeping with you, there's no doubt about that," Sam agreed.

"Tonight, though, I'll settle for a hug and a kiss," I reassured.

With that we went to bed and, to my amazement, the girls were already starting to sleep through the night. They only woke us up once.

In the coming days, Sam and I slipped back into our regular routine, except that now we had two little ones demanding our attention. I did my best to help Sam with their changing and feeding. Her stay in the hospital had left her unable to nurse, so formula was the order of the day. Needless to say, it was evident that our grocery bill was going to increase.

On Wednesday, the 23rd, I arrived at work early. If Katone had cases on the court docket, I wanted to try to prepare him in case anyone pled not guilty. As I walked into the building and headed for my office, the desk sergeant looked up just long enough to say, "Morning, sir, you're early today."

"Yes, Jake, I've got work to do," I replied. "Did you have any trouble last night?"

"None, sir," was the reply.

I walked up the steps to the desk area, and attached to the wall next to the clerk was a list of the court cases, prepared by Operations the day before, hanging by a thumbtack. I took it down and scanned it. I saw that Katone had cases in both the military and the civilian session. It was enough to make me want to groan.

I went into my office to call Katone, only to discover that the number was no longer in service. I went back out to the desk, where the clerk was talking on the phone and typing a journal entry at the same time. The sergeant was looking through some 19-32s. "Jake," I said, "the telephone number I have for Katone is disconnected. Do you have another one?"

"Sorry, sir, that's all we've got, too." He continued, "I heard that he had to move for non-payment of rent. He probably doesn't have a new phone number yet."

"I wanted to talk to him and prepare him for court this morning. You don't know where I can find him, by any chance?"

"I'm afraid not, sir." He then added, "If you can help that idiot, you'll be the first. Bingham gave up on him."

I then attended the morning briefing and afterward drove over to court. Maybe Katone would show up early. As I arrived, the clerk was arranging his paperwork.

"Seen Katone?" I asked.

"No, sir," was the reply.

"I sure hope he doesn't embarrass us this week," I said.

Before long, those with cases pending had arrived, so I took my place in the observer's seats.

At 0900 sharp the bailiff said, "All rise." As everyone stood up he continued, "Federal Magistrate's Court for the San Angelo District, military part is now in session, Judge Hartsell presiding." After the judge took his place, the bailiff continued, "Be seated."

As he did each week, Judge Hartsell explained the defendant's rights. Then, as each defendant agreed for the judge to hear his case, conveyor-belt justice was dispensed. The judge moved them out quickly, until the eighth case was called. That was Captain Rasmussen, whom I had seen in court before.

With the Vietnamese war winding down, fewer officers were needed, and the Pentagon was starting to send out RIF (reduction in force) notices to career officers they considered excess. The word was out that Rasmussen had received one, and I could see why. His appearance was unkempt. The fatigues he wore looked like he had slept in them, his boots hadn't been polished in some time, his shirttail was out in places and he needed a shave. He looked like a higher-ranking version of Katone.

Judge Hartsell said, "You are charged with speeding fifty-five miles per hour in a thirty-mile zone. How do you plead?"

"Not guilty."

Glancing down to see who had written the ticket, the judge said, "See if Sergeant Katone is available."

The bailiff walked to the door and called for Katone. Katone entered the courtroom. His appearance wasn't much better than that of Rasmussen. He walked up to the bench and the judge said, after both men had been sworn in, "Tell us, Sergeant Katone, the circumstances which resulted in your issuance of this citation."

"Well, Judge," he began, "last Wednesday afternoon I was driving down Baseline Road when I observed a vehicle I believed to be speeding. I followed the vehicle onto Texas Street and clocked the defendant doing fifty-five miles per hour. As the speed limit was thirty, I issued the ticket."

"Captain Rasmussen, you may state your case now," said the judge.

"Your Honor, I have a few questions of the sergeant," Rasmussen said.

"You may proceed."

"Sergeant, how long did you follow me to verify I was going fifty-five miles per hour/"

"Probably two blocks, sir," Katone replied.

"And what was your speed on Baseline Road?"

"The speed limit, thirty miles per hour," Katone said with a shrug.

"Then isn't it a fact that fifty-five was the speed you needed to increase to from your original thirty to catch up to me, and not my actual speed?" the captain said quickly.

A STATESIDE TOUR OF DUTY

Katone hesitated for a second and, before he could answer, Rasmussen asked another question. "If not, then what was your speed while you were catching up to me?"

"I'm not sure—"

I couldn't tell if Katone paused or the captain cut him off, or both, but Rasmussen rapidly fired another question.

"How far did you pursue me on Texas Street before you clocked me for those two blocks?"

"Probably two blocks?" Katone's answer sounded more like a question. I could tell he was getting rattled.

"Texas Street is six blocks long," said Rasmussen. "If you pursued me for two blocks and clocked me for two blocks, what did you do in the other two blocks?"

This irrelevant question left Katone confused. "I don't know," Katone said as he tried to think.

"Then isn't it possible that fifty-five was the chase speed and not the clocking speed? Before Katone could answer the captain asked, "It is possible to make a mistake, isn't it?"

Katone made the mistake of answering the second question first. "I guess so." Then realizing his mistake, Katone compounded it with, "Well, I don't know."

Now Rasmussen paused in his machine-gun questioning to smile and speak in a friendlier manner. "We all know that you try to do a good job, sergeant, and that you have a lot on your mind. Now, honestly, if you're not completely sure, then there's a chance you made a mistake. You are human, aren't you?"

Instead of collecting his thoughts, Katone answered that final silly question. "Yes, but—"

Before Katone could qualify his statement as to what he was answering, Rasmussen had cut him off with, "No further questions, Your Honor. I've heard enough."

At this point, Katone should have asked the judge for a few seconds to clarify some points, but he didn't. He stood just there looking shell-shocked and bewildered. After a moment, the judge slammed down his gavel and said, "Case dismissed."

As the clerk was reading off the name of the next defendant, I got up and left through the side door. I had seen enough. I went to Operations, where I detailed the events to Bingham.

"You're not telling me anything I don't already know, lieutenant. The man should not be on line duty," Bingham agreed.

"Come with me over to the company, sarge. Together we'll convince the CO to reassign him somewhere else."

"Works for me, sir," he agreed. "I've been trying to do this for a long time."

Bingham and I spent the next hour detailing problems to the CO, but he resisted. "None of the other sections will want him either," he argued. "Where can we put him?"

It was Steve who came to the rescue with an excellent idea. "Make him the official building beautification supervisor," Steve said.

"The what?" Lynch asked.

"A permanent CQ," Steve said.

"We can't do that," argued the CO.

"We can if there's a big title attached to it," Steve explained. "Make him 290th Military Police Building Beautification and Grounds Supervisor. That way he can supervise some AWOLs from time to time making the place look better."

"I don't know," the captain pondered.

"Sir," I interjected, "you know that the colonel is adamant that an appearance of professionalism be projected by our personnel at all times. If you approve this promotion for Katone, I know the colonel will agree."

"Okay then, that's what we'll do. But, the Operations officer will have to tell him of the reassignment," the CO ordered.

"I know he'll be happy to do it," Bingham said.

As we walked back to the PMO, I asked Bingham one question. "Do you really think that Buffalo Bob will be happy to give Katone the news of his reassignment?"

"No way. He'll delegate that duty to me, and I'll tell Katone if he has any questions to see the CO." As we entered the building, he added, "That was a touch of brilliance, the way you brought up the colonel. Lynch isn't going to argue with him."

"No, and he probably knew that we could get the colonel to approve this if he didn't."

"No question there, sir."

That afternoon, Katone was told of his new assignment. Additionally, due to his difficulty with off-post housing and maintaining a telephone in his name, he was also ordered to move into the barracks. He gave no argument on this last point. This was probably because he was running out of options. Any new prospective landlord who checked on potential tenants would not rent to Katone. His reputation was getting that bad. Now, with him living in the barracks, he would not have to worry about bills such as rent, utilities, phone, etc. Also, he would be available at all times for his new position.

CHAPTER THIRTY

One of the first orders of business after Sam's return was to get a picture taken in Colonel Sherman's office with Sam and the colonel pinning on my first lieutenant's bars. I had been promoted more than a month previously, but Sam needed a picture, for posterity, to record the event.

We quickly got back into our old routine. On Wednesday night, we played bingo at the officers' club, where the twins could be admired by dozens of people. The attention they received, along with lots of bottles, seemed to keep them from fussing. Of course, if they did act up, we were prepared to leave immediately so no other participant's evening would be ruined. We never seemed to win anything, but it was a night out and Sam enjoyed that.

Saturday night, we would have some neighbors over to play canasta or pinochle, and on Sunday afternoon we would go for a leisurely drive and a picnic. Sam wouldn't trust a baby-sitter with the newborns, so an evening at the movies or a restaurant was something we didn't dare attempt. We cursed others who brought small children to such locations, and we decided not to be hypocrites. Of course, Sam joked that I didn't mind not going to such places because I was also cheap.

On July 4, Fort McCulloch celebrated the nation's birthday in a proper fashion. In the morning, there was a huge parade that went down MacArthur road and ended on the parade field. The local residents of surrounding towns were invited and they turned out in droves. All the units on post took part. Even the 290th had a small detachment in the procession. With most of our military policemen providing traffic control or patrolling the post, only a few men, who would normally be off for the day, marched in the pageantry. As the Traffic officer, I had my choice of marching with the men or supervising the traffic-control efforts. I picked the latter.

At Fort Belvoir, during Officer Candidate School, the commanding general had ordered a parade every week. As near as I could figure, the lard-butt jerk had nothing to do each week except watch parades. That, and bore everybody with a speech afterward.

The first parade I marched in was great. We marched down the street with flags flying and bands playing, with people on both sides of the street applauding. It felt wonderful. We then marched around the parade field at Fort Belvoir to hear General Nuisance give a speech. Afterward, we passed in review for the general on the reviewing stand, and back down the street, to additional applause.

The next week was still okay, but as the months wore on, parades became drudgery. I grew to hate them. After six months of OCS, it was a good thing none of us in the Belvoir parades had any live ammo in our rifles. If we had, General Lard Butt would have been a dead man. As a result of that experience, I preferred to work half of the day instead of marching in the parade.

Shortly after noon, my duty ended and I joined Sam, who had watched the parade with some of the other wives who lived in the trailer park. "I wish you had been marching," she commented. "Everyone else's husband was in the parade."

"Sorry, honey, I don't do parades—if I can help it. I had a belly full of them in my training days."

"But that's my chance to show you off and brag that you're my husband," she said jokingly.

"If that is what you want, you can put me on display in a window at home and let people drive by and look at me."

Sam laughed again. "Only if I can charge admission, and make some money."

"You're out of luck. Nobody will pay to look at me."

Sam snapped her fingers. "Darn, I should have married a guy with four arms."

"You wouldn't like that. You would get fondled and grabbed twice as much," I commented.

Sam just laughed. She knew that was true.

We went home and at dusk returned to the post's old football field for a fireworks display. Many years before, Fort McCulloch had a post football team, and this field was a reminder of those days. From the bleachers, Sam and I watched the brilliant display of pyrotechnics that ended the Sunday holiday. While the explosions woke the twins up, they didn't cry as we held them over our shoulders and patted their backs. We were able to enjoy the celebration of America's 195th birthday.

At work, the next week, we had several people come into the Traffic section to report hit-and-run damage to their vehicles. The first, on Monday, was a specialist from one of the engineer companies. Gross picked up his clipboard and began to make a report. He immediately noticed that the damage was in an unusual circular pattern. No vehicle could make such an indentation. His examination turned up a black substance on the surface of the car. He wiped a bit of it off with his finger and smelled it. He recognized it immediately.

"That's creosote!" He then sarcastically said, "Specialist, your car was struck by a runaway telephone pole."

"Oh!" said the startled soldier. "Someone must have borrowed my car without my knowledge."

"How did they get your car keys?" asked Gross.

"Sometimes I leave them on the desk by my bunk. I guess somebody borrowed them." He then added, "I guess I had better go and find out who did that."

"That might be a good idea," answered Gross. "Just remember that filing a false report is a big offense."

"I wouldn't do that," said the soldier. "It was an honest mistake. I really thought someone hit my car." He got into his car and drove off.

"Should I make a report on this, sir?" Gross asked.

"Yes, a very short one," I said. "That way if he tries to file a claim with his insurance, they will find out he's a big liar when they request a copy of the report. I wouldn't be surprised if they canceled his policy."

"No problem, sir. One short report coming up. Case closed."

The next report came in Tuesday morning from Mrs. Dean, who helped run the post teen center. She reported that her car had been struck in the rear the previous evening.

Unfortunately, she had just noticed it. Sergeant Corley and Byrd went over to make a report. While there, Corley got a list of the people who were known to have been in the teen center the night before and began calling to see if anyone had noticed anything. After several calls, he looked over and commented, "You know, sir, Brown and I can't figure what type of vehicle hit her car. The damage is too high for any other car or even a pickup."

"Why don't we go take another look, sarge?"

"Good idea, sir."

Corley grabbed a measuring tape and we drove to the teen center for another look. Sure enough, the damage was high above the bumper, across the back of the car at the top of the trunk. There was still green paint from the object that had struck the car in the impression.

"Measure the height of the damage, sarge," I commanded. I looked around. The teen center was painted the same color as the flakes of paint. "Take a look, sarge," I said as I pointed that out to him.

"I'll be damned, sir. Why didn't I notice that?"

"You were thinking in terms of a vehicle, sarge. Let's look around."

As we walked around the building, we noticed that the ground sloped down, with the rear of the building supported on short cement pilings. It was clear that the area was used for additional parking, and the base of the building was the same height as the damage to Mrs. Dean's car. Another hit-and-run case solved.

We walked into the building to tell Mrs. Dean the results of our investigation. She sat quietly for a moment and then yelled, "Julie!"

Her teenage daughter came over and asked, "Yes, Mama?"

"Last night when you parked my car behind the building, you backed into it. Didn't you?"

Her daughter's face turned a pallid white. Then in a weak voice she answered, "Yes, Mama."

"Why didn't you tell me about it?"

"I'm sorry, Mama, but I was afraid that you wouldn't let me drive again. I hoped that nobody would find out what happened."

As her daughter continued to try to rationalize her actions, Mrs. Dean said to us, "I'm sorry to trouble you; I saw the damage this morning and thought someone had hit my car." Then turning her wrath on her daughter, she snapped, "You're grounded, young lady."

"I'm sorry, ma'am, but we will have to issue your daughter a ticket for improper backing," Corley explained.

Corley cited the sixteen-year-old girl into the civilian part of the next week's Magistrate's Court and we departed with Mrs. Dean still voicing her displeasure toward her daughter.

The next hit-and-run case was a young specialist who reported that someone had hit his car while it was parked at work. He had looked around and found a car that also had damage that looked like it could have been made from striking his car. The young soldier's car was blue, with red paint from the vehicle that struck it. The possible suspect's car was red, with blue paint from another vehicle embedded in damage on the fender.

I had my doubts that he had found the offender. At the Northwestern University Traffic Institute, I had learned that in an accident the softer paint rubs off onto the harder one. There is no mutual exchange of paint. Still, we took a few flakes of paint from the red Plymouth, along with a few others we scraped off the blue Pontiac, and sent them to the crime lab at Fort Sam Houston to see if they would match. We then informed the sergeant who owned the Plymouth that we were investigating him as a possible hit-and-run suspect. A check of our 19-51 file indicated that the wife of the young specialist had a previous accident and he had two tickets for speeding. It was clear that they needed someone to blame this accident on to prevent their insurance from being canceled. However, until we got the report back from the crime lab there was nothing further we could do.

Thursday, July the 8th, we had the first traffic accident fatality I would experience on Fort McCulloch. It was 1700 hours, and I was preparing to leave for home when the call was received. A National Guard lieutenant was dead on arrival at the post hospital—the apparent victim of a jeep rollover accident.

I went to the hospital with Byrd to investigate the accident. While he viewed the dead man's remains, I passed out witness statements to the men in the squad who had observed the accident.

A few seconds later, Byrd came out of the room where the lieutenant's body was resting and said, "No doubt about it, sir, the back of his head is smashed in, all right. He's deader than hell."

Since it was close to dinner time, and everything seemed so cut and dried, I didn't view the body myself. In retrospect, I realize this was a serious mistake on my part. Since I had not viewed the fatal injuries, I was unable to later ask intelligent questions as to how they might have been caused. All the witness statements were essentially identical. It was as if everyone had agreed beforehand what would be said, and this bothered me a little. However, I decided that since everyone had seen the same thing and they had probably talked about the event in some detail, then there was nothing to worry about.

After collecting the statements, we drove to the scene of the accident. It was a curve of a dirt road with deep ruts in it. Jeep rollovers are common, especially if someone takes a corner too fast. It was easy to see how everything happened. Everything seemed routine. I then told Byrd to go take pictures of the jeep and to note any damage it had incurred so he could finish his report. I then headed for home.

When I got to work the next morning, Byrd had been there for some time. He had the pictures of the jeep already developed and the news was not good.

"Sir," he began. "I think we're dealing with a murder."

"What makes you think so, Byrd?"

He began to show me the pictures of the interior of the jeep (the pictures were black and white). "You see all of these dark stains around the gear shift and on the floor of the jeep, sir?"

"Yes, what about them?"

"That's blood." He waited for my reaction, but I remained silent to hear any additional explanation he might have. "If the jeep just turned over and the lieutenant just struck his head somewhere, how in the hell did all of that blood get in there?"

"I don't know, Byrd, but we need to ask some more questions."

"Yes, sir, we sure do," he agreed. "But, guess what, sir? This unit leaves to return to Oklahoma tomorrow. When I tried to ask some more questions, all those men just said that they had told us everything and had nothing more to add. When I tried to press the issue, a full-bird colonel suggested that I stop bothering his men. I don't like it, sir. Something's not right." I agreed with that assessment.

I took the pictures up front to the morning briefing. I learned that the colonel was gone for a week's leave and that Major Disaster was in charge. I also learned that another man had died during the night from the same squad of the same platoon that the deceased lieutenant was a member of. Two men dead from the same squad in two days during National Guard training was an incident that was unprecedented. The company and battalion commanders of these men could probably kiss their careers good bye.

I showed the pictures and explained my suspicions. "If the lieutenant tried to enforce military discipline on these weekend warriors, it's possible someone took offense and killed him. We need to have these men held here past their departure date tomorrow to get to the bottom of this."

Everyone in the morning briefing agreed with me.

"We'll do it," said the major. "I'll call the general this morning and take steps to have these men kept here while we continue the investigation."

I then went over to the hospital to ask some more questions. There, I learned that the lieutenant's body had already been picked up by casualty branch, embalmed and shipped home. The doctor I dealt with was Major Williams of the Army Medical Corps, the second in command at the Fort McCulloch Army Hospital.

"Sir, what was the hurry? We haven't even finished our investigation yet."

The major look surprised. "That's not what the National Guard colonel I dealt with said. He insisted that it had been ruled an accident and that it was important to get the man home to his family for burial."

"National Guard colonel?"

"Yes, lieutenant, and he was a bird colonel at that." Williams then explained, "With no instructions to the contrary, I had to release the body."

The colonel the doctor mentioned sounded like the same one who had given Byrd trouble the night before when he tried to ask additional questions of the witnesses to the accident. On a hunch, I asked about the man who had died during the night. "What killed him?" I asked.

"Oddly enough, he died from overdrinking," replied the doctor. "The official cause was alcohol poisoning."

"Overdrinking?"

"Yes," continued the doctor. "It's very unusual, but it does happen. Most of the time a man will pass out before he imbibes enough to kill himself."

The whole case was getting more and more weird all the time. I drove back to the PMO and was told to see the major immediately. As I met with the major, it was clear that someone had applied pressure to him.

"Lieutenant, you are to finish up your investigation of the traffic fatality immediately," the major ordered.

"But, sir," I protested, "what about holding those men over for further questioning?"

"Unless you can provide hard evidence that a crime was committed, lieutenant, they will leave first thing in the morning. The United States government is not going to pay to keep them here while you conduct a fishing expedition."

"But, sir," I tried to explain, "we need to question those men to obtain the evidence we need."

"Not going to happen," the major said forcefully. "Close the case."

A STATESIDE TOUR OF DUTY

A National Guard colonel, who obviously had powerful friends, was going to sweep the entire episode under the rug to prevent it from harming his career. With Colonel Sherman on leave, there was no one I could appeal to. Major Disaster would not rock the boat and my only option was to close the case.

Before I returned to my desk in the Traffic section, I began to ask questions of the various MPs who worked the line-duty shifts. I told them that if anyone had seen anything unusual, they were to let me know. I quickly found what I was looking for.

Mabry and Crowe reported that the week before, while on the swing shift, they had observed a group of National Guardsmen goofing off in a jeep while on a training exercise near to where the accident had happened. There was a lieutenant with them who fit the description of the deceased man. They also mentioned that they had warned the Guardsmen that jeeps tip over easily.

Now I felt better. Maybe there wasn't any foul play at all. If the men were goofing off and the jeep tipped over, injuring the lieutenant, then the men would put him in the jeep and hurry to the hospital. That would account for the blood. In their scurrying to get medical attention, they probably rolled the jeep on the curve and decided to say that the entire accident happened there.

I helped Byrd write up a report that explained that the lieutenant had hit his head on the floor of the jeep during the accident and died as a result of his injuries. The routine jeep accident report satisfied Major Disaster and all my other superiors around the post. There would not be any bad publicity to embarrass the Army or the post commander. The only official notice was a small news item buried in the back pages of the newspapers. This mentioned that two National Guardsmen had died, one day apart, due to unfortunate (and accidental) circumstances.

Two weeks later, I had forgotten the entire incident, when Byrd asked me a very unusual question. We were sitting at our desks. I was reviewing accident reports and Byrd was typing up his latest report and smoking a cigarette. Suddenly, he stopped typing. "Sir, do you know anything about Mormons?" he asked.

I looked up and shrugged. "I met a few at college. They all seemed like nice enough people. Why do you ask?"

"Well, sir, as I understand it, Mormons don't smoke or drink. Is that right?"

"Well, Byrd," I expounded, "I guess any religion has a few adherents who don't follow the teaching of their denomination, but by and large Mormons don't smoke or drink. That's true. Why do you ask?"

"Do you remember that soldier who died from overdrinking?" Byrd asked.

"Yes, I do. What about him?"

"Well, sir, the morning that guard unit shipped out, I went out there to ask some more questions before they left. Like I said before, nobody in the dead man's squad would talk to me. As I was leaving, a man from one of the platoon's other squads asked me how the second man died. When I told him it was from overdrinking, he yelled 'Bullshit. That man was a devout Mormon who never touched a drop of liquor in his life.' What do you think about that?"

I was stunned. "What did you do then?" I asked.

"I talked to everyone else in the platoon I could find."

"And?"

"Everyone in the other three squads verified that the man never drank, but his fellow squad members claimed he had been drinking all night."

I picked up the phone and called Major Williams at the hospital. When I got him on the phone, I identified myself and asked, "Major, is it possible to murder someone and make it appear that the person died from overdrinking?"

"Sure," he answered. "That would be easy."

"How would you do it?"

He paused for a second then explained, "A syringe of 80-proof liquor injected into a main artery would be instantly fatal. A physician performing an autopsy would find alcohol in the circulatory system, and if that was compatible with the individual's conduct, then alcohol poisoning would be the presumptive cause of death."

"What about the needle mark where the syringe was injected?" I asked. "Wouldn't that cause questions?"

"It's doubtful that the physician would notice it unless he was specifically looking for it. Besides, there are too many places on the body to hide the injection point," he explained.

After talking to the doctor, I posed a possibility to Byrd. "Either through an accident caused by extreme negligence or outright homicide, the lieutenant was killed. The other men in the squad were worried that one member of the group was not going to keep his mouth shut, so they killed him, too, and used the drinking story to cover up the murder."

"That's the way I figure it, too, lieutenant."

With that, Byrd and I went up front to see the colonel. Maybe we could get the case reopened. Somewhere in Oklahoma, two men's families deserved to know the truth.

As we listed our facts and time line and voiced our suspicions to Colonel Sherman, he was sympathetic. Unfortunately, at this late date, that was nothing else he could do.

He called the post chief of staff, Colonel Rulon, and told him of my findings and my suspicions. It was a short phone call. The case would remain closed.

After hanging up the phone, the colonel passed along what he had been told. "Those men are scattered all over Oklahoma now, lieutenant. Without solid evidence to back up our suspicions, there is no way we can get the government to pay the expense to bring them back here. They should never have been allowed to leave until our investigation was finished in the first place."

"That's what I told the major, sir," I explained. "He just told me to close the case."

Sherman shook his head. "I wish I had been here. That worthless major will yield to the smallest amount of pressure. He has no backbone at all. Now that those Guardsmen are in another state back at their civilian jobs, they would have generals, congressmen and senators keeping us from bringing them back." He hesitated and then added, "And every one of them would claim to be saving taxpayer money."

"I understand, sir," I said.

Colonel Sherman was right. Both bodies had been returned to Oklahoma and buried. We had absolutely no evidence, only our hunches. It would take an act of Congress to get the bodies exhumed and the case reopened.

Colonel Sherman added one more thought. "When I was a captain at Fort Rucker years ago, we had two black soldiers killed, off post, by some rednecks. The local sheriff was a friend of the killers and claimed the soldiers were killed in self-defense. The commander at Rucker wanted to maintain good relations with the civilian authorities, and since we had no jurisdiction off post, I was told to drop the matter. I had to list the deaths as justifiable homicide. To this day, ending that investigation is the only thing in my Army career I regret. I wish I didn't have to tell you this, lieutenant, but we can't get justice for everybody. We do the best we can, but some things are beyond our control."

"Yes, sir," I said sadly.

"Another thing," he said. "When I mentioned your name, Rulon was not happy. I guess the higher-ups are still upset with you for trying to cause trouble for the Red Cross."

"They're still claiming that I'm not a team player?" I asked.

"Those were his exact words," the colonel said.

The next day the results came back on the paint samples we had sent to the lab. The result was exactly what I had expected. The red paint was a product used on Chevrolet vehicles. The sergeant who owned the Plymouth was in the clear.

Needless to say, the kid who owned the Pontiac was not happy. I explained that guilt must be proven in a court of law beyond a reasonable doubt, and with the lab results and what I knew about vehicle accidents, there was no way we could proceed in an investigation against the sergeant.

Likewise, I had the sergeant who owned the Plymouth come in and get the good news. He was no longer a suspect. Normally a report would be sent through channels to the man's company commander, explaining the situation, but I had a feeling that might not be appropriate in this case.

"Sergeant," I asked, "if I send this through channels, is there any chance it will cause you problems, even though it shows you were exonerated?"

"Yes, sir," he answered, I'm not real popular with my CO."

I turned around and dropped the file in the trash can. "Then consider it having gone through channels."

"Thank you, sir!" he said with a smile.

That night, Sam again brought up the subject of the two dead men for whom there would be no justice.

"Are you sure there is nothing you can do, honey?" She asked. "On *M.A.S.H.*, Trapper and Hawkeye are always able to find a way to solve every problem. There must be a way."

"You've been watching too much television, honey," I replied. "Writers on a television show can do whatever they want in a half an hour. In real life, it doesn't work out that way."

"I just keep thinking about that poor man's family being told that he drank himself to death when he was a teetotaler. It's not fair," she commented.

"A lot of things aren't fair, Sam. Look at the case of Captain Jeffery MacDonald."

"Who?"

It didn't surprise me that Sam had not heard about the MacDonald case. The brutal murders received little coverage in Phoenix, but anyone connected to the military police knew the story well. There were few in the MP Corps who didn't have an opinion on that investigation. It was an example of the most botched and shoddy police work imaginable.

I detailed for Sam how on the night of 17 February 1970 (while I was still in OCS) the wife and two daughters of Doctor Jeffery MacDonald at Fort Bragg had been murdered by intruders. MacDonald had also been stabbed in the back several times, hit over the head and left for dead. The apartment was a shambles and MacDonald told the story of how four hippie-like individuals had committed the crime.

Unfortunately, as many curious MPs walked through the house, evidence was destroyed. In addition, one new MP looked at a flower pot, dumping its contents on the floor and replacing the pot where he had found it. When CID investigators arrived, they took one look at the flower pot and decided that the entire event was staged. As they told it, if the flower pot was knocked over in a fight, the empty pot could not replace itself on the table. They then arrested MacDonald, who had been revived through mouth-to-mouth resuscitation, for the murder of his family. Investigators never looked at any other possible suspects.

The facts were that one of the investigators reported seeing a young woman who fit the description of one of the people in MacDonald's account, only a few blocks from the murder scene. Also, most competent medical authorities agreed that MacDonald could not have inflicted his injuries upon himself. Add to this the facts that MacDonald had absolutely no motive and that, as a doctor involved in the post's drug treatment program, he had made many enemies. At that point the fact that no other suspects were considered became ludicrous.

"That's terrible!" exclaimed Sam. "How often does that happen?"

"No one knows," I admitted, "but stories abound of people on death row who are found to be innocent after later evidence comes to light."

Sam was horrified. "That could happen to anyone—even us."

"Honey, if somebody murdered you and the kids and I couldn't prevent it, I would pray that I was one thousand miles away at the time of the crime. Hopefully I would be appearing on a television show with the President of the United States, the Pope, and Billy Graham. Unless I had an alibi that unbreakable, I would probably be arrested and the authorities would just try to pin the crime on me. Then I would be victimized a second time, as MacDonald was."

"Do you think they will convict the poor man?" Sam asked.

"Probably. All of the resources of the government are being thrown into the prosecution, and any evidence that might exonerate him had been destroyed by an incompetent investigation."

"That's *really* not fair."

"Sam, sweetheart, I've been told all of my life that life isn't fair. The more I work around here I'm finding out it is a definite fact—that life isn't fair. Come to think of it, you have a little experience in that regard."

She thought for a second. "Yes, I do." With that she changed the subject.

Alone, in the trailer, for much of the day, Sam needed more adult conversation, but mostly she needed somebody to listen. So I listened and let her do most of the talking. I was probably making her depressed anyway. As I burped Stacy, she continued to feed Tracy while she told me about her day. It was routine and not something I really wanted to hear, but Sam needed me to listen. So I did.

As we fed the babies that night, I hoped that when my children were grown, things might be different. The trouble is that in my heart, I knew that every generation of humans for the past million years had been wishing that same thing. Probably, my children would have the same wish for my grandchildren.

You do your best to make the world a better place. When problems come along, you confront them. As you experience hard knocks, you learn from them to make a better future and avoid having those problems again. The real tragedy, as I saw it, was that some people never learned from their mistakes and continued to make the same blunders over and over again. I saw examples of people doing that all the time in my work, and it was truly sad.

Another thing I was determined to do was to take everything I heard with a grain of salt. I would check out the facts, if possible, to determine the veracity of any statements. I knew there was a good chance that whatever news or gossip was being passed around was untrue. As my father had once told me, "Believe only half of what you see and none of what you hear." That was one piece of advice I passed along to anyone who might listen. Some called me cynical. How many listened and agreed with me, I will never know.

CHAPTER THIRTY-ONE

On Monday, the 12th, I received a letter from the post chief of staff, Colonel Rulon. Several weeks before, I had been put in charge of the collection for the Army Emergency Relief Fund. Each unit on post has an officer who must panhandle and shake down the members of his unit for money. The money collected goes to a military charity called by the before-mentioned name. The charity is a good one. It has no overhead to speak of and helps soldiers in need, often with few questions asked.

I had been a little lax in the collecting of funds, due to the other duties I was attending to. I quickly sent a reply to Colonel Rulon, apologizing for the failure to report any funds collected and promised to correct the situation immediately. After sending the letter, I went to everyone in the PMO and the orderly room, asking for donations. Before the next two weeks were over, I would have over $140 to report. Between my own efforts and others whom I designated to collect from personnel assigned elsewhere with AWOL App and PMI, I had donations from one hundred percent of our personnel.

As I was finalizing my report to Battalion, complete with the amount of money deposited, Buffalo Bob dropped into my office.

"Don't make the same mistake that a lieutenant I had serving under me at Fort Knox did," he admonished.

"What was that?" I asked.

"He deposited all of the donations for the Army Emergency Relief Fund into his personal account and then wrote a big check to the AER Fund for the amount donated. He then tried to deduct the entire amount off his taxes as a charitable donation, using his check as documentation."

"That's not a mistake, that's fraud," I said. "But let me guess—if you were part of a very large unit, then the amount was probably more than he could have made in a month. That made it easy to spot."

A STATESIDE TOUR OF DUTY

"That's right," replied Barker. "He wound up paying back taxes along with penalty and interest to the IRS and got an official reprimand in his 201 file."

"I'm not that stupid, or greedy," I said. I sat back in my chair. "What brings you over to Traffic?"

"I thought I would share a bit of information that just came my way," Barker said.

"What's that?"

"The last week Katone was on graveyard, he was helping out on the desk. He turned on the two-way communication system to the officers' club. As he did so, he heard a loud pounding noise. Instead of turning off the device and having a unit check it out, he yelled, 'Who's in there?' By the time Unit One could check it out, all they found was a window that had been forced open and a large sledgehammer by the safe in the office."

Sergeant Corley, who had been listening to the conversation, began to laugh hysterically. I shook my head with disbelief as I considered the situation. Communications equipment, allowing for two-way conversation, had been installed in the Finance office, the bank and the officers' club for after-hours monitoring. During the night, these could be turned on at the desk to see if anything unauthorized was happening at any of those locations. If a break-in or other unusual occurrence was in progress, then the monitoring device would be switched back off, in order to not tip off the intruder, and a unit would be dispatched to catch the perpetrators in the act. With Katone on the desk, the device had been useless.

"I bet that guy shit down both legs when Katone yelled at him," Corley guffawed. "Probably scared him out of ten years' growth."

As Sergeant Corley continued to laugh, I remained dumbfounded at Katone's incompetence. "I'm glad we took him off line duty," was my only comment.

"I am too, Nick," Barker agreed. "If he doesn't work out as a CQ, we won't accept him back. The colonel has already agreed to that."

Corley continued to roar with delight, and I couldn't blame him.

"Katone hears wham, wham, and wham, and does he send someone to investigate? Hell, no! He yells, 'Who's in there?' and tips the guy off." Corley continued to laugh uncontrollably.

It was funny. Somebody who thought he was alone to break open a safe hears a voice from the ethereal darkness and flees leaving his sledgehammer behind. Corley was right. The guy probably did defecate in his drawers on the way out.

On Tuesday morning, the 27th, Steve informed me that I was to chair the monthly OEO (Organizational Economic Opportunity) meeting. This was a race relations meeting that each Army unit was supposed to hold once each month. For years, the company XO had simply written up some fictional minutes for the meeting that was supposedly held, and forwarded them to Battalion. Unfortunately, word had reached the officer at Headquarters responsible for such records that the meetings were not being held. When Steve had reassured him that the required meetings were being held, the Battalion official stated his intention to attend the next one. It was scheduled for Thursday morning.

The meetings were a discussion on race relations that were to have an equal number of whites and blacks. With so few blacks in our unit, their turn to attend the meeting would come around so often that they lacked enthusiasm, and most of the white MPs thought it a waste of time. Personally, I felt that I had reached the point where I had enough to do. I know that race relations are important, but I had my doubts as to how much good these perfunctory meetings accomplished.

"Steve," I protested, "I have real work to do. Can't you or the CO chair this meeting?"

"Sorry, Nick, but we've been the chairman of record before. According to Battalion, it's your turn and they expect to see you there. Besides, according to those paper pushers at battalion headquarters, this is real work."

Sadly, I resigned myself to my fate. "Fine, you assign people to be there and I'll chair the meeting."

Steve smiled. "Thanks, Nick. You can spread BS better than anyone I know of. You'll do a great job."

"Yeah, thanks, buddy."

At 0900 hours Thursday morning, I went over to the company training classroom for the OEO meeting. Present for the meeting were six enlisted men (three white and three black), myself, Captain Maxfield (the battalion G2), and Steve. The three white soldiers were Sergeant Corley and specialists Woolhouse and Dobson. The three blacks were specialists Jackson and Dixon, with Sergeant Wallace. As we congregated for the meeting, they all seemed to be as excited about the meeting as I was. After all, this would normally have been a day off for most of them.

A STATESIDE TOUR OF DUTY

"The July OEO meeting for the 290th Military Police Company will come to order," I said. "Specialist Dobson will now read the minutes for the June meeting."

As Dobson read the minutes for the prior meeting, I was thankful that no one said anything about the meeting not actually being held. The fact that Steve had listed six different soldiers for June probably helped in that regard.

As Dobson finished, I said, "It is customary to ask if there are any necessary changes or deletions to the minutes, but as Lieutenant Bronson is the only one attending from last month's meeting, I guess we must rely on his recollection. That is, unless someone else knows of anything else that was discussed, from talking to others who were here."

While everyone else shook their heads, Steve requested a superficial change to the minutes. As Dobson (who was acting as secretary) made the correction, I asked, "Anything else?" After a moment, I asked, "Hearing none, do we have a motion to accept the minutes as corrected?"

"So moved," said Corley.

"Second the motion," Steve quickly added.

"Those in favor of accepting the minutes as corrected, signify by saying aye."

As the reply was unanimous, I then stated, "Since everyone agreed, we can now move on to new business." I was hoping for a short meeting. It was not to be.

Jackson raised his hand and I recognized him. "Sir," he began. "Why is it that all of the blacks in the company are on line duty? All of the choice sections, such as PMI, AWOL App and Traffic are all one hundred percent white."

"You raise a very valid point, Jackson. The Army is about forty per cent black, while most MP units are lucky if ten percent of their personnel are black. The leadership of the PMO and the company want to have as large a presence of black representation as possible to deal with the public, and consequently most blacks wind up on line duty. Until more blacks stop avoiding the MP corps, that's a problem we'll continue to have."

"That's still not right, sir."

"Nick," Steve interjected. "We should point out that there are no choice sections. Line duty is just as important, if not more so, than any other part of our organization. Without line duty, none of the other sections would even exist."

As Steve continued to pile it on with a big shovel, Jackson continued to protest. "The point is, sir, that most of us would prefer to work regular days than the rotating shifts of line duty."

"We did have a black in the Traffic section," I pointed out. "Cummings did an excellent job."

"He ETSed a while back, sir," Wallace noted. "Traffic is all white now."

"Unfortunately, that's true," I admitted. "He joined the NYPD, and that brings up another problem. Blacks in the MP Corps often don't re-up. They can join the civilian police force of their choice, so we often lose them."

Jackson's rebuttal was quick in coming. "Well, sir, if we're always going to be stuck on line duty, what do you expect?"

This was a no-win situation. The blacks in the company had a valid gripe. Unfortunately, they were desperately needed where they were, because other black soldiers desired to see other blacks patrolling the post. Their high profile on line duty was needed. I looked to Steve for help, but all he could do was add more crap about how there were no choice positions. Line duty was very important. After a lengthy discussion, I decided to change the subject.

"Let me explain it another way," I began. "When a black soldier gets stopped or questioned by a white MP, we often get complaints that the MP was overly aggressive. The same thing often happens when the situation is reversed. The white soldier often complains that he was treated with undue harshness. These complaints are usually filed in the trash can because you men have your life on the line and we don't question your professionalism. If all we got were complaints from black soldiers, we could wind up with a congressional investigation on our hands."

"You get complaints about us?" Dixon asked. "How come we don't know that?"

"In the absence of evidence of any wrongdoing on your part, there's no reason to pass them on," I replied. "If you wish, we can do that in the future. But, as far as I'm concerned, you men do a great job."

Everyone was silent for a few seconds. Then Wallace spoke up. "Maybe we could be rotated around to different sections. You know, spend a month on line duty, then a month in Traffic or PMI or something."

"That's an excellent idea," said Maxfield. "I can see that your company has some unique problems. You might put that into the company suggestion box."

A STATESIDE TOUR OF DUTY

That was just the kind of thought I would expect from some chair-warming Battalion official. The suggestion box had been up since I had arrived at Fort McCulloch, and most of the suggestions we received were anonymous recommendations that the CO do things to himself that were anatomically impossible. There had also been a comical proposal that the CQ Brasso the bullets for the personnel on line duty so the ammo would be bright and shiny, but most suggestions contained language only Sergeant Winters could appreciate.

I again took control of the meeting (or tried to). "Men," I stated firmly, "everyone here is important to this company. There isn't an officer who has served here that hasn't bemoaned the fact that we need a greater representation of black troops. Right now, the major has a notice in the *Daily Bulletin* that we are accepting OJTs to cross-train as MPs. If you have any friends in other companies you can talk into joining us, please do so."

"Most of my friends in other companies don't want anything to do with this line of work, sir," Jackson admitted.

"So, you see what we're up against, then," I answered.

"Is there anything else anyone would like to bring up?" Steve asked.

After a few moments of silence, I began to sum things up. "I won't lie to you, men. There is racism in the world and no one will deny it. However, no country in the world has done more than this one to try to overcome it. In the Army, everyone has the same opportunity at advancement and promotion. Also, my door and the doors of any other officers in the 290th are always open to anyone at any time. We really do believe in diversity and we have to be a team."

"You really think this country is trying to wipe out racism, sir?" Dixon asked.

"Yes, I do."

"Come on, sir! This is a racist country."

"Well, Dixon," I replied. "Let me put it this way. The USA is no more racist than any other country—"

"Name one," he interrupted.

"Almost every country in the world has problems between its various ethnic populations," I explained. "Look at Nigeria. It's the most populous black nation in the world. The Ibo people there felt discriminated against and formed the breakaway republic of Biafra. About a million people died as Nigeria completed their conquest of that territory. We don't have those kinds of problems here. Up in Canada, the French of Quebec are raising hell against their English-speaking neighbors. Every country on earth has similar problems, and every ethnic group of people on earth contains some racists or individuals who hate some other group of their fellow human beings."

I should have stopped while I was ahead. Now, my last statement was challenged by all three of the black MPs. Dixon, especially, claimed that blacks could not be racist.

"You really believe that?" I asked.

"Yes, sir, I do," Dixon stated emphatically.

I began to proceed logically. "Look, Dixon," I said. "Blacks usually call themselves 'soul brothers.' Define the term for us."

He looked around nervously then said, "Well, sir. We're 'brothers' because we share a common burden of discrimination, and 'soul' describes how we can empathize with the plight of the oppressed and long for a better world. It's a result of our traditions and social customs."

"Does anyone other than blacks possess soul?"

He thought for a second. "I guess maybe some Indians and a few Mexicans might."

"Do any whites have this quality of soul?" I questioned.

"No, sir. Usually not."

"My ancestors in Tennessee and South Carolina had everything they owned stolen and their houses burned in 1864. Couldn't they understand the oppressed?"

"That's different, sir," he countered. "They deserved it because they owned slaves."

"My ancestors didn't own any slaves, Dixon. They were just poor farmers who were in the way of General William T. Sherman's raping, marauding army."

Dixon was silent. Sergeant Wallace then said, "I think you're missing the point, sir."

"No, sergeant, I don't think so. Let me finish. If some white bigot says that all blacks are lazy and stupid, we all agree that his statement is racist and he is a bigot. Right?"

Everyone in the room nodded or otherwise agreed with the statement.

"So, if a black was to give a blanket statement that all whites were racist or couldn't empathize with the downtrodden or oppressed, that is likewise racist, right?"

The whites in the room agreed, while the blacks disagreed. Sergeant Wallace then changed the subject. "Maybe your family got inconvenienced by the Civil War, sir, but you have to admit it was a holy war. Without it, slaves in America would never have been freed."

"Sorry, sarge," I said. "But the facts don't bear that out. There was nothing holy about the Civil War. In fact, it never needed to be fought at all. Blacks in America would have been freed anyway and probably would be better off today if the war hadn't occurred."

"How in the hell do you figure that, sir?" Wallace countered.

"Well, first of all, Brazil (that's in South America)—" I hesitated, hoping that I hadn't insulted everyone's intelligence with that last comment. They remained quiet, so I continued. "Brazil had thirty times the number of slaves in the United States and freed them in 1889 without a war. The Industrial Revolution had made slavery obsolete in the Western world. If the Civil War had not been fought, slaves in this country would have been freed by 1890 also. In fact, many famous Southerners like Robert E. Lee and Judah P. Benjamin had already set their slaves free before the war.

"Second," I continued, "without the hard feelings of a conflict, Brazil saw marriages between the families of the former slave owners and families of former slaves within one generation after the manumission there. In Brazil, blacks and whites get along fine."

"Then why do we have so many problems here, sir?" Jackson asked.

"Because," I explained. "The economy of the South had been completely destroyed by the war. There was no Marshall Plan. People had to start over and rebuild everything. That pitted the poor whites and the blacks against each other and led to hatred, distrust, segregation and all of the other problems we have to solve today."

Everyone sat in silence. Either they were considering what I had just said, or they were just bored. I hoped that I had gotten everyone to start thinking.

"Thirdly," I began again, "in 1860, the Southern states were the richest states in the country. In 1870, after they were devastated and plundered, those states were the poorest. If the war had not been fought, the slaves would have been freed into the part of the country with the strongest economy and the best economic opportunities. As it was, they gained their freedom in an area that suffered a depression until the Second World War. In high school history, they probably told you that the Great Depression started with the crash of 1929. Actually, that was the rest of the country. In the South, we just continued the one we already had."

"What's your point, sir?" Wallace said.

"Just this, sergeant: If the American Civil War had never been fought the slaves would have been freed by 1890 anyway. We would probably all get along fine, and if your family lived where mine did, you and I might be in-laws today."

"I find that hard to believe, sir," Wallace replied.

"Apparently, Sergeant Wallace wouldn't want me for a brother-in-law," I joked.

"That would depend upon what your sister looked like, sir," he retorted. Everybody laughed.

Captain Maxfield, who had been looking at his watch, interjected a thought. "Perhaps you'll need to all agree to disagree, lieutenant." It was clear that he wanted to leave.

"Look, men," I said, "I don't have all of the answers." I hesitated. "Hell, I don't have any answers. I doubt if anyone other than God does. I can tell you that I personally don't have any race or creed prejudices. I don't care what color a man's skin is. I only care whether he does his job. I've had some great friends who were black and everyone who has back-stabbed me or done me dirt has been white." Now I was starting to feel like I was lecturing. It was time to stop.

"Does anyone have any comments they would like to add?" Everyone sat there like a bump on a log. "Does anyone have any questions?" Again, there was nothing. I decided to sum up and call it quits.

"Men, just remember this," I said. "Here in America, you can complain and disagree all you want, and nobody will bother you. Do that in China, Russia or Cuba and you'll be in jail. Please remember that. Is there anything else anyone wants to discuss?"

I looked around. "If not, then we need a motion to adjourn."

"So moved," said Corley.

"Second," said Steve.

"Those in favor, say aye." As everyone did so, I added, "We appreciate your input, men. Thank you all for coming."

As Maxfield began to critique the meeting I had just chaired, Steve asked, "Can I get you a cup of coffee, sir?"

"Yes, thanks. I'd appreciate it."

As Steve returned with the coffee, Maxfield was still elaborating on how important the OEO meetings were. Steve rolled his eyes as he entered the room. Finally, Maxfield left and Steve and I were left alone.

"Why didn't you help me in there?" I asked.

"I tried, but you wouldn't go along with me on how important line duty is."

"Oh, they knew that was a boatload of crap," I commented. "Even if it is true."

Steve smiled and said, "At least I didn't brownnose them about the great job they are doing."

"Well, you get this duty back next month, buddy," I said. "I'm not doing any more of those meetings."

"After the battle we had, I doubt if Maxfield will be back. Unless he does, there won't be a meeting next month," Steve stated. "We'll go back to just sending in the fabricated minutes that I make up."

I returned to the Traffic section, where Sergeant Corley was all smiles. "I told everyone how you shot down all of that racism crap, sir," he said.

I threw my hat onto my desk. "I sure could have used a little input from the rest of you men," I noted.

"No, sir. We might have been required to be there, but we weren't required to say anything. If you don't agree with what the black guys say in a meeting like that—then you're a racist. No, thank you. I wasn't going to say a word."

Corley, and the others, had a point. Any one of their black comrades might some day be their superior as a company first sergeant or battalion sergeant major or in some other capacity. There was no reason to piss off somebody you might be working for eventually. For that reason, in discussions between black and white soldiers, the conversation always avoided race. Of course, the black patrolmen did have a legitimate complaint. PMI or Traffic was a better situation than line duty, but the men were desperately needed where they were. Also, the white patrolmen on line duty coveted the other positions as well. There was no way on earth to make everyone happy. The thought occurred that perhaps I should have said that during the meeting.

As I headed home for lunch, the news and comment I normally listened to on the radio was preceded by an appeal to local voters for the special election set for August 10. It went as follows: "On August 10, please go to the polls and vote to keep the name for our new local high school as Bradshaw High School. Its great tradition of academic excellence is well known to all colleges and universities in the state of Texas and the name has been a part of Harrisville tradition for almost a hundred years. Remember, on August 10, vote for the name of Bradshaw

High School." It was followed by the quick comment, "Paid for by local citizens for Bradshaw High School."

As the political ad ended, I drove by the almost-completed new high school, only two blocks from the trailer court. For years, there had been two local high schools. One, Bradshaw, was mostly all white, and Harrisville High School was all black. With both falling apart, the local county had decided to build one to replace the two. The only problem was what to name the new school. The school board had three white members and two black members. So, when one of the white board members abstained from the vote because his grandfather had donated the land for the original school, the vote was deadlocked at 2–2. It was decided to put the issue to a countywide vote.

The campaign had been every bit as bitter and divisive as any political race I had ever witnessed. Walton Bradshaw, for whom the original school had been named in 1900, had been a slave owner prior to the Civil War. This made many of the black residents uneasy. However, the Bradshaw proponents countered that Alonzo Harris, for whom the town and consequently the black high school were named, had owned more slaves than Bradshaw did. To many black voters this was irrelevant, since the school had been named Harrisville High since 1921. They argued that the school was named for the town and not for Mr. Harris.

A number of city meetings on the subject had broken up in shouting matches. In one, a black man pointed out that the proposed school name was just Bradshaw, not specifically "Walton" Bradshaw. He also noted that Bradshaw was a common surname among longtime local black residents, and he was called an Uncle Tom, by other blacks, for his input. Likewise, whites that tried to be conciliatory and encourage the name of Harrisville High were called some racially charged epithets. Whoever invented the secret ballot had done the world a favor. The clear majority of voters, regardless of race, could remain silent and quietly vote their preference. Since Sam and I maintained our Arizona residence, we were not involved. We could watch the proceedings with no stake in the outcome.

As I walked in the door, I mentioned the ad I had just heard on the radio. "People around here sure get worked up about a name for a school," I said.

"Can you blame them, Nick? There are two schools that have been around forever, and everyone wants their kids to go to the one they went to."

"It's not the same school, Sam. It will just be a new one that had the old name transferred to it."

"You know what I mean, Nick. The tradition goes with the name. It means something to people."

"Honey," I replied, "they change the names of schools all the time. Michigan A&M became Michigan State. Texas Mines became the University of Texas, El Paso. Hell, I think ASU was once Arizona Normal or something. As long as you get a legal diploma from an accredited institution, who cares what school name is on it?"

"Believe it or not, Nick, a lot of people do. But that's just a poor girl talking, who never got to go to college."

I didn't know what had gotten Sam's dander up, but she seemed to want to argue with whatever I said that day. No matter what I said, she seemed to take issue with it. Even as I tried to give up and agree with whatever point she was stating, our argument continued. After all, I really didn't care what the new school name was.

I finally decided to change the direction of the conversation. Doing my best Humphrey Bogart impersonation, I asked, "Okay sweetheart, in the interest of tradition, which local school name should I support?"

"Don't make fun of me, Nick!" she snapped.

I threw my hands up in despair. "I'm not making fun of you, Sam! There are a lot of snobs out there who look down on anyone who didn't go to Harvard or Yale. I don't have time for such nonsense. Those elite places are no better, in my opinion, than ASU or Montana Tech, for that matter. In some ways, maybe they're not even as good. Tradition is fine, I guess, but anyone can begin a tradition at any time. I'm sorry if you thought I was making fun of you, and you're right—tradition is important."

She smiled and returned to making lunch. "And if someday I wanted to go to school and get a degree, would you have a problem with that?"

"No way! I think it would be wonderful for you to get a degree, if you want one." I then asked another question. "So that I can stay out of trouble around here, what name for the local school should I support?"

"I don't care," she laughed. "I didn't go to school here."

"Then what are we arguing for?" I asked.

"Because it's so much fun to make up afterward," she said.

If I live to be one hundred, I will never understand women. Apparently, Sam was starting to feel some inadequacy from her lack of higher education and needed to use an occasional argument to show her equality. Or, maybe she was just bored and needed an argument as some sort of mental stimulation. Whatever the reason, she was right about one thing: it was fun when we made up afterward. I would be late getting back to work after lunch, and I didn't care what the major thought.

Afterward, as I prepared to return to work, I told Sam about the morning meeting. I mentioned Wallace's comment.

"Why don't you put that guy's suggestion into practice, Nick? It seems that rotating the various jobs would be fair," Sam said.

"Honey," I explained, "trying to rotate all of the men in and out of line duty would be a nightmare. Everyone would be unhappy because they would feel that they were getting a raw deal. One man might miss more graveyard shifts and get more day shifts than the next and the complaints would be overwhelming. The colonel and Barker would never go for it, and I don't blame them."

"So, what can you do?"

"The only thing we can do is continue what we're doing. Besides, as I told them this morning, rank advancement and promotions have nothing to do with where someone works. They can get promoted on line duty just as rapidly as anywhere else."

"How do the black soldiers you have measure up with the white ones?" Sam asked.

I thought for a second. "Well, of the eight, three or four are among our best troops. Three are about average and the last one may not be the sharpest knife in the drawer, but he's a lot better than Joe Katone. At least he can follow instructions and get the job done."

As I returned to the office, Brown and Mabry were there waiting for me. Sergeant Corley had told them about the meeting that morning, and they both wanted to thank me for publicly pointing out that blacks could be racist, too—something they were afraid to do.

"Look, men," I said, "I figure the good Lord created us all and we need to look past our differences and learn to get along."

"Sometimes that's hard to do," said Brown. "Back home, the local drive-in showed a movie called *The Legend of Nigger Charley,* and the owner changed the title on the marquee to Negro. A few months later, *Ebony* magazine had an article belittling him and other white theater owners for doing so. If you use the word, you're a racist. If you avoid it, then you get disparaged, or called a coward, by those same people. We can't win."

"Well, Brown," I said, "I like to believe the world is getting better. I have some black neighbors and we get along fine. Twenty years ago, that would have been much more difficult in this country."

"It can't get better quickly enough for me," Brown commented.

"Sir," Mabry said, as he looked around, "a few days ago, my partner and I were patrolling over by the infantry battalion. As we stopped for a stop sign, a black soldier started taunting us. One thing he said was, 'Hi, pigs!' in a real insulting manner. I just looked back and smiled. I then answered, 'How are you doing, Nigger?' That shut him up as we drove off."

As Corley started to laugh, I said, "For the record, I never heard that. You were wise to smile as you spoke to him, but I'd avoid the use of that word in the future. If the wrong people hear you say it, it can cause you a lot of problems."

"Don't worry, sir," Mabry replied. "I always look around first."

"Just the same, it's always wise to avoid epithets. They never do any good." I didn't offer any additional advice to Mabry after that. I knew it wouldn't do any good. He would just disregard it. If I were a great philosopher or a genius, maybe I would have the answer to the hate that is so prevalent in the world, but I'm not. There was once a popular song that stated, "The French hate the Germans, the Germans hate the Poles . . . ," which pretty well describes life on the earth. In some parts of the world, the folks who live in the mountains even hate the flatlanders and vice versa. There seems no end to hatred in the world. I think you should live the best you can to set an example against racism and hope someone else follows it. At that point, I figured the best thing to do was to just end the conversation and get back to work.

By August 11, the vote totals for the countywide vote on the name of the new high school were made public. The local paper put out a special issue showing the breakdown by precinct. The name Bradshaw High School had won by 1,400 votes. I found it interesting that, while the name of Bradshaw was the choice of ninety percent in the mostly white areas, Harrisville High School had been the preference of eighty percent in the black precincts. It was black voters that made the difference. I thought that fact was interesting.

While few people said anything else on the subject, I believe most were relieved. If the results had been closer, there might have been demands for a recount or suspicion that something was not done properly, even though everyone of prominence, on both sides, agreed the results were fair. As it was, the fifty-five percent majority was accepted by all. Sam and I wished all the other problems in the world could be solved as easily.

CHAPTER THIRTY-TWO

On Saturday night, August 14, a major pornography bust was made in the barracks of Delta Company of the 55th Infantry. While most commanders would turn a blind eye to individuals collecting pornography for their own purposes, the sale and distribution of such material was a violation of the UCMJ (Uniform Code of Military Justice). In addition, the two individuals arrested had been showing stag movies in the barracks and charging admission. This was another infraction of the sale and distribution regulations.

By Monday morning, all the evidence seized had not yet been catalogued into evidence since the amount was so voluminous. There were seven large cardboard boxes of material to inventory for a possible court-martial. As Sergeant de la Vega was on leave, I was asked to help the PMI personnel process all the material. It was a disgusting job. There were twelve reels of 35-millimeter stag movies and more pictures than I wanted to count. The photographs depicted every imaginable sex act. After a few minutes, I made the decision to simply put the pictures in bundles with a generic description. That way it was not necessary to look at each picture. This saved a lot of time. The description simply said, "Miscellaneous pictures of various individuals and groups in innumerable poses. These include group orgies and couples involved in intercourse as well as sadomasochistic behavior, etc." By noon we had finished counting and locking away the evidence. I felt a need to wash my hands as I finished the task.

About 1400 hours, a captain came over from JAG. It was his assignment to view the evidence and determine if it fit the definition of pornography. I checked out the box containing the 35-millimeter erotica and walked over to the company with him. I directed Specialist Riley to set up the projector in the training room and then left. I ordered Riley to call me when the captain was through viewing the evidence. I would then come and get it and see that it was properly secured again.

After about two hours, I received a call that the viewing was over. As I walked into the orderly room, the captain was leaving. "What do you think, sir?" I asked. "Does it qualify as pornography?"

The captain shrugged and nonchalantly commented, "It would depend on who viewed the material and what their opinion was and possibly a number of other factors."

As he left, I then asked Riley, "Was it pornographic?"

His eyes were a big as saucers as he stated with exuberance, "Yes, sir! They did anything you can imagine. One movie had two couples who traded partners. Unfortunately, they traded partners a second time so the women were one couple and the men were the other. I got real grossed out, though, when those men started doing each other."

I simply took the material back to the evidence room and saw that it was locked up. What happened the next day was something I will never forget.

About 0830 hours, the entire JAG staff, from their colonel on down, arrived at the PMO. The colonel spoke for the delegation. "We've decided, lieutenant, that since two men's careers are on the line, the determination as whether this is pornographic or not must be a group determination."

The explanation was so ludicrous, I wanted to laugh. These individuals wanted to get their kicks this morning. However, I knew better than to laugh in the face of a full-bird colonel. "Yes, sir," I said.

I again checked out the films and hand-carried them over to the orderly room. "Riley!" I exclaimed, "Set up the projector."

"Yes, sir!" He was all smiles as he jumped up from his typewriter and headed for the training room.

It was after 1300 hours, when I had returned from lunch, before the JAG personnel were through viewing the evidence. As I again took possession of the box of films, I asked Riley, "How did it go this time?"

"Great, sir! This time, they watched them all. It was kind of like a stag party, except we didn't have any beer." He paused a second and added, "Of course they were more dignified than my buddies would have been. They spent a lot of time discussing legal definitions and such, but I could tell that they were enjoying the show."

That night, I mentioned the day's shenanigans to Sam. She was not impressed. "If a bunch of lowlifes want to show that trash in a latrine, they violate the law. But, if the legal eagles watch the same stuff to get their jollies, then it's okay? That makes no sense."

I smiled. I had decided this was a good time to facetiously play devil's advocate. Sometimes, Sam would complain that I could be obnoxious and, I suppose, this was one of those times.

"You have to understand, honey, that the legal staff was not charging admission; therefore, there was no violation of the UCMJ. Also, they were just doing their job. They had to make sure the films fit the definition of pornography."

"Get real, Nick! They didn't have to view them all, and you know it. They were just a bunch of dirty old men getting a thrill."

"So, if I had viewed it with them to familiarize myself with the case, you'd call me a dirty old man too?"

Sam folded her arms and smiled. She could tell I was trying to annoy her. "Nick, you are so full of crap it's incredible. Your job is to collect evidence, not to analyze it. Even I know that."

"But, if I don't view the films, how will I know that it is evidence? It could just be somebody's home movies of their vacation."

Sam grabbed my tie and pulled me close. "If I thought for one second that you were serious—husband of mine—I might get angry. We both know that people don't pay to watch boring home movies, and the legal staff didn't have to watch all the films. A couple of minutes are all you need to tell what the content is."

"So, you're telling me that it is okay for me to go and view a few minutes, then?"

"Tell you what, Nick. If you think it's necessary to view that smut, then bring it home and we can both see it."

I figured that I had better quit while I was ahead. I found something else to talk about while I helped Sam feed the twins. The rest of the workweek passed without incident.

On Friday, as I was preparing to leave for the day, I remembered what Sam had said several days before. As a joke, I checked out several of the films that had been seized in the upcoming pornography case from the evidence room. I then obtained the projector from the company. When I arrived at home I gave Sam a card that said "Happy Anniversary" and mentioned to her what I had done. Sam was always bluffing when it came to stuff like this, and I thought she would tell me to take it back to the evidence room.

"I'm not watching that garbage on my anniversary, Nick," she said defiantly. "Tom and Andrea have agreed to watch the twins for a couple of hours, and you're taking me to the officers' club for dinner."

At a time like this a wise man does not argue with his wife. Sam and I celebrated our first anniversary with a nice candlelight dinner at the officers' club and the reels of film were forgotten until the next night, after the babies were put to bed. I then asked Sam, "Shall we see what all of the legal fuss is about?"

"Why not, Nick?" she asked sarcastically. "I can just pop popcorn and we'll have Saturday night at the movies."

"Sounds good to me. I like popcorn. Of course, if you're a prude, I can always return them."

With a smirk, she answered, "Okay, Lieutenant Moultrie, we can watch these scummy movies. But next time, we will do what I want to do."

I hesitated. Doing what Sam wanted to do might be anything from an expensive dinner in a restaurant to a special vacation trip. I might wind up spending a lot of money. I almost considered taking the films back to the PMO, but I didn't.

"Okay, babe. Next weekend, you can decide what we're going to do."

She smiled. "Okay then, we'll watch those stupid movies tonight. Next weekend, we're going to the big city."

"Which one?" I asked.

"I haven't decided yet. I'll let you know when I do."

I set up the screen and the projector. In the close confines of our trailer it was difficult, but I soon had everything ready for a night at the cinema.

I quickly discovered that Riley was right. This stuff was pretty raw. However, I just tried to act indifferent, sit still and pretend that it had no effect on me. As we were watching the third or fourth film, I tried to critique the show in conversation with Sam. "The lighting in these films is terrible," I criticized.

"I don't believe for one minute that you're just seeing the lighting, Nick."

I ignored her statement. "There is no sound, and these things look like they were filmed in somebody's garage," I said.

"Then why are we watching them?" she asked.

"In MP school, they burned some marijuana for us one day so we could testify (if needs be), in court, as to what it smelled like without having used it," I explained. "I think the same principle applies here. Now I can verify that I know what pornography is."

"Uh-huh." She didn't sound convinced by that explanation. While watching a feature named *Club X*, we noticed that the participants looked like they had just gotten out of a concentration camp. "Why are some of these people so skinny, Nick?" she asked.

"They are probably drug addicts who are doing this to get money for their next fix. The ones in the other films who look healthy are just doing it for the money."

"You do realize that every girl in these films is somebody's daughter," she said. "How would you feel if our kids did something like this someday?"

Sam could really put things in perspective. The thought of one of my daughters doing this made my skin crawl. "I think they would be better off dead than to degrade themselves in this way," I told her.

"Then why are we watching this?" she asked again.

I had no answer for her. I just sat there in silence for a while and finally turned off the projector. "I'm sorry, Sam. I really expected you to refuse to watch them. At the same time, I've never seen a stag movie before. I hate to think that I've led something of a sheltered life, but that's the truth. I am embarrassed to say it, but I guess I really wanted to see one."

"Well, thank you for telling the truth. Do you have it out of your system now?"

"Yes, I do, Sam," I admitted.

"Good!" she said with a smile. "The next time you need to see a naked woman, just let me know. I can take my clothes off and show you one." We laughed for a bit and then she added, "I can't understand why people want to see more than one of these things, Nick. They're all the same."

I knew what she meant, but decided to disagree anyway. With a smile, I said, "They were not all the same, Sam. One film had two girls and a guy, one had two guys and a girl, one had a couple surrounded by mirrors, and one had—"

"You know what I mean," she snapped. "There are only so many things men and women can do sexually. If you see one of these movies, you have basically seen them all. It's just the same acts over and over."

"Honey," I teased. "You sure know how to take the fun out of a night of watching stag movies."

"Good!" she exclaimed. As she helped me put the furniture back in place, she added resolutely, "Don't ever bring that stuff into my home again, Nick. I think it shows a terrible disrespect for me as a woman and I'm sorry I ever watched it. There are so many things that I need to remember and can't that I don't need any of my mind cluttered up with any more of that trash."

"Don't worry, babe. I have no intention of ever bringing this stuff home again." As I put the films back into a cardboard box I asked, "Why did you watch them, Sam?"

"You suggested that I might be a prude. That made me a little angry. I'm not a prude, but I do have class and standards. There is a difference between prudishness and decency. A lot of people might not know that, but there is a difference. Besides, I love you. I even love you when you do stupid things like this."

Shortly afterward, as we were getting ready for bed, Sam asked a question that caught me by surprise. "I guess you want to make love tonight?"

"Honey, has there ever been a night when I didn't want to fool around? Why would tonight be any different?"

"Because, tonight I'll be wondering if you are getting excited by me or those movies we watched," she said.

"Those movies had no effect on me, Sam." I should have known better than to lie, since Sam knew better.

"Go get a big shovel, Nick, because it's getting deep in here. The look you had in your eyes while you were watching that junk tells me differently."

"I'm a red-blooded American male, Sam. If watching those shows made me think about us getting together later, what's wrong with that?"

"I always want to know that it's *my* body that you're excited about, Nick, not someone else's. If there is a possibility that you're thinking about someone else while you're making love to me, it ruins everything. I can't enjoy sex then."

"Didn't you feel anything while you were watching those films, honey?"

"Revulsion," she replied.

"Anything else?"

"Disgust, nausea, loathing," she said. "How many more feelings do you want?"

"You made your point," I agreed. "The stuff was awful. However, I won't think about it."

A STATESIDE TOUR OF DUTY

"How can you not think about it, Nick? I know it will be in my mind as long as I live. I don't think I will ever forget it. That is really disagreeable to me."

I decided to jokingly change the subject. "Honey, I will never watch that rot again. If I ever want to look at pornography again, then I will just set the timer on our camera and take naked pictures of us. Then it will only be you that I think about."

"Don't even think about that, Nick. It won't happen."

"Why not, babe? We could develop the pictures at the post hobby shop where they have a dark room and nobody would ever see them but us. We could pose for our own erotica. Then I would only think about you."

"And where would we keep the photos, Nick?"

I knew the question was rhetorical. Still, I looked around. If any burglar broke in and found the hypothetical pictures, we would be facing public humiliation or blackmail. If the kids found them when they got older, that would be a catastrophe. No, the only erotic pictures Sam and I would ever have of each other would remain mental. Only a pathetic individual with a weak mind would really require more of their spouse. I might make jokes, but that was never an actual option for me. Still, I tried to get in the last word. I felt the need to add one more comment. "We could always burn such pictures after we took them," I suggested.

"Stop being obnoxious, Nick. The world's biggest skinflint would waste money on film that would be burned afterward? I don't think so," she laughed.

Now I conceded on all points. "You win, honey. There will never be any more of this garbage in our house. All of our activities will remain G-rated from now on."

Sam giggled. "If you call what we do in our bedroom G-rated, Nick Moultrie, you are more warped than I thought."

"Excuse the hyperbole, honey," I said. "Let's go to bed and if you don't want to do anything, that's okay with me."

"Liar," she giggled again.

"I'm not lying," I said as I turned out the light. I got into bed and folded my arms. "You don't have to do anything if you don't want to."

"You are so cute when you pout," she noted.

"I'm not pouting," I said. "I just want to go to sleep."

"Yeah, right. You better go get that shovel, Nick, before we drown in the BS." Sam then got into bed and cuddled up to me. "I dare you to tell me later that the things we're about to do were G-rated," she said as she kissed me.

As I contemplated the material we had seen, I wondered how many rapes were committed by men whose perception of reality was skewed and distorted as a result of such viewing. In the fourteen months that I had been at Fort McCulloch, I had seen two cases of men arrested for child molestation and several rapes. Perhaps the perpetrators had seen stuff like this and perhaps not. If they had, it could not have helped. The fact that I had viewed it all revealed that I might have feet of clay, but it was a one-time event. I was not going to risk my marriage, or my family, by making it a regular event. However, pornography was not the only problem plaguing our society.

Earlier that day, a soldier had been arrested for possession (and use) of heroin. He had been placed in the detention cell, and by Monday morning he was suffering withdrawal. Since he might become a danger to himself or others, the desk requested that he be transported to the hospital, where he could be placed in a straitjacket and kept under observation. It took four men to handcuff him and get him into the car. One of the PMI personnel had called the subject's girlfriend in the mistaken belief that her presence would help calm him down. It didn't. She only added to the difficulty.

She kept trying to hug him while yelling, "It's okay, baby. I love you, baby. It'll be okay, baby."

He remained oblivious to her presence as he screamed obscenities and writhed in agony. The girlfriend only added extra dead weight while we were getting the guy into the car.

As I observed the turmoil, I occurred to me that it was not necessary to die to go to hell. The tracks on his arm told the tale. This man was already in hell while he was still alive. The whole scenario was terribly sad. A man with a life the starving masses of the world would die for had thrown it all away for the short-lived thrill of a heroin fix. It was possible that he might overcome his addiction but the odds were against it. The doctors at the hospital had told me that most people going through rehab usually just wanted to reduce their habit to where it would take fewer drugs to give them the results they desired. They claimed their goals were otherwise, but invariably they returned to treatment when their addiction got the best of them again. The result for military personnel was usually a dishonorable discharge.

A STATESIDE TOUR OF DUTY

In some ways, the heroin-addicted soldier was little different than the people shown in the films in the evidence closet. He cared for nothing except the substance that he craved. Like the people in the prurient filth, he had lost his self-respect, his dignity and a large part of his humanity. While some people might try to argue otherwise; the people in the stag reels were no different than mating animals. They were displaying the most basic of human conduct in exchange for money or drugs. For humans, some things were meant to remain personal and private.

When work ended on Friday, the 27th, Sam and I left for the weekend. We went to Galveston. I drove as fast as I could but, with two three-month-old babies in the car, the trip was not pleasant. Still, shortly before midnight we found a motel and settled in for the night. The little ones woke us up about 7:00 AM, but we kept the room dark, and after feeding them each a bottle we all went back to sleep. We woke up again shortly before noon. After getting something to eat, I called Stan. He and Kathy met us shortly after 2:00.

They drove us around town, so we could see all the local attractions, but it quickly became apparent that the only sites Sam wanted to see were the malls. "Where we live, we have access to a couple of five-and-dimes, a Montgomery Ward catalogue outlet and a PX," she said.

"So what?" I countered. "Just because a retail business is larger, doesn't make it better. What can you get here that you can't order from Monkey Ward?"

"Ignore him, Sam," Kathy interjected. "Men just don't understand. Stan is the same way."

"If you need something, you can go order it. Going into a place like this just makes you subject to impulse buying and all of the other retail traps that Madison Avenue dreams up," I explained. "Instead of obtaining needs, you wind up purchasing what you want."

"If Nick had his way, we would still be living in caves and cooking dinosaur meat over an open fire," Sam said as she rolled her eyes.

I began to count on my fingers, "No lawns to mow, no houses to maintain, no jobs to go to, no taxes to pay; sounds like we left paradise when we created the modern world," I rebutted. "Besides, when you wanted a nice fur coat for the winter; all I would have to do is go skin an animal. You would always be well dressed—by the standards of the time. And, there would be no more charge cards."

"Hell, yes!" Stan said enthusiastically. "Sign me up for that! It sounds great."

"What are we going to do with these guys, Sam?" Kathy asked.

"Since we love them, I guess we'll have to keep them, Kathy." The girls laughed for a moment at our expense, and then Sam gave her explanation. "When you go shopping, Nick, you need to be able to see the product, try it on and see how well it goes with whatever else you have. You can't do that with a catalogue. It's an overall much better shopping experience."

"I couldn't have said it better myself, Sam," Kathy agreed.

While the girls went from store to store, Stan and I found a coffee shop and made ourselves comfortable. The twins stayed with us and I rocked them back and forth in their stroller as we talked.

"How's it feel to be a dad, Nick?" he asked.

"I really like it. It's a lot more responsibility and pressure being accountable for other people, but I'm up to it. If nothing else, I know there will be another generation who remembers who I am. I just have to teach them to do better than I have. How about you and Kathy? When do you two plan to start a family?"

"We found out last week that Kathy is pregnant," Stan said. "So far, you're the first one I've told."

"Well congratulations, you old son of a gun. That's great!" I said. "Could you have imagined us as family men two or three years ago?"

"Not really. But, we've grown up a lot in the meantime."

We continued to discuss being or becoming family men, and then Stan changed the subject. "Kathy wants to quit her job when the baby is born."

"How do you feel about that?"

"Well," he answered, "with the promotion, I just got at work, we can make it okay. That is, of course, if Kathy will curb her spending. You can't believe how she loves to shop."

"Are you kidding?" I refuted. "I'm expecting Sam to get a personal thank-you letter from the White House for stimulating the economy. She's the queen of the shoppers."

"I guess all women are alike, aren't they Nick?"

"Yes," I agreed. "However, Sam is getting better. She grew up among people who didn't know how to budget, but she's getting it down pretty well now."

"How do you guys control your finances?"

Every month, Sam and I sit down and make a list of our expenses with about ten percent for savings and ten percent for miscellaneous and compare that to the income. If the expenses are larger than our income, then we have to make adjustments to the proposed expenses to get things in line. Since I'm the tight one, I control the checkbook after that."

"No way in hell Kathy would ever go for that."

"Every company has a controller or a chief financial officer," I explained. "A family should be no different. As long as Sam is kept informed and is included in all decisions, she's comfortable with the arrangement. Our budget includes some savings for our old age, which I try never to touch. I tell Sam that we either save some money or we go on welfare after we retire."

"Our problem is that we can both be prone to impulse buying," Stan admitted.

"That will destroy your budget," I said. "Anytime either I or Sam wants to buy something, I ask if we will die if we don't buy it. It has to be essential for us to buy it."

"Does that always work?" he asked.

"Not always," I admitted, "But it helps. As long as we can avoid any major new debts and have more going into savings than we take out—then I figure that's the best I can do."

Meanwhile, the girls were shopping. My wife later informed me that after learning of Kathy's pregnancy, Sam steered her to the maternity section. There weren't many styles Kathy liked, so she decided to wait until she was showing. The shoe department was different. As they were going through the shops carrying Kathy's purchases, Sam noticed that coats were on sale for the upcoming winter. She stopped in her tracks when she noticed one that was particularly appealing to her. It was a beautiful white one made of artificial fur. She began to examine it.

"It's not real fur, Kathy. No animals were killed making it," she said."

"Don't just stand there, Sam. Buy it. It will look great on you," Kathy said.

"I would have to put it on a charge card," she answered while looking at the price tag. "Nick will have a fit."

"If he's like Stan, he'll get over it. Besides," Kathy added, "Just show him a good time in bed tonight and he won't dare say a word."

Sam made a snorting sound as she stifled a laugh. "You do that too, huh?"

"Don't we all? Men are all basically alike. They're easy for us to control," Kathy joked.

Shortly afterward, the girls were entering the coffee shop after their conquest of the mercantile world.

"Look at the coat I bought for winter, honey," said Sam as she held up her new acquisition.

"How much did it cost?" I asked.

"Why is that always the first question men ask?" Kathy asked. No one answered the question.

"I'll tell you the price later," was Sam's answer.

Stan smiled. "If you won't die, you won't buy. I see that works real well."

"Like I said before, Stan—not always," I said ruefully.

"What are you guys talking about?" inquired Sam.

"I'll tell you about it later, honey," I grinned.

Afterwards, the four of us went to a restaurant. Sam and I held our breath, hoping the twins would not pick this time to start fussing and ruin the evening. With a diaper bag full of bottles and several other patrons showing them attention and saying how cute they were, we were successful. To add to the evening, Stan insisted on picking up the check. After a short (but friendly) disagreement, I let him do it.

On Sunday, we took a quick trip to the beach so Sam could see the Gulf of Mexico, and then we made the long trip back home. To me, the return ride home always seems to take longer than the initial journey. I don't know why that's true, but it always seems to be the case for me. It gave Sam and me a chance to do a lot more talking.

"When I got out of the shower last night, honey, the fact that you were waiting for me wearing nothing but that fur coat means that I'm not supposed to mention the price—right?" I asked.

"Something like that," she agreed.

"I just wish you would have talked to me first, before you bought it."

"Nick, winter is coming and I do need a new coat. Right?" she insisted.

"Agreed," I said reluctantly.

"And I don't remember you buying me a present on our anniversary," she added.

"That's true."

"So, just figure you bought it for me for our anniversary," she summed up.

"Very well, Sam. You win. But I'm telling you right now that there are to be no more budget busters between now and Christmas. I'm going to be damned insistent on that."

"Okay," she agreed. "I grew up with people who were always scared to answer the phone because it might be a bill collector. I've learned that the way you handle things is a lot better."

"So, you admit that I can do some things right?"

She put her hand on my shoulder. "Oh, Nick! I might tease you, but only because I know you can handle it. You do a lot of things right."

"Do you respect me, Sam?" I asked.

"Of course, Nick. Why would you ask such a stupid question?"

"You said the other day that I disrespected you as a woman to bring those movies home. It seems that you disrespect me by not sticking to our budget."

"That's ridiculous, Nick! There's a big difference between an occasional disagreement on budget priorities and bringing smut home that makes me feel like less of a human being." She then added, "If I didn't respect you, I wouldn't be married to you."

I smiled and winked at her.

"Kathy and I were talking about friends we know who married jerks. Losers who feel the need to beat their wives to think they're more of a man or ne'er-do-wells who can't hold a job. We both feel like we both did pretty well."

"I guess I can feel better now that I know I'm a keeper," I said with a smile. "I also have to admit that the joke you told about men fluffing the covers after farting in bed was pretty funny."

"I know that you are secure enough to laugh along with a joke rather than feel threatened, Nick. But while we're talking about jokes, Kathy and I decided you men are easy to control. All it takes is a little sex. In her words, 'Behind every great man is a woman rolling her eyes and occasionally spreading her legs for him.'"

"Sam, you make it sound like we're immature or a bunch of animals."

"Well, frankly, I think a lot of men are. Likewise, if you stated that a lot of women have similar faults, I would have to agree with that, too. We're lucky we found each other."

"I agree, honey."

It was past 10:00 PM when we finally got back home and put our fussy little ones in their beds. I barely had time to get a good night's sleep before I had to be back to work on Monday.

After arriving at work, I discovered that the subjects in the pornography case had accepted Article 15's to avoid a court-martial.

They were each reduced in rank by one stripe and required to forfeit $100 in pay.

Upon hearing the news, Sergeant de la Vega set up a fire barrel behind the PMO. Together we carried out the evidence which was no longer needed and started a fire. Cutting the strings that bound the bundles of photographs, we fed the contents into the flames. Finally, the only items left were the reels of film. Several men asked if there was any way they could take them.

"Sorry, boys!" I said. "By regulation evidence is kept, returned to the owners, or destroyed. Since Article 15's can't be appealed, we don't need it. It can't be returned and it's not ours to give away."

Sergeant Dee added with a smile, "You youngsters ought to know that this stuff will rot your brain. Let 'em burn."

"Amen, sarge," I said. "I couldn't have said it better myself." With that, I tossed the films into the fire.

CHAPTER THIRTY-THREE

On September 2, 1971, Sam and I moved from the trailer into post housing. Our apartment was a two-bedroom half of a duplex on Grant Court. The street was a large loop that contained twelve duplexes where company-grade officers lived.

From the housing warehouse we checked out some chests of drawers, a desk and a dining room table with chairs. At a garage sale we obtained some excellent deals on a couch, easy chair, coffee table and two end tables. We then purchased a bed from a local furniture store and we were ready to move in.

As we walked through our new home, Sam was ecstatic. She was so happy to be out of the confines of the cramped house trailer, she could hardly contain herself.

"This is like a real home," she cried. "I love it."

"Even though all of your neighbors will be snobby officers' wives?" I asked.

"I'll survive," she replied. "We need one more thing, though, Nick."

"What's that?"

She opened two folding doors in the hall to reveal the place for laundry hookups. "If you want clean clothes to wear, then you better buy me a washer and a dryer."

"We can go to a laundromat," I speculated.

"It won't take that many times at a laundromat to pay for the washer and dryer, Nick. That's false economy. Besides, I can't tend two babies and lug everything there, too. You will have to help me do the laundry each and every time. Do you know how much time that will waste for both of us?"

"Okay, Sam, let's buy a washer and I'll set up a clothes line in the back yard. We can dry them there. Sunshine is free."

"You want me to hang out clothes like a private's wife, when other officers' wives already look down on me for being friends with enlisted wives? Take a look around, Nick. Do you see any clotheslines behind any of these houses?"

"I thought you didn't care what they thought?" I asked.

"That was before I was surrounded by them, Nick. This way it will look like you don't love me as much as their husbands do." She folded her arms and didn't say anything further.

I could see that further discussion was futile. I cringed at the thought of additional expense, but it should be an outlay of money that wouldn't occur again for many years. After a few more seconds of contemplation, I said, "Okay, Sam, let's go buy them."

"Yes!" She exclaimed with a jump into the air. She gave me a big hug. "I knew you'd see it my way."

"I was afraid that if I made you go to the laundromat, you would cut me off for a long time."

She kissed me. "It always helps to have leverage in any negotiations," she noted with a smile. "Besides, that might have taught you a little discipline and would be good birth control."

I kissed her back. "If you want birth control, baby, just stay on the Pill. We get those at no cost."

"Whatever," she said. With that, she grabbed my hand and practically dragged me out the door. "Let's go buy them," she yelled.

After placing our girls on the back seat, we were off on another adventure in retail purchasing to obtain another budget buster.

We priced appliances at the locations in Harrisville where they were sold as well as the catalogue outlet. I complained about the prices, while Sam had difficulty finding exactly what she wanted. Finally, we drove to San Angelo. As we passed Sears, I said, "Why don't we stop here at Rears and Sawbuck? We have a credit card for them."

"What, more debt?" Sam asked with a smile.

"It's not a debt, honey. It's an investment to ensure that my little princesses have clean diapers and good hygiene," I joked. "Besides, I know good and well that you're itching to use the card. Don't pretend to protest."

As it turned out, appliances were on sale there that week and we got what Sam considered an excellent deal. There was only one problem. They wouldn't be able to deliver until the following Monday. We would have to make at least one trip to the laundromat. Sam got the thrill of

A STATESIDE TOUR OF DUTY

using a charge card and signing the receipt and I got to complain about the expense and we were on our way home.

After one trip to the laundromat, I realized that Sam was right. This had not been an option. Of course, I didn't tell her she was right. I was almost as happy as she was to see those machines delivered.

As we got our apartment the way we wanted it, Sam got to spend more money. There were curtains to buy. Sam also bought pictures for the wall, along with some throw rugs. I began to wish we could have stayed in the trailer.

For the most part, though, our life seemed to be idyllic at times. Even though I hated to spend money, I realized that most of Sam's purchases were necessary. An officer must maintain a certain image and a barren, spartan, empty apartment fails to reflect the proper appearance. I was not happy about that fact, but there was nothing I could do about it. Unfortunately, like all couples, we had our disagreements also.

A couple of weeks after we moved in, we got into an especially intense argument. Like most disputes, it was over some trivial, insignificant subject that we couldn't even remember the next day. Sadly, like many arguments, it also led to a shouting match. As Sam and I let our emotions get the better of us, the volume of our voices rose. Then the babies started crying to add to the confusion. Apparently, something I said was especially disagreeable to Sam. She picked up a case of canned soft drinks she had purchased at the commissary earlier that day and hurled it at me. I felt helpless and confused. In frustration, I lashed out at the wall with my fist and put a large hole in the drywall.

Immediately, I felt like an idiot. Grabbing a piece of the broken drywall, I started to leave.

"Where are you going?" Sam yelled.

"I have to go get something to patch that hole some dumb ass put in the wall," I shouted back.

"At least you know who did it," she screamed. As always, Sam got in the last word.

I drove to a hardware store and bought the supplies to patch the hole, along with some paint that appeared to match that on the piece of drywall.

When I arrived at home, Sam was crying. "What's the matter, honey? Why are you crying?" I asked.

"You scared me when you hit the wall. I've been sitting here thinking about what would happen if you hit me or one of our girls," she sobbed.

I pulled her close and gave her a hug.

"I'll never hit you, Sam. It's a man's job to protect his family, not abuse them. When you threw those cans at me I was so surprised and stunned that I felt helpless and confused. I just lashed out at the wall to release the anger I had, and felt like an imbecile afterward. I know that I can never do this again because I don't want to scare you and I can't afford any more repairs. They would be too hard to explain when we move out."

We continued to hold each other. "I can never use violence against you ,so it's only fair that you be held to the same standard. Neither of us can tolerate the other doing anything like this again." I began to wipe away her tears.

"You're absolutely right," she said. "I'm sorry."

"I'm sorry, too," I agreed. I then whispered into her ear with a snicker, "I thought love meant we never had to say we're sorry."

She playfully swatted my arm and grinned. "Oh, stop it! Maybe that movie line was dumb, but I still like it. I think it was kind of sweet."

"What in the world were we arguing about, anyway, Sam?" I asked.

"I don't remember. Let's just forget the whole thing."

I patched the hole and painted over the repair while Sam sang to the babies and fed them. As is always the case, the paint didn't quite match. That spot on the wall would be a reminder of how we should not act as long as we lived in that apartment. Sam would buy another picture to hang in that location to hide the mismatched paint, but we would always know it was there.

Among the most difficult and dangerous calls police personnel are required to answer are domestic disturbances. More policemen are killed dealing with these situations than any other. As the levels of violence rise between two domestic partners, anything can happen. When police are called by neighbors who are tired of the noise, they wind up between the two parties and usually find the wrath of both turned against them.

In the military, a soldier's career will be adversely affected if his name appears in the military police blotter too many times. In addition, the family gains a terrible reputation among the neighbors. They can become neighborhood pariahs. If the individual is an officer, his career is probably over after the first time the police are dispatched to his home. Sam knew this as well as I. In the future, we would have to be more mature and find other ways to solve our differences. If nothing else, we would have to keep our voices down. Of course, more important than

A STATESIDE TOUR OF DUTY

appearances was the fact we loved each other and did not want to hurt each other.

The most infamous couple at Fort McCulloch for domestic disturbances lived on Covington Street. Sergeant Rafael was a ten-year veteran of the Army and a returnee from Vietnam. Unfortunately, some five years before, during a tour in Korea, he had the misfortune to marry what had to be the meanest woman in the world. At the least provocation, his wife, Sue Ye, would beat him to a pulp. On numerous occasions MP units were called to their address and reported blood on the walls. All of it was his. She was only about half his size, and why he didn't seem to fight back was a mystery to all. Maybe he suspected that if he fought back, she would report him as an abuser and he might wind up in custody. Maybe, like me, he had always been taught not to hit women. Possibly, she had threatened to kill him if he did. Whatever the reason, his life must have been hell.

In retrospect, as I look back at my service at Fort McCulloch, one of the most horrific incidents of my service involved this couple. Those involved talked about it for some time. On that night, the desk received a call from neighbors that pitiful screams were coming from the Rafael residence. When the patrolmen responded, they found him lying on the floor in a pool of his own blood and Sue Ye standing over him wielding a large butcher knife.

"He come home drunk," she screamed. "No stand, no stand. He drunk. No excuse. No excuse."

Sergeant Lightfoot slowly placed his right hand on his .45-caliber pistol. "Drop the knife, ma'am," he stated with authority.

"He drunk. Teach lesson. Teach lesson," the woman screamed.

Once again Lightfoot forcefully stated, "I said drop the knife!"

"I have right," the woman screamed. "He drunk. He drunk." She held the knife up in her right hand toward Lightfoot as she screamed.

Specialist Kelly asked in a calm voice that belied the terror he felt, "Sarge, what do you want me to do?"

"Get your cuffs out, and hold your ground. Don't draw your weapon," replied the sergeant without taking his eyes off the woman. "Count slowly to ten and then distract her."

"Okay, sarge." Kelly then slowly pulled his handcuffs from the pouch on his belt.

Lightfoot took one step forward. "I told you to drop the knife, ma'am!"

She stepped toward Lightfoot. "You take his side. You black like him," she screamed. They were now within each other's reach.

"Ma'am," Kelly screamed as loud as he could.

As Kelly yelled, the startled woman looked in his direction. With lightening quickness Lightfoot reached out with his left hand and grabbed her right wrist with a vice-like grip. She started to swing at him with her left hand, but Lightfoot caught her fist in midair with his right.

"Get the cuffs on her, Kelly!" Lightfoot yelled.

Kelly quickly clamped his handcuffs to her left wrist. Lightfoot forced the knife from her right hand and Kelly rapidly had both of her hands cuffed behind her. He forced her to sit in a chair near the couch.

"Not right. Not right," she screamed at Lightfoot. "You take his side. You black like him."

By this time backup had arrived. Specialists Mabry and Crowe rushed in.

"Good heavens," Mabry exclaimed when he saw the blood.

While the woman continued to scream, Lightfoot directed his men. "Radio for an ambulance," he told Crowe. "Mabry, make sure their kids are okay. Kelly, check with the neighbors and see if they know of anyone who can watch these kids if we take their mother into custody."

The couple's two kids were cowering in a bedroom scared, but unhurt. All the neighbors had the same story. Because they were afraid of Sue Ye, they would not get involved and knew of no one who would take in the couple's kids. After the ambulance took her husband away, Lightfoot told the woman, "Ma'am, we're going to release you and leave. If you attack us, we will punish you. Do you understand?"

"I understand. Will not attack."

"If you harm your children, we will especially punish you," Lightfoot explained.

"Not harm children. They not bad. They not bad," she replied.

"Okay Kelly, take the cuffs off," the sergeant ordered.

As the MPs left, they went straight to the hospital. There, they were surprised to find out that Sergeant Rafael's injuries were not life-threatening. Despite the loss of blood, no internal organs had been damaged, no major arteries had been cut, and the sergeant would probably recover with no loss of use to his limbs. However, it had taken over four hundred stitches to sew up all the wounds.

After a night in the hospital, Rafael was afraid to go home, so he was allowed to stay in the MP barracks for a couple of nights. He refused to press charges against his wife, and counseling was arranged through the post chaplain's office.

The next afternoon, I conducted guard mount for the swing shift. Steve was the duty officer, but since he had a meeting at post headquarters, I filled in for him. After a quick inspection of shift personnel, I again took my place in front of the formation to say a few words. Having read the complete report of the previous incident, I felt what I had to say was apropos.

"Men, I want to compliment you all on some excellent work yesterday. Sergeant Lightfoot, the colonel especially wanted me to thank you for very professional and outstanding police work. Keep up the good work."

"Thank you, sir," replied Lightfoot.

As the men went to their cars to begin patrol, I again sought out Lightfoot. I put my hand on his shoulder and said, "I mean it, sarge. From what I have heard, that was very good work."

"Thanks again, sir," he said. "That woman picked the wrong man to pull a knife on."

"How's that?" I asked.

"My grandpa was a full-blooded Seminole who thought his boys should know how to use a knife. He taught my old man and dad taught me."

"That's right," I noted. "You are from Oklahoma."

"Yes, sir. After Basic training at Fort Polk, a few of us went down to New Orleans, where we got in a crap game in one of the bars. Some of the local Bloods thought they were going to show this hick from the country and his buddies how tough they were, and one made the mistake of pulling a knife. He's now missing three fingers for his trouble. That woman last night was no problem at all."

"Well, I understand the Seminole tribe was so tough that they never signed a treaty with the United States, so you come from rugged stock," I complemented.

"As near as I can figure, sir. I'm one-quarter Seminole, one-eighth white and five-eighths black, so I have a lot to draw from."

"Congratulations, sarge," I said. "That makes you a true American. It's good to work with you." With a smile, I held out my hand and he shook it.

"Thank you, sir. I appreciate that. Well, I have work to do."

He and his partner got into their car to begin patrol, and I returned to my office.

Some months ago, we had set up some training sessions to help the men on line duty deal with domestic disturbances. I had no idea how effective they were, but the PMO leadership figured that they couldn't hurt. When real trouble had occurred, though, what worked best of all was a quick-thinking man with fast hands. Some things you can't teach.

In my office, I chatted with Sergeant Corley as I cleared out the paperwork on my desk.

"Why in the hell would a man stay with a woman who did the things Rafael's wife does to him?" I wondered.

"Search me, sir." Corley replied. "I quit trying to figure people out years ago. Police work will do that to you."

"To stay with someone who beats you up and cuts you up just doesn't make sense," I continued.

"Well, sir. Just look at all the women who stay with men who beat them up. It's the same situation. Maybe he's afraid of losing his kids," Corley speculated.

"If she got custody, she could take them back to Korea, I suppose," I concurred.

"That's right, sir, and I'll tell you one more thing. He's not the only man that happens to. It's more common than people think."

"You're kidding!" I said.

"No, sir," Corley continued. "If a woman gets beat up, everyone feels sorry for her and is willing to help. If a man gets the same treatment, he faces public humiliation. So, men just keep quiet. One thing, though," he continued. "I don't blame that guy for getting drunk. Being married to that bitch would make you want to drink a lot."

As I continued to work, I remembered something I had read while in college. In the early days of his marriage, President Lincoln's wife was known to have violent temper tantrums. She was known to throw hot coffee into his face and storm out of the room at meal time. Lincoln spent his time on the road following circuit judges as a lawyer to avoid his wife much of the time. I pondered that such things happen to the rich and powerful as well as to the ordinary guys. A sad fact of life, I thought.

When I got home at the end of the day, Sam was waiting. "You won't believe what has happened, honey," she said.

"Why? What did happen?"

A STATESIDE TOUR OF DUTY

"Andrea just called. Last night Mr. Donaldson killed his wife and committed suicide. They will have a double funeral on Thursday."

I was stunned. Edward Donaldson and his wife Gail had been our landlords in the trailer court. Their trailer was only a few yards from ours. They never seemed to have any trouble. Why would a man do that? What problems did he have that he had kept hidden so well from others?

"You have got to be kidding," was all I could say.

"I wish I was honey. Everyone in the trailer court is pretty shook up over it."

I gave Sam a hug. "I feel sorry for him, honey. God have mercy on him."

"The girls in the trailer court want to go to the movies tonight to forget about it. They've invited me to go. You don't mind watching the babies, do you?" She waited for my answer.

"No. Go ahead. The kids will be okay with daddy tonight and daddy loves to spend time with his princesses. You spend some time with your friends."

"Thanks, honey." She got back to cooking supper. "You don't have any idea what is playing, do you?"

I smiled. Everyone at work had been talking about *Carnal Knowledge*. It was about two philandering bed-hoppers played by Jack Nicholson and Art Garfunkel. "Yes," I said with a straight face. "It's something called *Carnival Knowledge*."

"That sounds interesting. I think I'll enjoy that," Sam said.

A little after 7:00 PM our former neighbors picked Sam up and they went to the post theater to see what they thought was *Carnival Knowledge*. You would have thought that our babies knew about the joke I had played on their mother, from the way they acted. The little ones cried and fussed the entire time Sam was gone. I tried feeding them, rocking them and singing to them. Nothing worked. I was at my wits' end when Sam returned.

When Sam returned, she walked in with a funny look on her face. She slowly said the supposed name of the movie with emphasis on each syllable.

"*Car-ni-val Knowledge*? Nick, we were the only women in the theater. It was embarrassing."

"Did you enjoy it, honey?"

"I would have crawled under the seats, but some of my friends were already there. You are in big trouble."

I couldn't help laughing while Sam steamed. I could tell she was not appreciative of my humor.

"If it is any consolation, the girls have been crying since you left. I would have gone crazy if you had been gone longer," I said.

"They were just sticking up for Mama. Let that be a lesson to you. We girls stick together."

"Sam, when you ladies got to the theater, didn't you look at the name of the movie?"

She thought for a second. "I just thought that they had misspelled the word on the marquee. I really didn't think much about it," she said with a disconcerting look.

I couldn't help but continue to laugh. "I'm sorry, Sam. I really thought you would turn around when you saw the real title of the movie."

She shook her head. "Some day you will get yours," she said.

She picked up Stacy, who stopped crying immediately. "Mommy is home, girls," she said. Tracy quit crying also, upon hearing her mother's voice.

"I really expected that movie to be about a family involved with a circus or something," Sam said as a final thought.

The next night, Tom Cunningham and Eugene McPherson picked me up, and we went to the movie that our wives had seen the night before.

"I still can't believe they fell for that nonsense about *Carnival Knowledge*," Tom said. "That was funny. How did you think that one up, Nick?"

"I just used it as a play on words to Sam, and she then told your wives and they all sucked it down. It was funny, though," I explained.

"Jane was so embarrassed, I thought she was going to change color from black to red," Gene laughed.

It was nice for us to get a laugh at our wives' expense for once. Heaven knows, it seemed they liked to joke about us. It turned out that the movie wasn't that bad. At least we didn't think so. It was about two jerks who were unable to maintain a monogamous relationship. The losers each spent about twenty years going from one affair to another until by middle age one had a mistress young enough to be his daughter and the other was nearly impotent. Both were miserable. Had they built a relationship with someone they truly loved and not been such philanderers, they probably would have been much happier.

A STATESIDE TOUR OF DUTY

Unfortunately, most movie patrons probably missed the moral and saw only the skin that was displayed.

The next morning, Sam and I paid our respects at the Donaldson funeral. The event was closed-casket, as Donaldson had used a shotgun for the killings. The First Baptist Church of Harrisville was packed, and there were more flowers than I had ever seen. The eulogy was short and most attendees were left to wonder what could have driven Ed Donaldson to do what he had done.

An old Cherokee proverb goes that you should never judge a man until you have walked a mile in his moccasins. Considering the result, I didn't want to walk in Donaldson's moccasins. Whatever feelings he had before the murder-suicide should never be an option. It is a permanent solution to a temporary problem. I have always believed that as long as there is life, there is hope. Couples should grow old together loving and caring for one another. Maybe Sam and I were naive, but we were determined to keep that attitude for life. We knew that each of us was not perfect, but we could accept each other's faults. Unfortunately, there were others who couldn't make such a concession.

The week of October 3, I was duty officer. On that night, the desk sergeant, Staff Sergeant Harris, had the patrol supervisor cover the desk while he went on patrol with his men. A domestic disturbance call came in shortly before 2400 hours. I rode with him and Specialist Jackson to the residence. Sure enough, a buck sergeant named Pewett was using his wife as a punching bag. The wife demanded that we arrest her husband for beating her. Harris and Jackson handcuffed the man and were putting him in the patrol car when she apparently changed her mind.

She came running out with a cast-iron frying pan and hit Harris over the head with it. After screaming a string of obscenities, she yelled, "You pigs leave my husband alone! He's a good man."

"You are under arrest for assault, ma'am," I said.

"No, sir," said Harris. "I'm not pressing charges. She didn't hit me that hard, and I'm not pressing charges."

"She must have hit you harder than I thought, sarge," I said. "Why do you want to let her go?"

"What goes around comes around, sir. If she wants to get the hell beat out of her, then that's her problem." Harris straightened his hat and said, "Turn Pewett loose, Jackson."

Harris said little else on the way back to the station, but I could tell he was madder than hell.

Sometime later, I learned that a few days later the woman again called the desk to complain that her husband was trying to kill her. Harris took the call and had an answer for her.

That answer was, "I'm the man you hit in the head, with that frying pan for trying to arrest your husband, lady. If he does kill you, I'll see that he is prosecuted for your murder." He then hung up the phone.

After a few moments, he had a change of heart. He contacted Unit One and had them drive by the residence and explain to Pewett that future calls could result in his arrest for disturbing the peace, regardless of his wife's desires. He was also informed that his commanding officer would receive a copy of the report and he would be wise to schedule counseling through the chaplain's office. When asked about his decision to change the way he handled the situation he said, "I may have been pissed off, but I still have a job to do." When I was informed of his conduct, I was pleased that he placed professional conduct over personal anger or revenge.

Our neighbors quickly learned that I was an MP officer, and if I had to leave home in uniform after work hours, then something was happening. The wives would come over and try to find out from Sam what was going on. On Saturday night, I got a call from the desk that a bunch of people were in the station complaining of speeding tickets they didn't deserve. I left immediately.

When I got to work, I had each of the four people who were complaining write a statement about what happened. I then gave my usual spiel. "If I call the patrolman in and question him in front of you, he will feel his professionalism challenged. If he gets defensive, I may not be able to discover if a mistake was made, even if there was. I will conduct a full investigation and if any mistakes were made, it's to your benefit. We have to prove you guilty beyond a reasonable doubt. Therefore, if I found out that a mistake was made, we will void the ticket."

Some of the people were less than convinced, but they all left after giving me their statements. When I returned home shortly after eleven, five or six women were outside talking to Sam.

"What happened, honey?" she asked.

With a solemn look on my face I said, "They found a head sitting on a stump in the woods behind our houses."

All the women except Sam began to shriek with horror. Sam remained calm with a smile on her face.

I then said, "The head was singing, 'I ain't got no body.'"

All the women except one then had a look of exasperation on their face, knowing they had been fooled. However, one lady began to cry.

"You mean the poor man was so recently killed that he could still talk?" she sobbed.

Now everybody else busted out laughing. "What's so funny about a murder?" the poor woman cried.

It was a few minutes before we could explain the joke to her. She quickly retreated to her home in embarrassment.

Sam took my hand. "Let's go home, Nick. You've caused enough trouble for tonight," she said.

To the neighbors she said, "Call me tomorrow, girls, and I'll tell you what really happened."

Once we got inside our apartment, I asked one question. "How did you know that I was only telling a joke, Sam?"

"Nick, during the time I have been married to you, I have learned to tell when you are full of shit. Besides, if that had been true, you would have already called me and warned me to lock the door."

"Sam," I said, pretending to be shocked, "you're an officer's wife. I thought you had given up profanity."

"Tonight, Nick, I feel I was due for an exemption from that promise. There was no other way to describe what you did."

With that we both began laughing again. "Even after I told the punch line, she still didn't get it," I said.

"I know," Sam agreed. "I know I shouldn't laugh, but I can't help it."

Some couples go through life miserable and unhappy, others experience love and harmony, and many others are in between. Sam and I were hopeful that we would always be in the second group, experiencing love and harmony. We knew we would always have our difficulties and problems, but we could work through them together.

CHAPTER THIRTY-FOUR

Some things never change. There was a new football season, but Sergeant de la Vega continued his winning ways from the previous season. He didn't win the football pool every week, but it sure seemed like it.

Also, there will always be those people who swear that they don't deserve a speeding ticket. I began my workweek by talking with Gross about his work running VASCAR the previous Saturday night. I had him draw a diagram and describe in detail everything he had done. I listened closely, and then started asking questions.

"When you returned to the clocking location after you had stopped someone and wrote a ticket, did you park in the same exact location?" I asked.

"Yeah, I think so. Why? Does that matter?" he inquired.

"Yes, it does. Depending on a few factors, it can affect your results."

"I didn't know that, sir."

"After you set up to check people's speed from the side of the road, get some reference points. That way, you know exactly where you were and can park in that same spot next time."

He seemed dejected. "Maybe, it's possible that some of those people weren't speeding, sir."

"No sweat, Gross. Just use this as a learning experience. If you train someone else on this equipment, remember to teach them what you just learned. If nothing else, you're a better military policeman as a result."

"Yes, sir." He didn't sound convinced.

Of the eight tickets he had written on Saturday night, only four had complained. Unfortunately, all eight had to be thrown out. I called each person and explained that it was possible that there may have been an error in determining their speed. So, even if they were speeding, we could not prove it beyond the legal requirements. They could throw the tickets away. Each of the four who had complained came into the office during the day. If I was in the office, I told them, "If we made an error, we apologize; if not, you get the benefit of the doubt."

If I was not in, at the time, and they dealt with Sergeant Corley, his approach was a little different. In a gruff voice, he would say, "You were probably speeding; but if you were, we can't legally prove it. Therefore, you may disregard the ticket."

Toward the end of the day, I went over to the orderly room to talk to Steve. As I walked past the supply room, Winters was spewing forth his usual tirade of profanity. The volume of swearwords that man could generate in even the shortest conversation was prolific.

"How's everything going, Steve?" I asked.

"You really want to know?"

"Yeah, lay it on me," I replied.

He held up a single typewritten page. "We have spent the entire day typing this letter," he said. "Our entire staff has, as the total production for the day, this single page."

"How is that possible?" I asked.

"Lynch wanted this letter to post headquarters typed without any erasures or strikeovers of any kind. With all our personnel working at it, someone just finished the entire letter without a single mistake." He looked at the page again. "Our entire work effort for today is represented by this one page."

"Why didn't you just use correction tape?"

"The CO can spot that a mile away. He would just hold the letter up to the light and see the change. He wanted the letter to be perfect." Steve shook his head again. "Oh," he added, "I have another good one for you."

"What's that?"

"Lippman is being transferred to Germany. When I checked the property he is signed for, he was fifty bed sheets short. He brought me a bag of rags and tried to convince me that each rag was a sheet. I told him to bring me fifty sheets or we will have him pay for them."

"Good job. Don't let that crook get away with anything," I said.

"No way," he agreed. He got up and closed the door to his office. "Look, Nick, there's a few things you ought to know. I've applied for an early out. It looks like it's going to be approved."

"An early out? Why? When do you leave?"

"I will ETS January 2. Some of the local schools need teachers. I have received provisional certification to teach. After two years, it can be made permanent, just like I graduated with a teaching certificate. I start teaching ninth and tenth grade at the high school when the second semester starts. I'll get out four months early to do it."

"Wow," I said. "I'll miss you."

"When I'm gone, they are going to bring you over here to replace me."

"No problem," I said. "One office is as good as another around here."

"Well, not really. We get inspected semiannually, in addition to the annual IG inspection. In the past, the semiannual inspections were a joke. That's about to change."

"Why, what's happening?" I asked.

"With the war winding down, the Army is way over on the number of officers they have on active duty. That's why they approved my early out. They just brought in a bunch of prick captains from Fort Sam Houston to conduct the inspections. Word is these guys are tearing everyone a new asshole. You will have to really be on your toes when you get over here. It won't be easy."

I changed the subject. "So, you're going to teach school. What subjects?"

"History, civics, and world geography. I figure one or two days a week for show-and-tell or current events discussion and three days a week to cover the material, and I've got it made. No sweat. I'm actually looking forward to it."

"I'm happy for you. Sounds like you're getting out just in time," I said

"Another thing, Nick. I wanted you to be the first to know. I asked Barbara to marry me."

"And?" I asked.

"She said yes. We get married on December the 30th. I will ETS on my honeymoon. She slept over last night to celebrate."

"Congratulations, buddy, that's great!" I reached over and we grasped hands in a victory-type handshake. "Where was Charlie last night?" I asked as an afterthought.

"He's on leave," he replied. "He and Charlotte get married on December 17th."

"Wow! Sam will be delighted to hear that. We're both very happy for you and Barbara as well as Charlie and Charlotte."

A STATESIDE TOUR OF DUTY

As I continued to congratulate Steve on his upcoming marriage, Winters came into Steve's office to drop off some requisition forms to be signed. Every other word he said had four letters or one syllable. As he left, I got an idea.

"Let's get a pot together and guess how many swearwords Winters says in one day at work. The winner gets the money," I said

Steve began to laugh. "Nick, that is a great idea. I only wish I had thought of it. Of course, Winters can't be aware of what is going on."

"Right! How are we going to do it?" I asked.

He thought for a second. "I do a quarterly inventory of Supply to help get ready for the inspection in January, and stay on top of things. We can have a clerk with Winters all day. The clerk can keep track of the words, and I can rotate the clerks throughout the day so they can't juggle the total in their favor."

"How will you prevent it, Steve?"

"Simple, Nick. Each clerk will start with a new tally sheet so he won't know what the overall total is. You and I will simply total up the sheets at the end of the day."

"Good. We'll start first thing tomorrow. We just can't let Major Disaster know what we're doing," I said.

When I got home, I gave Sam the good news about Steve and Barbara. She was ecstatic. She telephoned Barbara immediately to congratulate her.

"If it wasn't for you and Nick, Sam, I wouldn't be getting married," Barbara explained. "I have you guys to thank."

"How's that, Barb?" Sam asked.

"Sunday night, Steve said that if Nick could be happy in marriage, then he figured that he could also. He then asked me to marry him."

"That's wonderful, Barb. Steve's a great guy. I'm sure that the two of you will be very happy," Sam gushed.

As the girls continued to talk, I turned on the television. The national news was coming on. As usual, there was continuing coverage of the war, even though the American role in it was winding down.

The next day, Steve and I went around to different personnel and explained what we were doing. There were many who wanted to participate. We stressed the need to keep the entire project top secret. If the major or the CO got wind of the endeavor, they would terminate it immediately. By the end of the week we had forty-six men who had entered the pool and given us their guess in a sealed envelope. We wrote down all the swearwords we could think of in order to produce tally sheets. The tally sheet was designed by Specialist Riley and several were reproduced on the Xerox machine. We would be ready first thing Monday morning.

When Winters arrived for work on the 18th of October, Steve and Riley were waiting for him. While officially doing inventory of the supply room, they began the clandestine tally of Winter's impious words. The scoring continued until Winters left for lunch and continued the second he arrived back at work at 1300 hours.

As Steve had planned, a new clerk found an excuse to be within earshot of winters every hour or so. When each clerk finished his duty, he brought his tally sheet to Steve or me. We had each clerk put their name and the time of checking on the sheet. If anyone questioned our honesty, we could show that all the hours of the workday were accounted for.

Finally, at 1705 hours, Steve and I met to total up the words and determine the winner. It was interesting. Winters had cursed Deity in some manner 942 times. He had described some form of intercourse (human, bestial or incestuous) 2,012 times. Illegitimate birth was recorded some 512 times and female canines (or their offspring) were mentioned 604 times. Minor cuss words like the common name for Hades and the curse to send someone there were lumped together and accounted for1, 906 of the words. Excrement or urine was mentioned 981 times. Winters had also described a performer of fellatio (or other miscellaneous sex acts) 52 times. There were also 34 words or combinations, which were listed as "other" or "unable to classify." The total was 7,243 profane words or combinations thereof.

When we opened the envelopes, we had five or six men looking on, each hopeful that he would take home the forty-six dollars. The winning guess, missing by only seven words, was 7,250. None other than Master Sergeant Walter de la Vega submitted it.

"Why in the hell did we even bother to count?" Steve said. "We should have just given him the money."

"At least this way there is no argument that he didn't win it fair and square," I commented. "Let's go home."

A few days later, Lippman transferred out of the unit. Before he did, he turned in fifty bed sheets to the company supply office. The next day, the supply sergeant from Bravo Company of the engineer battalion called. It seems his good friend George Lippman had borrowed fifty sheets from him for an inspection and had promised to return them the next day. He was informed that Lippman had left the post for Bad Kreuznach, Germany. The fifty sheets now belonged to the 290th MP Company. It goes without saying that the engineer supply sergeant was pissed.

With Lippman gone, Sergeant Corley took over the AWOL Apprehension section. As he cleaned out his desk, I bid him farewell. "It's been good working with you, sarge. Good luck in AWOL App," I said.

"Thanks, sir. It's been good working with you, too."

As he left the office, I thought to myself that I had only 209 more days left in the Army and I would be leaving also. Only I would be leaving the entire post, not just the Traffic section. The thought occurred to me that perhaps I should send out some résumés or otherwise look for a job for when I got out. Except for that, I was looking forward to becoming a civilian again.

On the 22nd of October I was told that the commanding general had ordered the formation of an ad hoc committee to do a staff study of on-post parking. Our former provost marshal, Colonel Cox, would oversee the committee. Apparently, this was how they would keep him busy until he retired at the end of November. Other members of the committee were First Sergeant Prince, myself, Sergeant Burk and two specialists from the engineer battalion, Specialist Byrd and Captain Warren of JAG. We were given offices in a building near the hospital.

On Monday, the 26th, the committee met and learned our mission. There would be big changes in the future for Fort McCulloch. The Department of the Army had a ten-year plan to completely revamp and renovate the entire post. Eventually, an entire mechanized infantry division would be stationed here and the communications school would be closed. We were to determine the location and size of the new parking lots for the new buildings. Parking lots had to be centrally located, to allow for the maximum number of troops to be able to go to the largest number of locations. In addition, entrances and egress had to provide for the best traffic flow.

The next four days were spent surveying and measuring different locations and studying maps. Captain Warren never met with us again, but was on call if we needed any legal opinion (which wasn't often) and Colonel Cox sat at his desk in his new office all day. That meant that as the only other officer, I was busy directing the men all day. Twice a day Sergeant Prince and I met with the colonel and kept him informed of our progress. The collection of data progressed rapidly. Actually, I enjoyed the new duties and was out of the office all day. Since I now had an additional office next to Colonel Cox's, I could come back from lunch a few minutes late and no one cared. The colonel gave me the freedom to come and go as I needed. If I got the job done and checked in with him twice daily, he didn't care how flexible my schedule was. If I worked late one day, I could come in later than normal the next to compensate. It was great to be rid of the major for a while.

Sadly, back on the 26th, another problem had occurred for the 290th MP Company. That night, fifteen of our younger MPs were busted while having a marijuana party at one of their residences in the housing area. Our military policemen had the unhappy duty of busting and booking fifteen of their comrades. Colonel Sherman immediately relieved all fifteen from duty. As the men were being questioned, it was discovered that another man, Jamal Ukpong, had known about the party, but did not participate. He wanted no part of the activity, but did not turn in his buddies. Sherman relieved him also for failure to report this violation of the law. This was unfortunate, as Specialist Ukpong was one of our best younger MPs.

The loss of so many men now meant that line duty would be composed of twelve-hour shifts. This was disastrous to company morale. The Traffic section was eliminated and its men reassigned to line duty. In addition, the loss of Ukpong meant there was one less black MP in our company. The 290th MP Company already had a smaller ratio of black personnel as compared to the Army in general, and the problem was now made worse.

The next day Ukpong caught up with me while we were making some notes near the hospital. The post master plan called for a large, new hospital, with a complex of other buildings across the street. I had several ideas to run by the colonel.

"Afternoon, sir, have you got a moment?" Ukpong called out as he saluted.

I returned the salute. "Sure, specialist. What's on your mind?"

"I guess you heard what happened?"

"Yes," I replied. "And it's a shame, because we were getting shorthanded as it was."

"Sir," Ukpong reassured, "I swear to you that I never smoked any dope with those guys."

A STATESIDE TOUR OF DUTY

"I believe you. If I was in charge, you would still be on duty. Unfortunately, the colonel is from the old school and sees toleration of violations as just another crime," I explained.

"Sir, I enjoy police work and would like to get my job back. Is there anything you can do?"

I collected my thoughts for a second. "Actually, there is. Colonel Sherman retires on Sunday. The major won't make any changes on his own, but we should have a new provost marshal within two weeks. When the new PM is assigned, we can go to the major and request that you be reassigned to the 290th. I'm sure I can convince him, and the new colonel will probably accept the recommendation of the major."

Ukpong looked relieved. "Do you really think so, sir?"

"Yes, I do. Good men are hard to find. We'll get you back on."

"Look, sir," the soldier explained. "All of my life, I've been told that you don't narc on your friends. I'm just not a stool pigeon."

"I understand. Pot is a lot more common today than it was just a few years ago. When I was in college, only the scumbags and hippies smoked it. Now you find it everywhere. That's why it's getting harder than ever to find good men for this job." I quickly decided to stop preaching and changed the subject. "Tell me about yourself. What's your background?"

"My grandfather was the Nigerian ambassador to the U.S. My father married an American and became naturalized. Mom was a schoolteacher. I was born in Washington, DC. I joined the Army to get a free college education and a career where I can retire while I'm still young, if I want to."

"Look, specialist," I said, "there is one more thing you have to do."

"What's that, sir?"

"Until we get you reinstated to the MP Company, you can't associate too much with your former buddies. You can remain friendly, but if you're seen in their company or fellowship very much, there is the problem of guilt by association." I hesitated before continuing. "It may get a bit lonely for the next couple of weeks, but it would be to your benefit."

"That will be tough, sir."

"True," I replied. "Don't act aloof or holier than thou. Just have something else to do if they get together."

"Thanks, sir."

"Okay, Ukpong. I'll see you in a week."

"I'll be there, sir. Thanks again." He saluted and I returned it as he walked away.

NEIL MITCHELL

At 1600, the PMO had a going away party for Colonel Sherman. Everyone congregated in the front office for cake and punch. When my turn came to shake hands with the colonel, he was very complimentary.

"Best of luck, Nick. It was nice to have you under my command. I wish you luck in whatever you choose to do in the future."

"Thank you, sir," I replied. "It has been an honor working for you. I sincerely mean that."

"I know you do, Nick. Thanks again," said the colonel.

I spent the remainder of the time talking to Steve, and at 1700 hours I decided to head for home. As I was walking past Susan's desk, I noticed some papers she was typing for Colonel Cox. Apparently, he had dropped them off for her to type if she got a little spare time.

The paperwork was addressed to the Indiana State Christian University. I recognized the name as a notorious diploma mill and examined the forms. The letter on top read as follows:

Dear Registrar:

I need a Bachelor's Degree by January 1st in order to begin work with the Texas State Department of Corrections. Please advise me as to whether the Bachelor of Criminal Justice or the Bachelor of Criminology Degree would be better. Enclosed is a check for $100 to cover the registration fee.

Sincerely,

Franklin R. Cox
Lt. Colonel MPC

The remaining papers were application forms to enroll Colonel Cox in the fictitious university. He needed a degree quickly to obtain a cushy job with the state of Texas. He would pay a few thousand dollars and receive a degree without ever attending a single class. For those of us who had spent four years getting our baccalaureate degree, this was a supreme insult. The state of Texas would look at the thirty-plus years he had spent in the Military Police Corps and overlook the fact that his degree wasn't worth what falls on the bottom of a bird cage. I placed the papers back on Susan's desk and left the building.

A STATESIDE TOUR OF DUTY

In addition to being Colonel Sherman's last day in the military, Sunday was also Halloween. This year I was not the duty officer, so I simply relaxed at home and passed out candy to the kids in costume until 1900, when trick-or-treating was required to be finished. I knew that somebody was having a busy night, but it wasn't me. The babies were learning to crawl, and Sam and I just relaxed at home with them.

The next week was relaxed. I continued to collect data for our staff study. Each afternoon, I would summarize the information to make the writing of the final report that much easier.

On November 8, our new provost marshal was welcomed into the PMO. His name was Lieutenant Colonel John W. Renfro. He was an inspector general and had no military police background. He was guided through the PMO and the company area by the major, who appeared to be in charge. I stood by my desk in the now-defunct Traffic section as he came through.

With Colonel Sherman's departure, we were back to wearing our reservation enforcement badges on our uniforms (the MP armbands had been eliminated, per the major's orders). I noticed that our new provost marshal was wearing one of the badges.

"Colonel, this is Lieutenant Moultrie. He is temporarily assigned to an ad hoc committee by the commanding general. He will become the Company XO in January."

I held out my hand. "How do you do, sir? It is an honor to meet you."

The colonel shook my hand, but from the aloof look on his face and the seeming desire to turn up his nose, I got the impression that he didn't want to. "How do you do, lieutenant?" He started to walk away, and then said, "I understand that you're not a team player."

I was stunned. "I beg your pardon, sir. With all due respect, I consider myself very much to be a team player, sir."

The colonel looked around and then ran his finger across a file cabinet. He held up his finger. "This place needs to be dusted," he said.

"This way, colonel," said the major. "Now I'll introduce you to our Operations personnel."

I stood there in disbelief. We were shorthanded as hell, and with all the things that had to be done, this nut job worried about dusting an office that had not been used in a week. This was not a good sign.

As the major and the colonel left for the orderly room, I went over to Operations. Bingham was standing at the door. "What do you think of our new provost marshal?" I asked.

"I will reserve judgment, sir," he replied. "One thing I will say, though, it is easy to see who is going to be in charge."

"The major?" I asked with a smile.

"Yes, sir. He's leading that guy around by the nose."

I decided to leave for the day. I had seen enough. I went to my other office to work on the staff study.

On Tuesday, I took Ukpong over to the PMO. We went to the major's office. "Excuse me, sir. Do you have a minute?" I asked.

"Yes, lieutenant. What can I do for you?"

"Specialist Ukpong would like very much to be reinstated to police work. Whereas he personally took no part in the criminal offense that has left us shorthanded, and his work has always been superior, I suggested that he plead his case to you and hopefully you will recommend reinstatement to the colonel." I paused to hear the major's reaction.

"Have him come in," said the major.

Ukpong entered the major's office and stood before his desk. "Do you need me to leave while you talk to the specialist, sir?" I asked.

"No, lieutenant. You can stay." He thought for a second and said to the soldier, "You know that you should have reported those men when you had knowledge of wrongdoing?"

"Yes, sir. I was just hoping it would be a one-time thing and they wouldn't do it again. I thought I would give them the benefit of the doubt."

"If something like that ever happened again, what would you do?" asked the major.

"I would report it in a heartbeat, sir. I've learned my lesson," replied the specialist.

"Have you asked Operations about this matter, lieutenant?" The major further inquired.

"Yes, sir. Captain Barker and Sergeant Bingham agree with me."

The major thought for a second. "Very well, I'll talk to the colonel. Unless you hear otherwise, Ukpong, plan on rejoining us next Monday."

Ukpong could hardly restrain himself. He appeared ready to jump and cheer. "Thank you, sir," he said. "Thank you very much."

"Just don't make that mistake again," the major said. "Dismissed."

"Yes, sir."

Ukpong thanked me again as he left the building. He was one happy soldier.

A STATESIDE TOUR OF DUTY

Toward the end of November, I was putting the finishing touches on the staff study. Having to split time between the staff study committee and the PMO was becoming tiresome, and I had put in extra hours to get it completed. There were eight people on the committee, but I was writing the report myself. I put in a quote from each of the other members, just so they could say that they had input, but otherwise the whole thing was my baby. It ran thirty pages in length, with fourteen additional pages of diagrams and pictures. I could have easily completed it using less than half of that amount of paper, but I knew that Headquarters would expect a long document to justify the amount of time spent completing it. A clerk typist was assigned from Headquarters and Headquarters Company to type it up, and we were ready to complete the project.

At 1300 hours on the 24th of November, the committee met for the last time. Each member of the committee had a copy of the staff study to look at while I went through it line by line. By the time had I finished, everyone else looked like they were ready to go to sleep.

When I had finished, the colonel asked, "Is everyone satisfied with this report?"

Everyone said, "Yes, sir," pretty much in unison.

Now the colonel signed the report, and everyone was free to go. I would never have to defend my work. Once Colonel Cox signed off on the staff study, it was no longer my report, it was the colonel's, and heaven help anyone who disagreed with its findings.

I could go home and enjoy Thanksgiving. Like the year before, we had Steve and Barbara over and the day was very enjoyable. Steve continued to warn me about the new inspectors for the semiannual inspection that was scheduled for January. I really didn't want to talk about work on a holiday, so I changed the subject. This was a day for enjoying good food and watching football.

Before our guests left, Steve had one more bit of information. "If Prince hadn't gotten in trouble over the Warren episode, he would still have been in big trouble," he said.

"How's that, Steve?"

"Remember how Prince guided big wigs on hunting trips?" he said with a smile.

"Yeah!"

"Well, on the last one he conducted, he had an antelope wired to a stake." He paused. "The idea was for the hunter to shoot the animal and Prince would retrieve it. Unfortunately, the hunter got excited and beat

Prince to the kill. He then discovered that the prey was a sitting duck that was unable to escape. He reported the incident to post headquarters. Prince was due for an Article 15 and forced retirement anyway."

"You're kidding!"

"No joke, Nick. Prince was willing to do anything to get a few brownie points with the higher-ups."

I could hardly stop laughing. "How did you find that out?"

"Charlie told me. It's common knowledge over at Headquarters."

With that, Steve and Barbara left. I started to relax in front of the television, but noticed Sam seemed very irritated.

"Are you going to help me clean up, Nick?" she asked in a less than congenial manner.

"Well, of course, honey. Why wouldn't I?"

"Earlier, you sat in there on your butt, like the lord of the manor. Thank heaven Barbara pitched in or we would have been eating late," she stated emphatically.

"I did help, Sam," I argued. "You had me peel the potatoes."

"You complained the entire time you were peeling them and that was all you did. If you want to have a big Thanksgiving dinner in the future, Nick, you better pitch in. I am your wife, not your servant."

"Yes, dear."

As Sam and I began to clean up after the meal, it occurred to me that those two simple words—yes, dear—avoided many an argument. If Sam was not in a good mood, all I had to do was to say them and her disposition improved immediately. However, I never mentioned to her that I had noticed that.

The day after Thanksgiving, I was informed that I would have to complete the CBR (chemical, biological and radiological) training that I had been avoiding so long. The class would start December 6 and last two weeks. I cleaned out my desk in the Traffic section and moved over to the company, where I would prepare to become the new XO. The Traffic section became the new break room, and the break room was converted into an arms room.

It had been decided some time before that the MP station provided better security for weapons than the orderly room, where only a CQ was available after work hours. A large metal door had been installed on the room and the weapons had been transferred over.

Saturday night, as Sam was reading the paper, she noticed that another book had recently been published on the Kennedy assassination.

Like most books on the subject, the author debunked the Warren Report and dealt in conspiracy theories. Sam was not impressed. "How could someone believe that important people like Earl Warren and Congressman Ford and the others lied in their report, Nick? It doesn't make any sense."

"A few months ago, I would have agreed with you. Sam. But, now I've learned how these things work," I explained.

She put down her paper. "How is that?" she asked with a puzzled look.

"Let me use the ad hoc committee I just served on as an example, Sam."

"Okay, honey, I'm listening," she said.

"Colonel Cox was in charge of the staff study, but he never collected any data. Hell, he never even read the report. He just depended on the briefings I gave him. But once he signed the report, he was ready to defend it against any criticism, since his name was on it. The Warren Commission worked the same way."

"Are you sure?" She asked.

"Yes. The Warren Commission was made up of busy people who had other things to do and didn't even want to serve on the delegation. They depended on their investigators, who, by the way, were lawyers and not real investigators."

"That sounds dumb," Sam noted.

"Remember, honey, we're dealing with the government here."

"Like I said, Nick—that sounds dumb."

"The lawyers were under intense pressure from LBJ to put out any explanation that might satisfy the American people as to what happened. The investigators slapped it together, and once the commission members signed it, their credibility was on the line. They will defend it until the day they die. I seriously doubt if any of them ever read it. Not all of it anyway."

"Have you ever read it, Nick?" she asked.

"A lot of it, but not all. I tried when I was in high school because one of my teachers claimed we shouldn't criticize it without reading it. The stupid thing is longer than a set of encyclopedias and just as boring. What I did read was a joke. Most researchers have shot it so full of holes that it isn't funny."

"So, we'll probably never find out what really happened and who really killed Kennedy?" she asked.

"That's right, but the same thing happened with Abraham Lincoln. Mary Sarrat was innocent, but to satisfy the public's lust for blood after the Lincoln assassination, the poor woman was convicted in a kangaroo court and hanged along with the real conspirators. Meanwhile, Edwin Stanton, the Secretary of War—whom many suspect was the real mastermind behind the assassination—continued to serve in the president's cabinet."

"Makes it hard to have faith in our government," Sam reflected.

"Well honey, the government is just made up of people. There is nothing special about them. Some are ambitious, some greedy and many are unscrupulous. It's just like everything else in life. The only difference is there is more money involved." I then added an afterthought, "Along with power and other people's lives."

"Too bad there isn't a better way," Sam lamented.

"Well, honey, this is still the only country in the world where people are beating down the door to get in. When you consider how much worse all the other governments are around the world, we still should be proud of our country. The USA may have its problems, but, I still think it's the best there is."

Sam smiled and agreed with me.

CHAPTER THIRTY-FIVE

For two weeks, beginning the 6th of December, I was back in school—sort of.

In the event of warfare, there is the likelihood that the enemy will use chemical, nuclear or biological weapons. Consequently, every military unit has an officer and NCO trained to prepare their men for that possibility. You learn how to spot such casualties and help your men avoid them. You learn how to monitor radioactivity, administer atropine in the case of a nerve gas attack, and so forth.

There were thirty-five men in the class. We had nine officers (two captains and seven lieutenants) and twenty-six NCOs ranging from buck sergeant to first sergeant. The classes started each morning at 0800, took a lunch break from 1200 to 1300 and ended at 1700. Unlike my college days, I didn't miss a class. When we finished on Friday, the 17th, my overall grade for CBR School was the third highest in the class. However, I was disappointed because I had not studied that hard. I had read all the material and completed all the assignments, but the thought occurred that with an hour of additional study at night I might have finished number one. In retrospect, a little additional effort would have taken me from very good to the best in the class. In short, I felt that I had let myself down. I should have worked harder.

That night, we went to Charlie and Charlotte's wedding. It was held in the post chapel, and her dress looked like it probably cost as much as some cars. I have never understood the tendency of women to pay so much for a dress that will be worn only once, but I kept that thought to myself. I knew Sam would defend the tradition, so I remained silent and just agreed with her when she made the comment, "They sure make a beautiful couple."

"According to Charlie, they have not been intimate before the wedding," I whispered to Sam.

"That is so neat, that he could respect her enough to wait until the honeymoon," Sam sighed.

"We waited until the honeymoon, after the second time we got engaged," I noted.

"It's not the same, Nick," she rebutted.

After the ceremony I introduced Sam to Charlie as we went through the reception line. Also it was the first time I got to meet Charlotte. She seemed down to earth and very friendly. It was no wonder Charlie had hit it off with her. I had to agree with Sam that they made a beautiful couple. We wished them well and left.

The next Monday, when I arrived at the orderly room, Captain Lynch asked, "How did you do in CBR School?"

"Not bad, sir," I replied. "I finished third in the class."

He smiled. "Out of how many? Three?"

"No, sir," I answered. "We started the class with thirty-five and thirty-one completed the course."

From his raised eyebrows, I could tell he was impressed. After a few seconds, he commented, "That's pretty good. Nothing wrong with that at all." He turned and went back into his office.

Steve began to fill me in on the reports that I was required to send to Battalion each month. About an hour later, Lynch looked into Steve's office. "Lieutenant!" he said. He then corrected himself by saying, "I guess I should say lieutenants. I need to go to Camp Price. I'll be back later this afternoon."

"No problem, sir," Steve replied. "We'll hold the fort down while you're gone."

As soon as the captain had driven off, Steve said, "To hell with it. Let's go play Ping-Pong."

"It's only 0915," I said, looking at my watch. "Isn't it a little early for that?"

"Are you kidding? The CO spends more than half of his time at Camp Price. I wondered what he did there, so I went up there and asked Jenkins about the workload."

"It's probably the same as whatever he did when Carter was there," I said. "Whatever that was."

"Yeah, Nick. Guess what Jenkins told me about Lynch's trips to Camp Price?"

A STATESIDE TOUR OF DUTY

"Search me," I replied.

"They do an inspection of the barracks, review paperwork for a few minutes and then go to the gym to play handball. If Lynch can spend his workday playing handball, we can damn sure play Ping-Pong."

"Works for me," I said.

We played six games before we got back to work. I won four.

On Tuesday, the 21st, the unit fund which I had overseen for the past year (another duty Steve and Raymond had passed off on me) was audited. I received a rating of excellent. It seemed everything was going my way.

Also on the 21st, the 290th Christmas party was held. It was originally scheduled for the orderly room, but with the weather unseasonably warm, it was held in large tent set up in the empty lot behind the orderly room. Some grills were set up to cook hamburgers and several kegs of beer were purchased. The sergeants planning it also hired two of the strippers who made bring-the-boss nights the bawdy success that they were. Steve and I decided it would be wise for us not to attend. We suspected that Sam and Barbara would not appreciate that.

The party would start at 1700 hours, and when that time came, I headed for home. When the party was being planned, I had told Sam that the families were not invited. She was disappointed, but expected me to put in a brief appearance before coming home.

When I came straight home from work, she was pleased. "So, you refused to go to the party in protest of the fact that wives weren't invited," she guessed.

"No, honey, actually I decided not to go because it will be a drunken assemblage with strippers."

"Strippers! You're kidding."

"No, honey, I'm afraid not. It was something I thought I should not attend."

"Oh!" She said. "Are these strippers or go-go dancers?"

"Sam, they are going to take off every stitch of clothing and give everyone a good look at their private parts. Steve and I decided not to go."

"I'm proud of you two, and I'm sure Barbara is also." She hesitated a second and asked, "How do you know what they do?"

"When I first got here, I was invited to bring-the-boss night at the NCO club. Sam, they were naked as jaybirds and made moves a contortionist would be proud of." As a frown came over Sam's face, I added, "We were not married then, and I haven't attended one of those bring-the-boss nights since."

"No wonder there are so many divorces around here," she said. "I knew strippers got naked in Las Vegas or San Francisco, but I didn't dream they did that here. Isn't this part of the Bible Belt?"

"Yes, it is. I guess it gives the preachers some sin to preach about." I quickly changed the subject. "From what I understand, many of the wives of the other men in the company don't care if their husbands go to those events," I noted.

"I'm sure they care, Nick. They probably don't tell their wives what's going on, or the poor women just know that they're married to scumbags," she countered. "If you went to something like that, I would be terribly disappointed. I would assume you were unhappy with me."

I smiled. "Since I prefer wedded bliss, I avoid parties like that." With a big, toothy grin, I added, "Does that entitle to a bonus tonight? The twins want a little brother."

Sam laughed. "My parents told me to marry a man with character and, instead, I married a man who is a character."

"It's part of my charm, honey."

"If you say so," Sam chuckled as she rolled her eyes and shook her head.

Very early the next morning, Sam and I left on leave. We went to Phoenix to spend Christmas with her family. Since our marriage, she had become closer with her father and, while she wasn't exactly a best friend with her stepmother, they could get along with each other now. I figured this trip would help to continue to improve those relationships. We would return on the 30th for Steve and Barbara's wedding, but I wouldn't sign in until the 31st.

As it turned out ,I discovered why Sam had trouble with her stepmother. She was extremely opinionated (worse than me) and had no tolerance for differing points of view. A couple of nights before we returned to Fort McCulloch, Clara (Sam's stepmother) mentioned that the teenage daughter of a neighbor had become pregnant. With disgust in her voice she opined that not only was premarital sex socially unacceptable but that sex was for procreative purposes only—regardless if the couple was married, or not. I was stunned by what I believed to be a very unreasonable opinion.

"The primary purposes of sex for a married couple are recreation, followed by communication," I said. "Procreation is a distant third on the list. In fact, I feel that procreation is more of a side effect of sex rather than a primary purpose." Sam looked at me and shook her head slightly. She clearly did not want me to react to Clara's statement.

The old gal did not like my opinion at all. Sam found a reason to leave the room. The discussion that followed got somewhat heated. She especially got upset when I admitted that Sam was on the Pill in order for us to do a little family planning.

"Using such birth control is a sin against God," she exclaimed. "The only acceptable birth control is abstinence and self-control."

Knowing Sam would cuss me out for getting into this argument, I said, "I apologize if what I said upset you. I think we need to agree to disagree." I then left the room and joined Sam in the bedroom we were using.

Sam was irritated. "Why didn't you ignore her, Nick?" she said. "Sometimes you need to keep your mouth shut and not share your opinions. She is entitled to her feelings, and we are free to ignore them."

"I'm sorry, Sam. I should have let the old battle-axe say her piece and be quiet. I feel sorry for your father, if that's her attitude." I looked at Sam and added, "Someday when we are through having kids, you aren't going to develop an attitude like that, are you? Our marriage will have problems if you do."

Sam smiled and put her arms around me. "I may not get horny as often as you do, but I love the closeness. I'm sure sex will always be a part of our relationship. In fact, if you promise not to pick any more fights with Clara and keep your mouth shut the rest of the time we're here, I'll give you a little tonight."

I laughed. "Do we dare do that?" I smiled. "She may check the sheets for semen stains after we leave."

"Nick, do you really care what she thinks? She is a religious fanatic. You need to let her opinions go in one ear and out the other."

"You're right, Sam. There will be no more trouble from me while we're here."

I kept my word and we had no more disagreements. Still, Sam's stepmother acted a little cool toward me until our departure.

When we returned to Fort McCulloch, I discovered that Steve and I were very wise in our decision not to attend the party. It seems that Sergeant Blanc had tipped the girls twenty dollars each to embarrass an officer. The CO, unaware of to the conspiracy, got a little too close to the strippers and they jumped on him. This knocked him off balance and he fell to the ground with the two naked girls on top of him.

In any event like this one, all sorts of rumors get started. Even people who were not there begin to tell what they claimed to have seen, and with each telling the stories get wilder and more exaggerated. All sorts of lurid stories of sex acts that were supposedly performed are told. However, all the stories are nonsense. In reality, the entire episode lasted only a couple of seconds, as the captain got up as quickly as possible and left the festivities immediately. The embarrassment from such an episode would be more than anyone should endure. However, the major was investigating whether the CO should be court-martialed for conduct unbecoming of an officer.

While Lynch could be an arrogant and pompous individual, I didn't believe any of the stories. No officer with any pride would do anything except try to get away in that instance. I felt sorry for our commanding officer. If Steve or I had been there, it could have been one of us that got ambushed and publicly humiliated.

The wild tales, about the party, being told by some of the men reminded me of a story I had heard in college. When I had been attending ASU, one of my fraternity buddies was from Tampa, Florida. He told me how two days before his assassination, President Kennedy had visited Tampa. During the trip, the rumor got started that the president's limo had picked up two hitchhikers. There is no way the Secret Service would allow such a thing, but that was the rumor. My friend said that during the next six years, he met at least a dozen guys in Tampa who claimed to be one of those two hitchhikers. Now, I took everything I heard with a huge grain of salt. The adage to not believe anything you heard and only half of what you see was becoming more of a cardinal rule for me all the time.

Upon our return to Fort McCulloch we attended Steve and Barbara's wedding. At the reception, after the wedding, I talked with Steve and we discussed how smart we had been to avoid the party. Otherwise one of us might have been the victim of the prank that had put Lynch in his current quandary. "Lynch may be a jerk, but I know for a fact that none of the stories are true," Steve said.

"I concur with that opinion," I agreed.

"It has been great working with you, Steve." I said.

"I feel the same way about you, Nick. We had to endure working with some real jerks, but it's behind us now."

A STATESIDE TOUR OF DUTY

We wished each other well, and he and Barbara left on their honeymoon.

With Steve on his honeymoon, I had to watch the New Year's Day bowl games by myself. As always, Sam complained and curled up with a good book as I watched the games. It was just as well that Steve was not there, because his Longhorns got thumped for the second year in a row. Penn State showed them how the sport should be played. I was sure that Steve was having a much better time on his honeymoon than watching that game. Later, as Nebraska was running roughshod over Alabama in the Orange Bowl, I turned off the television in disgust. I read some stories to the girls and later played gin rummy with Sam.

When I returned to work at the beginning of the new year, I spent all my time inventorying the company property book. I probably should have started the task sooner, as the CO had backdated my orders as property book officer and I now had ten days to complete the job. It took a few days to track down all the radios and other equipment assigned to the company. The hardest part was comparing the serial numbers and ensuring everything was accounted for. After a thorough inventory of the supply room, and the hand receipts that documented the items that personnel had checked out for their own use, I was confident that everything was accounted for. Steve and Winters had done an excellent job. I signed for everything on the last day available, as per regulations.

The next week saw two more changes in company personnel. Sergeant Winters transferred out and had his place taken by Staff Sergeant Thorn, and First Sergeant Reeves retired. First Sergeant Kenneth Newsome transferred in to take his place.

By the third week of January, the major had concluded his investigation into Captain Lynch's conduct at the Christmas party and determined that there was insufficient evidence of wrongdoing. Given the contradictory and conflicting versions of what happened, the result was not surprising. However, it had given the major something to do for a couple of weeks.

On the 19th of January, the prick captains Steve had warned me about descended on us for the semiannual inspection. Steve had warned me that they were failing units on their inspections, left and right. I should have listened. To hear them tell it, we weren't doing anything right. As they gigged us on one item after another, they made it seem like the entire free world would cease to exist due to us not fully complying with a few obscure and inconsequential regulations.

NEIL MITCHELL

The most irritating part of the inspection for me was of the unit fund. Whereas I had received an "Excellent" from post unit fund auditors just a few weeks previously, these jerks gave me a score of Barely Adequate. They marked me down for things that were not even regulation. While the unit fund passed the inspection, the company did not. When the inspectors were through, we were given thirty days to correct our deficiencies.

Steve had warned me that Lynch was always looking for a scapegoat to blame any problems on, and he was right. Through the grapevine, I quickly learned that Lynch had blamed the failed inspection on me. Never mind that I had just become XO and he had been the commanding officer for months. The buck did not stop with him. Somehow, the fault was all mine.

To add to our other problems, several of the men on line duty had sent letters to their congressmen complaining of the twelve-hour shifts. Lynch had at least five inquiring letters from those legislators on his desk requesting information on the subject. The more pressure Lynch had on him, the more things he demanded that I do. All I heard from him were complaints. It appeared that he felt it was his duty to just sit in his office like a little emperor and delegate everything to me.

Sam wasn't much happier than I was. While the neighbors might call, and try to pump her for good gossip, they usually avoided her for social occasions. This was obviously because she kept having contact with her enlisted friends from the trailer court. There was only one neighbor who stayed friendly to Sam. Tim and Joanne Harrison lived across the street. First Lieutenant Joanne Harrison was an officer herself, and a nurse who worked at the hospital. Her husband (a captain) was the commanding officer of the ordinance detachment. For some reason, Sam and Joanne hit it off and occasionally they went shopping together, since Sam's old friends didn't drop by as often.

It was nice to have each workday end, so I could go home and not have to hear Lynch bitch and complain until the next morning. The weekends were particularly nice. Unfortunately, on Monday I had to return to work.

Lynch asked me to prepare letters for the congressional inquiries, and I presented him with one, which read as follows:

A STATESIDE TOUR OF DUTY

Dear Congressman Finch,

The 290th Military Police Company is currently understaffed by forty-eight men according to our table of organization and equipment.

If you can go to the bathroom and shit me those forty-eight men I am short, I will be forever in your debt and so will Specialist Fourth Class Mabry.

Sincerely,

Robert G. Lynch
Captain, MPC

"Is this a joke, lieutenant?" yelled Lynch.

"Yes, sir! I thought it was apropos, and good for a laugh. Obviously, you disagree."

"Do I look like I'm laughing, lieutenant," he screamed.

I handed him the real letter. "No, sir. Apparently not. Here's the real letter."

He looked at the letter, which read as follows:

Dear Congressman Finch,

In reference to your letter of January 4th, the 290th Military Police Company is currently understaffed (according to our table Of Organization and Equipment) by forty-eight men.

This unfortunate scenario has necessitated the current situation where twelve-hour shifts are required to perform our mission.

We are hopeful that the Department of the Army will correct this predicament quickly, for us to return to the customary eight-hour shifts.

If there is anything you can do to help in this regard, all of our personnel would be very grateful.

Thank you for your time and attention.

Sincerely,

Robert G. Lynch
Captain, MPC

"This is more like it, lieutenant," he said after reading the letter. "If you would concentrate more on doing your job and less on silly bullshit like this phony letter, we would have this unit pass inspection more quickly."

I could not tell him what I was thinking in return. The simple fact was that if Lynch did something besides sit on his ass, brownnose the people at Battalion and play handball at Camp Price, we would pass inspection a lot quicker.

To add to my problems, Sergeant Thorn cleaned out the Supply office and threw away all the hand receipts for equipment that had been checked out from Sergeant Winters. He then complained that a great deal of property was missing. According to his account to Captain Lynch, "Lieutenant Moultrie could not have inventoried the property book, because so much stuff was missing."

This was the last straw. I went to Thorn's office. "I understand you threw out all of the hand receipts that were on file," I complained.

"Yes, sir," was the answer. "I like a clean office and I figured we needed to start fresh."

"Did you bother to have everyone who had something checked out come in and fill out a new one?"

"No, sir."

"Why the hell not? Those hand receipts documented where all of our property was."

"Oh," he said. "Those temporary forms are no good."

"Well, what do you propose to replace them with?"

He shrugged. "I don't know sir. I'll use a property log of something I can keep better control of."

"A property log?" I asked.

"Yes, sir. That way everything is accounted for in one large register."

I was steamed. "I don't give a damn how you keep track from now on. Just find all the property that was documented on the paperwork you threw away. I didn't inventory the property book just to have you give everything away."

Thorn went straight to Lynch and complained that I was harassing him. Shortly afterward Lynch called for me.

"Lieutenant, Sergeant Thorn says you are blaming him for your incompetence," Lynch said.

"Not at all," I said. "I inventoried the property book and he threw away paperwork that showed who had many of the items."

"You didn't inventory the property book," contradicted the CO. "You just took Lieutenant Bronson's word it was there and signed for it."

"I inventoried the entire property book," I reiterated again.

"No, you didn't. I know better," he said again.

To have the little bastard call me a liar to my face made me so mad that I wanted to punch him in the face and smash his teeth in. Maybe that's what he wanted. If I lost my temper and did anything disrespectful, it would be a court-martial offense. That would distract our superiors from his problems. Also, it would be that much easier to blame all his problems on me. I glared at him for a minute then asked, "Will that be all, sir?"

"Yes," he said. "You may go."

I went back to my office and called Lieutenant Jenkins at Camp Price. "Hello Dave," I said when I got him on the phone. "This is Moultrie. I have a question for you."

"Yeah, what is it?"

"Have you had difficulty keeping track of what property you've signed for since Thorn got here?" I asked.

"Man, I guess. He picks stuff up and drops stuff off so much that I don't have a clue what I have. I'm about to go crazy. Why do you ask?"

"He threw away all of my hand receipts that were left from the last Supply sergeant and has the CO convinced that I never inventoried the property book."

"Did you inventory it?"

"Hell, yes, I did," I said.

"Why do you think he's doing this, Nick?"

"My best guess is that he is trying to convince the CO that he is indispensable. If a couple of platoon leaders can't keep track of things and he can, then it makes himself look better," I guessed.

"The next time he comes up here, I'm going to lay down the law," Jenkins said. "This is bullshit."

"Be careful," I said. "I did that ,and he accused me of harassing him to the CO. You might want to be more tactful than I was."

"Thanks for the heads-up, Nick. I appreciate it," he said.

My assessment of the situation was correct. Within a few days, Thorn had accounted for all the property on the company's books. According to Lynch, "Thorn has saved your butt." In actuality, I figured he had kept a copy of those hand receipts so he could track down the items and have the people sign again for whatever they had.

NEIL MITCHELL

By the end of January, we had corrected the deficiencies from the last inspection. Of course, I knew that when the inspection team returned they would have found new regulations to attempt to flunk us over. That would be in June, after my ETS date, so I didn't have to worry about it.

One way I got rid of my frustrations was to play paddleball on Saturdays. This was a sport I had learned in high school and was very good at. Gene McPherson (our old neighbor from the trailer court) also played, and the two of us usually spent two or three hours playing on Saturday morning. Hitting the ball against the wall with the paddle was an excellent way to rid yourself of aggression and irritations. I noticed that some players were starting to buy fancy racquets to use instead of the usual wooden paddles. We played two of those guys that day, but the fancy racquets didn't help them. Gene and I still beat them badly at doubles.

"One day, guys like that will probably want to change the name of this sport to racquetball," I joked to Gene as we dispatched our latest victims.

"They can call it anything they want, as long as I can still win at it, Nick," he replied.

On that day, Sam had our car to go shopping with a friend, so Gene gave me a ride home. Like Sam and me, he and his wife now lived on post. They had a three-bedroom apartment in the enlisted section.

As he gave me a lift home he passed along some scuttlebutt he had heard at post headquarters. "There are people over there who don't like you, Nick. Something about making trouble for the Red Cross."

"I know. But a little over three months, and I'll be gone. After that, it won't matter what they think," I replied.

There was no doubt about it. With Sherman gone, the people I had pissed off at post headquarters were letting my superiors know of their dislike for me, and my bosses were passing it along. When I got home, I was still angry about the situation. I lay down on the couch to cool off while I waited for Sam to return.

It was my number one rule to never bring the job home with me. My home was my refuge as well as my castle. This day, however, the pressure got to me. Sam had bought some things I felt were unnecessary, and we got into an argument. After about an hour of total discord, Sam and I were both tired.

"What happened today to get you into such a foul mood?" she asked.

A STATESIDE TOUR OF DUTY

"Gene told me that the brass over at Headquarters are still pissed off about the Red Cross thing. That's the source of all my problems at work. It's being passed on through the major and Lynch."

"So why take it out on me?" she asked.

"I'm sorry, Sam. I really am. Let's forget the whole thing."

We hugged and I gave her a kiss, but I could tell the rest of the day would not be the same. Unlike other times when we made up, this time Sam seemed distant and a little cold. Sure enough, that night as we got ready for bed, Sam put on her red flannel nightgown.

"Honey, you don't need that tonight," I said.

"Yes, I do, Nick," she countered. "I don't feel like doing anything tonight. Just go to sleep and leave me alone tonight."

I had read a book on selling a few months before. I figured the knowledge might come in handy when I got out of the service. I might have to sell my abilities and myself to an employer or I may have a sales job someday. The book was adamant that you should never take no for an answer. I didn't know if the author meant for it to be used on unhappy wives, but I figured I could try the technique. I decided to give Sam my first sales presentation.

I quickly discovered that the information in the book did not pertain to unwilling wives. Despite my most amorous efforts, Sam was not interested. Nothing I could do would get her into a romantic mood. In fact, she was becoming quite irritated. Then I had what I thought was a great idea.

"What if I paid you, honey? What then?" I asked.

"With what? Monopoly money?" she questioned. "You keep everything in the bank. I know you don't have any money on you."

"I could write you a check," I suggested.

After a second, Sam answered, "From what you've told me, the pros downtown can get up to a hundred dollars for their services. I'm worth as much as they are. Is my cheap husband willing to pay that price?"

I began to think I was a genius. We could have a very passionate interlude and then we could have a laugh together and tear up the check. This would be a great game. "Sure, babe. If I received the same treatment some john gets downtown."

"Actually, Nick, the treatment would be better because it would come from someone who really cares about you and loves you."

I was a genius. We were in negotiations. My plan was working. After coming to agreement as to how much time Sam would be on the clock, I went and got the checkbook. She sat up in bed as I wrote out the check and gave it to her. She examined it for a second, then folded it in half and put in the drawer of the nightstand on her side of the bed.

With a smile, she patted my side of the bed and said, "Welcome to Sam's Cathouse, sir. Lie down right here, and our number one (and only) girl will be right with you."

"I've heard that men are supposed to have their choice of girls in a bordello," I joked.

Sam gave me a disdainful look. "In this one, buddy, it's me or you can do without."

"You win," I said as I turned off the lights, took off my shorts and I lay down on the bed.

Sam got up and slowly disrobed. She then walked to the dresser and picked up a brush and began combing her tresses, as I admired her body in the illumination which came through the blinds from the street lights. At first I assumed she was trying to create more anticipation for me. Then it occurred to me. She was psyching herself out. This was going to be a great night.

It had always amazed me that a great basketball player can score fifty points for a career record one night and not be able to throw a ball into the ocean the next. Life is like that in all things. One night, love-making can be all fireworks and excitement and the next night when you do the very same things, it is a disappointment. If I had been playing basketball this particular night, it would have been a fifty pointer. For me at least. As we lay in bed holding each other more than two hours later, I was convinced that I was a genius.

"Well, honey," I said. "Let's tear up the check and go to sleep."

"What are you talking about? I earned that money." Apparently, we had a difference of opinion.

"It was a joke, honey," I said. "A man doesn't pay his wife for sex."

"He does when she's not in the mood like I was tonight," she argued. "We made a deal, and you're going to stick to it. That money is mine."

"Okay, it's yours," I reasoned. "But we can keep it in the bank, until we really need it for something."

"No way, Nick!" she yelled. "That money is mine to do with as I please. Keep it in the bank, nothing. I'm cashing the check Monday, and I will do what I want to with it."

A STATESIDE TOUR OF DUTY

We argued for a while before Sam had an idea. "Tomorrow I will call Joanne. She can come over and hear both sides of this disagreement and decide who gets to keep the money."

I thought that was a great idea. That would give me time to prepare for the debate. I could prepare some arguments that Clarence Darrow would be proud of. "Okay, honey," I said. "I will abide by her decision."

The next afternoon, Sam called Joanne and asked her to settle our dispute. She came over, and as Sam described what had happened, Joanne busted out laughing. "The next time Tim wants a little when I'm not in the mood, I'll have to remember this," she snickered.

I could see that it was not going well. I should have known better than to agree to a female arbiter. "Seriously, Joanne," I said. "Men don't pay their wives for sex."

"Apparently, you did," she giggled.

"But, Joanne," I argued, "if Sam keeps the money, she's breaking the law. That's prostitution."

Joanne really roared with delight at that one. "Nice try, Nick." She chuckled. "You're not only consenting adults—you're married. There is no law that says a woman can't have sex with her husband and no law prevents him from giving her money." She continued to laugh as she said, "In fact, Tim can pay me anytime he wants to."

"Joanne, if we leave the money in savings it can grow to thousands of dollars by the time we retire. If Sam cashes the check, it will take longer for us to retire," I noted.

"You should have thought of that before you made the deal with Sam, Nick," Joanne said. "It sounds like you have buyer's remorse."

I continued to argue, but Joanne would not consider my logic. My debating points fell upon deaf ears. I could tell that my logic was not as well thought out as I had supposed.

Finally, she held up her hand and said, "Nick, let me ask you one question."

"Okay."

Her question was right to the heart of the matter. "Do you think that what Sam did was worth the money?"

To bolster my arguments, I was about to say no, when I thought better of it. That would be the worst thing I could say. I would be verbally sticking my foot in my mouth. Sam would probably not be in the mood again for a long time, and it would be a lie anyway. So I answered her question honestly. "To tell the truth, Joanne," I said. "Sam was worth every penny." Sam beamed with pride as she gave me a wink and smiled at me.

"You made a deal, Nick," our neighbor said. "You also admit you got your money's worth. The money is hers."

I knew that I was beaten, so I sat down to watch television while the girls went into the kitchen to gloat. As I did, I heard Joanne ask, "If I may ask, what did Nick get for the money?" The women lowered their voices so I didn't understand much after that until Joanne said, "Oh, you *did* show him a good time!"

They continued to laugh at my expense for a few more seconds while they planned to go shopping the next afternoon. As Joanne was leaving I heard her say, "Next time Tim wants me to do something like that maybe I'll have to charge him, too. Tell Nick he may have started something. I never would have thought of that."

"If you need any more ideas, let me know while we're shopping tomorrow," Sam said.

After Joanne left, I said, "Never again am I paying, Sam. Don't even think about it."

She gave me a hug. "Then we can both agree that last night was a one-time event." She kissed me and said, "Even though it was kind of fun, tonight will be on the house."

"If we do it on top of the house, we'll get arrested for indecent exposure," I said.

"Like I've said before," she giggled, "I married a character."

"And you wouldn't have it any other way," I whispered in her ear. For once, I got the last word.

CHAPTER THIRTY-SIX

That Saturday I was playing golf with three others. One member of our foursome mentioned the latest rumor circulating around the post.

"Want to hear a good one, Nick?"

"Sure," I replied. "What have you heard?"

"There is a story making the rounds that some officer pays his wife a thousand dollars for sex."

I laughed. "Uncle Sam doesn't pay any officer enough to do that. I don't believe that for a moment. Besides, no man would ever pay his own wife for sex."

"I know," he conceded. "But you have to admit that somebody has a great imagination to start a rumor like that."

"I think he just has too much time on his hands, if you want the truth."

With that, I teed off and the subject was forgotten.

A few days later, Katone was whining and complaining more than usual as he swept out the orderly room. I decided to talk to him and try to find out what his current problem was. I doubted if I could help, but I could at least try.

"Sit down, sergeant," I said. "What seems to be the problem?"

"Well, sir. I just don't like it here," he explained.

"Is there some place you would rather be?"

"Yes, sir," he said with a smile. "Vietnam."

Now my curiosity was piqued. "What did you like about Vietnam?"

"It was wonderful," he whined. "There were plenty of girls around who you could lay at any time. You could occasionally kill people, if the situation came up." He paused for a second. "Get mad and kill someone around here, and you'll go to jail. Try to get a little sex and the girl yells rape." He almost started crying as he whined, "I hate it here."

What he said stunned me. "Tell me more," I said.

He reached into the pocket of his fatigue shirt for what I thought was a pack of cigarettes. It wasn't. It was a large collection of photographs taken during his three tours in Vietnam. "Let me show you these, sir."

"Okay," I said as he laid out the snapshots on my desk.

"Here is me and some of my buddies on a LRRP," he began. "This picture shows us digging in on a night perimeter." He pointed to another picture. "This is after a firefight. That's four dead gooks we just shot."

Katone was the first man I had ever seen who enjoyed performing a LRRP (pronounced "lerp"). It stood for long-range reconnaissance patrol and required days in the jungle. Likewise, his language and matter-of-fact descriptions made me cringe, but I tried not to show any shock or disgust. That might cause him to withdraw into himself and stop talking. I just sat quietly and let him continue.

"Here's another pile of dead gooks that we killed with a claymore," he continued. "Here are two of my best friends. I sure miss them. I can't seem to make any friends here."

"What did you like about these guys?" I asked.

"They were just like me, sir. We got drunk all the time when we got in from patrol and took turns on some hooch maid. We don't have hooch maids around here. The girls downtown want fifty dollars or more each time. I don't have that kind of money."

Well, Katone," I said. "I think you are going to have to learn to control your urges a little more and learn to live in society. I can set you up with an appointment with the post psychologist over at the hospital if you wish. He might be able to help."

"I'm not crazy, sir," he protested.

"I didn't say you were. Sometimes it just helps to talk with others. It's all confidential. Nobody would have to know."

"No, sir! I ain't going to talk with no shrink." He got up and continued sweeping.

"If you change your mind, let me know," I said.

As the conversation ended, I wondered what would become of Katone. It was just a matter of time before he would be discharged. He had no chance to be promoted, and as soon as he was passed over two more times, the Army was sure to cut him loose. He was lucky that he gotten to serve this long. He would, most likely, eventually wind up in prison or on Skid Row somewhere. It was tragic that the only place he had ever felt normal or needed was in the middle of a combat zone. It was unlikely he could ever adapt to conventional society. I began to feel sorry for him. With his minimal IQ, lack of marketable skills, and lack of desire to change, his future was bleak.

Buffalo Bob was scheduled to be duty officer for the week of January 30. As he wished to be gone on leave that week, he traded with me. I would fill in for him and he would take my next turn on the week of February 20. For some reason, whenever I took someone else's turn as duty officer, I wound up regretting it. It would happen again.

The week literally started out with a bang. On Sunday night, shortly after guard mount, the desk received word of an accident. I accompanied the patrolmen out to investigate the mishap on Highway 142 East and discovered that a soldier driving a Volkswagen had hit a large wild boar (some of the locals called them peccaries). When you hit a hog with a car, they tend to roll and flip the car over. That happened this time. The car was a total loss, but the driver had no noticeable injuries. He was just shook up.

The impact had broken the hog's spine, but he was still alive and thrashing around, trying to get up. "Sir is it okay if I put that poor thing out of its misery?" the patrolman asked.

"Please do. Then we can get it out of the highway."

He pulled back the slide on his pistol to chamber a round. He then fired one shot into the animal's head. As it lay still, the MP and his partner and I pulled the beast off the highway so it would not constitute a danger to other drivers.

"Specialist South," I commented, "That was the first shot I have ever seen fired in the line of duty other than practice."

"Same here, sir," he said. With any luck, it will be my last."

Unfortunately, the late sixties and early seventies had seen the rise of domestic socialist terrorist groups. Members of the Weathermen, Republic of New Africa, May 19th Coalition and others largely filled the FBI's Ten Most Wanted list much of the time. Unbeknownst to us, one of these groups was headed to Fort McCulloch. Later events would tell me all about this group. They called themselves the Biracial American Militant Movement (BAMM). This small group had formed at a Midwest college town only a year before and earned a reputation by firebombing the local college ROTC building and robbing a bank. As the most recently formed member of the bellicose and anarchistic groups the FBI was attempting to monitor, they were determined to make a name for themselves.

They traveled across the country by constantly stealing vehicles. As they did so, they also changed the license plate with another on a nearby car. This way, the police were looking for a vehicle with a different tag number. The driver with the exchanged tag rarely noticed that his license plate had been changed. By the time he did, the group had usually already stolen a different vehicle and exchanged plates again.

By a stroke of luck, the group was spotted in Tucson, but by the time the police closed in, the group had escaped by only a few minutes. How they could evade capture so completely was a mystery at the time. Years later, when the Cold War ended, it was discovered how they did it. They called the Embassy for the Soviet Union in Mexico City and were told where they could find a safe house. They would lie low for a few days, until the authorities were convinced they had left the jurisdiction. In their haste to leave the last location, however, they had left behind maps and information about their future plans.

The maps and other papers had clearly shown that they planned to go to Army bases where helicopters and other aircraft were found, and vandalize them. Large posts like Fort Polk, Fort Bragg and Fort Benning were their targets of choice. Knowing that their plans were now known, these troublemakers apparently switched to plan B. It seems that they began to look for lesser-known targets that might not be expecting trouble. Subsequent events showed that when they discovered Fort McCulloch on the map, they began to make plans.

The week was unusually busy. We had more than our average amount of domestic disturbances, vandalism and even a rape and two robberies. The heavier workload, coupled with the twelve-hour shifts, was taking a toll on the line-duty personnel. Unless a driver was extremely careless or driving in an overly aggressive manner, they usually didn't have to worry about being stopped. Some patrolmen were not even writing tickets.

On Thursday night, I received a call from the message center. There was an urgent (and classified) message I needed to come over and look at. Since it was classified, I needed to do this in person.

"I'm Lieutenant Moultrie from the provost marshal's office. I understand you have a message I need to read," I said as I entered the building.

"Yes, lieutenant, you do have a security clearance?" the specialist asked.

"I have a Secret clearance. It is required, to be commissioned," I explained.

A STATESIDE TOUR OF DUTY

The soldier handed me the message, which had just been printed off and had the word "CONFIDENTIAL" in bold print at the top and bottom of the page. It read as follows:

> The FBI has issued a warning to all military bases that the Biracial American Militant Movement (BAMM) has threatened to blow up helicopters and other aircraft on military bases. All Military and Security Police should remain alert for any civilian individuals who show unusual interest in the location of military aircraft or their airstrips.

I handed the paper back to the specialist. "Thank you," I said. "I will alert my men to be on guard."

I went back to the PMO, where I had the desk sergeant call his men from off the road. I then briefed them on the situation. As I finished, I added, "Men, this is not for public dissemination. Please keep it to yourselves. Fortunately, these terrorists probably don't even know that Fort McCulloch exists. I doubt if we will run into them, but be on guard, because we never know what may happen."

At each guard mount, I briefed the men to be vigilant and mentioned the situation at the colonel's briefing the next morning. Since the message was classified, I did not tell Sam about the circumstances. By regulation, someone can only be told about classified material if they have the requisite security clearance and the need to know. Telling someone without a security clearance, even your wife, is a serious violation of the regulations.

We would later learn that the terrorists were able to drive onto Fort McCulloch with no problems. There were no gates on the back highways, and since the commencement of the twelve-hour shifts, the main gate was not manned at all. Fort McCulloch was now a completely open post. The terrorists had stolen a pickup with a large camper shell on the back. They had taken out the rear window of the cab so they could go from the camper into the cab and back without stopping the vehicle. After the fact, we also learned that the four men, two white and two black, had four M-16s and several large-caliber handguns with considerable ammunition. They also had a metal footlocker, which contained dynamite and blasting caps. After casing the post, they chose Saturday night as their time to strike. Most personnel would be off for the weekend and the airfields were distant from the cantonment area.

They would cut the phone lines and strike quickly. After setting their charges, they would steal another car to escape in. If the two or three guards they expected to encounter gave them any problems, they figured they could kill them quickly.

Sam had bought me a model airplane that was radio-controlled for Christmas, but I had not had many chances to use it yet. Now, with the company's inspection problems solved and my week as duty officer almost over, that would change. I was determined to take Sam and the girls on a picnic the next day and demonstrate what she called my "new toy."

The airplane had a very small two-stroke engine that ran on a mixture of regular gasoline and two-stroke engine oil. Since I didn't need much gas, I took a 28-ounce pop bottle with me to work to obtain what I needed. Sam dropped me off at the PMO shortly before noon to conduct the guard mount and left to do her weekly shopping. I would have a patrol car drop me off at home later.

After I had conducted guard mount, I had one of the patrols take me to the post gas station. I made a funnel out of cardboard and proceeded to fill the pop bottle. This is harder than it sounds. The opening of the gas nozzle is larger than the bottle opening and you must barely pull the handle on the gas nozzle to get gas into the bottle. Even with the funnel, if I applied too much pressure with my grip I wound up with spilt gas. Before I had filled the bottle and inserted a cork, it seemed that I had spilled more gas than I had in the container. The station attendant joked, "Sir, that doesn't look like a container approved by government regulations."

"Nobody will know that but you and me," I replied. "And, I'm not going to give myself a ticket."

"This may be the biggest sale I make all day," he joked again as I paid him the nine cents for my purchase.

Before going home, I remembered some paperwork I had not finished the day before. I figured I had better go and take care of it so Lynch wouldn't have a reason to bitch Monday morning. After finishing, I forgot my bottle of gas in the office.

At 2000 hours, I had Sam take me back to work. I would ride with the patrols and planned to return home after midnight. She would go over to Jane McPherson's house, where some women were playing canasta. Our daughters she left at our home with a teenager that lived nearby, as a baby-sitter. With the kids getting bigger, she now occasionally entrusted them to others.

"Keep the world safe for democracy," she said as she dropped me off.

"Okay, babe, and remember that the officer's wife is supposed to always win," I teased.

"Our games are played honestly, Nick. And, you should know that I don't need to be an officer's wife to win," she said before driving off.

Shortly before 2400 hours, I went back to the office to get my bottle of gas and ordered Ukpong and South to drive me home. As we were driving down Humbard Street, South noticed a pickup running a stop sign about one block up. Ukpong turned on the blue lights and stepped on the gas.

"We'll give him something to help him remember to stop for the next sign," Ukpong said.

The pickup immediately speeded up instead of stopping. South keyed the radio. "Fort McCulloch, this is Unit Two."

"This is Fort McCulloch," the desk acknowledged. "Go ahead, Unit Two."

"Fort McCulloch, we are in pursuit of a blue pickup north on Humbard. Subject has turned right onto Secord. We request immediate assistance and backup."

Before the desk could answer, Unit One came on the air. "This is Unit One, Fort McCulloch, we are on Secord. We will intercept."

"This is Fort McCulloch. Ten-four, Unit One. Did you copy, Unit Two?"

"Ten-four, Fort McCulloch. That is affirmative," South replied, as Ukpong turned our car to block the road behind them.

The subjects had made the mistake of turning onto Secord Drive, which was a narrow street flanked by ditches. As Unit One turned sideways to block the street, the pickup attempted to turn around. The driver got his rear wheels in the ditch. The ditch had a lot of water in it from a rain earlier that afternoon, and the wheels began to spin. The pickup did not have four-wheel drive and the subjects were stuck.

"No sweat, we have them now," said South.

As it turned out, what we had was a tiger by the tail. One of the subjects opened fire with a handgun.

"Holy shit!" yelled South, as the three of us scurried to get behind our vehicle. Suddenly all four subjects were shooting at us as Unit 11 (pronounced "One One") arrived. At least two of the subjects were using M-16s. We had them outnumbered seven to four, but we were hopelessly outgunned. It appeared that we had no chance.

The 1959 song "The Hanging Tree" had a line that said, "To really live, you must almost die." Once you have experienced the terror of dodging bullets, you can appreciate that thought. As we lay on the ground behind our car, I knew that we were all probably dead men unless we acted quickly. Had they rushed us with their automatic weapons, they could have finished us off quickly. We would have had no chance. Fortunately, the terrorists remained in their vehicle and blasted away at us. Then I remembered the bottle of gas that I had placed in the car.

I reached into the vehicle and retrieved the bottle and removed the cork. I quickly took out my handkerchief (all OCS officers are taught to have one available to dust off their shined boots or shoes, when necessary) and twisted it up. I inserted one end into the bottle of gas and removed it. Then, using my ballpoint pen as a ramrod, I inserted the other end into the gas.

"South, give me your lighter," I ordered.

"This is a hell of a time to take up smoking, sir," he said.

"I got a better idea. Give me the damned lighter."

"If it will help, here it is, sir," he said as he tossed it over to me.

I peered around the rear of the car. The subjects had knocked out the windows on the sides of the camper. If I could throw the lit bottle of gas through the window, on my side, and it broke, we had a chance. If I missed the window or if the bottle did not break, then we might soon all meet our maker. I don't think I have ever prayed as hard as I did at that moment.

"Cover me, men. Open fire on them," I yelled as I lit the improvised wick on my Molotov cocktail.

From around the front of the car, South and Ukpong opened fire. The four men in the cars opposite us seemed to take it as a signal and began firing as well. They seemed to draw most of the fire from our antagonists, so I had my chance. I took one last look at my target and hurled the bottle of gasoline. By some miracle, my aim was accurate. The bottle went through the open window and struck something solid and broke. The interior of the camper erupted into an inferno, from which emanated hideously pitiful and painful screams. Suddenly our enemies were more interested in saving their lives than fighting. The driver threw down his handgun and surrendered. Two of the men in the camper were made of sterner stuff. They came out armed. The first stumbled and dropped his rifle. As he attempted to pick it up, at least three MPs shot him. The second man's clothes were on fire and he was shooting wildly. Like his friend, he was quickly cut down, although he would survive his wounds. The fourth man never even made it out of the camper. Later, an autopsy showed he had committed suicide.

With the shooting over, I yelled, "Get your fire extinguishers and put out that fire before it sets off ammunition." I then added as an afterthought, "Also, see to those men."

Every MP vehicle carries a fire extinguisher and first aid kit in the trunk along with some blankets. Quickly, everyone was busy putting out the fire. Someone used a blanket to put out the burning man's clothes. The driver was handcuffed, and the situation was brought under control.

I radioed the desk. "Fort McCulloch, this is Delta Oscar Moultrie."

"This is Fort McCulloch. Go ahead, sir."

"Fort McCulloch, send an ambulance to 200 block of Secord Drive. We have severe injuries and possible fatalities."

"Ten-four, sir. We will comply and dispatch same. What is the situation, sir?"

"Fort McCulloch, the subjects opened up on us with automatic weapons. We have returned fire and have the situation under control. Check the notification chart. The Charlie Oscar and the provost marshal will probably need to be made aware of the circumstances."

"Ten-four, sir. What are the injuries to our personnel?"

"That news, Fort McCulloch, is excellent. We appear to have suffered no casualties. All of our men appear to be Oscar Kilo."

"Ten-four, sir. Fort McCulloch clear."

I now surveyed the hellish scene. The body of the fourth man (or what was left of him) was pulled out of the pickup camper. A blanket was placed over him and the other dead subject. An ambulance arrived and took the badly burned man away. Now I was beginning to breathe easier.

"Sir, you better look at this," Lightfoot yelled.

I walked over to the camper and looked inside. What I saw made me swallow hard. Lightfoot had opened a footlocker to reveal some dynamite and a box of blasting caps.

"The ammo they had was the least of our worries, sir," he said. "We were damned lucky."

"Yes, we were," I replied. "If those blasting caps had gone off, there would be a large crater where we're standing now."

"What do you suppose kept them from detonating, sir?" the sergeant asked.

"Either the good Lord didn't want us yet or, like you said, Lightfoot, we were damned lucky. Take your pick."

"Either way, sir, I'll be saying some prayers tonight for the first time in years," Lightfoot admitted.

"I'll have the desk call Ordinance Detachment to pick up the explosives," I said as I walked back to the car.

We spent the next three hours filling out reports to explain everything that had happened. In addition, I wrote up a flash report to Fifth Army and began a Blue Bell report. Even though I was no longer the Blue Bell reporting officer, I knew it would have to be done.

Lynch and Renfro both arrived at the PMO and began to get the details of the battle. They questioned Lightfoot first. The sergeant had great praise for me as he told of my weapons improvisation with the bottle of gas. Renfro's eyes got large at the mention of the gasoline.

"What were you men doing with a bottle of gasoline, Lightfoot?" he asked.

"Search me, sir," he said. "The lieutenant got it. It sure saved our butts."

The colonel turned on me. "Lieutenant, what were you doing with a bottle of gasoline in one of our squad cars? If it had been ignited from a cigarette or something, the men in the car might have been killed."

"I was taking it home to use in a model airplane, sir. If I didn't have it, we would all be dead now."

"A pop bottle is not a container that is approved by government regulations," the colonel said. "I expect my officers to follow the regulations."

"A lot of good men would be dead if I had not obtained that bottle of gas, sir," I reiterated.

The colonel threw up his arms. "You're missing the point, lieutenant. Just because things work out in your favor does not excuse you for violating regulations. Rules are meant to be obeyed. This is intolerable."

I was stunned. Sure, I violated some minor regulation. So what? The UCMJ and the other government regulations contain so many rules that most people can't get through the day without violating one. Would this dumb-ass colonel feel better if seven of us were lying dead on the road right now? I never dreamed that there could be someone more bureaucratic than the major, but there was. To this former inspector general, the rules were more sacrosanct than people's lives.

A STATESIDE TOUR OF DUTY

"What are you doing now?" asked the colonel.

"I'm preparing a Blue Bell report, sir. Fifth Army will want one right away."

"I will have Captain Barker do that, lieutenant," the colonel snapped as he pounded his fist on the desk. "You are relieved of duty. I only want competent officers filling out my reports. You appear to be incorrigible."

I was stunned. This was incredible. I knew better than to argue with the colonel, however. That might be viewed as insubordination and make matters worse. "Yes, sir," I answered. I put my pen back into my pocket. I then walked out to the main desk area. "Can I get a unit to take me home?" I dejectedly asked the desk sergeant.

"Yes, sir. Right away," he answered.

The patrolmen providing me with the ride were as surprised as I was. They couldn't understand the colonel's reasoning. It was clear that they now had very little regard for the colonel.

I did not criticize the colonel. I just replied that things would work out. In reality, I was not so sure.

When I got home, Sam was waiting up for me. "Where have you been, honey?" she asked. "I've been worried sick."

I explained what had happened and she got angry. "What does that idiot want, Nick? Dead men who follow the rules?"

"I guess so, honey. I'm tired. Let's go to bed." I looked at the clock. It was 0430 hours. It now appeared that I would be ending my Army career in disgrace and probably helping Geoffery maintain the golf course for the next couple of months. I had never been as depressed as I was right then. I felt like crying, but that was something I was determined not to do.

As I lay there I wondered if somehow it was some sort of karma. I might be receiving punishment for being disrespectful to some of my superiors. While I had been careful not to show my disdain to the major and some others to their face, others had heard me give my opinions of them when they were not around. I should have maintained respect for the position they held, irrespective of my personal feelings for the person holding the position. Maybe it was kismet or fate or something like that. I suppose that a good junior officer carries an incompetent superior and makes then look better than they are. I had not done that, and maybe I was paying a price for it. That was a passing thought as I drifted off to sleep.

By 0800 hours, the phone was ringing. The local stations were running constant news bulletins about the incident the night before. All the neighbors wanted to get the details. Sam turned on the television. It seemed that the colonel would have a news conference at 1000 hours. "I haven't had much sleep," I told each caller. "The news people probably know as much as I do. Let me get some shut-eye and I will get back to you."

The tenth or eleventh caller was a local reporter.

"Lieutenant Moultrie," he said. "I understand that you were the officer in charge last night."

"Yes, I was," I admitted. Then it hit me that this might be my one chance to get out of trouble. Hopefully I could use the media as an unknowing ally. I then went into detail about what happened, leaving out the part about the classified message.

"Sounds like you were a hero, lieutenant. You will probably get a medal for this," said the reporter.

"Not likely," I said. "The colonel relieved me of duty for violating regulations."

"He what?"

"I put gas in a non-regulation container. I broke the rules. Colonel Renfro has relieved me of duty. I could be court-martialed."

The reporter was incredulous. "That's the most stupid thing I have ever heard of," he said.

"Well, that is the Army, and Renfro was a former inspector general."

After I hung up the phone, Sam and I didn't answer it any more. We would not be going on a picnic, I would not be able to fly my model airplane, and this was going to be one lousy day.

At 1000, all three television channels were carrying the colonel's news conference. He made a statement about how our vigilant military policeman had done their job and he had the situation under control. He then asked for questions. He pointed to a reporter on the front row.

"Yes, colonel. I'm Steve Brown of KSAN news. It is my understanding that the officer who saved the lives of your men last night has been relieved of duty for having the bottle of gas on hand that saved everyone in the first place. Could you elaborate as to why you would punish him for saving lives?"

"You punished the man that saved everyone's lives? another reporter exclaimed. Yes, colonel, please explain that," said the person next to him.

"What?" asked numerous people in the room simultaneously.

A STATESIDE TOUR OF DUTY

"That's crazy," yelled another.

"Would you prefer that your men were killed?" another yelled.

Everyone seemed to be dumbfounded at the revelation of Mr. Brown. They now jumped to their feet and began to shout questions without being recognized. Now the room was chaos, as the news personnel demanded an explanation.

The colonel fidgeted and looked around.

"You have to understand," he yelled. "Lieutenant Moultrie violated a government regulation."

Another reporter yelled, "So what? He saved other people's lives last night."

Now all the reporters were not waiting for the colonel to recognize them. They were just yelling questions, and the colonel looked like he was about lose control of his anal sphincter muscle along with his news conference.

Suddenly, Buffalo Bob walked up to the podium and yelled for calm so the colonel could answer one person at a time.

"The colonel is eager to answer all of your questions and explain everything," he said. "Please raise your hands and he will answer your questions, one at a time."

The colonel whispered to Captain Barker as he placed his hand over the microphone, "I want to end this right now."

"If you do that, sir, the press will crucify us all, but I do have an idea that should solve the problem," Barker replied.

"Whatever it is, do it," the colonel ordered.

"Ladies and gentlemen of the press, you did not give Colonel Renfro a chance to explain the situation fully. Lieutenant Moultrie being relieved of duty was a technicality and a temporary procedural matter for violating a minor regulation. It is basically a formality. He will be back on duty Monday morning."

As Barker spoke, the colonel, at first, looked stunned. However, as the members of the press calmed down, Renfro apparently realized that Barker's explanation was the only way out. He regained his composure and answered about a dozen more questions, most of them pertaining to me. He was quickly aware that firing me was not an option.

As Sam and I watched the news conference, she said, "It serves the big jerk right. I hope they tear him to pieces."

A few minutes later, the colonel ended his news conference and shortly after that a patrol car pulled up outside. I went out to talk to the patrolman.

"Sir, the colonel needs to see you right now," the patrolman announced.

I dressed in my uniform and returned to the PMO, which right now stood for "pissed me off" (as far as I was concerned). I went straight to the colonel's office. He got right to the point.

"Lieutenant, why did you tell a reporter that I had relieved you of duty?" He demanded to know.

I should have answered the dumb question with, "Because you did." However, I resisted that impulse.

"Sir," I began. "He called and I explained I could not make a statement because I had been relieved of duty. I guess that he assumed the worst," I replied.

The colonel relaxed. "Very well, you are now reinstated. Do not violate any more regulations."

"Yes, sir," I replied. I decided the less said the better from that point on. "Will that be all, sir?" I asked.

"Yes, lieutenant. Dismissed."

I walked out of the PMO and drove home. Only eighty-five days left in the Army, I thought. I could do that standing on my head. I would just keep a low profile and stay out of trouble. There would be no more joking around for me. Everything I did from then on would be deadly serious and I would follow all regulations. No way was I going to give Renfro another chance to get rid of me. I would be polite and tactful at all times when dealing with my superiors, but I could never forgive the unfair treatment I had received. I was determined to keep that last thought to myself and always smile when dealing with them. They would not know that behind the smile was a wish for them all to go to hell.

As the company XO, there was no chance of having to attend the colonel's morning briefing unless Lynch was on leave, or otherwise unavailable, and I would avoid the PMO if at all possible. I would stay in my office and be as invisible as possible. The less the higher brass saw of me, the better.

When I got home, Sam said, "Remember when you asked if I would be nostalgic about leaving here? I don't think I will be. I will be very happy to leave."

"I will too, honey. There will be no argument from me." I didn't have much to say after that.

CHAPTER THIRTY-SEVEN

In the coming days, I tried to forget the shoot-out. Unfortunately, that was not possible. Sam complained that I had changed. I was not as jovial as I had been in the past. "Nick," she said. "If you allow these people to change you, then you're letting them beat you. Don't do it."

"No good deed goes unpunished, honey. I've always heard that and now I know it's true."

"You've always been a little cynical, Nick. However, you know that and usually try to give people the benefit of the doubt to make up for it. That's what I love about you. Don't change."

"Okay, honey, I'll try." Whatever other changes I went through, I was determined to keep my problems at work and not allow my relationship with Sam to suffer.

At work, all my duties were mundane and I was simply counting the days until I would become a civilian again. In Army parlance, I was a short-timer.

At the end of February, forty new men from the MP School at Fort Gordon arrived for duty with the company, and the twelve-hour shifts ended. In addition, the fact that I was close to my ETS date really became evident when my replacement joined the 290th Military Police Company.

Lieutenant Brenton C. Woodbury joined the staff on the 136th anniversary of the Battle of the Alamo, March 6, 1972. He was an ROTC graduate from Grambling University.

The black enlisted men were delighted to have a black officer in the company. Like me before him, he received the designation as the assistant Operations officer and began the task of writing up Blue Bell and Serious Incident reports. About two weeks after he arrived, I noticed that he seemed depressed.

"What's the matter, Brent?" I asked. "You seem down today."

"I really stepped in it, Nick, and my wife is fit to be tied."

"Why, what happened?"

"I didn't vol-indef and my orders for Vietnam are due to arrive any day now."

"Major Wilson at OPO told you that," I said. "Right?"

"He's Lieutenant Colonel Wilson," Woodbury replied with a puzzled look.

"That's because he sold the vol-indef program to so many suckers." I smiled at the stunned look on his face. "He told me that crap, he told Captain Tucker—whom I replaced—that same story. He also told the two previous men who had been sent here the same song and dance. You are here for two years, Brent. You can't get out of here. Lieutenant Bronson tried, and he spent his entire time here also."

He looked relieved. "Are you kidding me?" he asked.

"No, I'm not. You will never see Vietnam unless you go as a tourist," I explained.

"Thanks, Nick," he said. He headed for the nearest phone to tell his wife the good news.

In the coming weeks, I got to turn the mail room over to him; he had to take the CBR training, etc. Next, he became the property book officer. There was one duty he refused to accept. That was income tax officer. When I explained how I learned the job, he simply said, "If someone needs help with his taxes, I'll send them to H&R Block."

Next, he became court liaison officer. Two weeks of sitting with him through Kangaroo Court and the job was his. Right off, there was a big case.

A five-ton dump truck driver from the engineer battalion ran a stop sign right in front of a man riding a motorcycle. The man on the bike tried to turn out of the way, but as the motorcycle turned over on its side, it slid, together with the rider, under the wheels of the truck. This was only the second on-post fatality we had investigated since I had been here. He made sure that all the paperwork was in order and that the investigating officers were in court. For the charges of negligent homicide and running a stop sign, the driver was given a suspended sentence of six months in the penitentiary and fined one hundred dollars.

"You have had your baptism of fire," I told Woodbury. "It gets easier from here on."

On April 1, Sam took me to work. She said she had errands to run. I didn't think much about it. When she picked me up at 1700, she said, "I had a doctor's appointment today, honey."

"No kidding! What for?" I asked.

"I had to have a pregnancy test," she said with a smile.

Every muscle on my body froze. In a month and a half, I would leave the service. I had no job prospects, and we might have another mouth to feed. Now I was scared.

"And?" I asked.

"I am. The baby is due December 1st."

As I leaned back in my seat, Sam asked, "Are you happy, honey?"

"I'm delighted," I said. "I thought you were on the Pill?"

"I forgot to take one or two," she said. "The doctor said it happens all of the time."

I did not feel like talking as Sam continued to chatter away. She was as happy as can be.

"Are you sure you're happy, honey?" she asked. "You don't look happy."

"Yes, I'm happy," I said. "We'll get by somehow."

"Of course, we will, honey. Everything will be just fine," she said.

As we arrived at home, I helped the girls out of the back seat. The twins would turn one year old in a month and they were now walking. They were starting to get into everything and now we would have another one in diapers. I sat down on the floor to play with the girls as I began to contemplate the arrival of their sibling. I was determined not to be depressed.

"Oh!" said Sam. "There was another thing I needed to tell you."

"What is that?" I asked.

"I believe I'm supposed to say 'April fool.' Nick." She began to laugh. "You should have seen the look on your face. It was priceless."

"You little stinker!" I said. "After what you put me through, don't plan on wearing your red flannel nightgown tonight. Also, don't forget to take your pill."

"It's nice to see you laugh again, Nick," she said.

"It feels good, too," I admitted.

The four of us then spent a nice, quiet evening at home.

The two surviving terrorists were charged with attempted murder and resisting arrest, along with numerous weapons violations. Their trial took place in San Angelo and I had to travel back and forth to observe the proceedings and to testify. The man who had been badly burned in the inferno had third-degree burns over fifty percent of his body. He should have been in a hospital, but his lawyer had him brought into court in a wheelchair all wrapped in bandages. It was clearly a ploy to gain sympathy with the jury.

Their New York lawyer looked like a cartoon character. He had jet-black hair that was always in disarray. It appeared that when he got up each day, he gazed into the mirror and decided it was a new hairstyle and did not comb it. He described himself as a civil rights attorney, but I thought he was more of an anarchist or a Marxist revolutionary.

The person openly bragged that he had never criticized a socialist country or defended a police officer. He also claimed that he would defend, pro bono, anybody who killed a cop. The more I listened to him in court, the less I liked him.

To hear him tell it, his innocent clients were out for a leisurely drive when they were attacked by murderous MPs who wanted to burn them alive. The things he said were so humorous that I wanted to laugh aloud. Unfortunately, he was serious and hoped that the four blacks on the jury would hold out for acquittal or a hung jury. All he needed was for one to accept the absurd foolishness that he was presenting.

His big problem was that one of his clients was white. This made a mockery of the race-baiting rhetoric he was spewing forth. I hoped that the jury could see that these men were just criminals and not unfortunate victims fighting the oppressive establishment. The fact that they were from middle-income families and had dropped out of college did not help his case either.

The prosecution picked up points when Sergeant Lightfoot and Specialist Ukpong took the stand. They told of the terror that they had felt when the defendants fired at them with automatic weapons and how they only shot back in self-defense (with pistols). The screwball lawyer was unable to shake their testimony on cross-examination and it was time for me to be a witness.

The U.S. attorney had told me that it was imperative that I keep my cool. Telling what happened was easy. I just retold the facts from a night that was seared in my mind. I thought it would be easy to hold my temper under cross-examination, but as he asked his insulting questions, my blood pressure began to rise. Then I got an idea. I would pretend he was Captain Lynch or Colonel Renfro. At that point, I began to smile. After dealing with those bureaucratic assholes, this guy was a lightweight.

He continued to ask questions like, "Do you have any relatives who are racists?" He had already pointed out that I was from South Carolina.

A STATESIDE TOUR OF DUTY

I shrugged and said, "I probably do, but aren't they entitled to freedom of speech?"

The New York lawyer who looked like he stepped out of a B-grade movie went berserk. "Your honor, instruct this witness to only answer the question," he screamed.

The cross-examination continued. "Isn't it a fact, lieutenant, that you violated the law and had gas in an unauthorized container?"

I smiled again and answered, "I had a pop bottle full of gas. So what? They had a footlocker half full of dynamite." I pointed at the defendants as I said that. The goofball lawyer went berserk again. This was starting to be fun.

The judge admonished me to only answer the questions, but it was easy for me to see that His Honor was growing tired of this clown of a lawyer in the dark suit. While he did warn me, he would not punish me for verbally jousting with the defense attorney. He also was careful to give the guy lots of latitude in his cross-examination to avoid any reasons for an appeal.

I was on the stand for the better part of three days, as the lawyer, who insisted that his clients call him Bill, asked the inanest questions. The longer I was there, the easier it got. It was either this or my regular job. My remuneration was the same either way. Finally, at 1545 hours on the third day, he finished his interrogation.

"I have no further questions of this disgusting governmental hit man!" he yelled as he sat down. He had given up. I had won.

The U.S. attorney then skillfully asked a few questions in redirection to clarify a few points, and my part in the trial was over. I had a big, toothy grin on my face as I passed by the defense table. The defense team only scowled back.

The defense only took two days. Mister Lawyer did not allow his clients to testify. He knew they would be slaughtered on cross-examination. His whole case hung on discrediting us military policemen and he had been unable to do that. He had several character witnesses speak for the defendants. A former Scout leader, a former clergyman, and two college professors all told how the accused men had been as innocent as newborn lambs when they had known them.

On-cross examination, the U.S. attorney simply asked each man how long it had been since he had lost contact with the individual he was praising. The times ranged from three to ten years, plenty of time for these men to change. The prosecution also entered into evidence papers written by the accused men. These had been found in either Tucson or the pickup cab and showed their current opinions. The character witnesses were forced to admit that the defendants' mindset had changed since they had known them.

Finally, as the defense rested, it was time for the jury to take over. The deliberations went on for twelve hours over two days. Then came the suspense of waiting for the verdict to be read. The defendants were found guilty on all counts.

As the reporters met with jurors, it was learned that the only point of contention in the jury room was a technical point on one of the lesser charges. The jury foreman, who was black, turned out to be a veteran of the World War II Battle of the Bulge.

"I didn't fight Hitler just to let these friends of Brezhnev take over," he told the press.

The jury foreman, like Steve Bronson, Colonel Sherman, and so many others I had met, was probably someone his peers and protégés were proud to serve alongside. The good men I had dealt with more than made up for having to deal with the likes of Major Receiver or Colonel Renfro. No matter where one goes in life, they must deal with people they would rather avoid, as well as those they are pleased to know. My time in the Army was no different from any other occupation. It is best that we remember those who make life worthwhile and forget those who do not.

My final weeks were total boredom. The new first sergeant, Newsome, was a bigger hypochondriac than the major's wife was. He seemed to spend most of the day talking about his excrement. What color it was depended upon what ailment he had, according to him. When he started talking, I usually decided to be elsewhere. In my opinion, you go, you flush, and you do not look at it or check it out.

One morning, the clerks were talking about how easy it was to get Newsome to feel ill. I did not believe them until one decided to show me. Newsome walked into the orderly room as spry as a new recruit.

"Top of the morning, everybody," he said. He was clearly feeling well.

Riley walked over and kind of stared at him for a second.

"Excuse me, Top," he said. Then turning away, he added, "It must have been the light."

"What, what?" said Newsome.

"I thought you looked a little pale around the ears," said Riley. "But, it could be my imagination."

A STATESIDE TOUR OF DUTY

"To tell you the truth, I was feeling a little odd a while ago," Newsome said.

"I'll bet it's one of those twenty-four hour bugs that hits all of a sudden," said Riley.

"I don't feel so good," the first sergeant said.

"Yeah, sarge. You're really starting to look bad," said the clerk.

"Tell the CO I had to go to on sick call," said Top, and he staggered out of the door.

It was unbelievable. A man fit as a fiddle was deathly ill in a few seconds through the power of suggestion.

"Do you believe it now, sir?" Riley asked. "He's the biggest hypochondriac I've ever seen."

I had to agree.

When he was not talking about his health, Newsome was talking about his daughter. A senior at Bradshaw High School, she had run away from home. The thought that he did not know where she was in the world made him melancholy and added to his health problems.

It was common knowledge among the men where she was. She was shacked up with Sergeant Dimick. I had agonized over whether to tell him or not. Finally, I decided not to get involved in his personal problems. Hopefully, his daughter would eventually return home and they would reconcile. I kept quiet on the subject, and prepared to ETS.

About three weeks before my ETS date to leave the Army, a young man came to see me. He was a young soldier from one of the infantry companies.

"Sir," he began. "I understand that you know more about the traffic laws than anyone else around here."

"That's probably true," I admitted. "What can I do for you?"

"Two weeks ago, a woman ran a stop sign in town and totaled out my car. I only have liability insurance on my vehicle and the woman had no insurance of any kind. I went to a lawyer and he told me there was nothing he could do since the woman is on welfare."

"Soldier, the only thing you can do is to contact the state driver's license division and have them revoke her driver's license. Where she was driving without insurance and caused an accident, they will do that."

"That's all?" he asked. "Sir, she was driving a Cadillac!"

"If she has no assets other than the car, you are out of luck. That lawyer told the truth," I replied. "You can't garnishee a welfare check. But, if I were you, I would get her license revoked."

"Yes, sir," the man said sadly.

As he walked away, I wished I had better news for him. Unfortunately, some freeloaders lived off the fat of the land, letting others provide for them while buying fancy cars with their welfare checks. Those people were immune to lawsuits and could destroy the property of others with impunity. The only recourse anyone had was to inconvenience him or her by having his or her driver's license taken away.

Lawyers always make a big show of wanting people to be compensated for their troubles, but in reality the only ones fully compensated are usually the lawyers themselves. If there are no deep pockets to go after, they usually do not even try to help. I am sure there are exceptions, but my overall opinion of trial lawyers is mostly negative.

We spent the last ten days clearing quarters and checking out of the post. I had a list of places to go like the one I received when I had arrived. That was the easy part. We had to clean our apartment so that a white-glove inspector could not find a speck of dust anywhere in the place. In addition, the stove had to be disassembled and cleaned to the point where the various parts shined. We completed the task on the 21st and got a room in the post guest house. The only things the inspector found wrong were some streaks in the waxed floor and the spot of mismatched paint on the wall. Neither Sam nor I could remember what had caused it—at least that is what we told him.

The final evening was spent saying good-bye to our friends and neighbors. There were more than a few tears as Sam hugged the friends she had made over the past year and a half and told them to keep in touch. Finally, we returned to our room at the guest house for our last night's sleep in the military.

As we prepared for sleep, Sam asked me, "Honey, why do you always tell people that I'm the one who keeps you civilized?"

"It seems like a good humorous comment to start the conversation with. Besides, how do you know it's not true?"

"Oh Nick," She said. "Get real; you are as nice as they come. That's why I married you."

"So were the first Christian missionaries to New Guinea," I replied.

"Uh-oh," Sam said with a smile, "I hear another long story coming on."

"Do I ever have any other kind? Aren't you curious how that applies?" I waited for her answer.

"Okay, Nick," she said with a smile. "What do some missionaries in the Third World have to do with us?"

A STATESIDE TOUR OF DUTY

"Well, honey," I began. "Traditionally people in primitive places like New Guinea never wore any clothes, due to the hot climate. They ran around stark naked at all times."

"You can't do that here, honey. It's against the law," Sam said with a smile.

"Bear with me sweetie. Let me finish. You see, when the first Christian missionaries went to countries like that in the early nineteenth century, their clothes were very heavy and hot. They often quickly stopped wearing their coat and tie. Soon they quit wearing other items of their apparel, and many eventually began to live like the natives. To counter this trend, the denominations that sent them began to send married couples only. With their wives present, these men usually kept the standards of the Western world and continued to attempt to convert the indigenous people to Christianity. They were less likely to go native."

"So I prevent you from running around naked?" Sam asked with a laugh.

"Honey," I replied. "You convinced me to quit looking at *Playboy* and *Penthouse*, I don't dare tell off-color jokes in your presence and my social skills seem to improve when you are near. In reality, I do think you keep me civilized to some degree. While I make the comment as a bit of humor, I think there is some truth to it."

"Thank you, Nick. I'll take that as a compliment."

"You are quite welcome," I said as I kissed her,

I had come to Fort McCulloch as a twenty-two-year-old kid with a couple of suitcases. I was leaving as a twenty-four-year-old man with a wife and family. In retrospect, I had originally regarded Sam mostly as a sex object and someone to keep me from being lonely. Now, I recognized her as my equal and as an indispensable partner. She would help me raise the kids and would be the one with whom I would spend the rest of my life. What I had learned between July 1970 and May 1972, they do not teach in school. I do not know of very many places in the world where one can mature as quickly as I had in the past twenty-two months.

On the morning of May 22, 1972, I went to Finance and was paid for the last time. In addition to pay and allowances prorated for twenty-two days, I had accrued sixty days of unused leave. This gave me an additional two months of pay and allowances. The additional money for the unused leave amounted to just under two thousand dollars. We would be leaving the Army completely out of debt and with considerable savings for the future.

Uncle Sam had paid to move our household goods back to Phoenix, so once the suitcases were in the car, we were ready to go. We put some toys on the back seat to keep the twins occupied and, after one last look around to ensure nothing was overlooked, we proceeded. We drove out the main gate for the last time at 11:30 in the morning. While leaving, our eyes, thoughts, and plans were straight ahead contemplating the future. At Fort McCulloch, I had given the bureaucracy as much trouble as it had given me. I had not allowed myself to become corrupted by people or events around me.

In growing from a kid out of school into a man of experience, I had lived, learned, and survived. Now, my stateside tour of duty was completed. As Sam and I departed out of the main gate that morning, we did not look back.

EPILOGUE

Steve and Barbara Bronson live today in a suburb of Dallas, Texas. Steve retired as the principal of a large Dallas high school and Barbara served several terms on the local school board. She was recently elected to the local city council. They have two children.

Charlie and Charlotte Connerly now live in Omaha, Nebraska. Charlie retired from IBM in 2011 and enjoys fishing, while Charlotte owns (and runs) a boutique. They have three children.

Major Receiver died of Alzheimer's disease in 1997. His wife died soon afterward.

Colonel Cox was hired by the Texas Department of Corrections. He died at his desk from a stroke in 1988. His wife's whereabouts are unknown. She is believed to be living in France.

Colonel Sherman went fishing and enjoyed retirement. He took part in lobbying for a World War II memorial. He died two weeks before it was dedicated.

Colonel Renfro died in a traffic accident in Florida in 2002, killed by a drunk driver. I never liked the man, but no one deserves that fate.

Byron and Kathy Raymond now live near Boston, Massachusetts, where Byron is a successful building contractor. Kathy is his office manager. They never had any children.

Captain Lynch retired from the Army as a lieutenant colonel in 1994. He and his wife live near St. Louis, Missouri. They have two children. Sam thought his wife was one of the nicest people she had met at Fort McCulloch so, hopefully, the children are nothing like their father.

In May of 1975 Nick graduated from law school with a JD in corporate law. Nick and Sam Moultrie continued to reside in Phoenix, Arizona, where Nick retired from a law firm in 2012. Sam participated in extensive volunteer charity work and passed away shortly after her seventieth birthday, in 2017. They had two sons after leaving the service. Robert Bruce Moultrie and William Wallace Moultrie have both served as officers in the U.S. Army (they never did name a son Norris James Moultrie, Jr.). The youngest son, William, was wounded in action in Iraq in 2003.

Of the twin daughters, Tracy now works for an insurance company and Stacy has a home-based business.

Nick and Sam have sixteen grandchildren and three great-grandchildren. For a total of forty-six years they remained happily married, retained their sense of humor, and enjoyed life together. While all people deserve such a reward in life, sadly many fail to achieve it.

ECHOES OF VALOR:
Navigating Duty and Growth in Neil Mitchell's 'A Stateside Tour of Duty'

In Neil Mitchell's captivating novel, *A Stateside Tour of Duty*, readers are transported into the heart of American military life through the eyes of Norris James Moultrie, affectionately known as Nick. This compelling narrative, set against the backdrop of the Vietnam War era, explores themes of duty, patriotism, and personal growth. Mitchell masterfully crafts a story that is not just about the military experience but also delves into the complexity of human emotions and relationships.

Nick's journey from receiving his draft notice to navigating the intricacies of military service in the United States offers an authentic and nuanced portrayal of the challenges faced by those who serve. Through vivid descriptions and engaging dialogue, Mitchell provides a window into the day-to-day life of servicemen, from the camaraderie and conflicts to the mundane and the profound.

Mitchell's background, with its rich tapestry of experiences, from his father's military service to his own time in the army, infuses the narrative with authenticity and depth. His ability to draw from personal history and extensive knowledge of military life adds a layer of realism that is both enlightening and engaging.

A Stateside Tour of Duty transcends the genre of military fiction, offering insights into the era's social and political complexities. It is a testament to the resilience of the human spirit and the bonds forged in the face of adversity. For its heartfelt storytelling, meticulous attention to detail, and profound insights into the human condition. This novel is not just a read; it's an experience that resonates with the echoes of a pivotal era in American history.

This review awards *A Stateside Tour of Duty* the highest honor of a Gold review for its exceptional storytelling, authenticity, and emotional depth. Neil Mitchell's work stands as a remarkable contribution to the landscape of military fiction and beyond.

– Peter T. of MainSpring Books

www.ingramcontent.com/pod-product-compliance
Lightning Source LLC
Chambersburg PA
CBHW021409010826
48972CB00013B/950